Praise for *New York Times* bestselling author

NORA ROBERTS

"There's no mystery about why Roberts is a bestselling author of romances and mainstream novels: she delivers the goods with panache and wit."

—*Publishers Weekly*

"Move over, Sidney Sheldon: the world has a new master of romantic suspense, and her name is Nora Roberts."

—*Rex Reed*

"Roberts is indeed a word artist, painting her story and her characters with vitality and verve."

—*Los Angeles Daily News*

"Nora Roberts is the very best there is—she's superb in everything she does."

—*Romantic Times*

"Characters that touch the heart, stories that intrigue, romance that sizzles—Nora Roberts has mastered it all."

—*Rendezvous*

"Ms. Roberts is an enormously gifted writer whose incredible range and intensity guarantee the very best of reading. So move over, bestsellers. The new 'top gun' of contemporary fiction has arrived."

—*Rave Reviews*

"A consistently entertaining writer."

—*USA Today*

NORA ROBERTS

Multi-*New York Times* bestselling author of the finest in women's fiction, Nora Roberts is beloved by readers everywhere. A consummate storyteller, her generous spirit, humor, creativity and commitment to her characters, her writing and—most especially—her readers, have earned her fame all over the world. Today there are more than twenty-eight million Nora Roberts books in print worldwide. She was the first author ever to be inducted into the Romance Writers of America Hall of Fame and has received almost every award for excellence in the field. Nora Roberts is truly a publishing phenomenon.

NORA ROBERTS

THE Calhoun Women

Published by Silhouette Books
America's Publisher of Contemporary Romance

To my friend and neighbor, Ida Levy

 SILHOUETTE BOOKS

THE CALHOUN WOMEN

Copyright © 1996 by Harlequin Books S.A.

ISBN 0-373-48332-5

The publisher acknowledges the copyright holders of the individual works as follows:
COURTING CATHERINE
Copyright © 1991 by Nora Roberts
A MAN FOR AMANDA
Copyright © 1991 by Nora Roberts
FOR THE LOVE OF LILAH
Copyright © 1991 by Nora Roberts
SUZANNA'S SURRENDER
Copyright © 1991 by Nora Roberts

This edition published by arrangement with Harlequin Books S.A.

® and TM are trademarks of Harlequin Books S.A., used under license. Trademarks indicated with ® are registered in the United States Patent and Trademark Office, the Canadian Trade Marks Office and in other countries.

Printed in U.S.A.

CONTENTS

THE Calhoun Women
by Nora Roberts

COURTING CATHERINE

Prologue

Bar Harbor, Maine
June 12, 1912

I saw him on the cliffs overlooking Frenchman Bay. He was tall and dark and young. Even from a distance, as I walked with little Ethan's hand in mine, I could see the defiant set of his shoulders. He held the brush as though it were a saber, his palette like a shield. Indeed it seemed to me that he was dueling with his canvas rather than painting on it. So deep was his concentration, so fast and fierce the flicks of his wrist, one would have thought his life depended on what he created there.

Perhaps it did.

I thought it odd, even amusing. My image of artists had always been one of gentle souls who see things we mortals cannot, and suffer in their quest to create them for us.

Yet I knew, before he turned and looked at me, that I would not see a gentle face.

It seemed that he was the product of an artist himself. A rough sculptor who had shorn away at an oak slab, carving out a high brow, dark hooded eyes, a long straight nose and full sensual mouth. Even the sweep of his hair might have been hewn from some ebony wood.

How he stared at me! Even now I can feel the heat rise to my face and the dampness spring to my palms. The wind was in his hair, sweet and moist from the sea, and ruffled the loose shirt he wore that was splattered and streaked from his paint. With the rocks and sky at his back, he looked very proud, very angry, as if he owned this jut of land—or the entire island—and I was the intruder.

He stood in silence for what seemed like forever, his eyes so intense, so fierce somehow that my tongue cleaved to the roof of my mouth. Then little Ethan began to babble and tug at my hand. The angry glare in his eyes softened. He smiled. I know a heart does not stop at such moments. And yet . . .

I found myself stammering, apologizing for the intrusion, lifting Ethan into my arms before my bright and curious little boy could rush forward toward the rocks.

He said, "Wait."

And taking up pad and pencil began to sketch as I stood immobile and trembling for reasons I cannot fathom. Ethan stilled and smiled, somehow as mesmerized by the man as I. I could feel the sun on my back and the wind on my face, could smell the water and the wild roses.

"Your hair should be loose," he said, and, putting the pencil aside, walked toward me. "I've painted sunsets that were less dramatic." He reached out and touched Ethan's bright red hair. "You share the color with your young brother."

"My son." Why was my voice so breathless? "He is my son. I'm Mrs. Fergus Calhoun," I said while his eyes seemed to devour my face.

"Ah, The Towers." He looked beyond me then to where the peaks and turrets of our summer home could be seen on the higher cliff above. "I've admired your house, Mrs. Calhoun."

Before I could reply, Ethan was reaching out, laughing, and the man scooped him up. I could only stare as he stood with his back to the wind, holding my child, jiggling him easily on his hip.

"A fine boy."

"And an energetic one. I thought to take him for a walk to give his nanny a bit of a rest. She has less trouble with my two other children combined than with young Ethan."

"You have other children?"

"Yes, a girl, a year older than Ethan, and a baby, not quite one. We only arrived for the season yesterday. Do you live on the island?"

"For now. Will you pose for me, Mrs. Calhoun?"

I blushed. But beneath the embarrassment was a deep and dreamy pleasure. Still, I knew the impropriety and Fergus's temper. So I refused, politely, I hoped. He did not persist, and I am ashamed to say that I felt a keen disappointment. When he gave Ethan back to me, his eyes were on mine—a deep slate gray that seemed to see more than my face. Perhaps more than anyone had seen before. He bid me good day, so I turned to walk with my child back to The Towers, my home and my duties.

I knew as surely as if I had turned to look, that he watched me until I was hidden by the cliff. My heart thundered.

Chapter One

Bar Harbor
1991

Trenton St. James III was in a foul mood. He was the kind of man who expected doors to open when he knocked, phones to be answered when he dialed. What he did not expect, and hated to tolerate, was having his car break down on a narrow two-lane road ten miles from his destination. At least the car phone had allowed him to track down the closest mechanic. He hadn't been overly thrilled about riding into Bar Harbor in the cab of the tow truck while strident rock had bellowed from the speakers and his rescuer had sung along, off-key, in between bites of an enormous ham sandwich.

"Hank, you just call me Hank, ayah," the driver had told him then took a long pull from a bottle of soda. "C.C.'ll fix you up all right and tight. Best damn mechanic in Maine, you ask anybody."

Trent decided, under the circumstances, he'd have to take just-call-me-Hank's word for it. To save time and trouble, he'd had the driver drop him off in the village with directions to the garage and a grimy business card Trent studied while holding it gingerly at the corners.

But as with any situation Trent found himself in, he decided to make it work for him. While his car was being dealt with, he made half a dozen calls to his office back in Boston—putting the fear of God into a flurry of secretaries, assistants and junior vice-presidents. It put him in a slightly better frame of mind.

He lunched on the terrace of a small restaurant, paying more attention to the paperwork he took from his briefcase than the excellent lobster salad or balmy spring breeze. He checked his watch often, drank too much coffee and, with impatient brown eyes, studied the traffic that streamed up and down the street.

Two of the waitresses on lunch shift discussed him at some length. It was early April, several weeks before the height of the season, so the restaurant wasn't exactly hopping with customers.

They agreed that this one was a beaut, from the top of his dark blond head to the tips of his highly polished Italian shoes. They agreed that he was a businessman, and an *important* one, because of the leather briefcase and spiffy gray suit and tie. Plus, he wore cuff links. Gold ones.

They decided, as they rolled flatware into napkins for the next shift, that he was young for it, no more than thirty. Outrageously handsome was their unanimous vote while they took turns refilling his coffee cup and getting closer looks. Nice clean features, they agreed, with a kind of polished air that would have been just a tad slick if it hadn't been for the eyes.

They were dark and broody and impatient, making the waitresses speculate as to whether he'd been stood up by a woman. Though they couldn't imagine any female in her right mind doing so.

Trent paid no more attention to them than he would have to anyone who performed a paid service. That disappointed them. The whopping tip he left made up for it nicely. It would have surprised him that the tip would have meant more to the waitresses if he had offered a smile with it.

He relocked his briefcase and prepared to take the brisk walk to the mechanic at the end of town. He wasn't a cold man and wouldn't have considered himself aloof. As a St. James he had grown up with servants who had quietly and efficiently gone about the business of making his life simpler. He paid well, even generously. If he didn't show any overt appreciation or personal interest, it was simply because it never occurred to him.

At the moment, his mind was on the deal he hoped to close by the end of the week. Hotels were his business, with the emphasis on luxury and resorts. The summer before, Trent's father had located a particular property while he and his fourth wife had been yachting in Frenchman Bay. While Trenton St. James II's instincts as to women were notoriously skewed, his business instincts were always on target.

He'd begun negotiations almost immediately for the buy of the enormous stone house overlooking Frenchman Bay. His appetite had been whetted by the reluctance of the owners to sell what had to be a white elephant as a private home. As expected, the senior Trenton had been turning things his way, and the deal was on the way to being set.

Then Trent had found the whole business dumped into his lap as his father was once again tangled in a complicated divorce.

Wife number four had lasted almost eighteen months, Trent mused. Which was two months longer than wife number three. Trent accepted, fatalistically, that there was bound to be a number five around the corner. The old man was as addicted to marriage as he was to real estate.

Trent was determined to close the deal on The Towers before the ink had dried on this last divorce decree. As soon as he got his car out of the garage, he would drive up and take a firsthand look at the place.

Because of the time of year, many of the shops were closed as he walked through town, but he could see the possibilities. He knew that during the season the streets of Bar Harbor were crammed with tourists with credit cards and travelers' checks at the ready. And tourists needed hotels. He had the statistics in his briefcase. With solid planning, he figured The Towers would cull a hefty percentage of that tourist trade within fifteen months.

All he had to do was convince four sentimental women and their aunt to take the money and run.

He checked his watch again as he turned the corner toward the mechanic's. Trent had given him precisely two hours to deal with whatever malfunction the BMW had suffered. That, he was convinced, was enough.

Of course he could have taken the company plane up from Boston. It would have been more practical, and Trent was nothing if not a practical man. But he'd wanted to drive. Needed to, he admitted. He'd needed those few hours of quiet and solitude.

Business was booming, but his personal life was going to hell.

Who would have thought that Marla would suddenly shove an ultimatum down his throat? Marriage or nothing. It still baffled him. She had known since the beginning of their relationship that marriage had never been an option. He had no intention of taking a ride on the roller coaster his father seemed to thrive on.

Not that he wasn't—hadn't been—fond of her. She was lovely and well-bred, intelligent and successful in her field of fashion design. With Marla, there was never a hair out of place, and Trent appreciated that kind of meticulousness in a woman. Just as he had appreciated her practical attitude toward their relationship.

She had claimed not to want marriage or children or pledges of undying love. Trent considered it a personal betrayal that she suddenly changed her tune and demanded it all.

He hadn't been able to give it to her.

They had parted, stiff as strangers, only two weeks before. She was already engaged to a golf pro.

It stung. But even as it stung, it convinced him he had been right all along. Women were unstable, fickle creatures, and marriage was a bloodless kind of suicide.

She hadn't even loved him. Thank God. She had simply wanted "commitment and stability," as she had put it. Trent felt, smugly, that she would soon find out marriage was the last place to find either.

Because he knew it was unproductive to dwell on mistakes, he allowed thoughts of Marla to pass out of his mind. He would take a vacation from females, he decided.

Trent paused outside the white cinder-block building with its scatter of cars in the lot. The sign over the open garage doors read C.C.'s Automovation. Just beneath the title, which Trent found ostentatious, was an offer of twenty-four-hour towing, complete auto repairs and refinishing—foreign and domestic—and free estimates.

Through the doors, he could hear rock music. Trent let out a sigh as he went in.

The hood was up on his BMW, and a pair of dirty boots peeked out from beneath the car. The mechanic was tapping the toes of the boots together in time to the din of music. Frowning, Trent glanced around the garage area. It smelled of grease and honeysuckle—a ridiculous combination. The place itself was a disorganized and grimy mess of tools and auto parts, something that looked as though it might have been a fender, and a coffee maker that was boiling whatever was inside it down to black sludge.

There was a sign on the wall that stated No Checks Cashed, Not Even For You.

Several others listed services provided by the shop and their rates. Trent supposed they were reasonable, but he had no yardstick. There were two vending machines against a wall, one offering soft drinks, the other junk food. A coffee can held change that customers were free to contribute to or take from. An interesting concept, Trent thought.

"Excuse me," he said. The boots kept right on tapping. "Excuse me," he repeated, louder. The music upped its tempo and so did the boots. Trent nudged one with his shoe.

"What?" The answer from under the car was muffled and annoyed.

"I'd like to ask you about my car."

"Get in line." There was the clatter of a tool and a muttered curse.

Trent's eyebrows lifted then drew together in a manner that made his subordinates quake. "Apparently I'm the first in line already."

"Right now you're behind this idiot's oil pan. Save me from rich yuppies who buy a car like this then don't bother to find out the difference between a carburetor and a tire iron. Hold on a minute, buddy, or talk to Hank. He's around somewhere."

Trent was still several sentences back at "idiot." "Where's the proprietor?"

"Busy. Hank!" The mechanic's voice lifted to a roar. "Damn it. Hank! Where the devil did he take off to?"

"I couldn't say." Trent marched over to the radio and flicked off the music. "Would it be too much to ask you to come out from under there and tell me the status of my car?"

"Yeah." From the vantage point under the BMW, C.C. studied the Italian loafers and took an immediate dislike to them. "I got my hands full at the moment. You can come down here and lend one of yours if you're in such a hurry, or drive over to McDermit's in Northeast Harbor."

"I can hardly drive when you're under my car." Though the idea held a certain appeal.

"This yours?" C.C. sniffed and tightened bolts. The guy had a fancy Boston accent to go with the fancy shoes. "When's the last time you had this thing tuned? Changed the points and plugs, the oil?"

"I don't—"

"I'm sure you don't." There was a clipped satisfaction in the husky voice that had Trent's jaw tightening. "You know, you don't just buy a car, but a responsibility. A lot of people don't pull down an annual salary as rich as the sticker price on a machine like this. With reasonable care and maintenance, this baby would run for your grandchildren. Cars aren't disposable commodities, you know. People make them that way because they're too lazy or too stupid to take care of the basics. You needed a lube job six months ago.''

Trent's fingers drummed on the side of his briefcase. "Young man, you're being paid to service my car, not to lecture me on my responsibilities to it." In a habit as ingrained as breathing, he checked his watch. "Now, I'd like to know when my car will be ready, as I have a number of appointments.''

"Lecture's free." C.C. gave a push and sent the creeper scooting out from under the car. "And I'm not your young man.''

That much was quite obvious. Though the face was grimy and the dark hair cropped boyishly short, the body clad in greasy coveralls was decidely feminine. Every curvy inch of it. Trent wasn't often thrown for a loss, but now he simply stood, staring as C.C. rose from the creeper and faced him, tapping a wrench against her palm.

Looking beyond the smears of black on her face, Trent could see she had very white skin in contrast with her ebony hair. Beneath the fringe of bangs, her forest-green eyes were narrowed. Her full, unpainted lips were pursed in what, under different circumstances, would have been a very sexy pout. She was tall for a woman and built like a goddess. It was she, Trent realized, who smelled of motor oil and honeysuckle.

"Got a problem?" she asked him. C.C. was well aware that his gaze had drifted down from the neck of her coveralls to the cuffs and back again. She was used to it. But she didn't have to like it.

The voice had an entirely different effect when a man realized those dark, husky tones belonged to a woman. "You're the mechanic!''

"No, I'm the interior decorator.''

Trent glanced around the garage with its oil-splattered floor and cluttered worktables. He couldn't resist. "You do very interesting work.''

Letting the breath out between her teeth, she tossed the wrench onto a workbench. "Your oil and air filter needed to be changed. The timing was off and the carburetor needed some adjusting. You still need a lube job and your radiator should be flushed.''

"Will it run?''

"Yeah, it'll run." C.C. took a rag out of her pocket and began to wipe her hands. She judged him as the kind of man who took better care of his ties than he did of his car. With a shrug, she stuck the rag back into her pocket. It was no concern of hers. "Come through to the office and we can settle up.''

She led the way through the door at the rear of the garage, into a narrow hallway that angled into a glass-walled office. It was cramped with a cluttered desk, thick parts catalogues, a half-full gum ball machine and two wide swivel chairs. C.C. sat and, in the uncanny way of people who heap papers on their desk, put her hand unerringly on her invoices.

"Cash or charge?" she asked him.

"Charge." Absently he pulled out his wallet. He wasn't sexist. Trent assured himself he was not. He had meticulously made certain that women were given the same pay and opportunity for promotion in his company as any male on his staff. It never occurred to him to be concerned whether employees were males or females, as long as they were efficient, loyal and dependable. But the longer he looked at the woman who sat busily filling out the invoice, the more he was certain she didn't fit his or anyone's image of an auto mechanic.

"How long have you worked here?" It surprised him to hear himself ask. Personal questions weren't his style.

"On and off since I was twelve." Those dark green eyes flicked up to his. "Don't worry. I know what I'm doing. Any work that's done in my shop is guaranteed."

"Your shop?"

"My shop."

She unearthed a calculator and began to figure the total with long, elegantly shaped fingers that were still grimy.

He was putting her back up. Maybe it was the shoes, she thought. Or the tie. There was something arrogant about a maroon tie. "That's the damage." C.C. turned the invoice around and started down the list point by point.

He wasn't paying any attention, which was totally out of character. This was a man who read every word of every paper that crossed his desk. But he was looking at her, frankly fascinated.

"Any questions?" She glanced up and found her gaze locked with his. She could almost hear the click.

"You're C.C.?"

"That's right." She was forced to clear her throat. Ridiculous, she told herself. He had ordinary eyes. Maybe a little darker, a bit more intense than she had noted at first, but still ordinary. There was no earthly reason why she couldn't look away from them. But she continued to stare. If she had been of a fanciful state of mind—which she assured herself she was not—she would have said the air thickened.

"You have grease on your cheek," he said quietly, and smiled at her.

The change was astonishing. He went from being an aloof, annoying man to a warm and approachable one. His mouth softened as it curved, the impatience in his eyes vanished. There was humor there now, an easy, inviting humor that was irresistible. C.C. found herself smiling back.

"It goes with the territory." Maybe she'd been a tad abrupt, she thought, and made an effort to correct it. "You're from Boston, right?"

"Yes. How did you know?"

Her lips remained curved as she shrugged. "Between the Massachusetts plates and your speech pattern, it wasn't hard. We get a lot of trade from Boston on the island. Are you here on vacation?"

"Business." Trent tried to remember the last time he'd taken a vacation, and couldn't quite pin it down. Two years? he wondered. Three?

C.C. pulled a clipboard from under a pile of catalogues and scanned the next day's schedule. "If you're going to be around for a while, we could fit that lube job in tomorrow."

"I'll keep it in mind. You live on the island?"

"Yes. All my life." The chair creaked as she brought her long legs up to sit Indian-style. "Have you been to Bar Harbor before?"

"When I was a boy, I spent a couple of weekends here with my mother." Lifetimes ago, he thought. "Maybe you could recommend some restaurants or points of interest. I might squeeze in some free time."

"You shouldn't miss the park." After unearthing a sheet of memo paper, she began to write. "You really can't go wrong anywhere as far as seafood, and it's early enough in the season that you shouldn't have any problem with crowds and lines." She offered the paper, which he folded and slipped into his breast pocket.

"Thanks. If you're free tonight maybe you could help me sample some of the local seafood. We could discuss my carburetor."

Flustered and flattered, she reached out to accept the credit card he offered. She was on the point of agreeing when she read the name imprinted there. "Trenton St. James III."

"Trent," he said easily, and smiled again.

It figured, C.C. thought. Oh, it absolutely figured. Fancy car, fancy suit, fancy manners. She should have spotted it right off. She should have *smelled* it. Seething, she imprinted the card on the credit card form. "Sign here."

Trent took out a slim gold pen and signed while she rose and stalked over to a pegboard to retrieve his keys. He glanced over just as she tossed them to him. *At* him was more accurate. He managed to snag them before they hit his face. He jingled them lightly in his hand as she stood, hands on hips, face dark with fury.

"A simple no would have done the job."

"Men like you don't understand a simple no." C.C. turned to the glass wall, then whirled back. "If I'd known who you were, I'd have drilled holes in your muffler."

Slowly Trent slipped the keys into his pocket. His temper was renowned. It wasn't hot—that would have been easier to dodge. It was ice. As he stood it slid through him, frosting his eyes, tightening his mouth, coating his voice. "Would you like to explain?"

She strode toward him until they were toe to toe and eye to eye. "I'm Catherine Colleen Calhoun. And I want you to keep your greedy hands off my house."

Trent said nothing for a moment as he adjusted his thoughts. Catherine Calhoun, one of the four sisters who owned The Towers—and one who apparently had strong feelings regarding the sale. Since he was going to have to maneuver around all four of them, he might as well start here. And now.

"A pleasure, Miss Calhoun."

"Not mine." She reached down and ripped off his copy of the credit card receipt. "Get your butt back in your big, bad BMW and head back to Boston."

"A fascinating alliteration." Still watching her, Trent folded the paper and put it into his pocket. "You, however, are not the only party involved."

"You're not going to turn my house into one of your glossy hotels for bored debutantes and phony Italian counts."

He nearly smiled at that. "You've stayed in one of the St. James hotels?"

"I don't have to, I know what they're like. Marble lobbies, glass elevators, twenty-foot chandeliers and fountains spurting everywhere."

"You have something against fountains?"

"I don't want one in my living room. Why don't you go foreclose on some widows and orphans and leave us alone?"

"Unfortunately, I don't have any foreclosures scheduled this week." He held up a hand when she snarled. "Miss Calhoun, I've come here at the request of your liaison. Whatever your personal feelings, there are three other owners of The Towers. I don't intend to leave until I've spoken with them."

"You can talk until your lungs collapse, but . . . what liaison?"

"Mrs. Cordelia Calhoun McPike."

C.C.'s color fluctuated a bit, but she didn't back down. "I don't believe you."

Without a word, Trent set his briefcase down onto the piles of paper on her desk and flipped the combination. From one of his neatly ordered files he withdrew a letter written on heavy ivory paper. C.C.'s heart dropped a little. She snatched it from him and read.

Dear Mr. St. James,
The Calhoun women have taken your offer to The Towers under consideration. As this is a complex situation, we feel it would be in everyone's best interest to discuss the terms in person, rather than communicating by letter.

As their representative, I would like to invite you to The Towers— (*C.C. gave a strangled groan*)—for a few days. I believe this more personal approach will be of mutual benefit. I'm sure you'll agree that having a closer, more informal look at the property that interests you will be an advantage.

Please feel free to contact me, at The Towers, if you are amenable to the arrangement.

Very truly yours,
Cordelia Calhoun McPike

C.C. read it through twice, grinding her teeth. She would have crumpled the letter into a ball if Trent hadn't rescued it and slipped it back into its file.

"I take it you weren't apprised of the arrangement?"

"Apprised? Damn straight I wasn't apprised. That meddlesome old . . . Oh, Aunt Coco, I'm going to murder you."

"I assume Mrs. McPike and Aunt Coco are one and the same person."

"Some days it's hard to tell." She turned back. "But either way, both of them are dead."

"I'll sidestep the family violence, if you don't mind."

C.C. stuck her hands into her coverall pockets and glared at him. "If you still intend to stay at The Towers, you're going to be neck deep in it."

He nodded, accepting. "Then I'll take my chances."

Chapter Two

Aunt Coco was busily arranging hothouse roses in two of the Dresden vases that had yet to be sold. She hummed a current rock hit as she worked, occasionally adding a quick bum-bum-bum or ta-te-da. Like the other Calhoun women, she was tall, and liked to think that her figure, which had thickened only a little in the past decade, was regal.

She had dressed and groomed carefully for the occasion. Her short, fluffy hair was tinted red this week and pleased her enormously. Vanity was not a sin or character flaw in Coco's estimation, but a woman's sacred duty. Her face, which was holding up nicely, thank you, from the lift she'd had six years before, was scrupulously made up. Her best pearls swung at her ears and encircled her neck. Coco decided, with a quick glance in the hall mirror, that the black jumpsuit was both dramatic and sleek. The backless heels she wore slapped satisfactorily against the chestnut floor and had her teetering at six foot.

An imposing and, yes, regal figure, she bustled from room to room, checking and rechecking every detail. Her girls might be just a tiny bit upset with her for inviting company without mentioning it. But she could always claim absentmindedness. Which she did whenever it suited her.

Coco was the younger sister of Judson Calhoun, who had married Deliah Brady and sired four girls. Judson and Deliah, whom Coco had loved dearly, had been killed fifteen years before when their private plane had gone down over the Atlantic.

Since then, she had done her best to be father and mother and friend to her beautiful little orphans. A widow for nearly twenty years, Coco was a striking woman with a devious mind and a heart the consistency of marshmallow cream. She wanted, was determined to have, the best for her girls. Whether they liked it or not. With Trenton St. James's interest in The Towers, she saw an opportunity.

She didn't care a bit whether he bought the rambling fortress of a house. Though God knows how much longer they could hold on to it in any case, what with taxes and repairs and heating bills. As far as she was concerned, Trenton St. James III could take it or leave it. But she had a plan.

Whether he took or left it, he was going to fall head over bank account with one of the girls. She didn't know which one. She'd tried her crystal ball but hadn't come up with a name.

But she knew. She had known the moment the first letter had come. The boy was going to sweep one of her darlings away into a life of love and luxury.

She'd be damned if any one of them would have one without the other.

With a sigh, she adjusted the taper in its Lalique holder. She had been able to give them love, but the luxury... If Judson and Deliah had lived, things would have been different. Surely Judson would have pulled himself out of the financial difficulty he'd been suffering. With his cleverness, and Deliah's drive, it would have been a very temporary thing.

But they hadn't lived, and money had become an increasing problem. How she hated to have to sell off the girls' inheritance piece by piece just to keep the sagging roof they all loved over their heads.

Trenton St. James III was going to change all that by falling madly in love with one of her darling babies.

Maybe it would be Suzanna, she thought, plumping the pillows on the parlor sofa. Poor little dear with her heart broken by the worthless cur she had married. Coco's lips tightened. To think he had fooled all of them. Even her! He had made her baby's life a misery, then had divorced her to marry that busty bimbo.

Coco let out a disgusted breath then cast a beady eye on the cracked plaster in the ceiling. She would have to make sure that Trenton would suit as a father to Suzanna's two children. And if he didn't...

There was Lilah, her own lovely free spirit. Her Lilah needed someone who would appreciate her lively mind and eccentric ways. Someone who would nurture and settle. Just a bit. Coco wouldn't tolerate anyone who would try to smother her darling girl's mystical bent.

Perhaps it would be Amanda. Coco twitched a drapery so that it covered a mouse hole. Hardheaded, practical-minded Amanda. Now that would be a match! The successful businessman and woman, wheeling and dealing. But he would have to have a softer side, one that recognized that Mandy needed to be cherished, as well as respected. Even if she didn't recognize it herself.

With a satisfied sigh, Coco moved from parlor to sitting room, from sitting room to library, library to study.

Then there was C.C. Shaking her head, Coco adjusted a picture so that it hid—almost—the watermarks on the aging silk wallpaper. That child had inherited the Calhoun stubbornness in spades. Imagine, a lovely girl wasting her life diddling with engines and fuel pumps. A grease monkey. Lord save us.

It was doubtful that a man like Trenton St. James III would be interested in a woman who spent all of her time under a car. Then again, C.C. was the baby of the family at twenty-three. Coco felt that she had more than enough time to find her little girl the perfect husband.

The stage was set, she decided. And soon, Mr. St. James would be walking into Act One.

The front door slammed. Coco winced, knowing that the vibration would have pictures jittering on the walls and crockery dancing on tables. She worked her way through the winding maze of rooms, tidying as she went.

"Aunt Coco!"

Coco's hand lifted automatically to pat her breast. She recognized C.C.'s voice, and the fury in it. Now what could have happened to fire the girl up? she wondered, and put on her best sympathetic smile.

"Just coming, dear. I didn't expect you home for hours yet. It's such a pleasant..." She trailed off as she saw her niece, stripped down to fighting weight in torn jeans and a T-shirt, traces of grease still on her face and the hands she had fisted and jammed at her hips. And the man behind her—the man Coco recognized as her prospective nephew-in-law. "Surprise," she finished, and pasted the smile back into place. "Why, Mr. St. James, how lovely." She stepped forward, hand extended. "I'm Mrs. McPike."

"How do you do?"

"It's so nice to meet you at last. I hope you had a pleasant trip."

"An... interesting one, all in all."

"Even better than pleasant." She patted his hand before releasing it, approving his level gaze and well-pitched voice. "Please, come in. I believe a person should begin as they mean to go on, so I want you to begin to make yourself at home right now. I'll just fix us all some tea."

"Aunt Coco," C.C. said in a low voice.

"Yes, dear, would you like something other than tea?"

"I want an explanation, and I want it now."

Coco's heart hammered a bit, but she gave her niece an open, slightly curious smile. "Explanation? For what?"

"I want to know what the hell he's doing here."

"Catherine, really!" Coco tsk-tsked. "Your manners, one of my very few failures. Come, Mr. St. James—or may I call you Trenton—you must be a bit frazzled after the drive. You did say you were driving? Why don't we just go in and sit in the parlor?" She was easing him along as she spoke. "Marvelous weather for a drive, isn't it?"

"Hold it." C.C. moved quickly and planted herself in their path. "Hold it. Hold it. You're not tucking him up in the parlor with tea and small talk. I want to know why you invited him here."

"C.C." Coco gave a long-suffering sigh. "Business is more pleasant and more successful on all sides when it's conducted in person, and in a relaxed atmosphere. Wouldn't you agree, Trenton?"

"Yes." He was surprised that he had to hold back a grin. "Yes, I would."

"There."

"Not another step." C.C. flung out both hands. "We haven't agreed to sell."

"Of course not," Coco said patiently. "That's why Trenton is here. So we can discuss all the options and possibilities. You really should go up and wash before tea, C.C. You've engine grease or whatever on your face."

With the heel of her hand, C.C. rubbed at it. "Why wasn't I told he was coming?"

Coco blinked and tried to leave her eyes slightly unfocused. "Told? Why, of course, you were told. I would hardly have invited company without telling all of you."

Face mutinous, C.C. held her ground. "You didn't tell me."

"Now, C.C., I..." Coco pursed her lips, knowing—since she'd practiced in the mirror—that it made her look befuddled. "I didn't? Are you certain? I would have sworn I told you and the girls the minute I got Mr. St. James's acceptance."

"No," C.C. said flatly.

"Oh, my." Coco lifted her hands to her cheeks. "Oh, how awful, really. I must apologize. What a dreadful mix-up. And all my fault. C.C., I do beg your pardon. After all, this is your house, yours and your sisters'. I would never presume on your good nature and your hospitality by..."

Before Coco had trailed off again, the guilt was working away. "It's your house as much as ours, Aunt Coco. You know that. It's not as if you have to ask permission to invite anyone you like. It's simply that I think we should have—"

"No, no, it's inexcusable." Coco had blinked enough to have her eyes glistening nicely. "Really it was. I just don't know what to say. I feel terrible about the whole thing. I was only trying to help, you see, but—"

"It's nothing to worry about." C.C. reached out for her aunt's hand. "Nothing at all. It was just a little confusing at first. Look, why don't I make the tea, and you can sit with—him."

"That's so sweet of you, dear."

C.C. muttered something unintelligible as she walked down the hall.

"Congratulations," Trent murmured, sending Coco an amused glance. "That was one of the smoothest shuffles I've ever witnessed."

Coco beamed and tucked her arm through his. "Thank you. Now, why don't we go in and have that chat?" She steered him to a wing chair by the fireplace, knowing that the springs in the sofa were only a memory. "I must apologize for C.C. She has a very quick temper but a wonderful heart."

Trent inclined his head. "I'll have to take your word for it."

"Well, you're here and that's what matters." Pleased with herself, Coco sat across from him. "I know you'll find The Towers, and its history, fascinating."

He smiled, thinking he'd already found its occupants a fascination.

"My grandfather," she said, gesturing to a portrait of a dour-faced thin-lipped man above the ornate cherrywood mantel. "He built this house in 1904."

Trent glanced up at the disapproving eyes and lowered brows. "He looks...formidable," he said politely.

Coco gave a gay laugh. "Oh, indeed. And ruthless in his prime, so I'm told. I only remember Fergus Calhoun as a doddering old man who argued with shadows. They finally put him away in 1945 after he ried to shoot the butler for serving bad port. He was quite insane—Grandfather," she explained. "Not the butler."

"I . . . see."

"He lived another twelve years in the asylum, which put him well into his eighties. The Calhouns either have long lives or die tragically young." She crossed her long, sturdy legs. "I knew your father."

"My father?"

"Yes, indeed. Not well. We attended some of the same parties in our youth. I remember dancing with him once at a cotillion in Newport. He was dashingly handsome, fatally charming. I was quite smitten." She smiled. "You resemble him closely."

"He must have fumbled to let you slip through his fingers."

Pure feminine delight glowed in her eyes. "You're quite right," she said with a laugh. "How is Trenton?"

"He's well. I think if he had realized the connection, he wouldn't have passed this business on to me."

She lifted a brow. As a woman who followed the society and gossip pages religiously, she was well aware of the senior St. James's current messy divorce. "The last marriage didn't take?"

It was hardly a secret, but it made Trent uncomfortable just the same. "No. Should I give him your regards when I speak with him?"

"Please do." A sore point, she noted, and skimmed lightly over it. "How is it you ran into C.C.?"

Fate, he thought, and nearly said so. "I found myself in need of her services—or I should say my car needed them. I didn't immediately make the connection between C.C.'s Automovations and Catherine Calhoun."

"Who could blame you?" Coco said with a fluttering hand. "I hope she wasn't too, ah, intense."

"I'm still alive to talk about it. Obviously, your niece isn't convinced to sell."

"That's right." C.C. wheeled in a tea cart, steering it across the floor like a go-cart and stopping it with a rattle between the two chairs. "And it's going to take more than some slick operator from Boston to convince me."

"Catherine, there is no excuse for rudeness."

"That's all right." Trent merely settled back. "I'm becoming used to it. Are all your nieces so . . . aggressive, Mrs. McPike?"

"Coco, please," she murmured. "They're all lovely women." As she lifted the teapot, she sent C.C. a warning glance. "Don't you have work, dear?"

"It can wait."

"But you only brought out service for two."

"I don't want anything." She plopped down on the arm of the sofa and folded her arms over her chest.

"Well then. Cream or lemon, Trenton?"

"Lemon, please."

Swinging one long, booted leg, C.C. watched them sip tea and exchange small talk. Useless talk, she thought nastily. He was the kind of man who had been trained from diapers on the proper way to sit in a parlor and discuss nothing.

Squash, polo, perhaps a round of golf. He probably had hands like a baby's. Beneath that tailored suit, his body would be soft and slow. Men like him didn't work, didn't sweat, didn't feel. He sat behind his desk all day, buying and selling, never once thinking of the lives he affected. Of the dreams and hopes he created or destroyed.

He wasn't going to mess with hers. He wasn't going to cover the much-loved and much-cracked plaster walls with drywall and a coat of slick paint. He wasn't going to turn the drafty old ballroom into a nightclub. He wasn't going to touch one board foot of her wormy rafters.

She would see to it. She would see to him.

It was quite a situation, Trent decided. He parried Coco's tea talk while the Amazon Queen, as he'd begun to think of C.C., sat on a sagging sofa, swinging a scarred boot and glaring daggers at him. Normally he would have politely excused himself, headed back to Boston to turn the whole business over to agents. But he hadn't faced a true challenge in a long time. This one, he mused, might be just what he needed to put him on track.

The place itself was an amazement—a crumbling one. From the outside it looked like a combination of English manor house and Dracula's castle. Towers and turrets of dour gray stone jutted into the sky. Gargoyles—one of which had been decapitated—grinned wickedly as they clung to parapets. All of this seemed to sit atop a proper two-story house of granite with neat porches and terraces. There was a pergola built along the seawall. The quick glimpse Trent had had of it had brought a Roman bathhouse to mind for reasons he couldn't fathom. As the lawns were uneven and multileveled, granite walls had been thrown up wherever they were terraced.

It should have been ugly. In fact, Trent thought it should have been hideous. Yet it wasn't. It was, in a baffling way, charming.

The way the window glass sparkled like lake water in the sun. Banks of spring flowers spread and nodded. Ivy rustled as it inched its patient way up those granite walls. It hadn't been difficult, even for a man with a pragmatic mind, to imagine the tea and garden parties. Women floating over the lawns in picture hats and organdy dresses, harp and violin music playing.

Then there was the view, which even on the short walk from his car to the front door had struck him breathless.

He could see why his father wanted it, and was willing to invest the hundreds of thousands of dollars it would take to renovate.

"More tea, Trenton?" Coco asked.

"No, thank you." He sent her a charming smile. "I wonder if I might have a tour of the house. What I've seen so far is fascinating."

C.C. gave a snort Coco pretended not to hear. "Of course, I'd be delighted to show you through." She rose and with her back to Trent wiggled her eyebrows at her niece. "C.C., shouldn't you be getting back?"

"No." She rose and, with an abrupt change of tactics, smiled. "I'll show Mr. St. James through, Aunt Coco. It's nearly time for the children to be home from school."

Coco glanced at the mantel clock, which had stopped weeks before at ten thirty-five. "Oh, well . . ."

"Don't worry about a thing." C.C. walked to the doorway and with an imperious gesture of her hand waved Trent along. "Mr. St. James?"

She started down the hall in front of him then up a floating staircase. "We'll start at the top, shall we?" Without glancing back, she continued on and up, certain Trent would start wheezing and panting by the third flight.

She was disappointed.

They climbed the final circular set that led to the highest tower. C.C. put her hand on the knob and her shoulder to the thick oak door. With a grunt and a hard shove, it creaked open.

"The haunted tower," she said grandly, and stepped inside amid the dust and echoes. The circular room was empty but for a few sturdy and fortunately empty mouse traps.

"Haunted?" Trent repeated, willing to play.

"My great-grandmother had her hideaway up here." As she spoke, C.C. moved over to the curved window. "It's said she would sit here, on this window seat, looking out to sea as she pined for her lover."

"Quite a view," Trent murmured. It was a dizzying drop down to the cliffs and the water that slapped and retreated. "Very dramatic."

"Oh, we're full of drama here. Great-Grandmama apparently couldn't bear the deceit any longer and threw herself out this very window." C.C. smiled smugly. "Now, on quiet nights you can hear her pacing this floor and weeping for her lost lover."

"That should add something to the brochure."

C.C. jammed her hands into her pockets. "I wouldn't think ghosts would be good for business."

"On the contrary." His lips curved. "Shall we move on?"

Tight-lipped, C.C. strode out of the room. Using both hands, she tugged on the knob, then dug in a bit and prepared to put her back into it. When Trent's hand closed over hers, she jolted as though she'd been scalded.

It felt as though she had.

"I can do it," she muttered. Her eyes widened as she felt his body brush hers. He brought his other arm around, caging her, trapping her hands under his. C.C.'s heart bounded straight into her throat, then back-flipped.

"It looks like a two-man job." With this, Trent gave a hard tug that brought the door to and C.C. back smartly against him.

They stood there a moment, like lovers looking out at a sunset. He caught himself drawing in the scent of her hair while his hands remained cupped over hers. It passed through his mind that she was quite an armful—an amazingly sexy armful—then she jumped like a rabbit, slamming back against the wall.

"It's warped." She swallowed, hoping to smother the squeak in her voice. "Everything around here is warped or broken or about to disintegrate. I don't know why you'd even consider buying it."

Her face was pale as water, Trent noted, making her eyes that much deeper. The panicked distress in them seemed more than a warped tower door warranted. "Doors can be repaired or replaced." Curious, he took a step toward her and watched her brace as if for a blow. "What's wrong with you?"

"Nothing." She knew if he touched her again she would go off like a rocket through what was left of the roof. "Nothing," she repeated. "If you want to see anything else, we'd better go down."

C.C. let out a long, slow breath as she followed him down the circular stairs. Her body was still throbbing oddly, as if she'd brushed a hand over a live wire. Not enough to get singed, she thought, just enough to let you know there was power.

She decided that gave her two reasons to get rid of Trenton St. James quickly.

She took him through the top floor, through the servants' wing, the storage rooms, making certain to point out any cracked plaster, dry rot, rodent damage. It pleased her that the air was chill, slightly damp and definitely musty. It was even more gratifying to see that his suit was sprinkled with dust and his shoes were rapidly losing their shine.

Trent peered into one room that was crowded with furniture boxes, broken crockery. "Has anyone gone through all this stuff?"

"Oh, we'll get around to it eventually." She watched a fat spider sneak away from the dim light. "Most of these rooms haven't been opened in fifty years—since my great-grandfather went insane."

"Fergus."

"Right. The family only uses the first two floors, and we patch things up as we have to." She ran her finger along an inch-wide crack in the wall. "I guess you could say if we don't see it, we don't worry about it. And the roof hasn't crashed down on our heads. Yet."

He turned to study her. "Have you ever thought about turning in your socket wrench for a real estate license?"

She only smiled. "There's more down this way." She particularly wanted to show him the room where she had tacked up plastic to cover the broken windows.

He walked with her, gingerly across a spot where two-by-fours had been nailed over a hole in the floor. A high arched door caught his eyes, and before C.C. could stop him, he had his hand on the knob.

"Where does this lead to?"

"Oh, nowhere," she began, and swore when he pulled it open. Fresh spring air rushed in. Trent stepped out onto the narrow stone terrace and turned toward the pie-shaped granite steps.

"I don't know how safe they are."

He flicked a glance over his shoulder. "A lot safer than the floor inside."

With an oath, C.C. gave up and climbed after him.

"Fabulous," he murmured as he paused on the wide passageway between turrets. "Really fabulous."

Which was exactly why C.C. hadn't wanted him to see it. She stood back with her hands in her pockets while he rested his palms on the waist-high stone wall and looked out.

He could see the deep blue waters of the bay with the boats gliding lightly over it. The valley, misty and mysterious, spread like a fairy tale. A gull, hardly more than a white blur, banked over the bay and soared out to sea.

"Incredible." The wind ruffled his hair as he followed the passage, down another flight, up one more. From here it was the Atlantic, wild and windy and wonderful. The sound of her ceaseless war on the rocks below echoed up like thunder.

He could see that there were doors leading back in at various intervals, but he wasn't interested in the interior just now. Someone, one of the family, he imagined, had set out chairs, tables, potted plants. Trent looked out over the roof of the pergola, to the tumbling rocks below.

"Spectacular." He turned to C.C. "Do you get used to it?"

She moved her shoulders. "No. You just get territorial."

"Understandable. I'm surprised any of you spend time inside."

With her hands still tucked in her pockets, she joined him at the wall. "It's not just the view. It's the fact that your family, generations of them, stood here. Just as the house has stood here, through time and wind and fire." Her face softened as she looked down. "The children are home."

Trent looked down to see two small figures race across the lawn toward the pergola. The sound of their laughter carried lightly on the wind.

"Alex and Jenny," she explained. "My sister Suzanna's children. They've stood here, too." She turned to him. "That means something."

"How does their mother feel about the sale?"

She looked away then as worry and guilt and frustration fought for control. "I'm sure you'll ask her yourself. But if you pressure her." Her head whipped around, hair flying. "If you pressure her in any way, you'll answer to me. I won't see her manipulated again."

"I have no intention of manipulating anyone."

She gave a bark of bitter laughter. "Men like you make a career out of manipulation. If you think you've happened across four helpless women, Mr. St. James, think again. The Calhouns can take care of themselves, and take care of their own."

"Undoubtedly, particularly if your sisters are as obnoxious as you."

C.C.'s eyes narrowed, her hands fisted. She would have moved in then and there for the kill, but her name was murmured quietly behind her.

Trent saw a woman step through one of the doors. She was as tall as C.C., but willowy, with a fragile aura that kicked Trent's protective instincts into gear before he was aware of it. Her hair was a pale and lustrous blond that waved to her shoulders. Her eyes were the deep blue of a midsummer sky and seemed calm and serene until you looked closer and saw the heartbreak beneath.

Despite the difference in coloring, there was a resemblance—the shape of the face and eyes and mouth—that made Trent certain he was meeting one of C.C.'s sisters.

"Suzanna." C.C. moved between her sister and Trent, as if to shield. Suzanna's mouth curved, a look that was both amused and impatient.

"Aunt Coco asked me to come up." She laid a hand on C.C.'s arm, soothing her protector. "You must be Mr. St. James."

"Yes." He accepted her offered hand and was surprised to find it hard and callused and strong.

"I'm Suzanna Calhoun Dumont. You'll be staying with us for a few days?"

"Yes. Your aunt was kind enough to invite me."

"Shrewd enough," Suzanna corrected with a smile as she put an arm around her sister. "I take it C.C.'s given you a partial tour."

"A fascinating one."

"I'll be glad to continue it from here." Her fingers pressed lightly but with clear meaning into C.C.'s arm. "Aunt Coco could use some help downstairs."

"He doesn't need to see any more now," C.C. argued. "You look tired."

"Not a bit. But I will be if Aunt Coco sends me all over the house looking for the Wedgwood turkey platter."

"All right then." She sent Trent a last, fulminating glance. "We aren't finished."

"Not by a long shot," he agreed, and smiled to himself as she slammed back inside. "Your sister has quite an . . . outgoing personality."

"She's a fire-eater," Suzanna said. "We all are, given the right circumstances. The Calhoun curse." She glanced over at the sound of her children laughing. "This isn't an easy decision, Mr. St. James, one way or the other. Nor is it, for any of us, a business one."

"I've gathered that. For me it has to be a business one."

She knew too well that for some men business came first, and last. "Then I suppose we'd better take it one step at a time." She opened the door that C.C. had slammed shut. "Why don't I show you where you'll be staying?"

Chapter Three

"So, what's he like?" Lilah Calhoun crossed her long legs, anchoring her ankles on one arm of the couch and pillowing her head on the other. The half-dozen bracelets on her arm jingled as she gestured toward C.C. "Honey, I've told you, screwing your face up that way causes nothing but wrinkles and bad vibes."

"If you don't want me to screw my face up, don't ask me about him."

"Okay, I'll ask Suzanna." She shifted her sea-green eyes toward her older sister. "Let's have it."

"Attractive, well mannered and intelligent."

"So's a cocker spaniel," Lilah put in, and sighed. "And here I was hoping for a pit bull. How long do we get to keep him?"

"Aunt Coco's a little vague on the particulars." Suzanna sent both of her sisters an amused look. "Which means she's not saying."

"Mandy might be able to pry something out of her." Lilah wiggled her bare toes and shut her eyes. She was the kind of woman who felt there was something intrinsically wrong with anyone who stretched out on a couch and didn't nap. "Suze, have the kids been through here today?"

"Only ten or fifteen times. Why?"

"I think I'm lying on a fire engine."

"I think we ought to get rid of him." C.C. rose and, to keep her restless hands busy, began to lay a fire.

"Suzanna said you already tried to throw him off the parapet."

"No," Suzanna corrected. "I said I stopped her before she thought to throw him off the parapet." She rose to hand C.C. the fireplace matches she'd forgotten. "And while I agree it's awkward to have him here while we're all so undecided, it's done. The least we can do is give him a chance to say his piece."

"Always the peacemaker," Lilah said sleepily, and missed Suzanna's quick wince. "Well, it might be a moot point now that he's gone through the place. My guess is that he'll be making some clever excuse and zooming back to Boston."

"The sooner the better," C.C. muttered, watching the flames begin to lick at the apple wood.

"I've been dismissed," Amanda announced. She hurried into the room as she hurried everywhere. Pushing a hand through her chin-length honey-brown hair, she perched on the arm of a chair. "She's not talking, either." Amanda's busy hands tugged at the hem of her trim business suit. "But I know she's up to something, something more than real estate transactions."

"Aunt Coco's always up to something." Suzanna moved automatically to the old Belker cabinet to pour her sister a glass of mineral water. "She's happiest when she's scheming."

"That may be true. Thanks," she added, taking the glass. "But I get nervous when I can't get past her guard." Thoughtful, she sipped, then swept her gaze over her sisters. "She's using the Limoges china."

"The Limoges?" Lilah pushed up on her elbows. "We haven't used that since Suzanna's engagement party." And could have bitten her tongue. "Sorry."

"Don't be silly." Suzanna brushed the apology away. "She hasn't entertained much in the past couple of years. I'm sure she's missed it. She's probably just excited to have company."

"He's not company," C.C. put in. "He's nothing but a pain in the—"

"Mr. St. James." Suzanna rose quickly, cutting off the finale of her sister's opinion.

"Trent, please." He smiled at her, then with some wryness at C.C.

It was quite a tableau, he thought, and had enjoyed it for perhaps a minute before Suzanna had seen him in the doorway. The Calhoun women together, and separately, made a picture any man still breathing had to appreciate. Long, lean and leggy, they sat, stood or sprawled around the room.

Suzanna stood with her back to the window, so that the last lights of the spring evening haloed around her hair. He would have said she was relaxed but for that trace of sadness in her eyes.

The one on the sofa was definitely relaxed—and all but asleep. She wore a long, flowered skirt that reached almost to her bare feet and regarded him through dreamy amused eyes as she pushed back a curling mass of waist-length red hair.

Another sat perched on the arm of a chair as if he would spring up and into action at the sound of a bell only she could hear. Sleek, slick and professional, he thought at first glance. Her eyes weren't dreamy or sad, but simply calculating.

Then there was C.C. She'd been sitting on the stone hearth, chin on her hands, brooding like some modern-day Cinderella. But she had risen quickly, defensively, he noted, to stand poker straight with the fire behind her. This wasn't a woman who would sit patiently for a prince to fit a glass slipper on her foot.

He imagined she'd kick him smartly in the shins or somewhere more painful if he attempted it.

"Ladies," he said, but his eyes were on C.C. without him even being aware of it. He couldn't resist the slight nod in her direction. "Catherine."

"Let me introduce you," Suzanna said quickly. "Trenton St. James, my sisters, Amanda and Lilah. Why don't I fix you a drink while you—"

The rest of the offer was drowned out by a war whoop and storming feet. Like twin whirlwinds, Alex and Jenny barreled into the room. It was Trent's misfortune that he happened to be standing in the line of fire. They slammed into him like two missiles and sent him tumbling to the couch on top of Lilah.

She only laughed and said she was pleased to meet him.

"I'm so sorry." Suzanna collared each child and sent Trent a sympathetic glance. "Are you all right?"

"Yes." He untangled himself and rose.

"These are my children, Disaster and Calamity." She kept a firm maternal arm around each. "Apologize."

"Sorry," they told him. Alex, a few inches taller than his sister looked up from under a mop of dark hair.

"We didn't see you."

"Didn't," Jenny agreed, and smiled winningly.

Suzanna decided to go into the lecture about storming into rooms later and steered them both toward the door. "Go ask Aunt Coco if dinner's ready. Walk!" she added firmly but without hope.

Before anyone could pick up the threads of a conversation, there was a loud, echoing boom.

"Oh, Lord," Amanda said into her glass. "She's dragged out the gong again."

"That means dinner." If there was one thing Lilah moved quickly for, it was food. She rose, tucked her arm through Trent's and beamed up at him. "I'll show you the way. Tell me, Trent, what are your views on astral projection?"

"Ah..." He sent a glance over his shoulder and saw C.C. grinning.

Aunt Coco had outdone herself. The china gleamed. What was left of the Georgian silver that had been a wedding present to Bianca and Fergus Calhoun glittered. Under the fantasy light of the Waterford chandelier the rack of lamb glistened. Before any of her nieces could comment, she dived cleanly into polite conversation.

"We're dining formal style, Trenton. So much more cozy. I hope your room is suitable."

"It's fine, thank you." It was, he thought, big as a barn, drafty, with a hole the size of a man's fist in the ceiling. But the bed was wide and soft as a cloud. And the view... "I can see some islands from my window."

"The Porcupine islands," Lilah put in, and passed him a silver basket of dinner rolls.

Coco watched them all like a hawk. She wanted to see some chemistry, some heat. Lilah was flirting with him, but she couldn't be too hopeful about that. Lilah flirted with men in general, and she wasn't paying any more attention to Trent than she did to the boy who bagged groceries in the market.

No, there was no spark there. On either side. One down, she thought philosophically, three to go.

"Trenton, did you know that Amanda is also in the hotel business? We're all so proud of our Mandy." She looked down the rosewood table at her niece. "She's quite a businesswoman."

"I'm assistant manager of the BayWatch, down in the village." Amanda's smile was both cool and friendly, the same she would give to any harried tourist at checkout time. "It's not on the scale of any of your hotels, but we do very well during the season. I heard you're adding an underground shopping complex to the St. James Atlanta."

Coco frowned into her wine as they discussed hotels. Not only was there not a spark, there wasn't even a weak glow. When Trent passed Amanda the mint jelly and their hands brushed, there was no breathless pause, no meeting of the eyes. Amanda had already turned to giggle with little Jenny and mop up spilled milk.

Ah, there! Coco thought triumphantly. Trent had grinned at Alex when the boy complained that brussels sprouts were disgusting. So, he had a weakness for children.

"You don't have to eat them," Suzanna told her suspicious son as he poked through his scalloped potatoes to make sure nothing green was hidden inside. "Personally, I've always thought they looked like shrunken heads."

"They do, kinda." The idea appealed to him, as his mother had known it would. He speared one, stuck it into his mouth and grinned. "I'm a cannibal. Uga bugga."

"Darling boy," Coco said faintly. "Suzanna's done such a marvelous job of mothering. She seems to have a green thumb with children as well as flowers. All the gardens are our Suzanna's work."

"Uga bugga," Alex said again as he popped another imaginary head into his mouth.

"Here you go, little creep." C.C. rolled her vegetables onto his plate. "There's a whole passel of missionaries."

"I want some, too," Jenny complained, then beamed at Trent when he passed her the bowl.

Coco put a hand to her breast. Who would have guessed it? she thought. Her Catherine. The baby of her babies. While the dinner conversation bounced around her, she sat back with a quiet sigh. She couldn't be mistaken. Why, when Trent had looked at her little girl—and she at him— there hadn't just been a spark. There had been a sizzle.

C.C. was scowling, it was true, but it was such a *passionate* scowl. And Trent had smirked, but it was such a *personal* smirk. Positively intimate, Coco decided.

Sitting there, watching them, as Alex devoured his little decapitated heads, and Lilah and Amanda argued over the possibility of life on other planets, Coco could almost hear the loving thoughts C.C. and Trent sent out to each other.

Arrogant, self-important jerk.

Rude, bad-tempered brat.

Who the hell does he think he is, sitting at the table as if he already owned it?

A pity she doesn't have a personality to match her looks.

Coco smiled fondly at them while the "Wedding March" hummed through her head. Like a general plotting strategy, she waited until after coffee and dessert to spring her next offensive.

"C.C., why don't you show Trenton the gardens?"

"What?" She looked up from her friendly fight with Alex over the last bite of her Black Forest cake.

"The gardens," Coco repeated. "There's nothing like a little fresh air after a meal. And the flowers are exquisite in the moonlight."

"Let Suzanna take him."

"Sorry." Suzanna was already gathering a heavy-eyed Jenny into her arms. "I've got to get these two washed up and ready for bed."

"I don't see why—" C.C. broke off at the arched look from her aunt. "Oh, all right." She rose. "Come on then," she said to Trent and started out without him.

"It was a lovely meal, Coco. Thank you."

"My pleasure." She beamed, imagining whispered words and soft, secret kisses. "Enjoy the gardens."

Trent walked out of the terrace doors to find C.C. standing, tapping a booted foot on the stone. It was time, he thought, that someone taught the green-eyed witch a lesson in manners.

"I don't know anything about flowers," she told him.

"Or about simple courtesy."

Her chin angled. "Now listen, buddy."

"No, you listen, buddy." His hand snaked out and snagged her arm. "Let's walk. The children might still be within earshot, and I don't think they're ready to hear any of this."

He was stronger than she'd imagined. He pulled her along, ignoring the curses she tossed out under her breath. They were off the terrace and onto one of the meandering paths that wound around the side of the house. Daffodils and hyacinths nodded along the verge.

He stopped beneath an arbor where wisteria would bloom in another month. C.C. wasn't certain if the roar in her head was the sound of the sea or her own ragged temper.

"Don't you ever do that again." She lifted a hand to rub where his fingers had dug. "You may be able to push people around in Boston, but not here. Not with me or any of my family."

He paused, hoping and failing to get a grip on his own temper. "If you knew me, or what I do, you'd know I don't make a habit of pushing anyone around."

"I know exactly what you do."

"Foreclose on widows and orphans? Grow up, C.C."

She set her teeth. "You can see the gardens on your own. I'm going in."

He merely shifted to block her path. In the moonlight, her eyes glowed like a cat's. When she lifted her hands to shove him aside, he clamped his fingers onto her wrists. In the brief tug-of-war that followed, he noted—irrelevantly he assured himself—that her skin was the color of fresh cream and almost as soft.

"We're not finished." His voice had an edge that was no longer coated with a polite veneer. "You'll have to learn that when you're deliberately rude, and deliberately insulting, there's a price."

"You want an apology?" she all but spat at him. "Okay. I'm sorry I don't have anything to say to you that isn't rude or insulting."

He smiled, surprising both of them. "You're quite a piece of work, Catherine Colleen Calhoun. For the life of me I can't figure out why I'm trying to be reasonable with you."

"Reasonable?" She didn't spit the word this time, but growled it. "You call it reasonable to drag me around, manhandle me—"

"If you call this manhandling, you've led a very sheltered life."

Her complexion went from creamy white to bright pink. "My life is none of your concern."

"Thank God."

Her fingers flexed then balled into fists. She hated the fact, loathed it, that her pulse was hammering double time under his grip. "Will you let me go?"

"Only if you promise not to take off running." He could see himself chasing her, and the image was both embarrassing and appealing.

"I don't run from anyone."

"Spoken like a true Amazon," he murmured, and released her. Only quick reflexes had him dodging the fist she aimed at his nose. "I should have taken that into account, I suppose. Have you ever considered intelligent conversation?"

"I don't have anything to say to you." She was ashamed to have struck out at him and furious that she'd missed. "If you want to talk, go suck up to Aunt Coco some more." In a huff, she plopped down on the small stone bench under the arbor. "Better yet, go back to Boston and flog one of your underlings."

"I can do that anytime." He shook his head and, certain he was taking his life in his hands, sat beside her.

There were azaleas and geraniums threatening to burst into bloom around them. It should, he thought, have been a peaceful place. But as he sat, smelling the tender fragrance of the earliest spring blooms mixed with the scent of the sea, listening to some night bird call its mate, he thought that no boardroom had ever been so tense or hostile.

"I wonder where you developed such a high opinion of me." And why, he added to himself, it seemed to matter.

"You come here—"

"By invitation."

"Not mine." She tossed back her head. "You come in your big car and your dignified suit, ready to sweep my home out from under me."

"I came," he corrected, "to get a firsthand look at a piece of property. No one, least of all me, can force you to sell."

But he was wrong, she thought miserably. There were people who could force them to sell. The people who collected the taxes, the utility bills, the mortgage they'd been forced to take out. All of her frustration, and her fear, over every collection agency centered on the man beside her.

"I know your type," she muttered. "Born rich and above the common man. Your only goal in life is to make more money, regardless of who is affected or trampled over. You have big parties and summer houses and mistresses named Fawn."

Wisely he swallowed the chuckle. "I've never even known a woman named Fawn."

"Oh, what does it matter?" She rose to pace the path. "Kiki, Vanessa, Ava, it's all the same."

"If you say so." She looked, he was forced to admit, magnificent, striding up and down the path with the moonlight shooting around her like white fire. The tug of attraction annoyed him more than a little, but he continued to sit. There was a deal to be done, he reminded himself. And C. C. Calhoun was the foremost stumbling block.

So he would be patient, Trent told himself, and wily and find the hook. "Just how is it you know so much about my type?"

"Because my sister was married to one of you."

"Baxter Dumont."

"You know him?" Then she shook her head and jammed her hands into her pockets. "Stupid question. You probably play golf with him every Wednesday."

"No, actually our acquaintance is only slight. I do know of him, and his family. I'm also aware that he and your sister have been divorced for a year or so."

"He made her life hell, scraped away her self-esteem, then dumped her and his children for some little French pastry. And because he's a big-shot lawyer from a big-shot family, she's left with nothing but a miserly child-support check that comes late every month."

"I'm sorry for what happened to your sister." He rose as well. His voice was no longer sharp but fatalistic. "Marriage is often the least pleasant of all business transactions. But Baxter Dumont's behavior doesn't mean that every member of every prominent Boston family is unethical or immoral."

"They all look the same from where I'm standing."

"Then maybe you should change positions. But you won't, because you're too hardheaded and opinionated."

"Just because I'm smart enough to see through you."

"You know nothing about me, and we both know that you took an uncanny dislike to me before you even knew my name."

"I didn't like your shoes?"

That stopped him. "I beg your pardon?"

"You heard me." She folded her arms and realized she was starting to enjoy herself. "I didn't like your shoes." She flicked a glance down at them. "I still don't."

"That explains everything."

"I didn't like your tie, either." She poked a finger on it, missing the quick flare in his eyes. "Or your fancy gold pen." She tapped a fist lightly at his breast pocket.

He studied her jeans, worn through at the knees, her T-shirt and scuffed boots. "This from an obvious fashion expert."

"You're the one out of place here, Mr. St. James III."

He took a step closer. C.C.'s lips curved in a challenging smile. "And I suppose you dress like a man because you haven't figured out how to act like a woman."

It was a bull's-eye, but the dart point only pricked her temper. "Just because I know how to stand up for myself instead of swooning at your feet doesn't make me less of a woman."

"Is that what you call this?" He wrapped his fingers around her forearms. "Standing up for yourself?"

"That's right. I—" She broke off when he tugged her closer. Their bodies bumped. Trent watched the temper in her eyes deepen to confusion.

"What do you think you're doing?"

"Testing the theory." He looked down at her mouth. Her lips were full, just parted. Very tempting. Why hadn't he noticed that before? he wondered vaguely. That big, insulting mouth of hers was incredibly tempting.

"Don't you dare." She meant it to come out as an order, but her voice shook.

His eyes came back to hers and held. "Afraid?"

The question was just the one to stiffen her spine. "Of course not. It's just that I'd rather be kissed by a rabid skunk."

She started to pull back, then found herself tight against him, eyes and mouth lined up, warm breath mingling. He hadn't intended to kiss her—certainly not—until she'd thrown that last insult in his face.

"You never know when to quit, Catherine. It's a flaw that's going to get you in trouble, starting now."

She hadn't expected his mouth to be so hot, so hard, so hungry. She had thought the kiss would be sophisticated and bland. Easily resisted, easily forgotten. But she had been wrong. Dangerously wrong. Kissing him was like sliding into molten silver. Even as she gasped for air, he heightened the kiss, plunging his tongue deep, taunting, tormenting, teasing hers. She tried to shake her head but succeeded only in changing the angle. The hands that had reached for his shoulders in protest slid possessively around his neck.

He'd thought to teach her a lesson—about what he'd forgotten. But he learned. He learned that some women—this woman—could be strong and soft, frustrating and delightful, all at once. As the waves crashed far below, he felt himself battered by the unexpected. And the unwanted.

He thought, foolishly, that he could feel the starlight on her skin, taste the moondust on her lips. The groan he heard, vibrating low, was his own.

He lifted his head, shaking it, as if to clear the fog that had settled over his brain. He could see her eyes, staring up at his—dark, dazed.

"I beg your pardon." Stunned by his action, he released her so quickly that she stumbled back even as her hands slid away from him. "That was completely inexcusable."

She said nothing, could say nothing. Feelings, too many of them, clogged in her throat. Instead she made a helpless gesture with her hands that made him feel like a lower form of life.

"Catherine...believe me, I don't make a habit of—" He had to stop and clear his dry throat. Lord, he wanted to do it again, he realized. He wanted to kiss the breath from her as she stood there, looking lost and helpless. And beautiful. "I'm terribly sorry. It won't happen again."

"I'd like you to leave me alone." Never in her life had she been more moved. Or more devastated. He had just opened up a door to some secret world, then slammed it again in her face.

"All right." He had to stop himself from reaching out to touch her hair. He started back down the path toward the house. When he looked back, she was still standing as he had left her, staring into the shadows, with moonlight showering her.

His name is Christian. I have found myself walking along the cliffs again and again, hoping for a few words with him. I tell myself it's because of my fascination with art, not the artist. It could be true. It must be true.

I am a married woman and mother of three. And though Fergus is not the romantic husband of my girlish dreams, he is a good provider, and sometimes kind. Perhaps there is some part of me, some small defiant part that wishes I had not bent to my parents' insistence that I make a good and proper marriage. But this is foolishness, for the deed has been done for more than four years.

It's disloyal to compare Fergus with a man I hardly know. Yet here, in my private journal, I must be allowed this indulgence. While Fergus thinks only of business, the next deal or dollar, Christian speaks of dreams and images and poetry.

How my heart has yearned for just a little poetry.

While Fergus, with his cool and careless generosity, gave me the emeralds on the day of Ethan's birth, Christian once offered me a wildflower. I have kept it, pressing it here between these pages. How much lovelier I would feel wearing it than those cold and heavy gems.

We have spoken of nothing intimate, nothing that could be considered improper. Yet I know it is. The way he looks at me, smiles, speaks, is gloriously improper. The way I look for him on these bright summer afternoons while my babies nap is not the action of a proper wife. The way my heart drums in my breast when I see him is disloyalty in itself.

Today I sat upon a rock and watched him wield his brush, bringing those pink and gray rocks, that blue, blue water to life on canvas. There was a boat gliding along, so free, so solitary. For a moment I pictured the two of us there, faces to the wind. I don't understand why I have these thoughts, but while they remained with me, clear as crystal, I asked his name.

"Christian," he said. "Christian Bradford. And you are Bianca."

The way he said my name—as if it had never been said before. I will never forget it. I toyed with the wild grass that pushed itself through the cracks in the rocks. With my eyes cast down, I asked him why his wife never came to watch him work.

"I have no wife," he told me. "And art is my only mistress."

It was wrong for my heart to swell so at his words. Wrong of me to smile, yet I smiled. And he in return. If fate had dealt differently with me, if time and place could have been altered in some way, I could have loved him.

I think I would have had no choice but to love him.

As if we both knew this, we began to talk of inconsequential matters. But when I rose, knowing my time here was at an end for the day, he bent over and plucked up a tiny spike of golden heather and slipped it into my hair. For a moment, his fingers hovered over my cheek and his eyes were on mine. Then he stepped away and bid me good day.

Now I sit with the lamp low as I write, listening to Fergus's voice rumble as he instructs his valet next door. He will not come to me tonight, and I find myself grateful. I have given him three children, two sons and a daughter. By providing him with an heir, I have done my duty, and he does not often find the need to come to my bed. I am, like the children, to exist to be well dressed and well mannered, and to be presented at the proper occasions—like a good claret—for his guests.

It is not much to ask, I suppose. It is a good life, one I should be content with. Perhaps I was content, until that day I first walked along the cliffs.

So tonight, I will sleep alone in my bed, and dream of a man who is not my husband.

Chapter Four

When you couldn't sleep, the best thing to do was get up. That's what C.C. told herself as she sat at the kitchen table, watching the sunrise and drinking her second cup of coffee.

She had a lot on her mind, that was all. Bills, the dyseptic Oldsmobile that was first on her schedule that morning, bills, an upcoming dentist appointment. More bills. Trenton St. James was far down on her list of concerns. Somewhere below a potential cavity and just ahead of a faulty exhaust system.

She certainly wasn't losing any sleep over him. And a kiss, that ridiculous—*accident* was the best term she could use to describe it—wasn't even worth a moment's thought.

Yet she had thought of little else throughout the long, sleepless night.

She was acting as though she'd never been kissed before, C.C. berated herself. And, of course, she had, starting with Denny Dinsmore, who had planted the first sloppy mouth-to-mouth on her after their eighth-grade Valentine's dance.

Naturally there had been no comparison between Denny's fumbling yet sincere attempt and the stunning expertise of Trent's. Which only proved, C.C. decided as she scowled into her coffee, that Trent had spent a large part of his life with his lips slapped up against some woman's. Lots of women's.

It had been a rotten thing to do, she thought now. Particularly in the middle of what had been becoming a very satisfactory argument. Men like Trent didn't know how to fight fair, with wit and words and good honest fury. They were taught how to dominate, by whatever manner worked.

Well, it had worked, she thought, running a fingertip over her lips. Damn him and the horse he rode in on. It had worked like a charm, because for one moment, one brief, trembling moment she had felt something fine and lovely—something more than the exciting press of his mouth on hers, more than the possessive grip of his hands.

It had been inside her, beneath the panic and the pleasure, beyond the whirl of sensation—a glow, warm and golden, like a lamp in the window on a stormy night.

Then he had turned off that lamp, with one quick, careless flick, leaving her in the dark again.

She could have hated him for that alone, C.C. thought miserably, if she hadn't already had enough to hate him for.

"Hey, kid." Lilah breezed through the doorway, tidy in her park service khakis. Her mass of hair was in a neat braid down her back. Swinging at each ear was a trio of amber crystal balls. "You're up early."

"Me?" C.C. forgot her own mood long enough to stare. "Are you my sister or some clever imposter?"

"You be the judge."

"Must be an imposter. Lilah Maeve Calhoun's never up before eight o'clock, which is exactly twenty minutes before she has to rush out of the house to be five minutes late for work."

"God, I hate to be so predictable. My horoscope," Lilah told her as she rooted through the refrigerator. "It said that I should rise early today and contemplate the sunrise."

"So how was it?" C.C. asked as her sister brought a cold can of soda and a wicked slice of the Black Forest cake to the table.

"Pretty spectacular as sunrises go." Lilah shoveled cake into her mouth. "What's your excuse?"

"Couldn't sleep."

"Anything to do with the stranger at the end of the hall?"

C.C. wrinkled her nose and filched a cherry from Lilah's plate. "Guys like that don't bother me."

"Guys like that were created to bother women, and thank God for it. So..." Lilah stretched her legs out to rest her feet on an empty chair. The kitchen faucet was leaking again, but she liked the sound of it. "What's the story?"

"I didn't say there was a story."

"You don't have to say, it's all over your face."

"I just don't like him being here, that's all." Evading, C.C. rose to take her cup to the sink. "It's like we're already being pushed out of our own home. I know we've discussed selling, but it was all so vague and down some long, dark road." She turned back to her sister. "Lilah, what are we going to do?"

"I don't know." Lilah's eyes clouded. It was one of the few things she couldn't prevent herself from worrying about. Home and family, they were her weaknesses. "I guess we could sell some more of the crystal, and there's the silver."

"It would break Aunt Coco's heart to sell the silver."

"I know. But we may have to go piece by piece—or make the big move." She scooped up some more cake. "As much as I hate to say it, we're going to have to think hard, and practically, and seriously."

"But, Lilah, a hotel?"

Lilah merely shrugged. "I don't have any deep, moral problem with that. The house was built by crazy old Fergus to entertain platoons of guests, with all kinds of people racing around to serve meals and tidy linens. It seems to me that a hotel just about suits its original purpose." She gave a long sigh at C.C.'s expression. "You know I love the place as much as you do."

"I know."

What Lilah didn't add was that it would break her heart to have to sell it but that she was prepared to do what was best for the family.

"We'll give the gorgeous Mr. St. James a couple more days, then have a family meeting." She offered C.C. a bolstering smile. "The four of us together can't go wrong."

"I hope you're right."

"Honey, I'm always right—that's my little cross to bear." She took a swig of the sugar-ladened soft drink. "Now, why don't you tell me what kept you up all night?"

"I just did."

"No." Head cocked, she waved her fork at C.C. "Don't forget Lilah knows all and sees all—and what she doesn't she finds out. So spill it."

"Aunt Coco made me take him out in the garden."

"Yeah." Lilah grinned. "She's a wily old devil. I figured she was plotting some romance. Moonlight, flowers, the distant lap of water on rocks. Did it work?"

"We had a fight."

Lilah nodded, giving a go-ahead signal with her hand as she sipped. "That's a good start. About the house?"

"That..." C.C. began to pluck dried leaves from a withered philodendron. "And things."

"Like?"

"Names of mistresses," C.C. muttered. "Prominent Boston families. His shoes."

"An eclectic argument. My favorite kind. And then?"

C.C. jammed her hands into her pockets. "He kissed me."

"Ah, the plot thickens." She had Coco's love of gossip and, leaning forward, cradled her chin on her hands. "So, how was it? He's got a terrific mouth—I noticed it right off."

"So kiss him yourself."

After thinking it over a moment, Lilah shook her head—not without some regret. "Nope, terrific mouth or not, he's not my type. Anyway, you've already locked lips with him, so tell me. Was he good?"

"Yeah," C.C. said grudgingly. "I guess you could say that."

"Like on a scale of one to ten?"

The chuckle escaped before C.C. realized she was laughing. "I wasn't exactly thinking about a rating system at the time."

"Better and better." Lilah licked her fork clean. "So, he kissed you and it was pretty good. Then what?"

Humor vanished as C.C. blew out a long breath. "He apologized."

Lilah stared, then slowly, deliberately set down her fork. "He what?"

"Apologized—very properly for his inexcusable behavior, and promised it wouldn't happen again. The jerk." C.C. crumbled the dead leaves in her hand. "What kind of a man thinks a woman wants an apology after she's been kissed boneless?"

Lilah only shook her head. "Well, the way I see it, there are three choices. He *is* a jerk, he's been trained to be overly polite, or he was incapable of thinking rationally."

"I vote for jerk."

"Hmm. I'm going to have to think about this." She drummed her cerise-tipped fingers on the table. "Maybe I should do his chart."

"Whatever sign his moon is in, I still vote for jerk." C.C. walked over to kiss Lilah's cheek. "Thanks. Gotta go."

"C.C." She waited until her sister turned back. "He has nice eyes. When he smiles, he has very nice eyes."

Trent wasn't smiling when he finally managed to escape from The Towers that afternoon. Coco had insisted on giving him a tour of the cellars, every damp inch, then had trapped him with photo albums for two hours.

It had been amusing to look at baby pictures of C.C., to view, through snapshots, her growing up from toddler to woman. She had been incredibly cute in pigtails and a missing tooth.

During the second hour, his alarm bells had sounded. Coco had begun to pump him none too subtly about his views on marriage, children, relationships. It was then he'd realized that behind Coco's soft, misty eyes ticked a sharp, calculating brain.

She wasn't trying to sell the house but to auction off one of her nieces. And apparently C.C. was the front-runner, with him preselected as the highest bidder. Well, the Calhoun women were in for a rude awakening, Trent determined. They were going to have to look elsewhere on the marriage market for a suitable candidate—and good luck to him.

And the St. Jameses would have the house, Trent promised himself. By damn they would, with no strings or wedding veils attached.

He started down the steep, winding drive in a controlled fury. When he caught the sound of his own voice as he muttered to himself, Trent decided that he would take a long, calming drive. Perhaps to Acadia National Park where Lilah worked as a naturalist. Divide and conquer, he thought. He would seek out each of the women in their own work space and rattle their beautiful chains.

Lilah seemed to be receptive, he thought. Any one of them would be more so that C.C. Amanda appeared to be sensible. He was certain Suzanna was a reasonable woman.

What had gone wrong with sister number four?

But he found himself heading down to the village, past Suzanna's fledgling landscape and garden business, past the BayWatch Hotel. When he drove up to C.C.'s garage, he told himself that was what he'd meant to do all along.

He would start with her, the sharpest thorn in his side. And when he was done, she would have no illusions about trapping him into marriage.

Hank was climbing into the tow truck as Trent climbed out of the BMW. "'Lo." Grinning, Hank pulled on the brim of his gray cap. "Boss's inside. Got us a nice fender bender over at the visitor's center."

"Congratulations."

"Ayah, we've been needing a little bodywork 'round here. Now, once the season picks up, business'll boom." Hank slammed the door then leaned his head out of the window, disposed to chat.

For some reason, Trent found himself noticing the boy—really noticing him. He was young, probably about twenty, with a round, open face, a thick down-east accent and a shock of straw-colored hair that shot out in all directions.

"Have you worked for C.C. long?"

"Since she bought the place from old Pete. That'll be, ah, three years. Ayah. Three years, nearly. She wouldn't hire me till I finished high school. Funny that way."

"Is she?"

"Once she gets a bee in her bonnet ain't no shaking it loose." He nodded toward the garage. "She's a might touchy today."

"Is that unusual?"

Hank chuckled and switched the radio on high. "Can't say she's all bark and no bite, 'cause I've seen her bite a time or two. See ya."

"Sure."

When Trent walked in, C.C. was buried to the waist under the hood of a late-model sedan. She had the radio on again, but this time it was her hips rather than her boots keeping time.

"Excuse me," Trent began, then remembered they had been through that routine before. He walked up and tapped her smartly on the shoulder.

"If you'd just..." But she turned her head only enough to see the tie. It wasn't maroon today, but navy. Still, she was certain of its owner. "What do you want?"

"I believe it was a lube job."

"Oh." She went back to replacing spark plugs. "Well, leave it outside, put the key on the bench, and I'll get to it. It should be ready by six."

"Do you always do business so casually?"

"Yeah."

"If you don't mind, I think I'll hold on to my keys until you're less distracted."

"Suit yourself." Two minutes passed in humming silence broken only by the radio's prediction of thunderstorms that evening. "Look, if you're just going to stand around, why don't you do something useful? Get in and start her up."

"Start her up?"

"Yeah, you know. Turn the key, pump the gas." She cocked her head up and blew at her bangs. "Think you can handle it?"

"Probably." It wasn't exactly what he'd had in mind, but Trent walked around to the driver's side. He noted that there was a car seat strapped in the front, and something pink and gooey on the carpet. He slid in and turned the key. The engine turned over and purred, quite nicely, he thought. Apparently C.C. thought differently.

Taking up her timing light, she began to make adjustments.

"It sounds fine," Trent pointed out.

"No, there's a miss."

"How can you hear anything with the radio blasting?"

"How can you not hear it? Better," she murmured. "Better."

Curious, he got out to lean over her shoulder. "What are you doing?"

"My job." Her shoulders moved irritably, as if there were an itch between the blades. "Back off, will you?"

"I'm only expressing normal curiosity." Without thinking, he set a hand lightly on her back and leaned farther in. C.C. jolted, felt a flash of pain then swore like a sailor.

"Let me see." He grabbed the hand she was busy shaking.

"It's nothing. Take off, will you? If you hadn't been in my way, my hand wouldn't have slipped."

"Stop dancing around and let me see." He took a firm grip on her wrist and examined her scraped knuckles. The faint well of blood beneath the engine grease caused him a sharp and ridiculous sense of guilt. "You'll need something on this."

"It's just a scratch." God, why wouldn't he let go of her hand? "What I need to do is finish this job."

"Don't be a baby," he said mildly. "Where's the first-aid kit?"

"It's in the bathroom, and I can do it myself."

Ignoring her, he kept hold of her wrist as he walked around to shut the engine off. "Where's the bathroom?"

She jerked her head toward the hallway that separated the garage from the office. "If you'd just leave your keys—"

"You said it was my fault you hurt your hand, so I'll take the responsibility."

"I wish you'd stop pulling me around," she said as he hauled her toward the hallway.

"Then keep up." He pushed open a door into a white-tiled bathroom the size of a broom closet. Ignoring her protests, he held C.C.'s hand under a spray of cool water. The dimensions of the room had them standing hip to hip. They both did their level best to ignore that as he took the soap and, with surprising gentleness, began to clean her hand. "It isn't deep," he said, annoyed that his throat was dry.

"I told you, it's just a scratch."

"Scratches get infected."

"Yes, doctor."

With a retort on the tip of his tongue, he glanced up. She looked so cute, he thought, with grease on her nose and her mouth in a five-year-old's pout. "I'm sorry," he heard himself say, and the petulance faded from her eyes.

"It wasn't your fault." Wanting something to do, she opened the mirrored cabinet over the sink for the first-aid kit. "I can take care of it, really."

"I like to finish what I start." He took the kit from her and found the antiseptic. "I guess I should say this is going to sting."

"I already know it stings." C.C. let out a little hiss as he swabbed the cut. Automatically she leaned over to blow on the heat, just as he did the same. Their heads bumped smartly. Rubbing hers with her free hand, C.C. gave a half laugh. "We make a lousy team."

"It certainly looks that way." With his eyes on hers, Trent blew softly on her knuckles. Something flickered in those pretty green irises, he noted. Alarm, surprise, pleasure, he couldn't be sure, but he would have wagered half his stock options that C. C. Calhoun was totally ignorant of her aunt's romantic plotting.

He brought her hand to his lips—just a test, he assured himself—and watched what was definitely confusion darken her eyes. Her hand went limp in his. Her mouth opened and stayed that way, with no sound coming out.

"A kiss is supposed to make it better," he pointed out and, for purely selfish reasons, whispered his lips over her hand again.

"I think... it would be better if..." Lord, the room was small, she thought distractedly. And getting smaller all the time. "Thanks," she managed. "I'm sure it's fine now."

"It needs to be bandaged."

"Oh, well, I don't—"

"You'll only get it dirty." Enjoying himself enormously, he took a roll of gauze and began to wrap her hand.

Thinking it would put some distance between them, C.C. turned. As if following the moves of a dance, Trent turned as well. Now they were facing, rather than side-by-side. He shifted—there was room to do little else—and her back was against the wall.

"Hurt?"

She shook her head. She wasn't hurt, C.C. decided, she was crazy. A woman had to be crazy to have her heart pounding like a jackhammer because a man was wrapping gauze around her skinned knuckles.

"C.C." He taped the gauze competently in place. "Can I ask you a personal question?"

"I..." She lifted her shoulders and swallowed.

"What exactly is a lube job?"

She caught the amusement in his eyes, and, charmed by it, smiled back. "Forty-seven-fifty."

"Oh." They were as close as they had been the night before, when they'd been arguing. This, Trent decided, was much more pleasant. "Are you going to flush my radiator?"

"Absolutely."

"Then I'm forgiven for last night?"

Her brows lifted. "I didn't say that."

"I wish you'd reconsider." With her hand held between them, he shifted slightly closer. "You see, if I'm going to be damned for it, it's harder to resist the urge to sin again."

Flustered, she pressed back against the wall. "I don't think you're the least bit sorry about what you did."

He considered her a moment, the wide eyes, the tempting mouth. "I'm afraid you're right."

As she stood, torn between delight and terror, the phone began to shrill. "I've got to get that." Nimble as a greyhound, she streaked by him and out of the room.

He followed more slowly, surprised at himself. There was no doubt in his mind that she was as much victim of her aunt's fantasies as he. Another woman, certainly one with matrimony on her mind, would have smiled—or pouted. Would have slid her arms seductively around him—or held him sulkily away. But another woman would not have stood with her back planted against the wall as if facing a firing squad. Another woman would not have looked at him with big, helpless eyes and stammered.

Or looked so alluring while she did so.

C.C. snatched up the phone in her office, but her mind was blank. She stood, staring through the glass wall with the phone at her ear for ten silent seconds before the voice through the receiver brought her back.

"What? Oh, yes, yes, this is C.C. Sorry. Is that you, Finney?" She let out a long, pent-up breath as she listened. "Did you leave the lights on again? Are you sure? Okay, okay. It might be the starter motor." She ran a distracted hand through her hair and started to ease a hip down on the desk when she spotted Trent. She popped back up like a spring. "What? I'm sorry, could you say that again? Uh-huh. Why don't I come take a look at it on my way home? About six-thirty." Her lips curved. "Sure. I always have a taste for lobster. You bet. Bye."

"A mechanic who makes house calls," Trent commented.

"We take care of our own." Relax, she ordered herself. Relax right now. "Besides it's easy when there's the offer of an Albert Finney lob-stah dinner on the other end."

There was a tug of annoyance he tried mightily to ignore. "How's the hand?"

She wriggled her fingers. "Fine. Why don't you hang your keys on the pegboard?"

He did so. "Do you realize you've never called me by name?"

"Of course I have."

"No, you've called me names, but never by my name." He lifted a hand to gesture the thought away. "In any case, I need to talk to you."

"Listen, if it's about the house, this really isn't the time or place."

"It isn't, precisely."

"Oh." She looked at him, feeling that odd little jolt in her heart. "I'm really getting backed up. Can it wait until you pick up your car?"

He wasn't used to waiting for anything. "It won't take long. I feel I should warn you, as I believe you're as unaware as I was, of your aunt's plans."

"Aunt Coco? What plans?"

"The white-lace-and-orange-blossom type of plans."

Her expression went from baffled to stunned to suspicion. "Marriage? That's absurd. Aunt Coco's not planning to be married. She doesn't even see anyone seriously."

"I don't think she's the candidate." He walked toward her, keeping his eyes on her. "You are."

Her laugh was quick and full of fun as she sat on the edge of the desk. "Me? Married? That's rich."

"Yes, and so am I.'

Her laughter dried up. Using the palms of her hands, she levered herself off the desk. When she spoke, her voice was very cool, with licks of temper beneath. "Exactly what are you implying?"

"That your aunt, for reasons of her own, invited me here not only to look over the house, but her four very attractive nieces."

Her face went dead pale, as he now knew it did when she was desperately angry. "That's insulting."

"That's a fact."

"Get out." She gave him one hard shove toward the door. "Get out. Get your keys, your car and your ridiculous accusations and get out."

"Hold on and shut up for one minute." He took her firmly by the shoulders. "Just one minute, and when I'm done if you still think I'm being ridiculous, I'll leave."

"I know you're ridiculous. And conceited, and arrogant. If you think for one minute that I have—have designs on you—"

"Not you," he corrected with a little shake. "Your well-meaning aunt. 'Why don't you show Trenton the garden, C.C.? The flowers are exquisite in the moonlight.'"

"She was just being polite."

"In a pig's eye. Do you know how I spent my morning?"

"I couldn't be less interested."

"Looking through photo albums." He saw the anger turn to distress and pressed on. "Dozens of them. You were quite the adorable child, Catherine."

"Oh, God."

"And bright, too, according to your doting aunt. Spelling bee champ in the third grade."

With a strangled groan, she lowered to the desk again.

"Not a single cavity in your mouth."

"She didn't," C.C. managed.

"Oh, that and more. Top honors in your auto mechanics class in high school. Using the bulk of your inheritance to buy this shop from your employer. I'm told you're a very sensible woman who knows how to keep her feet on the ground. Then again, you come from excellent stock and were well-bred."

"Like a holstein," she muttered, firing up.

"As you like. Naturally, with your background, brains and beauty, you'd make the right man the most excellent of wives."

She was no longer pale, but blushing furiously. "Just because Aunt Coco's proud of me doesn't mean she's asking you to pick out a silver pattern."

"After she finished relating your virtues and showing me the pictures—quite lovely ones—of you in your prom dress."

"My—" C.C. only shut her eyes.

"She began to ask me my views on marriage and children. Dropping rather large, heavy hints that a man in my position needs a stable relationship with a stable woman. Such as yourself."

"All right, all right. Enough." She opened her eyes again. "Aunt Coco often gets ideas in her head about what's best for my sisters and me. If she goes overboard." C.C. set her teeth. "When she goes overboard, it's only because she loves us and feels responsible. I'm sorry she made you uncomfortable."

"I didn't tell you this to embarrass you or to have you apologize." Suddenly awkward, he slipped his hands into his pockets. "I thought it best if you knew the way her thoughts were headed before, well, something got out of hand."

"Got out of hand?" C.C. repeated.

"Or was misunderstood." Odd, he thought, it was usually so easy to lay the ground rules. He certainly couldn't remember fumbling before. "That is, after last night . . . I realize you've been sheltered to a certain degree."

The fingers of C.C.'s good hand began to drum on the knee of her coveralls.

Perhaps he should start again. "I believe in honesty, C.C., in both my business and my personal relationships. Last night, between temper and the moonlight, we—I suppose you could say we lost control for a moment." Why did that seem so pale and inadequate a description for what had happened? "I wouldn't want your lack of experience, and your aunt's fantasies to result in a misunderstanding."

"Let me see if I get this. You're concerned that because you kissed me last night, and my aunt brought up the subject of marriage along with my baby pictures this morning, that I might get some wild idea in my head that I might be the next Mrs. St. James."

Thrown off, he ran a hand over his hair. "More or less. I thought it would be better, certainly more fair, if I told you straight off so that you and I could handle it reasonably. That way you wouldn't—"

"Develop any delusions of grandeur?" she suggested.

"Don't put words in my mouth."

"How can I? There's no room with your foot in there."

"Damn it." He hated the fact that she was absolutely right. "I'm simply trying to be perfectly honest with you so that there won't be any misunderstanding when I tell you I'm very attracted to you."

She only lifted a brow, too furious to see that his own words had left him speechless. "Now, I take it, I'm supposed to be flattered."

"You're not supposed to be anything. I'm merely trying to lay out the facts."

"I'll give you some facts." She shoved a hand into his chest. "You're not attracted to me, you're attracted to the image of the perfect and enviable Trenton St. James III. My aunt's fantasies, as you call them, are a result of a wonderful loving heart. Something I'm sure you can't understand. And as far as I'm concerned, I wouldn't think about spending five minutes with you much less the rest of my life. You may end up with my home, but not with me, buster." She was revving up and feeling wonderful. "If you came crawling to me on your hands and knees with a diamond as big as my fist in your teeth, I'd laugh in your face. Those are the facts. I'm sure you can find your way out."

She turned and strode down the hall. Trent winced as the door slammed.

"Well," he murmured, pressing his fingers to his eyes. "We certainly cleared that up."

Chapter Five

Insufferable. It was the perfect word to describe him, C.C. decided, and hugged it to her throughout the rest of the day.

By the time she got home, the house was quiet and settled for the night. She could hear, faintly, the soft and haunting notes of the piano from the music room. Turning away from the stairs, she followed the music.

It was Suzanna, of course, who sat at the lovely old spinet. She had been the only one who had stuck with the lessons or shown any real talent. Amanda had been too impatient, Lilah too lazy. And C.C.... She looked down at her hands. Her fingers had been more at home smeared with motor oil than at the keys of a piano.

Still she loved to listen. There was nothing that soothed or charmed her more than music.

Suzanna, lost somewhere in her own heart, sighed a little as the last notes died.

"That was beautiful." C.C. walked over to kiss her sister's hair.

"I'm rusty."

"Not from where I'm standing."

Smiling, Suzanna reached back to pat her hand and felt the gauze. "Oh, C.C., what did you do?"

"Just scraped my knuckles."

"Did you clean it well? When was your last tetanus shot?"

"Slow down, Mommy. It's clean as a whistle and I had a tetanus shot six months ago." C.C. sat on the bench, facing out into the room. "Where is everyone?"

"The kids are fast asleep—I hope. Wiggle your fingers."

C.C. sighed and complied.

With a satisfied nod, Suzanna continued. "Lilah's out on a date. Mandy's looking over some ledger or other. Aunt Coco went up hours ago to have a bubble bath and put cucumber slices on her eyes."

"What about him?"

"In bed, I imagine. It's nearly midnight."

"Is it?" Then she smiled. "You were waiting up for me."

"I was not." Caught, Suzanna laughed. "Exactly. Did you fix Mr. Finney's truck?"

"He left his lights on again." She yawned hugely. "I think he does it on purpose just so I can come over and recharge his battery." She stretched her arms to the ceiling. "We had lobster and dandelion wine."

"If he wasn't old enough to be your grandfather, I'd say he has a crush on you."

"He does. And it's mutual. So, did I miss anything around here?"

"Aunt Coco wants to have a séance."

"Not again."

Suzanna ran her hands lightly over the keys, improvising. "Tomorrow night, right after dinner. She insists there's something Great-Grandmother Bianca wants us to know—Trent, too."

"What does he have to do with it?"

Suzanna brushed at C.C.'s bangs. "If we decide to sell him the house, he'll more or less inherit her."

"Is that what we're going to do, Suzanna?"

"It might be what we have to do."

C.C. rose to toy with the tassels of the floor lamp. "My business is doing pretty good. I could take out a loan against it."

"No."

"But—"

"No," Suzanna repeated. "You're not going to risk your future on the past."

"It's my future."

"And it's our past." She rose, as well. When that light came into Suzanna's eyes, even C.C. knew better than to argue. "I know how much the house means to you, to all of us. Coming back here after Bax—after things didn't work out," Suzanna said carefully, "helped keep me sane. Every time I watch Alex or Jenny slide down the banister, I remember doing it myself. I see Mama sitting here at the piano, hear Papa telling stories in front of the fire."

"Then how can you even think of selling?"

"Because I learned to face realities, however unpleasant." She lifted a hand to C.C.'s cheek. Only five years separated them. Sometimes Suzanna felt it was fifty. "Sometimes things happen to you, or around you, that you just can't control. When that happens, you gather up what's important in your life, and go on."

"But the house is important."

"How much longer do you really think we can hang on?"

"We could sell the lithographs, the Limoges, a few other things."

"And drag out the unhappiness." She knew entirely too much about that. "If it's time to let go, I think we should let go with some dignity."

"Then you've already made up your mind."

"No." Suzanna sighed and sat again. "Every time I think I have, I change it. Before dinner, the children and I walked along the cliffs." Eyes dreamy, she stared through the darkened window. "When I stand there, looking out over the bay, I feel something, something so incredible, it breaks my heart. I don't know what's right, C.C. I don't know what's best. But I'm afraid I know what has to be done."

"It hurts."

"I know."

C.C. sat beside her, rested her head on Suzanna's shoulder. "Maybe there'll be a miracle."

Trent watched them from the darkened hallway. He wished he hadn't heard them. He wished he didn't care. But he had heard, and for reasons he didn't choose to explore, he did care. Quietly he went back up the stairs.

"Children," Coco said with what she was certain was the last of her sanity, "why don't you read a nice book?"

"I want to play war." Alex swished an imaginary saber through the air. "Death to the last man."

And the child was only six, Coco thought. What would he be in ten years' time? "Crayons," she said hopefully, cursing rainy Saturday afternoons. "Why don't you both draw beautiful pictures? We can hang them on the refrigerator, like an art show."

"Baby stuff," Jenny said, a cynic at five. She hefted an invisible laser rifle and fired. "Z-z-zap! You're zapped, Alex, and totally disengrated."

"Disintergrated, dummy, and I am not either. I threw up my force field."

"Nuh-uh."

They eyed each other with the mutual dislike only siblings can feel after being cooped up on a Saturday. By tacit agreement, they switched to hand-to-hand combat. As they wrestled over the faded Aubusson carpet, Coco cast her gaze to the ceiling.

At least the match was taking place in Alex's room, so little harm could be done. She was tempted to go out and close the door, leaving them to finish up themselves, but she was, after all, responsible.

"Someone's going to get hurt," she began, in the age-old refrain of adult to child. "Remember what happened last week when Jenny gave you a bloody nose, Alex?"

"She did not." Masculine pride rose to the forefront as he struggled to pin his agile sister to the mat.

"Did too, did too," she chanted, hoping to do so again. She scissored her quick little legs over him.

"Excuse me," Trent said from the doorway. "I seem to be interrupting."

"Not at all." Coco fluffed her hair. "Just some youthful high spirits. Children, say hello to Mr. St. James."

"'Lo," Alex said as he struggled to get his sister into a headlock.

Trent's answering grin struck Coco with inspiration. "Trenton, might I ask you a favor?"

"Of course."

"All the girls are working today, as you know, and I have just one or two quick, little errands to run. Would you mind terribly keeping an eye on the children for a short time?"

"An eye on them?"

"Oh, they're no trouble at all." She beamed at him, then down at her grandniece and grandnephew. "Jenny, don't bite your brother. Calhouns fight fair." Unless they fight dirty, she thought. "I'll be back before you know I'm gone," she promised, easing past him.

"Coco, I'm not sure that I—"

"Oh, and don't forget about the séance tonight." She hurried down the steps and left him to fend for himself.

Jenny and Alex stopped wrestling to stare owlishly at him. They would fight tooth and nail but would unite without hesitation against an outside force.

"We don't like baby-sitters," Alex told him dangerously.

Trent rocked back on his heels. "I'm already sure I don't like being one."

Alex's arm was around his sister's shoulders now, rather than her neck. Hers slipped round his waist. "We don't like it more."

Trent nodded. If he could handle a staff of fifty, he could certainly handle two sulky children. "Okay."

"When we went back to Boston last summer for a visit, we had a sitter." Jenny eyed him with suspicion. "We made everybody's life a living hell."

Trent turned the chuckle into a cough. "Is that so?"

"Our father said we did," Alex corroborated. "And he was glad to see the back of us."

The infant profanity was no longer amusing. Trent struggled to keep the burn of anger out of his eyes and merely nodded. Baxter Dumont was obviously a prince among men. "I once locked my nanny in the closet and climbed out the window."

Alex and Jenny exchanged interested glances. "That's pretty good," Alex decided.

"She screamed for two hours," Trent improvised.

"We put a snake in our baby-sitter's bed and she ran out of the house in her nightgown." Jenny smiled smugly and waited to see if he could top it.

"Nicely done." What now? he wondered. "Have you any dolls?"

"Dolls are gross," Jenny said, loyal to her brother.

"Off with their heads!" Alex shouted, sending her into giggles. He sprang up, flourishing his imaginary sword. "I'm the evil pirate, and you're my prisoners."

"Uh-uh, I had to be prisoner last time." Jenny scrambled to her feet. "It's my turn to be the evil pirate."

"I said it first."

She gave him a hefty shove. "Cheater, cheater, cheater."

"Baby, baby, baby," he jeered, and pushed her back.

"Hold it!" Trent shouted before they could dive for each other. The unfamiliar masculine tone had them stopping in their tracks. "*I'm* the evil pirate," he told them, "and you're both about to walk the plank."

He enjoyed it. Their children's imagination might have been a bit bloody-minded, but they played fair when the rules were set. There would have been any number of people he knew socially who would have been stunned to see Trenton St. James III crawling around on the floor or firing a water pistol, but he could remember being closed in on rainy days himself.

The play went from pirates to space marauders to Indian rampage. At the end of a particularly gruesome battle, the three of them were sprawled on the floor. Alex, rubber tomahawk in hand, played dead so long he fell asleep.

"I won," Jenny said, then with her feather headdress falling over her eyes, cuddled against Trent's side. She, too, in the enviable way of children, was asleep in moments.

C.C. found them like that. The rain was patting gently at the windows. In the bath down the hall, a drip fell musically into a bucket. Otherwise there was only the sound of gentle, even breathing.

Alex was sprawled on his face, his fingers still clutched over his weapon. In addition to bodies, the floor was scattered with miniature cars, defeated action figures and a few plastic dinosaurs. Avoiding the casualties, she stepped inside.

She wasn't exactly sure what her feelings were at finding Trent sleeping on the floor with her niece and nephew. What she was certain of was that if she hadn't seen it for herself, she wouldn't have believed it.

His tie and shoes were gone, his hair mussed, and there was a streak of damp down his linen shirt.

The tug on her heart was slow and tender and very real. Why, he looked…sweet, she thought, then immediately jammed her hands into her pockets. That was absurd. A man like Trent was never sweet.

Maybe the kids had knocked him unconscious, she mused, and leaned over him. He opened his eyes, stared up at her for a moment, then made some kind of sleepy noise deep in his throat.

"What are you doing?" she whispered.

"I'm not completely sure." He lifted his head and looked around. Jenny was tucked into the curve of his arm, and Alex was down for the count on the other side. "But I think I'm the only survivor."

"Where's Aunt Coco?"

"Running a few errands. I'm keeping my eye on the kids."

She lifted a brow. "Oh, I can see that."

"I'm afraid there was a major battle, and many lives were lost."

C.C.'s lips twitched as she went to Alex's bed for a blanket. "Who won?"

"Jenny claimed victory." Gently he slipped his arm out from under her head. "Though Alex will disagree."

"Undoubtedly."

"What should we do with them?"

"Oh, we'll keep them, I suppose."

He grinned back at her. "No, I meant should they be put in bed or something?"

"No." Expertly she flipped open the blanket and spread it over both of them where they lay. "They'll be fine." She had a ridiculous urge to slip an arm around his waist and lay her head on his shoulder. She squashed it ruthlessly. "It was nice of you to offer to look after them."

"I didn't offer precisely. I was dragooned."

"It was still nice of you."

He caught up with her at the door. "I could use a cup of coffee."

C.C. hesitated only a moment. "All right. I'll fix it. It looks like you've earned it." She flicked a glance over her shoulder as she started down the stairs. "How'd your shirt get wet?"

"Oh." He brushed a hand over it, faintly embarrassed. "A direct hit with a death ray disguised as a water pistol. So, how was your day?"

"Not nearly as adventurous as yours." She turned into the kitchen and went directly to the stove. "I only rebuilt an engine."

When the coffee was started, she moved over to light a fire in the kitchen hearth. She had rain in her hair, Trent noticed. He wasn't a lyrical man, but he found himself thinking that the droplets of water looked like a shower of diamonds against the glossy cap.

He'd always preferred women with long hair, he reminded himself. Feminine, soft, wavy. And yet... the style suited C.C., showing off her slender neck, perfectly framing that glorious white skin.

"What are you staring at?"

He blinked, shook his head. "Nothing. Sorry, I was just thinking. It's ah... there's something comforting about a fire in the kitchen."

"Hmm." He looked weird, she thought. Maybe it was the lack of a tie. "Do you want milk in your coffee?"

"No, black."

Her arm brushed his as she walked to the stove. This time it was he who stepped back. "Did Aunt Coco say where she was going?"

Maybe there was static electricity in the air, he thought. That would explain the jolt he'd felt when he'd touched her. "Not exactly. It doesn't matter, the kids were entertaining."

She studied his face as she handed him a mug. "I think you mean it."

"I do. Maybe I haven't been around children enough to become jaded. Those two are quite a pair."

"Suzanna's a terrific mother." Comfortable, she leaned back against the counter as she sipped. "She used to practice on me. So, how's the car running?"

"Better than it has in months." He toasted her with the mug. "I'm afraid I didn't notice anything was off until after you'd worked on it. I don't really know anything about engines."

"That's all right. I don't know how to plot a corporate takeover."

"I was sorry you weren't there when I came around to pick it up. Hank said you'd gone to dinner. I guess you had a good time—you didn't get in until late."

"I always have a good time with Finney." She turned around to raid the cookie jar, then offered him one as he tried to ignore the little nip of jealousy.

"An old friend?"

"I guess you could say so." C.C. took a deep breath and prepared to launch into the speech she had practiced all day. "I'd like to straighten out the business you brought up yesterday."

"It isn't necessary. I got the picture."

"I could have explained things without being so hard on you."

He tilted his head, studying her thoughtfully. "You could have?"

"I like to think so." Determined to wipe the slate clean, she set the coffee aside. "I was embarrassed, and being embarrassed makes me angry. This whole situation is difficult."

He could still hear, very clearly, the unhappiness in her voice as she had spoken with Suzanna the night before. "I think I'm beginning to understand that."

Her eyes came back to his, and she sighed. "Well, in any case, I can't help but resent the fact that you want to buy The Towers, or that we might have to let you—but that's a separate thing from Aunt Coco's maneuvers. I think I realized, after I stopped being mad, that you were just as embarrassed as I was. You were just so damned polite."

"It's a bad habit of mine."

"You're telling me." She waved half a cookie at him. "If you hadn't brought up the kiss—"

"I understand that was an error in judgment, but since I'd already apologized for it, I thought we could deal with it reasonably."

"I didn't want an apology," C.C. muttered. "Then or now."

"I see."

"No, you don't. You certainly don't. What I meant was that an apology was unnecessary. I may be inexperienced by your standards, and I may not be sophisticated like the women you're used to dealing with, but I'm not foolish enough to start weaving daydreams out of one stupid kiss." She was getting angry again and was determined not to. After one deep, cleansing breath, she tried again. "I'd simply like to put that, and our conversation yesterday behind us, completely and totally. If it turns out that we will have business dealings, it would be wiser all around if we can be civilized."

"I like you this way."

"What way?"

"When you're not taking potshots at me."

She finished off her cookie and grinned. "Don't get used to it. All Calhouns have hideous tempers."

"So I've been warned. Truce?"

"I suppose. Want another cookie?"

He was staring again, she noted, and her own eyes widened when he reached out to brush his fingertips down her hair. "What are you doing?"

"Your hair's wet." He stroked it again, fascinated. "It smells like wet flowers."

"Trent—"

He smiled. "Yes?"

"I don't think this is the best way to handle things."

"Probably not." But his fingers trailed down through her hair to the nape of her neck. He felt her quick shudder. "I can't quite get you out of my mind. And I keep having these uncontrollable urges to get my hands on you. I wonder why."

"Because—" she wet her lips "—I irritate you."

"Oh, you do that, without question." He pressed those fingers at the back of her neck and had her moving forward an inch. "But not simply in the way you mean. It's not simple at all. Though it should be." His other hand skimmed over the collar of her denim work shirt, then cupped her chin. "Otherwise, why would I feel this irresistible need to touch you every time I get near you?"

"I don't know." His fingers, light as a feather, trailed down to where her pulse thudded at the base of her throat. "I wish you wouldn't."

"Wouldn't what?"

"Touch me."

He slid his hand down her sleeve to her bandaged hand, then lifted it to his lips. "Why?"

"Because you make me nervous."

Something lit in his eyes, turning them almost black. "You don't even mean to be provocative, do you?"

"I wouldn't know." Her eyes fluttered closed on a strangled moan when he brushed his lips over her jawline.

"Honeysuckle," he murmured, drawing her closer. He'd once thought it such a common flower. "I can all but taste it on you. Wild and sweet."

Her muscles turned to water as his mouth cruised over hers. So much lighter, so much gentler than the first time. It wasn't right that he could do this to her. The part of her mind that was still rational all but shouted it. But even that was drowned out by the flood of longing.

"Catherine." He had her face framed between his hands now as he nipped seductively at her lips. "Kiss me back."

She wanted to shake her head, to pull away and walk casually, even callously out of the room. Instead she flowed into his arms, her mouth lifting to his, meeting his.

His fingers tightened before he could prevent it, then slipped down to pull her more truly against him. He could think of nothing, wanted to think of nothing—no consequences, no rules, no code of behavior. For the first time in his memory, he wanted only to feel. Those sharp and sweet sensations she had racing through him were more than enough for any man.

She was strong—had always been strong—but not enough to prevent time from standing still. It was this one moment, she realized, that she had been waiting for all of her life. As her hands slid up his back, she held the moment to her as completely as she held him.

The fire crackled in the grate. The rain pattered. There was the light, spicy scent of the potpourri Lilah set everywhere about the house. His arms were so strong and sure, yet with a gentleness she hadn't expected from him.

She would remember it all, every small detail, along with the dark excitement of his mouth and the sound of her name as he whispered it against hers.

He drew her away, slowly this time, more shaken than he cared to admit. As he watched, she ran her tongue over her lips as if to savor a last taste. That small, unconscious gesture nearly brought him to his knees.

"No apology this time," he told her, and his voice wasn't steady.

"No."

He touched his lips to hers again. "I want you. I want to make love with you."

"Yes." It was a glorious kind of release. Her lips curved against his. "Yes."

"When?" He buried his face in her hair. "Where?"

"I don't know." She shut her eyes on the wonder of it. "I can't think."

"Don't." He kissed her temple, her cheekbone, her mouth. "This isn't the time for thinking."

"It has to be perfect."

"It will be." He framed her face again. "Let me show you."

She believed him—the words and what she saw in his eyes. "I can't believe it's going to be you." Laughing, she threw her arms around him, holding him close. "That I've waited all my life to be with someone. And it's you."

His hand paused on its way to her hair. "All of your life?"

Dreamily in love, she hugged him tighter. "I thought I'd be afraid the first time, but I'm not. Not with you."

"The first time." He shut his eyes. *Her* first time. How could he have been so stupid? He'd recognized the inexperience, but he hadn't thought, hadn't believed she was completely innocent. And he'd all but seduced her in her own kitchen. "C.C."

"I'm thirsty," Alex complained from the doorway, and had them springing apart like guilty children. He eyed them suspiciously. "What are you doing that stuff for? It's disgusting." He sent Trent a pained look, man-to-man. "I don't get why anybody wants to go around kissing girls."

"It's an acquired taste," Trent told him. "Why don't we get you a drink, then I need to talk to your aunt a minute. Privately."

"More mush stuff."

"What mush stuff?" Amanda wanted to know as she breezed in.

"Nothing." C.C. reached for the coffeepot.

"Lord, did I have a day," Amanda began, and grabbed a cookie.

Suzanna walked in two seconds later, followed by Lilah. As the kitchen filled with feminine laughter and scent, Trent knew his moment was lost.

When C.C. smiled at him across the room, he was afraid his head would be lost with it.

Chapter Six

It was Trent's first séance. He sincerely hoped it would be his last. There was simply no gracious way to decline attending. When he suggested that perhaps this was a family evening, Coco merely laughed and patted his cheek.

"My dear, we wouldn't think of excluding you. Who knows, it may be you the restless spirits choose to speak through."

The possibility did very little to cheer him up.

Once the children were tucked into bed for the evening, the rest of the family, along with the reluctant Trent, gathered around the dining room table. The stage had been set.

A dozen candles flickered atop the buffet. Dime-store holders cheek by jowl with Meissen and Baccarat. Another trio of white tapers glowed in the center of the table. Even nature seemed to have gotten into the spirit of things—so to speak.

Outside, the rain had turned into a wet fitful snow, blown about by a rising wind. As warm and cold air collided, thunder boomed and lightning flickered.

It was a dark and stormy night, Trent thought fatalistically as he took his seat.

Coco had not, as he'd secretly feared, worn a turban and a fringed shawl. As always, she was meticulously groomed. Around her neck, she did wear a large amethyst crystal, which she toyed with constantly.

"Now, children," she instructed. "Take hands and form the circle."

The wind knocked at the windows as C.C. slipped her hand into Trent's. Coco took his other. Directly across from him Amanda grinned, the amusement and sympathy obvious as she linked with her aunt and Suzanna.

"Don't worry, Trent," she told him. "The Calhoun ghosts are always well behaved around company."

"Concentration is essential," Lilah explained as she closed the gap between her eldest and youngest sister. "And very basic, really. All you have to do is clear your mind, particularly of any cynicism." She winked at Trent. "Astrologically, it's an excellent night for a séance."

C.C. gave his hand a quick, reassuring squeeze as Coco took over.

"We must all clear our minds and open our hearts." She spoke in a soothing monotone. "For some time I've felt that my grandmother, the unhappy Bianca, has wanted to contact me. This was her summer home for the last years of her young life. The place where she spent her most joyous and most tragic moments. The place where she met the man she loved, and lost."

She closed her eyes and took a deep breath. "We are here, Grandmama, waiting for you. We know your spirit is troubled."

"Does a spirit have a spirit?" Amanda wanted to know and earned a glare from her aunt. "It's a reasonable question."

"Behave," Suzanna murmured, and smothered a smile. "Go ahead, Aunt Coco."

They sat in silence, with only Coco's voice murmuring over the crackle of the fire and the moan of the wind. Trent's mind wasn't clear. It was filled with the way C.C. had fit in his arms, with the sweet and generous way her mouth had opened to his. The way she had looked at him, her eyes clouded and warm with emotions. Emotions he had recklessly stirred in her.

Guilt almost smothered him.

She wasn't like Marla or any of the women he had coolly romanced over the years. She was innocent and open and, despite a strong will and a sharp tongue, achingly vulnerable. He had taken advantage of that, inexcusably.

Not that it was entirely his fault, he reminded himself. She was, after all, a beautiful, desirable woman. And he was human. The fact that he wanted her—strictly on a physical plane—was only natural.

He glanced over just as she turned her head and smiled at him. Trent had to fight down a foolish urge to lift her hand to his lips and taste her skin.

She touched something in him, damn it. Something he was determined would remain untouched. When she smiled at him—even when she scowled at him—she made him feel more, want more, wish more, than any woman he'd ever known.

It was ridiculous. They were miles apart in every way. And yet, with her hand warm in his as it was now, he felt closer to her, more in tune with her, than he'd ever felt with anyone.

He could even see them sitting together on a sunny summer porch, watching children play on the grass. The sound of the sea was as soothing as a lullaby. The air smelled of roses climbing up the trellis. And of honeysuckle, growing wild where it chose.

He blinked, afraid his heart had stopped. The image had been so clear and so terrifying. It was the atmosphere, he assured himself. The candles flickering, the wind and lightning. It was playing games with his imagination.

He wasn't a man to sit on the porch with a woman and watch children. He had work, a business to run. The idea of him becoming involved with a bad-tempered auto mechanic was simply absurd.

Cold air seemed to slap him in the face. As he stiffened, he saw the flames of the candles lean dramatically to the left. A draft, he told himself, as the cold chilled him to the bone. The place was full of them.

He felt C.C.'s shudder. When he looked at her, her eyes were wide and dark. Her fingers curled tight around his.

"She's here!" There was both surprise and excitement in Coco's voice. "I'm sure of it."

In her delight, she nearly pulled her hands free and broke the chain. She had believed—well, had wanted to believe—but she had never actually felt a *presence* so distinctly.

She beamed down the table at Lilah, but her niece had her eyes closed and a faint smile on her lips.

"A window must have come open," Amanda said, and would have bolted up to check if Coco hadn't hissed at her.

"No such thing. Sit still, everyone. Sit still. She's here. Can't you feel it?"

C.C. did, and wasn't sure whether she should feel foolish or frightened. Something was different. She was certain that Trent sensed it, as well.

It was as though someone had gently closed a hand over her and Trent's joined ones. The cold vanished, replaced by a soothing, comforting warmth. So real was it that C.C. looked over her shoulder, certain she would see someone standing behind her.

Yet all she saw was the dance of fire and candlelight on the wall.

"She's so lost." C.C. let out a gasp when she realized it was she herself who had spoken. All eyes fixed on hers. Even Lilah's lazily opened.

"Do you see her?" Coco demanded in a whisper, squeezing C.C.'s fingers.

"No. No, of course not. It's just..." She couldn't explain. "It's so sad," she murmured, unaware that tears glistened in her eyes. "Can't you feel it?"

Trent could, and it left him speechless. Heartbreak, and a longing so deep it was immeasurable. Imagination, he told himself. The power of suggestion.

"Don't close it off." Coco searched desperately for the proper procedure. Now that something had actually happened, she hadn't a clue. A flash of lightning had her jolting. "Do you think she'll speak through you?"

At the opposite end of the table, Lilah smiled. "Just tell us what you see, honey."

"A necklace," C.C. heard herself say. "Two tiers of emeralds flanked by diamonds. Beautiful, brilliant." The gleam hurt her eyes. "She's wearing them, but I can't see her face. Oh, she's so unhappy."

"The Calhoun necklace," Coco breathed. "So, it's true."

Then, as if a sigh passed through the air, the candles flickered again, then ran straight and true. A log fell in the grate.

"Weird," Amanda said when her aunt's hand fell limply from hers. "I'll fix the fire."

"Honey." Suzanna studied C.C. with as much concern as curiosity. "Are you okay?"

"Yes." C.C. cleared her throat. "Sure." She shot Trent a quick look. "I guess the storm got to me."

Coco lifted a hand to her breast and patted her speeding heart. "I think we could all use a nice glass of brandy." She rose, more shaken than she wanted to admit, and walked to the buffet.

"Aunt Coco," C.C. began. "What's the Calhoun necklace?"

"The emeralds." She passed the snifters. "There was a legend that's been handed down through the family. You know part of it, how Bianca fell in love with another man, and died tragically. I suppose it's time I told you the rest of it."

"You kept a secret?" Amanda grinned as she swirled her drink. "Aunt Coco, you amaze me."

"I wanted to wait for the right time. It seems it's now." She took her seat again, warming the brandy between her hands. "Rumor was that Bianca's lover was an artist, one of the many who came to the island in those days. She would go to meet him when Fergus was away from the house, which was often. Theirs was not precisely an arranged marriage, but the next thing to it. She was years younger than he, and apparently quite beautiful. Since Fergus destroyed all pictures of her after her death, there's no way of knowing for sure."

"Why?" Suzanna asked. "Why would he do that?"

"Grief perhaps." Coco shrugged.

"Rage, more likely," Lilah put in.

"In any case." Coco paused to sip. "He destroyed all reminders of her, and the emeralds were lost. He had given Bianca the necklace when she gave birth to Ethan, her eldest son." She glanced at Trent. "My father. He was just a child at the time of his mother's death, so the events were never very clear in his mind. But his nanny, who had been fiercely loyal to Bianca, would tell him stories about her. And those he remembered. She didn't care for the necklace, but wore it often."

"As a kind of punishment," Lilah put in. "And a kind of talisman." She smiled at her aunt. "Oh, I've known about the necklace for years. I've seen it—just as C.C. did tonight." She lifted the brandy to her lips. "There are earrings to match. Emerald teardrops, like the stone in the center of the bottom tier."

"You're making that up," Amanda accused her, and Lilah merely moved her shoulders.

"No, I'm not." She smiled at C.C. "Am I?"

"No." Uneasy, C.C. looked to her aunt. "What does all this mean?"

"I'm not altogether sure, but I think the necklace is still important to Bianca. It was never seen after she died. Some believed Fergus threw it into the sea."

"Not on your life," Lilah said. "The old man wouldn't have thrown a nickel into the sea, much less an emerald necklace."

"Well..." Coco didn't like to speak ill of an ancestor, but she was forced to agree. "Actually, it would have been out of character. Grandpapa counted his pennies."

"He made Silas Marner look like a philanthropist," Amanda put in. "So, what happened to it?"

"That, my dear, is the mystery. My father's nanny told him that Bianca was going to leave Fergus, that she had packed a box, what the nanny called a treasure box. Bianca had secreted away what was most valuable to her."

"But she died instead," C.C. murmured.

"Yes. The legend is that the box, with its treasure, is hidden somewhere in the house."

"Our house?" Suzanna gaped at her aunt. "Do you really think there's some kind of treasure chest hidden around here for—what—eighty years, and no one's found it?"

"It's a very big house," Coco pointed out. "For all we know she might have buried it in the roses."

"If it existed in the first place," Amanda murmured.

"It existed." Lilah sent a nod toward C.C. "And I think Bianca's decided it's time to find it."

When everyone began to talk at once, arguments and suggestions bouncing around the table, Trent raised a hand. "Ladies. Ladies," he repeated, waiting for them to subside. "I realize that this is family business, but as I was invited to participate in this...experiment, I feel obligated to add a calming note. Legends are most often exaggerated and expanded over time. If there ever was a necklace, wouldn't it be more likely that Fergus sold it after the death of his wife?"

"He couldn't sell it," Lilah pointed out, "if he couldn't find it."

"Do any of you really think your great-grandfather buried treasure in the garden or hid it behind a loose stone?" One glance around the table told him that was precisely how they were thinking. Trent shook his head. "That kind of fairy tale's more suited for Alex and Jenny than for grown women." He spread his hands. "You don't even know for certain if there was a necklace in the first place."

"But I saw it," C.C. said, though it made her feel foolish.

"You imagined it," he corrected. "Think about it. A few minutes ago six rational adults were sitting around this table holding hands and calling up ghosts. All right as an odd sort of parlor game, but for anyone to actually believe in messages from the otherworld..." He certainly wasn't going to add that for a moment, he'd felt something himself.

"There's something appealing about a cynical, practical-minded man." Lilah rose to open one of the drawers of the buffet and unearthed a pad and pencil. After coming over to kneel by C.C.'s chair, she began to sketch. "I certainly respect your opinion, but the fact is not only did the necklace exist, I'm certain it still does."

"Because of a nanny's bedtime stories?"

She smiled at him. "No, because of Bianca." She slid the pad toward C.C. "Is that what you saw tonight?"

Lilah had always been a careless and clever artist. C.C. stared at the rough sketch of the necklace, two ornate and filigreed tiers studded with square-cut emeralds, sprinkled with diamond brilliants. From the bottom tier a large gem in the shape of a teardrop dripped.

"Yes." C.C. traced a fingertip over it. "Yes, this is it."

Trent studied the drawing. If indeed such a piece did exist, and Lilah's drawing was anywhere close to scale, it would undoubtedly be worth a fortune.

"Oh, my," Coco murmured as the pad was passed to her. "Oh, my."

"I think Trent has a point." Amanda gave the sketch a hard look before handing it to Suzanna. "We can hardly take the house apart stone by stone, even if we wanted to. Despite any sort of paranormal experience, the first order of business is to make certain—absolutely certain," she added when Lilah sighed, "that the necklace is a fact. Even eighty years ago, something like this had to cost an incredible amount of money. There has to be a record. If Lilah's famous vibes are wrong and it was sold again, there would be a record of that as well."

"Spoken like a true stick-in-the-mud," Lilah complained. "I guess this means we spend our Sunday pushing through a paper mountain."

C.C. didn't even try to sleep. She wrapped herself in her flannel robe and, with the house creaking around her, left her room for Trent's. She could hear the murmur of the late news from Amanda's room. Then the hum of sitars from Lilah's. It didn't occur to her to feel awkward or to hesitate. She simply knocked on Trent's door and waited for him to answer.

When he did, with his shirt open and his eyes a little sleepy, she felt her first frisson of nerves.

"C.C.?"

"I need to talk to you." She glanced toward the bed, then away. "Can I come in?"

How was a man to deal fairly when even flannel had become erotic? "Maybe it would be better if we waited until morning."

"I'm not sure I can."

The knots in his stomach tightened. "Okay. Sure." The sooner he explained himself to her, the better. He hoped. Trent let her in and closed the door. "Do you want to sit down?"

"Too much nervous energy." Hugging herself, she walked to the window. "It stopped snowing. I'm glad. I know Suzanna was worried about some of her flowers. Spring's so unpredictable on the island." She dragged a hand through her hair as she turned. "I'm making small talk, and I hate that." A deep breath settled her. "Trent, I need to know what you think about tonight. Really think about it."

"Tonight?" he said carefully.

"The séance." She rubbed her hands over her face. "Lord, I feel like an imbecile even saying it, but, Trent, something happened." Now she thrust those restless hands toward him, waiting for him to clasp them in his. "I'm very grounded, very literal minded. Lilah's the one who believes in all this stuff. But now... Trent, I need to know. Did you feel anything?"

"I don't know what you mean. I certainly felt foolish several times."

"Please." She gave his hands an impatient shake. "Be honest with me. It's important."

Isn't that what he'd promised himself he would do? "All right, C.C. Tell me what you felt."

"The air got very cold. Then it was as if something—someone—was standing behind us. Behind and between the two of us. It wasn't something that frightened me. I was surprised, but not afraid. We were holding hands, like this. And then..."

She was waiting for him to say it, to admit it. Those big green eyes demanded it. When he did so, it was with great reluctance. "It felt as though someone put a hand over ours."

"Yes." Eyes closed, she brought his hands to her curved lips. "Yes, exactly."

"Shared hallucination," he began, but she cut him off with a laugh.

"I don't want to hear that. No rational explanations." She pressed his hand to her cheek. "I'm not a fanciful person, but I know it meant something, something important. I *know*."

"The necklace?"

"Only a part of it—and not this part. All the rest—the necklace, the legend, we'll figure it out sooner or later. I think we'll have to because it's meant. But this, this was like a blessing."

"C.C.—"

"I love you." Eyes dark and brilliant, she touched his cheek. "I love you, and nothing in my life has ever felt so right."

He was speechless. Part of him wanted to step back, smile kindly and tell her she was letting the moment run away with her. Love didn't happen in a matter of days. If it happened at all, which was rare, it took years.

Another part, buried deep, wanted to hold her close so that the moment would never end.

"Catherine—"

But she was already moving into his arms. They seemed to be waiting for her. As if he had no control over them, they wrapped around her. The warmth, her warmth, seeped into him like a drug.

"I think I knew the first time you kissed me." She pressed her cheek to his. "I didn't want it, didn't ask for it, but it's never been like that for me before. I don't think I ever expected it to be. There you were, so suddenly, so completely in my life. Kiss me again, Trent. Kiss me now."

He was helpless to do otherwise. His lips were already burning for hers. When they met, the fire only sparked hotter. She was molten in his arms, sending white licks of flame shooting through his system. When he couldn't prevent his demand from increasing, she didn't hesitate, but strained against him, offering everything.

She slid her hands under his shirt, delighted to feel his quick, involuntary tremor. His muscles bunched under her fingers with the kind of strength she wanted, needed.

The wind sighed outside the windows as she sighed in his arms.

He couldn't get enough. He found himself wanting to devour her as his lips raced crazily over her face, down her throat where his teeth scraped lightly over her skin. The scent of honeysuckle wheeled in his head. She arched back, her low whimpers of pleasure pounding in his blood.

He had to touch her. He would go mad if he didn't. Mad if he did. When he parted her robe, he groaned, discovering she was naked for him beneath. Desperate, he filled his hand with her.

Now she knew what it was to have the blood swim. She could all but feel it racing under her skin, beating hot wherever he touched. There was a weakness here, a glorious one, mixed with a kind of manic strength. She wanted to give him both somehow and found the way when his mouth came frantically back to hers.

She trembled even as she answered. She surrendered even as she heated. As her head fell back and her fingers dug hard into his shoulders, he felt something move through him that was more than desire, deeper than passion.

Happiness. Hope. Love. As he recognized the feelings, terror joined them.

Breath heaving, he pulled away.

Her robe had fallen off one shoulder, baring it. Already his mouth had supped there. Her eyes were as brilliant as the emeralds she had imagined. Smiling, she lifted a trembling hand to his cheek.

"Do you want me to stay tonight?"

"Yes—no." Holding her at arm's length was the hardest thing he'd ever done. "Catherine..." He did want her to stay, he realized. Not just tonight, and not simply because of that glorious body of hers. The fact that he did made it all the more important to set things right. "I don't—I haven't been fair with you, and this has gotten out of hand so quickly." A long, unsteady breath escaped him. "Lord, you're beautiful. No," he said quickly when she smiled and started to step forward. "We need to talk. Just talk."

"I thought we had."

If she continued to look at him that way, he'd stop giving a damn about fairness. Or his own survival. "I haven't made myself clear," he began slowly. "If I had known—if I had realized how completely innocent you are, I wouldn't—well, I hope I would have been more careful. Now I can only try to make up for it."

"I don't understand."

"No, that's the problem." Needing some distance, he walked away. "I said I was attracted to you, very attracted. And that's obviously true. But I would never have taken advantage of you if I had known."

Suddenly cold, she drew the robe around her. "You're upset because I haven't been with a man before?"

"Not upset." Frustrated, he turned back. " 'Upset' isn't the word. I can't seem to find one. There are rules, you see." But she only continued to stare at him. "Catherine, a woman like you expects—deserves—more than I can give you."

She lowered her gaze to her hands as she carefully fastened the belt to her robe. "What is that?"

"Commitment. A future."

"Marriage."

"Yes."

Her knuckles were turning white. "I suppose you think this—what I said—is part of Aunt Coco's plans."

"No." He would have gone to her then if he'd dared. "No, of course I don't."

"Well." She struggled to make her fingers relax. "That's something, I suppose."

"I know your feelings are honest—exaggerated perhaps—but honest. And it's completely my fault. If this hadn't happened so quickly, I would have explained to you from the first that I have no intention of marrying, ever. I don't believe that two people can be loyal to each other, much less happy together for a lifetime."

"Why?"

"Why?" He stared at her. "Because it simply doesn't work. I've watched my father go from marriage to divorce to marriage. It's like watching a tennis match. The last time I heard from my mother, she was on her third marriage. It simply isn't practical to make vows knowing they'll only be broken."

"Practical," she repeated with a slow nod. "You won't let yourself feel anything for me because it would be impractical."

"The problem is I do feel something for you."

"Not enough." Only enough to cut out her heart. "Well, I'm glad we got that sorted out." Blindly she turned for the door. "Good night."

"C.C." He laid a hand on her shoulder before she could find the knob.

"Don't apologize," she said, praying her control would hold a few more minutes. "It isn't necessary. You've explained it all perfectly."

"Damn it, why don't you yell at me? Call me a few of the names I'm sure I deserve." He'd have preferred that to the quiet desolation he'd seen in her eyes.

"Yell at you?" She made herself turn and face him. "For being fair and honest? Call you names? How can I call you names, Trent, when I feel so terribly sorry for you?"

His hand slipped away from her. She held her head up. Under the hurt, just under it, was pride.

"You're throwing away something—no, not throwing," she corrected. "You're politely handing back something you'll never have again. What you've turned out of your life, Trent, would have been the best part of it."

She left him alone with the uneasy feeling that she was absolutely right.

* * *

There was a party tonight. I thought it would be good for me to fill the house with people and lights and flowers. I know that Fergus was pleased that I supervised all the details so carefully. I had wondered if he had noticed my distraction, or how often I walked along the cliffs these afternoons, or how many hours I have begun to spend in the tower, dreaming my dreams. But it does not seem so.

The Greenbaums were here, and the McAllisters and the Prentises. Everyone who summers on the island, that Fergus feels we should take note of, attended. The ballroom was banked with gardenias and red roses. Fergus had hired an orchestra from New York, and the music was both lovely and lively. I believe Sarah McAllister drank too much champagne, for her laugh began to grate on my nerves long before supper was served.

My new gold dress suited very well, I think, for it gathered many compliments. Yet when I danced with Ira Greenbaum, his eyes were on my emeralds. They hung like a shackle around my neck.

How unfair I am! They are beautiful, and mine only because Ethan is mine.

During the evening, I slipped up to the nursery to check on the children, though I know how doting Nanny is to all of them. Ethan woke and sleepily asked if I had brought him any cake.

He looks like an angel as he sleeps, he, and my other sweet babies. My love for them is so rich, so deep, that I wonder why it is my heart cannot transfer any of that sweet feeling to the man who fathered them.

Perhaps the fault is in me. Surely that must be so. When I kissed them good-night and stepped out into the hall again, I wished so desperately that rather than go back to the ballroom to laugh and dance, I could run to the cliffs. To stand at the cliffs with the wind in my hair and the sound and smells of the sea everywhere.

Would he come to me then, if I dared such a thing? Would he come so that we would stand there together in the shadows, reaching out for something we have no business wanting, much less taking?

I did not go to the cliffs. My duty is my husband, and it was to him I went. Dancing with him, my heart felt as cold as the jewels around my neck. Yet I smiled when he complimented me on my skill as a hostess. His hand at my waist was so aloof, but so possessive. As we moved to the music, his eyes scanned the room, approving what was his, studying his guests to be certain they were impressed.

How well I know what status and opinion mean to the man I married. And how little it seems they have come to mean to me.

I wanted to shout at him. "Fergus, for God's sake, look at me. Look at me and see. Make me love you, for fear and respect cannot be enough for either of us. Make me love you so that I will never again turn my steps toward the cliffs and what waits for me there."

But I did not shout. When he told me impatiently that it was necessary for me to dance with Cecil Barkley, I murmured my assent.

Now the music is done and the lamps are snuffed out. I wonder when I will see Christian again. I wonder what will become of me.

Chapter Seven

C.C. sat cross-legged in the center of an ocean of papers. Her assignment—whether or not she'd chosen to accept it—had been to go through all of the notes and receipts and scraps that had been stuffed into three cardboard boxes marked miscellaneous.

Nearby Amanda sat at a card table, with several more bulging boxes at her feet. With her hair clipped back and reading glasses sliding down her nose, she meticulously studied each paper before laying it on one of the various stacks she had started.

"This should have been done decades ago," she commented.

"You mean it should have been burned decades ago."

"No." Amanda shoved the glasses back into place. "Some of it's fascinating, and certainly deserves to be preserved. Stuffing papers into cardboard boxes is not my idea of preserving family history."

"Does a recipe for gooseberry jam rate as family history?"

"For Aunt Coco it does. That goes under kitchen, subheading menus."

C.C. shifted then waved away a cloud of dust. "How about a bill for six pair of white kid gloves and a blue silk parasol?"

"Clothing, by the date. Hmm, this is interesting. Aunt Coco's progress report from her fourth-grade teacher. And I quote, 'Cordelia is a delightfully gregarious child. However, she tends to daydream and has trouble finishing assigned projects.'"

"That's a news flash." Stiff, C.C. arched her back and rotated her head. Beside her, the sun was streaming through the smudges on the storeroom window. With a little sigh, she rested her elbows on her knees and studied it.

"Where the devil is Lilah?" Impatient as always, Amanda tapped her foot as she grumbled. "Suzanna had dispensation because she took the kids to the matinee, but Lilah's supposed to be on duty."

"She'll show up," C.C. murmured.

"Sure. When it's done." Digging into a new pile, Amanda sneezed twice. "This is some of the dirtiest stuff I've ever seen."

C.C. shrugged. "Everything gets dirty if it sits around long enough."

"No, I mean really dirty. It's a limerick written by Great-Uncle Sean. 'There was a young lady from Maine, whose large breasts drove the natives insane. They...' Never mind," Amanda decided. "We'll start a file on attempted pornography." When C.C. made no comment, she glanced over to see her sister still staring at a sunbeam. "You okay, sweetie?"

"Hmm? Oh, yeah. I'm fine."

"You don't look like you slept very well."

C.C. shrugged then busied herself with papers again. "I guess the séance threw me off."

"Not surprising." Her lips pursed as she sorted through more receipts. "I never put any stock in that business. Bianca's tower was one thing. I guess we've all felt something—well, something up there. But I always thought that it was because we knew Bianca had tossed herself out of the window. Then last night..." When the shiver caught her, she rubbed her chilled arms. "I know that you really saw something, really experienced something."

"I know the necklace is real," C.C. said.

"I'll agree it *was* real—especially when I have a receipt in my hand."

"Was and is. I don't think I would have seen it if it had been pawned or tossed into the sea. It might sound loony, but I know Bianca wants us to find it."

"It does sound loony." With a sigh, Amanda leaned back in the creaking chair. "And what's loonier is that I think so, too. I just hope nobody at the hotel finds out I'm spending my free time looking for a buried treasure because my long-dead ancestor told us to. Oh!"

"Did you find it?" C.C. was already scrambling up.

"No, no, it's an old date book. 1912. The ink's a bit faded, but the handwriting's lovely—definitely feminine. It must be Bianca's. Look. 'Send invitations.' And here's the guest list. Wow, some party. The Prentises." Amanda took off her glasses to gnaw on the earpiece. "I bet they were Prentise Hall—one of the cottages that burned in '47."

"'Speak to gardener about roses,'" C.C. read over her sister's shoulder. "'Final fitting on gold ball gown. Meet Christian, 3:00 p.m.' Christian?" She laid a tensed hand on Amanda's shoulder. "Could that have been her artist?"

"Your guess is as good as mine." Quickly Amanda pushed her glasses back on. "But look here. 'Have clasp on emeralds strengthened.' Those could be the ones."

"They have to be."

"We still haven't found any receipts."

C.C. gave a tired look at the papers littering the room. "What are our chances?"

Even Amanda's organizational skills quaked. "Well, they improve every time we eliminate a box."

"Mandy." C.C. sat on the floor beside her. "We're running out of time, aren't we?"

"We've only been at it for a few hours."

"That's not what I mean." She rested her cheek on Amanda's thigh. "You know it's not. Even if we find the receipt, we still have to find the necklace. It could take years. We don't have years. We're going to have to sell, aren't we?"

"We'll talk about it tomorrow night, at the family meeting." Troubled, she stroked C.C.'s hair. "Look, why don't you go take a nap? You really do look beat."

"No." She rose, pacing over the papers to the windows and back. "I'm better off keeping my mind and my hands busy. Otherwise, I might strangle someone."

"Trent, for instance?"

"An excellent place to start. No." With a sigh, she stuck her hands into her pockets. "No, this mess isn't really his fault."

"Are we still talking about the house?"

"I don't know." Miserable, she sat on the floor again. At least she could be grateful she'd cried herself dry the night before. "I've decided that all men are stupid, selfish and totally unnecessary."

"You're in love with him."

A wry smile curved her lips. "Bingo. And to answer your next question, no, he doesn't love me back. He's not interested in me, a future, a family, and he's very sorry he didn't make that clear to me before I made the mistake of falling for him."

"I'm sorry, C.C." After taking off her glasses, Amanda got up to cross the room and sit on the floor beside her sister. "I know how it must hurt, but you've only known him for a few days. Infatuation—"

"It's not infatuation." Idly she folded the recipe for jam into a paper airplane. "I've found out that falling in love doesn't have anything to do with time. It can take a year or an instant. It happens when it's ready to happen."

Amanda put an arm around C.C.'s shoulders and squeezed. "Well, I don't know anything about that. Fortunately, I've never had to worry about it." The fact made her frown, but only for a moment. "I do know this. If he hurt you, we'll make him sorry he ever crossed a Calhoun."

C.C. laughed then sent the gooseberry plane flying. "It's tempting, but I think it's more a matter of me hurting myself." She gave herself a little shake. "Come on, let's get back to work."

They'd barely gotten started again when Trent came in. He looked at C.C., met a solid wall of ice. When he turned to Amanda, he fared little better.

"I thought you might be able to use some help," he told them.

Amanda glanced at C.C., noted her sister was employing the silent treatment. A very effective weapon, in Amanda's estimation. "That's nice of you, Trent." Amanda gave him a smile that would have frosted molten lava. "But this is really a family problem."

"Let him help." C.C. didn't even bother to look up. "I imagine he's just terrific at pushing papers."

"All right then." With a shrug, Amanda indicated another folding chair. "You can use that if you like. I'm organizing according to content and year."

"Fine." He took the chair and sat across from her. They worked in frigid silence, with the crinkle of papers and the tap of Amanda's shoe.

"Here's a repair bill," he said—and was ignored. "For repairing a clasp."

"Let me see." Amanda had already snatched it out of his hand before C.C. made the dash across the room. "It doesn't say what kind of necklace," she muttered.

"But the dates are right." C.C. stabbed a finger on it. "July 16, 1912."

"Have I missed something?" Trent asked them.

Amanda waited a beat, saw that C.C. wasn't going to answer and glanced up herself. "We came across a date book of Bianca's. She had a note to take the emeralds to have the clasp repaired."

"This might be what you need." His eyes were on C.C., but it was Amanda who answered.

"It may be enough to satisfy all of us that the Calhoun necklace existed in 1912, but it's a long way from helping us find it." She set the receipt aside. "Let's see what else we can turn up."

In silence, C.C. went back to her papers.

A few moments later, Lilah called from the base of the stairs. "Amanda! Phone!"

"Tell them I'll call back."

"It's the hotel. They said it's important."

"Damn." She set down the glasses before sending Trent a narrowed look. "I'll be back in a few minutes."

He waited until the sound of her rapid footsteps had finished echoing. "She's very protective."

"We stick together," C.C. commented, and set a paper on a pile without a clue to its contents.

"I've noticed. Catherine . . ."

Braced, C.C. flicked him her coolest glance. "Yes?"

"I wanted to make certain you were all right."

"All right. In what way?"

She had dust on her cheek. He wanted, badly, to smile and tell her. To hear her laugh as she brushed it off. "After last night—I know how upset you were when you left my room."

"Yes, I was upset." She turned over another piece of paper. "I guess I made quite a scene."

"No, that's not what I meant."

"I did." She forced her lips to curve. "I guess I'm the one who should apologize this time. The séance, all that happened during it, went to my head." Not my head, she thought, but my heart. "I must have sounded like an idiot when I came to your room."

"No, of course not." She was so cool, he thought. So composed. And she baffled him. "You said you loved me."

"I know what I said." Her voice dropped another ten degrees, but her smile stayed in place. "Why don't we both chalk it up to the mood of the moment?"

That was reasonable, he realized. So why did he feel so lost. "Then you didn't mean it?"

"Trent, we've only known each other for a few days." Did he want to make her suffer? she wondered.

"But you looked so—devastated when you left."

She arched a brow. "Do I look devastated now?"

"No," he said slowly. "No, you don't."

"Well, then. Let's forget it." As she spoke, the sun lost itself behind the clouds. "That would be best for both of us, wouldn't it?"

"Yes." It was just what he'd wanted. Yet he felt empty when he stood up again. "I do want what's best for you, C.C."

"Fine." She studied the paper in her hand. "If you're going down, ask Lilah to bring up some coffee when she comes."

"All right."

She waited until she was sure he was gone before she covered her face with her hands. She'd been wrong, C.C. discovered. She hadn't nearly cried herself dry.

Trent went back to his room. His briefcase was there, stacked with work he had intended to do while away from his office. Taking a seat at the scarred kneehole desk, he opened a file.

Ten minutes later, he was staring out the window without having glanced at the first word.

He shook himself, picked up his pen and ordered himself to concentrate. He succeeded in reading the first word, even the first paragraph. Three times. Disgusted, he tossed the pen aside and rose to pace.

It was ridiculous, he thought. He had worked in hotel suites all over the world. Why should this room be any different? It had walls and windows, a ceiling—so to speak. The desk was more than adequate. He could even, if he chose, light a fire to add some cheer. And some warmth. God knew he could use some warmth after the thirty icy minutes he'd spent in the storeroom. There was no reason why he shouldn't be able to sit down and take care of some business for an hour or two.

Except that he kept remembering—how lovely C.C. had looked when she'd come into the room in her gray flannel robe and bare feet. He could still see the way her eyes had glowed when she had stood almost where he was standing now, smiling at him. Frowning, he rubbed at a dull pain around his heart. He wasn't accustomed to aches there. Headaches certainly. Never heartaches.

But the memory of the way she'd slipped into his arms haunted him. And her taste—why was it that it still hovered just a breath from his own lips?

It was guilt, that was all, he assured himself. He had hurt her, the way he was certain he'd never hurt another woman. No matter how cool she had been today, no matter how composed, that was a guilt he would live with for a long time.

Maybe if he went up and talked to her again. His hand was on the knob before he stopped himself. That would only make things worse, if possible. Just because he wanted to assuage some guilt was no excuse to put her in an uncomfortable position again.

She was handling it, better than he by all accounts. She was strong, obviously resilient. Proud. Soft, his mind wandered. Warm. Incredibly beautiful.

On an oath he began to pace again. It would be wiser for him to concentrate on the house rather than any of its occupants. The few days he'd spent in it might have caused a personal upheaval, but it had given him time and opportunity to formulate plans. From the inside. It had given him a taste of the mood and tone and the history. And if he could settle down for a few moments, he could put some of those thoughts on paper.

But it was hopeless. The minute he took his pen in hand, his mind went blank. He was feeling closed in, Trent told himself. He just needed some air. Snatching up a jacket, he did something he hadn't given himself time to do in months.

He took a walk.

Following instinct, he headed toward the cliffs. Down the uneven lawn, around a crumbling stone wall. Toward the sea. The air had a bite. It seemed that spring had decided to pick up her pretty skirts and retreat. The sky was gray and moody, with a few hopeful patches of blue. Wildflowers that had been brave enough to shove their way through rock and soil blew fitfully in the wind.

Trent walked with his hands in his pockets, and his head down. Depression wasn't a familiar sensation, and he was determined to walk it off. When he glanced back, he could just see the peaks of towers above and behind. He turned away and faced the sea—unknowingly mirroring the stance of a man who had painted there decades before.

Breathtaking. It was the only word that came to his mind. Rocks tumbled dizzily down, pink and gray where the wind buffeted them, black where the water struck and funneled. Bad-tempered whitecaps churned, slicing at the darker water. Smoky fog rolled and shredded, and the air held a fresh threat of rain.

It should have been gloomy. It was simply spectacular.

He wished she was with him. That she would be here, now, beside him before time passed or the wind changed. She would smile, he thought. Laugh, as she planted those long, gorgeous legs and lifted her face to the blow. If she had been there, the beauty of it wouldn't make him feel so lonely. So damned lonely.

The tingle at the base of his neck had him turning, nearly reaching out. He'd been so certain that he would look and see her walking toward him. There was nothing but the slope of rock, and the wind. Yet the feeling of another presence remained, very real, so that he almost called out.

He was a sensible man, Trent assured himself. He knew he was alone. Yet it seemed as though someone was there with him, waiting. Watching.

For a moment, he was certain he caught the light, drifting scent of honeysuckle.

Imagination, he decided, but his hand wasn't quite steady as he lifted it to push the blowing hair out his eyes.

Then there was weeping. Trent froze as he listened to the sad, quiet sound that sobbed just under the wind. It ebbed and flowed, like the sea itself. Something clenched inside his stomach as he strained to hear—though common sense told him there could be nothing to hear.

A nervous breakdown? he wondered. But the sound was real, damn it. Not a hallucination. Slowly, ears pricked, he climbed down a jumble of rocks.

"Who's there?" he shouted as the sound sighed and drifted on the wind. Chasing it, he hurried down, driven by an urgency that drummed through his blood. A shower of loose stones rattled into space, bringing him sharply back to reality.

What in God's name was he doing? Scrambling down a cliff wall after a ghost? He lifted his hands and saw that despite the brisk wind his palms were sweating. All he could hear now was the frantic pounding of his own heart. After forcing himself to stand still and take a few calming breaths, he looked around for the easiest form of assent.

He had just started back when the sound came again. Weeping. No, he realized. Whimpering. It was quite clear now and nearly under his feet. Crouching, Trent searched behind an outcrop of rock. It was a poor, pitiful sight, he thought. The little black puppy was hardly more than a ball of fur-covered bones. Relief poured through him, making him laugh out loud. He wasn't going crazy after all. As Trent studied it, the terrified pup tried to inch back, but there was nowhere to go. Its little frightened eyes fixed on Trent as it trembled. "Had a rough time, have you?" Cautiously Trent reached out, ready to snatch his hand back if the pup snapped. Instead it simply cowered and whined. "It's okay, fella. Relax. I won't hurt you." Gently he stroked the puppy between the ears with his fingertips. Still shivering, the pup licked Trent's hand. "Guess you're feeling pretty lonely." He sighed as he calmed the dog. "Me, too. Why don't we go back to the house?" He gathered the dog up, zipping it inside his jacket for the climb. When he was halfway to the top, Trent stopped then turned blindly around. It was at least fifty yards from where he had stood looking out to sea to where he had discovered the stray. His palms grew damp again when he realized it would have been impossible for him to have heard the puppy's whines from the ridge above. The distance and the wind would have smothered the whimpers. Yet he had heard ... something. And, hearing it, had climbed down to find the lost dog. "What the devil was it?" Trent murmured, and cuddling the pup closer, headed for home. He was just beginning to feel foolish when he crossed the lawn. What was he supposed to say to his hostesses? Look what followed me home? How about— Guess what? I decided to take my life in my hands and climb back down the cliff. Look what I found. Neither opening seemed quite suitable. The sensible thing would be to get in the car and drive the dog down to the village. There was bound to be an animal shelter or vet. He could hardly march into the parlor and dump his find on the rug. But he couldn't, Trent discovered. He simply couldn't turn the shivering ball of fur over to strangers. The little guy trusted him and was even now curling softly under his heart. As he stood hesitating, C.C. came out of the house.

Trent shifted and tried to look natural. "Hi."

'Hi." She paused to button her denim jacket. "We're out of milk. Do you need anything from the village?"

A can of dog food, he thought, and cleared his throat. "No, thanks. I, ah..." The pup wriggled against his shirt. "Did you find anything?"

"Lots of things, but nothing that tells us where to look for the necklace." Her misery turned to curiosity as she watched the ripples run along his jacket. "Is everything all right?"

"Fine. Just fine."Trent cleared his throat, folded his arms. "I took a walk."

"Okay." It was awful, she thought, just awful. He could hardly meet her eyes. "Aunt Coco's making a light lunch if you're hungry."

"Oh—thanks."

She started to move by him when a high-pitched yip stopped her in her tracks. "What?"

"Nothing." He smothered an involuntary chuckle as the puppy wiggled along his ribs.

"Are you all right?"

"Yes, yes, I'm fine." He gave her a sheepish smile as the dog poked his nose above the zipper of the jacket.

"What have you got?" C.C. forgot her vow to keep her distance and stepped closer to tug the zipper down. "Oh! Trent, it's a puppy."

"I found him down in the rocks," he began quickly. "I wasn't sure just what to—"

"Oh, you poor little thing." She was already cooing as she gathered the puppy to her. "Are you lost?" She rubbed her cheek over its fur, nuzzled nose to nose. "There now, it's all right." The puppy wagged his tail so fast and hard he nearly fell out of her grip.

"Cute, isn't he?" Grinning, Trent moved closer to stroke. "Looks like he's been on his own for a while."

"He's just a baby." She crooned and cuddled. "Where did you say you found him?"

"Down on the rocks. I was walking." And thinking of you. Before he could stop himself, Trent reached out to touch her hair. "I couldn't just leave him there."

"Of course not." She looked up and saw that she was all but in his arms. His hand was in her hair, his eyes on hers.

"Catherine—"

The pup yipped again and had her jolting back. "I'll take him in. He must be cold, and hungry."

"All right." The only place left for his hands was his pockets. "Why don't I run down and get the milk?"

"Okay." Her smile was strained as she backed toward the steps. She turned and, murmuring to the puppy, dashed inside.

By the time Trent returned, the stray had a place of honor by the kitchen hearth and the undivided attention of four beautiful women.

"Wait until Suze and the kids get back," Amanda was saying. "They'll flip. He sure goes for your liver pâté, Aunt Coco."

"Obviously a gourmet among dogs." Lilah, already on her hands and knees, leaned her nose against his. "Aren't you, cutie?"

"I'm sure he should have something more bland." Coco was also on the floor, charmed. "With the proper care, he'll be very handsome."

The pup, amazed at his good fortune, raced in circles. Spotting Trent, he gamboled over, tripping over his own feet. The women scrambled up, all asking him questions at the same time.

"Hold on." Trent set the grocery bag on the table, then crouched down to scratch the pup's belly. "I don't know where he came from. I found him when I was walking along the cliffs. He was hiding out. Weren't you, boy?"

"I suppose we should ask around, to see it anyone's lost him," Coco began, then held up a hand as her nieces voiced unanimous dissent. "It's only right. But it is up to Trent, since he found him."

"I think you should do what you think's best." He rose to pull the milk out of the bag. "He could probably use some of this."

Amanda already had a saucer and was arguing with Lilah on the proper amount to give their new guest.

"What else did you get?" C.C. poked at the bag.

"A few things." He moved his shoulders, then gave up. "I thought he should have a collar." Trent pulled out a bright red collar with silver studs.

C.C. couldn't hold back the grin. "Very fashionable."

"And a leash." Trent set that on the table, as well. "Puppy food."

"Uh-huh." C.C. began to go through the bag herself. "And puppy treats, rawhide bones."

"He'll want to gnaw," Trent told her.

"Sure, he will. A ball and a squeaky mouse." Laughing, she squeezed the rubber toy.

"He should have something to play with." He didn't want to add that he'd searched for a dog bed and cushion but hadn't come across them.

"I didn't know you were a softie."

He glanced down at the happily lapping puppy. "Neither did I."

"What's his name?" Lilah wanted to know.

"Well, I . . ."

"You found him, you get to name him."

"Do it quick," Amanda advised him. "Before Lilah sticks him with something like Griswold."

"Fred," Trent said on impulse. "He looks like a Fred to me."

Unimpressed with his christening, Fred plopped down with one ear in the saucer of milk and went to sleep.

"Well, that's settled." Amanda gave the pup one last pat before she rose. "Come on, Lilah, it's your turn to take a shift."

"I'll give you a hand." Instincts humming, Coco hustled her two nieces out of the room and left C.C. alone with Trent.

"I'd better go, too." C.C. started for the door. Trent laid a hand on her arm to stop her.

"Wait."

"What for?"

"Just... wait."

She stood, battling back hurt. "I'm waiting."

"I—how's your hand?"

"It's fine."

"Good." He felt like an idiot. "That's good."

"If that's all ..."

"No. I wanted to tell you... I noticed a rattle in the car when I drove down to the village."

"A rattle?" She pursed her lips. "What kind of rattle?"

An imaginary one, he thought, but shrugged. "Just a rattle. I was hoping you could take a look at it."

"All right. Bring it in tomorrow."

"Tomorrow?"

"My tools are at the shop. Is there anything else?"

"When I was walking, I kept wishing you were with me."

She looked away until she was sure she had rebuilt the chink he'd just knocked in her defensive wall. "We want different things, Trent. Let's just leave it at that." She turned toward the door. "Try to get your car in early," she added without looking around. "I've got an exhaust system to replace tomorrow."

Chapter Eight

C.C. fired up her torch, flipped down her faceplate and prepared to cut off the tail pipe on the rusted exhaust of a '62 Plymouth.

The day was not going well.

She wasn't able to get the scheduled family meeting off her mind. No other paperwork on the necklace had shown up, though they had gone through reams and reams of receipts and old ledgers. She knew, because of Amanda's refusal to talk, that the news wasn't good.

Added to that had been another restless night. She heard Fred's whimpering and had gone to check on him only to hear Trent's low murmuring soothing the puppy behind his bedroom door.

She'd stood there for a long time, listening.

The fact that he'd taken the stray into his room, cared enough to comfort and nurture only made C.C. love him more. And the more she loved, the more she hurt.

She knew she was hollow eyed this morning, because she'd made the mistake of looking at a mirror. That she could handle. Her looks had never been a major concern. The bills she had found in the morning mail were.

She'd been telling the truth when she'd told Suzanna the business was doing well. But there were still rough spots. Not all of her customers paid promptly, and her cash flow was too often merely a trickle. Six months, she thought as she cut through the old metal. She only needed six months. But that was too long, much too long to help keep The Towers.

Her life was changing, changing fast, and none of it seemed to be for the better.

Trent stood watching her. She had some battered hulk of a car up on the lift and stood under it, wielding a torch. While he watched, she shifted aside as a pipe clattered to the floor. She was wearing coveralls again, thick safety gloves and a helmet. The music she never seemed to be without jingled from the radio on the workbench.

Surely a man was over the edge when he thought how delightful it would be to make love on a concrete floor with a woman who was dressed like a welder.

C.C. changed positions, then saw him. Very carefully she shut off the torch before she lifted the shield of her helmet.

"I couldn't find anything wrong with your car. Keys are in the office. No charge." She flipped down the shield again.

"C.C."

"What?"

"How about dinner?"

She pushed back the shield and eyed him warily. "How about it?"

"I mean…" With a leery glance overhead, he stepped under the car with her. "I'd like you to have dinner with me tonight."

She shifted her weight. "I've had dinner with you every night for several nights." She flipped the shield down. Trent flipped it up again.

"No, I mean I want to take you out to dinner."

"Why?"

"Why not?"

She lifted a brow. "Well, that's very nice, but I'm a little pressed tonight. We're having a family meeting." She pulled down the shield again and prepared to relight the torch.

"Tomorrow then." Annoyed, Trent pushed the shield back up. "Do you mind? I like to see you when I talk to you."

"Yes, I mind because I've got work. And no, I won't have dinner with you tomorrow."

"Why?"

She blew out a long breath that ruffled her bangs. "Because I don't want to."

"You're still angry with me."

Her eyes, which had begun to heat, went flat. "We settled all that, so there's no reason to go out on a date."

"Just dinner," he said, finding he couldn't let go. "No one's calling it a date. One simple meal, as friends, before I go back to Boston."

"You're going back?" She felt her heart drop to her knees and turned away to rattle through some tools.

"Yes, I have meetings scheduled for the middle of the week. I'm expected in the office Wednesday afternoon."

Just like that, she thought as she picked up a pipe wrench and set it down again. I've got meetings scheduled, see you later. Sorry I broke your heart. "Well, then, have a nice trip."

"C.C." He laid a hand on her arm before she could hide behind the shield again. "I'd like to spend a little time with you. I'd feel a lot better about everything if I was sure we parted on good terms."

"You want to feel better about things," she muttered, then made herself relax her jaw. "Sure, why not? Dinner tomorrow night is fine. You deserve a send-off."

"I appreciate it. Really." He touched her cheek, started to lean toward her. C.C. pulled the shield down with a snap.

"Better stand back from the torch, Trent," she said sweetly. "You might get burned."

Family meetings with the Calhouns were traditionally noisy, argumentative and drenched with tears and laughter. This one was abnormally subdued. Amanda, in her capacity as adviser on finances, sat at the head of the table.

The room was silent.

Suzanna had already put the children to bed. It had been a little easier than usual as both of them had exhausted themselves with Fred—and vice versa.

Trent had excused himself discreetly, directly after dinner. It hardly mattered, C.C. thought. He would know the outcome soon enough.

She was afraid everyone knew it already.

"I guess we all know why we're here," Amanda began. "Trent's going back to Boston on Wednesday, and it would be best all around it we gave him our decision about the house before he left."

"It would be better if we concentrated on finding the necklace." Lilah's stubborn look was offset by the nervous way she twisted the obsidian crystals around her neck.

"We're all still looking for the papers." Suzanna laid a hand on Lilah's arm. "But I think we have to face the reality that finding the necklace could take a long time. Longer than we have."

"Thirty days is longer than we have." All eyes turned to Amanda. "I got a notice from the lawyer last week."

"Last week!" Coco put in. "Stridley contacted you and you didn't mention it?"

"I was hoping I could get an extension without worrying everyone." Amanda laid her hand on the file she set on the table. "No deal. We've been chipping away at the back taxes, but the hard fact is that we haven't been making enough headway. The insurance premiums are due. We can make them all right, and the mortgage—for the time being. The utility bills over the winter were higher than usual, and the new furnace and repairs to the roof ate up a lot of our principal."

C.C. held up a hand. "How bad is it?"

"As bad as it gets." Amanda rubbed at an ache in her temple. "We could sell off a few more pieces, and keep our head above water. Just. But taxes are due again in a couple months, and we'll be back where we started."

"I can sell my pearls," Coco began, and Lilah cut her off.

"No. Absolutely not. We agreed a long time ago that there were some things that couldn't be sold. If we're going to face facts," she said grimly, "then let's face them."

"The plumbing's shot," Amanda continued, and had to clear her tightening throat. "If we don't get the rewiring done, we could end up burning the place down around our ears. Suzanna's lawyer's fees—"

"That's my problem," Suzanna interrupted.

"That's *our* problem," Amanda corrected, and got a unanimous note of assent. "We're a family," she continued. "We've been through the very worst together, and we handled it. Six or seven years ago, it looked as if everything was going to be fine. But…taxes have gone up, along with the insurance, the repairs, everything. It's not as though we're paupers, but the house eats up every cent of spare cash, and then some. If I thought we could weather this, hang in for another year or two, I'd say sell the Limoges, or a few antiques. But it's like trying to plug a hole in a dam and watching others spring out while your fingers are slipping."

"What are you saying, Mandy?" C.C. asked her.

"I'm saying." Amanda pressed her lips together. "I'm saying the only realistic choice I see is for us to sell the house. With the offer from St. James, we can pay off the debts, keep most of what's important to all of us and buy another. If we don't sell, it's going to be taken away from us in any case within a few months." A tear trickled down her cheek. "I'm sorry. I just can't find a way out."

"It's not your fault." Suzanna reached out for her hand. "We all knew it was coming."

Amanda sniffled and shook her head. "What buffer we had, we lost in the stock market crash. We just haven't been able to recover. I know I made the investments—"

"*We* made the investments." Lilah leaned over to join hands, as well. "On the recommendation of a very reputable broker. If the bottom hadn't fallen through, if I'd won the lottery, if Bax hadn't been such a greedy bastard, maybe things would be different now. But they're not."

"We'll still be together." Coco added her hand. "That's what matters."

"That's what matters," C.C. agreed, and laid her hand on top. And that, if nothing else, felt right. "What do we do now?"

Struggling for composure, Amanda sat back. "I guess we ask Trent to come down and make sure the offer still stands."

"I'll get him." C.C. pushed away from the table to walk blindly from the room.

She couldn't believe it. Even as she walked through the huddle of rooms, into the hallway, up the steps with her hand trailing along the banister, she couldn't believe it. None of it would be hers much longer.

There would come a time very soon when she wouldn't be able to step from her room onto the high stone terrace and look out at the sea. She wouldn't be able to climb the steps to Bianca's tower and find Lilah curled on the window seat, dreaming out through the dusty glass. Or Suzanna working in the garden with the children racing on the lawn nearby. Amanda wouldn't come bolting down the stairs in a hurry to get somewhere, do something. Aunt Coco would no longer fuss over the stove in the kitchen.

In a matter of moments, the life she'd known was over. The one to come had yet to begin. She was somewhere in a kind of limbo, too stunned from the loss to ache.

Trent crouched beside the fire where Fred snored on the bright red cushion in his new wicker dog bed. He was going to miss the little devil, Trent realized. Even if he had the time or inclination for a pet back in Boston, he didn't have the heart to take Fred away from the children, or from the women, if it came to that.

He'd seen C.C. tossing the ball for the pup in the side yard that afternoon when she'd come home from work. It had been so good to hear her laugh, to see her wrestle with the dog and Suzanna's children.

Oddly it reminded him of the image he'd had—daydream, he corrected. The daydream he'd had when his mind had wandered the night of the séance. Of him and C.C. sitting on a sunny porch, watching children play in the yard.

It was foolishness, of course, but something had tugged at him that afternoon when he'd stood at the door and looked at her tossing a ball to Fred. A good something, he remembered, until she'd turned and had seen him. Her laughter had died, and her eyes had gone cool.

He straightened, studying the flames in the fire. It was crazy, but he wished with his whole heart that she would flare up, just once more. Throw another punch at him. Call him names. The worst kind of punishment was her steady, passionless politeness.

The sound of the knock on the door had Fred yipping quietly in his sleep. When Trent answered, finding C.C. on the other side of the threshold, twin twinges of delight and distress danced through his system. He wouldn't be able to turn her away this time. It wouldn't be possible to tell her, or himself, that it couldn't be. He had to... Then he looked into her eyes.

"What's wrong? What's happened?" He reached out to comfort, but she stepped stiffly away.

"We'd like you to come downstairs, if you don't mind."

"Catherine—" But she was already walking away, her stride lengthening in her hurry for distance.

He found them all gathered around the dining room table, their faces composed. He was astute enough to understand that he was facing one combined will.

The Calhouns had closed ranks.

"Ladies?"

"Trent, sit down, please." Coco gestured to the chair beside her. "I hope we didn't disturb you?"

"Not at all." He looked at C.C., but she was staring fixedly at the wall above his head. "Are we having another séance?"

"Not this time." Lilah nodded toward Amanda. "Mandy?"

"All right." She took a deep breath and was relieved when Suzanna's hand gripped hers under the table. "Trent, we've discussed your offer for The Towers, and have decided to accept it."

He gave her a blank look. "Accept it?"

"Yes." Amanda pressed her free hand to her quivering stomach. "That is, if your offer still stands."

"Yes, of course it does." He scanned the room, his gaze lingering on C.C. "You're certain you want to sell?"

"Isn't that what you wanted?" C.C.'s voice was clipped. "Isn't that what you came for?"

"Yes." But he'd gotten a great deal more than he'd bargained for. "My firm will be delighted to purchase the property. But...I want to be certain that you're all agreed. That this is what you want. All of you."

"We're all agreed." C.C. went back to staring at the wall.

"The lawyers will handle the details," Amanda began again. "But before we hand things over them, I'd like to review the terms."

"Of course." He named the purchase price again. Hearing it had tears burning in C.C.'s eyes. "There's no reason why we can't be flexible on the timing," he went on. "I realize you'll want to do some kind of inventory before you—relocate."

It was what they wanted, he reminded himself. It was business. It shouldn't make him feel as if he'd just crawled out from under a rock.

"I think we'd like to make the move quickly." Suzanna glanced around the table for confirmation. "As soon as we can find another house."

"If there's anything I can do to help you—"

"You've done enough," C.C. interrupted coolly. "We can take care of ourselves."

"I'd like to add a condition." Lilah leaned forward. "You're purchasing the house, and the land. Not the contents."

"No. Naturally the furniture, heirlooms, personal possessions remain yours."

"Including the necklace." She inclined her head. "Whether it's found before we leave, or after, the Calhoun necklace belongs to the Calhouns. I want that in writing, Trent. If anytime during your renovations, the necklace is recovered, it belongs to us."

"All right." The little clause would drive the lawyers crazy, he thought. But that was their problem. "I'll see that it's put in the contract."

"Bianca's tower." She spoke slowly, afraid her voice would break. "Be careful what you do with it."

"How about some wine?" Coco rose, hands fluttering. "We should have some wine."

"Excuse me." C.C. made herself stand slowly, fighting the impulse to race from the room. "If we're all through, I think I'll go up. I'm tired."

Trent stared after her, but Suzanna stopped him. "I don't think she'd be receptive right now. I'll go."

C.C. went to the terrace to lean out over the wall and let the cold wind dry the tears. There should be a storm, she thought. She wished there was a storm, something as angry and as passionate as her own heart.

Pounding a fist on the wall, she cursed the day she'd ever met Trent. He wouldn't take her love, but he would take her home. Of course, if he had accepted the first and returned it, he could never have taken the house.

"C.C." Suzanna stepped out to slip an arm around her shoulders. "It's cold. Why don't we go inside?"

"It's not right."

"No." She gathered her sister closer. "It's not."

"He doesn't even know what it means." She dashed the angry tears away. "He can't understand. He wouldn't want to."

"Maybe he doesn't. Maybe no one can but us. But it's not his fault, C.C. We can't blame him because we couldn't hang on." She looked away from the gardens she loved, toward the cliffs that always drew her. "I left here once before—it seems like a lifetime ago, but it was only seven years. Nearly eight now." She sighed. "I thought it was the happiest day of my life, leaving the island for my new home in Boston."

"You don't have to talk about that. I know it hurts you."

"Not as much as it once did. I was in love, C.C., a new bride with the future in the palm of my hand. And when I turned around and saw The Towers disappearing behind me, I cried like a baby. I thought it would be easier this time." As tears threatened, she closed her eyes. "I wish it were. What is it about this place that pulls us so?" she wondered.

"I know we can find another house." C.C. linked fingers with her sister. "I know we'll be all right, even happy. But it hurts. And you're right, it's not Trent's fault. But..."

"You have to blame someone." Suzanna smiled.

"He hurt me. I really hate to admit that, but he hurt me. I want to be able to say that he made me fall in love with him. Even that he let me fall in love with him. But I did it all by myself."

"And Trent?"

"He isn't interested."

"From the way he looks at you, I'd say you're wrong."

"Oh, he's interested," C.C. said grimly. "But love has nothing to do with it. He very politely refused to take advantage of my—my lack of experience, as he called it."

"Oh." Suzanna looked out toward the cliffs again. Rejection, she knew, was the sharpest blade of all. "It doesn't help much, but it might have been more difficult for you if he hadn't been—sensible."

"He's sensible, all right," C.C. said through her teeth. "And being a sensible and a civilized man, he'd like us to be friends. He's even taking me to dinner tomorrow so he can be certain I'm not pining away for him, and he can go back to Boston guilt free."

"What are you going to do?"

"Oh, I'll go to dinner with him. I can be just as damned civilized as he can." She set her chin. "And when I'm finished, he's going to be sorry he ever set eyes on Catherine Calhoun." She whirled toward her sister. "Do you still have that red dress? The beaded one that's cut down to sin?"

Suzanna's grin spread. "You bet I do."

"Let's go take a look at it."

Well, well, well, C.C. thought. What a difference a day and a tight silk dress could make. Lips pursed, she turned in front of the cracked cheval glass in the corner of her room. The dress was just a smidgen too small for her—even with the frantic alterations Suzanna had made. It only made more of a statement.

Don't you wish you had me, it said quite clearly. C.C. ran her hands over her hips. And he could wish until his head exploded.

The dress was a form-fitting glitter of flame that licked down from its plunging neckline to the abbreviated hem. Suzanna had ruthlessly slashed it off so that it hit C.C. midthigh. The long sleeves ended in points over her wrists. And she'd added Coco's rhinestone ear clips, with their wicked sparkle.

The thirty minutes she'd spent on makeup seemed to have paid off. Her lips were as red as the dress, thanks to Amanda's contribution. Her eyes were shadowed with copper and emerald, thanks to Lilah. Her hair was as glossy as a raven's wing and slicked back a bit at the temples.

All in all, C.C. thought as she turned, Trenton St. James III was in for a surprise.

"Suzanna said you needed some shoes." Lilah walked in and stopped in midyawn. The shoes dangled from her fingertips as she stared. "I must have passed through a parallel universe."

C.C. grinned and spun a circle. "What do you think?"

"I think Trent's going to need oxygen." Approving, she passed C.C. a pair of spiked snakeskin heels. "Kiddo, you look dangerous."

"Good." She pulled on the shoes. "Now if I can just walk in these without falling on my face."

"Practice. I've got to get Mandy."

A few moments later, all three sisters supervised C.C.'s walk. "You'll be having dinner," Amanda put in, wincing at each wobble. "So you'll be sitting down most of the time."

"I'm getting it," C.C. muttered. "I'm just not used to heels. How do you work in these things all day?"

"Talent."

"Walk slower," Lilah suggested. "More deliberately. As if you have all the time in the world."

"Take if from her," Amanda agreed. "She's an expert at slow."

"In this case—" Lilah gave Amanda an arched look "—slow is sexy. See?"

Taking her sister's advice, C.C. walked with a cautious deliberation that came off as slinky. Amanda held out her hands. "I stand corrected. What coat are you wearing?"

"I haven't thought of it."

"You can wear my black silk cape," Amanda decided. "You'll freeze but you'll look great doing it. Perfume. Aunt Coco's got some of that smoldering French stuff left from Christmas."

"No." Suzanna shook her head. "She should stick with her usual scent." Tilting her head, she studied her sister and smiled. "The contrast will drive him crazy."

Unaware of what was in store for him, Trent sat in the parlor with Coco. His bags were packed. His calls were made. He wished he could come up with a reasonable excuse to stay another few days.

"We've enjoyed having you," Coco told him when he'd expressed his appreciation for her hospitality. "I'm sure we'll be seeing each other again soon."

Her crystal ball didn't lie, she reminded herself. It still linked Trent up with one of her nieces, and she wasn't ready to wave surrender.

"I certainly hope so. I have to say, Coco, how much I admire you for raising four such lovely women."

"Sometimes I think we raised each other." She smiled mistily around the room. "I'm going to miss this place. To be honest I didn't think it mattered to me until . . . well, until now. I didn't grow up here as the girls did. We traveled quite a bit, you see, and my father only came back sporadically. I always thought it was the fact that his mother had died here that put him off. Then, of course, I spent my married life and the first few years of my widowhood in Philadelphia. Then when Judson and Deliah were killed, I came here for the girls." She sent him a sad, apologetic smile. "I'm sorry to get sentimental on you, Trenton."

"Don't apologize." He sipped thoughtfully at his aperitif. "My family has never been close, and as a result, there was never a home like this in my life. I think that's why I've begun to understand what it could mean."

"You should settle down," she said, cagily, she thought. "Find a nice girl, make a home and family of your own. Why, I can't think of anything lonelier than not having anyone to go home to."

Wanting to avoid that line of thought, he reached down to throw the ball for Fred. They both watched as the dog bounded after it, tripped himself up and went sprawling.

"Not particularly graceful," Trent mused. He rose and went over to retrieve the ball himself. Scratching the dog's belly, he glanced over. The first thing he saw was a pair of very slim black heels. Slowly his gaze traveled up a long, shapely pair of legs. With the breath backing up in his lungs, he sat back on his heels.

There was a sparkle of scarlet, snug and sleek over a curvy feminine form.

"Lose something?" C.C. asked as his eyes fixed on her face.

Her lips were curved and red and slick. Trent ran his tongue over his teeth to be certain he hadn't swallowed it. On unsteady legs, he rose.

"C.C.?"

"We were having dinner tonight, weren't we?"

"We . . . yes. You look wonderful."

"Do you like it?" She turned a circle so that he could see the back of the dress dipped even lower than the front. "I think red's a cheerful color." And powerful, she thought, still smiling.

"It suits you. I've never seen you in a dress before."

"Impractical when it comes to changing fuel pumps. Are you ready to go?"

"Go where?"

Oh, she was going to enjoy this. "To dinner."

"Right. Yes."

She inclined her head the way Suzanna had showed her and handed him her cape. It was a service he'd performed hundreds of times for dozens of women. But his hands fumbled.

"Don't wait up, Aunt Coco."

"No, dear." Behind their retreating backs, she grinned and raised her fists in the air. The moment the front door shut, the three remaining Calhouns exchanged high fives.

Chapter Nine

"I'm glad you talked me into going out tonight." C.C. reached for the door handle before she remembered to let Trent open the car for her.

"I wasn't sure you'd still be willing to go." He closed his hand over hers.

"Because of the house?" As casually as possible, C.C. slid her hand from under his and lowered herself into the car. "That's done. I'd rather not talk about it tonight."

"All right." He closed the door, rounded the hood. "Amanda recommended the restaurant." He had his hands on the keys but continued to stare at her.

"Something wrong?"

"No." Unless you counted his nervous system. After starting the car, he tried again. "I thought you might like dining near the water."

"Sounds fine." His radio was on a classical station. Not her usual style, she thought. But it wasn't a usual night. C.C. settled back and prepared to enjoy the ride. "Have you heard that rattle again?"

"What rattle?"

"The one you asked me to fix yesterday."

"Oh, that rattle." He smiled to himself. "No. It must have been my imagination." When she crossed her legs, his fingers tightened on the wheel. "You never told me why you decided to be a mechanic."

"Because I'm good at it." She shifted in her seat to face him. He caught a drift of honeysuckle and nearly groaned. "When I was six, I took apart our lawn mower's engine, to see how it worked. I was hooked. Why did you go into hotels?"

"It was expected of me." He stopped, surprised that that had been the first answer out of his mouth. "And I suppose I got good at it."

"Do you like it?"

Had anyone ever asked him that before? he wondered. Had he ever asked himself? "Yes, I guess I do."

"Guess?" Her brows lifted into her bangs. "I thought you were sure of everything."

He glanced at her again and nearly ran off the road. "Apparently not."

When they arrived at the waterfront restaurant, he was used to the transformation. Or thought he was. Then he went around to open the car door for her. She slid out, rose up. They were eye to eye, barely a whisper apart. C.C. held her ground, wondering if he could hear the way her heart was pounding against her ribs.

"Are you sure nothing's wrong?"

"No, I'm not sure." No one, he was certain, this impossibly sexy was meant to be resisted. He cupped a hand at the back of her neck. "Let me check."

She eased away the instant before his lips brushed hers. "This isn't a date, remember? Just a friendly dinner."

"I'd like to change the rules."

"Too late." She smiled and offered a hand. "I'm hungry."

"You're not the only one," he murmured, and took her inside.

He wasn't sure how to handle her. The smooth moves he'd always taken for granted seemed rusty. The setting was perfect, the little table beside the window with water lapping just outside. As the sun set away in the west, it deepened and tinted the bay. He ordered wine as she picked up her menu and smiled at him.

Under the table, C.C. gently eased out of her shoes. "I haven't been here before," she told him. "It's very nice."

"I can't guarantee the food will be as exceptional as your aunt's."

"No one cooks like Aunt Coco. She'll be sorry to see you go. She likes cooking for a man."

"Will you?"

"Will I what?"

"Be sorry to see me go."

C.C. looked down at the menu, trying to concentrate on her choices. The hard fact was, she had none. "Since you're still here, we'll have to see. I imagine you have a lot to catch up on in Boston."

"Yes, I do. I've been thinking that after I do, I may take a vacation. A real one. Bar Harbor might be a good choice."

She looked up, then away. "Thousands think so," she murmured, relieved when the waiter served the wine.

"If you could go anywhere you liked, where would it be?"

"That's a tough question, since I haven't been anywhere." She sipped, found the wine as smooth as chilled silk on her tongue. "Somewhere where I could see the sun set on the water, I think. Someplace warm." She shrugged. "I suppose I should have said Paris or London."

"No." He laid a hand on hers. "Catherine—"

"Are you ready to order?"

C.C. glanced quickly at the waiter who hovered beside them. "Yes." She slid her hand from Trent's and picked arbitrarily from the menu. Cautious, she kept one hand in her lap as she lifted her wine. The moment they were alone again, she started to speak. "Have you ever seen a whale?"

"I . . . no."

"You'll be coming back occasionally while you're—while you're having The Towers converted. You should take a day and go out on one of the whale-watch boats. The last time I managed it, I saw three humpback. You need to dress warmly though. Even in high summer it's cold once you get out on the Atlantic. It can be a rough ride, but it's worth it. You might even think about offering some sort of package yourself. You know, a weekend rate with a whale-watch tour included. A lot of the hotels—"

"Catherine." He stopped her by closing a hand over her wrist before she could lift her glass again. He could feel the rapid, unsteady beat of her pulse. Not passion this time, he thought. But heartache. "The papers haven't been signed yet," he said quietly. "There's still time to look for other options."

"There aren't any other options." He cared, she realized as she studied his face. It was in his eyes as they looked into hers. Concern, apology. It made it worse somehow, knowing he cared. "We sell to you now, or The Towers is sold later for taxes. The end result is the same, and there's a little more dignity doing it this way."

"I might be able to help. A loan."

She retreated instantly. "We can't take your money."

"If I buy the house from you, you're taking my money."

"That's different. That's business. Trent," she said before he could argue, "I appreciate the fact that you'd offer, especially since I know the only reason you're here is to buy The Towers."

It was, he thought. Or it had been. "The thing is, C.C., I feel like I'm foreclosing on those widows and orphans."

She managed a smile. "We're five strong, self-sufficient women. We don't blame you—or maybe I do, a little, but at least I know I'm being unfair when I do. My feelings for you don't make it easy to be fair.

"What are your feelings?"

She let out a little sigh as the waiter served the appetizers and lit the candle between them. "You're taking the house, you might as well take it all. I'm in love with you. But I'll get over it." With her head tilted slightly, she lifted her fork. "Is there anything else you want to know?"

When he took her hand again, she didn't pull back, but waited. "I never wanted to hurt you," he said carefully. How well her hand fit into his, he thought, looking down at it. How comforting it was to link his fingers with hers. "I'm just not capable of giving you—of giving anyone—promises of love and fidelity."

"That's sad." She shook her head as his eyes came back to hers. "You see, I'm only losing a house. I can find another. You're losing the rest of your life, and you only have one." She forced her lips to curve as she drew away from him. "Unless, of course, you subscribe to Lilah's idea that we just keep coming back. This is nice wine," she commented. "What is it again?"

"Pouilly Fumé."

"I'll have to remember that." She began to talk cheerfully as she ate the meal without tasting a thing. By the time coffee was served, she was wound like a top. C.C. knew that she would rather take an engine apart with her fingernails than face another evening such as this.

To love him so desperately, yet to have to be strong enough, proud enough to pretend she was capable of living without him. To sit, greedily storing each gesture, each word, while pretending it was all so casual and easy.

She wanted to shout at him, to rage and damn him for stirring her emotions into a frenzy then calmly walking away from the storm. But she could only cling to the cold comfort of pride.

"Tell me about your home in Boston," she invited. That would be something, she thought, to be able to picture him in his own home.

He wasn't able to take his eyes off her. The way the clusters at her ears shot fire. The way the candlelight flickered dreamily in her eyes. But all through the evening, he had felt as though she had blocked off a part of herself, the most important part of herself. And he might never see the whole woman again.

"My home?"

"Yes, where you live."

"It's just a house." It occurred to him quite suddenly that it didn't mean a thing to him. An excellent investment, that was all. "It's only a few minutes from the office."

"That's convenient. Have you lived there long?"

"About five years. Actually, I bought it from my father when he and his third wife split. They decided to liquidate some assets."

"I see." And she was very much afraid that she did. "Does your mother live in Boston, too?"

"No. She travels. Being tied down to one place doesn't agree with her."

"Sounds like Great-Aunt Colleen." C.C. smiled over the rim of her cup. "That's my father's aunt, or Bianca's oldest child."

"Bianca," he mused, and thought again of that moment when he'd felt that soft and soothing warmth over his and C.C.'s joined hands.

"She lives on cruise ships. Every now and again we get a postcard from some port of call. Aruba or Madagascar. She's eighty-something, obsessively single and mean as a shark with a hangover. We all live in fear that she might decide to visit."

"I didn't realize you had any relatives living other than Coco and your sisters." His brows drew together. "She might know something about the necklace."

"Great-Aunt Colleen?" Considering it, C.C. pursed her lips. "I doubt it. She was a child when Bianca died, and spent most of her girlhood in boarding schools." Without thinking, she pulled off her earrings and massaged the tender lobes. Desire spread like brushfire through Trent's blood. "Anyway, if we could find her—which isn't likely—and mentioned the whole business, she'd probably come steaming back to hack away at the walls. She doesn't have any love for The Towers, but she has a great deal for money."

"She doesn't sound like a relative of yours."

"Oh, we have a number of oddities in our family closet." After dropping the earrings into her bag, she leaned an elbow on the table. "Great-Uncle Sean—he was Bianca's youngest—was shot climbing out of his married paramour's window. One of his paramours, I should say. He survived, then took off for the West Indies, never to be heard of again. That was sometime during the thirties. Ethan, my grandfather, lost the bulk of the family fortune on cards and horses. Gambling was his weakness, and that's what killed him. He had a wager that he could sail from Bar Harbor to Newport and back within six days. He made it to Newport, and was heading back ahead of schedule when he ran into a squall and was lost at sea. Which meant he lost his last bet as well."

"They sound like an adventurous pair."

"They were Calhouns," C.C. explained, as if that said it all.

"I'm sorry the St. Jameses don't have anything to compare with it."

"Ah, well. I've always wondered if Bianca would have stepped back from that tower window if she'd known how messed up her children would become." C.C. looked thoughtfully out to where lights played on the dark water. "She must have loved her artist very much."

"Or was very unhappy in her marriage."

C.C. looked back. "Yes, there is that. Maybe we should head back. It's getting late." She started to rise, remembered, then slid her bare foot around the floor beneath the table.

"What is it?"

"I've lost my shoes." So much, she thought, for the sophisticated image.

Trent bent down to look himself and got an eyeful of long, slim leg. "Ah..." He cleared his throat and trained his eyes on the floor. "Here you go." He took both, then straightening, smiled at her. "Put your foot out. I'll give you a hand." He watched her as he slipped the shoes onto her feet and remembered that he'd once thought she would never stand for being a Cinderella. He trailed his finger up her instep and caught the flicker in her eyes. The flicker of desire that, no matter what common sense told him, he very much wanted.

"Have I mentioned that you have truly incredible legs?"

"No." She had one hand balled in a fist at her side and struggled to concentrate on it rather than the sensations his touch had spurting through her. "It's nice of you to notice."

"It's difficult not to. They're the only ones I've known that look sexy in coveralls."

Ignoring the thud of her own heart, she leaned toward him. "That reminds me."

He could kiss her now, he thought. He had only to shift a mere inch to have his mouth on hers, where he wanted it. "What?"

"I don't think your shocks have more than another couple thousand miles on them." With a smile, she rose. "I'd look into that when you get home." Pleased with herself, C.C. started out ahead of him.

When they settled in the car, she congratulated herself. A very successful evening all in all, she thought. Maybe he wasn't miserable, as she was, but she was damn sure she'd made him uncomfortable a time or two. He'd go back to Boston the next day.... She turned to stare out the window until she was certain she could deal with the pain. He'd go back, but he wouldn't forget her quickly or easily. His last impression of her would be one of a composed, self-contained woman in a sexy red dress. Better, C.C. decided, much better than the picture of a mechanic in coveralls with grease on her hands.

More importantly, she'd proven something to herself. She could love, and she could let go.

She looked up as the car started to climb. She could see the shadowy peaks of the two towers spearing into the night sky. Trent slowed the car as he looked, as well.

"The light's on in Bianca's tower."

"Lilah," C.C. murmured. "She often sits up there." She thought of her sister sitting by the window, looking out into the night. "You won't tear it down, will you?"

"No." Understanding more than she knew, he closed his hand over hers. "I promise you it won't be torn down."

The house disappeared as the road curved away, then all but filled the view. They could hear the beat and slap of the sea as they looked at it. Lights were sprinkled on throughout, glowing against the dull gray stone. A slender shadow moved in front of the tower window, stood for a moment, then slid away.

Inside, Lilah called down the stairs. "They're back."

Four women raced to the windows to peer out.

"We shouldn't spy on them," Suzanna murmured, but moved the curtain aside a bit more.

"We're not." Amanda strained her eyes. "We're just checking, that's all. Can you see anything?"

"They're still in the car," Coco complained. "How are we supposed to see what's going on if they're going to sit in the car?"

"We could use our imaginations." Lilah shook her hair back. "If that man isn't begging her to go to Boston with him, then he really is a jerk."

"To Boston?" Alarmed, Suzanna glanced over. "You don't think she'd go to Boston, do you?"

"She'd go to the Ukraine if he had the sense to ask her," Amanda commented. "Look, they're getting out."

"Maybe if we just cracked a window a little bit, we could hear—"

"Aunt Coco, that's ridiculous." Lilah clucked her tongue.

"You're right, of course." Color tinged Coco's cheek.

"Of course I'm right. They'd hear the windows creak if we tried." Grinning, she pressed her face against the glass. "We'll just have to read their lips."

"This was nice," C.C. said as she stepped out of the car. "I haven't been out to dinner in a while."

"You had dinner with Finney."

She gave him a blank look, then laughed. "Oh, Finney, sure." The breeze played with her bangs as she smiled. "You've got quite a memory."

"Some things seem to stick to it." The jealousy he felt was, unfortunately, no memory. "Doesn't he ever take you out?"

"Finney? No, I just go to his place."

Frustrated, Trent jammed his hands into his pockets. "He should take you out."

She smothered a chuckle as the image of old Albert Finney escorting her to a restaurant ran through her mind. "I'll be sure to mention it to him." She turned to start up the steps.

"Catherine, don't go in yet." He took her hands.

At the windows four pairs of eyes narrowed.

"It's late, Trent."

"I don't know if I'll see you again before I leave."

It took all her strength to keep her eyes steady. "Then we'll say goodbye now."

"I need to see you again."

"The shop's open at eight-thirty. I'll be there."

"Damn it, C.C., you know what I mean." His hands were on her shoulders now.

"No, I don't."

"Come to Boston." He blurted it out, shocking himself while she stood calmly waiting.

"Why?"

To give himself a moment to find control again, he stepped back. "I could show you around." How much more inane could he get? Trent wondered. How much more beautiful could she look? "You said you'd never been. We could...have some time together."

Inside her wrap, she shivered, but her voice was calm and smooth. "Are you asking me to come to Boston and have an affair with you?"

"No. Yes. Oh, Lord. Just wait." He turned to pace a few steps away and breathe.

Inside, Lilah smiled. "Why, he's in love with her after all, but he's too stupid to know it."

"Shh!" Coco waved a hand. "I can almost hear what they're saying." She had an ear at the base of the water glass she pressed up to the window.

At the bottom of the steps, Trent tried again. "Nothing I begin ends the way I expect it to when I'm with you." He turned back. She was still standing with the house behind her, the dress glimmering like liquid fire in the dark. "I know I have no business asking you, and I didn't intend to. I intended to say a very civil goodbye and let you go."

"And now?"

"Now I want to make love with you more than I want to go on breathing."

"To make love," C.C. repeated steadily. "But you don't love me."

"I don't know anything about love. I care for you." He walked back to touch a hand to her face. "Maybe that could be enough."

She studied him, realizing he didn't have any idea that he was breaking an already shattered heart. "It might be, for a day or a week or a month. But you were right about me, Trent. I expect more. I deserve more." Keeping her eyes on his, she slid her hands over his shoulders. "I offered myself to you once. That won't happen again. And neither will this."

She pressed her mouth against his, pouring every scrap of her tattered emotions into it. Her arms enfolded him even as her body swayed seductively toward his. With a sigh, her lips parted, inviting him to take.

Off balance, needy, he dragged her head back and plundered. Unsteady, his hands skimmed beneath her wrap, urgently seeking the warmth of her skin.

So many feelings, too many feelings, bombarded him. He wanted only to fill himself with the taste of her. But there was more. She wouldn't let him take only the kiss, but all the emotion that went with it. He felt he was drowning in it, but it was so strong and heady a flood, he couldn't fight.

Love me! Why can't you love me? Her mind seemed to scream it even as she was borne away on the tide of her own longings. Everything she wanted was here, inside the circle of her arms. Everything but his heart.

"Catherine." He couldn't get his breath. Dragging her closer, he pressed his mouth to her neck. "I can't get close enough."

She held him to her a moment longer, then slowly, painfully, pulled away. "Yes, you could. And that's what hurts the most." Turning, she dashed up the steps.

"Catherine."

She paused at the door. With her head high, she turned around. He was already coming after her when he saw the tears glittering in her eyes. Nothing else would have stopped him.

"Goodbye, Trent. I hope to God that keeps you up at night."

As he listened to the echo of the door slamming, he was certain it would.

It cannot go on. I can no longer pretend that I am disloyal to my husband only between the covers of this journal. My life, so calm and ordered during my twenty-four years, has become a lie this summer. One I must atone for.

As autumn approaches and we make our plans to return to New York, I thank God I will soon leave Mount Desert Island behind me. How close, how dangerously close I have come these past days to breaking my marriage vows.

And yet, I grieve.

In another week, we will be gone. I may never see Christian again. That is how it should be. How it must be. But in my heart I know that I would give my soul for one night, even one hour, in his arms. Imagining how it could be obsesses me. With him there would finally be passion, and love, even laughter. With him it would not simply be a duty, cold and silent and soon over.

I pray to be forgiven for the adultery I have committed in my heart.

My conscience has urged me to keep away from the cliffs. And I have tried. It has demanded that I be a more patient, loving and understanding wife to Fergus. I have done so. Whatever he has asked of me, I have done. At his request, I gave a tea for several of the ladies. We have gone to the theater, to countless dinner parties. I have listened until my head was throbbing to talk of business and fashion and the possibility of war. My smile never falters, for Fergus prefers that I look content at all times. Because it pleases him, I wear the emeralds when we go out in the evenings.

They are my penance now, a reminder that a sin is not always in the action, but in the heart.

I sit here in my tower now as I write. The cliffs are below, the cliffs where Christian paints. Where I go when I sneak from the house like a randy housemaid. It shames me. It sustains me. Even now I look down and see him. He faces the sea, and waits for me.

We have never touched, not once, though the ache is in both of us. I have learned how much passion there can be in silences, in long, troubled looks.

I will not go to him today, but only sit here and watch him. When I feel I have the strength, I will go to him only to say goodbye and wish him well.

While I live through the long winter that faces me, I will wonder if he will be here next summer.

Chapter Ten

"Here are the papers you asked for, Mr. St. James."

Oblivious to his secretary's presence, Trent continued to stand at the window, staring out. It was a habit he'd developed since returning to work three weeks before. Through the wide tinted glass, he could watch Boston bustling by below. Steel-and-glass towers glittered beside elegant brownstones in a architectural potpourri. Thick traffic weaved and charged on the streets. In sweats and colorful running shorts, joggers paced themselves along the path beside the river. Then there was the river itself, streaming with boats, sails puffed full of warm spring breezes.

"Mr. St. James?"

"Yes?" He glanced around at his secretary.

"I've brought you the papers you requested."

"Thank you, Angela." In an old habit, he looked at his watch. It occurred to him, painfully, that he had rarely thought of the time when he'd been with C.C. "It's after five. You should go home to your family."

Angela hesitated. She'd worked for Trenton for six years. It had only been during the past couple of weeks that he had begun calling her by her first name or inquiring about her family. The day before, he'd actually complimented her on her dress. The change in him had the entire staff baffled. As his secretary, she felt obligated to dig out the source of it.

"May I speak with you a minute?"

"All right. Would you like to sit down?"

"No, sir. I hope you won't consider this out of place, Mr. St. James, but I wanted to know if you're feeling well."

A ghost of a smile played around his mouth. "Don't I look well?"

"Oh, yes, of course. A little tired perhaps. It's just that since you returned from Bar Harbor, you seem distracted, and different somehow."

"You could say I am distracted. I am different, and to answer your original question, no, I don't think I am entirely well."

"Mr. St. James, if there's anything I can do..."

Studying her, he sat on the edge of his desk. He had hired her because she was efficient and quick. As he recalled, he had nearly passed her over because she'd had two small children. It had worried him that she wouldn't be able to balance her responsibilities, but he'd taken what he'd considered a chance. It had worked very well indeed.

"Angela, how long have you been married?"

"Married?" Thrown off, she blinked. "Ten years."

"Happily?"

"Yes, Joe and I are happy."

Joe, he mused. He hadn't even known her husband's name. Hadn't bothered to find it out. "Why?"

"Why, sir?"

"Why are you happy?"

"I . . . I suppose because we love each other."

He nodded, gesturing to prod her along. "And that's enough?"

"It certainly helps you get through the rough spots." She smiled a little, thinking of her Joe. "We've had some of them, but one of us always manages to pull the other through."

"You consider yourself a team then. So you have a great deal in common?"

"I don't know about that. Joe likes football and I hate it. He loves jazz, and I don't understand it." It wouldn't occur to her until later that this was the first time she'd felt completely at ease with Trent since she'd taken the job. "Sometimes I feel like wearing earplugs all weekend. Whenever I feel like shipping him out, I think about what my life would be without him. And I don't like what I see." Taking a chance, she stepped closer. "Mr. St. James, if this is about Marla Montblanc getting married last week, well, I'd just like to say that you're better off."

"Marla got married?"

Truly baffled, Angela shook her head. "Yes, sir. Last week, to that golf pro. It was in all the papers."

"I must have missed it." There had been other things in the papers that had captured his attention.

"I realize you'd been seeing her for quite a while."

Seeing her, Trent mused. Yes, that cool, passionless phrase described their relationship perfectly. "Yes, I had been."

"You're not—upset?"

"About Marla? No." The fact was he hadn't thought of her in weeks. Since he'd walked into a garage and spotted a pair of scarred boots.

Another woman, Angela realized. And if she'd had this kind of affect on the boss, she had all of Angela's support. "Sir, if someone—something else," she corrected cautiously, "is on your mind, you may be overanalyzing the situation."

The comment surprised him enough to make him smile again. "Do I overanalyze, Angela?"

"You're very meticulous, Mr. St. James, and analyze details finitely, which works very well in business. Personal matters can't always be dealt with logically."

"I've been coming to that same conclusion myself." He stood again. "I appreciate the time."

"My pleasure, Mr. St. James." And it certainly had been. "Is there anything else I can do for you?"

"No, thank you." He turned back to the window. "Good night, Angela."

"Good night." She was grinning when she closed the door at her back.

Trent stood where he was for some time. No, he hadn't noticed the announcement of Marla's wedding. The papers had also been full of the upcoming sale of The Towers. "Bar Harbor landmark to become newest St. James Hotel," he remembered. "Rumors of lost treasures sweeten the deal."

Trent wasn't certain where the leak had come from, though he wasn't surprised by it. As he'd expected, his lawyers had grumbled over the clause Lilah had insisted on. Whispers of emeralds had sneaked down the hallways. It was only natural that they would find their way onto the street and into print.

Newspapers and tabloids had been rife with speculation on the Calhoun emeralds for more than a week. They'd been termed priceless and tragic and legendary—all the right adjectives to ensure more newsprint.

Fergus Calhoun's business exploits had been rehashed, along with his wife's suicide. An enterprising reporter had even managed to track down Colleen Calhoun aboard a cruise ship in the Ionian Sea. The grande dame's pithy reply had been printed in italics.

"Humbug."

He wondered if C.C. had seen the papers. Of course, she had, he thought. Just as she'd probably been hounded by the press.

How was she taking it? Was she hurt and miserable, forced to answer questions when some nosy reporter stuck a tape recorder in her face? He smiled a little. *Forced?* He imagined she'd throw a dozen reporters out of the garage if they had the nerve to try.

God, he missed her. And missing her was eating him alive. He woke up each morning wondering what she was doing. He went to bed each night to toss restlessly as thoughts of her invaded his brain. When he slept, she was in his dreams. She was his dream.

Three weeks, he thought. He should have adjusted by now. Yet every day that he was here and she was somewhere else, it got worse.

The revised contracts for the sale of The Towers were sitting on his desk. He should have signed them days ago. Yet he couldn't make himself take that final step. The last time he had looked at them, he had only been able to focus on three words.

Catherine Colleen Calhoun.

He'd read it over and over, remembering the first time she'd told him her name, tossing it at him as though it had been a weapon. She'd had grease on her face, Trenton remembered. And fire in her eyes.

Then he would think of other times, odd moments, careless words. The way she had scowled at him from her perch on the arm of the sofa while he'd had tea with Coco. The look on her face when they'd stood on the terrace together, watching the sea. How perfectly her mouth had fit to his when he had kissed her under an arbor of wisteria not yet in bloom.

It would be blooming now, he mused. Those first fragrant flowers would be opening. Would she think of him at all when she walked there?

If she did, he was very much afraid the thoughts wouldn't be kind.

She'd cursed him when she'd seen him last. She'd leveled those deep green eyes at him and had hoped that the kiss, the last kiss they'd shared, would keep him up at night.

He doubted even she could know how completely her wish had come true.

Rubbing his tired eyes, he walked back to his desk. It was, as always, in perfect order. As his business was—as his life had been.

Things had changed, he was forced to admit. He had changed, but perhaps he hadn't changed so completely. Once again, he picked up the contracts to study them. He was still a skilled and organized businessman, one who knew how to maneuver a deal and make it work to his advantage.

He picked up his pen and tapped it lightly on the papers. A germ of an idea had rooted in his mind a few days before. Now he sat quietly and let it form, shift, realign.

It was unusual, he considered. Maybe even mildly eccentric, but...but, he thought as a smile began to curve his mouth, if he played his cards right, it could work. It was his job to make it work. Slowly he let out a long breath. It might just be the most important deal of his life.

He picked up the phone and, employing all of the St. James clout, began to turn the first wheels.

Hank finished sanding the fender on the '69 Mustang, then stood back to admire his work. "Coming along just fine," he called to C.C.

She glanced over, but her hands were full with the brake shoes she was replacing above her head. "It's going to be a beauty. I'm glad we got the shot at reconditioning it."

"You want me to start on the primer?"

She swore as brake fluid dripped onto her cheek. "No. You told me three times today that you've got a hot date tonight. Get cleaned up and take off."

"Thanks." But he'd been too well trained to leave without replacing tools and material. "You found another house yet?"

"No." She ignored the sudden ache in her stomach and concentrated on her work. "We're all going out tomorrow to look."

"Won't be the same, not having Calhouns in The Towers. Sure is something about that necklace, though. Papers are full of stories about it."

"They'll die down." She hoped.

"Guess if you find it, you'd be millionaires. You could retire and move to Florida."

Despite her mood, she had to chuckle. "Well, we haven't found it yet." Just the receipt, she mused, which Lilah had unearthed during her one and only shift in the storeroom. "Florida'll have to wait. The brakes won't."

"Guess I'll be going. Want me to lock up the office?"

"Go ahead. Have a good time."

He went out whistling, and C.C. stopped a moment to rest her arms and neck. She wished she'd been able to keep Hank around a while longer, for company, for the distraction. Even if he rambled on about the house and the necklace, he helped keep her mind occupied.

No matter how loudly she played the radio, once she was alone, there was too much silence.

They would hear from the lawyer any day. Perhaps Aunt Coco had gotten a call from Stridley that afternoon, telling her that the contracts had been signed and a settlement date set.

Would Trent come to the settlement? she wondered. No, no, of course not. He would send a representative, and that was for the best.

Besides, she had too much to do to worry about it. House hunting, the search through old papers for a clue to the emeralds' whereabouts, the classic Mustang she intended to baby along to gleaming perfection. She barely had a moment to catch her breath much less brood about seeing Trent over the settlement table.

If only it would stop hurting, even for a few moments.

It would get better, she told herself as she returned to the brake job. It had to. After they'd found a new house and settled in. After the talk of the necklace had died away. Everything would get back to normal—or what she would have to accept as normal. If the ache never completely went away, then she would learn to live with it.

She had her family. Together, they could handle anything.

Her shoulders were stiff by the time she'd finished. Rolling them a little, she started to step out from under the car when she realized the radio had stopped playing. She glanced over. And saw Trent standing by the workbench. The wrench she was holding clattered to the floor.

"What are you doing here?"

"Waiting for you to finish." She looked fabulous, was all he could think. Absolutely fabulous. "How are you?"

"Busy." Rocked from the pain, she turned to hit a button on the wall. The lift groaned as it brought the car down. "You're here about the house, I guess."

"Yes, you could say that's a large part of it."

"We've been expecting to hear from the lawyer."

"I know."

When the car was settled, she took a rag and wiped her hands, keeping her eyes on them. "Amanda's handling the details. She's at the Bay-Watch if you need to discuss anything."

"What I need to discuss concerns you. Us."

She looked up, then took a quick step back when she realized he'd moved over to stand next to her. "I really don't have anything else to say to you."

"Okay, then I'll do the talking. In just a minute."

He moved fast. Still, she was certain if she'd been expecting it, she could have evaded him. She wasn't certain she would have tried.

It felt so good, so right, to have his mouth covering hers, his hands framing her face. Her pride faltered long enough to have her reaching up to grasp his wrists, holding on as she let her needs flow into the kiss.

"I've thought about doing that for three and a half weeks," he murmured.

She squeezed her eyes tight. "Go away, Trent."

"Catherine—"

"Damn you, I said go away." She yanked free, then turned to brace her palms on the bench. "I hate you for coming here, for making a fool out of me again."

"You're not the fool. You never were."

When his hand brushed lightly over her shoulder, she snatched up a hammer and whirled. "If you touch me again, so help me, I'll break your nose."

He looked at her. The fire was in her eyes again. "Thank God. You're back." Delighted but cautious, he held up a hand. "Just listen, please. Business first."

"My business with you is settled."

"There's been a change in the plans." He plucked some change out of the can on the bench. "Can I buy you a drink?"

"No. Say what you have to say, then get out."

With a shrug, he strolled over to the soft drink machine and plugged in the change. It was then that C.C. noticed he was wearing scuffed high-tops.

"What are those?" she asked, staring at them.

"These?" Trent grinned as he popped the top on the can. "New shoes. What do you think?" When she simply gaped, he took a long drink. "I know, not quite the usual image, but things change. A number of things have changed. Would you mind putting down that hammer?"

"What? Oh. All right." She set it aside. "You said plans had changed. Does that mean you've decided not to buy The Towers?"

"Yes and no. Would you rather go into the office to discuss this?"

"Damn it, Trent, just tell me what's going on."

"All right. Here's the deal. We take one wing, the west, I think, so it doesn't involve Bianca's tower. We have it extensively remodeled. My preference is to salvage as much of the original material as possible and reconstruct, whenever possible, according with the original blueprints. It should maintain its turn-of-the-century feel. That will be part of the draw."

"The draw?" she repeated, lost.

"We can easily have ten suites without compromising the architecture. If memory serves, the billiard room would be excellent for dining, with the west tower remodeled for more intimate meals and private parties."

"Ten suites?"

"In the west wing," he agreed. "With an accent on aesthetics and intimacy. We'll have to put all the fireplaces back in working order. I think, with what we'll offer, we'll have year-round clientele rather than just seasonal."

"What are you going to do with the rest of the house?"

"That would be up to you, and your family." He set the drink aside and came toward her. "The way I see it, you could live very easily on the first two floors and the east wing. God knows there's plenty of room."

Confused, she pressed her fingers to her temple. "We'd be, what—renting it from you?"

"That's not exactly what I had in mind. I was thinking more of a partnership." He took her hand, examining it closely. "Your knuckles have healed."

"What kind of partnership?"

"The St. James Corporation fronts the money for the renovations, advertising and so forth. Once the retreat—I like retreat better than hotel in this case—once it's in operation, we split the profits, fifty-fifty."

"I don't understand."

"It's really very simple, C.C." He lifted her hand, kissed one finger. "We compromise. We have our hotel, you have your home. Nobody loses."

Afraid to feel it, she banked down the little flicker of hope. "I don't see how it could work. Why would anyone want to pay to stay in someone else's home?"

"A landmark," he reminded her, and kissed another finger. "With a legend, a ghost and a mystery. They'll pay very well to stay here. And when they get a taste of Coco's bouillabaisse—"

"Aunt Coco?"

"I've already offered her the position of chef. She's delighted. There's still the matter of a manager, but I think Amanda will fit the slot, don't you?" His eyes smiled as he brushed a kiss over her third finger.

"Why are you doing this?"

"I'm a businessman. It makes good business sense. I've already begun the market research." He turned her hand over and pressed his lips to the palm. "That's what I've told my board of directors. I think you know differently."

"I don't know anything." She pulled her hand away to walk to the open garage doors. "All I know is that you come back here with some sort of wild scheme—"

"It's a very solid plan," he corrected. "I'm not a wild-scheme sort of person. At least I never have been." He went to her again, taking her shoulders. "I want you to keep your home, C.C."

With her lips pressed tight, she closed her eyes. "So, you're doing it for me."

"For you, your sisters, Coco, even Bianca." Hands firm, he turned her to face him. "And I'm doing it for me. You wanted to keep me up at night, and you did."

She managed a weak smile. "Guilt works miracles."

"It has nothing to do with guilt. It never did. It has to do with love. With being in love. Don't pull away," he said quietly when she jerked against his hold. "Business is closed for the day. Now it's just you and me. This is as personal as it gets."

At her sides, her hands clenched into fists. "It's all personal with me, don't you understand? You came here and changed everything in my life, then waltzed away again. Now you come back and tell me you've altered the plans."

"You weren't the only one things changed for. Nothing's been the same for me since I met you." Panic snaked through him. She wasn't going to give him another chance. "I didn't ask for this. I didn't want it."

"Oh, you made it abundantly clear what you didn't want." She shoved against him and got nowhere. "You have no right to start this up again."

"The hell with rights." He gave her a hard shake. "I'm trying to tell you that I love you. That's a first for me, and you're not going to turn it into an argument."

"I'll turn it into whatever I want," she tossed back, furious when her voice broke. "I'm not going to let you hurt me again. I'm not going to—" Then she went still, eyes widening. "Did you say you were in love with me?"

"Just shut up and listen. I've spent three and a half weeks feeling empty and miserable without you. I went away because I thought I could. Because I thought that was right and fair and best for both of us. Logically, it was. It still is. We're nothing alike. I couldn't see any percentage in risking both our futures when you'd certainly be better off with someone else. Someone like Finney."

"Finney?" A shout of laughter escaped. "Oh, that's rich." While her emotions whirled, she knocked a fist against his chest. "Tell you what, why don't you take your percentages back to Boston and draw a graph? Now leave me alone. I've got work to do."

"I'm not finished." When she opened her mouth to swear at him, he let instinct rule and kissed her until she quieted. As breathless as she, he rested his brow against hers. "That has nothing to do with logic or percentages." Still holding on, he took a step back so that he could see her. "Catherine, every time I reminded myself that I didn't believe in love or marriage or lifetimes, I remembered the way I felt with you."

"How? How did you feel with me?"

"Alive. Happy. And I knew I was never going to feel that way again unless I came back." He let his hands slide away. "C.C., you told me once that what we had could be the best part of my life. You were right. I don't know if I can make it work, but I need to try. I need you."

He was afraid, she realized. Even more afraid than she was. With her eyes on his, she lifted a hand to his cheek. "I can give you a guarantee on a muffler, Trent. Not on this."

"I'd settle for you telling me you still love me, that you'll give me another chance."

"I still love you. But I can't give you another chance."

"Catherine—"

"Because you haven't taken the first one yet." She touched her lips to his once, then twice. "Why don't we take it together?" she asked, then laughed when he dragged her close. "Now you've done it. You'll have grease all over you."

"I'll have to get used to it." After one last spin, he drew away to study her face. Everything he needed was right there, in her eyes. "I love you, Catherine. Very much."

She brought his hand to her cheek. "I'll have to get used to it. Maybe if you said it a few hundred times."

He told her as he held her, as he traced kisses over her face, as he lingered over the taste of her mouth.

"I think it's working," she murmured. "Maybe we should close the garage doors."

"Leave them up." He stepped back again, struggling to clear his head. "I'm still St. James enough to want to do things in their proper order, but I'm running low on control."

"What order is that?" Smiling, she ran a finger up his shirt to toy with the top button.

"Wait." Churning, he put a hand over hers. "I thought about this all the way up from Boston. It played a lot of different ways—I'd take you out again. A little wine, a lot of candlelight. Or we'd walk in the garden again at dusk."

He glanced around the garage. Honeysuckle and motor oil, he thought. Perfect.

"But this seems like the right time, the right place." He reached in his pocket for a small box, then opening it, handed it to her. "You once said if I offered you a diamond, you'd laugh in my face. I thought I might have more luck with an emerald."

Tears backed up in her throat as she stared down at the deep green stone in its simple gold setting. It gleamed up at her, full of hope and promise. "If this is a proposal, you don't need any luck at all." Wet and brilliant, her eyes came back to his. "The answer was always yes."

He slid the ring onto her finger. "Let's go home."

"Yes." Her hand linked with his. "Let's go home."

* * * * *

A MAN FOR AMANDA

Prologue

Bar Harbor
June 8, 1913

In the afternoon, I walked to the cliffs. The day, our first day back in The Towers, was bright and warm. The rumble of the sea was as I had left it ten long months ago. There was a fishing boat chugging over the blue-green water, and a neat sloop gliding cheerfully along. So much was the same, and yet, one vital change dimmed the day for me.

He was not there.

It was wrong of me to wish to find him waiting where I had left him so many months ago. To find him painting as he always did, slicing the brush against canvas like a dueler in the heat of battle. It was wrong of me to wish to see him turn, look at me with those intense gray eyes—to see him smile, to hear him say my name.

Yet I did wish it.

My heart was dancing in my breast as I rushed from the house to race across the lawn, past the gardens and down the slope.

The cliffs were there, so high and proud, jutting up to the pure summer sky. The sea, almost calm today, mirrored the color so that it seemed I stood cupped in a lovely blue ball. The rocks tumbled down before me, down and down to where the waves slapped and hissed. Behind me, the towers of my summer home, my husband's home, speared up, arrogant and beautiful.

How strange that I should love the house when I have known such unhappiness inside it.

I reminded myself that I am Bianca Calhoun, wife of Fergus Calhoun, mother to Colleen and Ethan and Sean. I am a respected woman, a dutiful wife, a devoted mother. My marriage is not a warm one, but that does not alter the vows I took. There is no place in my life for romantic fancies and sinful dreams.

Still, I stood and I waited. But he did not come. Christian, the lover I have taken only with my heart, did not come. He may not even be on the island any longer. Perhaps he has packed up his canvases and brushes, moved from his cottage and gone on to paint some other sea, some other sky.

It would be best. I know it would be best. Since I met him last summer, I have hardly gone an hour without thinking of him. Yet I have a husband I respect, three children I love more than my life. It is to them I must be faithful, not to the memory of something that never was. And never could be.

The sun is setting as I sit and write by the window of my tower. In a short time I must go down and help Nanny put my babies to bed. Little Sean has grown so, and is already beginning to toddle. Soon he will be as quick as Ethan. Colleen, quite the young lady at four, wants a new pink dress.

It is of them I must think, my children, my precious loves, and not of Christian.

It will be a quiet night, one of very few we will have during our summer on Mount Desert Island. Fergus has already talked of giving a dinner dance next week. I must...

He is there. Down below on the cliffs. He is hardly more than a shadow with the distance and the dimming light. Yet I know it is he. Just as I knew, as I stood and pressed my hand to the glass, that he was looking up, looking for me. However impossible it is, I would swear I could hear him call my name. So softly.

Bianca.

Chapter One

He was a solid wall of denim and muscle. Ramming into him knocked the wind out of her lungs and the packages out of her hands. In her rush to get from one place to the next, she didn't even bother to glance at him but dove to save the flying boxes.

If he'd been looking where he'd been going, she wouldn't have run into him. Amanda managed to bite her tongue before she snapped out the thought, and scowled instead at the run-down heels of his boots. In a hurry, as usual, she knelt on the sidewalk outside the boutique where she'd been shopping, to gather up her scattered packages.

"Let me give you a hand, honey."

The slow southwestern drawl grated on her nerves. She had a million things to do, and scrambling on the sidewalk with a tourist wasn't on her schedule. "I've got it," she muttered, leaning over so that her chin-length hair drifted down to curtain her face. Everything was grating on her nerves today, she thought as she hurried to restack bags and boxes. This little irritation was the last in a long line.

"It's an awful lot for one person to carry."

"I can manage, thanks." She reached for a box just as her persistent helper did the same. The brief tug-of-war had the top slipping off and the contents spilling onto the sidewalk.

"Now, that's mighty pretty." There was amused, masculine approval in the voice as he scooped up a scrap of thin red silk that pretended to be a nightie.

Amanda snatched it from him and stuffed it into one of the bags. "Do you mind?"

"No, ma'am. I sure don't."

Amanda pushed back her tumbled hair and took her first good look at him. So far, all she'd seen were a pair of cowboy boots and the line of faded denim from knee to ankle. There was a great deal more of him. Even crouched down beside her he looked big. Shoulders, hands. Mouth, she thought nastily. Right now he was using it to grin at her. It might, under different circumstances, have been an engaging enough grin. But at the moment it was stuck in the middle of a face she'd decided to dislike on sight.

Not that it wasn't a good one, with its slashing warrior's cheekbones, velvet green eyes and deep tan. The curl of his reddish-blond hair over the collar of his denim shirt might have been charming. If he hadn't been in her way.

"I'm in a hurry," she told him.

"I noticed." He flipped a long finger through her hair to tuck it behind her ear. "Looked like you were on the way to a fire when you plowed into me."

"If you'd moved," she began, then shook her head. Arguing would take time she simply didn't have. "Never mind." Grabbing at packages, she rose. "Excuse me."

"Hold on."

He unfolded himself as she tapped her foot and waited. Disconcerted, she frowned up at him. At five feet ten inches, she was accustomed to meeting most men almost eye to eye. With this one she had several extra inches to go. "What?"

"I can give you a ride to that fire if you need it."

Her brow arched in her frostiest look. "That won't be necessary."

Using a fingertip, he pushed a box back in place before it could slide out of her grip. "You look like you could use a little help."

"I'm perfectly capable of getting where I'm going, thank you."

He didn't doubt it for a minute. "Then maybe you can help me." He liked the way her hair kept falling into her eyes, and the impatient way she kept blowing it away again. "I just got into town this morning." His gaze lazily skimmed her face. "I thought maybe you could make some suggestions about... what I should do with myself."

At the moment, she had a pocketful of them. "Try the chamber of commerce." She started by him, then whirled when his hand came down on her arm. "Look, buster, I don't know how they do things back in Tucson—"

"Oklahoma City," he corrected.

"Wherever, but around here, cops take a dim view of men who hassle women on the streets."

"That so?"

"You bet it's so."

"Well then, I'll have to watch my step since I plan to be around awhile."

"I'll hang out a bulletin. Now, excuse me."

"Just one more thing." He held up a pair of brief black panties embroidered with red roses. "I think you forgot this."

She grabbed the bikinis, then stalked off as she balled them into her pocket.

"Nice meeting you," he called after her, and laughed when she doubled her already hurried pace.

* * *

Twenty minutes later, Amanda gathered up her packages from the back seat of her car. Balancing some under her chin, she kicked the door closed with her foot. She'd nearly forgotten about the encounter already. There was too much on her mind. Behind her, the house rose up into the sky, its gray stones staid, its towers and peaks fanciful and its porches sagging. Next to her family, there was nothing Amanda loved more than The Towers.

She raced up the steps, avoided a rotting board then struggled to free a hand enough to open the towering front door. "Aunt Coco!" The moment she stepped into the hall, an oversize black puppy raced down the stairs. On the third from the bottom, he tripped, rolled and went sprawling onto the gleaming chestnut floor. "Almost made it that time, Fred."

Pleased with himself, Fred danced around Amanda's legs as she continued to call for her aunt.

"Coming. I'm coming." Tall and stately, Cordelia Calhoun McPike hurried in from the rear of the house. She wore peach linen slacks under a splattered white apron. "I was in the kitchen. We're going to try my new recipe for cannelloni tonight."

"Is C.C. home?"

"Oh, no, dear." Coco patted the hair she'd tinted the day before to Moonlit Blonde. In an old habit, she peeked into the hall mirror to make certain the shade suited her—for the moment. "She's down at her garage. Something about rocker arms, I think—though what rocking chairs have to do with cars and engines, I can't say."

"Great. Come upstairs, I want to show you what I got."

"Looks like you bought out the shops. Here, let me help you." Coco managed to grab two bags before Amanda dashed up the stairs.

"I had the best time."

"But you hate to shop."

"For myself. This was different. Still, everything took longer than I thought it would, so I was afraid I wouldn't get back and be able to stash it all before C.C. got home." She rushed into her room to dump everything onto the big four-poster bed. "Then this stupid man got in my way and knocked everything all over the sidewalk." Amanda stripped off her jacket, folded it, then laid it neatly over the back of a chair. "Then he had the nerve to try to pick me up."

"Really?" Always interested in liaisons, romances and assignations, Coco tilted her head. "Was he attractive?"

"If you go for the Wild Bill Hickok type. Anyway, I made it—no thanks to him."

As Amanda sorted through the bags, Fred tried twice, unsuccessfully, to leap onto the bed. He ended by sitting on the rug to watch.

"I found some wonderful decorations for the bridal shower." She began to pull out white-and-silver bells, crepe paper swans, balloons. "I love this frilly parasol," she went on. "Not C.C.'s style maybe, but I thought if we hung it up over…Aunt Coco." With a sigh, Amanda sat on the bed. "Don't start crying again."

"I can't help it." Already sniffling, Coco took an embroidered hankie from her apron pocket and dabbed carefully at her eyes. "She's the baby, after all. The youngest of my four little girls."

"There's not one of the Calhoun women who could be called little," Amanda pointed out.

"You're still my babies, and have been ever since your mother and father died." Coco used the hankie expertly. She didn't want to smear her mascara. "Every time I think of her being married—and in only a matter of days, really—I just fill up. I adore Trenton, you know." Thinking of her future nephew, she blew delicately into the hankie. "He's a wonderful man, and I knew they'd be perfect together right from the start, but it's all so fast."

"You're telling me." Amanda combed a hand through her sleek cap of hair. "I've barely had time to organize. How anyone expects to put on a wedding with barely three weeks notice—or why they'd want to try—is beyond me. They'd be better off eloping."

"Don't say that." Scandalized, Coco stuck her hankie back into her pocket. "Why, I'd be furious if they cheated me out of this wedding. And if you think you can when your time comes, think again."

"My time isn't going to come for years, if ever." Meticulously Amanda tidied the decorations again. "Men are as far down on my list of priorities as they can get."

"You and your lists." Coco clucked her tongue. "Let me tell you, Mandy, the one thing you can't plan in this life is falling in love. Your sister certainly didn't plan it, and look at her. Squeezing fittings for a wedding dress in between her carburetors and transmissions. Your time may come sooner than you think. Why just this morning when I was reading my tea leaves—"

"Oh, Aunt Coco, not the tea leaves."

Grandly Coco drew herself up to her considerable height. "I've read some very fascinating things in the tea leaves. After our last séance, I'd think you'd be a bit less cynical."

"Maybe something happened at the séance, but—"

"Maybe?"

"All right, something did happen." Letting out a deep breath, Amanda shrugged. "I know C.C. got an image—"

"A vision."

"Whatever—of Great-Grandmama Bianca's emerald necklace." And it had been spooky, she admitted to herself, the way C.C. had been able to describe it, though no one had seen the two tiers of emeralds and diamonds in decades. "And no one who's lived in this house could deny that they've felt some—some presence or something up in Bianca's tower."

"Aha!"

"But that doesn't mean I'm going to start gazing into crystal balls."

"You're just too literal minded, Mandy. I can't think where you get it from. Perhaps from my Aunt Colleen. Fred, we must not chew on the Irish lace," Coco cautioned as Fred began to gnaw on Amanda's bedspread.

"In any case, we were speaking of tea leaves. When I took a reading this morning, I saw a man."

Amanda rose to hide the decorations in her closet. "You saw a man in your teacup."

"You know very well it doesn't work precisely like that. I saw a man, and I had the strongest feeling that he's very close."

"Maybe it's the plumber. He's been underfoot for days."

"No, it's not the plumber. This man—he's close, but he's not from the island." She let her eyes unfocus as she did when she practiced looking psychic. "In fact he's from some distance away. He's going to be an important part of our lives. And—I'm quite sure of this—he's going to be vitally important to one of you girls."

"Lilah can have him," Amanda decided, thinking of her free-spirited older sister. "Where is she anyway?"

"Oh, she was meeting someone after work. Rod or Tod or Dominick."

"Damn it." Amanda scooped up her jacket to hang it neatly in the closet. "We were supposed to go through more of the papers. She knew I was counting on her. We have to find some lead as to where the emeralds are hidden."

"We'll find them, dear." Distracted, Coco poked through the other packages. "When the time is right. Bianca wants us to. I believe she'll show us the next step very soon."

"We need more than blind faith and mystic visions. Bianca could have hidden them anywhere." Scowling, she plopped down onto the bed again.

She didn't care about the money—though the Calhoun emeralds were reputed to be worth a fortune. It was the publicity that had resulted when Trent, her sister's fiancé, had contracted to buy The Towers, and the old legend had become public knowledge. Amanda's idea of an ordered existence had been thrown into chaos since the first story had hit.

It certainly made good print, Amanda mused as her aunt oohed and aahed over the lingerie she had bought for her sister's shower.

Early in the second decade of the century, when the resort of Bar Harbor was in its elegant heyday, Fergus Calhoun had built The Towers as an opulent summer home. There on the cliffs overlooking Frenchman Bay, he and his wife, Bianca, and their three children had vacationed, giving elaborate parties for other members of the well-heeled society.

And there, Bianca had met a young artist. They had fallen in love. It was said that Bianca had been torn between duty and her heart. Her marriage, which had been firmly supported by her parents, had been a cold one. With her heart leading her, she had planned to leave her husband and had packed away a treasure box that had contained the emeralds Fergus had given her on the birth of their second child and first son. The whereabouts of the necklace was a mystery as, according to legend, she had thrown herself from the tower window, overwhelmed with guilt and despair.

Now, eighty years later, interest in the necklace had been revived. Even as the remaining Calhouns searched through decades of papers and ledgers for a clue, reporters and hopeful fortune hunters had become a daily nuisance.

Amanda took it personally. The legend, and the people in it, belonged to her family. The sooner the necklace was located, the better. Once a mystery was solved, interest faded quickly.

"When is Trent coming back?" she asked her aunt.

"Soon." Sighing, Coco stroked the silky red chemise. "As soon as he ties things up in Boston, he'll be on his way. He can't stand being away from C.C. There will barely be enough time to begin the renovations on the west wing before they'll be off on their honeymoon." Tears filled her eyes again. "Their honeymoon."

"Don't start, Aunt Coco. Think of what a fabulous job you'll do catering the reception. It's going to be great practice for you. This time next year you'll be starting your new career as chef for The Towers Retreat, the most intimate of the St. James hotels."

"Imagine it." Coco patted her hand at her breast.

At the knock on the front door, Fred was up and howling.

"You stay here and imagine it, Aunt Coco. I'll go answer the door."

In a race with Fred, she clattered down the steps. When the dog's four legs tangled, sending him somersaulting, she laughed and gathered him up. She was snuggling the dog against her cheek when she opened the door.

"You!"

The tone of her voice had Fred quaking. Not so the man who stood at the threshold, grinning at her. "Small world," he said in the same slow drawl he'd used when they'd knelt on the sidewalk. "I'm liking it better all the time."

"You followed me."

"No, ma'am. Though it would've been a damn good idea. The name's O'Riley. Sloan O'Riley."

"I don't care what your name is, you can turn around and start walking." She started to slam the door in his face, but he slapped a hand against it and held it wide.

"I don't think that's such a good idea. I've come a long way to get a look at the house."

Her dark blue eyes narrowed. "Oh, have you? Well, let me tell you something, this is a home, a private home. I don't care what you've read in the papers and how badly you want a shot at looking under loose stones for the emeralds. This isn't Treasure Island, and I've had my fill of people like you who think they can just come knocking at the door, or sneaking into the garden at night with a pick and shovel."

She looked just fine, Sloan thought as he waited out the tirade. Every furious inch of her. She was tall for a woman and lean with it—but not too lean. She curved out nicely in all the right places. She looked as though she could ride hard all day and still have the energy to kick up her heels at night. Stubborn chin, he decided, and approved. When she jutted it out, her warm brown hair swayed with the movement. Big blue eyes. Even while they spit fire they reminded him of cornflowers. When it wasn't scowling or swearing, he imagined her full, shapely mouth would be soft.

Soft and tasty.

"You run down yet?" he asked when she stopped to take a breath.

"No, and if you don't leave right now, I'm going to let my dog loose on you."

Taking his cue, Fred leaped out of her arms. With neck fur bristling, he bared his teeth in a growl.

"Looks pretty fierce," Sloan commented, then hunkered down to hold out the back of his hand. Fred sniffed it, then his tail began to wag joyously as Sloan scratched his ears. "Yep, pretty fierce animal you got here."

"That's it." Amanda set her hands on her hips. "I'm getting the gun."

Before she could turn inside to look for the fictitious weapon, Coco came downstairs.

"Who is it, Amanda?"

"Dead meat."

"I beg your pardon?" She stepped up to the door. The moment she spotted Sloan her ingrained vanity took over. In the blink of an eye she whipped her apron off. "Hello." Her smile was warm and feminine as she extended a hand. "I'm Cordelia McPike."

"A pleasure, ma'am." Sloan brought her fingertips to his mouth. "As I was just telling your sister here—"

"Oh, my." Coco let out a trill of delighted laughter. "Amanda's not my sister. She's my niece. The third daughter of my late brother—my much older brother."

"My mistake."

"Aunt Coco, this jerk knocked me down outside of the boutique, then followed me home. He just wants to wheedle his way into the house because of the necklace."

"Now, Mandy, you mustn't be so harsh."

"That's partially true, Mrs. McPike." Sloan gave Amanda a slow nod. "Your niece and I did have a run-in. Guess I didn't get out of her way in time. And I am trying to get into the house."

"I see." Torn between hope and doubt, Coco sighed. "I'm terribly sorry, but I don't think it would be possible to let you in. You see we have so much to do with the wedding—"

Sloan's eyes whipped back to Amanda. "You getting married?"

"My sister," she said tightly. "Not that it's any of your business. Now if you'll excuse us?"

"I wouldn't want to intrude, so I'll just be on my way. If you'll tell Trent that O'Riley was by, I'd appreciate it."

"O'Riley?" Coco repeated, then fluttered her hands. "Goodness, are you Mr. O'Riley? Please come in. Oh, I do apologize."

"Aunt Coco—"

"This is Mr. O'Riley, Amanda."

"I realize that. Why the devil have you let him in the house?"

"*The* Mr. O'Riley," Coco continued. "The one Trenton called about this morning. Don't you remember—of course you don't remember, because I didn't tell you." She patted her hands to her cheeks. "I'm afraid I'm just so flustered after keeping you standing outside that way."

"Don't you worry about it," he said to Coco. "It's an honest mistake."

"Aunt Coco." Amanda stood with her hand on the doorknob, ready to pitch the intruder out bodily if necessary. "Who is this O'Riley and why did Trent tell you to expect him?"

"Mr. O'Riley's the architect," Coco said, beaming.

Eyes narrowing, Amanda studied him from the tip of his boots to his wavy, disordered hair. "This is an architect?"

"Our architect. Mr. O'Riley will be in charge of the renovations for the retreat, and our living quarters. We'll all be working with Mr. O'Riley—"

"Sloan," he said.

"Sloan." Coco fluttered her lashes. "For quite some time."

"Terrific." Amanda let the door slam.

Sloan hooked his thumbs in his jean pockets and gave her a slow smile. "My thoughts exactly."

Chapter Two

"Where are our manners?" Coco said. "Here we are keeping you standing in the hall. Please, come in and sit down. What can I offer you? Coffee, tea?"

"Beer in a long-necked bottle," Amanda muttered.

Sloan merely smiled at her. "There you go."

"Beer?" Coco ushered him into the parlor, wishing she'd had a moment to freshen the flowers in the vase and plump the pillows. "I have some very nice beer in the kitchen that I use for my spiced shrimp. Amanda, you'll entertain Sloan, won't you?"

"Sure. Why not?" Though she wasn't feeling particularly gracious, Amanda gestured to a chair, then took one across from him in front of the fireplace. "I suppose I should apologize."

Sloan reached down to pet Fred, who had followed them in. "What for?"

"I wouldn't have been so rude if I'd realized why you were here."

"Is that so?" As Fred settled down on the rug between them, Sloan eased back in his chair to study his unwilling hostess.

After a humming ten seconds, she struggled not to fidget. "It was a natural enough mistake."

"If you say so. What exactly are these emeralds you figured I was here to dig up?"

"The Calhoun emeralds." When he only lifted a brow, she shook her head. "My great-grandmother's emerald necklace. It's been in all the papers."

"I haven't had much time to read the papers. I've been in Budapest." He reached into his pocket and pulled out a long, slim cigar. "Mind?"

"Go ahead." Automatically she rose to fetch an ashtray from across the room. Sloan considered it a pleasure to watch that out-of-my-way walk of hers. "I'm surprised Trent didn't mention it."

Sloan struck a match and took his sweet time lighting the cigar. He took an appreciative drag, then blew out a lazy stream of smoke. All the while, he was taking stock of the room, with its sagging sofa, the glistening Baccarat, the elegant old wainscoting and the peeling paint.

"I got a cable from Trent telling me about the house and his plans, and asking me to take it on."

"You agreed to take a job like this without even seeing the property first?"

"Seemed like the thing to do at the time." She sure had pretty eyes, Sloan thought. Suspicious, but pretty. He wondered how they'd look if he ever managed to get a smile out of her. "Besides, Trent wouldn't have asked if he didn't think I'd get a kick out of it."

Her foot began to tap as it did when she had sat in one place too long. "You know Trent well then?"

"We go back a few years. We were at Harvard together."

"Harvard?" Her foot stopped tapping as she gaped at him. "You went to Harvard?"

Another man might have been insulted. Sloan was amused. "Why, shucks, ma'am," he murmured, exaggerating his drawl, then watching her cheeks flush.

"I didn't mean to... it's just that you don't really seem—"

"The Ivy League type?" he suggested before he took another pull on the cigar. "Guess appearances can be deceiving. Take the house here for instance."

"The house?"

"You take your first look at it from the outside and it's hard to figure if it's supposed to be a fortress, a castle or an architect's nightmare. But you take the time to look again, and you see it's not supposed to be anything but what it is. A timeless piece of work, on the arrogant side, strong, maybe stubborn enough to hold its own, but with just enough fancy to add some charm." He grinned at her. "Some people believe that a house reflects the personality of the people who live in it."

He rose when Coco came back in wheeling a tray. "Oh, sit down, please. It's such a treat to have a man in the house. Isn't it, Mandy?"

"I'm all aflutter."

"I hope the beer's all right." She lifted a brimming pilsner glass from the tray.

"I'm sure it's fine."

"Do try some of these canapés. Mandy, I've brought us some wine." Delighted with the chance to socialize, she smiled at Sloan over the rim of her glass. "Has Amanda been telling you about the house?"

"We were just getting to it." Sloan took a long swallow of beer. "Trent wrote that it's been in the family since the early part of the century."

"Oh, yes. With Suzanna's children—Suzanna's my eldest niece—we've had five generations of Calhouns at The Towers. Fergus—" she gestured to the portrait of a dour-faced man over the mantel "—my grandfather, built The Towers in 1904, as a summer home. He and his wife, Bianca, had three children before she threw herself out of the tower window." As always, the idea of dying for love had her sighing. "I don't believe Grandpapa was ever quite right after that. He went insane later in life, but we kept him in a very nice institution."

"Aunt Coco, I'm sure Mr. O'Riley isn't interested in the family history."

"Not interested," Sloan agreed as he tapped out his cigar. "Fascinated. Don't stop now, Mrs. McPike."

"Oh, call me Coco. Everyone does." She fluffed her hair. "The house passed along to my father, Ethan. He was their second child, but the first son. Grandpapa was very adamant about the Calhoun line. His—Ethan's—elder sister, Colleen, was miffed about the arrangement. She rarely speaks to any of us to this day."

"For which we're all eternally grateful," Amanda put in.

"Well, yes. She can be a bit—overwhelming. That left Uncle Sean, my father's younger brother. He had a spot of trouble with a woman and sailed off to the West Indies before I was born. When my father was killed, the house passed to my brother, Judson. After his marriage he and his wife decided to live here year-round. They adored the place." She glanced around the parlor with its cracked walls and faded curtains. "Judson had wonderful plans for revamping the house, but tragically he and Deliah were killed before he could begin to implement them. Then I came here to care for Amanda and her three sisters. Have another canapé."

"Thanks. Can I ask why you decided to convert part of your home into a hotel?"

"That was Trent's idea. We're all so grateful to him, aren't we, Amanda?"

Since she accepted the fact that there would be no winding down Aunt Coco, Amanda smiled. "Yes, we are."

Coco sipped delicately from her glass. "To be frank, we were in some financial distress. Do you believe in fate, Sloan?"

"I'm Irish and Cherokee." He spread his long fingers. "That doesn't give me any other choice."

"Well then, you'll understand. It was fated that Trent's father would see The Towers while he was sailing in Frenchman Bay, and seeing it, develop a deep desire for it. When the St. James's corporation offered to buy the house and turn it into a resort hotel, we were torn. It was our home after all, the only home my girls have ever known, but the upkeep..."

"I understand."

"Things happen for the best," Coco put in. "And it was really very exciting and romantic. We were on the brink, the very brink, of being forced to sell, when Trent fell in love with C.C. Of course he understood how much the house meant to her, and came up with this marvelous plan of converting the west wing into hotel suites. That way we can keep the house, and overcome the financial difficulty of maintaining it."

"Everyone gets what they want," Sloan agreed.

"Exactly." Coco leaned forward. "With your heritage, I imagine you also believe in spirits."

"Aunt Coco—"

"Now, Mandy, I know how practical minded you are. It baffles me," she said to Sloan. "All that Celtic blood and not a mystical bone in her body."

Amanda gestured with her glass. "I leave that for you and Lilah."

"Lilah's my other niece," Coco told Sloan. "She's very fey. But we were talking about the supernatural. Do you have an opinion?"

Sloan set his glass aside. "I don't think you could have a house like this without a ghost or two."

"There." Coco clapped her hands together. "I knew as soon as I saw you we'd be kindred spirits. Bianca's still here, you see. Why at our last séance I felt her so strongly." She ignored Amanda's groan. "C.C. did, too, and she's nearly as practical minded as Amanda. Bianca wants us to find the necklace."

"The Calhoun emeralds?" Sloan asked.

"Yes. We've been searching for clues, but the clutter of eight decades is daunting. And the publicity has been a bother."

"That's a mild word for it." Amanda scowled into her glass.

"It might turn up during the renovation," Sloan suggested.

"We're hoping." Coco tapped one carefully manicured finger against her lips. "I think another séance might be in order. I'm sure you're very sensitive."

Amanda choked on her wine. "Aunt Coco, Mr. O'Riley has come here to work, not to play ghosts and goblins."

"I like mixing business and pleasure." He toasted Amanda with his glass. "In fact, I make a habit of it."

A new thought jumped into Coco's mind. "You're not from the island, Sloan."

"No, Oklahoma."

"Really? That's quite a distance." She slid her gaze smugly toward Amanda. "As architect for the renovations, you'll be very important to all of us."

"I'd like to think so," he said, baffled by the arched look Coco sent her niece.

"Tea leaves," Coco murmured, then rose. "I must go check on dinner. You will join us, won't you?"

He'd planned on taking a quick look at the house then going back to the hotel to sleep for ten hours. The annoyed look on Amanda's face changed his mind. An evening with her might be a better cure for jet lag. "I'd be mighty pleased to."

"Wonderful. Mandy, why don't you show Sloan the west wing while I finish things up?"

"Tea leaves?" Sloan asked when Coco glided from the room.

"You're better off in the dark." Resigned, she rose and gestured to the doorway. "Shall we get started?"

"That's a fine idea." He followed her into the hall and up the curving staircase. "Which do you like, Amanda or Mandy?"

She shrugged. "I answer to either."

"Different images. Amanda's cool and composed. Mandy's... softer." She smelled cool, he thought. Like a quiet breeze on a hot, dusty day.

At the top of the stairs she stopped to face him. "What kind of image is Sloan?"

He stayed one step below her so that they were eye to eye. Instinct told him they'd both prefer it that way. "You tell me."

He had the cockiest grin she'd ever seen. Whenever he used it on her she felt a tremor that she was certain was annoyance. "Dodge City?" she said sweetly. "We don't get many cowboys this far east." She turned and was halfway down the hall when he took her arm.

"Are you always in such a hurry?"

"I don't like to waste time."

He kept his hand on her arm as they continued to walk. "I'll keep that in mind."

My God, the place was fabulous, Sloan thought as they started up a pie-shaped set of steps. Coffered ceilings, carved lintels, thick mahogany paneling. He stopped at an arched window to touch the wavy glass. It had to be original, he thought, like the chestnut floor and the fancy plaster work.

True, there were cracks in the walls—some of them big enough that he could slide his finger in to the first knuckle. Here and there the ceiling had given way to fist-sized holes, and portions of the molding were rotted.

It would be a challenge to bring it back to its former glory. And it would be a joy.

"We haven't used this part of the house in years." Amanda opened a carved oak door and brushed away a spider web. "It hasn't been practical to heat it during the winter."

Sloan stepped inside. The sloping floor creaked ominously as he walked across it. Somewhere along the line heavy furniture had been dragged in or out, scarring the floor with deep, jagged grooves. Two of the panes on the narrow terrace doors had been broken and replaced with plywood. Mice had had a field day with the baseboard. Above his head was a faded mural of chubby cherubs.

"This was the best guest room," Amanda explained. "Fergus kept it for people he wanted to impress. Supposedly some of the Rockefellers stayed here. It has its own bath and dressing room." She pushed open a broken door.

Ignoring her, Sloan walked to the black marble fireplace. The wall above it was papered in silk and stained from old smoke. The chip off the corner of the mantel broke his heart.

"You ought to be shot."

"I beg your pardon?"

"You ought to be shot for letting the place go like this." The look he aimed at her wasn't lazy and amused, but hot and quick as a bullet. "A mantelpiece like this is irreplaceable."

Flustered, she stared guiltily at the chipped Italian marble. "Well, I certainly didn't break it."

"And look at these walls. Plasterwork of this caliber is an art, the same way a Rembrandt is art. You'd take care of a Rembrandt, wouldn't you?"

"Of course, but—"

"At least you had the sense not to paint the molding." Moving past her, he peered into the adjoining bath. And began to swear. "These are hand-made tiles, for God's sake. Look at these chips. They haven't been grouted since World War I."

"I don't see what that's—"

"No, you don't see." He turned back to her. "You haven't got a clue to what you've got here. This place is a monument to early-twentieth-century craftsmanship, and you're letting it fall apart around your ears. Those are authentic gaslight fixtures."

"I know very well what they are," Amanda snapped back. "This may be a monument to you, but to me it's home. We've done everything we could to keep the roof on. If the plaster's cracked it's because we've had to concentrate on keeping the furnace running. And if we didn't worry about regrouting tiles in a room no one uses, it's because we had to repair the plumbing in another one. You've been hired to renovate, not to philosophize."

"You get both for the same price." When he reached out toward her, she rammed back into the wall.

"What are you doing?"

"Take it easy, honey. You've got cobwebs in your hair."

"I can do it," she said, then stiffened when he combed his fingers through her hair. "And don't call me 'honey.'"

"You sure fire up quick. I had a mustang filly once that did the same thing."

She knocked his hand aside. "I'm not a horse."

"No, ma'am." In an abrupt change of mood, he smiled again. "You sure aren't. Why don't you show me what else you've got?"

Wary, she eased to the side until she felt safe again. "I don't see the point. You haven't got a notebook."

"Some things stick in your mind." His gaze lowered to her mouth, lingered, then returned to her eyes. "I like to get the lay of the land first before I start worrying about . . . details."

"Why don't I draw you a map?"

He grinned then. "You always so prickly?"

"No." She inclined her head. It was true, she wasn't. She could hardly have made a success in her career as assistant manager in one of the resort's better hotels if she was. "Obviously you don't bring out the best in me."

"I'll settle for what I've got." He curled a hand around her arm. "Let's keep going."

She took him through the wing, doing her best to keep her distance. But he had a tendency to close in, blocking her in a doorway, maneuvering her into a corner, shifting unexpectedly to put them face-to-face. He had a slow and economical way of moving, wasting no gestures that would tip her off as to which way he was going to turn.

They were in the west tower the third time Amanda bumped into him. Every nerve was on edge when she stepped back. "I wish you wouldn't do that."

"Do what?"

"Be there." Annoyed, she shoved aside a cardboard box. "In my way."

"It seems to me you're in too much of a hurry to get someplace else to watch where you are."

"More homespun philosophy," she muttered, and paced to the curved window that overlooked the gardens. He bothered her, she was forced to admit, on some deep, elemental level. Maybe it was his size—those broad shoulders and wide-palmed hands. His sheer height. She was accustomed to being on a more even level with most men.

Maybe it was that drawl of his, slow and lazy and every bit as cocky as his grin. Or the way his eyes lingered on her face, persistent, with a half-amused gleam. Whatever it was, Amanda thought with a little shake, she would have to learn how to handle it.

"This is the last stop," she told him. "Trent's idea is to convert this tower into a dining room, more intimate than the one he wants on the lower level. It should fit five tables for two comfortably, with views of the garden or the bay."

She turned as she spoke, and an early evening sunbeam shot through the window to halo her hair and pool lustrously around her. Her hands gestured with her words, a graceful flow of movement underlined by nerves. She lifted one hand to her hair to push it back. The light streamed through the honey-brown tresses, tipping them with gold. In the single shaft of light, dust motes danced around her like minute flakes of silver.

His mind wiped clean as new glass, Sloan stood and stared.

"Is something wrong?"

"No." He took a step closer. "You sure are easy on the eyes, Amanda."

She took a step back. There wasn't amusement in his eyes now, or the quick flaring anger she had seen briefly earlier. What was there was a great deal more dangerous. "If you, ah, have any questions about the tower, or the rest of the wing—"

"That was a compliment. Maybe not as smooth as you're used to, but a compliment just the same."

"Thank you." Her eyes darted around the room for a means of dignified escape as she retreated another step. "I think we could—" She ended on a gasp as his arm snaked around her waist to draw her tight against him. "What the hell do you think you're doing?"

"Keeping you from taking the same jump as your great-grandma." He nodded toward the window at her back. "If you'd kept dancing backward, you might have gone right through the glass. Those panes don't look very strong."

"I wasn't dancing anywhere." But her heart was pounding as if she had just finished a fast rumba. "Let go."

"You're a real nice armful." He leaned closer to take a sniff of her hair. "Even with all those thorns." Enjoying himself, he kept his arm where it was. "You could've said thanks, Calhoun. I probably just saved your life."

Her pulse might have been jumping, but she refused to let herself be intimidated by some slow-talking cowboy with an attitude. "If you don't let me go, now, someone's going to have to save yours."

He laughed, delighted with her, and was tempted to scoop her up there and then. The next thing he knew, he was landing on his butt five feet away. With a smug smile, Amanda inclined her head.

"That concludes our tour for this evening. Now, if you'll excuse me." When she started by him, his hand snaked out and snagged her ankle. Amanda barely had time to shriek before she landed on the floor beside him. "Why, you—oaf," she decided, and tossed the hair out of her eyes.

"What's good for the goose is good for the gander." He tipped a fingertip under her chin. "More homespun philosophy. You've got quick moves, Calhoun, but you've got to remember to keep your eye on the target."

"If I were a man—"

"This wouldn't be half as much fun." Chuckling, he gave her a quick, hard kiss, then tilted his head back to stare at her while she gaped. "Well, now," he said softly while lightning bolts went off inside his chest. "I think we'd better try that again."

She would have shoved him away. She knew she would have. Despite the heat trembling along her spine. Regardless of the thick syrupy longing that seemed to have replaced the blood churning in her veins. She would have shoved him away, had even lifted a hand to do so—certainly not to bring him closer—when footsteps clattered on the iron steps that led to the tower.

Sloan glanced up to see a tall, curvy woman in the doorway. She wore jeans that were ripped through at the knee with a plain white T-shirt tucked in the waist. Her hair was short and straight, offset by a fringe of sassy bangs. Below them her eyes registered surprise, then amusement.

"Hi." She looked at Amanda, grinning as she noted her sister's flushed face and tousled hair. The one place you didn't expect to see business-first Amanda Calhoun was on the floor with a strange and very attractive man. "What's going on?"

"We were going for the best two out of three," Sloan told her. He rose, then hauled Amanda up by the arm. With what sounded like a snarl, Amanda jerked out of his hold, then busied herself brushing the dust from her slacks.

"This is my sister, C.C."

"And you must be Sloan." C.C. walked in, offering her hand. "Trent's told me about you." Green eyes dancing, she flicked a glance at her sister, then back again. "I guess he didn't exaggerate."

Sloan held the offered hand a moment. C. C. Calhoun was exactly the opposite of the kind of woman he'd expected his old friend to be involved with. And because Trent was his friend, Sloan couldn't have been more delighted. "I can see why Trent's got himself roped and corralled."

"That's one of Sloan's whimsical compliments," Amanda pointed out.

With a laugh, C.C. threw an arm around Amanda's shoulders. "I think I figured that out. I'm glad to meet you, Sloan. Really glad. When I went up to Boston with Trent a couple of weeks ago, everyone I met was so..."

"Stuffy?" He grinned.

"Well." A little embarrassed, she moved her shoulders. "I guess it's hard for some of them to accept that Trent's going to marry a mechanic who knows more about engines than opera."

"Looks to me like Trent's getting one hell of a deal."

"We'll see." She knew with the least encouragement she would get mushy and embarrass herself. "Aunt Coco said you were staying for dinner. I was hoping you'd take one of the guest rooms here while you're on the island."

Sloan couldn't see it, but he'd have bet the pot that Amanda bit her tongue. The idea of ruffling her feathers made it tempting to change his plans. "Thanks, but I'm all taken care of. Besides..." Now he grinned at Amanda. "I'm going to be underfoot enough as it is."

"However you're most comfortable," C.C. told him. "Just so that you know you're welcome here at The Towers."

"I'll go down and see if Aunt Coco needs any help." Amanda sent Sloan a cool nod. "C.C. will show you down when you're ready."

He winked at her. "Thanks for the tour, honey."

He could almost hear her grinding her teeth as she walked away.

"That's some sister you've got there."

"Yes, she is." C.C.'s smile was warm, and warning. "Trent tells me you're quite the ladies' man."

"He's still mad because I stole a woman out from under his nose when we were both still young and foolish." Sloan took C.C.'s hand as they walked through the doorway. "You sure you're stuck on him?"

She had to laugh. "Now I see why he told me to lock up my sisters."

"If they're anything like that one, I expect they can take care of themselves."

"Oh, they can. The Calhoun women are as tough as they come." She paused at the top of the iron circular stairs. "I'd better warn you. Aunt Coco claims she saw you in the tea leaves this morning."

"In the...aah."

She gave a half apologetic, half amused shrug. "It's kind of a hobby of hers. Anyway, she might start to try to manipulate, especially if she decides the fates have linked you with one of my sisters. She means well, but..."

"O'Rileys are pretty good at handling themselves, too."

It only took one long look at him to have her believing it. C.C. tapped his shoulder. "Okay then. You're on your own."

Sloan started down behind her. "C.C., are there any men Amanda's involved with who I'm going to have to hoist out of the way?"

C.C. stopped, studying him through the opposite side of the open stairs. "No," she said after a moment. "Amanda's done all the hoisting herself."

"That's fine." He was smiling to himself as he descended the winding stairs. When they reached the second floor, he heard an echo of high-pitched screams and the frantic yapping of the dog.

"My sister Suzanna's kids," C.C. explained before he could ask. "Alex and Jenny are your typical quiet, retiring children."

"I can hear that."

A sturdy pale-haired missile zoomed up the steps. In reflex, Sloan caught it and found himself staring into a curious little face with a pouty mouth and big blue eyes.

"You're big," Jenny said.

"Nah. You're just short."

At five, she was just beginning to learn the wiles of womanhood and sent him a beaming smile. "Can I have a piggyback ride?"

"Got a quarter?" Giggling, she shook her head. "Okay," he said, "the first one's free then." When she squirmed around to his back, he started down again. At the base of the steps, Amanda had a dark-haired little boy in a headlock.

"Suzanna?" C.C. asked.

"In the kitchen. I was drafted to watch these two." She narrowed her eyes at Jenny. "The little pig-nosed one got away from me."

"Oink, oink." From the tower of Sloan's back, Jenny giggled and snorted.

"Who's he?" Alex wanted to know.

"Sloan O'Riley." Sloan offered a hand, man to man, which Alex eyed dubiously before accepting it.

"You talk funny. Are you from Texas?"

"Oklahoma."

After a moment's consideration, Alex nodded. "That's almost as good. Did you ever shoot anybody dead?"

"Not lately."

"That's enough, you ghoul." C.C. took charge. "Come on, let's go get cleaned up for dinner." She swung Jenny from Sloan's back.

"Cute kids," Sloan commented when C.C. hauled them up the stairs.

"We like them." Amanda offered him a genuine smile. Seeing him with Jenny riding his back had softened her. "They'll be in school most of the day, so they shouldn't bother you while you're working."

"I don't figure they'd be a bother one way or the other. I've got a nephew of my own back home. He's a pistol."

"Those two can be shotguns, I'm afraid." But the affection came through. "It's nice for them to be around a man now and again."

"Your sister's husband?"

The smile faded. "They're divorced. You might know him. Baxter Dumont?"

A shutter seemed to come down over Sloan's eyes. "I've heard of him."

"Well, that's history. Dinner's nearly ready. Why don't I show you where to wash up?"

"Thanks." Distracted, Sloan followed her. He was thinking that there were some points of history that had an unfortunate habit of overlapping.

Chapter Three

Anticipating the shock, Amanda dove into the cold water of the pool. She surfaced with a delicious shiver then began the first of her usual fifty laps.

There was nothing she liked better than beginning a day with a vigorous workout. It ate away the old tension to make room for the new that would develop before the workday was done.

Not that she didn't enjoy her job as assistant manager of the BayWatch Hotel. Particularly since it gave her the privilege of using the hotel pool before the guests began to crowd in. It was the end of May and the season had begun to swing. Of course it was nothing compared to what it would be by midsummer, but most of the rooms in the hotel were occupied, which meant she had her hands full. This hour, which she gave herself whenever weather permitted, was prized.

As she approached one end of the pool, she curled, tucked and pushed off.

In another year, she thought as she sent beads of water flying, she would be manager of The Towers Retreat. A St. James hotel. The goal that she had worked and struggled for since she'd taken her first part-time job as a desk clerk at sixteen was about to be realized.

It nagged at her from time to time that she would have the job only because Trent was marrying her sister. Whenever it did, she became only more determined to prove that she deserved it, that she had earned it.

She would be managing an exclusive hotel for one of the top chains in the country. And not just any hotel, she thought, cutting cleanly through the water, but The Towers. A part of her own heritage, her own history, her own family.

The ten luxurious suites Trent intended to create out of the crumbling west wing would be her responsibility. If he was right, the St. James name and the legend of The Towers would keep those suites filled year-round.

She would do a good job. An exceptional one. Every guest who traveled home from The Towers would remember the excellent service, the soothing ambience, the silky smooth organization.

It was going to happen. There would be no more slaving for a demanding and unappreciative supervisor, no more frustration at doing the work and handing over the credit. At last the credit, and the failure, would be hers alone.

It was only a matter of waiting until the remodeling was done.

And that brought her thoughts ramming headfirst into Sloan O'Riley.

She certainly hoped Trent knew what he was doing. What baffled her most was how such a smooth and polished man such as Trenton St. James III had ever become friends with a throwback like O'Riley. The man had actually knocked her down. Of course, she'd knocked him down first, but that was entirely beside the point.

Amanda kicked off again. Her leanly muscled arms sliced through the water, her long legs scissored. She didn't regret, not for a minute, that she'd had the wit and the strength to get the best of him first. He'd been pushy and overfamiliar and too full of himself from the moment she'd met him. And he'd kissed her.

She turned her head up for air then slid her face into the water again.

She hadn't given him the least bit of encouragement. In fact, just the opposite. But he'd sat there, grinning like a fool, and had kissed her. The memory of it had her gasping for air again.

Not that she'd liked it, Amanda assured herself. If C.C. hadn't walked in, she would have given the arrogant Mr. O'Riley a piece of her mind. Except that she hadn't had one left.

Because she'd been angry, that's all. She wasn't a bit attracted to the rough, outdoorsy type with callused hands and dusty boots. She wasn't fool enough to fall for a pair of dark green eyes that crinkled at the corners when they smiled. Her image of the ideal man included a certain sophistication, smooth manners, culture, a quiet aura of success. If and when she became interested in a relationship, those would be her requirements. Slow-talking cowboys need not apply.

Maybe there had been something sweet about him when he'd talked to the children, but it wasn't enough to overcome the rest of the deficits in his personality.

She remembered the way he'd flirted and charmed Aunt Coco at dinner. He'd kept C.C. amused with stories of Trent's college days and had been tolerant and easy with Alex's and Jenny's questions about horses and Indians and six-shooters.

But he'd watched Suzanna a little too closely, a little too carefully for Amanda's liking. A woman chaser, Amanda decided. If Lilah had been at dinner, he probably would have flirted with her, as well. But Lilah could take care of herself where men were concerned.

Suzanna was different. She was beautiful, sensitive and vulnerable. Her ex-husband had hurt her deeply, and no one, not even the cocky Sloan O'Riley was going to get the chance to hurt Suzanna again. Amanda would make sure of it.

When she reached the edge of the pool this time, she gripped the coping and dipped her head back into the water to slick her hair out of her eyes. Surfacing, she found herself staring up into a watery image that was entirely too familiar.

"Morning." Sloan grinned down at her. The sun was at his back, bringing out the reddish tones in his untidy hair. "You got a nice form there, Calhoun."

She blinked her eyes clear. "What the hell are you doing here?"

"Here?" He glanced over his shoulder at the whitewashed hotel. "You could say I'm hanging my hat here." Watching her, he jerked a thumb up and back. "Room 320."

"You're a guest at the BayWatch?" Amanda propped her elbows on the coping. "It figures."

Agreeable, Sloan crouched down. She had the clear creamy Calhoun skin, he noted, particularly striking, and vulnerable, now washed clean of any cosmetics. "Nice way to start the day."

Her full damp mouth turned down in a frown. "It was."

"Since we're asking, what are you doing here?"

"I work here."

Things were becoming more and more interesting, he thought. "No fooling?"

"No fooling," she said dryly. "I'm assistant manager."

"Well, now." He dipped an experimental finger into the water. "Checking out the water temperature for the guests? That's dedication."

"The pool doesn't open until ten."

"Don't worry." He hooked his thumbs in the front pockets of his jeans. "I wasn't planning on taking a dip just yet." What he had been planning was to take a walk, a long solitary one. But that was before he'd spotted her doing laps. "So, I guess if I have any questions about the place, you're the one I talk to."

"That's right." Amanda moved over to the steps to climb out. The one-piece sapphire-colored suit clung like a second skin as water slid from her. "Is your room satisfactory?"

"Hmm?" She had legs designed to make a man sweat, he thought, slim and shapely and a yard long.

"Your room," she repeated as she reached for her towel. "It suits you?"

"It suits me fine. Just fine." He skimmed his gaze up those damp calves and thighs, over the slim hips on a lazy journey to her face. "The view's worth the price of admission."

Amanda hooked the towel around her neck. "The view of the bay's free—like the continental breakfast now being served in The Galley. You'll want to take advantage of it."

"I've found that a couple of croissants and a cup of coffee don't do much to stanch the appetite." Because he wasn't ready for her to walk away, he reached out to take both ends of the towel in a light grip. "Why don't you join me for a real breakfast?"

"Sorry." Her heart was beginning to thud uncomfortably. "Employees are discouraged from socializing with the guests."

"I reckon we could make an exception in this case, seeing as we're...old friends."

"We're not even new friends."

There was that smile again, slow, insistent and all too knowing. And then he said, "That's something we can fix over breakfast."

"Sorry. Not interested." She started to turn away, but he tightened his grip on the towel and held her in place.

"Where I come from people are a mite more friendly."

Since he wasn't giving her a choice, she held her ground. "Where I come from people are a great deal more polite. If you have any problems with the service during your stay at the BayWatch, I'll be more than happy to accommodate you. If you have any questions about The Towers, I'll make myself available to answer them. Other than that, we have nothing to discuss."

He watched her patiently, admiring the way she could coat her husky voice with frost even while her eyes glinted. This was a woman with plenty of control. And, though he was certain she'd snarl at the term, plenty of spunk.

"What time do you go on the clock here?"

She let out a hiss of breath. Obviously the man's head was as thick as his accent. "Nine o'clock, so if you'll excuse me, I'd like to go get dressed."

Sloan squinted up at the sun. "Looks to me like you've got about an hour before you punch in. The way you move, it won't take you half that to get yourself together."

Amanda shut her eyes briefly on a prayer for patience. "Sloan, are you trying to irritate me?"

"Don't figure I have to. It seems to come natural." Casually he wound the ends of the towel around his fists and had her jerking closer. He grinned as her chin shot up. "See?"

She resented bitterly the way her pulse was dancing, and the tight, clutching sensation deep in her stomach. "What's the matter with you, O'Riley?" she demanded. "I've made it absolutely plain that I'm not interested."

"I'll tell you how it is, Calhoun." He flipped his wrists again, shortening the towel farther. The humor she was used to seeing in his eyes changed into something else in the space of a heartbeat. And that something else was dark and dangerous. And exciting. "You're one long, cool drink of water," he murmured. "Every time I'm around you I get this powerful thirst." With a last jerk, he had her tumbling against him, her hands trapped tight between their bodies. "That little sip I had yesterday wasn't nearly enough." Bending down, he nipped at her bottom lip.

He felt her tremor, but as he kept his eyes on hers, he could see it wasn't from fear. A trace of panic maybe, but not fear. Still he waited to see if she would give him a flat-out no. That was something he would have to respect, however much the need churned through him.

But she said nothing, only stared at him with those wide wary eyes. Softly he brushed his lips over hers and watched the thick lashes flutter down. "I want more," he murmured. And took.

Her hands curled into fists between them, but she didn't use them to push him away. The struggle was all inside her, a wild and violent combat that jolted her system even as he bombarded her senses. Caught in the crossfire, her mind simply shut down.

His mouth wasn't lazy now. Nor were his hands slow. Hard and hot, his lips took from hers while his fingers pressed against her damp back. The scrape of his teeth had her gasping, then moaning when his tongue slid seductively over hers.

Her fingers uncurled to clutch at his shirt, then to claw their way up to his shoulder, into his hair. The desperation was new, terrifying, wonderful. It drove her to strain against him while her mouth burned with an urgency that matched his.

The change rocked him. He was used to having his senses clouded by a woman, to having his body throb and his blood burn. But not like this. In the instant she went from dazed surrender to fevered urgency, he knew a need so sharp, so jagged that it seemed to slice through his soul.

Then all he knew was her. All he could feel was the cool slick silk of her skin. All he could taste was the honeyed heat of her mouth. All he could want was more.

She was certain her heart would pound its way out of her breast. It seemed the heat from his body turned the water on her skin to steam, and the vapors floated through her brain. Nor did they clear when he eased her gently away.

"Amanda." He drew in a deep gulp of air but wasn't sure he'd ever get his breath back again. One look at her as she stood heavy eyed, her swollen lips parted, had the edgy desire cutting through him again. "Come up to my room."

"Your room?" She touched unsteady fingers to her lips, then her temple. "Your room?"

Lord, that throaty voice and those dazed eyes were going to have him on his knees. One thing he'd yet to do was beg for a woman. With her, he was afraid begging was inevitable.

"Come with me." Possessively he ran his hands over her shoulders. Somewhere along the line the towel had slid to the concrete. "We need to finish this in private."

"Finish this?"

On a groan, he brought his lips back to hers again in a last, long, greedy kiss. "Woman, I think you're going to be late for work."

He had her arm and had pulled her toward the gate before she shook her head clear. His room? she thought fussily. Finish this? Oh, Lord, what had she done? What was she about to do? "No." She jerked away and took a deep, cleansing breath that did nothing to stop the tremors. "I'm not going anywhere."

He tried to steady himself and failed. "It's a little late to play games." His hand snaked out to cup the back of her neck. "I want you. And there's no way in hell you're going to convince me you don't want me right back. Not after that."

"I don't play games," she said evenly, and wondered if he could hear her over the riot of her heartbeat. She was cold, so terribly cold. "I don't intend to start now." She was the sensible one, she reminded herself. She wasn't the kind of woman who raced into a hotel room to make love with a man she barely knew. "I want you to leave me alone."

"Not a chance." He struggled to keep his fingers light as temper and need warred inside him. "I always finish what I start."

"You can consider this finished. It had no business starting."

"Why?"

She turned away to snatch up her wrap. The thin terry cloth wasn't nearly enough to warm her again. "I know your type, O'Riley."

He reached deep for calm and rocked back on his heels. "Do you?"

Clumsy with temper, she fought to push her arms through the sleeves. "You swagger from town to town and fill a few free hours with an available woman having a quick roll between the sheets." She pulled the tie on the wrap tight. "Well, I'm not available."

"You figure you got me pegged, huh?" He didn't touch her, but the look in his eyes was enough to have her bracing. He didn't bother to explain that it was different with her. He hadn't yet explained it to himself. "You can take this as a warning, Calhoun. This isn't finished between us. I'm going to have you."

"Have me? *Have* me." Propelled by pride and fury, she took one long stride toward him. "Why you conceited self-absorbed sonofabitch—"

"You can save the flattery for later," he interrupted. "There will be a later, Amanda, when it's just you and me. And I promise you, it won't be quick." Because the idea appealed to him, he smiled. "No sir, when I make love with you, I'm going to take my time." He ran a finger down the collar of her wrap. "And I'm going to drive you crazy."

She slapped his hand away. "You already are."

"Thanks." He gave her a friendly nod. "I think I'll go see about that breakfast. You have a good day."

She would, she thought as he walked off whistling. She'd have a fine day if he was out of it.

It was bad enough that she had to work late, Amanda thought, without having to listen to one of Mr. Stenerson's droning lectures on efficiency. As manager of the BayWatch, Stenerson ruled his staff with fussy hands and whines. His preferred method of supervision was to delegate. In that way he could dole out blame when things went wrong, and gather in credit when things went right.

Amanda stood in his airy pastel office, staring at the top of his balding head as he ran through his weekly list of complaints.

"Housekeeping has been running behind by twenty minutes. In my spot check of the third floor, I discovered this cellophane wrapper under the bed of 302." He waved the tiny clear paper like a flag. "I expect you to have a better handle on things, Miss Calhoun."

"Yes, sir." *You officious little wienie.* "I'll speak to the housekeeping staff personally."

"See that you do." He lifted his ever-present clipboard. "Room service speed is off by eight percent. At this rate of deterioriation, it will lower to twelve percent by the height of the season."

Unlike Stenerson, Amanda had done time in the kitchen during the breakfast and dinner rush. "Perhaps if we hired another waiter or two," she began.

"The solution is not in adding more staff, but in culling more efficiency from those we have." He tapped a finger on the clipboard. "I expect to see room service up to maximum by the end of next week."

"Yes, sir." *You supercilious windbag.*

"I'll expect you to roll up your sleeves and pitch in whenever necessary, Miss Calhoun." He folded his soft white hands and leaned back. Before he'd opened his mouth again, Amanda knew what was coming. She could have recited the speech by rote.

"Twenty-five years ago, I was delivering trays to guests in this very hotel. It was through sheer determination and a positive outlook that I worked my way up to the position I hold today. If you expect to succeed, perhaps even take over in this office after my retirement, you must eat, sleep and drink the BayWatch. The efficiency of the staff directly reflects your efficiency, Miss Calhoun."

"Yes, sir." She wanted to tell him that in another year she would have her own staff, her own office and he could kiss his whipping boy goodbye. But she didn't tell him. Until that time, she needed the job and the weekly paycheck. "I'll have a meeting with the kitchen staff right away."

"Good, good. Now, I'll want you on call this evening, as I'll be incommunicado."

As always, she thought but murmured her agreement.

"Oh, and check the August reservations. I want a report on the ratio of Escape Weekends to Seven-Day Indulgences. Oh, and speak with the pool boy about missing towels. We're five short already this month."

"Yes, sir." Anything else? she wondered. Shine your shoes, wash your car?

"That'll be all."

Amanda opened the door and struggled to keep her unflappable professional mask in place. All she really wanted to do was knock her head against the wall for a few indulgent minutes. Before she could retreat to some private, quiet place to do so, she was called to the front desk.

Sloan took a seat in the lobby just to watch her. He was surprised to see that she was still working. He'd put in a full day at The Towers, and the scarred briefcase beside the chair was bulging with notes, measurements and sketches. He was ready for a tall beer and a rare steak.

But here she was, soothing guests, instructing desk clerks, signing papers. And looking just as cool and fresh as spring water. He watched her pull off an earring, jiggling it in her palm as she took a phone call.

It was one of life's small pleasures to watch her, he decided. All that drive and energy, the effortless control. Almost effortless, he thought with a grin. There was a line between her brows—frustration, he thought. Annoyance. Or just plain stubbornness. He had a powerful urge to go up to her and smooth it away. Instead, he gestured to a bellman.

"Yes, sir."

"Is there a florist around here?"

"Yes, sir, just down the street."

Still watching Amanda, Sloan dug out his wallet and pulled out a twenty. "Would you run down there and get me a red rose? A long-stemmed one that's still closed. And keep the change."

"Yes, *sir*. Thank you, sir."

While he waited, Sloan ordered a beer from the lobby bar and lighted a cigar. Stretching out his booted feet, he settled back to enjoy.

Amanda clipped on her earring then pressed a hand to her stomach. At least when she went down to give the kitchen staff a pep talk she could grab something to eat. A glance at her watch told her that she wouldn't have time to take her evening shift going through the paperwork, looking for a clue to the necklace. If there was any bright side to the enforced overtime, it was that Sloan wouldn't be at The Towers when she returned.

"Excuse me."

Amanda glanced up to see a trim, attractive man in a bone-colored suit. His dark hair was brushed back from a high forehead. Pale blue eyes smiled pleasantly as they looked into hers. The faint British accent added charm to his voice.

"Yes, sir. May I help you?"

"I'd like to speak with the manager."

Amanda felt her heart sink a little. "I'm sorry, Mr. Stenerson is unavailable. If there's a problem, I'll be glad to handle it for you."

"No problem, Miss—" his eyes flicked down to her name tag "—Calhoun. I'll be checking in for a few weeks. I believe I have the Island Suite."

"Of course. Mr. Livingston. We're expecting you." Quick and competent, she tapped the information into the computer herself. "Have you stayed with us before?"

"No." He smiled again. "Regrettably."

"I'm sure you'll find the suite very comfortable." She passed him a registration form as she spoke. "If there's anything we can do to make your stay more pleasant, don't hesitate to ask."

"I'm already certain it will be pleasant." He gave her another lingering look as he filled out the form. "Unfortunately, it must also be productive. I wanted to inquire about the possibility of renting a fax machine during my stay."

"We offer fax service for our guests' convenience," she said.

"I'll require my own." The diamond on his pinky winked as he slid the form across the counter. "I'm afraid I wasn't able to clear up all my business, as I had hoped. It simply wouldn't be practical for me to run down here every time I need to send or receive a document. Naturally, I'll be willing to pay whatever necessary for the convenience. If renting isn't feasible, perhaps I can purchase one."

"I'll see what I can arrange."

"I'd appreciate that." He offered her his credit card for an imprint. "Also, I'll be using the parlor in the suite as an office. I'd prefer if housekeeping left my papers and disarray undisturbed."

"Of course."

"Might I ask if you're familiar with the island?"

Smiling, she handed him his card and his keys. "I'm a native."

"Wonderful." His eyes on hers, he held her hand lightly. "Then I'll know to come to you if I have any questions. You've been very helpful, Miss Calhoun." He glanced at her name tag again. "Amanda. Thank you."

"You're quite welcome." Her pulse gave a quick jitter as she slid her hand from his to signal a bellman. "Enjoy your stay, Mr. Livingston."

"I already am."

As he walked away, the young desk clerk beside Amanda gave a low feminine sigh. "Who was that?"

"William Livingston." Amanda caught herself staring after him and pulled herself back to file the imprint.

"Gorgeous. If he had looked at me the way he looked at you, I'd have melted on the spot."

"Melting's not part of the job description, Karen."

"No." Dreamy eyed, Karen put her hand on a ringing phone. "But it sure is part of being a woman. Front desk, Karen speaking. May I help you?"

William Livingston, Amanda thought, tapping his registration form against her palm. New York, New York. If he could afford a couple of weeks in the Island Suite, that meant he had money as well as charm, good looks and impeccable taste in clothes. If she'd been looking for a man, he would have fit the bill nicely.

Opening up the phone book, Amanda reminded herself she was looking for a fax machine, not a man.

"Hey, Calhoun."

With her finger on Office Supplies in the business section, she glanced up. Sloan, his chambray shirt rolled up to the elbows, his hair curling untidily over its collar, leaned on the counter.

"I'm busy," she said dismissively.

"Working late?"

"Good guess."

"You sure look pretty in that little suit." He reached over the counter to rub a thumb and finger down the crisp red lapel of her jacket. "Kinda prim and proper."

Unlike the little bounce her pulse had given when William Livingstone had taken her hand, it went haywire at Sloan's touch. Annoyed, she brushed it away. "Do you have a problem with your room?"

"Nope. It's pretty as a picture."

"With the service?"

"Slick as a wet rock."

"Then if you'll excuse me, I've got work to do."

"Oh, I figured that. I've been watching you tow the mark here for the last half hour."

The line appeared between her brows. "You've been watching me?"

His gaze lingered on her mouth as he remembered just how it tasted. "It made the beer go down easy."

"It must be nice to have so much free time. Now—"

"It's not how much, it's what you do with it. Since you were . . . tied up for breakfast, why don't we have dinner?"

Well aware that her co-workers had their ears pricked, Amanda leaned closer and kept her voice low. "Can't you get it through your head that I'm not interested?"

"No." He grinned, then sent a wink toward Karen, who was hovering as close as discretion allowed. "You said you didn't like to waste time. So I figured we could have a little supper and pick up where we left off this morning."

In his arms, she thought, lost for a moment. With her mind fuddled and her blood racing. She was staring at his mouth when it curved and snapped her back to reality. "I'm busy, and I have no desire—"

"You've got plenty of that, Amanda."

She set her teeth, wishing with all her heart she could call him a liar and mean it. "I don't want to have dinner with you. Clear?"

"As glass." He flicked a finger down her nose. "I'll be upstairs if you get hungry. Three-twenty, remember?" He lifted the rose from behind the counter and put it into her hand. "Don't work too hard."

"Two winners in one night," Karen murmured, and watched Sloan walk away. "Lord, he sure knows how to wear jeans, doesn't he?"

Indeed he did, Amanda thought, then cursed herself. "He's crude, annoying and intolerable." But she brushed the rosebud against her cheek.

"Okay, I'll take bachelor number two. You can concentrate on Mister Beautiful from New York."

Damn it, why was she so breathless? "I'm going to concentrate on my job," Amanda corrected. "And so are you. Stenerson's on the warpath, and the last thing I need is some cowboy stud interrupting my routine."

"I wish he'd offer to interrupt mine," Karen murmured, then bent over her terminal.

She wasn't going to think about him, Amanda promised herself. She set the rose aside, then picked it up again. It wasn't the flower's fault, after all. It deserved to be put in water and appreciated for what it was. Softening a bit, she sniffed at it and smiled. And it had been sweet of him to give it to her. No matter how annoying he might be, she should have thanked him.

Absently she lifted the phone as it rang. "Front desk, Amanda speaking. May I help you?"

"I just wanted to hear you say that." Sloan chuckled into the phone. "Good night, Calhoun."

Biting back an oath, Amanda banged down the receiver. For the life of her she couldn't understand why she was laughing when she took the rose back into her office to find a vase.

* * *

I ran to him. It was as if another woman burst out into the twilight to race over the lawn, down the slope, over the rocks. In that moment there was no right or wrong, no duty but to my own heart. Indeed, it was my heart that guided my legs, my eyes, my voice.

He had turned back to the sea. The first time I had seen him he had been facing the sea, fighting his own personal war with paint and canvas. Now he only stared out at the water.

When I called to him, he spun around. In his face I could see the mirror of my own joy. There was laughter, mine and his, as he rushed toward me.

His arms went around me, so tightly. My dreams had known what it would be like to finally be held by them. His mouth fitted truly to mine, so sweet, so urgent.

Time does not stop. As I sit here and write this, I know that. But then, oh then, it did. There was only the wind and the sound of the sea and the sheer and simple glory of being in his arms. It was as if I had waited my entire life, sleeping, eating, breathing, all for the purpose of that single precious window of time. If I have another hundred years left to me, I will never forget an instant of it.

He drew away, his hands sliding down my arms to grip mine, then to bring them to his lips. His eyes were so dark, like gray smoke.

"I'd packed," he said. "I'd made arrangements to sail to England. Staying here without you was hell. Thinking you would come back, and that I'd never be able to touch you nearly drove me mad. Every day, every night, Bianca, I've ached for you."

My hands moved over his face, tracing it as I'd often longed to. "I thought I'd never see you again. I tried to pray that I wouldn't." As shame crept through my joy, I tried to turn away. "Oh, what you must think of me. I'm another man's wife, the mother of his children."

"Not here." His voice was rough, even as his hands were gentle. "Here you belong to me. Here, where I first saw you a year ago. Don't think of him."

He kissed me again, and I could not think, could not care.

"I've waited for you, Bianca, through the chill of winter, the warmth of spring. When I tried to paint, it was your image that haunted me. I could see you standing here, with the wind in your hair, the sunlight turning it copper, then gold, then flame. I tried to forget you." His hands were on my shoulders, holding me back while his eyes seemed to devour my face. "I tried to tell myself it was wrong, that for your sake if not my own, I should leave here. I would think of you, with him, dancing at a ball, attending the theater, taking him into your bed." His fingers tightened on my shoulders. "She is his wife, I would tell myself. You have no right to want her, to wish that she would come to you. That she could belong to you."

I lifted my fingers to his lips. His pain was my pain. I think it will always be so. "I have come to you," I told him. "I do belong to you."

He turned away from me, the struggle between conscience and love as strong in him as it was in me. "I have nothing to offer you."

"Your love. There is nothing else I want."

"It's already yours, has been yours from the first moment I looked at you." He came back to me to touch my cheek. *I could see the regret, and the longing, in those beautiful eyes. "Bianca, there is no future for us. I cannot and will not ask you to give up what you have."*

"Christian—"

"No. Whatever wrongs I do, I will not do that. I know you would give me what I ask, what I have no right to ask, then come to hate me for it."

"No." Tears came to my eyes then, bitter in the cooling wind. "I could never hate you."

"Then I would hate myself." He crushed my fingers against his lips again. "But I'll ask you for the summer, for a few hours when you can come here and we can pretend winter will never be." He smiled and kissed me softly. "Come here and meet me, Bianca, in the sunlight. Let me paint you. I'll be content with that."

And so tomorrow, and every day during this sweet, endless summer I will go to him. On the cliffs above the sea we will take what happiness we can.

Chapter Four

"Well, hello."

At the husky greeting, Sloan looked up from his notes on the billiard room to see a willowy gypsy in a flowing flowered robe. Long cables of red hair streamed down her shoulders and back. Dreamy green eyes assessed him before she glided into the room like a woman who had all the time in the world and was willing to spend it generously.

"Hi." Sloan caught the elusive scent—like crushed wildflowers—before she offered a hand.

"I'm Lilah." Her voice was as lazily flirtatious as her eyes. "We've missed each other the past couple of days."

If there was a man who didn't get a jolt from this one, Sloan thought, he was dead and buried. "I'm real sorry about that."

She laughed then gave his hand a companionable squeeze. First impressions ranked high with Lilah, and she'd already decided to like him. "Me, too. Especially now. What have you been up to?"

"Getting a feel for the place, and the people in it. How about you?"

"I've been busy trying to figure out if I was in love."

"And?"

"Nope." She moved her shoulders gently, but he caught the wistful look in her eyes before she turned to move around the room. "So, what's the plan here, Sloan O'Riley?"

"Elegant dining in a turn-of-the-century atmosphere." He kicked back in the Windsor armchair he'd been using and gestured toward the papers spread over the library table. "We take out part of that wall there, open up into the adjoining study, add a couple of glass pocket doors, and we've got a lounge."

"Just like that?"

"Just like that—after we deal with the structural hassles. I'll have some preliminary sketches for your family and Trent to look over in a couple of days."

"It seems strange," she murmured, running a finger along the old, dusty chair rail. "Thinking about this place being fresh and new again, having people in it." But if she closed her eyes, she could see it perfectly, the way it had once been. "They used to give huge parties, very elaborate, very chic. I can imagine my great-grandfather standing here beside a billiard table sipping Scotch, and wheeling and dealing." She turned back to Sloan. "Do you think about those things when you make your sketches and calculate stress and space?"

"As a matter of fact, I do. There's a burn mark on the floor right over there." He tipped his pencil toward the spot. "I imagine some fat guy in a dinner suit dropped his cigar while he was discussing the war in Europe. A couple of others were standing by the window, stripped down to their shirtsleeves and swirling brandy while they talked about the stock market."

Laughing, Lilah crossed back to him. "And the ladies were down in the parlor."

"Listening to piano music and gossiping about the latest fashions from Paris."

Lilah tilted her head. "Or discussing the possibility of being given the vote."

"There you go."

"I think you're just what The Towers needs," she decided. "Can I take a look at your drawings, or are you temperamental?"

"I make it a policy never to turn down a beautiful woman."

"Astute and clever." She went to lean over his shoulder and push through his papers. "Why, it's the Emperor's Room."

"The what?"

"The Emperor's Room, that's what I call the best guest room. Must be the harps and cherubs on the ceiling." Sliding her hair behind her shoulder, she leaned closer. "This is great."

The dressing room would be a cozy parlor, she noted, complete with a wet bar and an entertainment center that would be hidden behind the original paneling. The bath would remain almost as it was, with the addition of a private whirlpool tucked away in what had been an old storage closet.

"Both ends of one century," Lilah murmured. "You've hardly changed any of the original layout."

"Trent indicated he wanted to keep the luxury and convenience without altering the mood. We'll save most of the original materials, duplicate what's beyond hope."

"You're going to do it." And because she could see that as well, quite clearly, her eyes filled as she laid a hand on his shoulder. "My father wanted to. My mother and he used to talk about it all the time. I wish they could have seen this."

Touched, Sloan laid his hand over hers. Their fingers had linked when Amanda came to the door. Her first reaction was shock at seeing her sister with her cheek all but brushing Sloan's. Then came the spear of jealousy. There was no denying there was something private, even intimate passing between them. On the heels of that sharp green shaft, pride stepped in.

Hadn't she told herself he was a woman chaser?

"Excuse me." Her voice was a thin sheet of ice as she stepped into the room. "I've been looking for you, Lilah."

"You found me." She blinked back the tears but didn't bother to straighten. "I thought I'd come by and meet Sloan."

"I see you have." Determined to be casual if it killed her, Amanda jammed her hands into the pockets of her sweats. "It's your turn for a shift in the storeroom."

"That's what I get for having the day off." She wrinkled her nose, then sent Sloan a smile. "The Calhouns have become detectives, searching for clues to the hiding place of the elusive emeralds."

"So I've heard."

"Maybe you'll take a hack at one of the walls, and they'll fall out, looking as fabulous and glittery as the day Bianca hid them." With a sigh, she drew away. "Well, since duty calls, I'd better get dressed for it. Mandy, you ought to take a look at some of Sloan's sketches. They're great."

"I'll bet."

The tone would have been a direct tip-off, even if Lilah hadn't known her sister so well. So, Lilah thought with a lifted brow. That's the way it was. Since she'd never been able to resist teasing her sister, she leaned down to kiss Sloan's cheek. "Welcome to The Towers."

He didn't have a doubt as to what she was up to. The eyes might be dreamy, he thought, but there was a shrewd and devilish brain behind them. "Thanks. I'm feeling more at home every day."

"I'll meet you in the sweatshop in fifteen minutes," she said to Amanda, then grinned to herself as she went out.

"Is that your new uniform?" he asked Amanda as she stood scowling in the center of the room, her hands still fisted in the pockets of baggy gray sweats.

"I don't go in until two today."

"That's nice." He crossed his outstretched legs at the ankles. "I like your sister."

"That was obvious."

He only grinned. "What does she do, anyway?"

"If you mean professionally, she's a naturalist at Acadia National Park."

"Wildflowers and stuff. It suits."

As if the admiration in his voice didn't bother her in the least, she shrugged and walked to the terrace doors. "I thought you'd be taking measurements or something." Glancing over her shoulder, she shot him a narrow look. "Of the rooms, that is."

This time he laughed outright. "You're mighty cute when you're jealous, Calhoun."

Now she turned to look deliberately down her nose. "I don't know what you're talking about."

"Sure you do, but you can relax. I've already set my sights on you."

Did he expect her to be flattered? she wondered. The hell of it was that, in a odd way, she was. "Do I look like a target?"

"I'd say more like the grand prize." In a gesture of peace, he held up a hand as she sucked in her breath to swear at him. "Before you get more fired up, why don't we deal with business?"

"I am not fired up," she lied. "And I don't see what business we could have."

"Trent said you were the one I should . . . collaborate with, until he got back. Seeing as you're the one who handles most of the family business, and you've got a firsthand knowledge of hotels."

Because it was logical, she calmed enough to consider it. "What do you want to know?"

How long it's going to take me to knock down that wall around you, he thought. "I figured you'd want to take a look at what I've started. I'd like to get to the drawing board soon."

Actually she was dying to see, but kept her agreement grudgingly cool. "All right, but I only have a few minutes."

"I'll take what I can get."

He waited as she crossed the room. She didn't trust him worth spit, Sloan decided. And that was just fine for now.

"I've got two of the suites mapped out," he told her, shuffling papers. "Plus the tower and most of the dining room here."

She leaned closer, squinting a bit to focus without her reading glasses. As Lilah had been, she was impressed with the sketches. Not only were they competent, but they showed a quick understanding of mood, tone and the practicality necessary for smooth service.

"You work fast," she said, surprised.

"When it's called for." He enjoyed watching the way she lifted a hand to tuck back the swing of hair, not with the sinuous movements of her redheaded sister, but with a quick, absent flick. She smelled of soap and some cool sprinkle of scent.

"What's this?"

"What's what?" He was too busy with the way the sunlight showered on her hair to pay attention to anything else.

"This." She tapped a finger on a sketch.

"Hmm. That's an old servants' stairway. We bring this wall out here, to box it in." He took her finger to slide it along the sketch, the rough side of his palm fitting over the smooth skin of her hand. "It makes this suite two levels, the sitting room and bath down here, two bedrooms and a master bath up here. Since the stairs are already open, it gives us a separation of functions without closing off the flow of space."

"It's nice." Vaguely uneasy with the contact, she flexed her hand but only succeeded in tangling her fingers with his. "I suppose you're going to get estimates and bids."

"I've made some calls."

Something seemed to be happening to her legs from the knees down. They'd gone weak on her, as if she'd run a very long, very fast race. "Well, you..." She braced and turned her head to face him. His eyes were very close, very quiet, very calm. "Obviously you know what you're doing."

"Yeah, I do."

Oh, yeah, he did, she thought as she felt herself pulled toward him—not by his hand, but by something soft and warm and needy inside her. She had only to give in to it, to lean a little closer. Her mouth could be on his, and she would know, as she had known the day before, a kind of whippy excitement and dazzling pleasure. He was waiting, watching her, with those dark green eyes going from calm to intense, willing her to make that slight and significant move. As she began to slide toward him, she heard herself sigh.

Then she remembered.

He had been in almost this same position with Lilah just moments before. Faces close, fingers linked. Only a fool let herself be manipulated by a man who was that casual with a woman's feelings. And Amanda Kelly Calhoun was no fool.

She jerked back, tugging her hand from under his. Sloan felt the knots already winding through his stomach yank tighter.

"Did I miss something?" he asked with a casualness that cost him dearly.

"I don't know what you mean."

"The hell you don't. You were a hair's breadth away from kissing me, Mandy. Your eyes were full of it. Now you've got them frosted up again."

She wished it was as easy to put the ice back into her blood. "You're letting your ego get the best of you. But then, that's probably typical. If you want to take time out to flirt and snuggle with a woman, try Lilah again."

He was used to holding on to his temper. When a man had a dangerous one, he learned early to keep it chained down. But it wasn't easy, not with her, not with the way she so consistently racked his system. "Are you telling me that Lilah's available to any man who asks?"

She went from frost to fire so quickly he could only stare in amazed appreciation. "You don't know anything about my sister, O'Riley. Watch what you say or you'll find yourself on your butt again."

"I was asking what you said," he reminded her.

"I can say what I like, you can't. Lilah has a warm, generous heart. If you do anything to hurt her, I'll—"

"Hold on." Chuckling, he threw up both hands, palms out. "I don't mind you taking a chunk out of me, Calhoun, but I'd rather it be for something I did—or was at least planning to do. First, I'm not quite the tomcat you seem to think I am. And second, I'm not interested in—what was it—snuggling with Lilah."

Amanda's chin lifted a fraction higher. "What's the matter with her?"

Exasperated, he let his hands fall again. "Not a damn thing. Tell me, has your great-grandaddy's insanity trickled down or are you just being plain obstinate?"

"Take your pick." Now she was as embarrassed as she was angry and stalked over to the window to stare out. Whether he was a tomcat—as he'd put it—or not, it was no concerns of hers. It was her problem that she had overreacted to his meeting with Lilah. She was getting herself wound up over nothing, Amanda told herself. If she kept snapping at him every time they spent five minutes together, their business relationship would suffer. And business was, after all, her strongest suit. She gave herself another moment to be sure she'd regained some balance, then turned back.

"We seem to have gotten offtrack. Let's put this back on a professional level, and keep it there."

"You do that real well," he observed.

"What?"

"Pull yourself in. It can't be easy if being around me churns you up half as much as I get being around you." Then he grinned and recrossed his ankles. "Go ahead, be professional. I got real admiration for that side of you."

She wasn't sure whether to scream or laugh or just throw her hands up in defeat. Instead she shook her head and tried again. "I like your work."

"Thanks."

"Trent and I have discussed the budget for the project. He and C.C. may still be on their honeymoon when the bids start coming in. If that's the case, you and I will have to go over them. As far as the hotel section goes, you have a free hand. As to the other part of the house, the family part, we're only interested in essential repairs."

"Why? The place deserves a decent face-lift."

"Because the hotel is a business, and the Calhouns and St. Jameses will be partners. We have the property, he has the funds. We've all agreed that we won't take advantage of his generosity, or the fact that he's marrying C.C."

Sloan considered a moment. "Trent seems to have other ideas. And I've never known him to let anyone take advantage."

The smile softened her face. "I know, and we, all of us, appreciate that he's willing to help, but we feel strongly about this. The Towers, our part of it, is a Calhoun problem. Our position is that we'll accept the needed repairs to the plumbing, the wiring and other immediate necessities, then we'll pay him back from our share of the retreat. If business is good, we'll be able to take care of the rest ourselves within the next few years."

There was pride at stake here, he noted. And more, integrity. He nodded. "You work things out with Trent. Meanwhile, I'll concentrate on the west wing."

"Fine. If your schedule allows, you can take a look at the rest. It would be helpful if we had an idea what the budget will be on the family areas."

He started to point out that he was an architect not a contractor, then shrugged. It wouldn't hurt him to take a look. "Sure. I'll work up an estimate."

"I'd appreciate it. Once you do, I'd prefer if you gave it to me. Just me."

"You're the boss."

She lifted a brow. Odd, but she hadn't thought about it quite that way before. Her lips curved as she digested it. "Then we understand each other. One more thing."

He linked his hands behind his head. "We can have as many things as you want."

"Only one," she said, though her lips quivered. "When I was finalizing some of the wedding plans, I realized you were down as best man. I left your list with Aunt Coco."

"My list?"

"Yes, of the timetable, the duties you're responsible for, that sort of thing. There's also a copy of the necessary information—the name and phone number of the photographer, the contact for the musicians, the bartender we hired...oh, and I jotted down the names of three shops where you can rent a tux." Once again she took in the sheer size of him. "You really should get in for a fitting right away."

"I've got it covered." Impressed, he shook his head. "You're damn efficient, Calhoun."

"Yes, I am. Well then, I'll let you get back to work. I'll be in the third-floor storeroom in the other wing until about one. After that you can reach me at the BayWatch if you have any questions."

"Oh, I know where to find you, Calhoun. Good hunting."

He watched her walk away, and thought of her sitting in the storeroom, surrounded by dusty boxes and mounds of yellowing papers. She'd probably already found a way to put things in their tidy place, he thought with a grin. He wondered if she realized what a sweet contrast it was. She would stack and catalogue and file in the most practical way possible, while she searched through pieces of the past for an old dream.

Amanda found no dreams that morning. By the time she arrived at the BayWatch, she had already put in a five-hour day. When she had started the quest for the necklace weeks before, she had promised herself she wouldn't become discouraged, no matter how long it took or how little she found.

Thus far, they had come across the original receipt for the emeralds, and a date book where Bianca had mentioned them. It was enough, Amanda had decided, to prove the necklace had indeed existed, and to keep hope alive that it would be found again.

She often wondered about it, about what it had meant to Bianca Calhoun and why she had secreted it away. If indeed she had. Another old rumor was that Fergus had tossed the necklace into the sea. After all the stories Amanda had heard about Fergus Calhoun's abiding love of a dollar, it was hard to believe that he had willfully thrown away a quarter of a million in jewels.

Besides, she didn't want to believe it, Amanda admitted as she pinned on her name tag. Though she wouldn't have cared for anyone to know it, she had a strong streak of the romantic, and that part of her held tight to the notion that Bianca had hidden away the emeralds, like a gift or promise, waiting for the time they would be needed again.

It embarrassed her a little to know she felt that way. Amanda preferred the outward, and the logical, routine of sorting through papers and organizing them in the practical pursuit of a valuable heirloom.

Bianca herself remained as much a mystery to Amanda as the necklace. Her ingrained pragmatism made it impossible to understand a woman who had risked everything for, and ultimately had died for, love. Feelings that intense and that desperate seemed unlikely to her, unless they were in the pages of a book.

What would it be like to love that strongly? she wondered. To feel as though your life were so completely bound to another's that it was impossible to survive without him. Inconvenient, she decided. Uncomfortable and unwise. She could only be grateful that she hadn't inherited that dangerous kind of passion. Feeling smug about her own unbattered heart, she settled down to work.

"Amanda?"

She was halfway through the August reservations and held up a hand. "Minute," she murmured, and totaled her calculations to that point. "What is it, Karen? Wow." She pushed her glasses back up her nose and studied the luxurious spray of roses in the desk clerk's arms. "What did you do, win a beauty pageant?"

"They're not mine." Karen buried her face in them. "Don't I wish. They just came in, for you."

"Me?"

"You're still Amanda Calhoun," Karen pointed out as she offered the florist's card. "Though if you want to trade places until these three dozen long-stemmed beauties fade, I'm game."

"Three dozen?"

"I counted." Grinning, Karen laid them on the desk. "Three dozen and one," she added, nodded toward the single rose that stood beside them.

Sloan, Amanda thought, and felt her heart give a quick, catchy sigh. How was she supposed to get a handle on a man who did sweet, unexpected things every time she thought she'd made up her mind about him? How could he have known about her secret weakness for red roses? She hadn't even thanked him for the first one.

"Aren't you going to read the card?" Karen demanded. "If I have to go back to the desk without knowing who sent them, I'll be distracted and my work will suffer. The evil Albert Stenerson'll fire me, and it'll be your fault."

"I already know who they're from," she began, unaware of the softness in her eyes. "It was really so sweet of him to—oh." Baffled, she studied the name on the card. Not Sloan, she realized, with a cutting edge of disappointment that surprised her. They weren't from Sloan.

"Well? Do you want me to beg?"

Still puzzled, Amanda handed the card over.

"*With my appreciation. William Livingston.* Whew." Karen tossed back her long, dark hair. "What did you have to do to deserve this kind of gratitude?"

"I got him a fax machine."

"You got him a fax machine," Karen repeated, handing the card back to Amanda. "Last Sunday I cooked a pot roast with all the trimmings and all I got was a bottle of cheap wine."

Amanda continued to frown and tapped the card on the edge of her desk. "I guess I'd better thank him."

"I guess you'd better." Karen picked up one of the roses and sniffed. "Unless you'd rather delegate. I'd be glad to go up and express your appreciation to Mr. Eyes-To-Die-For Livingston."

"Thanks, but I'll handle it." She picked up the phone, then sent Karen an arched look. "Scram."

"Spoilsport." Laughing, she went out, discreetly shutting the door at her back as Amanda dialed the extension for the Island Suite.

"Livingston."

"Mr. Livingston, this is Amanda Calhoun."

"Ah, the efficient Miss Calhoun." There was a laugh in his voice, a pleasant and flattering one. "What can I do for you?"

"I wanted to thank you for the flowers. They're beautiful. It was very thoughtful of you."

"Just a small way of showing you that I appreciate your help, and the quick work."

"That's my job. Please let me know if I can be of any further assistance during your stay."

"As a matter of fact, there is something you could help me with."

"Of course." Automatically she picked up a pen and prepared to write.

"I'd like you to have dinner with me."

"Excuse me?"

"I'd like to take you to dinner. Eating alone is unappetizing."

"I'm sorry, Mr. Livingston, it's against hotel policy for the staff to socialize with the guests. It's kind of you to ask."

"Kindness has nothing to do with it. Can I ask if you'd consider it if hotel policy could be . . . bent?"

There was no chance of that, Amanda thought. Not with Stenerson. "I'd be happy to consider it," she said tactfully. "Unfortunately, as long as you're a guest at the BayWatch—"

"Yes, yes. I'll get back to you shortly."

Amanda blinked at the dead receiver, shrugged, then replaced it to get back to work. Ten minutes later, Stenerson was opening her door.

"Miss Calhoun, Mr. Livingston would like to have dinner with you." His mouth primed up even more than usual. "You're free to go. Naturally, I'll expect you to conduct yourself in a manner that will reflect properly on the hotel."

"But—"

"Don't make a habit of it."

"I—" But he was already shutting the door. Amanda was still staring at it when her phone rang. "Miss Calhoun."

"Shall we say eight o'clock?"

On a long breath, she sat back in her chair. She was on the point of refusing when she caught herself stroking the single rosebud Sloan had given her. Amanda snatched back her hand and balled it in her lap.

"I'm sorry, I'm on until ten tonight."

"Tomorrow then. Where shall I pick you up?"

"Tomorrow's fine," she said on impulse. "Let me give you directions."

Chapter Five

Sloan knew the minute Trent returned to The Towers. Even in the library at the end of a long corridor he could hear the high happy yaps of the dog, the shouts of children and the mix of laughter. Setting aside his notebook, he strolled out to see his old friend.

Trent had gotten no further than the foyer. Jenny was hanging on his legs as Fred circled and danced. Alex was jumping up and down in a bid for attention while Coco, Suzanna and Lilah all fired questions at once. C.C. only stood beaming, held snug against Trent's side. At a shout from above, Sloan looked up to see Amanda bolting down the stairs. Her laughter glowed in her face as he'd never seen it before. Squeezing through her sisters, she took her turn at a hug.

"If you hadn't come back today, I was sending out a team of mercenaries," she told Trent. "Four days before the wedding and you're down in Boston."

"I knew you could handle the details."

"She has miles of lists," Coco put in. "It's frightening."

"There, you see?" Trent gave Amanda a quick kiss.

"What did you bring me? What did you bring me?" Jenny demanded.

"Talk about mercenary." Laughing, Suzanna scooped her daughter up. When she spotted Sloan in the hallway, her easy smile faded. She tried to tell herself that it was her imagination that his eyes changed whenever he looked at her. It had to be. What possible reason would he have for disliking her on sight?

Sloan studied her another moment, a tall, slender woman with pale blond hair pulled back in a ponytail, a face blessed with classical beauty and sad blue eyes. Dismissing her, he looked back at Trent. His smile came naturally again.

"I hate to interrupt when you're surrounded by beautiful women, but time's wasting."

"Sloan." His arm still around C.C., Trent stepped forward to grip Sloan's hand. In all of his varied groups of acquaintances, associates and colleagues, this was the only man he considered a genuine friend. "On the job already?"

"Getting started."

"You look like you've just gotten back from a long vacation in the tropics instead of six weeks in Budapest. It's good to see you."

"Same here." Sloan sent a quick wink at C.C. "It's really good to see that you're finally developing some taste."

"I like him," C.C. said.

"Women tend to," Trent said. "How's your family?"

Sloan's gaze flicked to Suzanna again. "They're fine."

"You two must have a lot to catch up on." Feeling awkward, Suzanna took her son's hand. "We're going to take a walk before dinner."

Amanda waited until Coco had urged everyone along toward the parlor before she put a hand on Sloan's arm. "Wait."

He grinned at her. "I've been waiting, Calhoun."

She wasn't even tempted to rise to the bait. "I want to know why you look at Suzanna that way."

The humor faded from his eyes. "What way is that?"

"Like you detest her."

It annoyed him that those particular and very private feelings showed so clearly. "You've got more imagination than I gave you credit for."

"It's not my imagination." Baffled, she shook her head. "What could you possibly have against Suzanna? She's the kindest, most good-hearted person I know."

It was difficult not to sneer, but he kept his face bland. "I didn't say I had anything against her. You did."

"You didn't have to say it. Obviously I can't make you talk about it, but—"

"Maybe that's because I'd rather talk about us." Casually he set both hands on the banister behind her, caging her between.

"There is no us."

"Sure there is. There's you and there's me. That makes us. That's real basic grammar."

"If you're trying to change the subject—"

"You're getting that line between your eyebrows again." He lifted a thumb to rub at it. "That Calhoun line. How come you never smile at me the way you smiled at Trent?"

"Because I like Trent."

"It's funny, most people figure I'm an amiable sort of guy."

"Not from where I'm standing."

"Why don't you stand a little closer?"

She had to laugh. If there had been a contest for persistence, Sloan O'Riley would have won hands down. "This is close enough, thanks." More than close enough, she added silently when she had to fight back an urge to run her fingers through that untidy mane of reddish-blond hair. "*Amiable* isn't the word I would use. Now, *cocky, annoying, tenacious,* those might suit."

"I kind of like tenacious." He leaned closer to breathe in her scent. "A man doesn't get very far if he caves in every time he runs into a wall. You climb over, tunnel under, or just knock the whole damn thing down."

She put a hand to his chest before he could close that last inch of distance. "Or he keeps beating his head against it until he has a concussion."

"That's a calculated risk, and worth it if there's a woman behind the wall looking at him the way you look at me."

"I don't look at you any particular way."

"When you forget that you want to be professional, you look at me with those big blue eyes of yours all soft, and a little scared. A lot curious. Makes me want to scoop you up right there and carry you off to someplace real quiet so I can satisfy that curiosity."

She could imagine it all too clearly, feel it all too sharply. There was only one solution. Escape. "Well, this has been fun, but I've got to go change."

"Are you going back to work?"

"No." Agile, she swooped under his arm and swung up the steps. "I've got a date."

"A date?" he repeated, but she was already racing across the second floor.

He told himself he wasn't waiting for her, though he'd been pacing the foyer for a good twenty minutes. He wasn't going to hang around like an idiot and watch her go strolling off with some other man—after she'd tied him into knots by just standing there and looking at him. There was plenty for him to do, including enjoying the dinner Coco had invited him to, talking over old times and new plans with Trent, even sitting down at his drawing board. He wasn't about to spend the evening mooning over the fact that some obstinate woman preferred someone else's company to his.

After all, Sloan reminded himself as he paced the foyer, she was free to come and go as she pleased. The same as he was. Neither one of them was branded. Just because he had a hankering for her didn't mean he was going to get riled up when she spent a couple of hours with another man.

The hell it didn't.

Turning, he took the steps two at a time.

"Calhoun?" He strode down the corridor, banging on doors. "Damn it, Calhoun, I want to talk to you." He was at the far end of the hall and starting back when Amanda opened her door.

"What's going on?" she demanded.

He stared a moment as she stood in the stream of light that spilled out of the room behind her. She'd done something fancy to her hair, he noted, so that it looked sexily rumpled. Played with her face, too, in that damnably sultry way some women have a talent for. Her dress was a pale icy blue, full at the skirt, nipped at the waist with two skinny straps slinking over her shoulders. Chunky stones in a deeper blue glittered at her ears and throat.

She didn't look efficient, he thought furiously. She didn't look competent. She looked as delectable as a pretty white cake on a fancy tray. And he was damned if any other man was going to take even one small nibble.

Her foot was already tapping when he started toward her.

Amiable? she thought, and had to resist the urge to bolt back into her room and lock the door. No one would call him amiable now. He looked as though he'd just finished chewing a mountain of glass and was raring for the second course.

"What kind of date?" he snapped at her, and found himself further incensed by the fact that her skin smelled like glory.

Amanda inclined her head slowly. The hands she had fisted on her hips slid carefully to her sides. When you were facing a raging bull you didn't wave a red flag but tried to ease yourself over the fence. "The usual kind."

"Is that the way you dress for the usual kind?"

Irked, she glanced down and smoothed her skirts. "What's wrong with the way I'm dressed?"

For an answer, he took her arm and swung her around. He'd been right, he thought as his stomach clutched up. Those two little straps were all that were covering her back. Right down to the waist. "Where's the rest of it?"

"Rest of what?"

"The dress."

She turned back, still cautious, and examined his face. "Sloan, I think you've gone around the bend."

She didn't know how right she was, he thought. "I've got as much sense as any man can hang on to after ten minutes with you. Cancel."

"Cancel?" she repeated.

"The date, damn it." He nudged her none too gently toward her bedroom. "Go in and call him up and tell him you can't make it. Ever."

"You really are crazy." She forgot about bulls and red flags and cut loose. "I go where I please and with whom I please. If you think I'm going to break a date with an attractive, charming and intelligent man because some overbearing baboon tells me to, then think again."

"It's the date," he warned, "or that pretty stiff neck of yours."

Her eyes narrowed down to two slits of righteous blue fire. "Don't you threaten me, you pinhead. I have a dinner date with your antithesis. A gentleman." She elbowed him aside. "Now get out of my way."

"I'll get out of your way," he promised. "After I give you something to think about."

He had her back against the wall with his mouth covering hers before she could blink. She could taste the anger. That, she would have fought against to the last breath. But she could also taste the need, and that, she surrendered to. It was such a perfect echo of her own.

He didn't care if it was unreasonable. He didn't care if it was wrong or stupid or any of the other terms that could so easily apply to his actions. He wanted to curse her for making him behave like some reckless teenager. But he could only taste her, drowning in the flavor that he was coming to understand he would always crave. He could only pull her closer against him so that he could feel the instant heat that pumped from her body into his.

He could sense each change as it flowed through her.

First the anger that kept her rigid and aloof. Then the surrender, reluctant then melting so that her bones seemed to dissolve. And the passion overlapping so quickly it stole his breath. It was that he understood he couldn't live without.

Her arms went around him as if they belonged there. Strained against his, her body throbbed until it was one sweet ache. This was an ache that once felt could never be forgotten, would always be craved. Eager, she nipped at his mouth, knowing in another moment delirium could overtake her. Wanting it, wanting that liberating mindless whirl of desire only he could ignite inside her.

Only he.

In one long possessive stroke his hands ran from her shoulders to her wrists, holding there a moment while her pulse scrambled under his palms. When he lifted his head, she leaned back limply against the wall, watching him while she struggled to catch her breath. While she fought to break through the torrent of sensations and understand the feelings beneath them.

The thought of another man touching her, of looking into her face and seeing it flushed with passion as it was now, of seeing her eyes clouded with it, terrified him. Because he preferred good clean anger to fear, he gripped her shoulders again, all but lifting her off her feet.

"Think about that," he told her in a low dangerous voice. "You think about that good and hard."

What had he done to her to make her need so terribly? He had to know, just by looking at her, that he had only to pull her inside her room to take everything he claimed to want. He had only to touch her again to have her desperate to give. He wouldn't even have to ask. It shamed her to realize it, destroyed her to understand that anyone would have such complete power over her pride and her will.

"You made your point," she said unsteadily, infuriated that tears were stinging the back of her eyes and throat. "Do you want to hear me say that you can make me want you? Fine. You can."

The sparkle of tears in her eyes did what her fury couldn't. It beat him soundly. There was regret in his voice when he lifted a hand to her face. "Amanda—"

She stiffened and shut her eyes. If he was gentle—she knew if he showed her even a scrap of tenderness, she would crumble. "You've got your conquest, Sloan. Now I'd appreciate it if you'd let me go."

He let his hand slide to his side before he stepped back. "I'm not going to tell you I'm sorry." But the way she looked at him made him feel as though he had just shattered something small and fragile.

"That's all right. I'm sorry enough for both of us."

"Amanda." Lilah stood at the top of the stairs, watching them both with her sleepy-eyed curiosity. "Your date's here."

"Thanks." Frantic for escape, she turned into her room to grab her jacket and purse. Being careful not to look at Sloan, she hurried out again to rush downstairs. Lilah glanced after her, then walked down the hall to rest her hands on Sloan's shoulders.

"You know, big guy, you look like you could use a friend."

He couldn't begin to put a name to any of the emotions currently running riot through him. "Maybe I'll just go downstairs and throw him out a window."

"You could," Lilah agreed after a moment, "but Mandy's always been a sucker for the underdog."

Sloan swore then decided to work off some of the frustration by pacing the corridor. "So, who is he anyway?"

"I've never met him before. His name's William Livingston."

"And?"

Lilah gave a gentle shrug. "Tall, dark and handsome as the saying goes. Very faint, very charming British accent, Italian suit, upper-class manners. That patina of wealth and breeding without being ostentatious."

Sloan swore and considered punching a hole in the wall. "He sounds just dandy."

"Sounds," she agreed, but her look was troubled.

"What is it?"

"Bad vibes." Absently she ran a hand up and down her arm. "And he had a very muddy aura."

"Give me a break, Lilah."

With a little smile, she glanced back at him. "Don't knock it, Sloan. Remember, I'm on your side. I happen to think you're just what my take-it-all-too-seriously sister needs." In her easy way, she hooked a friendly arm through his. "Relax, Mr. William Livingston doesn't have a chance. Not her type." She laughed as she walked with him to the steps. "She thinks he is, but he's not. So let's go eat. There's nothing like Aunt Coco's Trout Amandine to put you in a good mood."

Pretending she had an appetite, Amanda studied her menu. The restaurant William had chosen was a lovely little place overlooking Frenchman Bay. Since the night was warm, they could enjoy the terrace service with candlelight flickering in the gentle sea breeze, and the fragile scent of spring flowers.

Amanda left the choice of wine up to him and tried to convince herself that she was about to have a delightful evening.

"Are you enjoying Bar Harbor?" she asked.

"Very much. I'm hoping to get some sailing in soon, but in the meantime, I've been content to enjoy the scenery."

"Have you been to the park?"

"Not yet." He glanced over at the bottle the waiter offered, perused the label, then nodded.

"You shouldn't miss it. The view from Cadillac Mountain is stupendous."

"So I'm told." He tasted the wine, approved, then waited for Amanda's to be poured. "Perhaps you'll find some time and act as my guide."

"I don't think—"

"Hotel policy's already been bent," he interrupted, and touched his glass lightly to hers.

"I wanted to ask you how you managed it."

"Very simply. I gave your Mr. Stenerson a choice. Either he could make an exception to his policy, or I could move to another hotel where it wouldn't be an issue."

"I see." She took a thoughtful sip of wine. "That seems a bit drastic just for a dinner."

"A very delightful dinner. I wanted to get to know you better. I hope you don't mind."

What woman could? she asked herself, and only smiled.

It was impossible not to relax, not to be charmed by his stories, flattered by his attentiveness. He did not, as so many successful men did, talk constantly of his business. As an antique dealer he'd traveled all over the world and, throughout the meal, gave Amanda glimpses of Paris and Rome, London and Rio.

When her thoughts drifted now and again to another man, she doubled her determination to enjoy herself where she was, and with whom.

"The rosewood chiffonier in your foyer," he commented as they lingered over coffee and dessert. "It's a beautiful piece."

"Thank you. It's Regency period—I think."

He smiled. "You think correctly. If I had run into it at an auction, I would have considered myself very fortunate."

"My great-grandfather had it shipped over from England when he built the house."

"Ah, the house." William's lips curved as he lifted his cup. "Very imposing. I half expected to see medieval maidens drifting about on the lawn."

"Or bats swooping out of the tower."

On a delighted laugh, he squeezed her hand. "No, but perhaps Rapunzel letting down her hair."

The image appealed and made her smile. "We love it, and always have. Maybe the next time you visit the island you'll stay at The Towers Retreat."

"The Towers Retreat," he murmured, tapping a finger thoughtfully against his lips. "Where have I heard that before?"

"A projected St. James hotel?"

His eyes cleared. "Of course. I read something a few weeks ago. You don't mean to say that your home is The Towers?"

"Yes, it is. We hope to have the retreat ready for occupancy in about a year."

"That is fascinating. But wasn't there some legend attached to the place? Something about ghosts and missing jewelry?"

"The Calhoun emeralds. They were my great-grandmother's."

With a half smile, he tilted his head. "They're real? I thought it was just a clever publicity gimmick. Stay in a haunted house and search for missing treasure. That sort of thing."

"No, in fact we're not at all pleased that the whole business leaked out." Even thinking about it annoyed her so that she began to drum her fingers on the table. "The necklace is real—was real in any event. We don't know where it might have been hidden. In the meantime we're forever bothered by reporters or having to chase erstwhile treasure hunters off the grounds."

"I'm sorry. That's very intrusive."

"We hope to find it soon, and put an end to all the nonsense. Once renovations start, it might turn up under a floorboard."

"Or behind the ubiquitous secret panel," he offered with a smile and made her laugh.

"We don't have any of those—at least that I know of."

"Then your ancestor was remiss. A place like that deserves at least one secret panel." He laid a hand over hers again. "Perhaps you'll let me help you look for it . . . or at least let me use it as an excuse to see you again."

"I'm sorry, but at least for the next few days I'm tied up. My sister's getting married on Saturday."

He smiled over their joined hands. "There's always Sunday. I would like to see you again, Amanda. Very much." He let the subject, and her hand slip gently away.

On the drive home he kept the topics general. No pressure, Amanda thought, grateful. No arrogant assumptions or cocky grins. This was the kind of man who knew how to treat a woman with the proper respect and attention. William wouldn't knock her to the ground and laugh in her face. He wouldn't stalk her down like a gunslinger and fire out demands.

So why was she so let down when they stopped in front of the house and Sloan's car was nowhere in sight? Shaking off the mood, she waited for William to come around and open her door.

"Thank you for tonight," she told him. "It was lovely."

"Yes, it was. And so are you." Very gently he placed his hands on her shoulders before touching his lips to hers. The kiss was very warm, very soft—an expert caress of lips and hands. And to her disappointment, it left her completely unmoved.

"Are you really going to make me wait until Sunday to see you again?"

His eyes told her that he had not been unmoved. Amanda waited for the banked desire in them to strike some chord. But there was nothing.

"William, I—"

"Lunch," he said, adding a charming smile. "Something very casual at the hotel. You can tell me more about the house."

"All right. If I can swing it." She eased away before he could kiss her again. "Thanks again."

"My pleasure, Amanda." He waited, as was proper, for her to go inside. As the door shut behind her, his smile changed ever so slightly, hardened, cooled. "Believe me, it will be my pleasure."

He walked back to his car. He would drive it well out of sight of The Towers. And then he would come back to do a quick and quiet tour of the grounds, to note down the most practical entrances.

If Amanda Calhoun could be his entryway into The Towers, that was all well and good—with the side benefit of romancing a beautiful woman. If she didn't provide him with a way in, he would simply find a different route.

One way or the other, he didn't intend to leave Mount Desert Island without the Calhoun emeralds.

"Did you have a good time?" Suzanna asked when Amanda came in the front door.

"Suze." Amused but not surprised, Amanda shook her head. "You waited up again."

"No, I didn't." To prove it, Suzanna gestured with the mug in her hand. "I just came down to make myself some tea."

Amanda laughed as she walked over to rest her hands on her sister's shoulders. "Why is it that we Irish-as-Paddy's-pig Calhouns can't tell a decent lie?"

Suzanna gave up. "I don't know. We should practice more."

"Honey, you look tired."

"Mmm." Exhausted was the word, but she didn't care for it. Suzanna sipped the tea as they started up the stairs together. "Springtime. Everybody wants their flowers done yesterday. I'm not complaining. It looks like the business is finally going to turn a real profit."

"I still think you should hire on some more help. Between the business and the kids you run yourself ragged."

"Now who's playing mama? Anyway, Island Gardens needs one more good season before I can afford anything but one part-time helper. Plus I like to be busy." Even though fatigue was dragging at her, she paused outside of Amanda's door. "Mandy, can I talk to you for a minute before you go to bed?"

"Sure. Come on in." Amanda left the door slightly ajar as she slipped out of her shoes. "Is something wrong?"

"No. At least nothing I can put my finger on. Can I ask you what you think of Sloan?"

"Think of him?" Stalling, Amanda set her shoes neatly in the closet.

"Impressions, I guess. He seems like a very nice man. Both kids are already crazy about him, and that's an almost foolproof barometer for me."

"He's good with them." Amanda took off her earrings to replace them in her jewelry box.

"I know." Troubled, she wandered the room. "Aunt Coco's set to adopt him. He's slipped right into an easy relationship with Lilah. C.C.'s already fond of him, and not just because he's a friend of Trent's."

Pouting a little, Amanda unclasped her necklace. "His type always gets along beautifully with women."

Distracted, Suzanna merely shook her head. "No, it's not a man-woman kind of thing at all. Just a kind of innate relaxation."

Amanda had no comment for that as she recalled the fevered tension in him a few hours earlier.

"He seems like an easygoing, friendly man."

"But?"

"It's probably my imagination, but whenever he looks at me, I get this wave of hostility." With a half laugh, she shrugged. "Now I sound like Lilah."

Amanda's eyes met her sister's in the mirror. "No, I sensed something myself. I can't explain it. I even called him on it."

"Did he say anything? I don't expect everyone to like me, but when I feel a dislike this strong, at least I want to know why."

"He denied it. I don't know what to say, Suzanna, except that I don't think he's the kind of man who would react that way to someone he doesn't even know." She made a helpless gesture with her hands. "He can certainly be annoying, but I don't think he's a man to be deliberately unfair. Maybe we're both being oversensitive."

"Maybe." Suzanna pushed the uncomfortable feelings away. "We're all a little crazed with C.C.'s wedding, and the renovations. Well, I won't lose any sleep over him." She kissed Amanda's cheek. "Good night."

"Night." As she eased down onto the bed, Amanda let out a long sigh. It was unfortunate, she thought. It was infuriating. But she already knew she'd be losing sleep over him.

Chapter Six

She was right on schedule. If there was one thing you could count on about Amanda Calhoun, Sloan thought, it was that she'd be on time. She was moving fast—typically—so he lengthened his stride and crossed the hotel patio to waylay her by the gate leading to the pool. His hand covered hers on the latch.

She jerked away, which was no less than he'd expected. "Don't you have anything better to do?" she asked.

"I want to talk to you."

"This is my time." She shoved open the gate, strode through then whirled around. "My personal time. I don't have to talk to you." To prove it, she slammed the gate smartly in his face.

Sloan took a long, slow breath, then opened the gate. "Okay, you can just listen." He caught up with her as she heaved her towel onto a deck chair.

"I'm not going to talk, and I'm not going to listen. There's absolutely nothing you have to say that could interest me." She stripped off her terry wrap, tossed it aside, then dove into the pool.

Sloan watched her through the first lap. She was mad enough to spit, he thought, then moved his shoulders. So, they'd do it the hard way.

With each kick and stroke, Amanda cursed him. She'd spent half the night replaying their last scene together over and over in her mind. It had made her miserable. It had made her furious. When she'd awakened that morning, she'd promised herself that he would never get the chance to touch her again. Certainly he would never get the chance to make her feel helpless and needy again.

Her life was just beginning to move along as she wanted. There was no way, no way in hell that Sloan O'Riley or anyone else was going to block her path.

She ran straight into him, a dud torpedo into a battleship. Sputtering, she surfaced to see him standing chest high in the water. Bare-chest high.

"What are you doing?"

"I figured I'd have a better chance of getting you to listen in here than I would if I stood on the side and yelled at you."

Eyes narrowed, she slicked the hair back from her face. There was a laugh bubbling in her throat that she refused to acknowledge. "The pool isn't open to guests until ten."

"Yeah, I think you mentioned that. What you didn't mention is that this water is freezing."

"Yeah." Now she did smile, and there was as much humor as smugness in the curve of her lips. "I know. That's why I like to keep moving."

She started off, slicing cleanly through the water. Less than a foot away, he was matching her stroke for stroke. He'd stripped off more than his shirt, she noted. The only thing covering that very long body was a pair of brief navy briefs. Each time her face went into the water, her eyes slid over to take another look.

His broad shoulders and chest tapered down to a narrow waist and hips. The skin was stretched taut over the bones there, without an ounce of excess flesh. His stomach was board flat, and...oh my. When she nearly sucked in water instead of air, Amanda forced her gaze to skip down several strategic inches to the hard, muscled thighs and calves.

The tough, weathered tan was over every inch of exposed flesh. His skin gleamed like wet copper. And what would it feel like to run her hands over it now? To feel those sleek, smooth muscles under her fingers? How could their bodies fit together now, if slick as otters, they slid against each other through the chill water?

Chill? she thought. The pool was beginning to feel like a sauna. Deliberately she pushed off hard and increased her pace. If she could outrace him, maybe she could outrace her own wayward thoughts.

He was still beside her, matching speed and stroke so that they crossed the pool in a kind of unstudied and effortless harmony. It was lovely, almost sensuous, the way their arms lifted and pulled at the same moment, the way their legs scissored and their bodies stretched...like making love, she thought dreamily, then shook herself to knock that hot image from her brain.

Amanda kicked in and put all that frustrated passion into speed. Still, their hands slapped the wall in unison. She began to enjoy it for what it was, an unstated competition between two people who were evenly matched. She'd lost track of the laps and didn't care. When her lungs were straining and her muscles weak, she gripped the edge of the pool to surface, laughing.

He knew she'd never looked more beautiful, with her hair and face drenched with water and her eyes filled with delight. More than anything he'd ever wanted, he wanted to pull her against him then, just to hold her while her laughter danced on the morning air. But he'd made a promise to himself sometime during his own sleepless night. He intended to keep it.

He sent her a friendly grin. "That warmed things up."

"You're pretty good. For an Okie."

"You're not bad yourself, for a female."

She laughed again and rested her head on the side of the pool to look at him. His hair was dark with water, curling over his brow and neck in a way that had her fingers itching to play with it. "I like to race."

"Race? Is that what we were doing? I thought we were just taking a nice, leisurely swim."

She tossed water into his eyes, then stood. "I have to get in."

"Are you going to let me talk to you now?"

The laughter faded from her eyes. "Let's just leave it," she suggested, and hitched herself up on the side of the pool.

He laid a hand on her leg. "Mandy—"

"I don't want to argue with you again. Since we've actually managed to get along for five minutes, why can't we just leave it at that?"

"Because I want to apologize."

"If you'd just—" She broke off to stare at him. "You what?"

"I want to apologize." He stood to put his hands lightly on her arms just beneath her shoulders. "I was out of line last night, way out, and I'm sorry."

"Oh." Disconcerted, she looked down and began to rub at the beads of water on her thigh.

"Now you're supposed to say, all right, Sloan, I accept your apology."

She looked up through wet, spiky lashes, then smiled. Things were suddenly too comfortable to cling to anger. "I guess I do. You acted like such a jerk."

He grimaced. "Thanks a lot."

"You did. Spouting off threats and orders. Then there was all that steam coming out of your ears."

"Want to know why?"

She shook her head and started to rise, but he held her in place. "You brought it up," he pointed out. "I couldn't stand the idea of you being with someone else. Look at me." Gently he cupped her chin, turning her face back to his. "You triggered something in me right off. I can't shake it. I don't much want to."

"I don't think—"

"Thinking has nothing to do with it. I know how I feel when I look at you."

She was losing fast. The quick skip of panic couldn't compete with the flood of pleasure. "I have to think," she murmured. "I'm made that way."

"Okay, well here's something new for you to think about. I'm falling in love with you."

Panic was more than a skip now, but a hard slap. It darted into her eyes as she stared at him. "You don't mean that."

"Yes, I do. And you know it or you wouldn't be sitting there looking like a rabbit caught in the high beams."

"I don't—"

"I'm not asking how you feel," he cut in. "I'm giving you my side of it, so you can get used to it."

She didn't think she would, ever, any more than she would get used to him. Certainly it would be impossible to get used to the feelings shooting off inside her. Is this what love was? she wondered. This edgy and bright sensation that could turn warm and soft without warning? "I don't—I'm not sure how..." She let out a huff of breath. "Did you do this just to make me crazy?"

It helped to be able to smile. "Yep. Give me a kiss, Calhoun."

She twisted and slid wetly out of his hold. "I'm not kissing you again, because it erases every intelligent thought from my head."

Now he grinned. "Honey, that's the nicest thing you've ever said to me." When he rose smoothly from the pool, Amanda snatched up her towel. She snapped it once, hard enough to make the air crack.

"Keep back. I mean it. You either give me time to figure all this out or I aim and fire. And I aim below the belt." There was both amusement and challenge in her eyes when she tilted her chin. "You don't have a lot of protection at the moment."

He ran his tongue around his teeth. "You've got me there. How about a drive after you get off work?"

It would be nice, she thought, to go driving with him up into the hills, with the windows open and the air streaming. But, regretfully, duty came first.

"I can't. C.C.'s shower's tonight. We're surprising her when she gets home from work." She frowned a little. "It's on your list."

"Guess it slipped my mind. Tomorrow then."

"I have the final meeting with the photographer, then I have to help Suzanna with the flowers. Not the next night, either," she said before he could ask. "Most of the out-of-town guests will be arriving, plus we've got the rehearsal dinner."

"Then the wedding," he said with a nod. "After the wedding, Calhoun."

"After the wedding, I'll..." She smiled, realizing she was enjoying herself. "I'll let you know." Grabbing her wrap, she headed for the gate.

"Hey. I haven't got a towel."

She tossed a laugh over her shoulder. "I know."

Late that afternoon, Sloan stood out on the lower terrace, making sketches of the exterior of The Towers. He wanted to add another outside stairway without disturbing the integrity of the building. He stopped when Suzanna came out carrying two wicker baskets pregnant with spring flowers.

"I'm sorry." She hesitated, then tried a smile. "I didn't know you were out here. I'm going to set things up for the shower."

"I'll be out of your way in a minute."

"That's all right." She set the basket down and went back inside.

Over the next few minutes, she went back and forth, carrying out chairs and paper decorations. They passed the time in nerve-racking silence until she finally set aside one of Amanda's swans and looked at him.

"Mr. O'Riley, have we met before?"

He kept right on sketching. "No."

"I wondered because you seemed to know me, and have a poor opinion of me."

His gaze lifted coldly to hers. "I don't know you—Mrs. Dumont."

"Then why—" She broke off. She hated confrontations, the way they tightened up her stomach muscles. Turning away, she started back inside. She could feel his eyes on her, icy and resentful. After bracing a hand on the jamb, she forced herself to turn back. "No, I'm not going to do this. You're in my home, Mr. O'Riley, and I refuse to walk on eggshells in my own home ever again. Now I want to know what your problem is."

He tossed his sketch pad onto a small glass-topped table. "The name doesn't ring any bells with you, Mrs. Dumont? O'Riley doesn't strike a chord?"

"No, why should it?"

His mouth tightened. "Maybe if I add a name to it. Megan. Megan O'Riley. Hear any bells now?"

"No." Frustrated, she pushed a hand through her hair. "Will you get to the point?"

"I guess it's easy for someone like you to forget. She wasn't anyone to you but a slight inconvenience."

"Who?"

"Megan. My sister, Megan."

Completely lost, Suzanna shook her head. "I don't know your sister."

The fact that the name meant nothing to her only infuriated him. Sloan stepped toward her, ignoring the quick fear in her eyes. "No, you never met her face-to-face. Why bother? You managed to see that she was pushed aside easily enough. Not that you ended up with any prize. Baxter Dumont was always a bastard, but she loved him."

"Your sister?" Suzanna lifted an unsteady hand to rub at her temple. "Your sister and Bax."

"Starting to get through?" When she started to turn away, he grabbed her arm and whirled her back. "Was it for love or money?" he demanded. "Either way, you could have shown some compassion. Damn it, she was seventeen and pregnant. Couldn't you have stood back far enough to let the spineless sonofabitch see his son?"

She'd gone a translucent shade of white. Under his hand, her arm seemed to turn to water. "Son," she whispered.

"She was just a kid, a terrified kid who'd believed every lie he'd told her. I wanted to kill him, but it would only have made it worse for Meg. But you, you couldn't even find it in your heart to give her the scraps from the table. You went right ahead with your fancy life as if she and the boy didn't exist. And when she called and begged you just to let him see the boy once or twice a year, you called her a whore and threatened to have her son taken away if she ever contacted your precious husband again."

She couldn't get her breath. Not since her last hideous argument with Bax had she found it so difficult to breathe. Weakly she batted at the hand that held her arm. "Please. Please, I need to sit down."

But he was staring at her. As the impetus of his own rage ebbed he could see that it wasn't shame in her eyes, it wasn't derision or even anger. It was pure shock. "My God," he said quietly, "you didn't know."

All she could do was shake her head. When his grip loosened, she turned and bolted into the house. Sloan stood for a moment, pressing his fingers against his eyes. All the disgust he had felt for Suzanna turned sharply on himself. He started after her and ran into a furious Amanda in the doorway.

"What did you do to her?" With both hands she shoved him back. "What the hell did you say to her to make her cry like that?"

The fist in his stomach squeezed tighter. "Where did she go?"

"You're not getting near her again. When I think that I'd begun to believe I could—damn you, O'Riley."

"There's nothing you can say to me that's worse than what I'm already thinking about myself. Now where is she?"

"You go to hell." She slammed the terrace door and flipped the lock.

Sloan gave brief thought to kicking it in then, swearing, went around to the stone steps on the side of the house. He found Suzanna standing on the second-floor balcony, looking out at the cliffs. He'd taken his first step toward her when Amanda burst out of the doors.

"You keep away from her." She already had a protective arm around her sister. "Just turn around and start walking. Don't stop until you get back to Oklahoma."

"This isn't any of your concern," Sloan told her, and Suzanna had to grab hold before Amanda sprang at him.

"It's all right." Suzanna squeezed Amanda's hand. "I need to talk to him, Mandy. Alone."

"But—"

"Please. It's important. Go down and finish setting up, will you?"

Reluctant, Amanda stepped back. "If it's what you want." She aimed a killing look at Sloan. "Watch your step."

When they were alone, Sloan struggled for the right words. "Mrs. Dumont. Suzanna—"

"What's his name?" she asked.

"What?"

"The boy. What's his name?"

"I don't—"

"Damn it, what's his name?" She whirled away from the wall. Shock had been replaced by angry tears. "He's half brother to my children. I want to know his name."

"Kevin. Kevin O'Riley."

"How old is he?"

"Seven."

Turning back to the sea, she shut her eyes. Seven years before she had been a new bride, full of hope and dreams and blind love. "And Baxter knew? He knew that she'd had his child?"

"Yes, he knew. Megan wouldn't tell anyone at first who the father was. But after she'd called and spoken to you...but she didn't speak to you, did she?"

"No." Suzanna continued to stare straight ahead. "Baxter's mother perhaps."

"I want to apologize."

"There's no need. If it had been one of my sisters, I would have struck out with more than a few hard words." To warm herself she cupped her elbows with her hands. "Go on."

She was tougher than she looked, Sloan thought, but it didn't ease his conscience. "After she'd called, she fell apart. That's when she finally told me everything. How she'd met Dumont when she'd gone to New York to visit some friends. He was there on some business and he started showing her around. She'd never been to New York before, and it—and he dazzled her. She was just a kid."

"Seventeen," Suzanna murmured.

"And naive with it. Well, she got over that quick enough." The bitterness came though. "He gave her all the usual bull about getting married, about how he'd come out to Oklahoma and meet her family. Once she got home, he never contacted her. She got through to him on the phone once or twice. He made excuses and more promises. Then she found out she was pregnant."

He steadied himself, trying not to remember how angry and frightened he'd been when he'd learned his baby sister was going to have a baby of her own.

"When she told him, he changed tactics fast. He said some pretty awful things to her, and she grew up fast. Too fast."

Suzanna understood that, more than he could know. "It must have been terribly difficult for her, having the child without having the father."

"She handled herself. I have a very supportive family. Well, you'd know about that."

"Yes."

"Luckily, money wasn't a problem, either, so she could get all the care she and the baby needed. She never wanted his money, Suzanna."

"No, I understand that, too."

He nodded slowly, seeing that she did. "And when Kevin was born...well, Meg was great. It was for his sake that she tried to contact Dumont again, and eventually decided to appeal to his wife. All she wanted was for her son to have some contact with his father."

"I understand." Steadier, she turned around to look at him. "Sloan, if I had any influence with Bax I'd use it." She lifted her hands and let them fall. "But I don't, not even when it concerns the children he's chosen to acknowledge."

"I figure Kevin's better off the way things are. Suzanna—" he dragged a hand through his disordered hair "—how the hell did a woman like you end up with Dumont?"

She smiled a little. "Once I was a young, naive girl who believed in happy ever after."

He wanted to take her hand but wasn't certain she'd accept it. "I know you said you didn't want an apology, but I'd feel a hell of a lot better if you'd take it just the same."

It was she who offered her hand. "It's easy to do when it's family. I guess in an odd way, that's what we are." She pressed her free hand to their joined ones. Later, she promised herself, she would find a few minutes alone to let the grief come. And to let it go. "I want to ask you a favor. I'd like for my children to know about Kevin, and unless it would upset your sister, for them to have a chance to meet each other."

"When I take a wrong turn, I take it big. It would mean a lot to her."

"Jenny and Alex are going to be thrilled." She looked at her watch. "Speaking of which, they're probably already home from school and driving Aunt Coco crazy. I'd better go."

He looked down the steps toward the terrace. And thought of Amanda. "Me, too. I've got other fences to mend."

Suzanna lifted a brow. "Good luck."

He had a feeling he was going to need it. By the time he'd reached the terrace, he was sure of it. Amanda was there, fastening streamers while Lilah leisurely tied balloons to the back of chairs. A long table was already covered with a frilly white cloth.

Amanda heard the scrape of boot heels on stone and turned to aim one deadly glare. Lilah didn't need another hint.

"Well." She flicked a balloon with a fingertip to send it dancing. "I think I'll go see if Aunt Coco's got any of those chocolate pastries ready." As she walked by Sloan, she paused. Unlike Amanda's, her eyes were cool, but the meaning was clear. "I'd hate to think I was wrong about you." She walked through the terrace doors and, after a brief hesitation, shut them to give her sister privacy.

Amanda didn't wait to pounce. "You've got a nerve, or maybe you're just plain stupid, showing your face here after what you did."

"You don't know anything about it. Suzanna and I worked it out."

"Oh, you think so?" Ready to joust, she slammed down a package of pretty pink-and-silver plates. "Not by a long shot. When I think that just a few hours ago you'd nearly convinced me you were the kind of man I could care about, then I come home and find my sister running away from you looking devastated. I want to know what you did."

"I ran with the wrong information. And I'm sorry about it."

"That's not good enough."

His own emotions were a bit too raw for reason. "Well, it's going to have to be. If you want to know more, you're just going to have to ask Suzanna."

"I'm asking you."

"And I'm telling you that what happened was between her and me. It doesn't have anything to do with you."

"That's where you're wrong." She crossed the terrace until they were toe to toe. "You mess with one Calhoun, you mess with them all. I may have to put up with you until after the wedding, since you're supposed to be best man. But when it's over, I'm going to do whatever I have to do to see to it that you go back where you came from."

Pushed to the end of his chain, he took her by the lapels. "I told you before, I finish what I start."

"You are finished, O'Riley. The Towers doesn't need you, and neither do I."

He was just about to prove her wrong when Trent opened the terrace doors. Trent took one look at his friend and future sister-in-law glaring daggers at each other and cleared his throat.

"Looks like I'm going to have to work on my timing."

"Your timing's perfect." Amanda rammed an elbow into Sloan's stomach before she pulled away. "We've got no time for men around here tonight. Why don't you take this jerk you've sicced on us and go do something manly." She shoved by Trent and stalked into the house.

"Well." Trent let out a long breath. "I don't think I mentioned the Calhoun temperament when I asked you to take on the job."

"No, you didn't." Scowling at the empty doorway, Sloan rubbed his stomach. "Is there a dark, noisy bar anywhere in this town?"

"I guess we could find one."

"Good. Let's go get drunk."

He found the bar, and he found the bottle. Sloan slumped in the corner booth and hissed through his teeth as the whiskey stung his throat. Over the first drink, and the second, he told Trent about his altercation with Suzanna.

"Baxter Dumont is Kevin's father? You never told me."

"I gave Meg my word I wouldn't tell anybody. Even our folks don't know."

Trent was silent a moment, sipping thoughtfully at his club soda. "It's hard to figure out how such a selfish bastard managed to father three terrific kids."

"It's a puzzle, all right." Sloan signaled for another round. "Then I go off and unload both barrels on Suzanna." He broke off and swore. "Damn it, Trent, I'm never going to forget the way she looked when I cut loose on her."

"She'll handle it. From what C.C.'s told me, she's dealt with worse."

"Yeah, maybe. Maybe. But I don't care much for slapping down women. I was already feeling like something you scrape off your shoe when Amanda lit into me."

"These women stick together."

"Yeah." Scowling, Sloan drank again. "Like a dirt clod."

"Why didn't you explain things to her?"

Sloan shrugged and knocked back more whiskey. He had his own share of pride. "It wasn't any of her business."

"You just explained it to me."

"That's different."

"Okay. Do you want some pretzels to go with that?"

"No."

They sat for a moment, nursing drinks, two dynamically different men, one in battered jeans, the other in tailored slacks; one slumped comfortably, the other comfortably alert. They'd both come from money—Trent from real estate, Sloan from oil, but their backgrounds and family lives had been opposites. Trent's first experience with real family ties had come through the Calhouns, and Sloan had known them always. They had almost nothing in common, and yet in their first semester in college they had become friends and had remained so for more than ten years.

Because he was feeling sorry for himself, Sloan enjoyed the sensation of getting steadily drunk. Because he recognized the symptoms, Trent stayed meticulously sober.

Over yet another drink, Sloan eyed his friend. "When'd you start wearing basketball shoes?"

Trent glanced down at his own feet and grinned to himself. They were a symbol of sorts of the way one hot-tempered brunette had changed his life. "They're not basketball shoes, they're running shoes."

"What's the difference?" Sloan narrowed his eyes. "And you're not wearing a tie. How come you're not wearing a tie?"

"Because I'm in love."

"Yeah." With a short oath, Sloan sat back. "See what it's doing to you? It makes you nuts."

"You hate ties."

"Exactly. Damn woman's been driving me crazy since the first time I saw her."

"C.C.?"

"No, damn it. We were talking about Amanda."

"Right." Settling back in the seat, Trent smiled. "Well, some woman's always driving you crazy. I've never seen anyone with a more...admirable affection for the gentler sex."

"Gentler my ass. First she runs into me, then she knocks me on my butt. I can hardly say two words without having her claw at me." After calling for another drink, he leaned across the table. "You've known me for over ten years. Wouldn't y'say that I was a kind of even-tempered, affable sort of man?"

"Absolutely." Trent grinned. "Except when you're not."

Sloan slapped a hand on the table. "There you go." Nodding agreement, he pulled out a cigar. "So what the hell's wrong with her?"

"You tell me."

"I'll tell you." He jabbed the cigar toward Trent's face. "She's got the devil's own temper and a mule's stubbornness to go with it. If a man can keep his eyes off her legs, it's plain enough to see." He picked up his fresh whiskey and scowled into it. "She sure enough has first-class legs."

"I've noticed. They run in the family." As Sloan downed the liquor, Trent winced. "Am I going to have to carry you home?"

"More'n likely." He settled back to let the whiskey spin in his head. "What you want to go and get yourself married for, Trent? We'd both be better off hightailing it outta here."

"Because I love her."

"Yeah." On a sigh, Sloan let out a lazy stream of smoke. "That's how they get you. They get you all tangled up so you can't think straight. Used to be I thought women were God's own pleasure, but I know better now. They've only got one reason for being here, and that's to make a man's life misery." He squinted over at Trent. "Have you seen the way her skirt jiggles when she walks—especially when she's in a hurry, like she always is."

On a chuckle, Trent lifted his glass again. "I take the Fifth on that one."

"And the sassy way her hair moves when she's yelling at you. Her eyes get all snappy. Then you grab ahold of her to shut her up, and God Almighty." He took another quick slug of whiskey, but it did nothing to put out the fire. "You ever missed your step and gone down on an electric fence?"

"Can't say I have."

"It burns," Sloan murmured. "Burns like fire and knocks you senseless for a minute. When you get your senses back, you're kind of numb and shaky."

Carefully Trent set down his drink and leaned closer to study his friend. "Sloan, is this leading where I think it's leading, or are you just drunk?"

"Not drunk enough." Annoyed, he shoved the glass aside. "I haven't had a decent night's sleep since I set eyes on her. And since I set eyes on her it's like there was never anyone else. Like there's never going to be anyone else." With his elbows propped on the table, he rubbed his hands over his face. "I'm crazy in love with her, Trent, and if I could get my hands on her right now, I'd strangle her."

"Calhoun women have a talent for that." He grinned at Sloan. "Welcome to the club."

It rained all day so I could not go down to the cliffs to see Christian. For most of the morning I played games with the children to keep them from becoming fussy about being kept indoors. They squabbled, of course, but Nanny distracted them with cookies. Even the boys enjoyed the tea party we had with Colleen's little china dishes. For me, it was one of those sweet, insular days that a mother always remembers—the way her children laugh, the funny questions they ask, the way they lay their heads on your lap when nap time approaches.

The memory of this single day is as precious to me as any I have had, or will have. They will not be my babies very long. Already Colleen is talking about balls and dresses.

It makes me wonder what my life would be like if it could be Christian who would stroll into the parlor. He would not nod absently as he opened the brandy decanter. He would not forget to ask about his children.

No, my Christian would come to me first, his hands outstretched to meet mine as I rose to kiss him. He would laugh, as I hear him laugh during our stolen hours at the cliff.

And I would be happy. Without this bittersweet pain in my heart. Without this guilt. There would be no need then for me to seek the quiet and solitude of my tower, or to sit alone watching the gray rain as I write my dreams in this book.

I would be living my dreams.

But it is all just a fancy, like one of the stories I tell the children at bed-time. A happy-ever-after story with handsome princes and beautiful maidens. My life is not a fairy tale. But perhaps, someday someone will open these pages and read my story. I hope they will have a kind and gen-erous heart, condemn me not for my disloyalty to a husband I have never loved, but rejoice for me in my joy in those few short hours with a man I will love even after death.

Chapter Seven

Sloan's head was filled with tiny little men wielding pick axes. To quiet them, he tried rolling over. A definite mistake, he realized, as the slight movement sent a signal to the army-navy band waiting in the wings to punch up the percussions. Gingerly he pulled a pillow over his face, hoping to smother the sound or—if that didn't work—himself.

But the noise kept booming until his abused system told him it was the door, not just the hangover. Giving up, he stumbled out of bed, grateful there was no one around to hear him whimper. With the road gang working away inside his temples, he turned the air between the bedroom and the parlor door a ribald shade of blue.

When he wrenched it open, Amanda took one look, noting the bloodshot eyes, night stubble and curled lip. He was wearing the jeans, unclasped, that he'd fallen asleep in, and nothing else.

"Well," she said primly, "you look like you had a delightful time last night."

And she looked as neat and crisp as a freshly starched shirt. It was, he was sure, reason enough for homicide. "If you came up here to ruin my day, you're too late." He started to swing the door shut, but she held it open and stepped inside.

"I have something to say to you."

"You've said it." Instantly he regretted turning sharply away. As his head throbbed nastily, he vowed to hold on to what was left of his dignity. He would not crawl away, but walk.

Because he looked so pitiful, she decided to help him out. "I guess you feel pretty lousy."

"Lousy?" He narrowed his eyes to keep them from dropping out of his head. "No, I feel dandy. Just dandy. I live for hangovers."

"What you need is a cold shower, a couple of aspirin and a decent breakfast."

After making an inarticulate sound in his throat, he groped his way toward the bedroom. "Calhoun, you're on dangerous ground."

"I won't be in your way long." Determined to accomplish her mission, she followed him. "I just want to talk to you about—" She broke off when he slammed the bathroom door in her face. "Well." Blowing out a huffy breath, she set her hands on her hips.

Inside, Sloan stripped off his jeans then stepped into the shower. With one hand braced on the tile, he turned the water on full cold. His single vicious curse bounced along the walls then slammed right back into his head. Still, he was a little steadier when he stepped out again, fought with the cap on the aspirin bottle and downed three.

His hangover hadn't gone away, he thought, but at least he was now fully awake to enjoy it. Wrapping a towel around his waist, he walked back into the parlor.

He'd thought she would have gotten the message, but there she was, hunched over his drawing board with glasses perched on her nose. She'd tidied up, too, he noted, emptying ashtrays, piling cups on the room service tray, picking up discarded clothes. In fact, she had her hands full of his clothes while she studied his drawings.

"What the hell are you doing?"

She glanced up and, determined to be cheerful, smiled. "Oh, you're back." The sight of him in nothing but a damp towel had her careful to keep her eyes strictly on his face. "I was just taking a look at your work."

"I don't mean that, I mean what are you doing picking up after me? It's not part of your job to play Sally Domestic."

"I didn't see how you could work in a sty," she shot back, "so I straightened up a little while I was waiting for you."

"I like working in a sty. If I didn't, I would've picked the damn stuff up myself."

"Fine." Incensed, she hurled his clothes into the air so that they scattered over the room. "Better?"

Slowly he pulled off the T-shirt that had landed on his head. "Calhoun, do you know what's more dangerous than a man with a hangover?"

"No."

"Nothing." He took one measured step toward her when there was another knock at the door.

"That's your breakfast." Amanda's voice was clipped as she strode toward the door. "I had them put a rush on it."

Defeated, Sloan sank onto the couch and put his head in his hands so that he could catch it easily when it fell off. "I don't want any damn breakfast."

"Well, you'll eat it and stop feeling sorry for yourself." She signed the check, then took the tray herself to place it on the table in front of him. "Whole wheat toast, black coffee and a Virgin Mary, heavy on the hot sauce. It'll take the edge off."

"An electric planer couldn't take the edge off." But he reached for the coffee.

Satisfied that she had made a good start, Amanda took off her glasses and slipped them into her pocket. He really did look pathetic, she thought.

His wet hair was dripping down his face. She had a strong urge to kneel down beside him and stroke those damp curls back. But he'd probably have snapped her hand off at the wrist, and she had an equally strong urge to survive.

"Trent mentioned that you did quite a bit of drinking last night."

After trying the spiced-up tomato juice, he eyed her narrowly. "So you came by to see the morning-after in person."

"Not exactly." Her fingers toyed with her name tag, then the top button on her jacket. "I thought since it was my fault you got into this condition, I should—"

"Hold it. If I get drunk, it's because my hand reaches for the bottle."

"Yes, but—"

"I don't want your sympathy, Calhoun, or your guilt any more than I want your maid service."

"Fine." Pride and temper went to war. Pride won. "I merely came by this morning to apologize."

He bit off another piece of toast. It did soothing things to the rocky sea of his belly. "What for?"

"For what I said, and the way I acted yesterday." Unable to stand still, she walked over to the window and pulled the shades open, ignoring Sloan's quick hiss of pain. "Although I still think I was perfectly justified. After all, I only knew that you'd said something to hurt Suzanna badly." But there was regret in her eyes when she turned back. "When she told me about your sister—about Bax—I realized how you must have been feeling. Damn it, Sloan, you could have told me yourself."

"Maybe. Maybe you could have trusted me."

She took her glasses out again, playing with the earpieces to keep her hands busy. "It wasn't really a matter of trust, but of automatic reflex. You don't know what Suzanna went through, how deeply she was hurt. Or if you do, because of your own sister, then you should understand why I couldn't bear to see her look like that again." She shoved the glasses away. When she looked at him, her eyes were damp. "And it was worse, because I have feelings for you."

If there was one thing he had no defense against, it was tears. Wanting to ward them off as much as he wanted to make peace, he rose to take her hands. "I made my share of mistakes yesterday." Smiling, he rubbed her knuckles over his cheek. It felt good—damn good. "I guess it's as hard for you to apologize as it is for me."

"If you mean it's like swallowing a lump of coal, then you're right."

"Why don't we call it even, all around?" But when he lowered his head to kiss her, she stepped back.

"I really need to think straight for a while."

He caught her hand again. "I really need to make love with you."

Her heart took a quick leap into her throat. For someone who moved so slowly, how did he get from one point to the next so fast? "I'm, ah, on duty. I'm already over my break, and Stenerson—"

"Why don't I give him a call?" Still smiling, he began to kiss her fingers. The hangover was down to a dull ache, not nearly as noticeable as another, more pleasant one in the pit of his stomach. "Tell him I need the assistant manager for a couple hours."

"I think—"

"There you go again," he murmured, brushing his lips lightly over hers.

"No, really, I have to..." Her mind clouded as he trailed those lips down her throat. "I really have to get back to my desk. And I—" She took a big, shuddering gasp of air. "I need to be sure." Scrambling for survival, she pulled away. "I have to know what I'm doing."

Sloan pressed a hand to the familiar burn that spread inside his gut. He had a feeling he was just going to have to live with it for a while longer. "Tell you what, Calhoun. You think about it, and think hard, until after the wedding. Like we said before." Before she could relax, he had her chin cupped firmly in his hand. "And after the wedding, if you don't come to me, you'd better run fast."

The line appeared between her brows. "That sounds like an ultimatum."

"No, that's a fact. If I were you, I'd get out that door now, while I still had the chance."

All dignity, she marched to it before turning back with a smile that should have tipped him off. "Enjoy your breakfast," she told him, then slammed the door with a vengeance. She could almost see him holding his battered head.

"I didn't think I'd be nervous." C.C. stared at the wedding dress of snowy silk and lace that hung on the back of her closet door. "Maybe it'd be better if I just wore regular clothes."

"Don't be ridiculous. And stop fidgeting." Amanda bent close to her sister to add a bit more blusher to her cheeks. "You're supposed to be nervous."

"Why?" Annoyed with herself, C.C. pressed a hand to her fluttery stomach. "I love Trent and want to get married. Why should I be nervous now that it's going to happen?" She looked back at the dress and swallowed. "Less than an hour from now."

Amanda grinned. "Maybe I should call Aunt Coco and have her give you a booster-shot course on the birds and the bees."

"Very funny." But the idea did amuse her enough to make her smile. "When's Suzanna coming back?"

"I told you, as soon as she has the kids dressed. Jenny might love the idea of being flower girl, but Alex is a most reluctant ring bearer. He'd rather be carrying a machine gun down the aisle than a satin pillow. And before you ask, again, Lilah is supposed to be downstairs making sure all the last-minute details go off properly. Though why we think we can trust her is beyond me."

"She'll be fine. She always handles things when it's important." C.C. laid a hand on Amanda's. "And it is important, Mandy."

"I know, honey. It's the most important day of your life." Misty-eyed, she laid her cheek against C.C.'s. "Oh, I feel as though I should say something profound, but I can only say be happy."

"I will be, and it's not as if I'll be really going away. We'll be living here most of the time, except when...when we're in Boston." Her throat filled up.

"Don't start," Amanda warned. "I mean it. After all the work I put in making you beautiful, you're not going out in the garden with red eyes and a runny nose." Blowing her own, she stepped back. "Now, let me help you get dressed."

When Suzanna came in a short time later, a child's hand in each of hers, she had to struggle with her own tears. "Oh, C.C., you look wonderful."

"Are you sure?" Fretting, she plucked at the lace at her throat. The dress was a slim column, elegantly simple with only that whisper of lace at the neck, and another whisper at the hem to adorn it. "Maybe I should have gone for something less formal."

"No, it's perfect." Suzanna bent down to her son, her own dress rustling with the movement. "Alex, stand still for five minutes, please."

He tried out the sneer he'd been practicing in the mirror. "I hate cummerbunds."

"I know, but if you don't want me to strap it around your mouth, you'll stand still." Tweeking his nose, she straightened. "I have something for you." She offered C.C. a small box. Inside was a single teardrop sapphire on a braided gold chain.

"Mama's necklace," C.C. whispered.

"Aunt Coco gave it to me when I—on my wedding day." She took it out to fasten around her sister's neck. "I want you to have it and wear it on yours."

C.C. lifted a hand to it, closing her fingers around the stone. "I'm not nervous anymore."

"Then that's my cue to panic." Afraid to say more, Amanda gave her a quick kiss. "I'll run downstairs and make sure everything's on schedule."

"Mandy—"

Amanda smiled over her shoulder. "Yes, I'll send Lilah up." She went out, hurrying downstairs while she ticked off duties in her mind. Taking a moment, she stopped by the hall mirror to adjust the spray of baby's breath over her ear.

"You look great." She glanced over and saw Sloan. "Just great."

"Thanks." They stood awkwardly a moment, a man in a tuxedo and a woman in a tea-length gown the color of ripe peaches. "I, uh, where's Trent?"

"He needed a couple of minutes to himself. His father came by with some advice." Relaxing slowly, Sloan grinned. "When a man's been married as many times as Mr. S.J., he comes up with some interesting viewpoints." He had to laugh at the expression on Amanda's face. "Don't worry, I nudged him along outside with a glass of champagne and Coco. Seems like they're old friends."

"I think she met him a long time ago." When Sloan took a step toward her, she began to talk rapidly. "You look terrific. I didn't expect you to look good in a tuxedo.'' Before he'd finished laughing, she was rambling on. "What I mean is I didn't expect it to suit you. I mean—''

"You're cute when you're flustered.''

She ended up smiling at him. As far as she could recall, he was the only person who had ever accused her of being cute. "I really have to go.'' Before she gave in to the urge to fuss with his tie or something equally mushy. "We'll be starting in a few minutes. Guests need to be seen to.''

"Most everybody's already in the garden.''

"The photographer.''

"All set up.''

"The champagne.''

"On ice.'' He took the last step toward her and tilted up her chin with a fingertip. "Weddings make you nervous, Calhoun?''

"This one does.''

"Going to save a dance for me?''

"Of course.''

He toyed with the flowers in her hair. "And later?''

"I...''

"C.C.'s ready!'' Alex bellowed from the top of the stairs. "Can we get this dumb thing over with.''

With a laugh, Sloan kissed her fingers. "Don't worry, I'll make sure the groom's in place.''

"All right, and—damn!'' She swore, then snatched up the ringing phone. "Hello? Oh, William, I really can't talk. We're about to start the wedding.... Tomorrow?'' She lifted a distracted hand to her hair. "No, of course. Umm...yes, that's fine. Late afternoon would be best. Three o'clock? I'll see you then.'' Still off balance, she turned to find Sloan watching her with very cool, measuring green eyes.

"You take big chances, Calhoun.''

"That wasn't what it sounded like.'' She caught herself trying to explain and frowned. "What do you mean, 'chances'?''

"That's something we'd better discuss later. We've got a wedding to get to.''

"You're absolutely right.'' They strode off in opposite directions.

Moments later, the Calhoun women took their turns walking down the garden path. First Suzanna, then Lilah, then Amanda, followed by a beaming Jenny and a thoroughly embarrassed Alex. They took their places with Amanda doing her best not to glance in Sloan's direction. Then she forgot everything as she watched C.C. come forward, a wispy veil over her hair. Beside her, prepared to give her youngest niece away, Coco held her arm and wept.

She watched her sister marry under an arbor of delicately fragrant wisteria. Through a mist of tears she looked on as the man who was now her brother-in-law slipped the circle of emeralds onto C.C.'s finger. The look that passed between them spoke more eloquently of promises than any of the vows exchanged. With her hands clasped with her sisters', she saw C.C.'s face lift to Trent's as they shared their first kiss as husband and wife.

"Is it finally over?" Alex wanted to know.

"No," Amanda heard herself say as her gaze drifted to Sloan's. "It's just beginning."

"Beautiful wedding." After Amanda was thoroughly kissed by Trent's father, she managed to nod in agreement. "Trent tells me you put most of it together."

"I'm good with details," she said, and offered him a plate for the buffet.

"So I hear." Trim, tanned and expansive, St. James smiled at her. "I've also heard that all of the Calhoun sisters are lovely. I can now corroborate that myself."

He was quite the elegant old flirt, Amanda mused but smiled back as he arranged food on his plate. "We're delighted to welcome you to the family."

"It's odd the way things have worked out," he said. "A year ago I looked up from my boat in the bay and saw this house. I simply had to have it. Now, not only is part of it a portion of my business, but it's a part of my family." He glanced over to see Trent and C.C. dancing on the terrace. "She's made him happy," he said quietly. "I never quite had the knack for that myself." With a vague movement of his shoulders, he brushed the thought aside. "Would you care to dance?"

"I'd love to."

They'd hardly taken three steps on the dance floor, when Sloan swung Coco around and smoothly switched partners.

"You might have asked," Amanda muttered as his arms slid around her.

"I did, before. Anyway, she'll flirt with him the way he wants instead of treating him like a distant relation."

"He is a distant relation." But she glanced over and saw that Coco already had St. James laughing. "Everything's going well, I think."

"Smooth as glass." Just as smoothly, he noted, as she fit into his arms. "You did a good job."

"Thanks, but I hope it's the last wedding I have to plan for quite a while."

"Don't you think about getting married yourself?"

She missed a step and nearly stumbled over his feet. "No—that is, yes, but not really."

"That's a definitive answer."

"What I mean is it's not in my short-range plans." No matter what longings had tugged at her when her gaze had locked with Sloan's under the arbor. "I'm going to be busy over the next few years with the retreat. I've always wanted to manage a first-class hotel, to make policy instead of just carrying it out. It's what I've been working for, and now that Trent's giving me the chance, I can't afford to divide my loyalties."

"An interesting way of seeing it. With me it's always been a matter of getting tied down with one person in one place, then finding out I made a mistake."

"There's that, too." Relieved that they weren't arguing, she smiled. "I never asked, but I guess you do a lot of traveling."

"Here and there. A drawing board's portable. You might like to do some traveling yourself, check out the hotel competition. Why don't we go somewhere quiet and talk about it?"

"Sorry, I'm on call. And if you want to be helpful, you'll play best man and go get a few more bottles of champagne from the kitchen." She tucked her arm through his. "I've got to run up and get the streamers anyway."

"Streamers?"

"To decorate the car. They're up in my room."

"Tell you what," Sloan began when they reached the kitchen. "Why don't I come up to your room and help you get the streamers?"

"Because I want to decorate the car before they get back from their honeymoon." With a laugh, she dashed away. Amanda was halfway down the hall on the second floor when the creak of a board overhead had her stopping. Tuned to the moans and groans of the old house, she frowned. Footsteps, she realized. Definitely footsteps. Wondering if one of the wedding guests had decided to take an impromptu tour, she started back toward the stairway. On the third-floor landing, she spotted Fred, curled up and sleeping.

"Fine watchdog," she muttered, bending down to shake him. He only rolled over with a groggy snore. "Fred?" Alarmed, she shook him again, but instead of bouncing up, ready to play, he lay still. When she picked him up, his head lolled onto her hand. Even as she gathered him up, someone shoved her from behind and sent her headfirst into the wall.

Stunned and sprawled on the dog, she struggled up to her knees. Someone was running down the stairs. With the wrath of the Calhouns filling her, she jumped up, Fred tucked under her arm like a furry football, and gave chase. She turned sharply on the second-floor landing, ears straining. On an oath she headed down to the main floor, heels clattering on wood. Sloan caught her as she stumbled on the last step.

"Whoa. What's the hurry?" Grinning, he scanned her tumbled hair and the spray of baby's breath now hanging to her shoulder. "What did you do, Calhoun, trip over the dog?"

"Did you see him?" she demanded, and broke out of Sloan's hold to rush to the door.

"See who?"

"There was somebody upstairs." Her heart was pumping fast and hard. She hadn't noticed it before. Or the fact that her legs were shaky. "Someone was sneaking around on the third floor. I don't know what they did to Fred."

"Hold on." Gently now, he guided her back to the stairs and eased her down. "Let's have a look." He took the dog, then pulling up an eyelid, swore. When he looked back at Amanda, there was a flat grimness in his eyes she'd never seen before. "Somebody drugged him."

"Drugged him?" Amanda gathered Fred back to her breast. "Who would drug a poor little dog?"

"Someone who didn't want him to bark, I imagine. Tell me what happened."

"I heard someone on the third floor and went up to see. I found Fred, just lying there." She nuzzled the puppy. "When I started to pick him up, someone pushed me into the wall."

"Are you hurt?" His hands were instantly on her face.

"No." She let out a disgusted breath. "If it hadn't stunned me for a minute, I would have caught him."

Eyes narrowed, Sloan sat back on his heels. "Didn't it occur to you to call for help?"

"No." The baby's breath was tickling her shoulder, so she pulled it away.

"Idiot."

"Look, O'Riley, nobody's going to poke around in my house, and hurt my dog and get away with it. If he hadn't had a start on me, I'd have caught him."

"And then what?" he demanded. "God Almighty, Amanda, don't you realize he would have given you more than a push."

Actually she hadn't thought of it. But that didn't change the bottom line. "I can take care of myself. It's bad enough when people come to the door, or sneak around the grounds, but when they start breaking into the house, they're going to answer for it." She gave a nod of satisfaction as she rose. "I scared him good, anyway. The way he was running, he's halfway to the village by now. I don't think he'll be coming back. What about Fred?"

"I'll take care of him." He took the sleeping puppy from her. "He just needs to sleep it off. And you need to call the police."

"After the wedding." She shook her head before he could object. "I'm not spoiling this for C.C. and Trent just because some jerk decided to do some treasure hunting. What I will do is check the third floor and see if anything's missing. Then I'm going to go back out and make sure everything runs smoothly until it's time to throw rice at the bride and groom. After that, I'll call the police."

"Got it all figured out, nice and tidy, as usual." The hot edge of his temper seeped into his voice. "Things don't always work that way."

"I'll make it work."

"Sure you will. Can't have something like attempted robbery and a little assault mess up all your short-term plans. Just like you can't have someone like me messing up your long-term ones."

"I don't see what you're so upset about."

"You wouldn't," he said tightly. "You hear somebody in the house where they shouldn't be, get hit in the head, but you don't even think about calling for me. You don't think about asking somebody for help, not even when that somebody's in love with you."

The tightness in her chest returned, making her voice clipped. "I was just doing what I had to do."

"Yeah," he agreed with a slow nod. "You go ahead and do what you have to do now. I'll get out of your way."

Chapter Eight

And he'd stay out of her way, Sloan promised himself. The woman had fuddled his brain long enough.

He stood out on the terrace off his bedroom, trying to enjoy the balmy May evening. He'd left The Towers as soon as it had been possible. Oh, he'd done his duty, he thought. Amanda wasn't the only one who could do what was expected of her. With the help of Suzanna and the children, he'd decorated the newlyweds' car. A smile plastered on his face, he'd tossed the rice. He'd even given Coco his handkerchief when her own proved inadequate for her happy tears. He'd waited with a worried Lilah until Fred had given his first groggy bark.

Then he'd gotten the hell out of there.

She didn't need him. The fact that he hadn't realized until now just how much he needed her to need him didn't make it any easier. Here he was, waiting to sweep her off her feet, and she was chasing after thieves or making dates with guys named William. Well, he was through making a fool of himself over her.

She had a job to do, and so did he. She had a life to live, and so did he. It was time he put things back in perspective. A man had to be crazy to think about saddling himself with an ornery, my-way-or-nothing female. A sane man wanted a nice, calm woman who'd give him some peace after a long day, not one who riled him up every time he took a breath.

So, he'd put Amanda Calhoun out of his mind and be a happier man for it.

"Sloan."

With one hand still braced on the railing, he turned. She was in the doorway, her fingers linked tight together. She'd changed the silk dress for a crisp cotton blouse and slacks. Very streamlined, very simple and certainly not sexy enough to make his heart start jumping as it was now.

"I knocked," she began, then with an uneasy movement of her shoulders, stepped onto the terrace. "I was afraid you wouldn't let me in, so I got a pass key."

"Isn't that against the rules?"

"Yes. I'm sorry, but I couldn't talk to you at home. I didn't even think I wanted to. Then after the police came and went, and everything was as close to normal as it gets, I couldn't settle down." She let out a long breath. Obviously he wasn't going to say anything to make it easier. He was just going to stand there, his white dress shirt unbuttoned and pulled out of the tuxedo pants, his feet bare and his eyes watchful. "I guess I'm not comfortable with unfinished business."

"All right." After lighting a cigar, he leaned back on the railing. "Finish it."

"It isn't as simple as that." A wayward breeze fluttered her hair. She shook it back impatiently. "I was upset and angry before—about there being someone in the house. My house. I know you were concerned and I was very abrupt with you. And after I'd calmed down some I realized you were hurt that I hadn't asked you to help."

He blew out smoke. "I'll get over it."

"It's just that—" She broke off to pace the narrow width of the balcony. No, he wasn't going to make it easier. "I'm used to handling things myself. I've always been the one who's been able to find the logical solution, or the straightest route. It's part of my makeup. When something needs to be done, I do it. I have to, I guess. It's not as though I don't ever want help. It's just...it's just that I'm more used to being asked for it, than asking for it myself."

"One of the things I admire about you, Amanda, is the way you get things done." His eyes stayed on hers as he took a long, contemplative drag. "Why don't you tell me what you're going to do about me?"

"I don't know what to do." When her voice rose, she struggled to calm it and started moving again. "I don't like that. I always know what to do if I reason it out long enough. But no matter how much I think it all through, I can't find an answer."

"Maybe that's because two and two don't always make four."

"But they should," she insisted. "They always have for me. All I know is that you make me feel...different than I've ever felt before. It scares me." When she whirled back, her eyes were wide and dark with anger. "I know it's easy for you, but not for me."

"Easy for me?" he repeated. "You think this is easy for me?" In two furious motions, he tossed the cigar onto the terrace and ground it out. "I've been on slow burn since the minute I laid eyes on you. That isn't easy on a man, Amanda, believe me."

Because she found it hard to breathe, her voice came out in a whisper. "No one's ever wanted me the way you do. That frightens me." She pressed her lips together. "I've never wanted anyone the way I want you. That terrifies me."

He reached out to snag her hand by the wrist. "Don't expect to say that to me, or look at me the way you look right now, then ask me to let you go."

While panic and excitement warred inside her, she shook her head. "That's not what I'm asking."

"Then spell it out."

"Damn it, Sloan, I don't want you to be reasonable. I don't want to think. I want you to make me stop thinking, right now." On a moan, she threw her arms around him, pressed her lips to his and took exactly what she wanted.

There was fear. She was afraid she was taking a giant step off the edge of a very steep cliff.

There was exhilaration. She was taking that step with her eyes wide open.

And he was with her, all the way. His body was free-falling with hers, caught in the crosswinds, soaring on the current.

"Sloan—"

"Don't say a word." His arms locked tight around her as he pressed his mouth to her throat. The pulse hammering there matched exactly the rhythm of his own. That was what he wanted. That unity. He realized he'd never found it with another woman. "Not a word. Just come inside."

He led her from the balcony to the bedroom, leaving the door open to let in the sunset and the scent of water and flowers. He touched her hair first, watching his own fingers tangle and stroke. Then softly, a whispering touch, his lips on hers. No, he didn't want words from her, because he wasn't certain he could ever find the right ones to tell her what was in his heart. But he could show her.

Unsteady, she braced her hands on his chest. She didn't want to be weak now, but strong. Yet as those lips roamed over her face, she trembled.

Very slowly, barely touching her, he unbuttoned her blouse and slid it from her shoulders. Beneath was a white cotton chemise that made him smile. He should have known that beneath her practical clothes his Amanda would have more practicality. Watching her, he unhooked her slacks so that they slipped to the floor. When she reached out, he took her hands.

"No, just let me touch you. Let me see what it does to you."

Helpless, she closed her eyes as his fingers skimmed, lightly tracing the curve of her breasts. As if she were fashioned of the most delicate glass, he swept those fingertips over her. Elegantly erotic, the fragile caress had the blood rushing under skin, heating it, sensitizing it until she thought she might die from sheer pleasure.

Her head fell back, a shuddering moan escaped as he continued those lazy explorations with patient, gentle hands. He saw the dark delight flicker over her face, felt it shivering through her body. As excitement rioted through him, he circled his thumbs in a whispering touch over the nipples that strained against the cotton. Then his tongue replaced his hands and she gripped frantically at his shoulders for balance.

"Please...I can't..."

Now she was falling fast and hard, but he was there to catch her. When her knees gave way, he lifted her, cradling her in his arms, covering her mouth with his before laying her on the bed.

"Nobody," she murmured against his lips. "Nobody's ever made love to me like this."

"I'm just getting started."

He was true to his word. With a leisurely pace he took her places she had never been, had her lingering there before gently urging her on. With each touch he opened doors always firmly locked, then left them wide so that light and wind tunneled through. Each time she arched against him, shuddering, he soothed her until she floated down again.

Her taste was enough. Honey here, whiskey there, then as delicate as spun sugar. He filled himself with it, nibbling her skin. Down her arms, her throat, those long, lovely legs. Whenever he was tempted to hurry, to take his own release, he found himself greedy for one more taste.

He skimmed his hands up her ribs, pushing her shirt up, then over her head. At last, at long last, he sampled the smooth skin of her breast. Her hands were in his hair, pressing him closer as colors seemed to shatter behind her eyes.

Slow burn. Is that what he'd said? she wondered frantically as his clever mouth inched lower, still lower. She understood now, now when her body was on fire from the inside, heating degree by degree. The sparks were shooting through her, little pinpoints of unspeakable pleasure as ancient as the first stars that winked to life in the sky beyond the window.

He was tugging the last barrier aside, and she could do nothing but writhe under his hands, the breath sobbing in her lungs.

When he flicked his tongue over her, she arched against him, her hands grabbing at the bedspread in taut fists. Sensations hammered her, too fast, too sharp. She struggled to separate them, but they were one wild maze without beginning or end.

Did she know she was calling out his name over and over? he wondered. Did she know that her body was moving in that slow, sinuous rhythm, as if he were already inside her? He slid up her gradually, savoring each instant, absorbing each ache, each need, each longing. Her eyes fluttered open, dark and dazed.

She could only see his face, so close to hers—his eyes so intense. Gracefully her arms lifted to brush his shirt aside, to touch as thoroughly as she had been touched. She rose to him, to press her lips to his chest, to glide them up to his throat.

The light grew dimmer, softer. The breeze quieted. In an easy dance she moved over him, undressing him, needing to show him what he had done to her heart as well as her body. Her lips curved against his flesh as she felt him tremble as she had trembled. The glory flowed through her like water, clear and bright, so that when her arms came around him, when her mouth opened willingly beneath his, she let it pour into the kiss.

With a murmuring sigh, he slid into her. Her breath caught, then released gently. They moved together, the pace deliberately slow, deliciously easy. The sweetness brought tears to her eyes that he kissed away.

Gradually sweetness became heat, and heat a fresh burning. As passion misted her vision, she felt his fingers link with hers, holding tight as she rode to the top of the crest. His name tumbled from her lips as he swept to the peak with her.

* * *

He lay with his lips pressed against her throat, still haunted by the taste of her. Beneath him she was quiet, her breathing deep and steady. He wondered if she slept, and started to ease his weight aside. But her arms slid up and around him again.

"Don't." Her voice was a husky whisper that sent his blood singing again. "I don't want it to end yet."

To satisfy them both, he rolled, reversing positions. Her hair brushed his cheek, a small thing that gave him tremendous happiness. "How's that?"

"Nice." She nuzzled her cheek against his. "It was all really, really nice."

"Is that the best you can do?"

"Umm. For right now. I don't think I've ever been this relaxed in my life."

"Good." Taking her hair in his hand, he pulled her head back to study her face. "It's getting too dark to see." Reaching over, he switched on the light.

Amanda brought up a hand to shield her eyes. "Why'd you do that?"

"Because I want to see you when we make love again."

"Again?" Chuckling, she dropped her head onto his shoulder. "You've got to be kidding."

"No, ma'am. I figure I might just get my fill of you by sunup."

Feeling deliciously lazy, she snuggled against him. "I can't stay the night."

"Wanna bet?"

"No, really." She arched like a cat when he stroked her back. "I wish I could, but I've got a whole list of things to do in the morning. Oh..." She shivered under his touch. "You've got such wonderful hands. Wonderful," she murmured as she lost herself in a long, dreamy kiss.

"Stay."

Her body shuddered as she felt him harden inside her. "Maybe for just a little while longer."

Drifting awake, she shifted. On a contented sigh, she reached out. Reluctantly she opened her eyes. Bright sunlight flooded the room, and she was alone in bed. Pushing her tumbled hair back, she sat up.

He'd gotten his way, she thought with a half smile. She had stayed the night, and he hadn't gotten enough of her—or she of him—until sunup.

It had been, she admitted freely, the most magnificent night of her life. And where the hell was Sloan?

On cue, he walked in, pushing a room service cart. "Morning."

"Good morning." She smiled, though she felt awkward with him dressed and her still naked and in bed.

"I ordered us some breakfast." Sensing her dilemma, he plucked up a white terry-cloth robe from a chair. "Compliments of the BayWatch," he said as he handed it to her, then leaned over a bit farther to give her a leisurely kiss. "Why don't we eat on the terrace?"

"That'd be nice. Give me a minute."

When she joined him outside, there were plates set on the pale azure cloth, and a single rose in a clear vase. It touched her deeply that he would take as much care with the morning as he had with the night.

"You think of everything."

"Just of you." He grinned as he sat across from her. "We can look at this like a first date, since I never could convince you to have a meal with me before."

"No." Her gaze lowered as she poured coffee for both of them. "I guess you couldn't." Picking up her napkin, she began to pleat it with her fingers. They were having breakfast, she thought, after a long night of feasting. And they'd never even ridden in the same car, shared a pizza, talked on the phone.

It was idiotic, she told herself. It was scary.

"Sloan, I realize this might sound stupid at this stage, but I . . . I don't make a habit of spending the night with men in hotel rooms. I'm not usually intimate with someone I've known such a short time."

"You don't have to tell me that." He closed a hand over hers until she looked at him. "It's been a fast trip for both of us. Maybe it's because what happened between us is special. I'm in love with you, Amanda. No, don't pull away." He tightened his grip. "Normally I'm a patient man, but I have to work hard on it with you. I'm going to do my best to give you time."

"If I said I was in love with you—" she let out a cleansing breath "—what would happen next?"

In his eyes, something flickered and sent her already unsteady pulse jumping. "Sometimes you can't work out the answers first. You've got to be willing to gamble."

"I've never been much of a gambler." She bit her lip, determined to get over that last skip of fear. "I wouldn't have come here last night if I hadn't been in love with you."

He lifted her hand to press his lips to the palm. Over it, he smiled at her. "I know."

The laugh was as much from relief as amusement. "You knew, but you just had to hear me say it."

"That's right." His eyes were suddenly very sober. "I had to hear you say it. Women aren't the only ones who need words, Amanda."

No, she thought, they weren't. "I love you, but I'm still a little scared of it. I'd like to take it slow, one step at a time."

"Fair enough. We can start by having our first date before the eggs get cold."

At ease, she buttered a piece of toast and split it with him. "You know, as long as I've worked here, I've never sat on one of those terraces and looked out at the bay."

"Never snuck into an empty room and played guest?" He laughed. "No, you wouldn't. You wouldn't even think about it. So, how does it feel, seeing it from the other side of the desk?"

"Well, the bed's comfortable, the hotel robes are roomy and the view's wonderful." There was laughter in her eyes, contented, easy laughter. "However, at The Towers Retreat, we'll offer all that and more. Private spas, romantic fireplaces, complimentary champagne with each reservation—I have to run that by Trent—*cordon bleu* meals prepared by Coco, world-renowned chef, all in a turn-of-the-century setting, complete with ghosts and a legendary hidden treasure." She rested her chin on her hand. "Unless we manage to get our hands on the emeralds before we open."

"Do you really believe they still exist?"

"Yes. Oh, not with any of the mystic business Aunt Coco or Lilah subscribe to. It's simple logic. They did exist. If anyone in the family had sold them, it would have come out. Therefore, they still exist. A quarter of a million in jewels doesn't just disappear."

His brow lifted. "They're that valuable?"

"Oh, probably more so by now—that's not even counting the aesthetic or intrigue value."

It changed the complexion of things for him entirely. "So what we've got is five women and two kids, who've been living alone in a house loaded with antiques, plus a fortune in jewels. And no security system."

She frowned a little. "It's not exactly loaded with antiques since we've had to sell off a lot over the years. And there's never been a problem. It's not as though any of us are helpless."

"I know. Calhoun women can take care of themselves. I'm beginning to think that besides being tough, they're stupid."

"Now, wait a minute—"

"No, you wait." To emphasize the point, he poked his fork at her. "First thing in the morning, we're going to see about an alarm system."

She'd already decided the same thing herself after yesterday's incident. But that didn't mean he could tell her to. "You're not going to start taking over my life."

"So, to be stubborn, you'll ignore the obvious, because I brought it up, and take a chance that someone might break in and hurt one of the kids."

"Don't put words in my mouth," she tossed back. "I've been checking into alarms for the past two weeks."

"Why didn't you just say so?"

"Because you were too busy handing out orders." She might have said more, but the horn on one of the tourist boats distracted her. "What time is it?"

"About one."

"One?" Her eyes went huge. "In the afternoon? That's not possible, we just got up."

"It's real possible when you don't get to sleep until morning."

"I've got a million things to do." She was already pushing back from the table. "All that mess from the wedding has to be cleaned up. Trent's father was coming for brunch two hours ago, and William's coming by at three.''

"Hold it.'' That brought him out of his chair. "You're not still going to see him?''

"Mr. St. James? He'll be gone by now. I can't believe I was so rude.''

"William,'' he corrected, snagging her arm. "The attractive, intelligent man you had dinner with the other night.''

"William? Well, of course I'm going to see him.''

"No.'' He tugged her closer. "You're not.''

The dangerous light in his eyes set off one in her own. "I just told you you weren't going to take over my life.''

"I don't give a damn what you told me. There's no way in hell I'm going to let you waltz out of my bed and on to a date with another man.''

With a little huff, she pulled her arm free. "You don't *let* me do anything. Get that straight. Next, it isn't a date. William Livingston is an antique dealer and I promised him I would show him through The Towers. He gets a busman's holiday, and I get a free assessment. Now move.'' She shoved past and headed for the shower. Muttering all the way, she slipped off the robe. She'd just finished adjusting the water temperature, stepping in and shutting the curtain when it was yanked open again.

"Damn it, Sloan!'' She slicked the wet hair out of her eyes and glared.

"He's an antique dealer?''

"That's what I said.''

"And he wants to look at furniture?''

"Exactly.''

He hooked his thumbs in his belt loops. "I'm going with you.''

"Fine.'' With a careless shrug, she picked up the soap and began to lather her shoulders. "Be a possessive bubblehead.''

"Okay.''

Telling herself she wasn't amused, she glanced over to see him pulling off his shirt. "What are you doing?''

Grinning, he tossed it aside. "I'll give you three guesses. A sharp lady like you should get it in one.''

She bit back a chuckle as he unsnapped his jeans. "I don't have time for water games right now.''

"Oh, I think we can sneak it in just under the wire.''

"Maybe.'' She squeezed the wet soap between her hands and shot it at him, nodding approval when he caught it, chest high. "If you wash my back first.''

Before stepping from his car, Livingston checked his microrecorder and the tiny camera in his pocket. He was very fond of technology and felt that the sophisticated equipment lent an air of elegance to the job. Since the moment he'd read about the Calhoun emeralds, he'd been obsessed by them, more than any other jewels he'd stolen in his long career. He was considered by Interpol, and indeed by himself, to be one of the most clever and elusive thieves on two continents.

The emeralds presented a challenge he couldn't resist. They weren't tucked in a vault or displayed in a museum. They weren't adoring some rich matron's neck. They were lying in wait somewhere in the odd old house, daring someone to find them. He intended to be that someone.

Though he wasn't opposed to employing violence in his work, he used it sparingly. He was sorry he'd had to use it on Amanda the day before, but he was much sorrier that she'd interrupted his search.

His own fault, he chided himself as he walked to the front door of The Towers. He'd been impatient and had decided that the wedding would be the perfect diversion, giving him the time and the privacy he required to case the interior of the house. Today, however, he would wander those rooms as a guest.

He might have been a thief from the South Side of Chicago, but when he put on a two-thousand-dollar suit, a trace of a British accent and polished manners, even the most discriminating invited him into their parlors.

He knocked and waited. The barking of the dog answered first, and Livingston's eyes hardened. He detested dogs, and the little bugger inside had nearly nipped him before he'd managed to give it a dose of phenobarbital.

When Coco answered the door, Livingston's eyes were clear and his charming smile already in place.

"Mr. Livingston, how nice to see you again." Coco started to offer a hand, then found it more judicious to grasp Fred's collar before the dog could leap at the man's calf. "Fred, stop that now. Mind your manners." Holding the snarling dog at bay, Coco offered a weak smile. "He really is a very gentle animal. He never acts like this, but he had an incident yesterday and isn't himself." After gathering Fred into her arms, she called for Lilah. "Let's go into the parlor, shall we?"

"I hope I'm not intruding on your Sunday, Mrs. McPike. I couldn't resist persuading Amanda to show me through your fascinating house."

"We're delighted to have you." Though she was becoming more disconcerted by the moment as Fred continued to snarl and snap. "Amanda's not here yet, though I can't think what's keeping her. She's always so prompt."

Lilah gave a half laugh as she came down the steps. "I can think exactly what's keeping her." There was no humor in her eyes as she studied their guest. "Hello again, Mr. Livingston."

"Miss Calhoun." He didn't care for the way she looked at him, as though she could see straight through the slick outer trappings to the ruthlessness inside.

"Fred's a bit high-strung today." With a quick pleading look, Coco passed the growling pup to Lilah. "Why don't you take him in the kitchen?" Her hands fluttered before she patted her hair. "Perhaps some herbal tea would soothe him."

"I'll take care of him." Lilah started down the hall, murmuring to the puppy, "I don't like him, either, Fred. Why do you suppose that is?"

"Well then." Relieved, Coco smiled again. "How about some sherry? You can enjoy it while I show you a particularly nice japanned cabinet. It's Charles II, I believe."

"I'd be delighted." He was also delighted to note that she was wearing an excellent set of pearls with matching earrings.

When Amanda arrived twenty minutes later, with Sloan stubbornly at her side, she found her aunt telling Livingston the family history while they admired an eighteenth-century credenza.

"William, I'm so sorry I'm late."

"Don't be." Livingston took one look at Sloan and concluded his entryway to The Towers wouldn't be Amanda after all. "Your aunt has been the most charming and informative of hostesses."

"Aunt Coco knows more about the furnishings than any of us," she told him. "This is Sloan O'Riley. Sloan is the architect who's designing the renovations."

"Mr. O'Riley." The handshake was brief. Sloan had already taken a dislike to the three-piece-suited, sherry-sipping antique dealer. "The work here must present quite a challenge."

"Oh, I'm getting by."

"I was just telling William how slow and tedious the job of sifting through all those old papers is. Not at all the exciting treasure the press makes it out to be." Coco beamed. "But I've decided to hold another séance. Tomorrow night, the first night of the new moon."

Amanda struggled not to groan. "Aunt Coco, I'm sure William isn't interested."

"On the contrary." He turned all his charm on Coco while a plan formed in his mind. "I'd love to attend myself, if I didn't have pressing business."

"The next time then. Perhaps you'd like to go upstairs—"

Before she could finish, Alex burst through the terrace doors, followed by a speeding Jenny and a laughing Suzanna. All three had dirt streaked on their hands and jeans. Eyes narrowed, Alex skidded to a halt in front of Livingston.

"Who's that?" he demanded.

"Alex, don't be a brat." Suzanna snagged his hand before he could spread any of his dirt over the buff-colored tailored pants. "I'm sorry," she began. "We've been in the garden. I made the mistake of mentioning ice cream."

"Don't apologize." Livingston forced his lips to curve. If he disliked anything more than dogs, it was small, grubby children. "They're... lovely."

Suzanna squeezed her son's hand before he could resort to violence at the term. "No, they're not," she said cheerfully. "But we're stuck with them. We'll just get out of your way." As she dragged them off to the kitchen, Alex shot a last look over his shoulder.

"He has mean eyes," he told his mother.

"Don't be silly." She tousled his hair. "He was just annoyed because you almost ran into him."

But Alex looked solemnly at Jenny, who nodded. "Like the snake on Rikki-Tikki-Tavi."

"You move, I strike," Alex said in a fair imitation of the evil cartoon voice.

"Okay, guys, you're giving me the creeps." She laughed off the quick shiver. "The last one in the kitchen has to wash the bowls." She gave them a head start while she rubbed the chill from her arms.

Chapter Nine

"There, you see." Amanda gave Sloan a quick kiss on the cheek. "That wasn't so bad."

He wasn't quite ready to be placated. "He hung around for five hours. I don't see why Coco had to invite him for dinner."

"Because he's a charming, and single man." She laughed and slipped her arms around his neck. "Remember the tea leaves."

They stood at the seawall, inside an ornate pergola. Sloan decided it was as good a time as any to nibble on her neck. "What tea leaves?"

"The ones that...mmm. The ones that told Aunt Coco that there would be a man coming along who'd be important to us."

He switched to her ear. "I thought that was me."

"Maybe." She gave a surprised yip when he bit her. "Savage."

"Sometimes the Cherokee in me takes over."

She leaned back to study his face. In the bleeding lights of sunset, his skin was almost copper, his eyes so dark a green they were nearly black. Yes, she could see both sides of his heritage, the Celtic and the Cherokee, both warriors, in those knife-edged cheekbones, the sculpted mouth, the wild reddish hair.

"I really don't know anything about you." Yet it hadn't been like making love to a stranger. When he had touched her, she'd known everything. "Just that you're an architect from Oklahoma who went to Harvard."

"You know I like beer and long-legged women."

"There's that."

Because he could see it was important to her, he sat on the wall, his back to the sea. "Okay, Calhoun, what do you want to know?"

"I don't want to interrogate you." The old nerves resurfaced, making it impossible for her to settle. "It's just that you know everything about me, really. My family, my background, my ambitions."

Because he enjoyed watching her move, he took out a cigar, lighted it, then began to speak. "My great-great-grandfather left Ireland for the New

World, and headed west to trap beaver. A genuine mountain man. He married a Cherokee woman, and hung around long enough to get three sons. One day he went off trapping and never came back. The sons started a trading post, did pretty well. One of them sent for a mail-order bride, a nice Irish girl. They had a passel of kids, including my grandfather. He was, and is, a wily old devil who bought up land while it was cheap enough, then hung on until he could sell it at a profit. Keeping up family tradition, he married Irish, a redheaded spitfire who supposedly drove him crazy. He must have loved her a lot, because he named the first oil well after her."

Amanda, who had been charmed thus far, blinked. "Oil well?"

"He called it Maggie," Sloan said with a grin as he blew out smoke. "She got such a kick out of it, he gave names to the rest of them, too."

"The rest of them," Amanda said faintly.

"My father took over the company in the sixties, but the old man hasn't stopped putting his two cents in. He's still ticked that I didn't go into the company, but I wanted to build, and I figured Sun Industries didn't need me."

"Sun Industries?" She nearly choked. It was one of the biggest conglomerates in the country. "You—I had no idea that you had money."

"My family does, anyway. Problem?"

"No. I just wouldn't want you to think that I . . ." She trailed off helplessly.

"That you were after the family fortune?" He let out a hoot of laughter. "Honey, I know you were after my body."

He had the uncanny ability to make her want to swear and laugh at the same time. "You really are a conceited jerk."

He tossed the cigar aside before making a grab for her. "But you love me."

"Maybe I do." With pretended reluctance, she slipped her arms around him. "A little." On a laugh, she lifted her lips to his. His mouth started off teasing, then heated with demands. His hands were light, then impatient, until she was wrapped tight around him, pouring herself mindlessly into the kiss.

"How do you do that to me?" she murmured as he nipped at her moist, parted lips.

"Do what?"

"Make me want you until it hurts."

On an unsteady moan, he pressed his lips to her throat. "Let's go inside. You can show me my room."

She tilted her head to give his busy mouth more freedom. "What room?"

"The room where we'll pretend I'm going to sleep when I'm sleeping with you."

"What are you talking about?"

"I'm talking about making love with you until we both need oxygen." Because he knew he was on the point of dragging her down on the hard, cold tiles, he set her away from him. "And I'm talking about the fact that I'm staying here until the alarm system's operational."

"But you don't need—"

"Oh, I need." He crushed his mouth to hers again to show her how much.

She waited for him, chiding herself for being as nervous as a new bride on her wedding night. Perhaps the waiting was more intense because she knew what they would bring to each other.

She slipped on a thin blue chemise, an impulsive extravagance that had been folded away for months. Unable to settle, she turned down the bed. There were candles she'd kept at the bedside and on the bureau for emergencies. But when she lighted them now, their glow was soft, romantic, and anything but practical. Suzanna had placed flowers in the room, as she always did. This time they were fragile lilies of the valley that added a haunting fragrance. Though there was no moonlight, she opened the terrace doors to let in the steady roar of the water on rocks.

Then he came to her, as she stood in the open doorway with the black night at her back.

The quick joke he'd meant to make melted from his mind. He could only stare, his hand growing damp on the knob, his heart bounding up to block his throat. To have her waiting for him, looking so desirable in the flicker of candlelight, to see that smile of welcome, was everything he'd ever wanted.

He wanted to be gentle with her, as he'd been so carefully gentle the night before. But when he crossed to her, the slow burn had already turned to fire. There was challenge instead of nerves in her eyes as she lifted her arms to take him in.

"I thought you'd never get here," she said, and, led by her own needs, crushed her mouth to his.

How could there be gentleness when there was such heat? How could there be patience when there was such urgency? Her body was already vibrating—Lord, he could feel each wild beat—as it fit itself to his. The flimsy material of her chemise teased the bare flesh of his chest, daring him to rip it aside and plunder. Her scent had wrapped itself around his system, taunting with dark secrets, seducing with fevered promises.

In that moment he was so full of her, he couldn't find himself.

Breathless, disoriented, he lifted his head. He knew his hands were big and could be rough if his heart didn't guide them. He knew his needs were huge and could be ruthless if he didn't retain control.

"Wait." He needed a moment to get back his breath and his sanity, but she was shaking her head.

"No." Her hands clutched in his hair, and she pulled him back to her.

She didn't know when the recklessness had burst through her, but it held sway now, as she fell with him onto the bed. Aggressive and desperate, her hands streaked over him. No weakness this time. No submission. She wanted the power, the power of knowing she could make him careless, make him as mindless and vulnerable as he made her.

In a tangle of arms and legs they rolled over the bed. Each time he tried to pull back, she was there, her mouth greedy, her low, sultry laughter pounding in his blood.

Her busy fingers rushed to unsnap his jeans, then tugged the denim over his hips. His muscles jumped and quivered when she danced those fingertips across his stomach. He swore, snatching her hands before she could drag him over that last jagged edge.

Breath heaving, he stared down at her, her wrists trapped in his hand. Her eyes were like cobalt, glistening dark in the shifting light. He could hear, over his own ragged breaths, the steady ticking of the bedside clock.

Then she smiled, a slow, lazy smile full of knowledge. And he heard nothing but the roar of his own needs.

Hot with hunger, his mouth fused with hers. Reckless with passion, his hands sought and took. She answered, demand for demand, pleasure for pleasure. Control snapped—he could almost hear the chain break as he sated himself with her. This was liberation, a world without reason. Desperate to feel her, he tore the chemise aside. Her quick gasp of surprise only fueled the fires.

Tossed in the whirlwind, she gave herself over to the speed, surrendered herself to the fury. No thought. No question. Only hot, damp flesh, ravenous, searching lips, quick, greedy hands.

His eyes open, fixed on hers, he drove himself into her, letting the shock of pleasure fill them both. Then she was rising up to meet him so that they drove each other into the dark.

"Yes, Mr. Stenerson." Amanda hummed a tune in her head as her supervisor droned on. And on. Ten more minutes, and she was off duty. Even the upcoming séance didn't dim her pleasure.

She would be with Sloan soon. Maybe there would be time for a walk before dinner.

"You don't seem to have your mind on your work, Miss Calhoun."

That brought her back with a jolt of guilt. "You were concerned about Mr. and Mrs. Wicken's complaint."

Glaring, he tapped his pencil on the desk. "I'm very concerned that one of our waiters spilled an entire tray of drinks in Mrs. Wicken's lap."

"Yes, sir. I arranged to have her slacks cleaned, and for a complimentary dinner for them any evening during their stay. They were satisfied."

"And you've fired the waiter?"

"No, sir."

His eyebrows rose up, wiggling like worms. "May I ask why not, when I specifically requested you do so?"

"Because Tim has been with us for three years, and could hardly be blamed for spilling the tray when the little Wicken boy stuck out his foot and tripped him. Several other waiters, and several of the guests saw it happen."

"Be that as it may, I gave you a specific order."

"Yes, sir." The cheerful little tune in her head became a throbbing headache. She'd meant to go over all of this with Stenerson before. "And after a closer review of the circumstances, I chose to handle it differently."

"Need I remind you who is in charge of this hotel, Miss Calhoun?"

"No, sir, but I would think after all the years I've worked at the BayWatch, you would trust my judgment." She took a deep breath, and a big risk. "If you don't, it might be best if I turned in my resignation."

He blinked three times, then cleared his throat. "Don't you feel that's a bit rash?"

"No, sir. If you don't feel I'm competent to make certain decisions, it undermines the system."

"It isn't your competence, but your lack of experience. However," he added, holding up a hand, "I'm sure you did what you felt was best in this case."

"Yes, sir."

By the time she left his office, her jaw was clenched. Amanda forced it to relax when William stopped her in the lobby.

"I just wanted to tell you again how much I enjoyed the tour of your home, and the wonderful meal."

"It was our pleasure."

"I have the feeling if I asked you to dinner again, you would have a different reason than hotel policy for saying no."

"William, I—"

"No, no." He patted her hand. "I understand. I'm disappointed, but I understand. I suppose Mr. O'Riley will attend the séance tonight?"

She laughed. "Whether he wants to or not."

"I really am sorry I'll miss it." He gave her hand a final squeeze. "It's at eight, did you say?"

"No, nine, sharp. Aunt Coco will have us all gathered around the dining table holding hands and sending out alpha waves or whatever."

"I hope you'll let me know if you receive any messages from…the other side."

"It's a deal. Good night."

"Good night." He glanced at his watch as she left. He had more than enough time to get ready.

"I thought I'd find you here." Amanda stepped into the large circular room the family called Bianca's tower. Lilah was curled on the window seat, as she often was, looking out to the cliffs.

"Yeah, just me and fierce Fred." Coming out of a private dream, she ruffled the dozing dog's fur. "We're getting in tune for tonight's séance."

"Spare me." Amanda plopped onto the seat beside her.

"Well, what's wiped off that satisfied smile you had on your face this morning? Did you fight with Sloan?"

"No."

"Then it must be the dastardly Stenerson." At Amanda's brief oath, Lilah grinned. "Right the second time. Why do you put up with him, Mandy? The man's a weasel."

"Because I work for him."

"So quit."

"Easy for you to say." She shot Lilah an impatient look. "We can't all drift around from day to day like dreamy forest sprites." She cut herself off, letting out a disgusted breath. "Sorry."

Lilah only shrugged. "It sounds like you've got more needling you than Stenerson."

"He started it. He said I didn't have my mind on my work, and he was right."

"So your mind was wandering. Big deal."

"It is a big deal. Damn it, I like my job, and I'm good at it. But I haven't been concentrating, not on that or the necklace, or anything, since..."

"Since the big gun swaggered in from the West."

"It's not funny."

"Sure it is." Lilah wrapped her arms around her knees and rested her chin on them. "So you lose a little concentration, misplace one of your lists or miss an appointment by five minutes. So what?"

"I'll tell you so what. He's changing me and I don't know what to do about it. I have responsibilities, obligations. Damn it, I have goals. I have to think about tomorrow, and five years from tomorrow." The trouble was, when she did, she thought of Sloan. "What if he's just a glitch? A wonderful, exciting glitch that throws off everything I've planned out? A few weeks from now, he finishes up here and heads back to Oklahoma, and my life's a mess."

"What if he asks you to go with him?"

"That's worse." Flustered, Amanda rose to wander in distracted circles. "What am I supposed to do? Throw away everything I've worked for, everything I've hoped for just because he says saddle up?"

"Would you?"

Amanda shut her eyes. "I'm afraid I would."

"Then why don't you talk to him?"

"I can't." She sat again. "We haven't talked about the future. I guess neither of us wants to think about it. It was just that today, I started thinking—"

"You would get back to it."

"I started thinking," Amanda repeated, "that a month ago I didn't even know him. It's crazy to start planning my life around someone I've only known such a short time."

"And you've always been the sensible one," Lilah put in.

"Well, yes."

"Then relax." For encouragement she patted Amanda's shoulder. "When the time comes, you're bound to do the sensible thing."

"I hope you're right," Amanda murmured, then forced herself to add a decisive nod. "Of course, you're right. I'm going to work in the store-room until dinner."

"See you're back on track already." Lilah chuckled to herself when Amanda strode out. "Come on, Fred." She nuzzled his nose. "Let's go see if we can derail her."

Sloan walked into the storeroom, armed with a bottle of champagne, a wicker basket and some of Lilah's sisterly advice. *Keep her off balance, big guy. The one thing you can't let her do is get logical on you.*

Though he wasn't exactly sure what had prompted Lilah's visit, he approved the spirit of it. Just as he approved the way Amanda looked, hunched over a desk in the storeroom, glasses on her nose, hair clipped back. There were neatly labeled file boxes stacked behind her, dozens of dusty cardboard boxes scattered alongside her and several fat piles of paper in front of her.

"Hey, Calhoun, ready for a break?"

"What?" Her head came up quickly, but it took a moment for her eyes to focus. "Oh, hi. I didn't hear you come in."

"Where were you?"

She lifted a ledger. "Back in 1929. It seems my illustrious great-grandpapa made a little pin money running liquor in from Canada during Prohibition."

"Good old Fergus."

"Greedy old Fergus," she corrected. "But a businessman through and through. If he kept such meticulous books of his illegal activities, he certainly would have a record of sale if he sold the emeralds."

"I thought Bianca hid them."

"That's the legend." She leaned back to rub her tired eyes. "I'd rather have the facts. I had this thought that maybe he put them in a safe-deposit box he didn't tell anyone about. But I can't find any record of that, either."

"Maybe you're looking in the wrong place." He set the bottle and basket down as he stood behind her. Gently he began to massage her neck muscles. "Maybe you should concentrate on Bianca. It was her necklace after all."

"We don't have a lot of information about Bianca." When her eyes started to drift closed, she popped them open again. "Great-Grandpapa destroyed all of her pictures, her letters, just about everything concerning her. We've only come across one of her date books so far."

"He must have been crazy mad."

"Crazy, anyway. Grieving, I'd think."

"No." Bending, he kissed the top of her head. "If he'd been grieving, he would have kept everything."

"Maybe it hurt to remember."

"If he'd loved her, he would have wanted to remember. He would have needed to. When you love someone, everything about them's precious." He felt her muscles knot under his fingers. "What's the problem, Amanda? You're all tied up."

"I've been sitting too long, that's all."

"Then my timing's perfect." He stepped back to pick up the champagne."

"What's that for?"

"Most people drink it." Sloan released the cork. After the pop came the seductive hiss. "I don't know about you, but I worked my butt off today. I thought we'd take a first-class coffee break."

She didn't need champagne to cloud her brain. He did that all by himself. And that, she reminded herself as she rose, was exactly what she needed to avoid. "It's a nice thought, but I should go help Aunt Coco with dinner."

"Lilah's helping her."

"Lilah?" Amanda's brows shot up. "You've got to be kidding."

"Nope." He opened the basket to take out two fluted glasses. "Suzanna's doing homework with the kids, and you and I are having dinner alone."

"Sloan, I'm really not dressed to go out."

"I like you in sweats." He poured the wine and, setting the bottle aside, lifted both glasses. "And we're not going anywhere."

"You just said—"

"I said we were having dinner alone, and we are. Right here."

"Here?" She gestured. "In the storeroom?"

"Yep. I got some of your aunt's pâté, some cold chicken and asparagus, and fresh strawberries." He tapped his glass against hers before drinking. "I've been thinking about you all day."

He didn't even have to try to make her knees weak. When he did sweet things, said sweet things, she dissolved into a puddle of love. "Sloan, we have to talk."

"Sure." But he bent down to rub his lips lazily over hers. "Why don't we get comfortable first?"

"What?" Already dizzy, she stared at him as he took out a blanket and spread it over the floor.

"Come on."

"I really think it would be better if we . . ." But he was already pulling her down to the blanket.

He took the glass from her hand, setting it on the floor before nuzzling her mouth. "This is better," he murmured. "Much better."

"The children are home," she managed as his hands slid under her shirt. "If someone came in—"

"I locked the door." Gently he skimmed the rough pad of his thumb over her nipples. "Pay attention, Calhoun, I'm going to show you how to relax."

She was so relaxed, she didn't think she could move. Heavy, her eyes fluttered partway open when Sloan lay a smidgen of pâté on her tongue.

"It's good," he told her, then spread a dab on her bare shoulder so he could lick it off. "Here." He lifted her, cradling her against his chest before he handed her the glass of champagne. "We were supposed to drink this first, but I got distracted."

It tasted like sin on her tongue. She sipped again, then opened her mouth obediently when he fed her more pâté, this time on a conventional cracker.

"More?"

She sighed her assent. They began to feed each other tidbits from the basket between kisses. Replete, she watched him pour the last of the champagne. "We're going to be late for the séance."

"Nope." He drew her back more comfortably against his chest. "Coco decided that the vibes weren't right. Something about interference from a dark presence."

"Sounds just like my levelheaded aunt."

"Now she wants to wait until the last night of the new moon." He nuzzled her neck. "We can stay in here all night."

She was beginning to believe that with him, anything was possible. "That would make it my first all-night picnic."

"After we're married, we'll make it a regular event."

Champagne slopped over her hand and onto his leg as she jolted straight.

"Easy, Calhoun, don't waste it."

She struggled around to face him. "What do you mean, married?"

"You know, like man and wife, that kind of thing."

With deliberate care, she set the glass down. Just like that, she thought, both panicked and angry. Just as she'd expected. With him it was *saddle up, Calhoun. We're getting hitched.* "What gave you the idea that we were getting married?"

He didn't like the fact that the line was back between her brows. "I love you, you love me. You're the logical one, Amanda. The next step's marriage from my point of view."

"It may be a step from your point of view, but it's a big leap from mine. You can't just assume I'm going to take it."

"Why not?"

"Because you can't. In the first place, I'm not planning on marriage for years yet. I've got my career to think about."

"What's one got to do with the other?"

"Everything. You've already messed up my concentration, had me shuffling around my priorities." Knowing it sounded foolish, she stopped to drag a hand through her hair. "Look at me," she demanded. "Just look at me. I'm sitting on the storeroom floor, naked, and arguing with a man I've only known for two weeks. This isn't me."

With deceptive laziness, he skimmed his gaze down, then up again. "Then who the hell is it?"

"I don't know." Frantic, she snatched up her sweats and began to pull them on. "I don't know who I am anymore, and it's your fault. Nothing's made sense since you ran into me on the sidewalk."

"You ran into me."

"That's beside the point." Shaken to the core, she yanked the sweatshirt over her head. "I'm daydreaming when I'm supposed to be working. I'm making love with you when I should be keeping appointments. I'm having naked picnics when I should be filing papers. It's got to stop."

"Maybe I should've just hit you over the head with the bottle of champagne instead of letting you drink it." Baffled, he scratched his head. "Why don't you sit down, Calhoun, and we'll talk this thing out?"

"No, I will not sit down. You'll start on me again, and I won't be able to think. You're not going to make plans for the rest of my life without consulting me, without even having the courtesy to ask. I'm taking back control of my life."

He rose then, naked and furious. "You're mad because I want you to marry me."

The breath hissed out between her clenched teeth. "You're just stupid." She grabbed the closest thing handy and ended up hurling her glasses at him. "Too stupid for words." With this she strode to the door, fought with and cursed the lock until she managed to open it. "You can take your incredibly romantic proposal and stuff it."

The hot and hazy afternoon was perfect for pleasure. Christian surprised me with a little basket of wine and cold ham. Together we sat in the wild grass beyond the rock and watched the boats glide by below. The light was so golden, like something poured out of a gilded pitcher. But it is always so when I'm with him. In this lovely fantasy of afternoons, there is nothing but sunlight and warm, fragrant air.

We talked of everything and nothing as he sketched me. He has already done two paintings of me since the summer began. Without risking modesty I can say he made me look beautiful. What woman is not when she is in love? And it was his eyes that studied me, his hands that drew my face, my hair. His feelings that guided his brush.

If I had not believed before how deep and true his love is for me, I would have seen it in the portraits he painted.

Will someone buy my portrait from him? It saddens me to think of it. Yet it makes me proud. That would be one way I could at last declare my feelings. Hanging on some pretty wall, the portrait of a woman whose eyes are filled with love for the man who painted her.

I say we talked of everything and nothing. We do not mention how quickly the days fly into weeks. There are so little of those weeks left before I must leave the island, and Christian. I think something in me will die this time.

Fergus and I attended a dinner dance tonight. He was very jolly, though there was much talk of war. He said that clever men know that there will always be war, and money to be made from it. I was stunned to hear him speak so, but he only brushed aside my concern.

"It's for you to think of how to spend the money, and for me to make it," he told me.

It upset me because it was not for money I married him, nor is it for money I stay with him. Both were for duty. Yet I have lived under his roof, eaten his food, taken his gifts without a thought.

It scrapes at my conscience to know that I appreciated the little picnic Christian brought to me so much more than I have ever appreciated all the sumptuous dinners Fergus's money has paid for.

Because it always pleases him, I wore the emeralds, and I have not yet put them away. They lie in the shadowed light, glinting at me, reminding me of both my grief and my joy.

If it were not for the children... but I can't think of it. There are the children. Whatever sins I commit, I will never desert them. They have needs that neither Christian nor I have a right to ignore. I know, in the loneliness ahead of me, they will be solace. Being blessed with them, it is not right to grieve for the child Christian and I must never conceive.

Yet, I do.

Tonight when I turn off the lamp I'll try to sleep quickly. For then it will be morning, and morning will become the golden afternoon, when I can see Christian again.

Chapter Ten

The only thing that prevented Amanda from slamming the door was the fact that Suzanna would have already put the children to bed. But she did kick it.

Limping and muttering and occasionally sending a furious look over her shoulder, she started down the hallway. At that point, she wasn't certain if she was more angry with Sloan for taking her assent for granted, or with herself for wanting to give it to him. Marriage hadn't been in her plans, but damn it, she was good at taking the unexpected and making it work. But if he thought she would give him the satisfaction of just hopping on board because he said so, then he didn't know Amanda Kelly Calhoun.

When we get married, she fumed. Not if, not will you or would you. And the problem, the big problem was that under the instant panic and anger had been a thrill. She paused outside of her bedroom door as her own soft sigh caught up with her. Oh, Lord, she did want to marry him. Despite all the good, solid, sensible reasons against it, marrying him was exactly what she wanted. Living with him would mean living with the constant threat of upheaval. She smiled to herself. And what more satisfying life could there be for a woman so skilled at putting things back in place?

With her hand on the doorknob, she hesitated, debating whether she would go back, give in to the urge to throw herself laughing into his arms and say... yes!

No. Resolute, Amanda pushed open the door. She wasn't about to make it that easy for him. If he wanted her, really wanted her, then he was going to have to work a little harder. When he got it right—if he got it right— she corrected as she shut the door behind her, she would smile, slide her arms around him and say—

An arm whipped around her throat and cut off her breath. Instinctively she struggled, throwing both hands up to the barrier to yank and scratch as she fought to drag in the air to scream. Until the hard, cold barrel of a gun pressed against her temple.

"Don't." The voice was only a harsh whisper at her ear. "Be very still, and very quiet, and I won't have to hurt you."

Obediently she let her arms fall limply to her sides, but her mind was speeding. The children were just down the hall. Their safety came first. And Sloan...Sloan could come along at any moment, furiously demanding a showdown.

"That's better." The pressure on her windpipe eased slightly. "If you scream, people are going to get hurt—starting with you. I don't think you want that." She shook her head. "Good. Now—" He swore and tightened his grip again as Sloan bellowed in the corridor.

"Calhoun. I'm not finished with you."

"Be absolutely quiet," the man warned as he dragged her back. "Or I'll kill him."

Amanda shut her eyes and prayed.

Sloan shoved open the door of her room, but it was pitch-dark and silent inside. While he stood in the doorway, swearing, Amanda was pressed back into the corner, knowing the gun was now aimed in Sloan's direction. Her stomach seemed to be packed with ice as she stood, not even daring to breathe, willing him to turn and go. And when he did, when she heard his boots clanging on the stairs, she wondered if she would ever see him again.

"Now that we have a little privacy, we can talk." But the arm stayed around her throat and the gun at her temple. "About the emeralds."

"I don't know where they are."

"Yes. Initially I had trouble believing that, but now I'm sure you don't. So we'll play this a different way. We'll have to move quickly. First the storeroom. I'll take the papers you've yet to sort through. Then, to add a little flare to the trip, we'll fetch Coco's pearls, and a few of the smaller, more portable items."

"You'll never get out of the house."

"You just leave that up to me." There was a faint lilt of pleasure in the voice now, as if he would enjoy the challenge. "Now we're going to move quietly, and very quickly to the storeroom. If you try anything heroic, I'll regret shooting you."

She didn't dare, not with the children so close. But the storeroom, she thought, as she started out with him directly behind her. That was a different matter.

Sloan had left the lights on. The remnants of their picnic were spread over the floor. The air smelled, ever so lightly, of strawberries and champagne.

"Very sweet," Livingston murmured, then shut the door behind them. "It would have been more convenient for me if you had had the séance instead of a tryst." He loosened his hold so that she could step away, but kept his gun level.

Amanda stared at the man she knew as William Livingston. He was all in black with a soft leather pouch worn crosswise over his chest. On his hands were thin surgical gloves. The gun he carried was small, but she didn't doubt it was lethal, not when she looked into his eyes.

"No recriminations, Amanda?" His brow lifted when she said nothing. "I'd hoped you and I could enjoy each other while I was conducting business, but...let's not waste time." From his pouch he pulled out a denim duffel bag. "Just the papers from those boxes there. I'm sure you're too efficient to have filed away anything useful."

She bent to pick up the bag he'd tossed at her. "You've lost your accent."

"It's lost its purpose. Be quick, Amanda." His eyes narrowed as he gestured with the gun. "Very quick."

She began to stuff papers into the bag. He was stealing her history, she thought furiously. Her family. "These won't do you any good."

"I doubt you believe that, or you wouldn't be wasting your time with them." His posture seemed almost relaxed now as he stood between Amanda and the door. "You're much too practical. In my profession, it pays to do your homework. I know your family quite well." To hurry her along, he waved the gun. "Which is why I chose to concentrate on you, the most efficient and straightforward of the Calhoun women."

If his ego was the only thing she could strike at, she'd take her best shot. "I hope you weren't expecting me to fall for you." She flicked a coolly dismissive glance over him. "You're not my type—then or now."

It hit the mark. His vanity was as huge as his ambition. "It's a pity that the lack of time prevents me from testing that. Perhaps when I come back, we'll pick up where we left off."

"Even if you get away tonight, you'll never get back in this house again."

He only smiled. "We'll see. Running into you like this complicates my plans, but it doesn't alter the final goal. The necklace. I want it very badly. Some jewels have power, and I have a feeling about this necklace. A strong feeling."

The air in the room was suddenly cold, bone-chilling cold. The expression in Livingston's eyes changed. "Drafts," he muttered uneasily. "The place is full of drafts."

But Amanda felt it, too, and was Calhoun enough to recognize it.

"It's Bianca," she said, and despite the gun, despite the odds, felt completely safe. "If you've done your homework, then you'll know she's still here." The darting nerves in his eyes made her smile. "I don't think she wants you to have the papers, or the necklace."

"Ghosts?" he laughed, but the sound was strained. Though he could see with his own eyes that nothing had changed, he was no longer sure he was alone in the room with Amanda. "That's unworthy of you."

"Then why are you frightened?"

"I'm not frightened, I'm in a hurry. That's enough." He found himself desperate to get out of the room, out of the house. Despite the eerie chill, a line of sweat dribbled down his back. "You carry the bag. Since this has taken longer than expected, we'll have to forgo Coco's pearls, for now." Impatient, he waved the gun at her. "Out the terrace doors."

Amanda debated heaving the duffel bag at him and running. But then he would have the papers. Instead, she struggled with it, then fumbled at the door. "It's stuck."

She was braced when he came up behind her to fight with the old latch. The minute the door opened, she stuck a foot behind him, threw her weight against him, then ran.

Wanting to lead him away from her family, she headed toward the west wing. As she hit the first set of stone stairs, she shouted for Sloan. The heavy bag bumped each step as she dragged it with her. She could hear him behind her, closing in, and zigged around a corner as the first bullet pinged off granite.

She didn't stop to catch her breath, though her lungs were beginning to burn. The May night was warm, oppressively warm after the cold of the storeroom. The air was heavy with the threat of rain.

The sensation of safety she had felt in the storeroom had vanished. There was no protection now, except for her knowledge of the complex layout of the terraces and stairs. But she was straining, fighting her way through the dark and through the sudden certainty that she could not handle this alone.

Then she saw Sloan, heading toward her from the opposite direction. The relief lasted only an instant before she heard another shot.

Lights were flashing everywhere inside the house. Sloan shouted at her before he came forward like a charging bull. Unarmed, Amanda realized, blind with fury, and straight into a loaded gun.

Without hesitation, she whirled away from Sloan and heaved the bag of papers at Livingston. As he snatched it up, she could hear raised voices from inside, Jenny's crying, the dog's frantic barks. Wanting to protect as much as be protected, Amanda raced toward Sloan. When she reached him, arms outstretched, he shoved her aside.

"Get in the house."

"He's got a gun," she said, desperately clinging to his arm. "Just let him go."

"I said get inside." He shook her off, then before her astonished eyes, leaped over the wall.

With her heart in her throat, she raced to it, to see him scrambling up from the terrace below. Even as Lilah burst through a door, Amanda was giving chase.

"What the hell's going on?" Lilah shouted after her.

"Call the police." After the single order, Amanda saved her breath for running, following the sound of stampeding feet and Fred's furious barks.

There was no moonlight to guide her, but she plunged heedlessly into the dark, screaming for Sloan when she heard the explosion of gunfire. She flew down the steps, tearing around the house in a dead run. Over her own ragged gasps, she heard a shouted curse, then the sound of tires squealing on asphalt.

In her hurry, she stumbled once, scrambling back up from the drive-way with gravel stinging her palms. Then for an instant, a terrifying instant, there was only the sound of the sea and the wind and her own thundering pulse.

Her legs trembled as she dashed down the slope, so blind with fear that she didn't see Sloan until she rammed into him.

"Oh, God." Her hands were instantly on his face. "I thought he'd killed you."

He was too infuriated at having lost his quarry to appreciate her concern. "Not for lack of trying. Are you all right?"

"Yes, yes, I'm fine. It was—"

"You're bleeding." Every other thought in his head vanished. "There's blood on your hands."

"I fell." She dropped her head onto his shoulder. "It was so dark, and I couldn't see." Fighting tears, she held on to him as Fred whined at their feet. In an abrupt change of mood, she pulled back, pushing at his chest with her sore hands. Her damp eyes sizzled. "Are you crazy, chasing after him that way? I told you he had a gun. He could have shot you."

"He damn near shot you," Sloan retorted. "And didn't I tell you to stay inside?"

"I don't take orders from you," she began.

"You're both alive," Lilah commented. Flashlight in hand, she strolled toward them. "I could hear you arguing from the end of the driveway." The light shot across papers scattered in the road. "What's all this?"

"Oh, God, he must have dropped some." Amanda was already down on her hands and knees, gathering them up.

"Must've been when Fred bit his leg." Far from pacified, Sloan bent to snatch up a paper before it blew away.

"Fred bit him?" Amanda and Lilah said in unison.

"Good and hard from the sound of it." It was a small but sweet satisfaction. "We might have had him, too, but he had a car stashed down the road."

"And he might have shot both of you," Amanda retorted.

"Excuse me." Lilah felt she was doing her part by shining the light so they could see to find papers. "Who is he?"

"Livingston," Sloan told her, then added a string of curses. "You'll have to get the details from your sister."

"Inside," Lilah suggested. "The rest of the family is in an uproar."

"You called the police?"

"Yes." Right before she'd rushed out of the house, barefoot, to chase her sister down the graveled driveway. When Fred stopped to perk his ears then give a long, ululant howl, she laughed. "And I'd say they're on the way. Fred already hears the sirens."

Because her arms were full, Amanda pushed the papers into Lilah's arms, then began to pick up more as they started back. "He didn't get everything," she muttered, then thought of that moment in the storeroom when the air had changed. "I knew he wouldn't."

At the door of the house Suzanna stood, a slim gladiator, armed with a fireplace poker. "Is everyone all right?"

"Fine." Amanda let out an exhausted breath. "The kids?"

"In the parlor with Aunt Coco. Oh, honey, your hands."

"I just scraped them."

"I'll get some antiseptic."

"And some brandy," Lilah added, before laying the papers on a table in the hallway.

Twenty minutes later, the story had been related to the police, and the family was left alone to absorb it. Sloan paced behind the sofa while the Calhoun women huddled together.

"We had that—that thief to dinner." Coco glared into her brandy. "I baked a chocolate soufflé. And all the time he was plotting to steal from us."

"The police will shoot him," Alex piped up. "Bang! Between the eyes."

"I think we've had enough excitement for one night." Suzanna kissed the top of his head. Less sure of himself than he wanted to be, Alex slipped a hand into hers and held tight.

"He got most of the papers." With a sigh, Amanda reached for the pile she'd tossed onto the coffee table. "I hope Fred took a good chunk out of him."

"Good boy, Fred." Lilah cuddled the dog in her lap. "I don't think they'll do Livingston—or whoever he is—any good. He's not meant to find the emeralds. We are."

"He won't get the chance," Sloan said grimly. "Not with the security system I'm putting in." He shot a look at Amanda, daring her to argue, but she was staring at one of the papers.

"It's a letter," she murmured. "A letter from Bianca to Christian."

"Oh, my dear." Coco leaned forward. "What does it say?"

Amanda read,

"My love,

I'm writing this as the rain continues to fall and keeps me from you. I wonder what you are doing, if you paint today in the gloomy light and think of me. When I'm alone like this in my tower, separated from the reality of my duties, I let the memories sweep over me. Of the first time I saw you, standing on the cliffs. Of the last time I touched you. I'm praying for the sun, Christian, so that we can make more memories. I cannot tell you how you have changed me, how much more my eyes see, now that they see with my heart. I can't imagine how empty my life would have been without this time we had together. I know now that love is very rare, very precious. It is something to be cherished and held on to tightly while too often it is smothered, or brushed carelessly away. Remember, even when our time together ends, I will hold your love. It will live in my heart long after that heart stops beating.

Bianca."

Coco let out a long, dreamy sigh. "Oh, how much they must have loved each other."

"Yucky," Alex said sleepily, and rested his head on his mother's breast.

Amanda smoothed the letter out, hating the fact that it had become crumpled. "I guess she never got the chance to send it to him. All these years it's been mixed up with receipts and account sheets."

"And tonight *we* found it, not Livingston," Lilah reminded her.

"Luck," Amanda murmured.

"Fate," her sister insisted.

When the phone rang, Amanda was the first up to answer. "It's the police," she said, then settled back to listen. "I see. Yes, thank you for letting us know." She hung up, blowing out a disgusted breath. "Looks like he got away. He didn't go back to the BayWatch for any of his things, or he slipped in and took what he wanted and left the rest."

"Do they think he'll come back?" Alarmed, Coco patted her chest.

"No, but they're going to keep an eye on the house until they're sure he's left the island."

"I imagine he's halfway to New York by now." Suzanna shifted the drowsy children on her lap. "And if he comes back, we'll be ready for him."

"More than ready," Amanda agreed. "They have an APB out, but…I guess that's all that can be done for tonight."

"No." Sloan crossed the room to her. "There's a little more that has to be done." He nodded to the rest of the room as he pulled her toward the doorway. "You'll excuse us."

"They might, but I don't," Amanda told him. "Let go of my arm."

"Okay." He did, then nipping her by the waist, hauled her over his shoulder. "It's always the hard way with you."

"I will not be slung around like a sack of potatoes." As he climbed the stairs, she wriggled, trying for one clear shot with her foot.

"We left some loose ends before you stormed off to go tangle with an armed robber. Now we're damn well going to tie them up. You like straight talk, Calhoun, and you're about to get some."

"You don't know what I like." She slammed a fist into his back. "You don't know anything."

"Then it's time I found out." He kicked open the door of her room, stalked over and dumped her onto the bed. When she scrambled up, fists raised, he shoved her down again. "You sit where I put you. So help me, we're going to have this out once and for all."

Amanda stunned them both by covering her face with her hands and bursting into tears. She couldn't stop them. Everything that had happened in the past few hours reared up to set off an emotional jag that knocked her flat. On an oath, Sloan stepped toward her, then away, then dragged a helpless hand through his hair.

"Don't do that, Mandy."

She only shook her head and continued to sob.

"Come on now, please." His voice gentled as he crouched in front of her. "I didn't mean to make you cry." Lost, he stroked her hair, patted her shoulder. "I'm sorry, honey. I know you've been through hell tonight. I should have waited to start on this." Cursing himself, he rubbed her arm. "Look, you can hit me if it'd make you feel better."

She sniffled, drew in a hitching breath, then clipped him hard enough to send him sprawling. Through a veil of tears, she studied him as he dabbed at his mouth with the back of his hand.

"I forgot how literal minded you were." He sat where he was as they watched each other. "You finished crying?"

"I think so." Sniffling again, she dug into her pocket for a tissue. "Your lip's bleeding."

"Yeah." He started to reach for the tissue, but she was wiping her face with it. Laughing, he sat back again. "God Almighty, you're a piece of work."

"I'm glad you think this whole thing is a big joke. Men breaking into the house, waving guns around. You're lucky I didn't find you facedown in the road with a hole in your head."

He saw the tears welling again and took her hands. "Is that what this is about?" He pressed a kiss to her freshly bandaged palms. "You're upset because I went after him?"

"I told you not to."

"Hey." His gaze fixed on hers, he raised a hand to cup her chin. "Do you think I could stand around after he'd taken a potshot at you? The only thing I regret is that I didn't catch up with him, so I could rearrange that pretty face of his."

"That's just stupid machismo," she said, but turned her cheek into his hand.

"That's the second time tonight you've called me stupid. I'd like to get back to the first time."

Instantly she pulled back and pokered up. "I don't want to talk about it."

"Too bad. That little chase was quite a diversion, but it's done now. We're not. How come you jumped all over me when I mentioned marriage?"

"Mentioned it? You ordered it."

"I just said that—"

"You just assumed," she interrupted, then pushed by him to stand up. "Just because I love you, just because I've made love with you, doesn't give you any right to take me for granted. I told you before that I make my own plans."

"I've had it with your plans, Calhoun." He took her arm to hold her still. "I've got plans, too, and needs. It so happens they all include you. I love you, damn it." He emphasized the point with a quick, frustrated shake. "You're the only woman I've ever needed, really needed. The only woman I've ever wanted to spend my life with, have children with, make a home with. God knows why when you're as ornery as a mule with two heads, but that's the way it is."

"Then why didn't you just ask?"

Baffled, he shook his head. "Ask what?"

She made a strangled sound and began to pace again. "It's not like I'm asking for Byron or Shelley. I don't expect you to get down on your knees with a hand over your heart. Maybe a little violin music wouldn't have hurt," she muttered. "Or some candlelight."

"Violin music?"

"Forget it." She stopped, hands on her hips, to face him down. "Do you think just because I'm sensible and organized that I don't need any trappings, any romance? You come here, change my entire life, make me love you so much I can't see straight, then you don't even have the good sense to do it right."

"Hold on." He held up a hand before she could stride by him again. "Are you saying you're mad because I didn't ask you fancy enough?"

The sound came again, louder this time. Her face was flushed with temper, her eyes glowing with it. "You didn't ask at all, but why should you? You already know the answer."

Trying to figure women, he thought while he rubbed his hands over his face, was like...trying to figure women. "You wait here," he told her, and strode out.

"Typical," Amanda called after him, then plopped down onto the bed. She was still stewing, her chin on her hand, when he came back in. "Now what?" she demanded.

"Just shut up a minute." He set the tape recorder he'd borrowed on her dresser, then pulled out a pack of matches. Systematically he began to light candles, moving from one part of the room to another while she scowled at him. When he was satisfied, he turned off the lights.

"What are you doing?"

"I'm getting things ready so I can ask you to marry me without having you throw something at me again."

Chin up, she jumped out of bed. "Now you're making fun of me."

"No, I'm not. Damn it, woman, are you going to argue with me all night or let me try to do this right?"

There was enough exasperation in his voice to make her stop and consider him. He didn't look terribly comfortable, she noted. And because he didn't, she wanted to smile. He was doing it for her, she realized. Because he loved her.

"I guess I'll let you try. What's that?" he asked, gesturing to the tape recorder.

"It's Lilah's." He punched the Play button. The soft, weeping sound of violins flowed into the room. Now she did smile, though her heart was beginning to thud.

"It's lovely."

"So are you, I should have made a point of telling you that more often." Stepping toward her, he held out a hand.

"Now's a good time to start." She placed her hand in his.

"I love you, Amanda." Very gently, he touched his lips to hers. "I love everything about you. The woman who makes lists and lines up her shoes in the closet. The woman who goes swimming in freezing water, just so she can be alone for a while. I love the incredibly sexy woman I found in bed, and the tough one, who knows her own mind. It's all the things you are I don't want to live without."

"I love you, too." She lifted a hand to his face. "I meant it when I said you'd changed my life. Tonight, when I read Bianca's letter, I understood how she felt. I'll never feel about anyone the way I feel about you. I'll never want to."

Smiling, he caught her wrist, turning it so that he could brush a kiss over her hand. "Then you're going to marry me?"

She laughed as she threw her arms around him. "I thought you'd never ask."

*   *   *   *   *

FOR THE LOVE OF LILAH

Prologue

Bar Harbor, 1913

The cliffs call to me. High and fierce and dangerously beautiful, they stand and beckon as seductively as a lover. In the morning, the air was as soft as the clouds that rode the sky to the west. Gulls wheeled and called, a lonely sound, like the distant ring of a buoy that carried up on the wind. It brought an image of a church bell tolling a birth. Or a death.

Like a mirage, other islands glinted and winked through the faint mist the sun had yet to burn from the water. Fishermen piloted their sturdy boats from the bay and out to the rolling sea.

Even knowing he would not be there, I couldn't stay away.

I took the children. It can't be wrong to want to share with them some of the happiness that I always feel when I walk in the wild grass that leads to the tumbled rocks. I held Ethan's hand on one side, and Colleen's on the other. Nanny gripped little Sean's as he toddled through the grass after a yellow butterfly that fluttered just beyond his questing fingers.

The sound of their laughter—the sweetest sound a mother can hear—lifted through the air. They have such bright and depthless curiosity, such unquestioning trust. As yet, they are untouched by the worries of the world, of uprisings in Mexico, of unrest in Europe. Their world does not include betrayals or guilt or passions that sting the heart. Their needs, so simple, are immediate and have nothing to do with tomorrow. If I could keep them so innocent, so safe and so free, I would. Yet I know that one day they will face all of those churning adult emotions and worries.

But today there were wildflowers to be picked, questions to be answered. And for me, dreams to be dreamed.

There is no doubt that Nanny understands why I walk here. She knows me too well not to see into my heart. She loves me too well to criticize. No one would be more aware than she that there is no love in my marriage. It is, as it has always been, a convenience to Fergus, a duty to me. If not for the children, we would have nothing in common. Even then, I fear he considers them worthwhile possessions, symbols of his success, such as our home in New York, or The Towers, the castlelike house he built for summers on the island. Or myself, the woman he took as wife, one whom he considers attractive enough, well-bred enough to share the Calhoun name, to grace his dinner table or adorn his arm when we walk into the society that is so important to him.

It sounds cold when I write it, yet I cannot pretend there has been warmth in my marriage to Fergus. Certainly there is no passion. I had hoped, when I followed my parents' wishes and married him, that there would be affection, which would deepen into love. But I was very young. There is courtesy, a hollow substitute for emotion.

A year ago perhaps, I could convince myself that I was content. I have a prosperous husband, children I adore, an enviable place in society and a circle of elegant friends. My wardrobe is crowded with beautiful clothes and jewelry. The emeralds Fergus gave me when Ethan was born are fit for a queen. My summer home is magnificent, again suited to royalty with its towers and turrets, its lofty walls papered in silk, its floors gleaming beneath the richest of carpets.

What woman would not be content with all of this? What more could a dutiful wife ask for? Unless she asked for love.

It was love I found along these cliffs, in the artist who stood there, facing the sea, slicing those rocks and raging water onto canvas. Christian, his dark hair blowing in the wind, his gray eyes so dark, so intense, as they studied me. Perhaps if I had not met him I could have gone on pretending to be content. I could have gone on convincing myself that I did not yearn for love or sweet words or a quiet touch in the middle of the night.

Yet I did meet him, and my life has changed. I would not go back to that false contentment for a hundred emerald necklaces. With Christian I have found something so much more precious than all the gold Fergus so cleverly accumulates. It is not something I can hold in my hand or wear around my throat, but something I hold in my heart.

When I meet him on the cliffs, as I will this afternoon, I will not grieve for what we can't have, what we dare not take, but treasure the hours we've been given. When I feel his arms around me, taste his lips against mine, I'll know that Bianca is the luckiest woman in the world to have been loved so well.

Chapter One

A storm was waiting to happen. From the high curving window of the tower, Lilah could see the silver tongue of lightning licking at the black sky to the east. Thunder bellowed, bursting through the gathering clouds to send its drumbeat along the teeth of rock. An answering shudder coursed through her—not of fear, but of excitement.

Something was coming. She could feel it, not just in the thickening of the air but in the primitive beating of her own blood.

When she pressed her hand to the glass, she almost expected her fingers to sizzle, snapped with the power of the electricity building. But the glass was cool and smooth, and as black as the sky.

She smiled a little at the distant rumble of thunder and thought of her great-grandmother. Had Bianca ever stood here, watching a storm build, waiting for it to crash over the house and fill the tower with eerie light? Had she wished that her lover had stood beside her to share the power and the unleashed passion? Of course she had, Lilah thought. What woman wouldn't?

But Bianca had stood here alone, Lilah knew, just as she herself was standing alone now. Perhaps it had been the loneliness, the sheer ache of it, that had driven Bianca to throw herself out of that very window and onto the unforgiving rocks below.

Shaking her head, Lilah took her hand from the glass. She was letting herself get moody again, and it had to stop. Depression and dark thoughts were out of character for a woman who preferred to take life as it came—and who made it a policy to avoid its more strenuous burdens.

Lilah wasn't ashamed of the fact that she would rather sit than stand, would certainly rather walk than run and saw the value of long naps as opposed to exercise for keeping the body and mind in tune.

Not that she wasn't ambitious. It was simply that her ambitions ran to the notion that physical comfort had priority over physical accomplishments.

She didn't care for brooding and was annoyed with herself for falling into the habit over the past few weeks. If anything she should be happy. Her life was moving along at a steady if unhurried pace. Her home and her family, equally important as her own comfort, were safe and whole. In fact, both were expanding along very satisfactory lines.

Her youngest sister, C.C., was back from her honeymoon and glowing like a rose. Amanda, the most practical of the Calhoun sisters, was madly in love and planning her own wedding.

The two men in her sisters' lives met with Lilah's complete approval. Trenton St. James, her new brother-in-law, was a crafty businessman with a soft heart under a meticulously tailored suit. Sloan O'Riley, with his cowboy boots and Oklahoma drawl, had her admiration for digging beneath Amanda's prickly exterior.

Of course, having two of her beloved nieces attached to wonderful men made Aunt Coco delirious with happiness. Lilah laughed a little, thinking how her aunt was certain she'd all but arranged the love affairs herself. Now, naturally, the Calhoun sisters' long-time guardian was itching to provide the same service for Lilah and her older sister Suzanna.

Good luck, Lilah wished her aunt. After a traumatic divorce, and with two young children to care for—not to mention a business to run—Suzanna wasn't likely to cooperate. She'd been badly burned once, and a smart woman didn't let herself get pushed into the fire.

For herself, Lilah had been doing her best to fall in love, to hear that vibrant inner click that came when you knew you'd found the one person in the world who was fated for you. So far, that particular chamber of her heart had been stubbornly silent.

There was time for that, she reminded herself. She was twenty-seven, happy enough in her work, surrounded by family. A few months before, they had nearly lost The Towers, the Calhoun's crumbling and eccentric home that stood on the cliffs overlooking the sea. If it hadn't been for Trent, Lilah might not have been able to stand in the tower room she loved so much and look out at the gathering storm.

So she had her home, her family, a job that interested her and, she reminded herself, a mystery to solve. Great-Grandmama Bianca's emeralds, she thought. Though she had never seen them, she was able to visualize them perfectly just by closing her eyes.

Two dramatic tiers of grass-green stones accented with icy diamonds. The glint of gold in the fancy filigree work. And dripping from the bottom strand, that rich and glowing teardrop emerald. More than its financial or even aesthetic value, it represented to Lilah a direct link with an ancestor who fascinated her, and the hope of eternal love.

The legend said that Bianca, determined to end a loveless marriage, had packed a few of her treasured belongings, including the necklace, into a box. Hoping to find a way to join her lover, she had hidden it. Before she had been able to take it out and start a life with Christian, she had despaired and leaped from the tower window to her death.

A tragic end to a romance, Lilah thought, yet she didn't always feel sad when she thought of it. Bianca's spirit remained in The Towers, and in that high room where Bianca had spent so many hours longing for her lover, Lilah felt close to her.

They would find the emeralds, she promised herself. They were meant to.

It was true enough that the necklace had already caused its problems. The press had learned of its existence and had played endlessly on the hidden-treasure angle. So successfully, Lilah thought now, that the annoyance had gone beyond curious tourists and amateur treasure hunters, and had brought a ruthless thief into their home.

When she thought of how Amanda might have been killed protecting the family's papers, the risk she had taken trying to keep any clue to the emeralds out of the wrong hands, Lilah shuddered. Despite Amanda's heroics, the man who had called himself William Livingston had gotten away with a sackful. Lilah sincerely hoped he found nothing but old recipes and unpaid bills.

William Livingston, alias Peter Mitchell, alias a dozen other names wasn't going to get his greedy hands on the emeralds. Not if the Calhoun women had anything to do about it. As far as Lilah was concerned, that included Bianca, who was as much a part of The Towers as the cracked plaster and creaky boards.

Restless, she moved away from the window. She couldn't say why the emeralds and the woman who had owned them preyed so heavily on her mind tonight. But Lilah was a woman who believed in instinct, in premonition, as naturally as she believed the sun rose in the east.

Tonight, something was coming.

She glanced back toward the window. The storm was rolling closer, gathering force. She felt a driving need to be outside to meet it.

Max felt his stomach lurch along with the boat. Yacht, he reminded himself. A twenty-six-foot beauty with all the comforts of home. Certainly more than his own home, which consisted of a cramped apartment, carelessly furnished, near the campus of Cornell University. The trouble was, the twenty-six-foot beauty was sitting on top of a very cranky Atlantic, and the two seasickness pills in Max's system were no match for it.

He brushed the dark lock of hair away from his brow where, as always, it fell untidily back again. The reeling of the boat sent the brass lamp above his desk dancing. Max did his best to ignore it. He really had to concentrate on his job. American history professors weren't offered fascinating and lucrative summer employment every day. And there was a very good chance he could get a book out of it.

Being hired as researcher for an eccentric millionaire was the fodder of fiction. In this case, it was fact.

As the ship pitched, Max pressed a hand to his queasy stomach and tried three deep breaths. When that didn't work, he tried concentrating on his good fortune.

The letter from Ellis Caufield had come at a perfect time, just before Max had committed himself to a summer assignment. The offer had been both irresistible and flattering.

In the day-to-day scheme of things, Max didn't consider that he had a reputation. Some well-received articles, a few awards—but that was all within the tight world of academia that Max had happily buried himself in. If he was a good teacher, he felt it was because he received such pleasure from giving both information and appreciation of the past to students so mired in the present.

It had come as a surprise that Caufield, a layman, would have heard of him and would respect him enough to offer him such interesting work.

What was even more exciting than the yacht, the salary and the idea of summering in Bar Harbor, to a man with Maxwell Quartermain's mindset, was the history in every scrap of paper he'd been assigned to catalogue.

A receipt for a lady's hat, dated 1932. The guest list for a party from 1911. A copy of a repair bill on a 1935 Ford. The handwritten instructions for an herbal remedy for the croup. There were letters written before World War I, newspaper clippings with names like Carnegie and Kennedy, shipping receipts for Chippendale armoires, a Waterford chandelier. Old dance cards, faded recipes.

For a man who spent most of his intellectual life in the past, it was a treasure trove. He would have shifted through each scrap happily for nothing, but Ellis Caufield had contacted him, offering Max more than he made teaching two full semesters.

It was a dream come true. Instead of spending the summer struggling to interest bored students in the cultural and political status of America before the Great War, he was living it. With the money, half of which was already deposited, Max could afford to take a year off from teaching to start the book he'd been longing to write.

Max felt he owed Caufield an enormous debt. A year to indulge himself. It was more than he had ever dared to dream of. Brains had gotten him into Cornell on a scholarship. Brains and hard work had earned him a Ph.D. by the time he'd been twenty-five. For the eight years since then, he'd been slaving, teaching classes, preparing lectures, grading papers, taking the time only to write a few articles.

Now, thanks to Caufield, he would be able to take the time he had never dared to take. He would be able to begin the project he kept secret inside his head and heart.

He wanted to write a novel set in the second decade of the twentieth century. Not just a history lesson or an oratory on the cause and effect of war, but a story of people swept along by history. The kind of people he was growing to know and understand by reading through their old papers.

Caufield had given him that time, the research and the opportunity. And it was all gilded by a summer spent luxuriously on a yacht. It was a pity

Max hadn't realized how much his system would resent the motion of the sea.

Particularly a stormy one, he thought, rubbing a hand over his clammy face. He struggled to concentrate, but the faded and tiny print on the papers swam then doubled in front of his eyes and added a vicious headache to the grinding nausea. What he needed was some air, he told himself. A good blast of fresh air. Though he knew Caufield preferred him to stay below with his research during the evenings, Max figured his employer would prefer him healthy rather than curled up moaning on his bed.

Rising, he did moan a little, his stomach heaving with the next wave. He could almost feel his skin turn green. Air, definitely. Max stumbled from the cabin, wondering if he would ever find his sea legs. After a week, he'd thought he'd been doing fairly well, but with the first taste of rough weather, he was wobbly.

It was a good thing he hadn't—as he sometimes liked to imagine—sailed on the *Mayflower*. He never would have made it to Plymouth Rock.

Bracing a hand on the mahogany paneling, he hobbled down the pitching corridor toward the stairs that led above deck.

Caufield's cabin door was open. Max, who would never stoop to eavesdropping, paused only to give his stomach a moment to settle. He heard his employer speaking to the captain. As the dizziness cleared from Max's head, he realized they were not speaking about the weather or plotting a course.

"I don't intend to lose the necklace," Caufield said impatiently. "I've gone to a lot of trouble, and expense, already."

The captain's answer was equally taut. "I don't see why you brought Quartermain in. If he realizes why you want those papers, and how you got them, he'll be trouble."

"He won't find out. As far as the good professor is concerned, they belong to my family. And I am rich enough, eccentric enough, to want them preserved."

"If he hears something—"

"Hears something?" Caufield interrupted with a laugh. "He's so buried in the past he doesn't hear his own name. Why do you think I chose him? I do my homework, Hawkins, and I researched Quartermain thoroughly. He's an academic fossil with more brains than wit, and is curious only about what happened in the past. Current events, such as armed robbery and the Calhoun emeralds are beyond him."

In the corridor, Max remained still and silent, the physical illness warring with sick suspicion. *Armed robbery.* The two words reeled in his head.

"We'd be better off in New York," Hawkins complained. "I cased out the Wallingford job while you were kicking your heels last month. We could have the old lady's diamonds inside of a week."

"The diamonds will wait." Caufield's voice hardened. "I want the emeralds, and I intend to have them. I've been twenty years in the business of stealing, Hawkins, and I know that only once in a lifetime does a man have the chance for something this big.''

"The diamonds—"

"Are stones." Now the voice was caressing and perhaps a little mad. "The emeralds are a legend. They're going to be mine. Whatever it takes."

Max stood frozen outside of the stateroom. The clammy illness roiling inside of his stomach was iced with shock. He hadn't a clue what they were talking about or how to put it together. But one thing was obvious—he was being used by a thief, and there was something other than history in the papers he'd been hired to research.

The fanaticism in Caufield's voice hadn't escaped him, nor had the suppressed violence in Hawkins's. And fanaticism had proved itself throughout history to be a most dangerous weapon. His only defense against it was knowledge.

He had to get the papers, get them and find a way off the boat and to the police. Though whatever he could tell them wouldn't make sense. He stepped back, hoping he could clear his thoughts by the time he got to his stateroom. A wicked wave had the boat lurching and Max pitching through the open doorway.

"Dr. Quartermain." Gripping the sides of his desk, Caufield lifted a brow. "Well, it seems as though you're in the wrong place at the wrong time."

Max grasped the doorjamb as he stumbled back, cursing the unsteady deck beneath his feet. "I—wanted some air."

"He heard every damn word," the captain muttered.

"I'm aware of that, Hawkins. The professor isn't blessed with a poker face. Well then," he began as he slid a drawer open, "we'll simply alter the plans a bit. I'm afraid you won't be granted any shore leave during our stay in Bar Harbor, Doctor." He pulled out a chrome-plated revolver. "An inconvenience, I know, but I'm sure you'll find your cabin more than adequate for your needs while you work. Hawkins, take him back and lock him in."

A crash of thunder vibrated the boat. It was all Max needed to uproot his legs. As the boat swayed, he rushed back into the corridor. Pulling himself along by the handrail, he fought the motion of the boat. The shouts behind him were lost as he came above deck into the howl of the wind.

A spray of saltwater dashed across his face, blinding him for a moment as he frantically looked for a means of escape. Lightning cracked the black sky, showing him the single stab of light, the pitching seas, the distant, angry rocks and the vague shadow of land. The next roll nearly felled him, but he managed through a combination of luck and sheer will to stay upright. Driven by instinct, he ran, feet sliding on the wet deck. In the next flash of lightning he saw one of the mates glance over from his post. The man called something and gestured, but Max spun around on the slippery deck and ran on.

He tried to think, but his head was too crowded, too jumbled. The storm, the pitching boat, the image of that glinting gun. It was like being caught in someone else's nightmare. He was a history professor, a man who lived in books, rarely surfacing long enough to remember if he'd eaten or picked up his cleaning. He was, he knew, terminally boring, calmly pacing himself on the academic treadmill as he had done all of his life. Surely he couldn't be on a yacht in the Atlantic being chased by armed thieves.

"Doctor."

His erstwhile employer's voice was close enough to cause Max to turn around. The gun being held less than five feet away reminded Max that some nightmares were real. Slowly he backed up until he rammed into the guardrail. There was nowhere left to run.

"I know this is an inconvenience," Caufield said, "but I think it would be wise if you went back to your cabin." A bolt of lightning emphasized the point. "The storm should be short, but quite severe. We wouldn't want you to... fall overboard."

"You're a thief."

"Yes." Legs braced against the rolling deck, Caufield smiled. He was enjoying himself—the wind, the electric air, the white face of the prey he had cornered. "And now that I can be more frank about just what I want you to look for, our work should go much more quickly. Come now, Doctor, use that celebrated brain of yours."

From the corner of his eye, Max saw that Hawkins was closing in from the other side, as steady on the heeling deck as a mountain goat on a beaten path. In a moment, they would have him. Once they did, he was quite certain he would never see the inside of a classroom again.

With an instinct for survival that had never been tested, he swung over the rail. He heard another crack of thunder, felt a burning along his temple, then plunged blindly beneath the dark, swirling water.

Lilah had driven down, following the winding road to the base of the cliff. The wind had picked up, was shrieking now as she stepped out of her car and let it stream through her hair. She didn't know why she'd felt compelled to come here, to stand alone on this narrow and rocky stretch of beach to face the storm.

But she had come, and the exhilaration streamed into her, racing just under her skin, speeding up her heart. When she laughed, the sound hung on the wind then echoed away. Power and passion exploded around her in a war she could delight in.

Water fumed against the rock, spouting up, spraying her. There was an icy feel to it that made her shiver, but she didn't draw back. Instead she closed her eyes for a moment, lifted her face and absorbed it.

The noise was huge, wildly primitive. Above, closer now, the storm threatened. Big and bad and boisterous. The rain, so heavy in the air you could taste it, held up, but the lightning took command, spearing the sky, ripping through the dark while the boom of thunder competed with the crash of water and wind.

She felt as though she were alone in a violent painting, but there was no sense of loneliness and certainly none of fear. It was anticipation that prickled along her skin, just as a passion as dark as the storm's beat in her blood.

Something, she thought again as she lifted her face to the wind, was coming.

If it hadn't been for the lightning, she wouldn't have seen him. At first she watched the dark shape in the darker water and wondered if a dolphin had swum too close to the rocks. Curious, she walked over the shale, dragging her hair away from the greedy fingers of wind.

Not a dolphin, she realized with a clutch of panic. A man. Too stunned to move, she watched him go under. Surely she'd imagined it, she told herself. She was just caught up in the storm, the mystery of it, the sense of immediacy. It was crazy to think she'd seen someone fighting the waves in this lonely and violent span of water.

But when the figure appeared again, floundering, Lilah was kicking off her sandals and racing into the icy black water.

His energy was flagging. Though he'd managed to pry off his shoes, his legs felt abominably heavy. He'd always been a strong swimmer. It was the only sport he had had any talent for. But the sea was a great deal stronger. It carried him along now rather than his own arms and legs. It dragged him under as it chose, then teasingly released him as he struggled to break free for one more gulp of air.

He couldn't even remember why he was fighting. The cold that had long since numbed his body granted the same favor to his brain. His thrashing movements were merely automatic now and growing steadily weaker. It was the sea that guided him, that trapped him, that would, he was coming to accept, kill him.

The next wave battered him, and exhausted, he let it take him under. He only hoped he would drown before he bashed into the rocks.

He felt something wrap around his neck and, with the last of his strength, pushed at it. Some wild thought of sea snakes or grasping weeds had him struggling. Then his face was above the surface again, his burning lungs sucking air. Dimly he saw a face close to his own. Pale, stunningly beautiful. A glory of dark, wet hair floated around him.

"Just hang on," she shouted at him. "We'll be all right."

She was pulling him toward shore, fighting the backwash of wave. Hallucinating, Max thought. He had to be hallucinating to imagine a beautiful woman coming to his aid a moment before he died. But the possibility of a miracle kicked into his fading sense of survival, and he began to work with her.

The waves slammed into them, dragging them back a foot for every two exhausting feet of progress they made. Overhead the sky opened to pour out a lashing rain. She was shouting something again, but all he could hear was the dull buzzing in his own head.

He decided he must already be dead. There certainly was no more pain. All he could see was her face, the glow of her eyes, the water-slicked lashes. A man could do worse than to die with that image in his mind.

But her eyes were bright with anger, electric with it. She wanted help, he realized. She needed help. Instinctively he put an arm around her waist so that they were towing each other.

He lost track of the times they went under, of the times one would pull the other up again. When he saw the jutting rocks, fangs spearing up through the swirling black, he turned his weary body without thought to shield hers. An angry wave flicked them waist high out of the water, as easily as a finger flicks an ant from a stone.

His shoulder slammed against rock, but he barely felt it. Then there was the grit of sand beneath his knees, biting into flesh. The water fought to suck them back, but they crawled onto the rocky shore.

The initial sickness was hideous, racking through him until he was certain his body would simply break apart. When the worst of it passed, he rolled, coughing, onto his back. The sky wheeled overhead, black, then brilliant. The face was above his again, close. A hand moved gently over his brow.

"You made it, sailor."

He only stared. She was eerily beautiful, like something he might have conjured if he'd had enough imagination. In the flickering lightning he could see her hair was a rich, golden red. She had acres of it. It flowed around her face, down her shoulders, onto his chest. Her eyes were the mystical green of a calm sea. As the water ran from her onto him, he reached up to touch her face, certain they would pass through the image. But he felt her skin, cold, wet and soft as spring rain.

"Real." His voice was a husky croak. "You're real."

"Damn right." She smiled, then cupping his face in her hands, laughed. "You're alive. We're both alive." And kissed him. Deeply, lavishly, until his head spun with it. There was more laughter beneath the kiss. He heard the joy in it, but not the simple relief.

When he looked at her again, she was blurring, that ethereal face fading until all he could see were those incredible, glowing eyes.

"I never believed in mermaids," he murmured before he lost consciousness.

Chapter Two

"**P**oor man." Coco, splendid in a flowing purple caftan, hovered beside the bed. She kept her voice low and watched, eagle eyed, as Lilah bandaged the shallow crease on their unconscious guest's temple. "What in the world could have happened to him?"

"We'll have to wait and ask." Her fingers gentle, Lilah studied the pale face on the pillow. Early thirties, she guessed. No tan, though it was mid-June. The indoor type, she decided, despite the fact that he had fairly good muscles. His body was well toned, if a bit on the lanky side—the weight of it had given her more than a little trouble when she'd dragged him to the car. His face was lean, a little long, nicely bony. Intellectual, she thought. The mouth was certainly engaging. Rather poetic, like the pallor. Though his eyes were closed now, she knew they were blue. His hair, nearly dry, was full of sand and long and thick. It was dark and straight, like his lashes.

"I called the doctor," Amanda said as she hurried into the bedroom. Her fingers tapped on the footboard as she frowned down at the patient. "He says we should bring him into Emergency."

Lilah looked up as the lightning struck close to the house and the rain slashed against the windows. "I don't want to take him out in this unless we have to."

"I think she's right." Suzanna stood on the other side of the bed. "I also think Lilah should have a hot bath and lie down."

"I'm fine." At the moment she was wrapped in a chenille robe, warmed by that and a healthy dose of brandy. In any case, she was feeling much too proprietary about her charge to turn him over.

"Crazy is what you are." C.C. massaged Lilah's neck as she lectured her. "Diving into the ocean in the middle of a storm."

"I guess I could've let him drown." Lilah patted C.C.'s hand. "Where's Trent?"

C.C. sighed as she thought of her new husband. "He and Sloan are making sure the new construction's protected. The rain's coming down pretty hard and they were worried about water damage."

"I think I should make some chicken soup." Coco, maternal instincts humming, studied the patient again. "That's just what he needs when he wakes up."

He was already waking up, groggily. He heard the distant and lovely sound of women's voices. Low pitched, smooth, soothing. Like music, it lulled him in and out of dreams. When he turned his head, Max felt the gentle feminine touch on his brow. Slowly, he opened eyes still burning from saltwater. The dimly lit room blurred, tilted, then slid into soft focus.

There were five of them, he noted dreamily. Five stupendous examples of womanhood. On one side of the bed was a blonde, poetically lovely, eyes filled with concern. At the foot was a tall, trim brunette who seemed both impatient and sympathetic. An older woman with smoky-blond hair and a regal figure beamed at him. A green-eyed, raven-haired Amazon tilted her head and smiled more cautiously.

Then there was his mermaid, sitting beside him in a white robe, her fabulous hair falling in wild curls to her waist. He must have made some gesture, for they all came a little closer, as if to offer comfort. The mermaid's hand covered his.

"I guess this is heaven," he managed through a dry throat. "It's worth dying for."

With a laugh, Lilah squeezed his fingers. "Nice thought, but this is Maine," she corrected. Lifting a cup, she eased brandy-laced tea through his lips. "You're not dead, just tired."

"Chicken soup." Coco stepped forward to tidy the blanket over him. She was vain enough to take an instant liking to him for his waking statement. "Doesn't that sound good, dear?"

"Yes." The thought of something warm sliding down his aching throat sounded glorious. Though it hurt to swallow, he took another greedy gulp of tea. "Who are you?"

"We're the Calhouns," Amanda said from the foot of the bed. "Welcome to The Towers."

Calhouns. There was something familiar about the name, but it drifted away, like the dream of drowning. "I'm sorry, I don't know how I got here."

"Lilah brought you," C.C. told him. "She—"

"You had an accident," Lilah interrupted her sister, and smiled at him. "Don't worry about it right now. You should rest."

It wasn't a question of should, but must. He could already feel himself drifting away. "You're Lilah," he said groggily. As he drifted to sleep, he repeated the name, finding it lyrical enough to dream on.

* * *

"How's the lifeguard this morning?"

Lilah turned from the stove to look at Sloan, Amanda's fiancé. At six-four, he filled the doorway, was so blatantly male—and relaxed with it—she had to smile.

"I guess I earned my first merit badge."

"Next time try making a pot holder." After crossing the room, he kissed the top of her head. "We wouldn't want to lose you."

"I figure jumping into a stormy sea once in my life is enough." With a little sigh, she leaned against him. "I was petrified."

"What the hell were you doing down there with a storm coming?"

"Just one of those things." She shrugged, then went back to fixing tea. For now, she preferred to keep the sensation of being sent to the beach to herself.

"Did you find out who he is?"

"No, not yet. He didn't have a wallet on him, and since he was in pretty rough shape last night, I didn't want to badger him." She glanced up, caught Sloan's expression and shook her head. "Come on, big guy, he's hardly dangerous. If he was looking for a way into the house to have a shot at finding the necklace, he could have taken an easier route than drowning."

He was forced to agree, but after having Amanda shot at, he didn't want to take chances. "Whoever he is, I think you should move him to the hospital."

"Let me worry about it." She began to arrange plates and cups on a tray. "He's all right, Sloan. Trust me?"

Frowning, he put a hand on hers before she could lift the tray. "Vibes?"

"Absolutely." With a laugh, she tossed back her hair. "Now, I'm going to take Mr. X some breakfast. Why don't you get back to knocking down walls in the west wing?"

"We're putting a few up today." And because he did trust her, he relaxed a little. "Aren't you going to be late for work?"

"I took the day off to play Florence Nightingale." She slapped his hand away from the saucer of toast. "Go be an architect."

Balancing the tray, she left Sloan to start down the hallway. The main floor of The Towers was a hodgepodge of rooms with towering ceilings and cracked plaster. In its heyday, it had been a showplace, an elaborate summer home built by Fergus Calhoun in 1904. It had been his symbol of status with gleaming paneling, crystal doorknobs, intricate murals.

Now the roof leaked in too many places to count, the plumbing rattled and the plaster flaked. Like her sisters, Lilah adored every inch of chipped molding. It had been her home, her only home, and held memories of the parents she had lost fifteen years before.

At the top of the curving stairs, she paused. Muffled with distance came the energetic sound of hammering. The west wing was getting a much needed face-lift. Between Sloan and Trent, The Towers would recapture at least part of its former glory. Lilah liked the idea and, as a woman who considered napping a favored pastime, enjoyed the sound of busy hands.

He was still sleeping when she walked into the room. She knew he had barely stirred through the night because she had stretched out on the foot of the bed, reluctant to leave him, and had slept there, patchily, until morning.

Quietly Lilah set the tray on the bureau and moved over to open the terrace doors. Warm and fragrant air glided in. Unable to resist, she stepped out to let it revitalize her. The sunlight sparkled on the wet grass, glittered on the petals of shell-pink peonies still heavy headed from rain. Clematis, their saucer-sized blossoms royally blue, spiraled on one of the white trellises in a race with the climbing roses.

From the waist-high terrace wall, she could see the glint of the deep blue water of the bay and the greener, less serene, surface of the Atlantic. It hardly seemed possible that she had been in the water just last night, grasping a stranger and fighting for life. But muscles, unaccustomed to the exercise, ached enough to bring the moment, and the terror, back.

She preferred concentrating on the morning, the generous laziness of it. Made tiny as a toy by the distance, one of the tourist boats streamed by, filled with people clutching cameras and children, hoping to see a whale.

It was June, and the summer people poured into Bar Harbor to sail, to shop, to sun. They would gobble up lobster rolls, haunt the ice cream and T-shirt shops and pack the streets, searching for the perfect souvenir. To them it was a resort. To Lilah, it was home.

She watched a three-masted schooner head out to sea and allowed herself to dream a little before going back inside.

He was dreaming. Part of his mind recognized it as a dream, but his stomach muscles still fisted, and his pulse rate increased. He was alone in an angry black sea, fighting to make his arms and legs swim through the rising waves. They dragged at him, pulling him under into that blind, airless world. His lungs strained. His own heartbeat roared in his head.

His disorientation was complete—black sea below, black sky above. There was a hideous throbbing in his temple, a terrifying numbness in his limbs. He sank, floating down, fathoms deep. Then she was there, her red hair flowing around her, twining around lovely white breasts, down a slender torso. Her eyes were a soft, mystical green. She spoke his name, and there was a laugh in her voice—and an invitation in the laugh. Slowly, gracefully as a dancer, she held out her arms to him, folding him in. He tasted salt and sex on her lips as she closed them over his.

With a groan, he came regretfully awake. There was pain now, ripe and throbbing in his shoulder, sharp and horrible in his head. His thought patterns skidded away from him. Concentrating, he worked his way above the pain, focusing first on a high, coffered ceiling laced with cracks. He shifted a little, acutely aware that every muscle in his body hurt.

The room was enormous—or perhaps it seemed so because it was so scantily furnished. But what furnishings. There was a huge antique armoire with intricately carved doors. The single chair was undoubtedly Louis Quinze, and the dusty nightstand Hepplewhite. The mattress he lay on sagged, but the footboard was Georgian.

Struggling up to brace on his elbows, he saw Lilah standing in the open terrace doors. The breeze was fluttering those long cables of hair. He swallowed. At least he knew she wasn't a mermaid. She had legs. Lord, she had legs—right up to her eyes. She wore flowered shorts, a plain blue T-shirt and a smile.

"So, you're awake." She came to him and, competent as a mother, laid a hand on his brow. His tongue dried up. "No fever. You're lucky."

"Yeah."

Her smile widened. "Hungry?"

There was definitely a hole in the pit of his stomach. "Yeah." He wondered if he'd ever be able to get more than one word out around her. At the moment he was lecturing himself for having imagined her naked when she'd risked her life to save his. "Your name's Lilah."

"That's right." She walked over to fetch the tray. "I wasn't sure you'd remember anything from last night."

Pain capered through him so that he gritted his teeth against it and struggled to keep his voice even. "I remember five beautiful women. I thought I was in heaven."

She laughed and, setting the tray at the foot of the bed, came to rearrange his pillows. "My three sisters and my aunt. Here, can you sit up a little?"

When her hand slid down his back to brace him, he realized he was naked. Completely. "Ah..."

"Don't worry, I won't peek. Yet." She laughed again, leaving him flustered. "Your clothes were drenched—I think the shirt's a lost cause. Relax," she told him as she set the tray on his lap. "My brother-in-law and future brother-in-law got you into bed."

"Oh." It looked as though he was back to single syllables.

"Try the tea," she suggested. "You probably swallowed a gallon of sea water, so I'll bet your throat's raw." She saw the intense concentration in his eyes and the nagging pain behind it. "Headache?"

"Vicious."

"I'll be back." She left him, trailing some potently exotic scent in her wake.

Max used the time alone to build back what little strength he had. He hated being weak—a leftover obsession from childhood when he'd been puny and asthmatic. His father had given up in disgust on building his only and disappointing son into a football star. Though he knew it was illogical, sickness brought back unhappy memories of childhood.

Because he'd always considered his mind stronger than his body, he used it now to block the pain.

Moments later, she was back with an aspirin and witch hazel. "Take a couple of these. After you eat, I can drive you into the hospital."

"Hospital?"

"You might want to have a doctor take a look."

"No." He swallowed the pills. "I don't think so."

"Up to you." She sat on the bed to study him, one leg lazily swinging to some inner tune.

Never in his life had he been so sexually aware of a woman—of the texture of her skin, the subtle tones of it, the shape of her body, her eyes, her mouth. The assault on his senses left him uneasy and baffled. He'd nearly drowned, he reminded himself. Now all he could think about was getting his hands on the woman who'd saved him. Saved his life, he remembered.

"I haven't even thanked you."

"I figured you'd get around to it. Try those eggs before they get any colder. You need food."

Obediently he scooped some up. "Can you tell me what happened?"

"From the time I came into it." Relaxed, she brushed her hair behind her shoulder and settled more comfortably on the bed. "I drove down to the beach. Impulse," she said with a lazy movement of her shoulders. "I'd been watching the storm build from the tower."

"The tower?"

"Here, in the house," she explained. "I got the urge to go down, watch it roll in from sea. Then I saw you." In a careless gesture, she brushed the hair back from his brow. "You were in trouble, so I went in. We sort of pulled each other to shore."

"I remember. You kissed me."

Her lips curved. "I figured we both deserved it." She touched a gentle hand to the bruise spreading on his shoulder. "You hit the rocks. What were you doing out there?"

"I..." He closed his eyes to try to clear his fuzzy brain. The effort had sweat pearling on his brow. "I'm not sure."

"Okay, why don't we start with your name?"

"My name?" He opened his eyes to give her a blank look. "Don't you know?"

"We didn't have the chance to introduce ourselves formally. Lilah Calhoun," she said, and offered a hand.

"Quartermain." He accepted her hand, relieved that much was clear. "Maxwell Quartermain."

"Drink some more tea, Max. Ginseng's good for you." Taking the witch hazel, she began to rub it gently over the bruise. "What do you do?"

"I'm, ah, a history professor at Cornell." Her fingers eased the ache in his shoulder and cajoled him into relaxing.

"Tell me about Maxwell Quartermain." She wanted to take his mind off the pain, to see him relax into sleep again. "Where are you from?"

"I grew up in Indiana..." Her fingers slid up to his neck to unknot muscles.

"Farm boy?"

"No." He sighed as the tension eased and made her smile. "My parents ran a market. I used to help out after school and over the summer."

"Did you like it?"

His eyes were growing heavy. "It was all right. It gave me plenty of time to study. Annoyed my father—always had my face in a book. He didn't understand. I skipped a couple grades and got into Cornell."

"Scholarship?" she assumed.

"Hmm. Got my doctorate," The words were slurred and weighty. "Do you know how much man accomplished between 1870 and 1970?"

"Amazing."

"Absolutely." He was nearly asleep, coaxed into comfort by her quiet voice and gentle hands. "I'd like to have been alive in 1910."

"Maybe you were." She smiled, amused and charmed. "Take a nap, Max."

When he awakened again, he was alone. But he had a dozen throbbing aches to keep him company. He noted that she had left the aspirin and a carafe of water beside the bed, and gratefully swallowed pills.

When that small chore exhausted him, he leaned back to catch his breath. The sunlight was bright, streaming through the open terrace doors with fresh sea air. He'd lost his sense of time, and though it was tempting just to lie back and shut his eyes again, he needed to take back some sort of control.

Maybe she'd read his mind, he thought as he saw his pants and someone else's shirt neatly folded at the foot of the bed. He rose creakily, like an old man with brittle bones and aching muscles. His body sang a melody of pain as he picked up the clothes and peeked through a side door. He eyed the claw-footed tub and chrome shower works with pleasure.

The pipes thudded when he turned on the spray, and so did his muscles as the water beat against his skin. But ten minutes later, he felt almost alive.

It wasn't easy to dry off—even that simple task had his limbs singing. Not sure the news would be good, he wiped the mist from the mirror to study his face.

Beneath the stubble of beard, his skin was white and drawn. Flowering out from the bandage at his temple was a purpling bruise. He already knew there were plenty more blooming on his body. As a result of salt water, his eyes were a patriotic red, white and blue. Though he'd never considered himself a vain man—his looks had always struck him as dead average—he turned away from the mirror.

Wincing and groaning and swearing under his breath, he struggled into the clothes.

The shirt fit fairly well. Better, in fact, than many of his own. Shopping intimidated him—rather salesclerks intimidated him with their bright, impatient smiles. Most of the time Max shopped out of catalogues and took what came.

Glancing down at his bare feet, Max admitted that he'd have to go shopping for shoes—and soon.

Moving slowly, he walked out onto the terrace. The sunlight stung his eyes, but the breezy, moist air felt like heaven. And the view... For a moment he could only stop and stare, hardly even breathing. Water and rock and flowers. It was like being on top of the world and looking down at a small and perfect slice of the planet. The colors were vibrant—sapphire, emerald, the ruby red of roses, the pristine white of sails pregnant with wind. There was no sound but the rumble of the sea and then, far off, the musical gong of a buoy. He could smell hot summer flowers and the cool tang of the ocean.

With his hand braced on the wall, he began to walk. He didn't know which direction he should take, so wandered aimlessly and with no little effort. Once, when dizziness overtook him, he was forced to stop, shut his eyes and breathe his way through it.

When he came to a set of stairs leading up, he opted to climb them. His legs were wobbly, and he could already feel fatigue tugging at him. It was pride as much as curiosity that had him continuing.

The house was built of granite, a sober and sturdy stone that did nothing to take away from the fancy of the architecture. Max felt as though he were exploring the circumference of a castle, some stubborn bulwark of early history that had taken its place upon the cliffs and held it for generations.

Then he heard the anachronistic buzz of a power saw and a man's casual oath. Walking closer, he recognized the busy noises of construction in progress—the slap of hammer on wood, the tinny music from a portable radio, the whirl of drills. When his path was blocked by sawhorses, lumber and tarps, he knew he'd found the source.

A man stepped out of another set of terrace doors. Reddish-blond hair was tousled around a tanned face. He squinted at Max, then hooked his thumbs in his pockets. "Up and around, I see."

"More or less."

The guy looked as if he'd been kicked by a team of mules, Sloan thought. His face was dead white, his eyes bruised, his skin sheened with the sweat of effort. He was holding himself upright through sheer stubbornness. It made it tough to hold on to suspicions.

"Sloan O'Riley," he said, and offered a hand.

"Maxwell Quartermain."

"So I hear. Lilah says you're a history professor. Taking a vacation?"

"No." Max's brow furrowed. "No, I don't think so."

It wasn't evasion Sloan saw in his eyes, but puzzlement, laced with frustration. "Guess you're still a little rattled."

"I guess." Absently he reached up to touch the bandage at his temple. "I was on a boat," he murmured, straining to visualize it. "Working." On what? "The water was pretty rough. I wanted to go on deck, get some air..." Standing at the rail, deck heaving. Panic. "I think I fell—" Jumped, was thrown. "—I must have fallen overboard."

"Funny nobody reported it."

"Sloan, leave the man alone. Does he look like an international jewel thief?" Lilah strolled lazily up the steps, a short-haired black dog at her heels. The dog jumped at Sloan, tripped, righted himself and managed to get his front paws settled on the knees of Sloan's jeans.

"I wondered where you'd wandered off to," Lilah continued, and cupped a hand under Max's chin to examine his face. "You look a little better," she decided as the dog started to sniff at Max's bare toes. "That's Fred," she told him. "He only bites criminals."

"Oh. Good."

"Since you have his seal of approval, why don't you come down? You can sit in the sun and have some lunch."

He would dearly love to sit, he realized and let Lilah lead him away. "Is this really your house?"

"Hearth and home. My great-grandfather built it just after the turn of the century. Look out for Fred." The dog dashed between them, stepped on his own ear and yelped. Max, who'd gone through a long clumsy stage himself, felt immediate sympathy. "We're thinking of giving him ballet lessons," she said as the dog struggled back to his feet. Noting the blank look on Max's face, she patted his cheek. "I think you could use some of Aunt Coco's chicken soup."

She made him sit and kept an eye on him while he ate. Her protective instincts were usually reserved for family or small, wounded birds. But something about the man tugged at her. He seemed so out of his element, she thought. And helpless with it.

Something was going on behind those big blue eyes, she thought. Something beyond the fatigue. She could almost see him struggle to put one mental foot in front of the other.

He began to think that the soup had saved his life as surely as Lilah had. It slid warm and vital into his system. "I fell out of a boat," he said abruptly.

"That would explain it."

"I don't know what I was doing on a boat, exactly."

In the chair beside him she brought up her limber legs to settle in the lotus position. "Taking a vacation?"

"No." His brow furrowed. "No, I don't take vacations."

"Why not?" She reached over to take one of the crackers from his plate. She wore a trio of glittering rings on her hand.

"Work."

"School's out," she said with a lazy stretch.

"I always teach summer courses. Except..." Something was tapping at the edges of his brain, tauntingly. "I was going to do something else this summer. A research project. And I was going to start a book."

"A book, really?" She savored the cracker as if it were laced with caviar. He had to admire her basic, sensual enjoyment. "What kind?"

Her words jerked him back. He'd never told anyone about his plans to write. No one who knew him would have believed that studious, steady-as-she-goes Quartermain dreamed of being a novelist. "It's just something I've been thinking of for a while, but I had a chance to work on this project...a family history."

"Well, that would suit you. I was a terrible student. Lazy," she said with a smile in her eyes. "I can't imagine anyone wanting to make a career out of a classroom. Do you like it?"

It wasn't a matter of liking it. It was what he did. "I'm good at it." Yes, he realized, he was good at it. His students learned—some more than others. His lectures were well attended and well received.

"That's not the same thing. Can I see your hand?"

"My what?"

"Your hand," she repeated, and took it, turning it palm up. "Hmm."

"What are you doing?" For a heady moment, he thought she would press her lips to it.

"Looking at your palm. More intelligence than intuitiveness. Or maybe you just trust your brains more than your instincts."

Staring at the top of her bent head, he gave a nervous laugh. "You don't really believe in that sort of thing. Palm reading."

"Of course—but it's not just the lines, it's the feeling." She glanced up briefly with a smile that was at once languid and electric. "You have very nice hands. Look here." She skimmed a finger along his palm and had him swallowing. "You've got a long life ahead of you, but see this break? Near-death experience."

"You're making it up."

"They're your lines," she reminded him. "A good imagination. I think you'll write that book—but you'll have to work on that self-confidence."

She looked up again, a trace of sympathy on her face. "Rough childhood?"

"Yes—no." Embarrassed, he cleared his throat. "No more than anyone's, I imagine."

She lifted a brow, but let it pass. "Well, you're a big boy now." In one of her casual moves, she slid her hair back then studied his hand again. "Yes, see, this represents careers, and there's a branch off this way. Things have been very comfortable for you professionally—you've hoed yourself a nice little rut—but this other line spears off. Could be that literary effort. You'll have to make the choice."

"I really don't think—"

"Sure you do. You've been thinking about it for years. Now here's the Mound of Venus. Hmm. You're a very sensual man." Her gaze flicked up to his again. "And a very thorough lover."

He couldn't take his eyes off her mouth. It was full, unpainted and curved teasingly. Kissing her would be like sinking into a dream—the dark and erotic kind. And if a man survived it, he would pray never to wake up.

She felt something creep in over her amusement. Something unexpected and arousing. It was the way he looked at her, she thought. With such complete absorption. As though she were the only woman in the world—certainly the only one who mattered.

There couldn't be a female alive who wouldn't weaken a bit under that look.

For the first time in her life she felt off balance with a man. She was used to having the controls, of setting the tone in her own unstudied way. From the time she'd understood that boys were different from girls, she had used the power she'd been born with to guide members of the opposite sex down a path of her own choosing.

Yet he was throwing her off with a look.

Struggling for a casualness that had always come easily, she started to release his hand. Max surprised them both by turning his over to grip hers.

"You are," he said slowly, "the most beautiful woman I've ever seen."

It was a standard line, even a cliché, and shouldn't have had her heart leaping. She made herself smile as she drew away. "Don't get out much, do you, Professor?"

There was a flicker of annoyance in his eyes before he made himself settle back. It was as much with himself as with her. He'd never been the hand-holding Casanova type. Nor had he ever been put so neatly back in his place.

"No, but that was a simple statement of fact. Now, I guess I'm supposed to cross your palm with silver, but I'm fresh out."

"Palm reading's on the house." Because she was sorry she'd been so glib and abrupt, she smiled again. "When you're feeling better, I'll take you up for a tour of the haunted tower."

"I can't wait."

His dry response had her laughing. "I have a feeling about you, Max. I think you could be a lot of fun when you forget to be intense and thoughtful. Now I'm going downstairs so you can have some quiet. Be a good boy and get some more rest."

He might have been weak, but he wasn't a boy. Max rose as she did. Though the move surprised her, she gave him one of her slow, languid smiles. His color was coming back, she noted. His eyes were clear and, because he was only an inch or so taller than she, nearly on level with hers.

"Is there something else I can get you, Max?"

He felt steadier and took a moment to be grateful. "Just an answer. Are you involved with anyone?"

Her brow lifted as she swept her hair over her shoulder. "In what way?"

"It's a simple question, Lilah, and deserves a simple answer."

The lecturing quality of his tone had her frowning at him. "If you mean am I emotionally or sexually involved with a man, the answer is no. At the moment."

"Good." The vague irritation in her eyes pleased him. He'd wanted a response, and he'd gotten one.

"Look, Professor, I pulled you out of the drink. You strike me as being too intelligent a man to fall for that gratitude transference."

This time he smiled. "Transference to what?"

"Lust seems appropriate."

"You're right. I know the difference—especially when I'm feeling both at the same time." His own words surprised him. Maybe the near-death experience had rattled his brains. For a moment she looked as though she would swipe at him. Then abruptly, and beautifully, she laughed.

"I guess that was another simple statement of fact. You're an interesting man, Max."

And, she told herself as she carried the tray inside, harmless.

She hoped.

Chapter Three

Even after he'd arranged to have funds wired from his account in Ithaca, the Calhouns wouldn't consider Max's suggestion that he move to a hotel. In truth, he didn't put up much of a fight. He'd never been pampered before, or fussed over. More, he'd never been made to feel part of a big, boisterous family. They took him in with a casual kind of hospitality that was both irresistible and gracious.

He was coming to know them and appreciate them for their varied personalities and family unity. It was a house where something always seemed to be happening and where everyone always had something to say. For someone who had grown up an only child, in a home where his bookishness had been considered a flaw, it was a revelation to be among people who celebrated their own, and each others', interests.

C.C. was an auto mechanic who talked about engine blocks and carried the mysterious glow of a new bride. Amanda, brisk and organized, held the assistant manager's position at a nearby hotel. Suzanna ran a gardening business and devoted herself to her children. No one mentioned their father. Coco ran the house, cooked lavish meals and appreciated male company. She'd only made Max nervous when she'd threatened to read his tea leaves.

Then there was Lilah. He discovered she worked as a naturalist at Acadia National Park. She liked long naps, classical music and her aunt's elaborate desserts. When the mood struck her, she could sit, sprawled in a chair, prodding little details of his life from him. Or she could curl up in a sunbeam like a cat, blocking him and everything else around her out of her thoughts while she drifted into one of her private daydreams. Then she would stretch and smile and let them all in again.

She remained a mystery to him, a combination of smoldering sensuality and untouched innocence—of staggering openness and unreachable solitude.

Within three days, his strength had returned and his stay at the The Towers was open-ended. He knew the sensible thing to do was leave, use his funds to purchase a one-way ticket back to New York and see if he could pick up a few summer tutoring jobs.

But he didn't feel sensible.

It was his first vacation and, however he had been thrust into it, he wanted to enjoy it. He liked waking up in the morning to the sound of the sea and the smell of it. It relieved him that his accident hadn't caused him to fear or dislike the water. There was something incredibly relaxing about standing on the terrace, looking across indigo or emerald water and seeing the distant clumps of islands.

And if his shoulder still troubled him from time to time, he could sit out and let the afternoon sun bake the ache away. There was time for books. An hour, even two, sitting in the shade gobbling up a novel or biography from the Calhoun library.

His life had been full of time tables, never timelessness. Here, in The Towers, with its whispers of the past, momentum of the present and hope for the future, he could indulge in it.

Underneath the simple pleasure of having no schedule to meet, no demands to answer, was his growing fascination with Lilah.

She glided in and out of the house. Leaving in the morning, she was neat and tidy in her park service uniform, her fabulous hair wound in a neat braid. Drifting home later, she would change into one of her flowing skirts or a pair of sexy shorts. She smiled at him, spoke to him, and kept a friendly but tangible distance.

He contented himself with scribbling in a notebook or entertaining Suzanna's two children, Alex and Jenny, who were already showing signs of summer boredom. He could walk in the gardens or along the cliffs, keep Coco company in the kitchen or watch the workmen in the west wing.

The wonder of it was, he could do as he chose.

He sat on the lawn, Alex and Jenny hunched on either side of him like eager frogs. The sun was a hazy silver disk behind a sheet of clouds. Playful and brisk, the breeze carried the scent of lavender and rosemary from a nearby rockery. There were butterflies dancing in the grass, easily eluding Fred's pursuits. Nearby a bird trilled insistently from the branch of a wind-gnarled oak.

Max was spinning a tale of a young boy caught up in the terrors and excitement of the revolutionary war. In weaving fact with fiction, he was keeping the children entertained and indulging in his love of storytelling.

"I bet he killed whole packs of dirty redcoats," Alex said gleefully. At six, he had a vivid and violent imagination.

"Packs of them," Jenny agreed. She was a year younger than her brother and only too glad to keep pace. "Single-handed."

"The Revolution wasn't all guns and bayonets, you know." It amused Max to see the young mouths pout at the lack of mayhem. "A lot of battles were won through intrigue and espionage."

Alex struggled with the words a moment then brightened. "Spies?"

"Spies," Max agreed, and ruffled the boy's dark hair. Because he had experienced the lack himself, he recognized Alex's hunger for a male bond.

Using a teenage boy as the catalyst, he took them through Patrick Henry's stirring speeches, Samuel Adams's courageous Sons of Liberty, through the politics and purpose of a rebellious young country to the Boston Tea Party.

Then as he had the young hero heaving chests of tea into the shallow water of Boston Harbor, Max saw Lilah drifting across the lawn.

She moved with languid ease over the grass, a graceful gypsy with her filmy chiffon skirt teased by the wind. Her hair was loose, tumbling free over the thin straps of a pale green blouse. Her feet were bare, her arms adorned with dozens of slim bracelets.

Fred raced over to greet her, leaped and yipped and made her laugh. As she bent to pet him, one of the straps slid down her arm. Then the dog bounded off, tripping himself up, to continue his fruitless chase of butterflies.

She straightened, lazily pushing the strap back into place as she continued across the grass. He caught her scent—wild and free—before she spoke.

"Is this a private party?"

"Max is telling a story," Jenny told her, and tugged on her aunt's skirt.

"A story?" The array of colored beads in her ears danced as she lowered to the grass. "I like stories."

"Tell Lilah, too." Jenny shifted closer to her aunt and began to play with her bracelets.

"Yes." There was laughter in her voice, an answering humor in her eyes as they met Max's. "Tell Lilah, too."

She knew exactly what effect she had on a man, he thought. Exactly. "Ah . . . where was I?"

"Jim had black cork all over his face and was tossing the cursed tea into the harbor," Alex reminded him. "Nobody got shot yet."

"Right." As much for his own defense against Lilah as for the children, Max put himself back on the frigate with the fictional Jim. He could feel the chill of the air and the heat of excitement. With a natural skill he considered a basic part of teaching, he drew out the suspense, deftly coloring his characters, describing an historical event in a way that had Lilah studying him with a new interest and respect.

Though it ended with the rebels outwitting the British, without firing a shot, even the bloodthirsty Alex wasn't disappointed.

"They won!" He jumped up and gave a war hoot. "I'm a Son of Liberty and you're a dirty redcoat," he told his sister.

"Uh-uh." She sprang to her feet.

"No taxation without restoration," Alex bellowed, and went flying for the house with Jenny hot on his heels and Fred lumbering after them both.

"Close enough," Max murmured.

"Pretty crafty, Professor." Lilah leaned back on her elbows to watch him through half-closed eyes. "Making history entertaining."

"It is," he told her. "It's not just dates and names, it's people."

"The way you tell it. But when I was in school you were supposed to know what happened in 1066 in the same way you were supposed to memorize the multiplication tables." Lazily she rubbed a bare foot over her calf. "I still can't remember the twelves, or what happened in 1066—unless that was when Hannibal took those elephants across the Alps."

He grinned at her. "Not exactly."

"There, you see?" She stretched, long and limber as a cat. Her head drifted back, her hair spreading over the summer grass. Her shoulders rolled so that the wayward strap slipped down again. The pleasure of the small indulgence showed on her face. "And I think I usually fell asleep by the time we got to the Continental Congress."

When he realized he was holding his breath, he released it slowly. "I've been thinking about doing some tutoring."

Her eyes slitted open. "You can take the boy out of the classroom," she murmured, then arched a brow. "So, what do you know about flora and fauna?"

"Enough to know a rabbit from a petunia."

Delighted, she sat up again to lean toward him. "That's very good, Professor. If the mood strikes, maybe we can exchange expertise."

"Maybe."

He looked so cute, she thought, sitting on the sunny grass in borrowed jeans and T-shirt, his hair falling over his forehead. He'd been getting some sun, so that the pallor was replaced by the beginnings of a tan. The ease she felt convinced her that she'd been foolish to be unsteady around him before. He was just a nice man, a bit befuddled by circumstances, who'd aroused her sympathies and her curiosity. To prove it, she laid a hand on the side of his face.

Max saw the amusement in her eyes, the little private joke that curved her lips before she touched them to his in a light, friendly kiss. As if satisfied with the result, she smiled, leaned back and started to speak. He circled a hand around her wrist.

"I'm not half-dead this time, Lilah."

Surprise came first. He saw it register then fade into a careless acceptance. Damn it, he thought as he slid a hand behind her neck. She was so certain there would be nothing. With a combination of wounded pride and fluttery panic, he pressed his lips to hers.

She enjoyed kissing—the affection of it, the elemental physical enjoyment. And she liked him. Because of it, she leaned into the kiss, expecting a nice tingle, a comforting warmth. But she hadn't expected the jolt.

The kiss bounced through her system, starting with her lips, zipping to her stomach, vibrating into her fingertips. His mouth was very firm, very serious—and very smooth. The texture of it had a quiet sound of pleasure escaping, like a child might make after a first taste of chocolate. Before the first sensation could be fully absorbed, others were drifting through to tangle and mix.

Flowers and hot sun. The scent of soap and sweat. Smooth, damp lips and the light scrape of teeth. Her own sigh, a mere shifting of air, and the firm press of his fingers on the sensitive nape of her neck. There was something more than simple pleasure here, she realized. Something sweeter and far less tangible.

Enchanted, she lifted her hand from the carpet of grass to skim it through his hair.

He was reexperiencing the sensation of drowning, of being pulled under by something strong and dangerous. This time he had no urge to fight. Fascinated, he slid his tongue over hers, tasting those secret flavors. Rich and dark and seductive, they mirrored her scent, the scent that had already insinuated itself into his system so that he thought he would taste that as well, each time he took a breath.

He felt something shift inside him, stretch and grow and heat until it gripped him hard by the throat.

She was outrageously sexual, unabashedly erotic, and more frightening than any woman he had known. Again he had the image of a mermaid sitting on a rock, combing her hair and luring helplessly seduced men to destruction with the promise of overwhelming pleasures.

The instinct for survival kicked in, so that he drew back. Lilah stayed as she was, eyes closed, lips parted. It wasn't until that moment that he realized he still held her wrist and that her pulse was scrambling under his fingers.

Slowly, holding on to that drugging weightlessness a moment longer, she opened her eyes. She skimmed her tongue over her lips to capture the clinging flavor of his. Then she smiled.

"Well, Dr. Quartermain, it seems history's not the only thing you're good at. How about another lesson?" Wanting more, she leaned forward, but Max scrambled up. The ground, he discovered, was as unsteady as the deck of a ship.

"I think one's enough for today."

Curious, she swung her hair back to look up at him. "Why?"

"Because..." Because if he kissed her again, he'd have to touch her. And if he touched her—and he desperately wanted to touch her—he would have to make love with her, there on the sunny lawn in full sight of the house. "Because I don't want to take advantage of you."

"Advantage of me?" Touched and amused, she smiled. "That's very sweet."

"I'd appreciate it if you wouldn't make me sound like a fool," he said tightly.

"Was I?" The smile turned thoughtful. "Being a sweet man doesn't make you a fool, Max. It's just that most men I know would be more than happy to take advantage. Tell you what, before you take offense at that, why don't we go inside? I'll show you Bianca's tower."

He'd already taken offense and was about to say so when her last words struck a chord. "Bianca's tower?"

"Yes. I'd like to show you." She lifted a hand, waiting.

He was frowning at her, struggling to fit the name "Bianca" into place. Then with a shake of his head, he helped her to her feet. "Fine. Let's go."

He'd already explored some of the house, the maze of rooms, some empty, some crowded with furniture and boxes. From the outside, the house was part fortress, part manor, with sparkling windows, graceful porches married to jutting turrets and parapets. Inside, it was a rambling labyrinth of shadowed hallways, sun-washed rooms, scarred floors and gleaming banisters. It had already captivated him.

She took him up a set of circular stairs to a door at the top of the east wing.

"Give it a shove, will you, Max?" she asked, and he was forced to thud the wood hard with his good shoulder. "I keep meaning to ask Sloan to fix this." Taking his hand, she walked inside.

It was a large, circular room, ringed with curving windows. A light layer of dust lay softly on the floor, but someone had tossed a few colorful pillows onto the window seat. An old floor lamp with a stained and tassled shade stood nearby.

"I imagine she had lovely things up here once," Lilah began. "To keep her company. She used to come up here to be alone, to think."

"Who?"

"Bianca. My great-grandmother. Come look at the view." Feeling a need to share it with him, she drew him to the window. From there it was all water and rock. It should have seemed lonely, Max thought. Instead it was exhilarating and heartbreaking all at once. When he put a hand to the glass, Lilah glanced over in surprise. She had done the same countless times, as if wishing for something just out of reach.

"It's...sad." He'd meant to say beautiful or breathtaking, and frowned.

"Yes. But sometimes it's comforting, too. I always feel close to Bianca in here."

Bianca. The name was like an insistent buzz in his head.

"Has Aunt Coco told you the story yet?"

"No. Is there a story?"

"Of course." She gave him a curious look. "I just wondered if she'd given you the Calhoun version rather than what's in the press."

A faint throbbing began in his temple where the wound was healing. "I don't know either version."

After a moment, she continued. "Bianca threw herself through this window on one of the last nights of summer in 1913. But her spirit stayed behind."

"Why did she kill herself?"

"Well, it's a long story." Lilah settled on the window seat, her chin comfortably propped on her knees, and told him.

Max listened to the tale of an unhappy wife, trapped in a loveless marriage during the heady years before the Great War. Bianca had married Fergus Calhoun, a wealthy financier, and had borne him three children. While summering on Mount Desert Island, she had met a young artist. From an old date book the Calhouns had unearthed, they knew his name had been Christian, but nothing more. The rest was legend, that had been passed down to the children from their nanny who had been Bianca's confidante.

The young artist and the unhappy wife had fallen in love, deeply. Torn between duty and her heart, Bianca had agonized over her choice and had ultimately decided to leave her husband. She had taken a few personal items, known now as Bianca's treasure, and had hidden them away in preparation. Among them had been an emerald necklace, given to her on the birth of her first son and second child, Lilah's grandfather. But rather than going to her lover, Bianca had thrown herself through the tower window. The emeralds have never been found.

"We didn't know the story until a few months ago," Lilah added. "Though I'd seen the emeralds."

His mind was whirling. Nagged by the pain, he pressed his fingers to his temple. "You've seen them?"

She smiled. "I dreamed about them. Then during a séance—"

"A séance," he said weakly, and sat.

"That's right." She laughed and patted his hand. "We were having a séance, and C.C. had a vision." He made a strangled sound in his throat that had her laughing again. "You had to be there, Max. Anyway, C.C. saw the necklace, and that's when Aunt Coco decided it was time to pass on the Calhoun legend. To get where we are today, Trent fell in love with C.C. and decided not to buy The Towers. We were in pretty bad shape and were on the point of being forced to sell. He came up with the idea of turning the west wing into a hotel, with the St. James's name. You know the St. James hotels?"

Trenton St. James, Max thought. Lilah's brother-in-law owned one of the biggest hotel corporations in the country. "By reputation."

"Well, Trent hired Sloan to handle the renovations—and Sloan fell for Amanda. All in all, it couldn't have worked out better. We were able to keep the house, combine it with business, and culled two romances out of the bargain."

Annoyance flickered into her eyes, darkening them. "The downside has been that the story about the necklace leaked, and we've been plagued with hopeful treasure hunters and out-and-out thieves. Just a few weeks ago, some creep nearly killed Amanda and stole stacks of the papers we'd been sorting through to try to find a clue to the necklace."

"Papers," he repeated as a sickness welled in his stomach. It was coming back now and with such force he felt as though he were being battered on the rocks again. Calhoun, emeralds, Bianca.

"What's wrong, Max?" Concerned, Lilah leaned over to lay a hand on his brow. "You're white as a sheet. You've been up too long," she decided. "Let me take you down so you can rest."

"No, I'm fine. It's nothing." He jerked away to rise and pace the room. How was he going to tell her? How could he tell her, after she had saved his life, taken care of him? After he'd kissed her? The Calhouns had opened their home to him, without hesitation, without question. They had trusted him. How could he tell Lilah that he had, however inadvertently, been working with men who were planning to steal from her?

Yet he had to. Marrow-deep honesty wouldn't permit anything else.

"Lilah . . ." He turned back to see her watching him, a combination of concern and wariness in her eyes. "The boat. I remember the boat."

Relief had her smiling. "That's good. I thought it would come back to you if you stopped worrying. Why don't you sit down, Max? It's easier on the brain."

"No." The refusal was sharp as he concentrated on her face. "The boat—the man who hired me. His name was Caufield. Ellis Caufield."

She spread her hands. "And?"

"The name doesn't mean anything?"

"No, should it?"

Maybe he was wrong, Max thought. Maybe he was letting her family story meld in his mind with his own experience. "He's about six foot, very trim. About forty. Dark-blond hair graying at the temples."

"Okay."

Max let out a frustrated breath. "He contacted me at Cornell about a month ago and offered me a job. He wanted me to sort through, catalogue and research some family papers. I'd get a generous salary, and several weeks on a yacht—plus all my expenses and time to work on my book."

"So, seeing as you're not brain damaged, you took the job."

"Yes, but damn it, Lilah, the papers—the receipts, the letters the ledgers. They had your name on them."

"Mine?"

"Calhoun." He jammed his useless hands into his pockets. "Don't you understand? I was hired, and worked on that boat for a week, researching your family history from the papers that were stolen from you."

She only stared. It seemed a long time to Max before she unfolded herself from the window seat and stood. "You're telling me that you've been working for the man who tried to kill my sister?"

"Yes."

She never took her eyes from his. He could almost feel her trying to get into his thoughts, but when she spoke, her voice was very cool. "Why are you telling me this now?"

Frazzled, he dragged a hand through his hair. "I didn't remember it all until now, until you told me about the emeralds."

"That's odd, isn't it?"

He watched the shutter come down over her eyes and nodded. "I don't expect you to believe me, but I didn't remember. And when I took the job, I didn't know."

She continued to watch him carefully, measuring every word, every gesture, every expression. "You know, it seemed strange to me that you hadn't heard about the necklace, or the robbery. It's been in the press for weeks. You'd have to be living in a cave not to have heard."

"Or a classroom," he murmured. Caufield's mocking words about having more intelligence than wit came back to him and made him wince. "Look, I'll tell you whatever I can before I leave."

"Leave?"

"I can't imagine any of you will want me to stay after this."

She considered him, instinct warring against common sense. With a long sigh, she lifted a hand. "I think you'd better tell the whole story to the whole family, all at once. Then we'll decide what to do about it."

It was Max's first family meeting. He hadn't grown up in a democracy, but under his father's uncompromising dictatorship. The Calhouns did things different. They gathered around the big mahogany dining room table, so completely united that Max felt like an intruder for the first time since he'd awakened upstairs. They listened, occasionally asking questions as he repeated what he had told Lilah in the tower.

"You didn't check his references?" Trent asked. "You just contracted to do a job with a man you'd never met, and knew nothing about?"

"There didn't seem to be any reason to. I'm not a businessman," he said wearily. "I'm a teacher."

"Then you won't object if we check yours." This from Sloan.

Max met the suspicious eyes levelly. "No."

"I already have," Amanda put in. Her fingers were tapping against the wood of the table as all eyes turned to her. "It seemed the logical step, so I made a couple of calls."

"Leave it to Mandy," Lilah muttered. "I guess it never occurred to you to discuss it with the rest of us."

"No."

"Girls," Coco said from the head of the table. "Don't start."

"I think Amanda should have talked about this." The Calhoun temper edged Lilah's voice. "It concerns all of us. Besides, what business does she have poking into Max's life?"

They began to argue heatedly, all four sisters tossing in opinions and objections. Sloan kicked back to let it run its course. Trent closed his eyes. Max merely stared. They were discussing him. Didn't they realize they were arguing about him, tossing him back and forth across the table like a Ping-Pong ball?

"Excuse me," he began, and was totally ignored. He tried again and earned his first smile from Sloan. "Damn it, knock it off!" It was his annoyed professor's voice and did the trick. All of the women stopped to turn on him with irritated eyes.

"Look, buster," C.C. began, but he cut her off.

"You look. In the first place, why would I be telling you everything if I had some ulterior motive? And since you want to corroborate who I am and what I do, why don't you stop pecking at each other long enough to find out?"

"Because we like to peck at each other," Lilah told him grandly. "And we don't like anyone getting in the way while we're at it."

"That'll do." Coco took advantage of the lull. "Since Amanda's already checked on Max—though it was a bit impolite—"

"Sensible," Amanda objected.

"Rude," Lilah corrected.

They might have been off and running again, but Suzanna held up a hand. "Whatever it was, it's done. I think we should hear what Amanda found out."

"As I was saying." Amanda flicked a glance over Lilah. "I made a couple of calls. The dean of Cornell speaks very highly of Max. As I recall the terms were 'brilliant' and 'dedicated.' He's considered one of the foremost experts on American history in the country. He graduated magna cum laude at twenty, and had his doctorate by twenty-five."

"Egghead," Lilah said with a comforting smile when Max shifted in his seat.

"Our Dr. Quartermain," Amanda continued, "comes from Indiana, is single and has no criminal record. He's been on the staff at Cornell for over eight years, and has published several well-received articles. His most recent was an overview of the social-political atmosphere in America prior to World War I. In academic circles, he's considered a wunderkind, serious minded, unflaggingly responsible, with unlimited potential." Sensing his embarrassment, Amanda softened her tone. "I'm sorry for intruding, Max, but I didn't want to take any chances, not with my family."

"We're all sorry." Suzanna smiled at him. "We've had an unsettling couple of months."

"I understand that." And they certainly couldn't know how much he detested the term *wunderkind*. "If my academic profile eases your minds, that's fine."

"There's one more thing," Suzanna continued. "None of this explains what you were doing in the water the night Lilah found you."

Max gathered his thoughts while they waited. It was easy to take himself back now, as easy as it was for him to put himself into the Battle of Bull Run or Woodrow Wilson's White House.

"I'd been working on the papers. A storm was coming in so the sea was rough. I guess I'm not much of a sailor. I was trying to crawl out on deck, for some air, when I heard Caufield talking to Captain Hawkins."

As concisely as he could, he told them what he had heard, how he had realized what he'd gotten into.

"I don't know what I was going to do. I had some wild idea about getting the papers and getting off the boat so I could take them to the police. Not very brilliant considering the circumstances. In any case, they caught me. Caufield had a gun, but this time the storm was on my side. I got up on deck, and took my chances in the water."

"You jumped overboard, in the middle of a storm?" Lilah asked.

"It wasn't very smart."

"It was very brave," she corrected.

"Not when you consider he was shooting at me." Frowning, Max rubbed a hand over the bandage on his temple.

"The way you describe this Ellis Caufield doesn't fit." Amanda tapped her fingers again as she thought it through. "Livingston, the man who stole the papers was dark haired, only about thirty."

"So, he dyed his hair." Lilah lifted her hands. "He couldn't come back using the same name and the same appearance. The police have his description."

"I hope you're right." A slow, humorless smile spread over Sloan's face. "I hope the sonofabitch is back so I can have another go at him."

"So we all can have another go at him," C.C. corrected. "The question is, what do we do now?"

They began to argue about that, with Trent telling his wife she wasn't going to do anything—Amanda reminding him it was a Calhoun problem—Sloan suggesting hotly that she keep out of it. Coco decided it was time for brandy and was ignored.

"He thinks I'm dead," Max murmured, almost to himself. "So he feels safe. He's probably still close by, on the same boat. The *Windrider*."

"You remember the boat?" Lilah held up a hand, signaling for silence. "You can describe it?"

"In detail," Max told her with a small smile. "It was my first yacht."

"So we take that information to the police." Trent glanced around the table, then nodded. "And we do a little checking ourselves. The ladies know the island as well as they know this house. If he's on it, or around it, we'll find him."

"I'm looking forward to it." Sloan glanced over at Max and went with his instincts. "You in, Quartermain?"

Surprised, Max blinked, then found himself smiling. "Yeah, I'm in."

I went to Christian's cottage. Perhaps it was risky as I might have been seen by some acquaintance, but I wanted so badly to see where he lived, how he lived, what small things he kept around him.

It's a small place near the water, a square wooden cottage with its rooms crowded with his paintings and smelling of turpentine. Above the kitchen is a sun-drenched loft for his studio. It seemed to me like a doll's house with its pretty windows and low ceilings—old leafy trees shading the front and a narrow porch dancing along the back where we could sit and watch the water.

Christian says that at low tide the water level drops so that you can walk across the smooth rocks to the little glade of trees beyond. And at night, the air is full of sound. Musical crickets, the hoot of owls, the lap of temperate water.

I felt at home there, as quietly content as I have been in my life. It seemed to me that we had lived there together for years. When I told Christian, he gathered me close, just to hold me.

"I love you, Bianca," he said. "I wanted you to come here. I needed to see you in my house, watch you stand among my things." When he drew me away, he was smiling. "Now, I'll always see you here, and I'll never be without you."

I wanted to swear to him I would stay. God, the words leaped into my throat only to be blocked there by duty. Wretched duty. He must have sensed it for he kissed me then, as if to seal the words inside.

I had only an hour with him. We both knew I would have to go back to my husband, to my children, to the life I had chosen before I met him. I felt his arms around me, tasted his lips, sensed the straining need inside him that was such a vibrant echo of my own.

"I want you." I heard my own whisper and felt no shame. "Touch me, Christian. Let me belong to you." My heart was racing as I pressed wantonly against him. "Make love to me. Take me to your bed."

How tightly his arms gripped me, so tightly I couldn't get my breath. Then his hands were on my face, and I felt the tremor in his fingertips. His eyes were nearly black. So much could be read there. Passion, love, desperation, regret.

"Do you know how often I've dreamed of it? How many nights I've lain awake aching for you?" Then he released me to stride across the room to where my portrait hung on his wall. "I want you, Bianca, every time I take a breath. And I love you too much to take what can't be mine."

"Christian—"

"Do you think I could let you go if I'd ever touched you?" There was anger now, ripe and violent as he whirled back. "I hate knowing that we sneak like sinners just to spend an hour together, as innocent as children. If I don't have the strength to turn away from you completely, then I will have enough to keep you from taking a step you'd only regret."

"How could I regret belonging to you?"

"Because you already belong to someone else. And every time you go back to him, I dream of killing him with my bare hands if only because he can look at you when I can't. If we took this last step, I'd leave you no choice. There would be no going back to him, Bianca. No going back to your home, or your life."

And I knew it was true, as he stood between me and the image of me he'd created.

So I left him to come home, to tie a ribbon in Colleen's hair, to chase a ball with Ethan, to dry Sean's tears when he scraped his knee. To dine in miserable politeness with a husband who is more and more of a stranger to me.

Christian's words were true, and it is a truth I must face. The time is coming when I will no longer be able to live in both worlds, but must choose one, only one.

Chapter Four

"I have the most marvelous idea," Coco announced. Like a ship in full sail, she streamed into the kitchen where Lilah, Max, Suzanna and her family were having breakfast.

"Good for you," Lilah said over a bowl of chocolate-chip ice cream. "Anyone who can think at this hour deserves a medal, or should be committed."

Like a mother hen, Coco checked the herbs she had potted on the window. She clucked over the basil before she turned back. "I have no idea why I didn't think of it before. It's really so—"

"Alex is kicking me under the table."

"Alex, don't kick your sister," Suzanna said mildly. "Jenny, don't interrupt."

"I wasn't kicking her." Milk dribbled down Alex's chin. "She got her knee in the way of my foot."

"Did not."

"Did too."

"Turkey face."

"Booger head."

"Alex." Suzanna bit down on the inside of her lip to maintain the properly severe maternal disapproval. "Do you want to eat that cereal or wear it?"

"She started it," he muttered.

"Did not," Jenny said under her breath.

"Did too."

Another glance at their mother had them subsiding to eye each other with grim dislike over their cereal bowls.

"Now that that's settled." Amused, Lilah licked her spoon. "What's your marvelous idea, Aunt Coco?"

"Well." She fluffed her hair, absently checking her reflection in the toaster, approving it, then beaming. "It all has to do with Max. Really it's so obvious. But, of course, we were worried about his health, then it's so difficult to think clearly with this construction going on. Do you know one of those young men was out on the terrace this morning in nothing but a pair of jeans and a tool belt? Very distracting.'' She peeked out of the kitchen window, just in case.

"I'm sorry I missed it." Lilah winked at Max. "Was it the guy with the long blond hair tied back with a leather thong?"

"No, the one with dark curly hair and a mustache. I must say, he's extremely well built. I suppose one would keep fit swinging hammers or whatever all day. The noise is a bother, though. I hope it doesn't disturb you, Max.''

"No." He'd learned to flow with Coco's rambling thought patterns. "Would you like some coffee?"

"Oh, that's sweet of you. I believe I will.'' She sat while he got up to pour her a cup. "They've literally transformed the billiard room already. Of course, we've a long way to go—thank you, dear,'' she added when Max set a cup of coffee in front of her. "And all those tarps and tools and lumber make things unsightly. But it will all be worth it in the end.'' As she spoke, she doctored her coffee with cream and heaps of sugar. "Now, where was I?"

"A marvelous idea," Suzanna reminded her, putting a restraining hand on Alex's shoulder before he could fling any soggy cereal at his sister.

"Oh, yes." Coco set her cup down without taking a sip. "It came to me last night when I was doing the tarot cards. There were some personal matters I'd wanted to resolve, and I'd wanted to get a feel for this other business.''

"What other business?" Alex wanted to know.

"Grown-up business." Lilah dug a knuckle into his ribs to make him laugh. "Boring."

"You guys better go find Fred." Suzanna checked her watch. "If you want to go with me today, you've got five minutes."

They were up and shooting out of the room like little bullets. Surreptitiously Max rubbed his shin where Alex's foot had connected.

"The cards, Aunt Coco?" Lilah said when the explosion was over.

"Yes. I learned that there was danger, past and future. Disconcerting.'' She cast a worried look over both her nieces. "But we're to have help dealing with it. There seemed to be two different sources of aid. One was cerebral, the other physical—potentially violent." Uneasy, she frowned a little. "I couldn't place the physical source, though it seemed I should because it was from someone familiar. I thought it might be from Sloan. He's so, well, Western. But it wasn't. I'm quite sure it wasn't." Brushing that aside, she smiled again. "But naturally the cerebral source is Max.''

"Naturally." Lilah patted his hand as he shifted uncomfortably in his chair. "Our resident genius."

"Don't tease him." Suzanna rose to take bowls to the sink.

"Oh, he knows I don't just like him for his brain. Don't you, Max?"

He was mortally afraid he would blush in a minute. "If you keep interrupting your aunt, you'll be late for work."

"And so will I," Suzanna pointed out. "What's the idea, Aunt Coco?"

She'd started to drink again, and again set the coffee down untouched. "That Max should do what he came here to do." Smiling, she spread her manicured hands. "Research the Calhouns. Find out as much as possible about Bianca, Fergus, everyone involved. Not for that awful Mr. Caufield or whatever his name is, but for us."

Intrigued, Lilah thought the idea over. "We've already been through the papers."

"Not with Max's objective, and scholarly eye," Coco pointed out. Already fond of him, she patted his shoulder. Her interpretation of the cards also had indicated that he and Lilah would suit very well. "I'm sure if he put his mind to it, he could come up with all kinds of wonderful theories."

"It's a good idea." Suzanna came back to the table. "How do you feel about it?"

Max considered. Though he didn't put any stock in tarot cards, he didn't want to hurt Coco's feelings. Besides, however she had come up with the idea, it was sound. It would be a way of paying them back and a way to justify staying on in Bar Harbor a few more weeks.

"I'd like to do something. There's a good chance that even with the information I gave them the police won't find Caufield. While everyone's looking for him, I could be concentrating on Bianca and the necklace."

"There." Coco sat back. "I knew it."

"I'd wanted to check out the library, the newspaper, interview some of the older residents, but Caufield shut down the idea." The more he thought about it, the more Max liked the notion of working on his own. "Claimed he wanted everything to come out of the family papers, or his own sources." He moved his cup aside. "Obviously he couldn't give me a free hand or I'd find out the truth."

"Now you have a free hand," Lilah put in. It amused her that she could already see the wheels turning. "But I don't think you'll find the necklace in a library."

"But I may find a photograph of it, or a description."

Lilah simply smiled. "I've already given you that."

He didn't put much stock in dreams and visions, either, and shrugged. "All the same, I might find something tangible. And I'll certainly find something on Fergus and Bianca Calhoun."

"I suppose it'll keep you busy." Unoffended by his lack of faith in her mystical beliefs, Lilah rose. "You'll need a car to get around. Why don't you drop me off at work and use mine?"

Irked by her lack of faith in his research abilities, Max spent hours in the library. As always, he felt at home there, among stacks of books, in the center of the murmuring quiet, with a notebook at his elbow. To him, research was a quest—perhaps not as exciting as riding a white charger. It was a mystery to be solved, though the clues were less adventurous than a smoking gun or a trail of blood.

But with patience, cleverness and skill, he was a knight, or a detective, carefully working his way to an answer.

The fact that he had always been drawn to such places had disappointed his father bitterly, Max knew. Even as a boy he had preferred mental exercise over the physical. He had not picked up the torch to follow his father's blaze of glory on the high school football field. Nor had he added trophies to the shelf.

Lack of interest and a long klutzy adolescence had made him a failure in sports. He had detested hunting, and on the last outing his father had pressured him into had come up with a vicious asthma attack rather than a buck.

Even now, years later, he could remember his father's disgusted voice creeping into his hospital room.

"Damn boy's a pansy. Can't understand it. He'd rather read than eat. Every time I try to make a man out of him, he ends up wheezing like an old woman."

He'd gotten over the asthma, Max reminded himself. He'd even made something out of himself, though his father wouldn't consider it a man. And if he never felt completely adequate, at least he could feel competent.

Shrugging off the mood, he went back to his quest.

He did indeed find Fergus and Bianca. There were little gems of information peppered through the research books. In the familiar comfort of a library, Max took reams of notes and felt the excitement build.

He learned that Fergus Calhoun had been self-made, an Irish immigrant who through grit and shrewdness had become a man of wealth and influence. He'd landed in New York in 1888, young, poor and, like so many who had poured into Ellis Island, looking for his fortune. Within fifteen years, he had built an empire. And he had enjoyed flaunting it.

Perhaps to bury the impoverished youth he had been, he had surrounded himself with the opulent, muscling his way into society with wealth and will. It was in polite, exclusive society that he had met Bianca Muldoon, a young debutante of an old, established family with more gentility than money. He had built The Towers, determined to outdo the other vacationing rich, and had married Bianca the following year.

His golden touch had continued. His empire had grown, and so had his family with the birth of three children. Even the scandal of his wife's suicide in the summer of 1913 hadn't affected his monetary fortune.

Though he had become somewhat of a recluse after her death, he had continued to wield his power from The Towers. His daughter had never married and, estranged from her father, had gone to live in Paris. His youngest son had fled, after a peccadillo with a married woman, to the West Indies. Ethan, his eldest child had married and had two children of his own, Judson, Lilah's father, and Cordelia Calhoun, now Coco Mc-Pike.

Ethan had died in a sailing accident, and Fergus had lived out the last years of his long life in an asylum, committed there by his family after several outbursts of violent and erratic behavior.

An interesting story, Max mused, but most of the details could have been gleaned from the Calhouns themselves. He wanted something else, some small tidbit that would lead him in another direction.

He found it in a tattered and dusty volume titled *Summering in Bar Harbor.*

It was such a flighty and poorly written work that he nearly set it aside. The teacher in him had him reading on, as he would read a student's ill-prepared term paper. It deserved a C- at best, Max thought. Never in his life had he seen so many superlatives and cluttered adjectives on one page. Glamorously to gloriously, magnificent to miraculous. The author had been a wide-eyed admirer of the rich and famous, someone who saw them as royalty. Sumptuous, spectacular and splendiferous. The syntax made Max wince, but he plodded on.

There were two entire pages devoted to a ball given at The Towers in 1912. Max's weary brain perked up. The author had certainly attended, for the descriptions were in painstaking detail, from fashion to cuisine. Bianca Calhoun had worn gold silk, a flowing sheath with a beaded skirt. The color had set off the highlights in her titian hair. The scooped bodice had framed . . . the emeralds.

They were described in glowing and exacting detail. Once the adjectives and the romantic imagery were edited, Max could see them. Scribbling notes, he turned the page. And stared.

It was an old photograph, perhaps culled from a newspaper print. It was fuzzy and blurred, but he had no trouble recognizing Fergus. The man was as rigid and stern faced as the portrait the Calhouns kept over the mantel in the parlor. But it was the woman sitting in front of him that stopped Max's breath.

Despite the flaws of the photo, she was exquisite, ethereally beautiful, timelessly lovely. And she was the image of Lilah. The porcelain skin, the slender neck left bare with a mass of hair swept up in the Gibson style. Oversize eyes he was certain would have been green. There was no smile in them, though her lips were curved.

Was it just the romance of the face, he wondered, or did he really see some sadness there?

She sat in an elegant lady's chair, her husband behind her, his hand on the back of the chair rather than on her shoulder. Still, it seemed to Max that there was a certain possessiveness in the stance. They were in formal wear—Fergus starched and pressed, Bianca draped and fragile. The stilted pose was captioned, Mr. and Mrs. Fergus Calhoun, 1912.

Around Bianca's neck, defying time, were the Calhoun emeralds.

The necklace was exactly as Lilah had described to him, the two glittering tiers, the lush single teardrop that dripped like emerald water. Bianca wore it with a coolness that turned its opulence into elegance and only intensified the power.

Max trailed a fingertip along each tier, almost certain he would feel the smoothness of the gems. He understood why such stones become legends, to haunt men's imaginations and fire their greed.

But it eluded him, a picture only. Hardly realizing what he was doing, he traced Bianca's face and thought of the woman who had inherited it.

There were women who haunt and inflame.

Lilah paused in her stroll down the nature path to give her latest group time to photograph and rest. They had had an excellent crowd in the park that day, with a hefty percentage of them interested enough to hike the trails and be guided by a naturalist. Lilah had been on her feet for the best part of eight hours, and had covered the same ground eight times—sixteen if she counted the return trip.

But she wasn't tired, yet. Nor did her lecture come strictly out of a guidebook.

"Many of the plants found on the island are typically northern," she began. "A few are subarctic, remaining since the retreat of the glaciers ten thousand years ago. More recent specimens were brought by Europeans within the last two hundred and fifty years."

With a patience that was a primary part of her, Lilah answered questions, distracted some of the younger crowd from trampling the wildflowers and fed information on the local flora to those who were interested. She identified the beach pea, the seaside goldenrod, the late-blooming harebell. It was her last group of the day, but she gave them as much time and attention as the first.

In any case she always enjoyed this seaside stroll, listening to the murmur of pebbles drifting in the surf or the echoing call of gulls, discovering for herself and the tourists what treasures lurked in the tide pools.

The breeze was light and balmy, carrying that ancient and mysterious scent that was the sea. Here the rocks were smooth and flat, worn to elegance by the patient ebb and flow of water. She could see the glitter of quartz running in long white rivers down the black stone. Overhead, the sky was a hard summer blue, nearly cloudless. Under it, boats glided, buoys clanged, orange markers bobbed.

She thought of the yacht, the *Windrider,* and though she searched as she had on each tour, she saw nothing but sleek tourist boats or the sturdy crafts of lobstermen.

When she saw Max hiking the nature trail down to join the group, she smiled. He was on time, of course. She'd expected no less. She felt a slow tingle of warmth when his gaze lifted from his feet to her face. He really had wonderful eyes, she thought. Intent and serious, and just a little shy.

As always when she saw him, she had an urge to tease him and an underlying longing to touch. An interesting combination, she thought now, and one she couldn't remember experiencing with anyone else.

She looked so cool, he thought, the mannish uniform over the willowy feminine form. The military khaki and the dangle of gold and crystal at her ears. He wondered if she knew how suited she was to stand before the sea while it bubbled and swayed at her back.

"At the intertidal zone," she began, "life has acclimated to tidal change. In spring, we have the highest and lowest tides, with a rise and fall of 14.5 feet."

She went on in that easy, soothing voice, talking of intertidal creatures, survival and food chains. Even as she spoke, a gull glided to perch on a nearby rock to study the tourists with a beady, expectant eye. Cameras clicked. Lilah crouched down beside a tide pool. Fascinated by her description of life there, Max moved to see for himself.

There were long purple fans she called dulse, and she had the children in the group groaning when she told them it could be eaten raw or boiled. In the dark little pool of water, she found a wealth of living things, all waiting, she said, for the tide to come in again before they went back to business.

With a graceful fingertip she pointed out the sea anemones that looked more like flowers than animals, and the tiny slugs that preyed on them. The pretty shells that were mollusks and snails and whelks. She sounded like a marine biologist one moment and a stand-up comedian the next.

Her appreciative audience bombarded her with questions. Max caught one teenage boy staring at her with a moony kind of lust and felt instant sympathy.

Tossing her braid behind her back, she wound up the tour, explaining about the information available at the visitors center, and the other naturalist tours. Some of the group started to meander their way back along the path, while others lingered behind to take more pictures. The teenager loitered behind his parents, asking any question his dazzled brain could form on the tide pools, the wildflowers and, though he wouldn't have looked twice at a robin, the birds. When he'd exhausted all angles, and his mother called impatiently for the second time, he trudged reluctantly off.

"This is one nature walk he won't forget any time soon," Max commented.

She only smiled. "I like to think they'll all remember some pieces of it. Glad you could make it, Professor." She did what her instincts demanded and kissed him fully, softly on the mouth.

Looking back, the teenager experienced a flash of miserable envy. Max was simply knocked flat. Lilah's lips were still curved as she eased away.

"So," she asked him, "how was your day?"

Could a woman kiss like that then expect him to continue a normal conversation? Obviously this one could, he decided and took a long breath. "Interesting."

"Those are the best kind." She began to walk up the path that would lead back to the visitors center. Arching a brow, she glanced over her shoulder. "Coming?"

"Yeah." With his hands in his pockets, he started after her. "You're very good."

Her laugh was light and warm. "Why, thank you."

"I meant—I was talking about your job."

"Of course you were." Companionably she tucked an arm through his. "It's too bad you missed the first twenty minutes of the last tour. We saw two slate-colored juncos, a double-crested cormorant and an osprey."

"It's always been one of my ambitions to see a slate-colored junco," he said, and made her laugh again. "Do you always do the same trail?"

"No, I move around. One of my favorites is Jordan Pond, or I might take a shift at the Nature Center, or hike up in the mountains."

"I guess that keeps it from getting boring."

"It's never boring, or I wouldn't last a day. Even on the same trail you see different things all the time. Look." She pointed to a thatch of plants with narrow leaves and faded pink blooms. "Rhodora," she told him. "A common azalea. A few weeks ago it was at peak. Stunning. Now the blooms will die off, and wait until spring." She brushed her fingertips over the leaves. "I like cycles. They're reassuring."

Though she claimed to be an unenergetic woman, she walked effortlessly along the trail, keeping an eye out for anything of interest. It might be lichen clinging to a rock, a sparrow in flight or a spray of hawkweed. She liked the scent here, the sea they were leaving behind, the green smell of trees that began to crowd in to block the view.

"I didn't realize that your job kept you on your feet most of the day."

"Which is why I prefer to stay off them at all other times." She tilted her head to look at him. "Tell you what though, the next time I have an afternoon, I'll give you a more in-depth tour. We can kill two birds with one stone, so to speak. Take in the scenery, and poke around for your friend, Caufield."

"I want you to stay out of it."

The statement took her so off guard that she walked another five feet before it registered. "You what?"

"I want you to stay out of it," he repeated. "I've been giving it a lot of thought."

"Have you?" If he had known her better, he might have recognized the hint of temper in the lazy tone. "And just how did you come to that particular conclusion?"

"He's dangerous." The voice, laced with hints of fanaticism came back clearly. "I think he might even be unbalanced. It's certain that he's violent. He's already shot at your sister, and at me. I don't want you getting in his way."

"It's not a matter of what you want. It's family business."

"It's been mine since I took a swim in a storm." Caught between sunlight and shade on the path, he stopped to put his hands on her shoulders. "You didn't hear him that night, Lilah. I did. He said nothing would stop him from getting the necklace, and he meant it. This is a job for the police, not for a bunch of women who—"

"A bunch of women who what?" she interrupted with a gleam in her eyes.

"Who are too emotionally involved to react cautiously."

"I see." She nodded slowly. "So it's up to you and Sloan and Trent, the big, brave men to protect us poor, defenseless women and save the day?"

It occurred, a bit too late, that he was on very shaky ground. "I didn't say you were defenseless."

"You implied it. Let me tell you something, Professor, there isn't one of the Calhoun women who can't handle herself and any man who comes swaggering down the road. That includes geniuses and unbalanced jewel thieves."

"There, you see?" His hands lifted from her shoulders, then settled again. "Your reaction is pure emotion without any logic or thought."

The heated eyes narrowed. "Do you want to see emotion?"

Besides brains, he prided himself on a certain amount of street smarts. Cautious, he eased back. "I don't think so."

"Fine. Then I suggest you take care with your phrasing, and think twice before you tell me to keep out of something that is wholly my concern." She brushed by him to continue toward the voices around the visitors center.

"Damn it, I don't want you hurt."

"I don't intend to get hurt. I have a very low threshold for pain. But I'm not going to sit around with my hands folded while someone plots to steal what's mine."

"The police—"

"Haven't been a hell of a lot of help," she snapped. "Did you know that Interpol has been looking for Livingston, and his many aliases, for fifteen years? No one was able to trace him after he shot at Amanda and stole our papers. If Caufield and Livingston are one in the same, then it's up to us to protect what's ours."

"Even if it means getting your brains bashed in?"

She tossed a look over her shoulder. "I'll worry about my brains, Professor. You worry about yours."

"I'm not a genius," he muttered, and surprised a smile out of her.

The exasperation on his face took the edge off her temper. She stepped off the path. "I appreciate the concern, Max, but it's misplaced. Why don't you wait out here, sit on the wall? I've got to go in and get my things."

She left him muttering to himself. He only wanted to protect her. Was that so wrong? He cared about her. After all, she had saved his life. Scowling, he sat on the stone wall. People were milling in and out of the building. Children were whining as parents tugged, dragged or carried them to cars. Couples were strolling along hand in hand while others pored eagerly through guide books. He saw a lot of skin broiled Maine lobster red by the sun.

He glanced at his own forearms and was surprised to see that they were tanned. Things were changing, he realized. He was getting a tan. He had no schedule to keep, no itinerary to follow. He was involved in a mystery, and with an incredibly sexy woman.

"Well..." Lilah adjusted the strap of her purse on her arm. "You're looking very smug."

He looked up at her and smiled. "Am I?"

"As a cat with feathers in his mouth. Want to let me in on it?"

"Okay. Come here." He rose, gave her one firm yank and closed his mouth over hers. All of his new and amazed feelings poured into the kiss. If he took the kiss deeper than expected, it only added to the dawning pleasure of discovery. If kissing her made the people walking around them disappear, it only accented the newness. Starting fresh.

It was happiness rather than lust she felt from him. It confused her. Or perhaps it was the way his lips slid over hers that dimmed coherent thought. She didn't resist. The reason for her earlier irritation was already forgotten. All she knew now was that it felt wonderful, somehow perfect, to be standing with him on the sunny patio, feeling his heart thud against hers.

As his mouth slipped from hers, she let out a long, pleased sigh, opening her eyes slowly. He was grinning at her, and the delighted expression on his face had her smiling back. Because she wasn't sure what to do with the tender feelings he tugged from her, she patted his cheek.

"Not that I'm complaining," she began. "But what was that for?"

"I just felt like it."

"An excellent first step."

Laughing, he swung an arm around her shoulder as they started toward the parking lot. "You've got the sexiest mouth I've ever tasted."

He didn't see the cloud come into her eyes. If he had, she couldn't have explained it. It always came down to sex, she supposed and made an effort to shrug the vague disappointment away. Men usually saw her just that way, and there was no reason to let it start bothering her now, particularly when she'd enjoyed the moment as much as he.

"Glad I could oblige," she said lightly. "Why don't you drive?"

"All right, but first I've got something to show you." After settling into the driver's seat, he picked up a manilla envelope. "I went through a lot of books in the library. There are several mentions of your family in histories and biographies. There was one in particular I thought would interest you."

"Hmm." She was already stretched out and thinking of a nap.

"I made a copy of it. It's a picture of Bianca."

"A picture?" She straightened again. "Really? Fergus destroyed all her pictures after she died, so I've never seen her."

"Yes, you have." He drew the copy out and handed it to her. "Every time you look in the mirror."

She said nothing, but with her eyes focused on the grainy copy she lifted a hand to her own face. The same jaw, the same mouth, nose, eyes. Was this why she felt the bond so strongly? she wondered, and felt tears burn her throat.

"She was beautiful," Max said quietly.

"So young." The words came out as a sigh. "Younger than I when she died. She'd already fallen in love when this was taken. You can see it, in her eyes."

"She's wearing the emeralds."

"Yes, I know." As he had, she traced a fingertip over them. "How difficult it must have been for her, tied to one man, loving another. And the necklace—a symbol of one man's hold on her, and a reminder of her children."

"Is that how you see it, a symbol?"

"Yes. I think her feelings for it, about it, were terribly strong. Otherwise, she wouldn't have hidden it." She slipped the paper back into the envelope. "A good day's work, Professor."

"It's just a beginning."

As she looked at him, she linked her fingers with his. "I like beginnings. Everything that follows has such possibilities. We'll go home and show this to everyone, after we make a couple of stops."

"Stops?"

"It's time for another beginning. You need some new clothes."

He hated shopping. He told her, repeatedly and firmly, but she blithely ignored him and strolled from shop to shop. He held his ground on a fluorescent T-shirt, but lost it again over one depicting a lobster dressed like a maître d'.

She wasn't intimidated by clerks, but sailed through the process of selection and purchase with a languid air of pure relaxation. Most of the merchants called her by name, and during the chats that accompanied the buying and selling, she would casually ask about a man fitting Caufield's description.

"Are we finished yet?" There was a plea in his voice that made her chuckle as they stepped out onto the sidewalk again. It was teeming with people in bright summer clothes.

"Not quite." She turned to study him. Harassed, definitely. Adorable, absolutely. His arms were full of bags and his hair was falling into his eyes. Lilah brushed it back. "How are you fixed for underwear?"

"Well, I . . ."

"Come on, there's a shop right down here that has great stuff. Tiger prints, obscene sayings, little red hearts."

"No." He stopped dead. "Not on your life."

It was a struggle, but she kept her composure. "You're right. Completely unsuitable. We'll just stick with those nice white briefs that come three to a package."

"For a woman with no brothers, you sure know a lot about men's underwear." He shifted the bags, and as an afterthought, shoved half of them into her arms. "But I think I can handle this one on my own."

"Okay. I'll window-shop."

She was easily diverted by a window filled with crystals of different sizes and shapes. They dangled from wire, shooting colored light behind the glass. Beneath them was a display of handmade jewelry. She was on the point of stepping inside to wrangle over a pair of earrings when someone bumped her from behind.

"Sorry." The apology was terse. Lilah glanced up at a burly man with a weathered face and graying hair. He looked a great deal more irritated than the slight bump warranted, and something about the pale eyes had her taking a step back. Still, she shrugged and smiled.

"It's all right."

Frowning after him a moment, she started to turn back into the shop. She spotted Max a few feet away, staring in shock. Then he was moving fast, and the expression on his face had her catching her breath.

"Max—"

With one hard shove, he had her in the shop. "What did he say to you?" he demanded with an edge to his voice that had her eyes widening. "Did he touch you? If the bastard put his hands on you—"

"Hold on." Since they had most of the people in the shop staring, Lilah kept her voice low. "Calm down, Max. I don't know what you're talking about."

There was a violence trembling through his blood he'd never experienced before. The echo of it in his eyes had several tourists edging back out the door. "I saw him standing next to you."

"That man?" Baffled, she glanced out the window, but he had long since moved on. "He just bumped into me. The sidewalks are crowded in the summer."

"He didn't say anything to you?" He didn't even realize that his hands had firmed into fists and that the fists were ready to do damage. "He didn't hurt you?"

"No, of course not. Come on, let's go sit down." Her tone was soothing now as she nudged him out. But instead of taking one of the benches that lined the street, Max kept Lilah behind him and searched the crowd. "If I'd known buying underwear would put you in such a state, Max, I wouldn't have brought it up."

There was fury in his eyes when he whirled around. "It was Hawkins," he said grimly. "They're still here."

Chapter Five

She didn't know what to make of him. Alone, with the lamplight glowing gold, Lilah sat in the tower room, watching night fall gently over water and rock. And thought of Max. He wasn't nearly as simple a man as she had believed at first—and as she was certain he believed of himself.

One moment he was shy and sweet and easily intimidated. The next he was as fierce as a Viking, the mild blue eyes electric, the poet's mouth grim. The metamorphosis was as fascinating as it was baffling, and left Lilah off balance. It wasn't a sensation she cared for.

After he had seen the man he called Hawkins, Max had all but dragged her to the car—muttering under his breath all the way—bundled her inside, then had driven off. Her idea about following Hawkins had been briskly and violently vetoed. Back at The Towers, he'd called the police, relating the information as calmly as he would list assigned reading for a student. Then, in a typical male move had powwowed with Sloan and Trent.

The authorities had not yet located Caufield's boat, nor, from Max's descriptions, had they identified either Caufield or Hawkins.

It was much too complicated, Lilah decided. Thieves and aliases and international police. She preferred the simple. Not the humdrum, she thought, but the simple. Life had been anything but since the press had begun their love affair with the Calhoun emeralds, and things had become only more convoluted since Max had washed up on the beach.

But she was glad he had. She wasn't sure why. Certainly she'd never considered the shy and brainy sort her type. It was true that she enjoyed men in general, simply for being men. An offshoot, she supposed, from living in a female household most of her life. But when she dated, she most often looked for fun and easy companionship. Someone to dance with or to laugh with over a meal. She'd always hoped she would fall in love with one of those carefree, uncomplicated men and start a carefree, uncomplicated life.

Sober college professors with outdated notions of chivalry and serious minds hardly met the qualifications.

Yet he was so sweet, she thought with a little smile. And when he kissed her, there was nothing sober or cerebral about it.

With a little sigh, she wondered just what she should do about Dr. Maxwell Quartermain.

"Hey." C.C. poked her head through the doorway. "I thought I'd find you in here."

"Then I must be becoming too predictable." Happy to have company, Lilah curled up her legs to make room on the window seat. "What's going on with you, Mrs. St. James?"

"Nearly finished the reconditioning on that Mustang." She sighed as she sat. "Lord, what a honey. I had an electrical system that gave me fits today, and two tune-ups." An unaccustomed fatigue was dragging at her, making her close her eyes and think about an early night. "Then all this excitement at home. Imagine, you bumping into one of the characters the cops are after."

"The curse and blessing of small towns."

"I cruised around a little before I came home." C.C. rolled her tired shoulders. "Down to Hulls Cove and back."

"You shouldn't be poking around alone."

"Just looking." C.C. shrugged. "Anyway, I didn't see anything. Our fearless men are out right now on search and destroy."

A quick bolt of alarm shot into Lilah. "Max went with them?"

On a yawn, C.C. opened her eyes. "Sure. Suddenly, they're the Three Musketeers. Is there anything more annoying than machismo?"

"Tooth decay," Lilah said absently, but there were nerves bumping along in her system she didn't care for. "I thought Max was going to stick to the research books."

"Well, he's one of the boys now." She patted Lilah's ankle. "Don't worry, honey. They can handle themselves."

"For heaven's sake, he's a history professor. What if they actually run into trouble?"

"He already has," C.C. reminded her. "He's tougher than he looks."

"What makes you think so?" Unreasonably distressed, Lilah got up to pace. The unaccustomed show of energy had C.C. lifting a brow.

"The man jumped out of a boat in the middle of a storm and almost made it to shore, despite the fact he'd been grazed by a bullet. The next day, he was on his feet again—looking like hell, but on his feet. There's a stubborn streak behind those quiet eyes. I like him."

Restless, Lilah moved her shoulders. "Who doesn't? He's a likable man."

"Well, with everything that Amanda found out—the wonder boy stuff—you'd expect him to be conceited, or stiff-necked. But he's not. He's sweet. Aunt Coco's ready to adopt him."

"He is sweet," Lilah agreed as she sat again. "And I don't want him to get hurt because of some misguided sense of gratitude."

C.C. leaned forward to look into her sister's eyes. There was more than casual concern in them, she thought, and smiled to herself. "Lilah, I know you're the mystic in the family, but I'm getting definite vibes. Are you getting serious about Max?"

"Serious?" The word had Lilah's nerves stretching. "Of course not. I'm fond of him, and I feel a certain responsibility toward him." And when he kisses me, I go directly to meltdown. She frowned a little. "I enjoy him," she slowly added.

"He's very attractive."

"You're a married woman now, kiddo."

"But not blind. There's something appealing about all that intelligence, those romantic and scholarly looks." She waited a beat. "Don't you think?"

Lilah sat back. Her lips were curved again to match the amusement in her eyes. "Are you apprenticing with Aunt Coco as matchmaker?"

"Just checking. I guess I'm so happy I want everyone I love to feel the same way."

"I am happy." She took a long, limbering stretch. "I'm too lazy not to be."

"Speaking of lazy, I feel like I could sleep for a week. Since Trent's out playing Hardy Boys, I think I'll go to bed." C.C. started to rise when a wave of dizziness had her plopping down again. Lilah was up like a shot and bending over her.

"Hey. Hey, honey. Are you all right?"

"Got up too fast, that's all." As the light grayed, she lifted a hand to her spinning head. "I feel a little . . ."

Moving fast, Lilah shoved C.C.'s head between her knees. "Just breathe slow. Take it easy."

"This is stupid." But she did as she was told until the faintness passed. "I'm just overtired. Maybe I'm coming down with something, damn it."

"Mmm." Because she suspected just what C.C. had come down with, Lilah's lips curved. "Tired? Have you been feeling sick?"

"Not really." Steadier, C.C. straightened. "Out of sorts, I guess. A little queasy the past couple of mornings, that's all."

"Honey." With a laugh, Lilah tapped her knuckles on her sister's head. "Wake up and smell the baby powder."

"Huh?"

"Hasn't it occurred to you that you could be pregnant?"

"Pregnant?" The dark green eyes widened like saucers. "Pregnant? Me? But we've only been married a little over a month."

Lilah laughed again and cupped C.C.'s face in her hands. "You haven't spent all that time playing pinochle, have you?"

C.C.'s mouth opened and closed before she managed to form a word. "It just never crossed my mind. . . . A baby." Her eyes changed, misting, softening. "Oh, Lilah."

"Could be Trenton St. James IV."

"A baby," C.C. repeated, and laid a hand over her stomach in a gesture that was filled with awe and protectiveness. "Do you really think?"

"I really think." She slid back on the seat to hug C.C. tight. "I don't have to ask you how you feel about it. It's all over your face."

"Don't say anything to anyone yet. I want to be sure." Laughing, she squeezed Lilah against her. "Suddenly I don't feel tired at all. I'll call the doctor first thing in the morning. Or maybe I should pick up one of those tests from the drugstore. I could do both."

Lilah let her ramble. Long after C.C. had gone, the echoes of her joy remained in the room.

It was what the tower needed, Lilah thought. That jolt of pure happiness. She stayed where she was, content now, watching the moon rise. Half-full, bone white, it hung in the sky and had her dreaming.

What would it be like, being with someone, smugly married, having a child growing inside you? Making a life with someone who would know you so well. Know every part of you and love you despite the flaws. Maybe because of them.

Lovely, she thought. It would be simply lovely. And if she had yet to find that for herself, she had only to look at C.C. and Amanda to know it could happen.

With some regret she switched off the light and started downstairs to her room. The house was quiet now. She imagined it must be at least midnight, and everyone had gone to bed. A wise choice, she mused, but she couldn't seem to shake the restlessness.

To comfort herself, she indulged in a long, fragrant bath before slipping into her favorite robe. Those were the little things that always pleased her—hot, scented water, cool, thin silk. Still unsettled, she walked out onto the terrace to see if the night air would lull her.

It was much too romantic, she thought. The glitter of moonlight silvering the trees, the quiet whoosh of water on rock, the scents from the garden. As she stood, a bird, as restless as she, began a lonely night song. It made her long for something. For someone. A touch, a whisper in the dark. An arm around her shoulders.

A mate.

Not just the physical, but the emotional, the spiritual partner. She had had men desire her and knew that could never be enough. There had to be someone who could look beyond the color of her hair or the shape of her face and into her heart.

Perhaps she was asking for too much, Lilah thought with a sigh. But wasn't that better than asking for too little? In the meantime she would have to concentrate on other things and leave her heart in fate's capricious hands.

She had started to turn back into her room when a movement caught her eye. In the swaying moonlight she saw two shadows bent low, moving with silent swiftness across the lawn. Before she could do more than register the shapes, they had melted into the garden.

She didn't even think about it. A home was meant to be defended. Her bare feet were noiseless on the stone steps as she walked down them. Whoever was trespassing on Calhoun territory was about to get the scare of their lives.

Like a ghost, she slipped into the garden, the robe floating around her. There were voices, muffled and excited, a faint yellow beam of a flashlight. There was a laugh, quickly smothered, then the sound of a shovel striking earth.

That more than anything brought the Calhoun temper bubbling to the surface. With the courage of the righteous, she strode forward.

"What the hell do you think you're doing?"

The shovel clanged on stone as it was dropped. The flashlight went spiraling into the azaleas. Two teenagers, wound up with the treasure hunt, looked around wildly for the source of the voice. They saw the pale figure of a woman draped in white. Summing up her quarry, Lilah lifted her arms for effect, knowing the full sleeves would billow nicely.

"I am guardian of the emeralds." She nearly chuckled, pleased with the way her voice floated. "Do you dare to face the curse of the Calhouns? Hideous death is certain for any who defile this ground. Run, if you value your lives."

They didn't have to be told twice. The treasure map they had paid ten bucks for fluttered to the ground as they raced back down the path, shoving each other and tripping over their own scrambling feet. Chuckling to herself, Lilah picked up the map.

She'd seen its like before. Some enterprising soul was making them up and selling them to gullible tourists. After shoving it into her pocket, she decided to give her two uninvited guests a little extra boost. She dashed after them. Ready to send up a ghostly wail, she burst out of the garden.

The wail turned into a grunt as she rammed into another shadow. Stopped in a dead run, Max overbalanced, swore, then went tumbling to the ground on top of her.

"What the hell are you doing?"

"It's me," she managed, then sucked in a breath. "What the hell are you doing?"

"I saw someone. Stay here."

"No." She grabbed his arms and held on. "It was just a couple of kids with a treasure map. I scared them off."

"You—" Furious, he braced on an elbow. Despite the dark, the anger shone clearly in his eyes. "Are you out of your mind?" he demanded. "You came out here, alone, to face down two intruders?"

"Two terrified teenagers with a treasure map," she corrected. Her chin lifted. "It's my house."

"I don't give a damn whose house it is. It might have been Caufield and Hawkins. It might have been anyone. No one with an ounce of sense follows potential robbers into a dark garden alone, in the middle of the night.''

She had her breath back and studied him blandly. ''What were you doing?''

''I was going after them,'' he began, then caught her expression. ''That's different.''

''Why? Because I'm a woman?''

''No. Well, yes.''

''That's stupid, untrue and sexist.''

''That's sensible, factual and sexist.'' They'd been arguing in furious whispers. Now he sighed. ''Lilah, you might have been hurt.''

''The only one who hurt me was you, with that flying tackle.''

''I didn't tackle you,'' he muttered. ''I was watching them and didn't see you. And I certainly didn't expect to find you out here sneaking around in the dark.''

''I wasn't sneaking.'' She blew hair out of her eyes. ''I was playing ghost, and very effectively.''

''Playing ghost.'' He shut his eyes. ''Now I know you're out of your mind.''

''It worked,'' she reminded him.

''That's beside the point.''

''It's precisely the point, the other being that you knocked me down before I could finish the job.''

''I've already apologized.''

''No, you haven't.''

''All right. I'm sorry if I...'' He started to push himself off her and made the mistake of glancing down. Her robe had come loose during the fall and lay open to the waist. Like alabaster, her breasts glowed in the moonlight. ''Oh, Lord,'' he managed to say through suddenly dry lips.

She'd lost her breath again. Lying still, she watched his eyes change. Irritation to shock, shock to wonder, wonder to a deep and dark desire. As his gaze skimmed up, came back to hers, every muscle in her body melted like hot wax.

No one had ever looked at her just that way. There was such intensity in his eyes, the same focused concentration they had held when he'd struggled to block out pain. They roamed to her mouth, lingering there until her lips trembled apart on his name.

It was like moving into a dream, he thought as he lowered himself onto her again. Everything was just one click out of focus, soft and fuzzy. His hands were in her hair, lost in it. Beneath his, her lips were warm, beautifully warm. Her arms came around him as if they had been waiting. He heard her sigh, long and deep.

His mouth was so gentle on hers, as if he were afraid she might vanish if he dared too much too soon. Yet she could feel the tension in the way he held himself, the way his hands fisted in her hair, the way his breath shuddered out as he brushed his lips over hers.

Her limbs grew heavy, her head light. Though she wanted to keep her eyes open, as his were, they drifted closed. The most pleasant of aches coursed through her as he nibbled delicately at her parted lips. Her murmur mixed with his, indecipherable.

The grass whispered as she shifted beneath him. Its cool, fresh fragrance seemed perfectly suited to him. As his fingers slid softly over her breast, she heard her own quiet moan of acceptance.

She was unbelievably perfect, he thought dizzily. Like some fantasy conjured on a lonely night. Long slender limbs, silky skin, an avid and generous mouth. The sheer physical pleasure of her was like a drug, and he was already addicted.

Murmuring her name, he skimmed his lips to her throat. There her pulse beat like thunder, heating her skin so that her scent tangled with each breath he took. Tasting her was like dining on sin. Touching her was paradise. He brought his lips back to hers to lose himself on that glorious edge between heaven and hell.

She could almost feel herself floating an inch above the cool grass. Her body felt free as air, soft as water. When his mouth met hers again, she let herself drift into the new kiss. Then it happened.

It was not the sweet click of a door opening that she had been hoping for. It was a rushing roar, like a gust of wind sweeping through her body. Behind it, speeding in its wake, was a pain, sharp, sweet and stunning. She stiffened against it, her cry of protest muffled against his lips.

If she had slapped him, his passion wouldn't have cooled more quickly. He jerked back to see her staring at him, her eyes wide and filled with fear and confusion. Appalled by his behavior, he scrambled to his knees. He was trembling, he realized, So was she. Small wonder. He had acted like a maniac, knocking her down, pawing her.

Lord help him, he wanted to do it again.

"Lilah..." His voice was a husky rasp, and he struggled to clear it. She didn't move a muscle. Her eyes never left his. He wanted to stroke her cheek, to gather her close and hold her, but was afraid to touch her again. "I'm sorry. Very sorry. You looked so beautiful. I guess I lost my head."

She waited for a moment, for the balance and ease that was so much a part of her. But it didn't come. "Is that it?"

"I..." What did she want him to say? he wondered. He felt like a monster already. "You're an incredibly desirable woman," he said carefully. "But that's no excuse for what happened just now."

What had happened? She was afraid she had fallen in love with him, and if she had, love hurt. She didn't like it one damn bit. "You want me, physically."

He cleared his throat. *Want* wasn't the word. *Craved* was closer, but still fell pitifully short of the mark. As gently as he would for a child, he brought her robe together again. "Any man would," he said, nerves straining.

Any man, she thought and closed her eyes on the slash of disappointment. She hadn't been waiting for any man, but for one man. "It's all right, Max." Her voice was a shade overbright as she sat up. "No harm done. It's just a matter of us finding the other physically attractive. Happens all the time."

"Yes, but—" Not to him, he thought. Not like this. He frowned down at a blade of grass. It was easier for her, he supposed. She was so open, so uninhibited. There had probably been dozens of men in her life. Dozens, he thought on a jolt of fury that had him tearing the blade in two. "What do you suggest we do about it?"

"Do about it?" Her smile was strained, but he wasn't even looking at her. "Why don't we just see if it passes. Like the flu."

He looked at her then, with something dangerous edging his eyes. "It won't. Not for me. I want you. A woman like you would know just how badly I want you."

The words brought both a thrill and an ache. "A woman like me," she repeated softly. "Yes, that's the crux of it, isn't it, Professor?"

"The crux of what?" he began, but she was already on her feet.

"A woman who enjoys men, and who's very generous with them."

"I didn't mean—"

"One who'll wrestle half-naked on the grass. A little bohemian for you, Dr. Quartermain, but you're not above experimenting a little bit here and there—with a woman like me."

"Lilah, for God's sake—" He too was on his feet, baffled.

"I wouldn't apologize again if I were you. There's certainly no need." Hurt beyond measure, she tossed back her hair. "Not when it concerns a woman like me. After all, you've got me pegged, don't you?"

Good Lord, were those tears in her eyes? He gestured helplessly. "I haven't got a clue."

"Right again. All you understand about this is your own wants." She swallowed the tears. "Well, Professor, I'll take them under consideration and let you know."

Completely lost, he watched her gather the skirts of her robe and dart up the stairs. Moments later her terrace doors closed with an audible click.

She didn't cry. Lilah reminded herself it was an exhausting experience that usually left her with a miserable headache. She couldn't think of a single man who was worth the trouble. Instead, she dragged open the drawer of her nightstand and pulled out her emergency bar of chocolate.

After plopping down onto the bed, she took a healthy bite and stared at the ceiling.

Sexy. Beautiful. Desirable. Big damn deal, she thought and bit off another hunk. For all his celebrated brains, Maxwell Quartermain was as big a jerk as any other man. All he saw was a pretty package, and once he'd unwrapped it, that would be that. He wouldn't see any substance, any of the softer needs.

Oh, he was more polite than most. A gentleman to the last, she thought in disgust. She hadn't had to untangle herself. God knew he'd been in a hurry to do that for himself.

Lost his head. At least he was honest, she thought, and brushed impatiently at a tear that sneaked past her guard.

She knew the kind of image she projected. It rarely bothered her what people thought of her. She understood herself, was comfortable with Lilah Maeve Calhoun. There certainly was no shame in the fact that she enjoyed men. Though she hadn't enjoyed them to the extent that others, including, she supposed, her family might think.

Uninhibited? Perhaps, but that wasn't synonymous with promiscuity. Did she flirt? Yes, it came naturally to her, but it wasn't done with malice or guile.

If a man flirted with women he was suave. If a woman flirted, she was a tease. Well, as far as she was concerned the game between the sexes was a two-way street, and she enjoyed playing. And as for the good professor...

She curled up into a tight, defensive ball. Oh, God, he'd hurt her. All that stuttering, apologizing, explaining. And all the time he looked so appalled.

A woman like you. The phrase played back in her head.

Couldn't he see what he'd done to her with that careful tenderness? Hadn't he been able to feel how deeply he'd affected her? All she had wanted was for him to touch her again, to smile in that sweet, shy way of his and tell her that he cared. About who she was, what she was, how she felt inside. She'd wanted comfort and reassurance, and he'd given her excuses. She had looked up at him, with the stab of love still streaking through her, the terror of it still trembling, and he'd jerked back as if she'd clipped him on the jaw.

She wished she had. If this was love, she didn't want her share after all.

Because it was quiet, or perhaps because her ears were tuned for him, she heard Max come up the steps, sensed him hesitate near her doors. She stopped breathing, though her heart picked up a quick beat. Would he come in now, push those doors open and come to her, tell her what she wanted so badly to hear? She could almost see his hand reach for the knob. Then she heard his footsteps again as he moved on down the terrace to his own room.

Her breath came out in a sigh. It wouldn't fit his principles to enter her bedroom uninvited. Outside, on the grass, he'd been following his instincts rather than his intellect, she admitted. No one was more in favor of that than Lilah. For him, it had been the moment, the moon, the mood. It was difficult to blame him, certainly impossible to expect him to feel as she felt. Want as she wanted.

She sincerely hoped he didn't sleep a wink.

She sniffled, swallowed chocolate, then began to think. Only two months before, C.C. had come to her, hurt and infuriated because Trent had kissed her, then apologized for it.

Pursing her lips, Lilah rolled onto her back again. Maybe it was typical male stupidity. It was difficult to fault the breed for something they were born with. If Trent had apologized because he'd cared about her sister, then it could follow that Max had played the same cards.

It was an interesting theory, and one that shouldn't be too difficult to prove. Or disprove, she thought with a sigh. Either way, it was probably best to know before she got in any deeper. All she needed was a plan.

Lilah decided to do what she did best, and slept on it.

Chapter Six

It wasn't difficult in a house the size of The Towers to avoid someone for a day or two. Max noted that Lilah had effortlessly stayed out of his way for that amount of time. He couldn't blame her, not after how badly he had botched things.

Still, it irked him that she wouldn't accept a simple and sincere apology. Instead she'd turned it into... damned if he knew what she'd turned it into. The only thing he was sure of was that she'd twisted his words, and their meaning, then had stalked off in a snit.

And he missed her like crazy.

He kept busy enough, buried in his research books, poring over the old family papers that Amanda had meticulously filed according to date and content. He found what he considered the last public sighting of the necklace in a newspaper feature covering a dinner dance in Bar Harbor, August 10, 1913. Two weeks before Bianca's death.

Though he considered it a long shot, he began a list of every servant's name he came across who had worked at The Towers the summer of 1913. Some of them could conceivably be alive. Tracking them or their families down would be difficult but not impossible. He had interviewed the elderly before on their memories of their youth. Quite often, those memories were as clear as crystal.

The idea of talking to someone who had known Bianca, who had seen her—and the necklace—excited him. A servant would remember The Towers as it had been, would have knowledge of their employers' habits. And, he had no doubt, would know their secrets.

Confident in the notion, Max bent over his lists.

"Hard at work, I see."

He glanced up, blinking, to see Lilah in the doorway of the storeroom. She didn't have to be told she'd dragged him out of the past. The blank, owlish look he gave her made her want to hug him. Instead she leaned lazily against the jamb.

"Am I interrupting?"

"Yes—no." Damn it, his mouth was watering. "I was just, ah, making a list."

"I have a sister with the same problem." She was wearing a full-skirted sundress in sheer white cotton, her gypsy hair like cables of flames against it. Long chunks of malachite swung at her ears when she crossed the room.

"Amanda." Because the pencil had gone damp in his hand, he set it aside. "She did a terrific job of cataloging all this information."

"She's a fiend for organization." Casually she rested a hip on the card table he was using. "I like your shirt."

It was the one she'd chosen for him, with the cartoon lobster. "Thanks. I thought you'd be at work."

"It's my day off." She slid off the table to round it and lean over his shoulder. "Do you ever take one?"

Though he knew it was ridiculous, he felt his muscles bunch up. "Take what?"

"A day off." Brushing her hair aside, she turned her face toward his. "To play."

She was doing it deliberately, there could be no doubt. Maybe she enjoyed watching him make a fool out of himself. "I'm busy." He managed to tear his gaze away from her mouth and stared down at the list he was making. He couldn't read a word. "Really busy," he said almost desperately. "I'm trying to note down all the names of the people who worked here the summer Bianca died."

"That's quite an undertaking." She leaned closer, delighted with his reaction to her. It had to be more than lust. A man didn't fight so hard against basic lust. "Do you want some help?"

"No, no, it's a one-man job." And he wanted her to go away before he started to whimper.

"It must have been a terrible time here, after she died. Even worse for Christian, hearing about it, reading about it, and not being able to do anything. I think he loved her very much. Have you ever been in love?"

Once again, she drew his eyes back to hers. She wasn't smiling now. There was no teasing light in her eyes. For some reason he thought it was the most serious question she had ever asked him.

"No."

"Neither have I. What do you think it's like?"

"I don't know."

"But you must have an opinion." She leaned a little closer. "A theory. A thought."

He was all but hypnotized. "It must be like having your own private world. Like a dream, where everything's intensified, a bit off balance and completely yours."

"I like that." He watched her lips curve, could almost taste them. "Would you like to take a walk, Max?"

"A walk?"

"Yes, with me. Along the cliffs."

He wasn't even sure he could stand. "A walk would be good."

Saying nothing, she offered him her hand. When he rose, she led him through the terrace doors.

The wind was up, pushing the clouds across a blue sky. It tore at Lilah's skirts and sent her hair flying. Unconcerned, she strolled into it, her hand lightly clasped in his. They crossed the lawn and left the busy sounds of building behind.

"I'm not much on hiking," she told him. "Since I spend most days doing just that, but I like to go to the cliffs. There are very strong, very beautiful memories there."

He thought again of all the men who must have loved her. "Yours?"

"No, Bianca's, I think. And if you don't choose to believe in such things, the view's worth the trip."

He started down the slope beside her. It felt easy, simple, even friendly. "You're not angry with me anymore."

"Angry?" Deliberately she lifted a brow. She had no intention of making things too simple. "About what?"

"The other night. I know I upset you."

"Oh, that."

When she added nothing else, he tried again. "I've been thinking about it."

"Have you?" Her eyes, mysterious with secrets, lifted to his.

"Yes. I realize I probably didn't handle it very well."

"Would you like another chance?"

He stopped dead in his tracks and made her laugh.

"Relax, Max." She gave him a friendly kiss on the cheek. "Just give it some thought. Look, the mountain cranberry's blooming." She bent to touch a spray of pink bell-shaped flowers that clung to the rocks. Touch, but not pick, he noted. "It's a wonderful time for wildflowers up here." Straightening, she tossed her hair back. "See those?"

"The weeds?"

"Oh, and I thought you were a poet," With a shake of her head, she had her hand tucked back in his. "Lesson number one," she began.

As they walked, she pointed out tiny clumps of flowers that pushed out of crevices or thrived in the thin, rocky soil. She showed him how to recognize the wild blueberry that would be ripe and ready the following month. There was the flutter of butterfly wings and the drone of bees deep in the grass. With her, the common became exotic.

She snipped off a thin leaf, crushing it to release a pungent fragrance that reminded him of her skin.

He stood with her on a precipice thrown out over the water. Far below, spray fumed on the rock, beating them smooth in a timeless war. She helped him spot the nests, worked cleverly onto narrow ridges and clinging tenaciously to faults in the rocks.

It was what she did every day for groups of strangers, and for herself. There was a new kind of pleasure in sharing it all with him, showing him something as simple and special as the tiny white sandwort or the wild roses that grew as tall as a man. The air was like wine, freshened by the wind, so that she sat on a huddle of rock to drink it with each breath.

"It's incredible here." He couldn't sit. There was too much to see, too much to feel.

"I know." She was enjoying his pleasure as much as the sun on her face and the wind in her hair. It was in his as well, streaming through the shaggy locks. There was fascination in his eyes, darkening them to indigo as the faint smile curved his lips. The wound on his temple was healing, but she thought it would leave a slight scar that would add something rakish to the intelligent face.

As a thrush began to trill, she circled her knee with her arms. "You look good, Max."

Distracted, he glanced over his shoulder. She was sitting easily on the rocks, as relaxed as she would have been on a cushy sofa. "What?"

"I said you look good. Very good." She laughed as his jaw dropped. "Hasn't anyone ever told you you're attractive?"

What game was she playing now? he wondered, and shrugged uncomfortably. "Not that I remember."

"No star-struck undergraduate, no clever English Lit professor? That's very remiss. I imagine more than one of them tried to catch your eye—and a bit more than that—but you were too buried in books to notice."

His brows drew together. "I haven't been a monk."

"No." She smiled. "I'm already aware of that."

Her words reminded him vividly of what had happened between them two nights before. He had touched her, tasted her, had managed, barely, to pull himself back before taking her right there on the grass. And she had rushed off, he remembered, furious and hurt. Now she was taunting him, all but daring him to repeat the mistake.

"I never know what to expect from you."

"Thank you."

"That wasn't a compliment."

"Even better." Her eyes slanted, half-closed now against the sun. When she spoke, her voice was almost a purr. "But you like predictability, don't you, Professor? Knowing what happens next."

"Probably as much as you like irritating me."

Laughing, she held out a hand. "Sorry, Max, sometimes it's irresistible. Come on, sit down. I promise to behave."

Wary, he sat on the rock beside her. Her skirts fluttered teasingly around her legs. In a gesture he felt was almost maternal, she patted his thigh.

"Want to be pals?" she asked him.

"Pals?"

"Sure." Her eyes danced with amusement. "I like you. The serious mind, the honest soul." He shifted, making her laugh. "The way you shuffle around when you're embarrassed."

"I do not shuffle."

"The authoritative tone when you're annoyed. Now you're supposed to tell me what you like about me."

"I'm thinking."

"I should have added your dry wit."

He had to smile. "You're the most self-possessed person I've ever met." He glanced at her. "And you're kind, without making a fuss about it. You're smart, but you don't make a fuss about that, either. I guess you don't make a fuss about anything."

"Too tiring." But his words had a glow spreading around her heart. "It's safe to say we're friends then?"

"Safe enough."

"That's good." She gave his hand a gentle squeeze. "I think it's important for us to be friends before we're lovers."

He nearly fell off the rock. "Excuse me?"

"We both know we want to make love." When he began to stammer she gave him a patient smile. She'd thought it through very carefully and was sure—well, nearly sure—this was right for both of them. "Relax, it isn't a crime in this state."

"Lilah, I realize I've been . . . that is, I know I've made advances."

"Advances." Desperately in love, she laid a hand on his cheek. "Oh, Max."

"I'm not proud of my behavior," he said stiffly, and had her hand sliding away. "I don't want . . ." His tongue tied itself into knots.

The hurt was back, a combination of rejection and defeat she detested. "You don't want to go to bed with me?"

Now his stomach was in knots, as well. "Of course I do. Any man—"

"I'm not talking about any man." They were the poorest two words he could have chosen. It was him, only him she cared about. She needed to hear him say he wanted her, if nothing else. "Damn it, I'm talking about you and me, right here, right now." Temper pushed her off the rock. "I want to know about your feelings. If I wanted to know how any man felt, I'd pick up the phone or drive into the village and ask any man."

Keeping his seat, he considered her. "For someone who does most things slowly, you have a very quick temper."

"Don't use that professorial tone on me."

It was his turn to smile. "I thought you liked it."

"I changed my mind." Because her own attitude confused her, she turned away to look out over the water. It was important to remain calm, she reminded herself. She was always able to remain calm effortlessly. "I know what you think of me," she began.

"I don't see how you can, when I'm far from sure myself." He took a moment to gather his thoughts. "Lilah, you're a beautiful woman—"

She whirled back, eyes electric. "If you tell me that again, I swear, I'll hit you."

"What?" Completely baffled, he threw his hands up and rose. "Why? Good God, you're frustrating."

"That's much better. I don't want to hear that my hair's the color of sunset, or that my eyes are like sea foam. I've heard all that. I don't care about that."

He began to think that being a monk, completely divorced from the mysterious female, had its advantages. "What do you want to hear?"

"I'm not going to tell you what I want to hear. If I do, then what's the point?"

At wit's end, he raked both hands through his hair. "The point is, I don't know what the point is. One minute you're telling me about sand-warts—"

"Sandwort," she said between her teeth.

"Fine. We're talking about flowers and friendship, and the next you're asking me if I want to take you to bed. How am I supposed to react to that?"

Her eyes narrowed. "You tell me."

He went on a mental search for safe ground and found none. "Look, I realize you're used to having men..."

Her narrowed eyes glinted. "Having them what?"

If he was going to sink, Max decided, he might as well go down with a flourish. "Just shut up." He grabbed her arms, dragged her hard against him and crushed his mouth to hers.

She could taste the frustration, the temper, the edgy passion. It seemed that what he was feeling was a reflection of her own emotions. For the first time, she struggled against him, fighting to hold back her response. And for the first time, he ignored the protest and demanded one.

His hand was in her billowing hair, pulling her head back so that he could plunder mindlessly. Her body was arched, straining away from him, but he locked her closer, so close even the wind couldn't slip between them.

This was different, she thought. No man had ever forced her to...feel. She didn't want this ache, these needs, this desperation. Since the last time they had been together she had convinced herself that love could be painless, and simple and comfortable, if only she were clever enough.

But there was pain. No amount of passion or desire could completely coat it.

Furious with both of them, he tore his mouth from hers, but his hands dug into her shoulders. "Is that what you want?" he demanded. "Do you want me to forget every rule, every code of decency? You want to know how I feel? Every time I'm around you I itch to get my hands on you. And when I do I want to drag you off somewhere and make love to you until you forget that there was ever anyone else."

"Then why don't you?"

"Because I care about you, damn it. Enough to want to show you some respect. And too much to want to be just the next man in your bed."

The temper faded from her eyes to be replaced by a vulnerability more poignant than tears. "You wouldn't be." She lifted a hand to his face. "You're a first for me, Max. There's never been anyone else like you." He said nothing, and the doubt in his eyes had her hand slipping to her side again. "You don't believe me."

"I've found it difficult to think clearly since I met you." Abruptly he realized he was still gripping her shoulders, and gentled his hold. "You could say you dazzle me."

She looked down. How close she had come, she realized, to telling him everything that was in her heart. And humiliating herself, embarrassing him. If it was just to be physical between them, then she would be strong enough to accept it. "Then we'll leave it at that for now." She managed a smile. "We've been taking ourselves too seriously anyway." To comfort herself, she gave him a soft, lingering kiss. "Friends?"

He let out a long breath. "Sure."

"Walk back with me, Max." She slipped a hand into his. "I feel like a nap."

An hour later, he sat on the sunny terrace outside of his room, the notebook on his lap forgotten and his mind crowded with thoughts of her.

He didn't come close to understanding her—was certain he couldn't come closer if he had several decades to consider the problem. But he did care, enough to add a good jolt of fear to the rest of the emotions she pulled out of him. What did he, a painfully middle-class college professor, have to offer a gorgeous, exotic and free-spirited woman who exuded sex like other women exuded perfume?

He was so pitifully inept that he was stuttering around her one minute and grabbing her like a Neanderthal the next.

Maybe the best thing for him was to remember that he was more comfortable and certainly more competent with his books than with women.

How could he tell her that he wanted her so badly he could hardly breathe? That he was terrified to act on his needs because, once done, he knew he'd never be free of her? An easy summer romance for her, a life-altering event for him.

He was falling in love with her, which was ridiculous. He couldn't have a place in her life, and hoped he was smart enough to get a grip on his emotions before they carried him too far. In a few weeks, he would go back to his nicely ordered routine. It was what he wanted. It had to be.

And he couldn't survive it if she haunted him.

"Max?" Trent, taking the circular route to the west wing, stopped. "Interrupting?"

"No." Max glanced down at the blank sheet on his lap. "Nothing to interrupt."

"You looked like you were trying to puzzle out a particularly difficult problem. Anything to do with the necklace?"

"No." Max looked up, squinted against the sun. "Women."

"Oh. Good luck." He lifted a brow. "Particularly if it's a Calhoun woman."

"Lilah." Weary, Max rubbed his hands over his face. "The more I think about her, the less I understand."

"A perfect start in a relationship." Because he was feeling smug about his own, Trent took a moment and sat down. "She's a fascinating woman."

"I've decided the word's *unstable.*"

"Beautiful."

"You can't tell her that. She bites your head off." Intrigued, he studied Trent. "Does C.C. threaten to hit you if you tell her she's beautiful?"

"Not so far."

"I thought it might be a family trait." He began to tap his pencil against the pad. "I don't know very much about women."

"Well then, I should tell you all I know." Steepling his fingers, Trent sat back. "They're frustrating, exciting, baffling, wonderful and infuriating."

Max waited a moment. "That's it?"

"Yeah." He glanced up, lifting a hand in salute as Sloan approached.

"Coffee break?" Sloan asked, and finding the idea appealing, took out a cigar.

"A discussion on women," Trent informed him. "You might like to add something to my brief dissertation."

Sloan took his time lighting the cigar. "Stubborn as mules, mean as alley cats and the best damn game in town." He blew out smoke and grinned at Max. "You've got a thing for Lilah, don't you?"

"Well, I—"

"Don't be bashful." Sloan's grin widened as he poked out with the cigar. "You're among friends."

Max wasn't accustomed to discussing women, and certainly not his feelings toward a particular woman. "It would be difficult not to be interested."

Sloan gave a hoot of laughter and winked at Trent. "Son, you'd be dead if you weren't interested. So what's the problem?"

"I don't know what to do about her."

Trent's lips curved. "Sounds familiar. What do you want to do?"

Max slanted Trent a long, slow look that had him chuckling.

"Yeah, there is that." Sloan puffed contentedly on his cigar. "Is she, ah, interested?"

Max cleared his throat. "Well, she's indicated that she—that is, earlier we took a walk up on the cliffs, and she...yeah."

"But?" Trent prompted.

"I'm already in over my head."

"Then you might as well go under for the third time," Sloan told him, and eyed the tip of his cigar. "'Course, if you make the lady unhappy, I'd have to pound your face in." He stuck the cigar back into his mouth. "I'm right fond of her."

Max studied him a moment, then laid his head back and laughed. "There's no way to win here. I think I finally figured that out."

"That's the first step." Trent shifted. "Since we've got a minute here without the ladies I thought you both should know that I finally got a report on this Hawkins character. Jasper Hawkins, smuggler, out of Miami. He's a known associate of our old friend Livingston."

"Well, well," Sloan murmured, crushing out the cigar.

"It begins to look like Livingston and Caufield are one in the same. No sign of the boat yet."

"I've been thinking about that," Max put in. "It might be that they covered their tracks there. Even if they figured I was dead, they'd have to consider that the body would wash up eventually, be identified. Questions would be asked."

"So they ditched the boat," Trent mused.

"Or switched it." Max spread his hands. "They won't back off. I'm sure of that. Caufield, or whoever he is, is obsessed with the necklace. He'd change tactics, but he wouldn't give up."

"Neither will we," Trent murmured. The three men exchanged quiet looks. "If the necklace is in this house, we'll find it. And if that bastard—" He cut himself off as he spotted his wife racing through the doors at the far end of the terrace. "C.C." He was up quickly, starting toward her. "What's wrong? What are you doing home?"

"Nothing. Nothing's wrong." With a laugh, she threw her arms around him. "I love you."

"I love you, too." But he drew away to study her face. Her cheeks were flushed, her eyes brilliant and wet. "Well, it must be good news." He brushed her hair back, checking her brow as he did so. He knew she hadn't been feeling quite herself for the past week.

"The best." She glanced over at Sloan and Max. "Excuse us." Gripping Trent's hand, she pulled him down the terrace toward their room where she could tell him in private. Halfway there, she exploded. "Oh, I can't wait. I know I broke the sound barrier getting home after the test came in."

"What test? You're sick?"

"I'm pregnant." She held her breath, watching his face. Concern to shock, shock to wonder.

"You—pregnant?" He gaped down at her flat stomach, then back into her face. "A baby? We're having a baby?"

Even as she nodded, he was scooping her up, to swing her around and around as she clung to him.

"What the hell's with them?" Sloan wondered.

"Men." Behind Max, Lilah glided from another room. "You're all so dense." With a sigh, she laid a hand on Max's shoulder, watching her sister and Trent through misty eyes. "We're having a baby, you dummies."

"I'll be damned." After a whoop, Sloan headed down to slap Trent on the back and kiss C.C. Hearing the sniffle behind him, Max rose.

"You okay?"

"Sure." She brushed a tear from her lashes, but another fell. "She's my baby sister." She sniffed again, then gave a watery laugh when Max offered her a handkerchief. "Trust you." She dabbed her eyes, blew her nose then sighed. "I'm going to keep it awhile, okay? We're all going to cry buckets when we go down and make the announcement to the rest of the family."

"That's all right." Unsure of himself, he stuck his hands into his pockets.

"Let's go down and see if there's any champagne in the fridge."

"Well, I think I should stay up here. Out of the way."

With a shake of her head, she took his hand firmly in hers. "Don't be a jerk, Like it or not, Professor, you're part of the family."

He let her lead him away and discovered he did like it. He liked it a lot.

It was the stray puppy that started it. Such a poor, bedraggled little thing. Homeless and helpless. I have no idea how he found his way to the cliffs. Perhaps someone had disposed of an unwanted litter, or the pup had become separated from its mother. But we found him, Christian and I, on one of our golden afternoons. He was hiding in a huddle of rocks, half-starved and whimpering, a tiny black bundle of bones and scruffy black fur.

How patiently Christian lured him out, with a gentle voice and bits of bread and cheese. It touched me to see this sweetness in the man I love. With me, he is always tender, but I have seen the fierce impatience in him, for his art. I have felt the near-violent passion fighting for freedom when he holds me in his arms.

Yet with the puppy, the poor little orphan, he was instinctively kind. Perhaps sensing this, the pup licked his hand and allowed himself to be petted even after the meager meal had been gobbled down.

"A scrapper." Christian laughed as he took his beautiful artist's hands over the dirty fur. "Tough little fellow, aren't you?"

"He needs a bath," I said, but laughed as well when the dusty paws streaked my dress. "And a real meal." Delighted with the attention, the pup licked my face, his whole body trembling with delight.

Of course, I fell in love. He was such a homely little bundle, so trusting, so needy. We played with him, as charmed as children, and had a laughing argument over what to call him.

We named him Fred. He seemed to approve as he yipped and danced and tumbled in the dirt. I will never forget the sweetness of it, the simplicity. My love and I sitting on the ground with a little lost pup, pretending that we would take him home together, care for him together.

In the end, I took Fred with me. Ethan had been asking for a pet, and I felt he was old enough now to be both appreciative and responsible. What a clamor there was when I brought the puppy to the nursery. The children were wide-eyed and excited, each taking turns holding and hugging until I'm sure young Fred felt like a king.

He was bathed and fed with a great deal of ceremony. Stroked and cuddled and tickled until he fell asleep in exhausted euphoria.

Fergus returned. The excitement over Fred had caused me to forget our plans for the evening. I'm sure my husband was right to be annoyed that I was far from ready to go out and dine. The children, unable to contain their delight, raced about, adding to his impatience. Little Ethan, proud as a new father, carried Fred into the parlor.

"What the devil have you got?" Fergus demanded.

"A puppy." Ethan held the wriggling bundle up for his father's inspection. "His name is Fred."

Noting my husband's expression, I took the puppy from my son and began to explain how it had come about. I suppose I'd hoped to appeal to Fergus's softer side, to the love, or at least the pride he felt for Ethan. But he was adamant.

"I'll not have a mongrel in my house. Do you think I have worked all my life to own such things only to have some flea-ridden mutt relieving himself on the carpets, chewing on the draperies?"

"He'll be good." Lip quivering, Colleen hugged my skirts. "Please, Papa. We'll keep him in the nursery and watch him."

"You'll do no such thing, young lady." Fergus dismissed Colleen's tears with a glance and turned to Ethan, whose eyes were also brimming. There was a fractional softening in his expression. After all this was his first son, his heir, his immortality. "A mongrel's no pet for you, my lad. Why any fisherman's son might own a mongrel. If it's a dog you want, we'll look into it when we get back to New York. A fine dog, with a pedigree."

"I want Fred." With his sweet face crumbling, Ethan looked up at his father. Even little Sean was crying now, though I doubt he understood.

"Out of the question." With his temper obviously straining, Fergus walked to the whiskey decanter and poured. "It's completely unsuitable. Bianca, have one of the servants dispose of it."

I know I paled as quickly as the children. Even Fred whimpered, pressing his face to my breast. "Fergus, you can't be so cruel."

There was surprise in his eyes, I have no doubt of it. It had never occurred to him that I would speak to him so, and in front of the children. "Madam, do as I bid."

"Mama said we could keep him," Colleen began, her youthful temper lifting her voice. "Mama promised. You can't take him away. Mama won't let you."

"I run this home. If you don't wish a strapping, mind your tone."

I found myself clutching Colleen's shoulders, as much to suppress her as to protect. He would not lift a hand to my children. Fury at the thought of it blinded me to all else. I know I trembled as I bent to her, to shift Fred back into her arms.

"Go upstairs to Nanny now," I said quietly. "Take your brothers."

"He won't kill Fred." Is there a rage more poignant than that of a child? "I hate him, and I won't let him kill Fred."

"Shh. It will be all right, I promise you. It will be all right. Go up to Nanny."

"A poor job you've done, Bianca," Fergus began when the children had left us. "The girl is old enough to know her place."

"Her place?" The fury had my heart roaring in my head. "What is her place, Fergus? To sit quietly in some corner, her hands folded, her thoughts and feelings unspoken until you have bartered her off into a suitable marriage? They are children. Our children. How could you hurt them so?"

Never in our marriage had I used such a tone with him. Never had I thought to. For a moment I was certain that he would strike me. It was in his eyes. But he seemed to pull himself back, though his fingers were white as marble against the glass he held.

"You question me, Bianca?" His face was very pale with his rage, his eyes very dark. "Do you forget whose house you stand in, whose food you eat, whose clothes you wear?"

"No." Now I felt a new kind of grief, that our marriage should be brought down to only that. "No, I don't forget. I can't forget. I would sooner wear rags and starve than see you hurt my children so. I will not allow you to take that dog from them and have him destroyed."

"Allow?" He was no longer pale, but crimson with fury. "Now it is you who forget your place, Bianca. Is it any wonder the children openly defy me with such a mother?"

"They want your love, your attention." I was shouting now, beyond restraint. "As I have wanted it. But you love nothing but your money, your position."

How bitterly we argued then. The names he called me I can't repeat. He dashed the glass against the wall, shattering the crystal and his own control. There was a wildness in his eyes when his hands came around my throat. I was afraid for my life, terrified for my children. He shoved me aside so that I fell into a chair. He was breathing quickly as he stared down at me.

Very slowly, with great effort, he composed himself. The violent color faded from his cheeks. "I can see now that I've been too generous with you," he said. "From this point, it will change. Don't think you will continue to go your own way as you choose. We will cancel our plans for this evening. I have business in Boston. While I'm there, I will interview governesses. It's time the children learned respect, and how to appreciate their position. Between you and their nanny, they have become spoiled and willful." He took his watch from his pocket and studied the time. "I will leave tonight and be gone two days. When I return I expect you to have remembered your duties. If the mongrel is still in my house when I return, both you and the children will be punished. Am I clear, Bianca?"

"Yes." My voice shook. "Quite clear."

"Excellent. In two days then."

He walked out of the parlor. I did not move for an hour. I heard the carriage come for him. Heard him instruct the servants. In that time my head had cleared and I knew what I had to do.

Chapter Seven

"What the hell good is messing with all these papers?" Hawkins paced the sun-washed room in the rented house. He had never been a patient man and preferred to use his fists or a weapon rather than his brain. His associate, now going by the name of Robert Marshall, sat at an oak desk, carefully leafing through the papers he had stolen from The Towers a month before. He had dyed his hair a nondescript brown and had grown a credible beard and mustache that he tinted the same shade.

If Max Quartermain had seen him, he would have called him Ellis Caufield. Whatever name he chose, whatever disguise he employed, he was a thief whose unscrupulous mind had centered on the Calhoun emeralds.

"I went through a great deal of trouble to get these papers," Caufield said mildly. "Now that we've lost the professor, I'll have to decipher them myself. It will simply take a little longer."

"This whole job stinks." Hawkins stared out the window at the thick trees that sheltered the house. It was tucked behind a grove of quaking aspen, and the cool leaves quivered continually in the breeze. With the windows of the study thrown open, the scents of pine and sweet peas wafted into the room. He could only smell his own frustration. The bright glint of blue that was the bay didn't lift his mood. He'd spent enough time in prison to feel shut in, however lovely the surroundings.

Cracking his knuckles, he turned away from the view. "We could be stuck in this place for weeks."

"You should learn to appreciate the scenery. And the room." His partner's nervous habit was an annoyance, but he tolerated it. For the time being, he needed Hawkins. After the emeralds had been found...well, that was another matter. "I certainly prefer the house to the boat for the long term. And finding the right accommodations across the bay on this island was difficult and expensive."

"That's another thing." Hawkins pulled out a cigarette. "We're spending a bundle, and all we've got to show for it is a bunch of old papers."

"I assure you, the emeralds will be more than worth any overhead."

"If the bloody things exist."

"They exist." Caufield waved the smoke away in a fussy gesture, but his eyes were intense. "They exist. Before the summer ends, I'm going to hold them in my hands." He lifted them. They were smooth and white and clever. He could all but see the glittery green stones dripping from his palms. "They're going to be mine."

"Ours," Hawkins corrected.

Caufield looked up and smiled. "Ours, of course."

After dinner, Max went back to his lists. He told himself he was being responsible, doing what needed to be done. In truth he'd needed to put some distance between himself and Lilah. He couldn't delude himself into thinking it was only desire he felt for her. That was a basic biological reaction and could be triggered by a face on a television screen, a voice on the radio.

There was nothing so simple or so easily dismissed about his reaction to Lilah.

Every day he was around her his emotions became more tangled, more unsteady and more ungovernable. It had been difficult enough when he had looked at her and wanted her. Now he looked at her and felt his needs meld with dreams that were unrealistic, foolish and impossible.

He'd never given much thought to falling in love, and none at all to marriage and family. His work had always been enough, filling the gaps nicely. He enjoyed women, and if he fell far short of being the Don Juan of Cornell, he had managed a few comfortable and satisfying relationships. Still, he'd never felt a burning need to race to the altar or to start building picket fences.

Bachelorhood had suited him, and when he had thought about the future, he had imagined himself getting crusty, perhaps taking up the pipe and buying a nice dog for companionship.

He was an uncomplicated man who lived a quiet life. At least until recently. Once he had helped the Calhouns locate the emeralds, he would go back to that quiet life. And he would go back alone. While things might never be exactly the same for him, he knew that she would forget the awkward college professor before the winter winds blew across the bay.

And he figured the sooner he finished what he had agreed to do and went away, the easier it would be to go. Gathering his lists, he decided it was time to take the next step toward ending the most incredible summer of his life.

He found Amanda in her room, going over her own lists. These were for her wedding, which would take place in three weeks.

"I'm sorry to interrupt."

"That's okay." Amanda pushed her glasses back up her nose and smiled. "I've got everything under control here except my nerves." She tapped her papers together and set them aside on the slant-top desk. "I was all for eloping, but Aunt Coco would have murdered me."

"I guess weddings take a lot of work."

"Even planning a small family ceremony is like plotting a major offensive. Or being in the circus," she decided, and laughed. "You end up juggling photographers with color schemes and fittings and floral arrangements. But I'm getting good at it. I took care of C.C.'s, I ought to be able to do the same for myself. Except..." Pulling her glasses off, she began to fold and unfold the earpieces. "The whole thing scares the good sense right out of me. So, take my mind off it, Max, and tell me what's on yours."

"I've been working on this. I don't know how complete it is." He set his list in front of her. "The names of all the servants I could find, the ones who worked here the summer Bianca died."

Lips pursed, Amanda slid her glasses back on. She appreciated the precise handwriting and neat columns. "All of these?"

"According to the ledger I went through. I thought we could contact the families, maybe even luck out and find a few still alive."

"Anyone who worked here back then would have to be over the century mark."

"Not necessarily. A lot of the help could have been young. Some of the maids, the garden and kitchen help." When she began to tap her pencil on the desk, he shrugged. "It's a long shot, I know, but—"

"No." Her gaze still on the list, she nodded. "I like it. Even if we can't reach anyone who actually worked here then, they might have told stories to their children. It's a safe bet some of them were local—maybe still are." She looked up at him. "Good thinking, Max."

"I'd like to help you try to pin some of the names down."

"I can use all the help I can get. It's not going to be easy."

"Research is what I'm best at."

"You've got yourself a deal." She held out a hand to shake. "Why don't we split the list in half and start tomorrow? I imagine the cook, the butler, the housekeeper, Bianca's personal maid and the nanny all traveled with them from New York."

"But the day help, and the lower positions were hired locally."

"Exactly. We could divide the list in that way, then cross-reference..." She trailed off as Sloan came in through the terrace doors carrying a bottle of champagne and two glasses.

"Leave you alone for five minutes and you start entertaining other men in your room." He set the wine aside. "And talking about cross-referencing, too. Must be serious."

"We hadn't even gotten to alphabetizing," Amanda told Sloan.

"Looks like I got here just in time." He took the pencil out of her hand before drawing her to her feet. "In another minute you might have been hip deep in correlations."

They certainly didn't need him, Max decided. By the way they were kissing each other, it was apparent they'd forgotten all about him. On his way out, he cast one envious look over his shoulder. They were just smiling at each other, saying nothing. It was obvious that they were two people who knew what they wanted. Each other.

Back in his room, Max decided he would spend the rest of the evening working on notes for his book. Or, if he could gather up the courage, he could sit in front of the old manual typewriter Coco had unearthed for him. He could take that step, that big one, and begin writing the story instead of preparing to write it.

He took one look at the battered Remington and felt his stomach clutch. He wanted to sit down, to lay his fingers on those keys, just as desperately as a man wants to hold a loved and desired woman in his arms. He was as terrified of facing the single blank sheet of paper as he would have been of a firing squad. Maybe more so.

He just needed to prepare, Max told himself. His reference books needed to be positioned better. His notes had to be more easily accessible. The light had to be adjusted.

He thought of dozens of minute details to be perfected before he could begin. Once he had accomplished that, had tried and failed to think of more, he sat.

Here he was, he realized, about to begin something he'd dreamed of doing his entire life. All he had to do was write the first sentence, and he would be committed.

His fingers curled into fists on the keys.

Why did he think he could write a book? A thesis, a lecture, yes. That's what he was trained to do. But a book, God, a novel wasn't something anyone could be taught to do. It took imagination and wit and a sense of drama. Daydreaming a story and articulating it on paper were two entirely different things.

Wasn't it foolish to begin something that was bound to lead to failure? As long as he was preparing to write the book, there was no risk and no disappointment. He could go on preparing for years without any sense of shame. If he started it, really started it, there would be no more hiding behind notes and research books. When he failed, he wouldn't even have the dream.

Wound tight, he ran his fingers over the keys while his mind jumped with dozens of excuses to postpone the moment. When the first sentence streaked from his brain to his fingers and appeared on the blank sheet of paper, he let out a long, unsteady breath.

Three hours later, he had ten full sheets. The story that had swum through his head for so long was taking shape with words. His words. He knew it was probably dreadful, but it didn't seem to matter. He was writing, actually writing. The process of it fascinated and exhilarated. The sound of it, the clatter and thud of the keys, delighted him.

He'd stripped off his shirt and shoes and sat bent over, his brows together, his eyes slightly unfocused. His fingers would race over the keys then stop while he strained to find the way to take what was in his head and put it on paper.

That was how Lilah found him. He'd left his terrace doors open for the breeze, though he'd long since stopped noticing it. The room was dark but for the slant of light from the lamp on the desk. She stood watching him, aroused by his total concentration, charmed by the way his hair fell into his eyes.

Was it any wonder she had come to him? she thought. She was so completely in love with him, how could she stay away? It couldn't be wrong to want to have a night with him, to show him that love in a way he might understand and accept. She needed to belong to him, to forge a bond that would matter to both of them.

Not sex, but intimacy. It had begun the moment he had lain half-drowned on the shingle and lifted a hand to her face. There was a connection she couldn't escape. And as she had risen from her own bed to come to his, one that she no longer wanted to escape.

Her instinct had led her to his room tonight as surely as it had led her to the beach during the storm.

The decision was hers, she knew. However badly he wanted her, he wouldn't take what wasn't offered. And he would hesitate to take even that because of his rules and his codes. Perhaps if he'd loved her... But she couldn't let herself think of that. In time, he would love her. Her own feelings were too deep and too strong not to find their match.

So she would take the first step. Seduction.

His concentration was so intense that a shout wouldn't have broken it. But her scent, whispering across the room on the night breeze, shattered it. Desire pumped into his blood before he glanced up and saw her in the doorway. The white robe fluttered around her. Caught in the fanning air, her hair danced over her shoulders. Behind her the sky was a black canvas, and she had—illusion to reality—stepped out of it. She smiled and his fingers went limp on the keys.

"Lilah."

"I had a dream." It was true, and speaking the truth helped calm her nerves. "About you and me. There was moonlight. I could almost feel the light on my skin until you touched me." She stepped inside, the movement causing the silk to make a faint shushing sound, like water rippling over water. "Then I didn't feel anything but you. There were flowers, the fragrance very light, very sweet. And a nightingale, that long liquid call for a mate. It was a lovely dream, Max." She stopped beside his desk. "Then I woke up, alone."

He was certain the ball of tension in his stomach would rip free any moment and leave him helpless. She was more beautiful than any fantasy, her hair like wildfire across her shoulders, her graceful body silhouetted enticingly beneath the thin, shifting silk.

"It's late." He tried to clear the huskiness from his throat. "You shouldn't be here."

"Why?"

"Because . . . it's—"

"Improper?" she suggested. "Reckless?" She brushed the hair from his brow. "Dangerous?"

Max lurched to his feet to grasp the back of the chair. "Yes, all of that."

There were age-old women's secrets in her eyes. "But I feel reckless, Max. Don't you?"

Desperate was the word. Desperate for just one touch. His fingers whitened on the chair back. "There's a matter of respect."

Her smile was suddenly very warm and very sweet. "I respect you, Max."

"No, I mean . . ." She looked so lovely when she smiled that way, so young, so fragile. "We decided to be friends."

"We are." With her eyes on his, she lifted her hand to smooth back her hair. Her rings glittered in the lamplight.

"And this is—"

"Something we both want," she finished. When she stepped toward him, he jerked back. The chair tumbled over. Her laughter wasn't mocking, but warm and delighted. "Do I make you nervous, Max?"

"That's a mild word for it." He could barely drag air through his dry throat. At his sides his hands were fisted, twins of the fists in the pit of his stomach. "Lilah, I don't want to ruin what we have together. Lord knows I don't want you to break my heart."

She smiled, feeling a surge of hope through her own nerves. "Could I?"

"You know you could. You've probably lost track of the hearts you've broken."

There it was again, she thought as disappointment shuddered through her. He still saw her, would likely always see her, as the careless siren who lured men, then discarded them. He didn't understand that it was her heart on the line, had been her heart on the line all along. She wouldn't let it stop her—couldn't. Tonight, being with him tonight, was meant. She felt it too strongly to be wrong.

"Tell me, Professor, do you ever dream of me?" She stepped toward him; he backed up. Now they stood in the shadows beyond the lamplight. "Do you ever lie in the dark and wonder what it would be like?"

He was losing ground fast. His mind was so full of her there wasn't room for anything but need. "You know I do."

Another step and they were caught in a slash of moonlight as white as her robe, and as seductive. "And when you dream of it, where are we?"

"It doesn't seem to matter where." He had to touch her, couldn't resist, even if it was only to brush his fingertips over her hair. "We're alone."

"We're alone now." She slid her hands over his shoulders to link them behind his neck. "Kiss me, Max. The way you did the first time, when we were sitting on the grass in the sunlight."

His fingers were in her hair, taut as wires. "It won't end there, Lilah. Not this time."

Her lips curved as they lifted to his. "Just kiss me."

He fought to gentle his grip, to keep his mouth easy as it cruised over hers. Surely he was strong enough to hold back this clawing need to ravage. He wouldn't hurt her. He swore it. And clung to the dim hope that he could have this one night with her and emerge unscathed.

So sweet, she thought. So lovely. The tenderness of the kiss was all the more poignant as she could feel the tremble of repressed passion in both of them. Her heart, already brimming with love, overflowed. When their lips parted, there were tears glittering in her eyes.

"I don't want it to end there." She touched her lips to his again. "Neither of us do."

"No."

"Make love with me, Max," she murmured. She kept her eyes on his as she stepped back, unbelting her robe. "I need you tonight." The robe slithered to the floor.

Beneath it her skin was as white and smooth as marble. Her long slender limbs might have been carved and polished by an artist's hands. She stood, cloaked only in moonlight, and waited.

He'd never seen anything more perfect, more elegant or fragile. Suddenly his hands felt big and clumsy, his fingers rough. His breath tore raggedly through his lips as he touched her. Though his fingers barely floated over her skin, he was terrified he would leave bruises behind. Fascinated, he watched his hand skim over her, tracing the slope of her shoulders, sliding down the graceful arms and back again. Carefully, very carefully, brushing over the water-soft skin of her breasts.

First her legs went weak. No one had ever touched her like this, with such drugging gentleness. It was as though she were the first woman he had ever seen and he was memorizing her face and form through his fingertips. She had come to seduce, yet her arms lay weighted at her sides. And she was seduced. Her head fell back in an involuntary gesture of surrender. He had no way of knowing that this surrender was her first.

That vulnerable column of her throat was impossible to resist. He pressed his mouth against it even as his palm brushed lightly over the point of her breast.

The combination had a bolt of sensation shooting through her. Stunned by it, she jolted and gasped out his name.

He retreated instantly, cursing himself. "I'm sorry." He was half-blind with needs and shook his head to clear it. "I've always been clumsy."

"Clumsy?" In a haze of longing, she swayed toward him, running her lips over his shoulder, his throat, down his chest. "Can't you feel what you're doing to me? Don't stop." Her mouth found his and lingered. "I think I'd die if you did."

The barrage on his system nearly felled him. Her hands streaked over him, impatient and greedy. Her mouth, Lord her mouth was hot and quick, searing his skin with every breathy kiss. He couldn't think, could barely breathe. There was nothing to do but feel.

Straining for control, he lifted her face to his, calming her lips, drugging them and her as he centered all of his needs into that one endless kiss. Yes, he could feel what he was doing to her, and it amazed him. On a low, throaty groan, she went limp in a surrender more erotic than any seduction. Her body seemed to melt into his in total pliancy, total trust. When he lifted her into his arms she made a small, lazy sound of pleasure.

Her eyes were nearly closed. He could see the glint of green under the cover of her lashes. As he carried her to the bed he felt as strong as Hercules. Gently, watching her face, he laid her on the covers.

There was moonlight here, streaming through the windows like liquid silver. He could hear the wind sighing through the trees and the distant drum of water on rock. Her scent, as mysterious as Eve, reached for him as easily as her arms.

He took her hands. Struck by the romance of the night, he brought them to his lips, skimming his mouth over her knuckles, down her fingertips, over her palms. All the time, he watched her as he scraped lightly with his teeth, soothed and aroused with his tongue. He heard her breath quicken, watched her eyes cloud with dazed pleasure and confusion as he made love to her hands. He felt the thunder of her pulse when he pressed his lips to her wrist.

He was bringing her something she hadn't prepared for. Total helplessness. Did he know how completely she was in his power? she wondered hazily. The drunk and weighty pleasure was flowing from her fingertips into every part of her. When his lips slid down her arm to nuzzle the inside of her elbow, a moan was wrenched from her.

She wasn't even aware that she was moving under him, inviting him to take anything, everything he wanted. When his mouth came to hers at last, his name was the only word she could form.

He fought back greed. It was impossible not to feel it, with her body so hot, so soft, so agile beneath his. But he refused to give in to it. Tonight, for there might only be tonight, would last. He wanted more than that fast and frantic union his body ached for. He wanted the dazzling pleasure of learning every inch of her, of discovering her secrets, her weaknesses. With patience he could brand in his brain what it was like to touch her and feel her tremble, what it was like to taste and hear her sigh. When her hands moved over him, he knew she was as lost in the night as he.

He slid down her slowly, searing her flesh with openmouthed kisses, whispering fingertips. With torturous patience he lingered at her breasts until they were achingly full with pleasure. Down, gradually down, while her fingers clenched and unclenched in his hair. He could hear her now, soft, incoherent pleas, gasping sighs as he trailed his mouth down her torso, nipped teasing teeth across her hip. She felt his breath flutter against her thigh and cried out, rearing up as the first hot wave slammed into her.

She flew over the edge then cartwheeled down as he roamed relentlessly to her knee.

He couldn't get enough. Every taste of her was more potent than the last. He sated himself on it as the tension began to roar in his temples, burn in his blood. Grasping her flailing hands, he drove himself mad by pushing her to peak again. When her body went lax, when her breath was sobbing, he brought his mouth back to hers.

She was willing to beg, but she couldn't speak. Sensation after sensation tore through her, leaving her weak and giddy and aching for more. Desperate for him, she fumbled with the catch of his jeans. She would have screamed with frustration if his mouth hadn't seduced hers into a groan.

Tugging, gasping, she dragged the denim over his hips, too delirious to know that her urgent fingers were making him shudder. Damp flesh slid over damp flesh as they pulled the jeans aside.

"Wait." The word came harshly through his lips as he fought to hold on to the last of his control. "Look at me." His fingers tightened in her hair as she opened her eyes. "Look at me," he repeated. "I want you to remember."

Muscles trembling with the effort to go slowly, he slipped into her. Her eyes went cloudy but remained on his as they set an easy rhythm. She knew as he filled her, with himself, with such perfect beauty, that she would always remember.

It was so sweet, so natural, the way his head rested between her breasts. Lilah smiled at the sensation as she stroked his hair. One hand was still linked with his as it had been when they'd slid over the crest together. Half-dreaming now, she imagined what it would be like to fall asleep together, just like this, night after night.

He could feel her relax beneath him, her body warm and pliant, her skin still sheened with the dew of passion. Her heartbeat was slowing gradually. For a moment he could pretend that this was one night among many. That she could belong to him in that complex and intimate way a woman belonged to a man.

He knew he'd given her pleasure, and that for a time they had been as bound together as two people could be. But now, he hadn't an idea what he should say—because all he wanted to say was that he loved her.

"What are you thinking?" she murmured.

He steadied himself. "My brain's not working yet."

Her laugh was low and warm. She shifted, wriggling down until they were face-to-face. "Then I'll tell you what I'm thinking." She brought her mouth to his in a languid, lingering kiss. "I like your lips." Teasingly she nipped the lower one. "And your hands. Your shoulders, your eyes." As she spoke, she trailed a fingertip up and down his spine. "In fact, at the moment I can't think of anything I don't like about you."

"I'll remind you of that the next time I irritate you." He combed her hair back because he enjoyed seeing it spread over his sheets. "I can't believe I'm here with you, like this."

"Didn't you feel it, Max, almost from the beginning?"

"Yes." He traced her mouth with a fingertip. "I figured it was wishful thinking."

"You don't give yourself enough credit, Professor." She traced light, lazy kisses over his face. "You're an attractive man with an admirable mind and a sense of compassion that's irresistible." Her eyes didn't light with amusement when he shifted. Instead she lay a hand on his cheek. "When you made love with me tonight, it was beautiful. The most beautiful night of my life."

She saw it in his eyes. Not embarrassment now, but plain disbelief. Because she was defenseless, stripped to the soul, nothing could have hurt her more. "Sorry," she said tightly and moved away. "I'm sure that sounds trite coming from me."

"Lilah..."

"No, it's fine." She pressed her lips together until she was certain her voice would be light and breezy again. "No use complicating things." As she sat up, she tossed her hair back. "There aren't any strings here, Professor. No trapdoors, no fine print. We're two consenting adults who enjoy each other. Agreed?"

"I'm not sure."

"Let's just say we'll take it a day at a time. Or a night at a time." She leaned over to kiss him. "Now that we've got that settled, I'd better go."

"Don't." He took her hand before she could slip off the bed. "Don't go. No strings," he said carefully as he studied her. "No complications. Just stay with me tonight."

She smiled a little. "I'll just seduce you again."

"I was hoping you'd say that." He pulled her against him. "I want you with me when the sun comes up."

Chapter Eight

When the sun came up to pour golden light through the windows and chase away the last dusky shadows, she was in his arms. It seemed incredible to him that her head would be resting on his shoulder, her hand fisted lightly over his heart. She slept like a child, deeply, curled toward him for warmth and comfort.

Though the night was over, he lay still, loath to wake her. The birds had begun their morning chorus. It was so quiet, he could hear the wind breathing through the trees. He knew that soon the sound of saws and hammers would disrupt the peace and bring reality back. So he clung to this short interlude between the mystery of the night and the bustle of day.

She sighed and settled closer as he stroked her hair. He remembered how generous she had been in those dark sleepy hours. It seemed he had only to think, to wish, and she would turn toward him. Again and again they had loved, in silence and with perfect understanding.

He wanted to believe in miracles, to believe that it had been as special and monumental a night for her as it had been for him. He was afraid to take her words at face value.

No one's ever made me feel the way you do.

Yet they had played over and over in his head, giving him hope. If he was careful and patient and weighed each step before it was taken, maybe he could make a miracle.

Though he didn't feel suited to the role of prince, he tilted her face to his to wake her with a kiss.

"Mmm." She smiled but didn't open her eyes. "Can I have another?"

Her voice, husky with sleep, sent desire shivering along his skin. He forgot to be careful. He forgot to be patient. His mouth took hers the second time with an edgy desperation that had her system churning before she was fully awake.

"Max." Throbbing, she locked herself around him. "I want you. Now. Right now."

He was already inside her, already dragging her with him where they both wanted to go. The ride was fast and furious, shooting them both to the top where they clung, breathless and giddy.

When her hands slid off his damp back, she still hadn't opened her eyes. "Good morning," she managed. "I just had the most incredible dream."

Though he was still light-headed, he braced on his forearms to look down at her. "Tell me about it."

"I was in bed with this very sexy man. He had big blue eyes, dark hair that was always falling in his face." Smiling, she opened her eyes and brushed it back for him. "This long, streamlined body." Still watching him, she moved her hands deliberately over him. "I didn't want to wake up, but when I did, it was even better than the dream."

Afraid he was crushing her, he rolled to reverse their positions. "What are the chances of spending the rest of our lives in this bed?"

She dropped a kiss on his shoulder. "I'm game." Then she groaned when the drone of power tools cut through the morning quiet. "It can't be seven-thirty."

As reluctant as she, he glanced at the clock beside the bed. "I'm afraid it can."

"Tell me it's my day off."

"I wish I could."

"Lie," she suggested, laying her cheek on his chest.

"Will you let me take you to work?"

She winced. "Don't say that word."

"Go for a drive with me after?"

She lifted her head again. "Where?"

"Anywhere."

Tilting her head, she smiled. "My favorite place."

Max kept his mind off Lilah—or tried to—by focusing on the multilayered task of locating people to go with the names on his list. He checked court records, police records, church records and death certificates. His meticulous legwork was rewarded with a handful of addresses.

When he felt he'd exhausted all the leads for that day, he drove by C.C.'s garage. He found her buried to the waist under the hood of a black sedan.

"I'm sorry to interrupt," he shouted over the din jingling out of a portable radio.

"Then don't." There was a streak of grease over her brow, but her scowl disappeared when she looked up and saw Max. "Hi."

"I could come back."

"Why, just because I snapped your head off?" She grinned, taking a rag out of her coveralls to wipe her hands. "Buy you a drink?" She jerked her head toward a soft drink machine.

"No, thanks. I just stopped by to ask you about a car."

"You're driving Lilah's, aren't you? Is it acting up?"

"No. The thing is I might be doing a lot of driving in the next few days, and I don't feel right using her car. I thought you might know if there's anything for sale in the area."

C.C. pursed her lips. "You want to buy a car?"

"Nothing extravagant. Just some convenient transportation. Then when I get back to New York..." He trailed off. He didn't want to think about going back to New York. "I can always sell it later."

"It so happens I do know somebody with a car for sale. Me."

"You?"

Nodding, she stuffed the rag back into her pocket. "With a baby coming, I've decided to turn in my Spitfire for a family car."

"Spitfire?" He wasn't sure what that was, but it didn't sound like the kind of car a dignified college professor would drive.

"I've had her for years, and I sure would feel better selling her to someone I know." She already had his hand and was pulling him outside.

There it sat, a fire-engine red toy with a white rag top and bucket seats. "Well, I..."

"I rebuilt the engine a couple of years ago." C.C. was busy opening the hood. "She drives like a dream. There's less than ten thousand miles on the tires. I'm the original owner, so I can guarantee she's been treated like a lady. And there's..." She glanced up and grinned. "I sound like a guy in a plaid sports jacket."

He could see his face in the shiny red paint. "I've never owned a sports car."

The wistfulness in his voice made C.C. smile. "Tell you what, leave me Lilah's car, drive her around. See how she suits you."

Max found himself behind the wheel, trying not to grin like a fool as the wind streamed through his hair. What would his students think, he wondered, if they could see sturdy old Dr. Quartermain tooling around in a flashy convertible? They'd probably think he'd gone around the bend. Maybe he had, but he was having the time of his life.

It was a car that would suit Lilah, he thought. He could already see her sitting beside him, her hair dancing as she laughed and lifted her arms to the wind. Or kicked back in the seat, her eyes closed, letting the sun warm her face.

It was a nice dream, and it could come true. At least for a while. And maybe he wouldn't sell the car when he got back to New York. There was no law that said he had to drive a practical sedan. He could keep it to remind him of a few incredible weeks that had changed his life.

Maybe he'd never be sturdy old Dr. Quartermain again.

He cruised up the winding mountain roads, then back down again to try out the little car in traffic. Delighted with the world in general, he sat at a light, tapping his fingers against the wheel to the beat of the music on the radio.

There were people jamming the sidewalks, crowding the shops. If he'd seen a parking place, he might have whipped in, strolled into a shop himself just to test his endurance. Instead, he entertained himself by watching people scout for that perfect T-shirt.

He noticed the man with dark hair and a trim dark beard standing on the curb, staring at him. Full of himself and the spiffy car, Max grinned and waved. He was halfway down the block before it hit him. He braked, causing a bellow of bad-tempered honking. Thinking fast, he turned a sharp left, streaked down a side street and fought his way through traffic back to the intersection. The man was gone. Max searched the street but couldn't find a sign of him. He cursed low and bitterly over the lack of a parking space, over his own slow-wittedness.

The hair had been dyed, and the beard had hid part of the face. But the eyes...Max couldn't forget the eyes. It had been Caufield standing on the crowded sidewalk, looking at Max not with admiration or absent interest, but with barely controlled rage.

He had himself under control by the time he picked Lilah up at the visitors' center. He had made what he considered the logical decision not to tell her. The less she knew, the less she was involved. The less she was involved, the better chance there was that she wouldn't be hurt.

She was too impulsive, he reflected. If she knew Caufield had been in the village, she would try to hunt him down herself. And she was too clever. If she managed to find him... The idea made Max's blood run cold. No one knew better than he how ruthless the man could be.

When he saw Lilah coming across the lot toward the car, he knew he'd risk anything, even his life, to keep her safe.

"Well, well, what's this?" Brows lifted, she tapped a finger on the fender. "My old heap wasn't good enough, so you borrowed my sister's?"

"What?" Foolishly he'd forgotten the car and everything else since he'd recognized Caufield. "Oh, the car."

"Yes, the car." She leaned over to kiss him, and was puzzled by his absent response and the pat on her shoulder.

"Actually, I'm thinking of buying it. C.C.'s in the market for a family car, so..."

"So you're going to buy yourself a snappy little toy."

"I know it's not my usual style," he began.

"I wasn't going to say that." Her brows drew together as she studied his face. Something was going on in that complicated mind of his. "I was going to say good for you. I'm glad you're giving yourself a break." She hopped in and stretched. Her lifted hand reached for his, but he only gave it a light squeeze, then released it. Telling herself she was being oversensitive, she fixed a smile in place. "So, how about that drive? I was thinking we could cruise down the coast."

"I'm a little tired." He hated lying, but he needed to get back to talk to Trent and Sloan, to feed the new description to the police. "Can I have a rain check?"

"Sure." She managed to keep her smile in place. He was so polite, so distant. Wanting some echo of their previous intimacy, she put a hand over his when he slipped into the car beside her. "I'm always up for a nap. Your room or mine?"

"I'm not . . . I don't think that's a good idea."

His hand was tense over the gearshift, and his fingers made no move to link with hers. He wouldn't even look at her, hadn't really looked at her, she realized, since she'd crossed the lot.

"I see." She lifted her hand from his and let it fall in her lap. "Under the circumstances, I'm sure you're right."

"Lilah—"

"What?"

No, he decided. He needed to do this his way. "Nothing." Reaching for the keys, he switched on the ignition.

They didn't speak on the way home. Max continued to convince himself that lying to her was the best way. Maybe she was miffed because he'd put off the drive, but he'd make it up to her. He just had to keep out of her way until he'd handled a few details. In any case his mind was crowded with possibilities that he needed time and space to work through. If Caufield and Hawkins were both still on the island, both of them bold enough to stroll through the village, did that mean they had found something useful in the papers? Were they still looking? Had they, as he had, dipped into the resources at the library to find out more?

They knew he was alive now. Would they manage to connect him with the Calhouns? If they considered him a liability, would his relationship with Lilah put her in danger?

That was a risk he couldn't afford to take.

He turned up the winding road that brought the peak of The Towers into view.

"I may have to go back to New York sooner than I expected," he said, thinking out loud.

To keep from protesting, she pressed her lips tight. "Really?"

He glanced over, cleared his throat. "Yes . . . ah, business. I could continue to do my research from there."

"That's very considerate of you, Professor. I'm sure you'd hate to leave a job half-done. And you wouldn't have any awkward relationships to interfere."

His mind was already focused on what needed to be done, and he made an absent sound of agreement.

By the time they pulled up at The Towers, Lilah had managed to turn the hurt into anger. He didn't want to be with her, and by his attitude it was plain he regretted that they'd ever been together. Fine. She wasn't about to sit around and sulk because some highbrow college professor wasn't interested in her.

She resisted slamming the car door, barely resisted biting his hand off at the wrist when he set it on her shoulder. "Maybe we can drive down the coast tomorrow."

She glanced at his hand, then at his face. "Don't hold your breath."

He jammed his hands into his pockets as she strolled up the steps. Definitely miffed, he thought.

By the time he had relayed his information to the other men and had fought his way through the pecking order at the police station, he really was tired. It might have been tension or the fact that he'd only had a couple hours' sleep the night before, but he gave in, stretched across his bed and tuned out until dinner.

Feeling better, he wandered downstairs. He thought about finding Lilah, asking her to walk in the gardens after the meal. Or maybe they'd take a drive after all, in the moonlight. It hadn't been a very big lie, and now that he'd unburdened himself to the police, he wouldn't have to dwell on it. In any case, if he decided it was best to leave, he might not have another evening with her.

Yes, a drive. Maybe he could ask her if she'd consider visiting him in New York—or just going away for a weekend somewhere. It didn't have to end, not if he started taking those careful steps.

He strolled into the parlor, found it empty and strolled out again. Just the two of them, watching the moon on the water, maybe pulling over to walk along the beach. He could begin to court her properly. He imagined she'd be amused by the term, but it was what he wanted to do.

He followed the sound of a piano into the music room. Suzanna was alone, playing for herself. The music seemed to match the expression in her eyes. There was a sadness in them, too deep for anyone else to feel. But when she saw him, she stopped and smiled.

"I didn't mean to interrupt."

"That's all right. It's time to get back to the real world anyway. Amanda took the kids into town so I was taking advantage of the lull."

"I was just looking for Lilah."

"Oh, she's gone."

"Gone?"

Suzanna was pushing back from the piano when Max barked the word and had her rising slowly. "Yes, she went out."

"Where? When?"

"Just a little while ago." Suzanna studied him as she crossed the room. "I think she had a date."

"A—a date?" He felt as though someone had just swung a sledgehammer into his solar plexus.

"I'm sorry, Max." Concerned, she laid a comforting hand on his. She didn't think she'd ever seen a man more miserably in love. "I didn't realize. She may have just gone out to meet friends, or to be by herself."

No, he thought, shaking his head. That would be worse. If she was alone, and Caufield was anywhere close... He shook off the panic. It wasn't Lilah the man was after, but the emeralds.

"It's all right, I only wanted to talk to her about something."

"Does she know how you feel?"

"No—yes. I don't know," he said lamely. He saw his romantic dreams about moonlight and courtship go up in smoke. "It doesn't matter."

"It would to her. Lilah doesn't take people or their feelings lightly, Max."

No strings, he thought. No trapdoors. Well, he'd already fallen through the trapdoor, and his feelings were the noose around his neck. But that wasn't the point. "I'm just concerned about her going out alone. The police haven't caught Hawkins or Caufield yet."

"She went out to dinner. I can't see anyone popping up in a restaurant and demanding emeralds she doesn't have." Suzanna gave his hand a friendly squeeze. "Come on, you'll feel better when you've eaten. Aunt Coco's lemon chicken should be about ready."

He sat through dinner, struggling to pretend that he had an appetite, that the empty place at the table didn't bother him. He discussed the progress of the servant's list with Amanda, dodged Coco's request to read his cards and felt generally miserable. Fred, sitting on his left foot, benefited from his mood by gobbling up the morsels of chicken Max slipped to him.

He considered driving into town, casually cruising, stopping at a few clubs and restaurants. But decided that would make him look like as a big a jerk as he felt. In the end he retreated to his room and lost himself in his book.

The story didn't come as easily as it had the night before. Now it was mostly fits and starts with a lot of long pauses. Still he found even the pauses constructive as an hour passed into two, and two into three. It wasn't until he glanced at his watch and saw it was after midnight that he realized he hadn't heard Lilah come home. He'd deliberately left his door ajar so that he would know when she passed down the hall.

There was a good chance he'd been engrossed in his work and hadn't noticed when she'd walked by to her room. If she'd gone out to dinner, surely she'd be home by now. No one could eat for five hours. But he had to know.

He went quietly. There was a light in Suzanna's room, but the others were dark. At Lilah's door, he hesitated, then knocked softly. Feeling awkward, he put his hand on the knob. He'd spent the night with her, he reminded himself. She could hardly be offended if he looked in to see if she was asleep.

She wasn't. She wasn't even there. The bed was made; the old iron head- and footboards that had probably belonged to a servant had been painted a gleaming white. The rest was color, so much it dazzled the eyes.

The spread was a patchwork quilt, expertly made from scraps of fabrics. Polka dots, checks, stripes, faded reds and blues. It was piled high with pillows of varied shapes and sizes. The kind of bed, Max thought, a person could sink into and sleep the day away. It suited her.

The room was huge, as most were in The Towers, but she'd cluttered it and made it cozy. On the walls that were painted a dramatic teal were sketches of wildflowers. The bold signature in the corners told him she'd done them herself. He hadn't even known she could draw. It made him realize there was quite a bit he didn't know about the woman he was in love with.

After closing the door behind him, he wandered the room, looking for pieces of her.

A baker's rack was packed with books. Keats and Byron jumbled with grisly murder mysteries and contemporary romances. A little sitting area was grouped in front of one of her windows, a blouse tossed carelessly over the back of a Queen Anne chair, earrings and glittering bracelets scattered over a Hepplewhite table. There was a bowl of smooth gemstones beside a china penguin. When he picked the bird up, it played a jazzy rendition of "That's Entertainment."

She had candles everywhere, in everything from elegant Meissen to a tacky reproduction of a unicorn. Dozens of pictures of her family were scattered throughout. He picked up one framed snapshot of a couple, arms around each other's waists as they laughed into the camera. Her parents, he thought. Lilah's resemblance to the man, Suzanna's to the woman were strong enough to make him certain of it.

When the cuckoo in the clock on the wall jumped out, he jolted and realized it was twelve-thirty. Where the hell was she?

Now he paced, from the window where she'd hung faceted crystals to the brass urn filled with dried flowers, from bookcase to bureau. Nerves humming, he picked up an ornate cobalt bottle to sniff. And smelled her. He set it down hastily when the door opened.

She looked...incredible. Her hair windblown, her face flushed. She wore some sheer drapey dress that swirled around her legs in bleeding colors. Long multicolored columns of beads danced at her ears. She lifted a brow and closed the door.

"Well," she said. "Make yourself at home."

"Where the hell have you been?" The demand shot out, edged with frustration and worry.

"Did I miss curfew, Daddy?" She tossed a beaded bag onto the bureau. She'd lifted a hand to remove an earring when he whirled her around.

"Don't get cute with me. I've been worried sick. You've been out for hours. No one knew where you were." Or who you were with, he thought, but managed to bite that one back.

She jerked her arm free. He saw the temper flash hot into her eyes, but her voice was cool and slow and unmoved. "It may surprise you, Professor, but I've been going out on my own for a long time."

"It's different now."

"Oh?" Deliberately she turned back to the bureau. Taking her time, she unfastened an earring. "Why?"

"Because we..." Because we're lovers. "Because we don't know where Caufield is," he said with more control. "Or how dangerous he might be."

"I've also been looking out for myself for a long time." Deceptively sleepy, her eyes met his in the mirror. "Is the lecture over?"

"It's not a lecture, Lilah, I was worried. I have a right to know your plans."

Still watching him, she slid bracelets from her arms. "Just how do you figure that?"

"We're—friends."

The smile didn't reach her eyes. "Are we?"

He jammed impotent hands into his pockets. "I care about you. And after what happened last night, I thought we...I thought we meant something to each other. Now, twenty-four hours later you're out with someone else. Looking like that."

She stepped out of her shoes. "We went to bed last night, and enjoyed it." She nearly choked over the bitterness lodged in her throat. "As I recall we agreed there'd be no complications." Tilting her head, she studied him. Her easy shrug masked the fact that her hands were balled tight. "Since you're here, I suppose we could arrange a repeat performance." Her voice a purr, she stepped closer to run a finger down the front of his shirt. "That's what you want from me, isn't it, Max?"

Furious, he pushed her hand aside. "I don't care to be the second act of the evening."

The flush vanished, leaving her cheeks pale before she turned away. "Congratulations," she whispered. "Direct hit."

"What do you want me to say? That you can come and go as you please, with whomever you please, and I'll sit up and beg for the scraps from the table?"

"I don't want you to say anything. I just want you to leave me alone."

"I'm not going anywhere until we've straightened this out."

"Fine." The cuckoo chirped out again as she unzipped her dress. "Stay as long as you like. I'm getting ready for bed."

She stepped out of the dress, tossed it aside, then walked over to her vanity in a lacy, beribboned chemise. Sitting, she picked up her brush to drag it through her hair.

"What are you so angry about?"

"Angry." She set her teeth as she slapped the bristles against her scalp. "What makes you think I'm angry? Just because you're waiting for me in my room, incensed that I had the nerve to make plans of my own when you didn't have the time or inclination to spend an hour with me. Unless it was in the sack."

"What are you talking about?" He took her arm, then yelped when she rapped the brush hard on his knuckles.

"I'll let you know when I want to be touched."

He swore, grabbed the brush and tossed it across the room. Too enraged to see the surprise in her eyes, he hauled her to her feet. "I asked you a question."

She cocked her chin. "If you've finished your temper tantrum—" He nearly lifted her off her feet.

"Don't push," he said between his teeth.

"You hurt me." The words exploded out of her. "Last night, even this morning, I was worth a little of your time and attention. As long as there was sex. Then this afternoon, you couldn't even look at me. You couldn't wait to dump me off here and get away from me."

"That's crazy."

"That's just what happened. Damn you, you made up lame excuses and practically patted me on the head. And tonight, you've got an itch and you're annoyed that I wasn't here to scratch it."

He was as pale as she now. "Is that what you think of me?"

She sighed then, and the anger dropped out of her voice. "It's what you think of me, Max. Now let me go."

His grip loosened so that she slipped away. "I had something on my mind this afternoon. It wasn't that I didn't want to spend time with you."

"I don't want excuses." She went to the terrace doors to fling them open. Maybe the wind would blow the tears away. "You've made it clear how you feel."

"Obviously I haven't. The last thing I wanted to do was hurt you, Lilah." But he'd lied to her, he thought. That had been his first mistake. "Just before I came to pick you up, I saw Caufield in the village."

She spun around. "What? You saw him? Where?"

"I was waiting at a light, and I saw him on the sidewalk. He's dyed his hair and grown a beard. By the time I'd realized, I was caught up in traffic and had to double back. He was gone."

"Why didn't you tell me you'd seen him?"

"I didn't want to worry you, and I wasn't going to have you getting some lamebrained idea about hunting him up yourself. You have a habit of acting on impulse, and I—"

"You jerk." The flush was back in her cheeks when she stepped forward to give him a shove. "That man is determined to take something from my family, and you don't have the sense to tell me you've seen him a few miles from here. If I'd known I might have been able to find him."

"Exactly my point. I'm not having you involved any more than necessary. That's why I thought it might be best if I went back to New York. They know I'm here now, and I'm not having you caught in the middle."

"You're not having?" She would have shoved him again, but he caught both her hands.

"That's right. You're going to stay out of it."

"Don't tell me—"

"I am telling you," he interrupted, pleased when she gaped at him. "What's more, you're not going to go wandering off at night until he's in custody. After I thought it over, I decided it was best if I stayed close and watched out for you. I'm going to take care of you whether you like it or not."

"I don't like it, and I don't need to be taken care of."

"Nonetheless." And he considered the argument closed.

It was her turn to stutter. "Why, you arrogant, self-important—"

"That's enough," he said in his best professor's voice and had her blinking. "There's no use arguing when the most intelligent decision's been made. Now, I think it's best if I take you to work every day. Whenever you make other plans, you'll let me know."

Her anger turned to simple shock. "I will not."

"Yes," he said mildly, "you will." He moved her hands behind her back to bring her closer. "About tonight," he began when their bodies brushed. "Clearly, you're laboring under a misconception concerning my motives, and my feelings."

She arched back, more surprised than annoyed when he didn't release her. "I don't want to talk about it."

"No, you prefer yelling about it, but that's unconstructive, and not my style." Both his hands and his voice were very firm. "To be precise, I didn't come here because I had an itch, though I certainly have every intention of making love with you."

Baffled, she stared at him. "What the devil's gotten into you?"

"I've suddenly realized that the best way to handle you is the way I handle difficult students. It takes more than patience. It requires a firm hand and a clear-cut outline of intentions and goals."

"A difficult—" She took a deep breath to hold on to her temper. "Max, I think you'd better go take some aspirin and lie down."

"As I was saying." He whispered a kiss over her cheek. "It isn't just a matter of sex, despite the fact that that aspect is incredibly satisfying. It's more of a matter of my being completely bewitched by you."

"Don't," she said weakly when he leaned close to nip at her ear.

"Maybe I've made the mistake of indicating that it's only the way you look, the way you feel under my hands, the way you taste that attracts me." He drew her bottom lip into his mouth, sucking gently until her eyes unfocused. "But it's more than that. I just don't know how to tell you." Her pulse beat fast and hard against his hands as he walked her backward. "There's never been anyone like you in my life. I intend to keep you there, Lilah."

"What are you doing?"

"I'm taking you to bed."

She struggled to clear her head as his lips skimmed down her throat. "No, you're not." She was angry with him about something. But the reason floated just out of reach as his mouth seduced her.

"I need to show you how I feel about you." Still toying with her lips, he lowered her to the mattress.

Her hands were free now and slipped under his shirt to run along the warm flesh beneath. She didn't want to think. There were so many feelings to be absorbed, and she drew him closer, eager.

"I was jealous," he murmured as he slid one lacy strap from her shoulder and replaced it with his mouth. "I don't want another man touching you."

"No." He was touching her now, long, lingering strokes up and down her trembling body. "Just you."

He sank into a kiss, spinning it out, wallowing in the flavor, the texture, until he was drunk on it. Then, like an addict, he went back for more.

This was comfort and care and romance, she thought hazily. To float together like this, with a sweet breeze blowing over heated bodies, soft murmurs muffled against clinging lips. Desire so perfectly balanced with affection. Nothing mattered so much as this—holding on to the hope of love.

She lifted his shirt over his head and let her hands roam. He was strong. It was more than the subtle ridge of muscles over his back and shoulders. It was the strength inside that aroused her. The integrity, the dedication to do what was right. He would be strong enough to be loyal and honest and gentle with those he loved.

He shifted her so that she was cocooned by pillows. Kneeling beside her, he began to untie each tiny ribbon down the center of the ivory silk. The contrast of patient fingers and hungry eyes left her breathless. He parted the material, caressing the newly exposed flesh with his lips. It amazed and humbled him that her skin should be as soft as the silk.

As patiently as he, she undressed him. Though the need to hurry was clawing at both of them, they held back, the understanding spoken.

She rose, wrapping her arms around his neck until they were torso to torso, thigh to thigh. With the bright light showering around them, they explored each other. A shudder then a sigh, a request and an answer. Questing lips sought out new secrets. Eager hands discovered new pleasures.

When she locked herself around him, he filled her. Glorying in the sensation, she arched back, taking him deeper, gasping out his name as the first shock waves struck. He could see her, her willowy body bowed, her skin glowing in the light while her bright hair rained down her back. As she shuddered, the stunned pleasure rushed into her face.

Then his vision grayed, his own body trembled. His hands slid down to grip her hips. She was wrapped tight around him when they shot over the peak together.

Chapter Nine

Max was whistling as he poured his coffee. It was the penguin's natty little tune and suited his mood. He had plans. Big ones. A drive along the coast, dinner at some out-of-the-way spot, then a nice long walk on the beach.

He sipped, scalded his tongue and grinned.

He was having a romance.

"Well, it's nice to see someone in such a bright mood so early in the morning." Coco sailed into the kitchen. She'd dyed her hair a raven black the night before, and the result had put her in a cheerful state of mind. "How about some blueberry pancakes?"

"You look terrific."

She beamed and reached for a frilly apron. "Why, thank you, dear. A woman needs a change now and again, I always say. Keeps men on their toes." After taking a large mixing bowl from the cupboard, she glanced back at him. "I must say, Max, you're looking rather well yourself this morning. The sea air or . . . something must agree with you."

"It's wonderful here. I'll never be able to thank you enough for letting me stay."

"Nonsense." In her haphazard way she began dumping ingredients into the bowl. It never failed to amaze Max how anyone could cook so carelessly with such exquisite results. "It was meant, you know. I knew it the moment Lilah brought you home. She was always one for bringing things home. Wounded birds, baby rabbits. Even a snake once." The memory of that made her pat her breast. "This was the first time she brought in an unconscious man. But that's Lilah," she continued, gaily mixing as she talked. "Always the unexpected. Quite talented, too. She knows all those Latin terms for weeds and the migratory habits of birds and things. When she's in the mood, she can draw beautifully."

"I know. I saw the sketches in her room."

She slanted him a look. "Did you?"

"I . . ." He took a quick gulp of coffee., "Yes. Do you want a cup?"

"No, I'll have my coffee when this is done." Oh, my, my, she thought, things were moving along just beautifully. The cards didn't lie. "Yes, our Lilah's quite a fascinating girl. Headstrong like the others, but in such a casual, deceptively amiable sort of way. I've always said that the right sort of man would recognize how special she is." Keeping an eye on Max, she rinsed and drained blueberries. "He'd need to be patient, but not malleable. Strong enough to keep her from veering off course too far, and wise enough not to try to change her." Gently folding the berries into the batter she smiled. "But then, if you love someone why would you want to change her?"

"Aunt Coco, are you pumping poor Max?" Lilah strolled in, yawning.

"What a thing to say." Coco heated the griddle and clucked her tongue. "Max and I were having a nice conversation. Weren't we, Max?"

"It certainly was a fascinating one."

"Really?" Lilah took the cup from him, and since he didn't make the move, leaned over to kiss him good morning. Watching, Coco all but rubbed her hands together. "I'll take that as a compliment, and since I see blueberry pancakes on the horizon, I won't complain."

Because the kiss had delighted her, Coco hummed as she got out dishes. "You're up early."

"It's becoming a habit of mine." Sipping Max's coffee, Lilah sent him a lazy smile. "I'll have to break it soon."

"The rest of the brood will be trooping down any minute." And Coco liked nothing better than to have all of her chicks in one place. "Lilah, why don't you set the table?"

"I'll definitely have to break it." With a sigh, she handed Max back his coffee. But she kissed Coco's cheek. "I like your hair. Very French."

With what sounded almost like a giggle, Coco began to spoon up batter. "Use the good china, dear. I feel like celebrating."

Caufield hung up the phone and went into a small, nasty rage. He pounded the desk with his fists, tore a few pamphlets to bits and ended by smashing a crystal bud vase against the wall. Because he'd seen the mood before, Hawkins hung back until it passed.

After three calming breaths, Caufield sat back. The glaze of blank violence faded from his eyes as he steepled his fingers. "We seem to be victims of fate, Hawkins. The car our good professor was driving is registered to Catherine Calhoun St. James."

On an oath, Hawkins heaved his bulk away from the wall. "I told you this job stinks. By rights he should be dead. Instead he plops right down in their laps. He'll have told them everything by now."

Caufield tapped the tips of his fingers together. "Oh, assuredly."

"And if he recognized you—"

"He didn't." Exercising control, Caufield laced his fingers then laid them on the desk. "He never would have waved in my direction. He doesn't have the wit for it." Feeling his fingers tighten, he deliberately relaxed them. "The man's a fool. I learned more in one year on the streets than he in all of his years in higher institutions. After all, we're here, not on the boat."

"But he knows," Hawkins insisted, viciously cracking his knuckles. "Now they all know. They'll take precautions."

"Which only adds spice to the game and it's time to begin playing. Since Dr. Quartermain has joined the Calhouns, I believe I'll pay one of the ladies a call."

"You're out of your mind."

"Have a care, old friend," Caufield said mildly. "If you don't like my rules, there's nothing holding you here."

"I'm the one who paid for the damn boat." Hawkins dragged a hand through his short wiry hair. "I've put over a month in this job already. I've got an investment."

"Then leave it to me to make it pay off." Thinking, Caufield rose to go to the window. There were pretty summer flowers in neat borders just outside. It reminded him that he'd come a long way from the tenements of south Chicago. With the emeralds, he'd go even further.

Perhaps a nice villa in the South Seas where he could relax and refresh himself while Interpol ran in circles looking for him. He already had a new passport, a new background, a new name in reserve—and a tidy sum gathering interest in a discreet Swiss account.

He'd been in the business most of his life, quite successfully. He didn't need the emeralds for the percentage of their value he'd cull by fencing them. But he wanted them. He intended to have them.

As Hawkins paced and abused his knuckles, Caufield continued to gaze out of the window. "Now, as I recall, during my brief friendship with the lovely Amanda, she mentioned that her sister Lilah knew the most about Bianca. Perhaps she knows the most about the emeralds, as well."

This, at least, made some sense to Hawkins. "Are you going to grab her?"

Caufield winced. "That's your style, Hawkins. Credit me with a little more finesse. I believe I'll pay a visit to Acadia. They say the naturalist tours are very informative."

Lilah had always preferred the long, sunny days of summer. Though she felt there was something to be said for the long stormy nights of winter, as well. In truth, it was time she preferred. She didn't wear a watch. Time was something to be appreciated just for its existence, not as something to keep track of. But for the first time in her memory, she wished time would hurry.

She missed him.

It didn't matter how foolish it made her feel. She was in love and giddy with it. When the feeling was so strong, she resented every hour they weren't together.

It was stronger. She had fallen in love with his sweetness, his basic goodness. She had recognized his insecurity and, as she had with broken wings and damaged paws, had wanted to fix it.

She still loved all of those things, but now she had seen a different side of him. He'd been—masterful. She cringed at the term that entered her head and would have sworn she found it offensive. But it hadn't been offensive, not in Max. It had been illuminating.

He had taken charge. He had taken her, she thought with a quick flash of excitement. Though she still resented being compared to a difficult student, she had to admire his technique. He'd simply stated his intentions and moved on them.

She'd be the first to admit that she'd have frozen another man in his tracks with a few well-chosen words if he'd attempted the same thing. But Max wasn't any other man.

She hoped he was beginning to believe it.

While her mind wandered, she kept an eye on her group. Jordan Pond was a favored spot and she had a full load.

"Please, don't disturb the plant life. I know the flowers are tempting, but we have thousands of visitors who'll want to enjoy them, in their natural setting. The bottle-shaped flower you see in the pond is yellow cow lily, or spatterdock. The leaves floating on the surface are bladderwort, and common to most Acadia ponds. It is their tiny bladders that help the plant float, and that trap small insects."

In his ripped jeans and tattered backpack, Caufield listened to her lecture. Behind his dark glasses, his eyes were watchful. He paid attention, though the talk of bog and pond plants meant nothing to him. He held back a sneer when the group gasped as a heron glided overhead to wade in the shallows several yards away.

As if fascinated, he lifted the camera strapped around his neck and snapped pictures of the bird, the wild orchards, even of a bullfrog who had come out to bask on a floating leaf.

Most of all, he bided his time.

She continued to lecture, tirelessly answering questions as they moved along the trail beside the glassy water. She spelled a weary mother by hitching a toddler on her hip and pointing out a family of black ducks.

When the lecture was over, the group was free to follow the circular trail around the pond or retreat to their cars.

"Miss Calhoun?"

Lilah glanced around. She'd noticed the bearded hiker in the group, though he hadn't asked any questions during the lecture. There was a hint of the South in his voice.

"Yes?"

"I wanted to tell you how terrific your talk was. I teach high school geography and reward myself every summer with a trip through a national park. You're really one of the best guides I've come across."

"Thank you." She smiled, and though it was a natural gesture for her, felt reluctant to offer her hand. She didn't recognize the sweaty, bearded hiker, but she picked up something disturbing. "You'll have to visit the Nature Center while you're here. Enjoy your stay."

He put a hand on her arm. It was a casual move, far from demanding, but she disliked it intensely.

"I was hoping you could give me a little one-on-one, if you've got a minute. I like to give the kids a full-scale report when school starts in the fall. A lot of them never see the inside of a park."

She forced herself to shake off the mood. It was her job, she reminded herself, and she appreciated talking to someone with a genuine interest. "I'd be happy to answer any questions."

"Great." He pulled out a notebook he'd been careful to scribble in.

She relaxed a little, giving him a more in-depth talk than the average group required.

"This is so kind of you. I wonder, could I buy you some coffee, or a sandwich?"

"That isn't necessary."

"But it would be a pleasure."

"I have plans, but thanks."

He kept his smile in place. "Well, I'll be around for a few more weeks. Maybe some other time. I know this is going to sound strange, but I'd swear I'd seen you before. Have you ever been to Raleigh?"

Her instincts were humming, and she wanted to get away from him. "No, I haven't."

"It's the darnedest thing." As if puzzled, he shook his head. "You seem so familiar. Well, thanks again. I'd better start back to camp." He turned, then stopped. "I know. The papers. I've seen your picture. You're the woman with the emeralds."

"No. I'm afraid I'm the woman without them."

"What a story. I read about it down in Raleigh a month or two ago, and then...well, I have to confess, I'm just addicted to those supermarket tabloids. Comes from living alone and reading too many essays." He gave her a sheepish smile that would have charmed her if her senses hadn't been working overtime.

"I guess the Calhouns have been lining a lot of bird cages lately."

He rocked back on his heels and laughed. "Pays to keep a sense of humor. I guess it's a hassle, but it gives people like me a lot of vicarious excitement. Missing emeralds, jewel thieves."

"Treasure maps."

"There's a map?" His voice sharpened and he worked hard at easing it again. "I hadn't heard."

"Sure, you can pick them up in the village." She reached in her pocket and drew the latest one out. "I've been collecting them. A lot of people are spending hard-earned money only to find out too late that x doesn't mark the spot."

"Ah." He had to fight against clenching his jaw. "Capitalism."

"You bet. Here, a souvenir." She handed it to him, careful for reasons she couldn't quite place not to brush his fingers. "Your students might get a kick out of it."

"I'm sure they will." To give himself time, he folded it and slipped it into his pocket. "I really am fascinated by the whole thing. Maybe we can have that sandwich soon and you can give me a firsthand account of what it's like to look for buried treasure."

"Mostly, it's tedious. Enjoy your stay in the park."

Knowing there was no safe way to detain her, he watched her go. She had a long, graceful body, he noted. He certainly hoped he wouldn't have to damage it.

"You're late." Max met her on the trail when she was still twenty yards from the parking area.

"It seems to be my day for teachers." She leaned into the kiss, pleased with how warm and solid it was. "I was detained by a Southern gentleman who wanted information on flora for his geography class."

"I hope he was bald and fat."

She didn't quite manage the laugh and rubbed the chill from her arms instead. "No, actually, he was quite trim and had an abundance of hair. But I turned down his request that I become the mother of his children."

"Did he make a pass at you?"

"No." She held a hand up before he could rush by her. And did laugh. "Max, I'm kidding—and if I wasn't, I can dodge passes all by myself."

He didn't feel as foolish as he might have even a day before. "You haven't been dodging mine."

"I can intercept them, too. Now what's behind your back?"

"My hands."

She laughed again and gave him a delighted kiss. "What else?"

He held out a clutch of painted daisies. "I didn't pick them," he said, knowing her feelings. "I bought them from Suzanna. She said you had a weakness for them."

"They're so cheerful," she murmured, absurdly touched. She buried her face in them, then lifted it to his. "Thanks."

As they began to walk, he draped an arm around her shoulders. "I bought the car from C.C. this afternoon."

"Professor, you're full of surprises."

"I thought you might like to hear about the progress Amanda and I are making on those lists. We could drive down the coast, have some dinner. Be alone."

"It sounds wonderful, but my flowers'll wilt."

He grinned down at her. "I bought a vase. It's in the car."

When the sun was setting behind the hills to the west, they walked along a cobble beach that formed a natural seawall on the southern point of the island. The water was calm, barely murmuring over the mounds of smooth stones. With the approach of dusk, the line between the sky and sea blurred until all was a soft, deep blue. A single gull, heading home, soared overhead with one long, defiant cry.

"This is a special place," Lilah told him. With her hand in his, she walked down the slope of cobbles to stand close to the verge of water. "A magic one. Even the air's different here." She closed her eyes to take a deep breath of it. "Full of stored energy."

"It's beautiful." Idly he bent to pick up a rock, just to feel the texture. In the near distance an island melted into the twilight.

"I often drive down here, just to stand and feel. I think I must have been here before."

"You just said you'd been here before."

Her eyes were soft and dreamy as she smiled. "I mean a hundred years ago, or five hundred. Don't you believe in reincarnation, Professor?"

"Actually, I do. I did a paper on it in college and after completing the research, I found it was a very viable theory. When you apply it to history—"

"Max." She framed his face with her hands. "I'm crazy about you." Her lips were curved when they met his, curved still when she drew away.

"What was that for?"

"Because I can see you, waist deep in thick books and cramped notes, your hair falling into your face and your eyebrows all drawn together the way they get when you're concentrating, doggedly pursuing truth."

Frowning, he tossed the cobble from hand to hand. "That's a pretty boring image."

"No, it's not." She tilted her head, studying him. "It's a true one, an admirable one. Even courageous."

He gave a short laugh. "Boxing yourself into a library doesn't take courage. When I was a kid, it was a handy escape. I never had an asthma attack reading a book. I used to hide there, in books," he continued. "It was fun imagining myself sailing with Magellan, or exploring with Lewis and Clark, dying at the Alamo or marching across a field at Antietam. Then my father would..."

"Would what?"

Uncomfortable, he shrugged. "He'd hoped for something different. He was a high school football star. Wide receiver. Played semipro for a while. The kind of man who's never been sick a day in his life. Likes to toss back a few beers on Saturday night and hunt on weekends during the season. I'd start wheezing as soon as he put a thirty-thirty in my hands." He tossed the cobble aside. "He wanted to make a man out of me, and never quite managed it."

"You made yourself." She took his hands, feeling a trembling anger for the man who hadn't appreciated or understood the gift he'd been given. "If he isn't proud of you, the lack is in him, not in you."

"That's a nice thought." He was more than a little embarrassed that he'd pulled those old, raw feelings out. "In any case, I went my own way. I was a lot more comfortable in a classroom than I was on a football field. And the way I figure it, if I hadn't hidden in the library all those years, I wouldn't be standing here with you right now. This is exactly where I want to be."

"Now that's a nice thought."

"If I tell you you're beautiful, are you going to hit me?"

"Not this time."

He pulled her against him, just to hold her as night fell. "I need to go to Bangor for a couple of days."

"What for?"

"I located a woman who worked as a maid at The Towers the year Bianca died. She's living in a nursing home in Bangor, and I made arrangements to interview her." He tilted Lilah's face to his. "Come with me."

"Just give me time to rearrange my schedule."

When the children were asleep, I told Nanny of my plans. I knew she was shocked that I would speak of leaving my husband. She tried to soothe. How could I explain that it wasn't poor Fred who had caused my decision. The incident had made me realize how futile it was to remain in an unhappy and stifling marriage. Had I convinced myself that it was for the children? Their father didn't see them as children who needed to be loved and coddled, but as pawns. Ethan and Sean he would strive to mold in his image, erasing every part of them he considered weak. Colleen, my sweet little girl, he would ignore until such time as he could marry her for profit or status.

I would not have it. Fergus, I knew, would soon wrench control from me. His pride would demand it. A governess of his choosing would follow his instructions and ignore mine. The children would be trapped in the middle of the mistake I had made.

For myself, he would see that I became no more than an ornament at his table. If I defied him, I would pay the price. I have no doubt that he meant to punish me for questioning his authority in front of our children. Whether it would be physical or emotional, I didn't know, but I was sure the damage would be severe. Discontent I might hide from the children, open animosity I could not.

I would take them and go, find somewhere we could disappear. But first I went to Christian.

The night was moon washed and breezy. I kept my cloak pulled tight, the hood over my hair. The puppy was snuggled at my breast. I had the carriage take me to the village, then walked to his cottage through the quiet

*streets with the smell of water and flowers all around. My heart was
pounding in my ears as I knocked. This was the first step, and once taken,
I could never go back.*

*But it wasn't fear, no, it wasn't fear that trembled through me when he
opened the door. It was relief. The moment I saw him I knew the choice
had already been made.*

"Bianca," he said. "What are you thinking of?"

*"I must talk to you." He was already pulling me inside. I saw that he'd
been reading in the lamplight. Its warm glow and the scent of his paints
soothed me more than words. I set the pup down and he immediately began to explore, sniffing into corners and making himself at home.*

*Christian made me sit, and no doubt sensing my nerves, brought me a
brandy. As I sipped, I told him of the scene with Fergus. Though I struggled to remain calm, I could see his face, the violence in it, as his hands had
closed over my throat.*

*"My God!" With this, Christian was crouching beside my chair, his
fingers skimming up my throat. I hadn't known there were bruises there
where Fergus's thumbs had pressed.*

*Christian's eyes went black. His hands gripped the arms of the chair
before he lunged to his feet. "I'll kill him for this."*

*I jumped up to stop him from storming out of the cottage. My fear was
such I'm not sure what I said, though I know I told him that Fergus had
left for Boston, that I couldn't bear more violence. In the end it was my
tears that stopped him. He held me as though I was a child, rocking and
comforting while I poured out my heart and my desperation.*

*Perhaps I should have been ashamed to have begged him to take me and
the children away, to have thrust that kind of burden and responsibility on
him. If he had refused, I know I would have gone on alone, taken my three
babies to some quiet village in Ireland or England. But Christian wiped
away my tears.*

*"Of course we'll go. I'll not see you or the children spend another night
under the same roof with him. He'll never lay a hand on any of you again.
It will be difficult, Bianca. You and the children won't have the kind of life
you're used to. And the scandal—"*

*"I don't care about the scandal. The children need to feel loved and
safe." I rose then, to pace. "I can't be sure what's right. Night after night
I've lain in bed asking myself if I have the right to love you, to want you.
I took vows, made promises, and was given three children." I covered my
face with my hands. "A part of me will always suffer for breaking those
vows, but I must do something. I think I'll go mad if I don't. God may
never forgive me, but I can't face a lifetime of unhappiness."*

*He took my hands to pull them away from my face. "We were meant to
be together. We knew it, both of us, the first time we saw each other. I was
content with those few hours as long as I knew you were safe. But I'll not
stand by and see you give your life to a man who'll abuse you. From to-*

night, you're mine, and will be mine forever. Nothing and no one will change that.''

I believed him. With his face close to mine, his fine gray eyes so clear and sure, I believed. And I needed.

"Then tonight, make me yours."

I felt like a bride. The moment he touched me, I knew I had never been touched before. His eyes were on mine as he took the pins from my hair. His fingers trembled. Nothing, nothing has ever moved me more than knowing I had the power to weaken him. His lips were gentle against mine even as I felt the tension vibrating through his body. There in the lamplight he unfastened my dress, and I his shirt. And a bird began to sing in the brush.

I could see by the way he looked at me that I pleased him. Slowly, almost torturously he drew off my petticoats, my corset. Then he touched my hair, running his hands through it, and looking his fill.

"I'll paint you like this one day," he murmured. "For myself."

He lifted me into his arms, and I could feel his heart pounding in his chest as he carried me to the bedroom.

The light was silver, the air like wine. This was no hurried coupling in the dark, but a dance as graceful as a waltz, and as exhilarating. No matter how impossible it seems, it was as though we had loved countless times before, as though I had felt that hard, firm body against mine night after night.

This was a world I had never experienced, yet it was achingly, beautifully familiar. Each movement, each sigh, each need was as natural as breath. Even when the urgency stunned me, the beauty didn't lessen. As he made me his, I knew I had found something every soul searches for. Simple love.

Leaving him was the most difficult thing I have ever done. Though we told each other it would be the last time we were separated, we lingered and loved again. It was nearly dawn before I returned to The Towers. When I looked at the house, walked through it, I knew I would miss it desperately. This, more than any place in my life, had been home. Christian and I, with the children, would make our own, but I would always hold The Towers in my heart.

There was little I would take with me. In the quiet before sunrise, I packed a small case. Nanny would help me put together what the children would need, but this I wanted to do alone. Perhaps it was a symbol of independence. And perhaps that is why I thought of the emeralds. They were the only things Fergus had given me that I considered mine. There were times I had detested them, knowing they had been given to me as a prize for producing a proper heir.

Yet they were mine, as my children were mine.

I didn't think of their monetary value as I took them out, held them in my hands and watched them gleam in the light of the lamp. They would be a legacy for my children, and their children, a symbol of freedom, and of hope. And with Christian, of love.

As dawn broke, I decided to put them, together with this journal, in a safe place until I joined Christian again.

Chapter Ten

The woman seemed ancient. She sat, looking as frail and brittle as old glass, in the shade of a gnarled elm. Close by, pert young pansies basked in a square of sunlight and flirted with droning bees. Residents made use of the winding stone paths through the lawns of the Madison House. Some were wheeled by family or attendants; others walked, in pairs or alone, with the careful hesitance of age.

There were birds trilling. The woman listened, nodding to herself as she plied a crochet hook and thread with fingers that refused to surrender to arthritis. She wore bright pink slacks and a cotton blouse that had been a gift from one of her great-grandchildren. She had always loved vivid colors. Some things don't fade with age.

Her skin was nut-brown, as creased and lined as an old map. Until two years before, she had lived on her own, tending her own garden, cooking her own meals. But a fall, a bad one that had left her helpless with pain on her kitchen floor for nearly twelve hours, had convinced her it was time to change.

Stubborn and set in her ways, she had refused offers by several members of her large family to live with them. If she couldn't have her own place, she'd be damned if she would be a burden. She'd been comfortably off, well able to afford a good home and good medical care. At the Madison House, she had her own room. And if the days of puttering in her garden were past, at least she could enjoy the flowers here.

She had company if she wanted it, privacy if she didn't. Millie Tobias figured that at ninety-eight and counting, she'd earned the right to choose.

She was pleased that she was having visitors. Yes, she thought as she worked her needle, she was right pleased. The day had already started off well. She'd awakened that morning with no more than the usual sundry aches. Her hip was twitching a bit, which meant rain on the way. No matter, she mused. It was good for the flowers.

Her hands worked, but she rarely glanced at them. They knew what to do with needle and thread. Instead, she watched the path, her eyes aided by thick, tinted lenses. She saw the young couple, the lanky young man with shaggy dark hair; the willowy girl in a thin summer dress, her hair the color of October leaves. They walked close, hand in hand. Millie had a soft spot for young lovers and decided they looked pretty as a picture.

Her fingers kept moving as they walked off the path to join her in the shade.

"Mrs. Tobias?"

She studied Max, saw earnest blue eyes and a shy smile. "Ayah," she said. "And you'd be Dr. Quartermain." Her voice was a crackle, heavy with down-east. "Making doctors young these days."

"Yes, ma'am. This is Lilah Calhoun."

Not a shy bone in this one, Millie decided, and wasn't displeased when Lilah sat on the grass at her feet to admire the crocheting.

"This is beautiful." Lilah touched a fingertip to the gossamer blue thread. "What will it be?"

"What it wants to. You're from the island."

"Yes, I was born there."

Millie let out a little sigh. "Haven't been back in thirty years. Couldn't bear to live there after I lost my Tom, but I still miss the sound of the sea."

"You were married a long time?"

"Fifty years. We had a good life. We made eight children, and saw all of them grown. Now I've got twenty-three grandchildren, fifteen great-grandchildren and seven great-great-grandchildren." She let out a wheezy laugh. "Sometimes I feel like I've propagated this old world all on my own. Take your hands out of your pockets, boy," she said to Max. "And come on down here so's I don't have to crane my neck." She waited until he was settled. "This here your sweetheart?" she asked him.

"Ah...well..."

"Well, is she or isn't she?" Millie demanded, and flashed her dentures in a grin.

"Yes, Max." Lilah sent him an amused and lazy smile. "Is she or isn't she?"

Cornered, Max let out a little huff of breath. "I suppose you could say so."

"Slow to make up his mind, is he?" she said to Lilah and winked. "Nothing wrong with that. You've got the look of her," she said abruptly.

"Of whom?"

"Bianca Calhoun. Isn't that what you came to talk to me about?"

Lilah laid a hand on Millie's arm. The flesh was thin as paper. "You remember her."

"Ayah. She was a great lady. Beautiful with a good and kind heart. Doted on her children. A lot of the wealthy ladies who came summering on the island were happy to leave their children to nursemaids and nannies, but Mrs. Calhoun liked to see to them herself. She was always taking them for walks, or spending time in the nursery. Saw them off to bed herself, every night, unless her husband made plans that would take her out before their bedtime. A good mother she was, and nothing better can be said of a woman than that."

She gave a decisive nod and perked up when she saw that Max was taking notes. "I worked there three summers, 1912, '13 and '14." And with the odd trick of old age, she could remember them with perfect clarity.

"Do you mind?" Max took out a small tape recorder. "It would help us remember everything you tell us."

"Don't mind a bit." In fact, it pleased her enormously. She thought it was just like being on a TV talk show. Her fingers worked away as she settled more comfortably in the chair. "You live in The Towers still?" she asked Lilah.

"Yes, my family and I."

"How many times I climbed up and down those stairs. The master, he didn't like us using the main staircase, but when he wasn't about, I used to come down that way and fancy myself a lady. Aswishing my skirts and holding my nose in the air. Oh, I was a pistol in those days, and not hard to look at either. Used to flirt with one of the gardeners. Joseph was his name. But that was just to make my Tom jealous, and hurry him along a bit."

She sighed, looking back. "Never seen a house like it, before or since. The furniture, the paintings, the crystal. Once a week we'd wash every window with vinegar so they'd sparkle like diamonds. And the mistress, she'd like fresh flowers everywhere. She'd cut roses and peonies out of the garden, or pick the wild orchids and lady's slippers."

"What can you tell us about the summer she died?" Max prompted.

"She spent a lot of time in her tower room that summer, looking out the window at the cliffs, or writing in her book."

"Book?" Lilah interrupted. "Do you mean a journal, a diary?"

"I suppose that's what it was. I saw her writing in it sometimes when I brought her up some tea. She'd always thank me, too. Call me by name. 'Thank you, Millie,' she would say, 'it's a pretty day.' Or. 'You didn't have to trouble, Millie. How is your young man?' Gracious, she was." Millie's mouth thinned. "Now the master, he wouldn't say a word to you. Might as well have been a stick of wood for all he noticed."

"You didn't like him," Max put in.

"Wasn't my place to like or dislike, but a harder, colder man I've never met in all my years. We'd talk about it sometimes, me and one of the other girls. Why did such a sweet and lovely woman marry a man like that? Money, I would have said. Oh, the clothes she had, and the parties, the jewelry. But it didn't make her happy. Her eyes were sad. She and the master would go out in the evenings, or they'd entertain at home. He'd go his own way most other times, business and politics and the like, hardly paying any mind to his wife, and less to his children. Though he was partial to the boy, the oldest boy."

"Ethan," Lilah supplied. "My grandfather."

"A fine little boy, he was, and a handful. He liked to slide down the banisters and play in the dirt. The mistress didn't mind him getting dirty, but she made certain he was all polished up when the master got home. A tight ship he ran, Fergus Calhoun. Was it any wonder the poor woman looked elsewhere for a little softness?"

Lilah closed a hand over Max's. "You knew she was seeing someone?"

"It was my job to clean the tower room. More than once I looked out that window and saw her running out to the cliffs. She met a man there. I know she was a married woman, but it wasn't for me to judge then, or now. Whenever she came back from seeing him, she looked happy. At least for a little while."

"Do you know who he was?" Max asked her.

"No. A painter, I think, because there were times he had an easel set up. But I never asked anyone, and never told what I saw. It was the mistress's secret. She deserved one."

Because her hands were tiring, she let them still in her lap. "The day before she died, she brought a little puppy home for the children. A stray she said she'd found out on the cliffs. Lord, what a commotion. The children were wild about that dog. The mistress had one of the gardeners fill up a tub on the patio, and she and the children washed the pup themselves. They were laughing, the dog was howling. The mistress ruined one of her pretty day frocks. After, I helped the nanny clean up the children. It was the last time I saw them happy."

She paused a moment to gather her thoughts while two butterflies danced toward the pansies. "There was a dreadful fight when the master came home. I'd never heard the mistress raise her voice before. They were in the parlor and I was in the hall. I could hear them plain. The master wouldn't have the dog in the house. Of course, the children were crying, but he said, just as cold, that the mistress was to give it to one of the servants and have it destroyed."

Lilah felt her own eyes fill. "But why?"

"It wasn't good enough, you see, being a mutt. The little girl, she stood right up to him, but she was only a wee thing, and it made no difference to him. I thought he might strike her—his voice had that meanness in it— but the mistress told the children to take the dog and go up to their nanny. It got worse after that. The mistress was fit to be tied. I wouldn't have said she had a temper, but she cut loose. The master said terrible things to her, vicious things. He said he was going to Boston for a few days, and that she was to get rid of the dog, and to remember her place. When he came out of the parlor, his face—I'll never forget it. He looked mad, I said to myself, then I peeked into the parlor and there was the mistress, white as a ghost, just sitting in a chair with her hand pressed to her throat. The next night, she was dead."

Max said nothing for a moment. Lilah was looking away, her eyes blind with tears. "Mrs. Tobias, had you heard anything about Bianca planning to leave her husband?"

"Later I did. The master, he dismissed the nanny, even though those poor babies were wild with grief. She—Mary Beals was her name—she loved the children and the mistress like they were her own. I saw her in the village the day they were to take the mistress back to New York for burying. She told me that her lady would never have killed herself, that she would never have done that to the children. She insisted that it had been an accident. And then she told me that the mistress had decided to leave, that she'd come to see she couldn't stay with the master. She was going to take the children away. Mary Beals said she was going to New York herself and that she was going to stay with the children no matter what Mr. Calhoun said. I heard later that she'd gotten her position back."

"Did you ever see the Calhoun emeralds, Mrs. Tobias?" Max asked.

"Oh, ayah. Once seen, you'd never forget them. She would wear them and look like a queen. They disappeared the night she died." A faint smile moved her mouth. "I know the legend, boy. You could say I lived it."

Composed again, Lilah looked back. "Do you have any idea what happened to them?"

"I know Fergus Calhoun never threw them into the sea. He wouldn't so much as flip a penny into a wishing well, so close with his money he was. If she meant to leave him, then she meant to take them with her. But he came back, you see."

Max's brows drew together. "Came back?"

"The master came back the afternoon of the day she died. That's why she hid them. And the poor thing never had a chance to take them, and her children, and get away."

"Where?" Lilah murmured. "Where could she have put them?"

"In that house, who could say?" Millie picked up her work again. "I went back to help pack up her things. A sad day. Wasn't one of us dry-eyed. We put all her lovely dresses in tissue paper and locked them in a trunk. We were told to clear the room out, even her hair combs and perfume. He wanted nothing left of her in there. I never saw the emeralds again."

"Or her journal?" Max waited while Millie pursed her lips. "Did you find the journal in her room?"

"No." Slowly she shook her head. "There was no diary."

"How about stationery, or cards, letters?"

"Her writing paper was in the desk, and the little book she kept her appointments in, but I didn't see a diary. We put everything away, didn't even leave a hairpin. The next summer, he came back. He kept her room locked up, and there wasn't a sign of the mistress in the house. There had been photographs, and a painting, but they were gone. The children hardly laughed. Once I came across the little boy standing outside his mother's room, just staring at the door. I gave my notice in the middle of the season. I couldn't bear to work in that house, not with the master. He'd grown even colder, harder. And he took to going up to the tower room and sitting for hours. I married Tom that summer, and never went back to The Towers.''

Later Lilah stood on the narrow balcony of their hotel room. Below she could see the long blue rectangle of the pool, hear the laughter and splashing of families and couples enjoying their vacation.

But her mind wasn't on the bright summer sun or the shouts and rippling water. It was on the days eighty years past, when women wore long, graceful dresses and wrote their dreams in private journals.

When Max came up quietly behind her to slip his arms around her waist, she leaned back into him, comforted.

"I always knew she was unhappy," Lilah said. "I could feel that. Just as I could feel she was hopelessly in love. But I never knew she was afraid. I never picked up on that."

"It was a long time ago, Lilah." Max pressed a kiss to her hair. "Mrs. Tobias might have exaggerated. Remember, she was a young, impressionable woman when it all happened."

Lilah turned to look quietly, deeply into his eyes. "You don't believe that."

"No." He stroked his knuckles over her cheek. "But we can't change what happened. We can't help her now."

"But we can, don't you see? By finding the necklace, and the journal. She must have written everything she felt in that book. Everything she wanted, and feared. She wouldn't have left it where Fergus would find it. If she hid the emeralds, she hid the book, too."

"Then we'll find them. If we follow Mrs. Tobias's account, Fergus came back before Bianca expected him. She didn't have the opportunity to get the emeralds out of the house. They're still there, so it's only a matter of time before we find them."

"But—"

He shook his head, cupping his hands around her face. "Aren't you the one who says to trust your feelings? Think about it. Trent comes to The Towers and falls in love with C.C. Because of his idea to renovate and turn part of the house into a retreat, the old legend comes out. Once it's made public, Livingston or Caufield or whatever we choose to call him develops an obsession. He makes a play for Amanda, but she's already hooked on Sloan—who's also there because of the house. Caufield's impatient, so he steals some of the papers. That brings me into it. You fish me out of the water, take me into your home. Since then we've been able to piece more together. We've found a photograph of the emeralds. We've located a woman who actually knew Bianca, and who's corroborated the fact that she hid the necklace in the house. It's all connected, every step. Do you think we'd have gotten this far if we weren't meant to find them?"

Her eyes softened as she linked her hands over his wrists. "You're awfully good for me, Professor. A little optimistic logic's just what I need right now."

"Then I'll give you some more. I think the next step is to start tracking down the artist."

"Christian? But how?"

"You leave it to me."

"All right." Wanting his arms around her, she laid her head on his shoulder. "There's another connection. You might think it's out of left field, but I can't help thinking about it."

"Tell me."

"A couple of months ago, Trent was walking the cliffs. He found Fred. We've never been able to figure out what the puppy was doing out there all alone. It made me think of the little dog Bianca brought to her children, the one she and Fergus argued about so bitterly only a day before she died. I wonder what happened to that dog, Max." She let out a long sigh. "Then I think about those children. It's difficult to imagine one's grandfather as a little boy. I never even knew him because he died before I was born. But I can see him, standing outside of his mother's door, grieving. And it breaks my heart."

"Shh." He tightened his arms around her. "It's better to think that Bianca had some happiness with her artist. Can't you see her running to him on the cliffs, stealing a few hours in the sun, or finding some quiet place where they could be alone?"

"Yes." Her lips curved against his throat. "Yes, I can. Maybe that's why I love sitting in the tower. She wasn't always unhappy there, not when she thought of him."

"And if there's any justice, they're together now."

Lilah tilted her head back to look at him. "Yes, you are awfully good for me. Tell you what, why don't we take advantage of that pool down there? I'd like to swim with you when it wasn't a matter of life or death."

He kissed her forehead. "You've got a deal."

She did more floating than swimming. Max had never seen anyone who could actually sleep on the water. But Lilah could—her eyes comfortably closed behind tinted glasses, her body totally relaxed. She wore two tiny scraps of leopard-print cloth that raised Max's blood pressure—and that of every other male within a hundred yards. But she drifted, hands moving gently in the water. Occasionally she would kick into a lazy sidestroke, her hair flowing out around her. Now and again, she would reach out to link her hand with his, or twine her arms around his neck, trusting him to keep her buoyant.

Then she kissed him, her lips wet and cool, her body as fluid as the water around them.

"Time for a nap," she said, and left him in the pool to stretch out on a chaise under an umbrella.

When she awoke, the shadows were long and only a few diehards were left in the water. She looked around for Max, vaguely disappointed that he hadn't stayed with her. Gathering up her wrap, she went back inside to find him.

The room was empty, but there was a note on the bed in his careful handwriting.

Had a couple of things to see to. Be back soon.

With a shrug, she tuned the radio to a classical station and went in to take a long, steamy shower.

Revived and relaxed, she toweled off, then began to cream her skin in long, lazy strokes. Maybe they could find some cozy little restaurant for dinner, she mused. Someplace where there were dim corners and music. They could linger over the meal while the candles burned down, and drink cool, sparkling wine.

Then they would come back, draw the drapes on the balcony, close themselves in. He would kiss her in that thorough, drugging way until they couldn't keep their hands off each other. She picked up her bottle of scent, spritzing it onto her softened skin. They would make love slowly or frantically, gently or desperately, until, tangled together, they slept.

They wouldn't think about Bianca or tragedies, about emeralds or thieves. Tonight they would only think about each other.

Dreaming of him, she stepped out into the bedroom.

He was waiting for her. It seemed he'd been waiting for her all of his life. She paused, her eyes darkened by the candles he'd lit, her damp hair gleaming with the delicate light. Her scent wafted into the room, mysterious, seductive, to tangle with the fragrance of the clutch of freesias he'd bought her.

Like her, he had imagined a perfect night and had tried to bring it to her.

The radio still played, low romantic strings. On the table in front of the open balcony doors two slender white tapers glowed. Champagne, just poured, frothed in tall tulip glasses. Behind the table, the sun was sinking in the sky, a scarlet ball, bleeding into the deepening blue.

"I thought we'd eat in," he said, and held out a hand for hers.

"Max." Emotion tightened her throat. "I was right all along." Her fingers linked with his. "You are a poet."

"I want to be alone with you." Taking one of the fragile blooms, he slipped it into her hair. "I'd hoped you wouldn't mind."

"No." She let out a shaky breath when he pressed his lips to her palm. "I don't mind."

He picked up the glasses, handed her one. "Restaurants are so crowded."

"And noisy," she agreed, touching her glass to his.

"And someone might object if I nibbled on you rather than the appetizers."

Watching him, she took a sip. "I wouldn't."

He slid a finger up her throat, then tilted her chin so that their lips met. "We'd better give dinner a try," he said after a long moment.

They sat, close together to watch the sun set, to feed each other little bites of lobster drenched with sweet, melted butter. She let champagne explode on her tongue, then turned her mouth to his where the flavor was just as intoxicating.

As a Chopin prelude drifted from the radio, he pressed a light kiss to her shoulder, then skimmed more up her throat.

"The first time I saw you," he said as he slipped a bite of lobster between her lips, "I thought you were a mermaid. And I dreamed about you that first night." Gently he rubbed his lips over hers. "I've dreamed about you every night since."

"When I sit up in the tower, I think about you—the way I imagine Bianca once thought about Christian. Do you think they ever made love?"

"He couldn't have resisted her."

Her breath shuddered out between her lips. "She wouldn't have wanted him to." With her eyes on his, she began to unbutton his shirt. "She would have ached needing him, wanting to touch him." On a sigh, she ran her hands over his chest. "When they were together, alone together, nothing else could have mattered."

"He would have been half-mad for her." Taking her hands, he brought her to her feet. He left her for a moment, to draw the shades so that they were closed in with music and candlelight. "Thoughts of her would have haunted him, day and night. Her face..." He skimmed his fingers over Lilah's cheeks, over her jaw, down her throat. "Every time he closed his eyes, he would have seen it. Her taste..." He pressed his lips to hers. "Every time he took a breath it would be there to remind him what it was like to kiss her."

"And she would have lain in bed, night after night, wanting his touch." Heart racing, she pushed the shirt from his shoulders, then shivered when he reached for the belt of her robe. "Remembering how he looked at her when he undressed her."

"He couldn't have wanted her more than I want you." The robe slithered to the floor. His arms drew her closer. "Let me show you."

The candles burned low. A single thread of moonlight slashed through the chink in the drapes. There was music, swelling with passion, and the scent of fragile flowers.

Murmured promises. Desperate answers. A low husky laugh, a sobbing gasp. From patience to urgency, from tenderness to madness, they drove each other. Through the dark, endless night they were tireless and greedy. A gentle touch could cause a tremor; a rough caress a soft sigh. They came together with generous affection, then again like warriors.

Each time they thought they were sated, they would turn to each other once more to arouse or to soothe, to cling or to stroke, until the candles gutted out and the gray light of dawn crept into the room.

Chapter Eleven

Hawkins was sick and tired of waiting around. As far as he was concerned every day on the island was a day wasted. Worse, he'd given up a tidy little job in New York that would have earned him at least ten grand. Instead, he'd invested half that much in a heist that looked more and more like a bust.

He knew Caufield was good. The fact was, there were few better at lifting locks and dancing around the police. In the ten years of their association, they had pulled off some very smooth operations. Which was why he was worried.

There was nothing smooth about this job. Damn college boy had messed things up good and proper. Hawkins resented the fact that Caufield wouldn't let him take care of Quartermain. He knew Caufield didn't think he had any finesse, but he could have arranged a nice, quiet accident.

The real problem was that Caufield was obsessed with the emeralds. He talked about them day and night—and he talked as though they were living things rather than some pretty sparklers that would bring in some good, crisp cash.

Hawkins was beginning to believe that Caufield didn't intend to fence the emeralds after all. He smelled the double cross and had been watching his partner like a hawk. Every time Caufield went out, Hawkins would pace the empty house, looking for some clue to his partner's true intentions.

Then there were the rages. Caufield was well-known for his unstable temper, but those ugly tantrums were becoming more frequent. The day before, he had stormed into the house, white-faced and wild-eyed, his body trembling with fury because the Calhoun woman hadn't been at her station in the park. He'd trashed one of the rooms, hacking away at furniture with a kitchen knife until he'd come to himself again.

Hawkins was afraid of him. Though he was a stocky man with ready fists, he had no desire to match Caufield physically. Not when the man got that gleam in his eyes.

His only hope now, if he wanted his rightful share and a clean escape, was to outwit his partner.

With Caufield out of the house again, haunting the park, Hawkins began a slow, methodical search. Though he was a big man, often considered dull witted by his associates, he could toss a room and hardly raise the dust. He sifted through the stolen papers, then turned away in disgust. There was nothing of use there. If Caufield had found anything, he would never have left it in plain view. He decided to start with the obvious, his partner's bedroom.

He shook out the books first. He knew Caufield liked to pretend he was educated, even erudite, though he'd had no more schooling than Hawkins himself. There was nothing in the volumes of Shakespeare and Steinbeck but words.

Hawkins searched under the mattress, through the drawers in the bureau. Since Caufield's pistol wasn't around, he decided the man had tucked it into his knapsack before setting off to find Lilah. Patient, Hawkins looked behind the mirrors, behind drawers, beneath the rug. He was beginning to think he had misjudged his partner when he turned to the closet.

There, in the pocket of a pair of jeans, he found the map.

It was crudely drawn on yellowed paper. For Hawkins, there was no mistaking its meaning. The Towers was clearly depicted, along with direction and distance and a few out-of-proportion landmarks.

The map to the emeralds, Hawkins thought as he smoothed out the creases. A bitter fury filled him while he studied each line and marker. The double-dealing Caufield had found it among the stolen papers and hidden it away for himself. Well, two could play that game, he thought. He slipped out of the room as he tucked the paper into his own pocket. Wouldn't Caufield have a fine rage when he discovered his partner had snatched the emeralds out from under his nose. Hawkins thought it was almost a pity that he wouldn't be around to see it.

He found Christian. It was so much easier than Max had supposed that he could only sit and stare at the book in his hand. In less than a half day in the library, he'd stumbled across the name in a dusty volume titled *Artists and Their Art: 1900-1950.* He had patiently dug away through the A's, was meticulously slogging through the B's, when there it was. Christian Bradford, 1884-1976. Though the given name had caused Max to perk up, he hadn't expected it to be so easy. But it all fell into place.

Though Bradford did not come to enjoy any real success until his last years, his early work has become valuable since his death.

Max skimmed over the treatise on the artist's style.

Considered a gypsy in his day, due to his habit of moving from one location to another, Bradford often sold his work for room and board. A prolific artist, he would often complete a painting in a matter of days. It is said he would work for twenty hours straight when the mood was on him. It remains a mystery why he produced nothing during the years between 1914 and 1916.

Oh God, Max thought, and rubbed his damp palms on his slacks.

Married in 1925 to Margaret Doogan, Bradford had one child, a son. Little more is known about his personal life, as he remained an obsessively private man until his death. He suffered a debilitating heart attack in the late sixties, but continued to paint. He died in Bar Harbor, Maine, where he had kept a cottage for more than a half century. He was survived by his son and a grandson.

"I've found you," Max murmured. Turning the page, he studied the reproduction of one of Bradford's works. It was a storm, fighting its way in from the sea. Passionate, violent, frenzied. It was a view Max knew— the view from the cliffs beneath The Towers.

An hour later, a half-dozen books under his arm, he arrived home. There was still an hour before he could pick up Lilah at the park, an hour before he could tell her they had jumped the next hurdle. Giddy with success, he greeted Fred so exuberantly that the dog raced up and down the hall, running into walls and tripping on his tail.

"Goodness." Coco trotted down the stairs. "What a commotion."

"Sorry."

"No need to apologize, I wouldn't know what to do if a day went by without a commotion. Why, Max, you look positively delighted with yourself."

"Well, as it happens, I—"

He broke off when Alex and Jenny came bounding down, firing invisible laser pistols. "Dead meat!" Alex shouted. "Dead meat!"

"If you must kill something," Coco said, "please do it outside. Fred needs an airing anyway."

"Death to the invaders," Alex announced. "We'll fry them like bacon."

In total agreement, Jenny aimed her laser at Fred and sent the dog scampering down the hall again. Deciding he made a handy invader, they raced after him. Even with the distance, the sound of the back door slamming boomed through the house.

"I don't know where they get those violent imaginations," Coco commented with a relieved sigh. "Suzanna's so mild tempered, and their father..." Something dark came into her eyes when she trailed off. "Well, that's another story. So tell me, what has you so happy?"

"I was just in the library, and I—"

This time it was the phone that interrupted. Coco slipped off an earring as she picked up the receiver. "Hello. Yes. Oh, yes, he's right here." She cupped a hand over the mouthpiece. "It's your dean, dear. He'd like to speak to you."

Max set the books on the telephone stand as Coco began to straighten pictures a few discreet feet away. "Dean Hodgins? Yes, I am, thank you. It's a beautiful spot. Well, I haven't really decided when I'm coming back... Professor Blake?"

Coco glanced back at the alarm in his voice.

"When? Is it serious? I'm sorry he's ill. I hope... I beg your pardon?" Letting out a long breath, Max leaned back against the banister. "I'm very flattered, but—" He lapsed into silence again, dragging a hand through his hair. "Thank you. Yes, I understand that. If I could have a day or two to consider. I appreciate it. Yes, sir. Goodbye."

When he simply stood, staring into space, Coco cleared her throat. "I hope it wasn't bad news, dear."

"What?" He focused on her, then shook his head. "No, well, yes. That is, the head of the history department had a heart attack last week."

"Oh." Immediately sympathetic, Coco came forward. "How dreadful."

"It was mild—if you can term anything like that mild. The doctors consider it a warning. They're recommending that he cut back on his work load, and he's taken them seriously, because he's decided to retire." He gave Coco a baffled look. "It seems he's recommended me to take over his position."

"Well now." She smiled and patted his cheek, but she was watching him carefully. "That's quite an honor, isn't it?"

"I'd have to go back next week," he said to himself. "To take over as acting head of the department until a final decision's made."

"Sometimes it's difficult to know what to do, which fork in the road to take. Why don't we have a nice cup of tea?" she suggested. "Then I'll read the leaves and we'll see."

"I really don't think—" The next interruption relieved him, and Coco clucked her tongue as she went to answer the banging on the door.

"Oh, my" was all she said. With her hand pressed to her breast, she said it again. "Oh, my!"

"Don't just stand there with your mouth hanging open, Cordelia," a crisp, authoritative voice demanded. "Have someone deal with my bags."

"Aunt Colleen." Coco's hand fluttered to her side. "What a... lovely surprise."

"Ha! You'd as soon see Satan himself on the doorstep." Leaning on a glossy, gold-tipped cane, she marched across the threshold.

Max saw a tall, rail-thin woman with a mass of luxurious white hair. She wore an elegant white suit and gleaming pearls. Her skin, generously lined, was as pale as linen. She might have been a ghost but for the deep blue eyes that scanned him.

"Who the hell is this?"

"Um. Um."

"Speak up, girl. Don't stutter." Colleen tapped the cane impatiently. "You never kept a lick of the sense God gave you."

Coco began to wring her hands. "Aunt Colleen, this is Dr. Quartermain. Max, Colleen Calhoun."

"Doctor," Colleen barked. "Who's sick? Damned if I'm going to stay in a contagious house."

"That's a Ph.D., Miss Calhoun." Max offered a cautious smile. "It's nice to meet you."

"Ha." She sniffed and glanced around the hall. "Still letting the place fall down around your ears. Best if it was struck by lightning. Burned to the ground. See to those bags, Cordelia, and have someone bring me some tea. I've had a long trip." So saying, she clumped off toward the parlor.

"Yes, ma'am." Hands still fluttering, Coco sent Max a helpless look. "I hate to ask..."

"Don't worry about it. Where should I take her luggage?"

"Oh, God." Coco pressed her hands to her cheeks. "The first room on the right on the second floor. We'll have to stall her so that I can prepare it. Oh, and she won't have paid the driver. Tightfisted old... I'll call Amanda. She can warn the others. Max—" she clutched his hands "—if you believe in prayer, use it now and pray that this is a very short visit."

"Where's the damn tea?" Colleen demanded in a bellow and thumped her cane.

"Just coming." Coco turned and raced down the hall.

Pulling all her rabbits out of her hat, Coco plied her aunt with tea and petits fours, dragged Trent and Sloan away from their work and begged Max to fall in. Arrangements were made for Amanda to pick up Lilah and for Suzanna to close early and pitch in to prepare the guest room.

It was like preparing for an invasion, Max thought as he joined the group in the parlor. Colleen sat, erect as a general, while she measured her opponents with the same steely eye.

"So, you're the one who married Catherine. Hotels, isn't it?"

"Yes, ma'am," Trent answered politely while Coco fluttered around the room.

"Never stay in 'em," Colleen said dismissively. "Got married quick, wouldn't you say?"

"I didn't want to give her a chance to change her mind."

She almost smiled, then sniffed and aimed at Sloan. "And you're the one who's after Amanda."

"That's right."

"What's that accent?" she demanded, eyes sharpening. "Where are you from?"

"Oklahoma."

"O'Riley," she mused for a moment, then pointed a long white finger. "Oil."

"There you go."

"Humph." She lifted her tea to sip. "So you've got some harebrained notion about turning the west wing into a hotel. Better off burning it down and claiming the insurance."

"Aunt Colleen." Scandalized, Coco gaped at her. "You don't mean that."

"I say what I mean. Hated this place most of my life." She shifted to brood up at the portrait of her father. "He'd have hated seeing paying guests in The Towers. It would have mortified him."

"I'm sorry, Aunt Colleen," Coco began. "But we have to make the best of things."

"Did I ask for an apology?" Colleen snapped. "Where the hell are my grand-nieces? Don't they have the courtesy to pay their respects?"

"They'll be along soon." Desperate, Coco poured more tea. "This was so unexpected, and we've—"

"A home should always be prepared for guests," Colleen retaliated with relish, then frowned at the doorway when Suzanna came in. "Which one is this?"

"I'm Suzanna." Dutifully she came forward to kiss her great-aunt's cheek.

"You favor your mother," Colleen decided with a grudging nod. "I was fond of Deliah." She shot a look at Max. "You after her?"

He blinked as Sloan struggled to turn a laugh into a cough. "Ah, no. No, ma'am."

"Why not? Something wrong with your eyes?"

"No." He shifted in his chair as Suzanna grinned and settled on a hassock.

"Max is visiting for a few weeks," said Coco, coming to the rescue. "He's helping us out with a little—historical research."

"The emeralds." Eyes gleaming, Colleen sat back. "Don't take me for a fool, Cordelia. We get newspapers aboard ship. Cruise ships," she said to Trent. "Much more civilized than hotels. Now, tell me what the hell is going on around here."

"Nothing, really." Coco cleared her throat again. "You know how the press blows things out of proportion."

"Was there a thief in this house, shooting off a gun?"

"Well, yes. It was disturbing, but—"

"You." Colleen hefted her cane and poked it at Max. "You with the Ph.D. I assume you can articulate clearly. Explain the situation, briefly."

At the pleading glance from Coco, Max set his unwanted tea aside. "The family decided, after a series of events, to investigate the veracity of the legend of the Calhoun emeralds. Unfortunately, news of the necklace leaked, causing interest and speculation among various people, some of them unsavory. The first step was to catalogue old family papers, to verify the existence of the emeralds."

"Of course they existed," Colleen said impatiently. "Haven't I seen them with my own eyes?"

"You were difficult to reach," Coco began, and was silenced with a look.

"In any case," Max continued. "The house was broken into, and a number of the papers stolen." Max skimmed over his involvement to bring her up to date.

"Hmm." Colleen frowned at him. "What do you do, write?"

Max's brow lifted in surprise. "I teach. History. At, ah, Cornell University."

Colleen sniffed again. "Well, you've made a mess of it. The lot of you. Bringing thieves under the roof, splashing our name all over the press, nearly getting yourselves killed. For all we know the old man sold the emeralds."

"He'd have kept a record," Max put in, and had Colleen studying him again.

"You're right there, Mr. Ph.D. He kept account of every penny he made, and every penny he spent." She closed her eyes a moment. "Nanny always told us she hid them away. For us." Fierce, her eyes opened again. "Fairy tales."

"I love fairy tales," Lilah said from the doorway. She stood, flanked by C.C. and Amanda.

"Come in here where I can see you."

"You first," Lilah muttered to C.C.

"Why me?"

"You're the youngest." She gave her sister a gentle shove.

"Throwing a pregnant woman to the wolves," Amanda muttered.

"You're next."

"What's that on your face?" Colleen demanded of C.C.

C.C. wiped a hand over her cheek. "Motor oil, I guess."

"What's the world coming to? You've got good bones," she decided. "You'll age well. You pregnant yet?"

Dipping her hands in her pockets, C.C. grinned. "As a matter of fact, yes. Trent and I are expecting in February."

"Good." Colleen waved her away. Steeling herself, Amanda stepped forward.

"Hello, Aunt Colleen. I'm glad you decided to come for the wedding."

"Might, might not." Lips pursed, she studied Amanda. "You know how to write a proper letter, in any case. It reached me last week, with the invitation." She was a lovely thing, Colleen thought, like her sisters. She felt a sense of pride in that, but would have bitten off her tongue before admitting it. "Any reason you couldn't marry a man from a nice Eastern family?"

"Yes. None of them annoyed me as much as Sloan."

With what might have been a laugh, Colleen waved her away.

When she focused on Lilah, her eyes burned and she had to press her lips tight to keep them from quivering. It was like looking at her mother, with all the years, and all the hurt wiped away.

"So, you're Lilah." When her voice cracked, she lowered her brows, looking so formidable that Coco trembled.

"Yes." Lilah kissed both her cheeks. "The last time I saw you I was eight, I think. And you scolded me for going barefoot."

"And just what are you doing with your life?"

"Oh, as little as possible," Lilah said blithely. "How about you?"

Colleen's lips twitched, but she rounded on Coco. "Haven't you taught these girls manners?"

"Don't blame her." Lilah sat on the floor at Max's feet. "We're incorrigible." She glanced over her shoulder, smiled at Max, then set a companionable hand on his knee.

Colleen didn't miss a trick. "So, you've got your eye on this one."

Tossing back her hair, Lilah smiled. "I certainly do. Cute, isn't he?"

"Lilah," Max muttered. "Give me a break."

"You didn't kiss me hello," she said quite clearly.

"Leave the boy alone." More amused than she would have admitted, Colleen thumped her cane. "At least he has manners." She waved a hand at the tea things. "Take this business away, Cordelia, and bring me a brandy."

"I'll get it." Lilah unfolded herself and strolled over to the liquor cabinet. She winked at Suzanna as her sister wheeled over the tea cart. "How long do you think she plans to make our lives a living hell?"

"I heard that."

Undaunted, Lilah turned with the brandy snifter. "Of course you did, Auntie. Papa always told us you had ears like a cat."

"Don't call me 'Auntie.'" She snatched the brandy. Colleen was used to deference—her personality and her money had always demanded it. Or to fear—the kind she easily instilled in Coco. But she enjoyed, tremendously, irreverence. "The trouble is your father never lifted a hand to any of you."

"No," Lilah murmured. "He didn't have to."

"No one loved him more than I," Colleen said briskly. "Now, it's time to decide what to do about this mess you've gotten yourselves into. The sooner mended, the sooner I can rejoin my cruise."

"You don't mean—" Coco caught herself and hastily rephrased. "Do you plan to stay with us until the emeralds are found?"

"I plan to stay until I'm ready to leave." Colleen aimed a look, daring disagreement.

"How lovely," Coco said between unsteady lips. "I believe I'll go in and see about dinner."

"I dine at seven-thirty. Precisely."

"Of course." Even as Coco rose, the familiar chaos could be heard racing down the hall. "Oh, dear."

Suzanna sprang to her feet. "I'll head them off." But she was a bit late as both children came barreling into the room.

"Cheat, cheat, cheat," Jenny accused, eyes brimming.

"Crybaby." But Alex was near tears himself as he gave her a brotherly shove.

"Who are these hooligans?" Colleen asked, interest perking.

"These hooligans are my children." Suzanna studied them both and saw that though she had tidied them herself less than twenty minutes before, they were both grimy and grim faced. Obviously her idea that they spend a quiet hour playing a board game had been a disaster.

Colleen swirled her brandy. "Bring them here. I'll have a look at them."

"Alex, Jenny." The warning tone worked very well. "Come meet Aunt Colleen."

"She isn't going to kiss us, is she?" Alex muttered as he dragged his feet across the room.

"I certainly will not. I don't kiss grubby little boys." She had to swallow. He looked so like her baby brother, Sean. Formally she offered a hand. "How do you do?"

"Okay." Flushing a bit, he touched the thin-boned hand.

"You're awfully old," Jenny observed.

"Quite right," Colleen agreed before Suzanna could speak. "If you're lucky, the same problem will be yours one day." She would have liked to have stroked the girl's shiny blond hair, but it would have shattered her image. "I'll expect you to refrain from shouting and clattering about while I'm in the house. Furthermore..." She trailed off when something brushed her leg. Glancing down, she saw Fred sniffing the carpet for crumbs. "What is that?"

"That's our dog." Seized with inspiration, Alex reached down to heft the fat puppy in his arms. "If you're mean to us, he'll bite you."

"He'll do no such thing." Suzanna put a hand on Alex's shoulder.

"He might." Alex pouted. "He doesn't like bad people. Do you, Fred?"

Colleen's skin went even whiter. "What is his name?"

"His name is Fred," Jenny said gaily. "Trent found him on the cliffs and brought him home for us." She struggled the dog away from her brother to hold him out. "And he doesn't bite. He's a good dog."

"Jenny, put him down before he—"

"No." Colleen waved Suzanna's warning aside. "Let me see him." Fred wriggled, smearing dirt on Colleen's pristine white suit as she sat him in her lap. Her hands shook as they stroked his fur. "I had a dog named Fred once." A single tear spilled over and down her pale cheek. "I only had him for a little while, but I loved him very much."

Saying nothing, Lilah groped for Max's hand and held tight.

"You can play with him, if you want," Alex told her, appalled that someone so old would cry. "He doesn't really bite."

"Of course he won't bite." Recovering, Colleen set the dog on the floor, then straightened painfully. "He knows I'd just bite him back. Isn't someone going to show me to my room, or do I have to sit here all day and half the damn night?"

"We'll take you up." Lilah tugged on Max's hand so that he rose to help her to her feet.

"Bring the brandy," Colleen said imperiously, and started out stumping with her cane.

"Delightful relatives you have, Calhoun," Sloan murmured.

"Too late to back out now, O'Riley." Amanda heaved a relieved breath. "Come on, Aunt Coco, I'll help you in the kitchen."

"Which room have you stuck me in?" Only slightly breathless, Colleen paused on the second-floor landing.

"The first one, here." Max opened the door, then stepped back.

The terrace doors had been opened to let in the breeze. The furniture had been hastily polished, a few extra pieces dragged in from storage. Fresh flowers sat atop the rosewood bureau. The wallpaper was peeling, but paintings had been culled from other rooms to hide the worst of it. A delicate lace spread had been unfolded from a cedar chest and adorned the heavy four-poster.

"It'll do," Colleen muttered, determined to fight the nostalgia. "Make sure there are fresh towels, girl. And you, Quartermain, is it? Pour me another dose of that brandy and don't be stingy."

Lilah peeked into the adjoining bath and saw all was as it should be. "Is there anything else, Auntie?"

"Mind your tone, and don't call me 'Auntie.' You can send a maid up when it's time for dinner."

Lilah stuck her tongue in her cheek. "I'm afraid it's the staff's year off."

"Unconscionable." Colleen leaned heavily on her cane. "Are you telling me you haven't even day help?"

"You know very well we've been under the financial gun for some time."

"And you'll still not get a penny from me to put into this cursed place." She walked stiffly to the open doors and looked out. God, the view, she thought. It never changed. How many times over how many years had she envisioned it? "Who has my mother's room?"

"I do," Lilah said, lifting her chin.

Very slowly, Colleen turned. "Of course, you would." Her voice had softened. "Do you know how much you favor her?"

"Yes. Max found a picture in a book."

"A picture in a book." Now the bitterness. "That's all that's left of her."

"No. No, there's much more. A part of her is still here, will always be here."

"Don't talk nonsense. Ghosts, spirits—that's Cordelia's influence, and it's a load of hogwash. Dead's dead, girl. When you're as close to it as I am, you'll know that."

"If you'd felt her as I've felt her, you'd know differently."

Colleen closed herself in. "Shut the door behind you. I like my privacy."

Lilah waited until they were out in the hall to swear. "Rude, bad-tempered old bat." Then with a lazy shrug, she tucked her arm through Max's. "Let's go get some air. To think I'd actually felt something for her downstairs when she held Fred."

"She's not so bad, Lilah." They passed through his room and onto the terrace. "You may be just as crotchety when you're eighty-something."

"I'll never be crotchety." She closed her eyes, tossed back her hair and smiled. "I'll have a nice rocking chair set in the sun and sleep old age away." She ran a hand up his arm. "Are you ever going to kiss me hello?"

"Yes." He cupped her face and did so thoroughly. "Hello. How was your day?"

"Hot and busy." But now she felt delightfully cool and relaxed. "That teacher I told you about was back. He seems overly earnest to me. Gives me the willies."

Max's smile disappeared. "You should report him to one of the rangers."

"What, for sending off bad vibrations?" She laughed and hugged him. "No, there's just something about him that hits me wrong. He's always wearing dark glasses, as if I might see something he didn't want seen if he took them off."

"You're letting your..." His grip tightened. "What does he look like?"

"Nothing special. Why don't we take a nap before dinner? Aunt Colleen exhausted me."

"What," Max said very precisely, "does he look like?"

"He's about your height, trim. Somewhere around thirty, I'd guess. Wears the hiker's uniform of T-shirt and ripped jeans. He doesn't have a tan," she said, frowning suddenly. "Which is odd seeing as he said he'd been camping for a couple of weeks. Average sort of brown hair, well over the collar. A very neat beard and mustache."

"It could be him." His fingers dug in as the possibility iced through him. "My God, he's been with you."

"You think—you think it's Caufield." The idea left her shaken so that she leaned back against the wall. "What an idiot I've been. I had the same feeling, the same feeling with this man as I did when Livingston came to take Amanda out for dinner." She ran both hands through her hair. "I must be losing my touch."

Max's eyes were dark as he stared out at the cliffs. "If he comes back, I'll be ready for him."

"Don't start playing hero." Alarmed, she grabbed his arms. "He's dangerous."

"He's not getting near you again." The complete and focused intensity was back on his face. "I'll be taking your shift with you tomorrow."

Chapter Twelve

He never let her out of his sight. Though they had given the authorities the description, Max took no chances. By the time the day was over, he knew more about the intertidal zone than anyone could want to know. He could recognize Irish moss from rockweed—though he still grimaced at Lilah's claim that the moss made excellent ice cream.

But there hadn't been a sign of Caufield.

On the off chance that he had been speaking the truth about camping in the park, the rangers had made a quiet and thorough search but had found no trace of him.

No one had seen the bearded man watching the fruitless search through field glasses. No one had seen the rage come into his eyes when he realized his cover had been blown.

As they drove home, Lilah unwound her braid. "Feel better?" she asked Max.

"No."

She pushed her hands under her hair to let the wind catch it. "Well, you should. It was sweet of you to worry about me, though."

"It has nothing to do with sweetness."

"I think you're disappointed that you didn't get to go into hand-to-hand combat."

"Maybe I am."

"Okay." She leaned over to nip at his ear. "Want to rumble?"

"It's not a joke," he muttered. "I'm not going to feel right until he's taken care of."

Lilah snuggled back in the seat. "If he had any sense he'd give up and go away. We live in the house and we've hardly made any progress."

"That's not true. We verified the existence of the emeralds. We found a photograph of them. We located Mrs. Tobias, and have her eyewitness account of what happened the day before Bianca died. And we've identified Christian."

"We've what?" She sprang up straight. "When did we identify Christian?"

Max grimaced as he glanced over at her. "I forgot to tell you. Don't look like that. First your great-aunt invades the house and sets everyone on their ears. Then you tell me about the man in the park. I thought I had told you."

She inhaled, then exhaled deeply to keep her patience. "Why don't you tell me now?"

"It was in the library yesterday," he began, and filled her in on what he'd found.

"Christian Bradford," Lilah said, trying out the name to see how it fit. "There's something familiar about it. I wonder if I've seen some of his paintings. It wouldn't be surprising if there were some in this area, since he lived here on and off. Died here."

"Didn't you study art in college?"

"I didn't study at all unless I was boxed in. Mostly I drifted through, and art was always more a hobby than anything else. I didn't want to work at it because I liked playing at it better. And I wanted to be a naturalist all along."

"An ambition?" He grinned. "Lilah, you'll ruin your image."

"Well, it was my only one. Everybody's entitled. Bradford, Bradford," she repeated, gnawing at the word. "I'd swear it rings a bell." She closed her eyes on it, opening them again when they pulled up at The Towers. "Got it. We knew a Bradford. He grew up on the island. Holt, Holt Bradford. The dark, broody, surly sort. He was a few years older—probably in his early thirties now. He left ten or twelve years ago, but it seems to me I heard he was back. He owns a cottage in the village. My God, Max, if he's Christian's grandson, it would be the same cottage."

"Don't get ahead of yourself. We'll look into it, one step at a time."

"If you have to be logical, I'll talk to Suzanna. She knew him a little better. I remember that she knocked him off his motorcycle the first week she had her license."

"I did not knock him off his motorcycle," Suzanna denied, and sank her aching body into a hot, frothy tub. "He fell off his motorcycle when he failed to yield. I had the right-of-way."

"Whatever." Lilah sat on the edge of the tub. "What do we know about him?"

"He has a nasty temper. I thought he was going to murder me that day. He wouldn't have scraped himself all up if he'd been wearing protective gear."

"I mean his background, not his personality."

Weary, Suzanna opened her eyes. Ordinarily the bathroom was the only place she could find true peace and privacy. Now even that had been invaded. "Why?"

"I'll tell you after. Come on, Suze."

"All right, let me think. He was ahead of me in school. Three or four years, I think. Most of the girls were crazy about him because he looked dangerous. His mother was very nice."

"I remember," Lilah murmured. "She came to the house after..."

"Yes, after Mom and Dad were killed. She used to do handwork. She'd done some lovely pieces for Mom. We still have some of them, I think. And her husband was a lobsterman. He was lost at sea when we were teenagers. I really don't remember that much."

"Did you ever talk to him?"

"Who, Holt? Not really. He'd sort of swagger around and glare. When we had that little accident he mostly swore at me. Then he went off somewhere—Portland. I remember because Mrs. Marsley was talking about him just the other day when I was selling her some climbing roses. He was a cop for a while, but there was some kind of incident, and he gave it up."

"What kind of incident?"

"I don't know. Whenever she starts I just let it flow in one ear and on out. I think he's repairing boats or something."

"He never talked about his family with you?"

"Why in the world should he? And why would you care?"

"Because Christian's last name was Bradford, and he had a cottage on the island."

"Oh." Suzanna let out a long breath as she absorbed the information. "Isn't that just our luck?"

Lilah left her sister to soak, and set off to find Max. Before she could go into his room, Coco waylaid her.

"Oh, there you are."

"Darling, you look frazzled." Lilah kissed her cheek.

"And who wouldn't be? That woman..." Coco took a deep calming breath. "I'm doing twenty minutes of yoga every morning just to cope. Be a dear and take this in to her."

"What is it?"

"Tonight's menu." Coco set her teeth. "She insists on treating this as though it's one of her cruises."

"As long as we don't have to play shuffleboard."

"Thank you, dear. Oh, did Max tell you his news?"

"Hmm? Oh, yes, belatedly."

"Has he decided? I know it's a wonderful opportunity, but I hate to think he'll be leaving so soon."

"Leaving?"

"If he takes the position, he'll have to go back to Cornell next week. I was going to read the cards last night, but with Aunt Colleen, I just couldn't concentrate."

"What position, Aunt Coco?"

"Head of the history department." She gave Lilah a baffled look. "I thought he'd told you."

"I was thinking of something else." She struggled to keep her voice even. "He's going to leave in a few days?"

"He'll have to decide." Coco cupped a hand under Lilah's chin. "You'll both have to decide."

"He hasn't chosen to bring me in on this one." She stared down at the menu until the words blurred. "It's a terrific opportunity, one I'm sure he's hoped for."

"There are a lot of opportunities in life, Lilah."

She only shook her head. "I couldn't do anything to discourage him from doing something he wants. Not if I loved him. It has to be his decision."

"Who the hell is jabbering out there?" Colleen thumped her cane on the floor.

"I'd like to take that cane and—"

"More yoga," Lilah suggested, forcing a smile. "I'll deal with her."

"Good luck."

"You bellowed, Auntie," Lilah said as she breezed through the door.

"You didn't knock."

"No, I didn't. Tonight's menu, Miss Calhoun. We hope it meets with your approval."

"Little snip." Colleen snatched the paper away, then frowned up at her grand-niece. "What's wrong with you, girl? You're white as a sheet."

"Pale skin runs in the family. It's the Irish."

"It's temper that runs in the family." She'd seen eyes that had looked like that before, she thought. Hurt, confused. But then she had been only a child, unable to understand. "Trouble with your young man."

"What makes you say so?"

"Just because I never tied myself down with a man doesn't mean I don't know them. I dallied in my day."

"Dallied." This time the smile came more easily. "A nice word. I suppose some of us are meant to dally through life." She ran a finger down the bedpost. "Just as there are some women men love but don't fall in love with."

"You're jabbering."

"No, I'm trying to be realistic. I'm not usually."

"Realism is cold comfort."

Lilah's brow lifted. "Oh, Lord, I'm afraid I'm more like you than I realized. What a scary thought."

Colleen disguised a chuckle. "Get out of here. You give me a headache. Girl," she said, and Lilah paused at the door, "any man who puts that look into your eyes is worth everything or nothing at all."

Lilah gave a short laugh. "Why, Auntie, you're absolutely right."

She went to his room, but he wasn't there. She'd yet to decide whether to confront Max about his plans or to wait until he told her himself. For better or worse, she thought she would follow her instincts. Idly she picked up a shirt he'd left at the foot of his bed. It was the silly screenprint she'd talked him into on that first shopping trip. The shirt, and the memory, still made her smile. Setting it aside, she crossed to his desk.

He had it piled with books—thick volumes on World War I, a history of Maine, a treatment on the Industrial Revolution. She lifted a brow over a book on fashion in the 1900s. He'd picked up one of the pamphlets from the park that gave a detailed map of the island.

In another pile were the art books. Lilah picked up the top one and opened it to where Max had marked it. As he had, she felt the quick thrill of discovery on reading Christian Bradford's name. Lowering into the chair in front of the typewriter, she read the brief biography twice.

Fascinated, excited, she set the book down to reach for another. It was then she noticed the typed pages, neatly stacked. More reports, she thought with a faint smile. She remembered how tidily he had typed up their interview with Millie Tobias.

From the top of the high tower of rock, she faced the sea.

Curious, Lilah settled more comfortably and read on. She was midway through the second chapter when Max came in. Her emotions were so ragged she had to brace before she could speak.

"Your book. You started your book."

"Yeah." He shoved his hands into his pockets. "I was looking for you."

"It's Bianca, isn't it?" Lilah set down the page she was holding. "Laura—she's Bianca."

"Parts of her." He couldn't have explained how it felt to know that she had read his words—words that had come not so much from his head as from his heart.

"You've set it here, on the island."

"It seemed right." He didn't move toward her, he didn't smile, but only stood looking uncomfortable.

"I'm sorry." The apology was stiff and overly polite. "I shouldn't have read it without asking, but it caught my eye."

"It's all right." With his hands still balled in his pockets, he shrugged. She hated it, he thought. "It doesn't matter."

"Why didn't you tell me?"

"There wasn't really anything to tell. I only have about fifty pages, and it's rough. I thought—"

"It's beautiful." She fought back the hurt as she rose.

"What?"

"It's beautiful," she repeated, and found that hurt turned quickly to anger. "You've got enough sense to know that. You've read thousands of books in your life, and know good work from bad. If you didn't want to share it with me, that's your business."

Still stunned, he shook his head. "It wasn't that I—"

"What was it then? I'm important enough to share your bed, but not to be in on any of the major decisions in your life."

"You're being ridiculous."

"Fine." Rolling easily with her temper, she tossed back her hair. "I'm being ridiculous. Apparently I've been ridiculous for some time now."

The tears crowding her voice confused as much as unnerved him. "Why don't we sit down and talk this through?"

She went with her instincts and shoved the chair at him. "Go ahead. Have a seat. But there's no need to talk anything through. You've started your book, but didn't think it was necessary to mention it. You've been offered a promotion, but didn't consider it worth bringing up. Not to me. You've got your life, Professor, and I've got mine. That's what we said right from the beginning. It's just my bad luck that I fell in love with you."

"If you'd just—" Her last words sank in, dazzling him, dazing him, delighting him. "Oh, God, Lilah." He started to rush forward, but she threw up both hands.

"Don't touch me," she said so fiercely, he stopped, baffled.

"What do you expect me to do?"

"I don't expect anything. If I had stuck to that from the beginning, you wouldn't have been able to hurt me like this. As it is, it's my problem. Now, if you'll excuse me."

He grabbed her arm before she reached the door. "You can't say things like this, you can't tell me you're in love with me then just walk away."

"I'll do exactly as I please." Eyes cold, she jerked her arm free. "I don't have anything more to say to you, and there's nothing you can say I want to hear right now."

She walked out of his room into her own and locked the door behind her.

Hours later, she sat in her room, cursing herself for losing her pride and her temper so completely. All she had succeeded in accomplishing was embarrassing herself and Max, and giving herself a vicious headache.

She'd slashed at him, and that had been wrong. She'd pushed him, and that had been stupid. Any hope she'd had of steering him gently into love had been smashed because she'd demanded things he hadn't wanted to give. Now, more than likely, she had ruined a friendship that had been vitally important to her.

There could be no apologizing. No matter how miserable she felt, she couldn't apologize for speaking the truth. And she could never claim to be sorry to have fallen in love.

Restless, she walked out on the terrace. There were clouds over the moon. The wind shoved them across the sky so that the light glimmered for a moment then was smothered. The heat of the day was trapped; the night almost sultry. Fireflies danced over the black carpet of lawn like sparks from a dying fire.

In the distance thunder rumbled, but there was no freshening scent of rain. The storm was out at sea, and even if the capricious wind blew it to land, it might be hours before it hit and relieved the hazy heat. She could smell the flowers, hot and heady, and glanced toward the garden. Her thoughts were so involved that she stared at the glimmer of light for a full minute before it registered.

Not again, she thought, and was almost depressed enough to let the amateur treasure hunters have their thrill. But Suzanna worked too hard on the gardens to have some idiot with a map dig up her perennials. In any case, at least chasing off a trespasser was constructive.

She moved quietly down the steps and into the deeper gloom of the garden. It was simple enough to follow the beam of light. As she walked toward it, Lilah debated whether to use the Calhoun curse or the old The Police Are On Their Way. Both were reliable ways of sending trespassers scurrying. Any other time the prospect might have amused her.

When the light blinked out, she stopped, frowning, to listen. There was only the sound of her own breathing. Not a leaf stirred, and no bird sang in the brush. With a shrug, she moved on. Perhaps they had heard her and had already retreated, but she wanted to be certain.

In the dark, she nearly fell over the pile of dirt. All amusement vanished when her eyes adjusted and she saw the destruction of Suzanna's lovely bed of dahlias.

"Jerks," she muttered, and kicked at the dirt with a sandaled foot. "What the hell is wrong with them?" On a little moan, she bent down to pick up a trampled bloom. Her fingers clenched over it when a hand slapped against her mouth.

"Not a sound." The voice hissed at her ear. Reacting to it, she started to struggle, then froze when she felt the point of the knife at her throat. "Do exactly what I say, and I won't cut you. Try to yell, and I'll slice this across your throat. Understand?"

She nodded and let out a long careful breath when his hand slid away from her mouth. It would have been foolish to ask what he wanted. She knew the answer. But this wasn't some adventure-seeking tourist out for a late-night lark.

"You're wasting your time. The emeralds aren't here."

"Don't play games with me. I've got a map."

Lilah closed her eyes and bit back a hysterical and dangerous laugh.

Max paced his room, scowled at the floor and wished he had something handy to kick. He'd messed things up beautifully. He wasn't exactly sure how he'd managed it, but he'd hurt Lilah, infuriated her and alienated her all in one swoop. He'd never seen a woman go through so many emotions in such a short time. From unhappiness to fury, from fury to frost—hardly letting him get in a single word.

He could have defended himself—if he'd been totally certain of the offense. How could he have known that she'd be offended he hadn't mentioned the book? He hadn't wanted to bore her. No, that was a lie, he admitted. He hadn't told her because he'd been afraid. Plain and simple.

As far as the promotion went, he'd meant to tell her, but it had slipped his mind. How could she believe that he'd have accepted the position and left without telling her?

"What the hell was she supposed to think, you jerk?" he muttered, and plopped down into a chair.

So much for all his careful plans, his step-by-step courtship. His tidy little itinerary for making her fall in love with him had blown up in his face. She'd been in love with him all along.

She loved him. He dragged a hand through his hair. Lilah Calhoun was in love with him, and he hadn't had to wave a magic wand or implement any complicated plan. All he'd had to do was be himself.

She'd been in love with him all along, but he'd been too stupid to believe it even when she'd tried to tell him. Now she'd locked herself in her room and wouldn't listen to him.

As far as he could see, he had two choices. He could sit here and wait until she cooled off, then he could beg. Or he could get up right now, beat down her door and demand that she hear him out.

He liked the second idea. In fact, he thought it was inspired.

Without taking the time to debate with himself, he went through the terrace doors. Since it was two in the morning, it made more sense to rattle the glass than beat on the inside door and wake up the household. And it was more romantic. He'd shove open those doors, stride across the room and drag her into his arms until she...

His erotic dream veered off as he caught a glimpse of her just before she disappeared into the garden.

Fine, he thought. Maybe better. A sultry garden in the middle of the night. Perfumed air and passion. She wasn't going to know what hit her.

"You know where they are." Hawkins dragged her head back by the hair and she nearly cried out.

"If I knew where they were, I'd have them."

"It's a publicity stunt." He whirled her around, laying the edge of the knife against her cheek. "I figured it out. You've just been playing games to get your names in the paper. I've put time and money into this deal, and it's going to pay off tonight."

She was too terrified to move. Even a tremor might have the blade slicing over her skin. She recognized rage in his eyes, just as she recognized him. This was the man Max had called Hawkins. "The map," she began, then heard Max call her name. Before she could take a breath, the knife was at her throat again.

"Make a sound and I kill you, then him."

He'd kill them both anyway, she thought frantically. It had been in his eyes. "The map," she said in a whisper. "It's a fake." She gasped when the blade pricked her skin. "I'll show you. I can show you where they are."

She had to get him away, away from Max. He was calling her again, and the frustration in his voice had tears welling in her eyes.

"Down that way." She gestured on impulse and let Hawkins drag her down the path until Max's voice faded. At the side edge, the garden gave way to the rocks where the smell and sound of the sea grew stronger. "Over there.'' She stumbled as he pulled her over the uneven ground. Beside her, the slope ran almost gently to a ridge. Below that, dizzying feet below, were the jagged teeth of rocks and the temperamental sea.

When the first flash of lightning struck, she jolted, then looked desperately over her shoulder. The wind had come up, but she hadn't noticed. The clouds still hid the moon and smothered the light.

Was she far enough away? she wondered. Had Max given up looking for her and gone back inside? Where it was safe.

"If you're trying to pull something on me—"

"No. They're here." She tripped on a jumble of rocks and went down hard. "Under here. In a box under the rocks."

She would inch away slowly, she told herself as every instinct screamed for her to run. While he was involved, she would inch away, then spring up and race to the house. He grabbed the hem of her skirt, ripping it.

"One wrong move, and you're dead." She saw the gleam of his eyes as he bent close. "If I don't find the box, you're dead."

Then his head went up, like a wolf scenting. Out of the dark with a vicious oath, Max leaped.

She screamed then as she saw the wicked edge of the knife glint in the flash of lightning. They hit the ground beside her, rolling over dirt and rock. She was still screaming when she jumped on Hawkins's back to grope for his knife hand. The blade sliced into the ground an inch from Max's face before she was bucked off.

"Damn it, run!" Max shouted at her, gripping Hawkins's beefy wrist with both hands. Then he grunted as a fist grazed his temple.

They were rolling again, the impetus taking them down the slope and onto the ridge. She did run, but toward them, sliding along the loose dirt and sending a shower of pebbles to rain over the struggling bodies. Panting for breath, she grabbed a rock. Her next scream sliced the air as Max's leg dangled over the edge into space.

All he could see was the contorted face above his. All he could hear was Lilah shouting his name. Then he saw stars when Hawkins rammed his head against the rock. For an instant, Max teetered on the edge, the brink between sky and sea. His hand slipped down the sweaty forearm. When the knife came down, he smelled the blood and heard Hawkins's grunt of triumph.

There was something else in the air—something passionate and pleading—as insubstantial as the wind but as strong as bedrock. It slammed into him like a fist. The understanding went through him that he wasn't only fighting for his life, but for Lilah's and the life they would make together.

He wouldn't lose it. With every ounce of strength, he smashed his fist into the face grinning over his. Blood spouted out of Hawkins's nose, then they were grappling again with the knife wedged between them.

Lilah lifted the rock in both hands, started to bring it down when the men at her feet reversed positions. Sobbing, she scrambled back. There were shouts behind her and wild barking. She held tight to the only weapon she had and prayed that she would have the chance to use it.

Then the struggling stopped, and both men went still. With a grunt, Max pushed Hawkins aside and managed to gain his knees. His face was streaked with dirt and blood, his clothes splattered with it. Weakly he shook his head to clear it and looked up at Lilah. She stood like an avenging angel, hair flying, the rock gripped in her hands.

"He rolled on the knife," Max said in a distant voice. "I think he's dead." Dazed, he stared down at his hand, at the dark smear that was the blood of the man he'd killed. Then he looked up at her again. "Are you hurt?"

"Oh, Max. Oh, God." The rock slipped from her fingers as she tumbled to her knees beside him.

"It's okay." He patted her shoulder, stroked her hair. "It's okay," he repeated though he was deathly afraid he would faint.

The dog got there first, then the others came thundering down the slope in nightgowns or robes and hastily pulled-on jeans.

"Lilah." Amanda was there, desperate hands running over her sister's body in a search for wounds. "Are you all right? Are you hurt?"

"No." But her teeth were starting to chatter in the sultry night. "No, he was—Max came." She looked over to see Trent crouched beside him, examining a long gash down his arm. "You're bleeding."

"Not much."

"It's shallow," Trent said between his teeth. "I imagine it hurts like hell."

"Not yet," Max murmured.

Trent looked over as Sloan walked back from the man sprawled on the ridge. Tight-lipped, Sloan shook his head. "It's done," he said briefly.

"It was Hawkins." Max struggled to his feet and stood, swaying. "He had Lilah."

"We'll discuss this later." Her voice uncharacteristically crisp, Coco took Max's good arm. "They're both in shock. Let's get them inside."

"Come on, baby." Sloan reached down to gather Lilah into his arms. "I'll give you a ride home."

"I'm not hurt." From the cradle of his arms she swiveled her head around to look for Max. "He's bleeding. He needs help."

"We'll fix him up," Sloan promised her as they started across the lawn. "Don't you worry, sweetie, the teacher's tougher than you think."

Up ahead, The Towers was ablaze with lights. Another roll of thunder walked the sky above its peaks, then echoed into silence. Abruptly, a tall, thin figure appeared on the second-floor terrace, a cane in one hand, a glinty chrome revolver in the other.

"What the hell is going on around here?" Colleen shouted. "How is a body supposed to get a decent night's sleep with all this hoopla?"

Coco sent one weary glance upward. "Oh, be quiet and go back to bed."

For some reason, Lilah laid her head on Sloan's shoulder and began to laugh.

It was nearly dawn when things settled. The police had come and gone, taking away their grisly package. Questions had been asked and answered—asked and answered again. Lilah had been plied with brandy, fussed over and ordered into a hot bath.

They hadn't let her tend Max's wound. Which might have been for the best, she thought now. Her hands hadn't been steady.

He'd bounced back from the incident remarkably well, she mused as she curled on the window seat in the tower room. While she had still been numb and shaky, he had stood in the parlor, his arm freshly bandaged, and given the investigating officer a clear and concise report of the whole event.

He might have been lecturing one of his classes on the cause and effect of the German economy on World War I, she thought with the ghost of a smile. It had been obvious that Lieutenant Koogar had appreciated the precision and clarity.

Lilah liked to think that her own account had been calm enough, though she hadn't been able to control the trembling very well even when her sisters had joined ranks around her.

Suzanna had finally told the lieutenant enough was enough and had bundled Lilah upstairs.

But despite the bath and brandy, she hadn't been able to sleep. She was afraid if she closed her eyes that she would see it unfolding again, see Max teetering on the edge of the ridge. They'd hardly spoken since the whole horrible business had happened. They would have to, of course, she reflected. She wanted to clear her thoughts and find just the right words.

But then he walked in, while the sky behind her was being gilded with sunrise, and she was afraid she would never find them.

He stood awkwardly, favoring his left arm, his face shadowed by fatigue. "I couldn't sleep," he began. "I thought you might be up here."

"I guess I needed to think. It's always easier for me to think up here." Feeling as awkward as he, she smoothed back her hair. It fell untamed, the color of the young sun, against the white shoulders of her robe. "Would you like to sit?"

"Yeah." He crossed the room and eased his aching muscles down onto the seat beside her. The silence dragged on, one minute, then two. "Some night," he said at length.

"Yes."

"Don't," he murmured when her eyes filled.

"No." She swallowed them back and stared out at the quiet dawn. "I thought he would kill you. It was like a nightmare—the dark, the heat, the blood."

"It's done now." He took her hand, curled strong fingers around hers. "You led him away from the garden. You were trying to protect me, Lilah. I can't thank you for it."

Off guard, she looked back at him. "What was I supposed to do, let him jump out of the petunias and stab you in the dark?"

"You were supposed to let me take care of you."

She tried to jerk her hand free, but he held firm. "You did, didn't you? Whether I wanted you to or not. You came rushing out like a crazy man, jumping on a maniac with a knife and nearly—" She broke off, struggling for composure while he only sat watching her with those patient eyes. "You saved my life," she said more calmly.

"Then we're even, aren't we?" She shrugged and went back to watching the sky. "The oddest thing happened during those last few minutes I was fighting with Hawkins. I felt myself slipping, losing ground. Then I felt something else, something incredibly strong. I'd say it was simple adrenaline, but it didn't come from me. It was something—other," he said, studying her profile. "I suppose you could call it a force. And I knew that I wasn't meant to lose, that there were reasons I couldn't. I guess I'll always wonder if that force, if that feeling came from you, or from Bianca."

Her lips curved as she looked back at him. "Why, Professor, how illogical."

He didn't smile. "I was coming to your room, to make you listen to me, when I saw you go into the garden. Normally I would consider it only right—or logical—to back off and give you time to recover after what's happened. But things change, Lilah. You're going to listen now."

For a moment she leaned her brow on the cool glass. Then she nodded. "All right, you're entitled. But first I'd like to say that I know I was angry earlier—about the book. It was the wrong reaction—"

"No, it wasn't. You trusted me with a great deal, and I didn't trust you. I was afraid you'd be kind."

"I don't understand."

"Writing's something I've wanted to do most of my life, but I . . . well, I'm not used to taking risks."

She had to laugh and, going with instinct, leaned over to kiss the bandage on his arm. "Max, what a thing to say now of all times."

"I haven't been used to taking risks," he corrected. "I thought if I told you about the book and got up the courage to show you a few pages, you'd see it as a pipe dream and be kind."

"It's stupid to be so insecure about something you have such talent for." Then she sighed. "And it was stupid for me to take it so personally. Take it from someone who isn't particularly kind. It's going to be a wonderful book, Max. Something you can be very proud of."

He cupped a hand behind her neck. "Let's see if you say that after I make you read several hundred more pages." He leaned toward her, touched his lips gently to hers. But when he started to deepen the kiss, she jumped up.

"I'll give you the first critique when it's published." Nerves humming, she began to pace.

"What is it, Lilah?"

"Nothing. So much has happened." She took a deep breath before she turned, smile firmly in place. "The promotion. I was so involved with myself before that I didn't even congratulate you."

"I wasn't keeping it from you."

"Max, let's not go over all of that again. The important thing is it's a wonderful honor. I think we should have a party to celebrate before you go."

A smile ghosted around his mouth. "Do you?"

"Of course. It isn't every day you get made head of your department. The next thing you know, you'll be dean. It's only a matter of time. And then—"

"Lilah, sit down. Please."

"All right." She clung to the desperate gaiety. "We'll have Aunt Coco bake a cake, and—"

"You're happy about the offer then?" he interrupted.

"I'm very proud of you," she said, and brushed the hair from his brow. "I like knowing that the powers that be appreciate how valuable you are."

"And you want me to accept?"

Her brows drew together. "Of course. How could you refuse? This is a wonderful opportunity for you, something you've worked for and earned."

"That's a pity." He shook his head and leaned back, still watching her. "I've already declined."

"You did what?"

"I declined, with appreciation. It's one of the reasons I never mentioned the whole business to you. I didn't see it as an issue."

"I don't understand. A career opportunity like this isn't something you casually turn aside."

"It depends on your career. I also tendered my resignation."

"You—you quit? But that's crazy."

"Yes, probably." And because it was, he had to grin. "But if I went back to Cornell to teach, the book would end up in a file somewhere gathering dust." He held out his hand, palm up. "You looked at this once and told me I'd have to make a choice. I've made it."

"I see," she said slowly.

"You only see part of it." He glanced around the tower. The light was pearly now, slowly going gold. There couldn't be a better time or a better place. He took both of her hands.

"I've loved you from the first moment I saw you. I couldn't believe that you could ever feel the same way, no matter how much I wanted it. Because I didn't, I made things more difficult than they might have been. No, don't say anything, not yet. Just listen." He pressed their joined hands to his lips. "You've changed me. Opened me. I know that I was meant to be with you, and if it took deceit and a necklace that's been lost the best part of a century, then that's what it had to take. Whether or not we'll ever find the emeralds, they brought you to me, and you're all the treasure I'll ever need."

He brought her close to kiss her mouth as morning rose and washed the last shadows from the room.

"I don't want this to be a dream," she murmured. "I've sat here before thinking of you, wishing for this."

"This is real." He framed her face then kissed her again to prove it.

"You're all I want, Max. I've been looking for you for such a long time." Gently she combed her fingers through the hair on his brow. "I was so afraid you wouldn't love me back, that you'd go away. That I'd have to let you go away."

"This has been home since the first night. I can't explain it."

"You don't have to."

"No." He turned his lips into her palm. "Not to you. One last thing." Again he took her hands. "I love you, Lilah, and I have to ask if you're willing to take the risk of marrying an unemployed former teacher who thinks he can write a book."

"No." She smiled and linked her arms around his neck. "But I'm going to marry a very talented and brilliant man who is writing a wonderful book."

With a laugh, he rested his brow on hers. "I like your way better."

"Max." She snuggled into the crook of his arm. "Let's go tell Aunt Coco. She'll be so thrilled she'll fix us blueberry pancakes for an engagement breakfast."

He eased her back against the pillows. "How about an engagement brunch?"

She laughed and flowed into the kiss. "This time I like your way better."

* * * * *

SUZANNA'S SURRENDER

Prologue

Bar Harbor, 1965

*T*he moment I saw her, my life was changed. More than fifty years have passed since that moment, and I'm an old man whose hair has turned white, whose body has grown frail. Yet my memories are full of color and strength.

Since my heart attack, I am to rest every day. So I have come back here to the island—her island—where it all began for me. It has changed, as I have. The great fire in '47 destroyed much. New buildings, new people have come. Cars crowd the streets without the charm of the jingling carriages. But I am lucky to be able to see it as it was, and as it is.

My son is a man now, a good one who chose to make his living from the sea. We have never understood each other, but have dealt together well enough. He has a quiet, lovely wife and a son of his own. The boy, young Holt, brings me a special kind of joy. Perhaps it is because I can see myself in him so clearly. The impatience, the fire, the passions that were once mine. Perhaps he, too, will feel too much, want too much. Yet I can't be sorry for it. If I could tell him one thing, it would be to grab hold of life and take.

My life has been full, and I'm grateful for the years I had with Margaret. I was no longer young when she became my wife. What we shared was not a blaze, but the quiet warmth of a banked fire. She brought me comfort, and I hope I gave her happiness. She's been gone for nearly ten years, and my memories of her are sweet.

Yet it is the memory of another woman that haunts me. This memory is so painfully clear, so complete. No amount of time could dull it. The years have not faded my image of her, nor have they altered by a single degree the desperate love I felt. Yes, feel still—will always feel though she is lost to me.

Perhaps now that I have brushed so close to death, I can open myself to it again, let myself remember what I have never been able to forget. Once it was too painful, and I lost the pain in a bottle. Finding no comfort there, I at last buried my misery in my work. Painting again, I traveled. But always, always, was pulled back here where I had once begun to live. Where I know I will one day die.

A man loves that way only once, and only if he is fortunate. For me, it was Bianca. It has always been Bianca.

It was June, the summer of 1912, before the Great War ripped the world apart. The summer of peace and beauty, of art and poetry, when the village of Bar Harbor opened itself to the wealthy and gave refuge to artists.

She came to the cliffs where I worked, her hand holding that of a child. I turned from my canvas, the brush still in my hand, the mood of the sea and the painting still on me. There she was, slender and lovely, the sunset hair swept up off her neck. The wind tugged at it, and at the skirts of the pale blue frock she wore. Her eyes were the color of the sea I was so frantically trying to recreate on canvas. They watched me, curious, wary. She had the pale and luminous skin of the Irish.

The moment I saw her, I knew I had to paint her. And I think I knew, as we stood in the wind, that I would have to love her.

She apologized for interrupting my work. The faint and musical lilt of Ireland was in the soft, polite voice. The child now in her arms was her son. She was Bianca Calhoun, another man's wife. Her summer home was on the ridge above. The Towers, the elaborate castle Fergus Calhoun had built. Even though I had only been on Mount Desert Island a short time, I had heard of Calhoun, and his home. Indeed I had admired the arrogant and fanciful lines of it, the turrets and peaks, the towers and parapets.

Such a place suited the woman who stood before me. She had a timeless beauty, a quiet steadiness, a graciousness that could never be taught, and banked passions simmering in her large green eyes. Yes, I was already in love, but then it was only with her beauty. As an artist, I wanted to interpret that beauty in my own way, with paint or pencils. Perhaps I frightened her by staring so intently. But the child, his name was Ethan, was fearless and friendly. She looked so young, so untouched, that it was difficult to believe the child was hers, and that she had two more besides.

She didn't stay long that day, but took her son and went home to her husband. I watched her walk through the wild roses, the sun in her hair.

I couldn't paint the sea anymore that day. Her face had already begun to haunt me.

Chapter One

She wasn't looking forward to this. It had to be done, of course. Suzanna dragged a fifty-pound bag of mulch over to her pickup, then muscled it into the bed. That small physical task wasn't the problem. In fact, she was pleased to be able to make the delivery her second stop on her way home.

It was the first stop she wished she could avoid. But for Suzanna Calhoun Dumont, duty could never be avoided.

She'd promised her family that she would speak to Holt Bradford, and Suzanna kept her promises. Or tried to, she thought, and wiped a forearm over her sweaty brow.

But damn it, she was tired. She'd put in a full day in Southwest Harbor, landscaping a new house, and she had a full schedule the next day. That wasn't taking into account that her sister Amanda was getting married in little more than a week, or that The Towers was mass confusion in preparation for the wedding and with the remodeling of the west wing. It didn't even begin to deal with the fact that she had two energetic children at home who would want, and deserved, their mother's time and attention that evening. Or the paperwork that was piling up on her desk—or the fact that one of her part-time employees had quit just that morning.

Well, she'd wanted to start a business, Suzanna reminded herself. And she'd done it. She glanced back at her shop, locked for the night with the display of summer blooms in the window, at the greenhouse just behind the main building. It belonged to her—and the bank, she thought with a little smile—every pansy, petunia and peony. She'd proven she wasn't the incompetent failure her ex-husband had told her she was. Over and over again.

She had two beautiful children, a family who loved her and a landscaping-and-gardening business that was holding its own. She didn't even suppose Bax's claim that she was dull could apply now. Not when she was in the middle of an adventure that had started eighty years before.

There certainly wasn't anything mundane about searching for a price-less emerald necklace, or being dogged by international jewel thieves who would stop at nothing to get their hands on her great-grandmother Bianca's legacy.

Not that she'd been much more than a supporting player so far, Suzanna mused as she climbed into the truck. It had been her sister C.C. who had started it by falling in love with Trenton St. James III, of the St. James Hotels. It had been his idea to turn part of the financially plagued family home into a luxury retreat. In doing so, the old legend of the Calhoun emeralds had leaked to the ever-eager press and had set off a chain reaction that had run a course from the absurd to the dangerous.

It had been Amanda who had nearly been killed when the desperate and obsessed thief going by the name of William Livingston had stolen family papers he'd hoped would lead him to the lost emeralds. And it had been her sister Lilah who had had her life threatened during the latest attempt.

In the week that had passed since that night, the police hadn't turned up a trace of Livingston, or his latest known alias, Ellis Caufield.

It was odd, she thought as she joined the stream of traffic, how The Towers and the lost emeralds had affected the entire family. The Towers had brought C.C. and Trent together. Then Sloan O'Riley had come to design the retreat and had fallen in love with Amanda. The shy history professor, Max Quartermain, had lost his heart to Suzanna's free-spirited sister, Lilah, and both of them had nearly been killed. Again, because of the emeralds.

There were times Suzanna wished they could forget about the necklace that had belonged to her great-grandmother. But she knew, as they all knew, that the necklace Bianca had hidden away before her death was meant to be found.

So they continued, following up every lead, exploring every dusty path. Now it was her turn. During his research, Max had uncovered the name of the artist Bianca had loved.

It was a story that never failed to make Suzanna wistful, but it was just her bad luck that the connection with the artist led to his grandson.

Holt Bradford. She sighed a little as she drove through the traffic-jammed streets of the village. She couldn't claim to know him well—wasn't sure anyone could. But she remembered him as a teenager. Surly, bad tempered and aloof. Of course, girls had been attracted by his go-to-hell attitude. The attraction helped along, no doubt, by the dark, brooding looks and angry gray eyes.

Odd she should remember the color of his eyes, she mused. But then again, the one time she had seen them up close and personal he'd all but burned her alive with them.

He'd probably forgotten the altercation, she assured herself. She hoped so. Altercations made her shaky and sweaty, and she'd had enough of them in her marriage to last a lifetime. Certainly Holt wouldn't still hold a grudge—it had been more than ten years. After all, he hadn't been hurt very much when he'd taken a header off his motorcycle. And it had been his fault, she thought, setting her chin. She'd had the right of way.

In any case, she had promised Lilah she would talk to him. Any connection with Bianca's lost emeralds had to be followed up. As Christian Bradford's grandson, Holt might have heard stories.

Since he'd come back to Bar Harbor a few months before, he had taken up residence in the same cottage his grandfather had lived in during his romance with Bianca. Suzanna was Irish enough to believe in fate. There was a Bradford in the cottage and Calhouns in The Towers. Surely between them, they could find the answers to the mystery that had haunted both families for generations.

The cottage was on the water, sheltered by two lovely old willows. The simple wooden structure made her think of a doll's house, and she thought it a shame that no one had cared enough to plant flowers. The grass was freshly mowed, but her professional eye noted that there were patches that needed reseeding, and the whole business could use a good dose of fertilizer.

She started toward the door when the barking of a dog and the rumble of a man's voice had her skirting around to the side.

There was a rickety pier jutting out above the calm, dark water. Tied to it was a neat little cabin cruiser in gleaming white. He sat in the stern, patiently polishing the brass. He was shirtless, his tanned skin taut over bone and muscle, and gleaming with sweat. His black hair was curled past where his collar would be if he'd worn one. Apparently he didn't find it necessary to cover himself with anything more than a pair of ripped and faded cutoffs. She noticed his hands, limber, long fingered, and wondered if he had inherited them from his artist grandfather.

Water lapped quietly at the boat. Behind it, she saw a fish hawk soar then plummet. It gave a cry of triumph as it rose up again, a silver fish caught wriggling in its claws. The man in the boat continued to work, untouched by or oblivious to the drama of life and death around him.

Suzanna fixed what she hoped was a polite smile on her face and walked toward the pier. "Excuse me."

When his head shot up, she stopped dead. She had the quick but vivid impression that if he'd had a weapon, it would have been aimed at her. In an instant, he had gone from relaxed to full alert, with an edgy kind of violence in the set of his body that had her mouth going dry.

As she struggled to steady her heartbeat, she noted that he had changed. The surly boy was now a dangerous man. There was no other word that came to mind. His face had matured so that it was all planes and angles, sharply defined. The stubble of a two-day beard added to the rough-and-ready look.

But it was his eyes once again, that dried up her throat. A man with eyes that sharp, that potent, needed no weapon.

He squinted at her but didn't rise or speak. He had to give himself a moment to level. If he'd been wearing his weapon, it would have been out and in his hand. That was one of the reasons he was here, and a civilian again.

He might have forced himself to relax—he knew how—but he remembered her face. A man didn't forget that face. God knows, he hadn't. Timeless. In one of his youthful fantasies, he'd imagined her as a princess, lost and lovely in flowing silks. And himself as the knight who would have slain a hundred dragons to have her.

The memory made him scowl.

She'd hardly changed, he thought. Her skin was still pale Irish roses and cream, the shape of her face still classically oval. Her mouth had remained full and romantically soft, her eyes that deep, deep, dreamy blue, luxuriously lashed. They were watching him now with a kind of baffled alarm as he took his time looking her over.

She'd pulled her hair back in a smooth ponytail, but he remembered how it had flowed, long and loose and gleaming blond over her shoulders.

She was tall—all the Calhoun women were—but she was too thin. His scowl deepened at that. He'd heard she'd been married and divorced, and that both had been difficult experiences. She had two children, a boy and girl. It was difficult to believe that the slender wand of a woman in grubby jeans and a sweaty T-shirt had ever given birth.

It was harder to believe, harder to accept, that she could jangle his nerves just by standing ten feet away.

With his eyes still on hers, he went back to his polishing. "Do you want something?"

She let out the breath she hadn't been aware she was holding. "I'm sorry to just drop in this way. I'm Suzanna Dumont. Suzanna Calhoun."

"I know who you are."

"Oh, well..." She cleared her throat. "I realize you're busy, but I'd like to talk with you for a few minutes. If this isn't a good time—"

"What about?"

Since he was being so gracious, she thought, annoyed, she'd get right to the point. "About your grandfather. He was Christian Bradford, wasn't he? The artist?"

"That's right. So?"

"It's kind of a long story. Can I sit down?"

When he only shrugged, she walked to the pier. It groaned and swayed under her feet, and she lowered herself carefully.

"Actually, it started back in 1912 or '13, with my great-grandmother, Bianca."

"I've heard the fairy tale." He could smell her now, flowers and sweat, and it made his stomach tighten. "She was an unhappy wife with a rich and difficult husband. She compensated by taking a lover. Somewhere along the line, she supposedly hid her emerald necklace. Insurance if she got up the guts to leave. Instead of taking off into the sunset with her lover, she jumped out of the tower window, and the emeralds were never found."

"It wasn't precisely—"

"Now your family's decided to start a treasure hunt," he went on as if she hadn't spoken. "Got a lot of press out of it, and more trouble than I imagine you bargained for. I heard you had some excitement a couple weeks ago."

"If you can call my sister being held at knife point excitement, yes." The fire had come into her eyes. She wasn't always good at defending herself, but when it came to her family, she was a scrapper. "The man who was working with Livingston, or whatever the bastard's calling himself now, nearly killed Lilah and her fiancé."

"When you've got priceless emeralds with a legend attached, the rats gnaw through the woodwork." He knew about Livingston. Holt had been a cop for ten years, and though he'd spent most of that time in Vice, he'd read reports on the slick and often violent jewel thief.

"The legend and the emeralds are my family's business."

"So why come to me? I turned in my shield. I'm retired."

"I didn't come to you for professional help. It's personal." She took another breath, wanting to be clear and concise. "Lilah's fiancé used to be a history professor at Cornell. A couple of months ago, Livingston, going under the name of Ellis Caufield, hired him to go through the family's papers he'd stolen from us."

Holt continued to polish the brightwork. "Doesn't sound like Lilah developed any taste."

"Max didn't know the papers were stolen," Suzanna said between her teeth. "When he found out, Caufield nearly killed him. In any case, Max came to The Towers and continued his research for us. We've documented the emeralds' existence, and we've even interviewed a servant who worked at The Towers the year Bianca died."

Holt shifted and continued to work. "You've been busy."

"Yes. She corroborates the story that the necklace was hidden, and that Bianca was in love, and planning to leave her husband. The man she was in love with was an artist." She waited a beat. "His name was Christian Bradford."

Something flickered in his eyes then was gone. Very deliberately he set down his rag. He pulled a cigarette from a pack, flicked on a lighter then slowly blew out a haze of smoke.

"Do you really expect me to believe that little fantasy?"

She'd hoped for surprise, even amazement. She'd gotten boredom. "It's true. She used to meet him on the cliffs near The Towers."

He gave her a thin smile that was very close to a sneer. "Saw them, did you? Oh, I've heard about the ghost, too." He drew in more smoke, lazily released it. "The melancholy spirit of Bianca Calhoun, drifting through her summer home. You Calhouns are just full of—stories."

Her eyes darkened, but her voice remained very controlled. "Bianca Calhoun and Christian Bradford were in love. The summer she died, they met often on the cliffs just below The Towers."

That touched a chord, but he only shrugged. "So what?"

"So there's a connection. My family can't afford to overlook any connection, particularly one so vital as this one. It's very possible she told him where she put the emeralds."

"I don't see what a flirtation—an unsubstantiated flirtation—between two people some eighty years ago has to do with emeralds."

"If you could get past this prejudice you seem to have toward my family, we might be able to figure it out."

"Not interested in either part." He flipped open the top of a small cooler. "Want a beer?"

"No."

"Well, I'm fresh out of champagne." Watching her, he twisted off the top, tossed it toward a plastic bucket, then drank deeply. "You know, if you think about it, you'd see it's a little tough to swallow. The lady of the manor, well-bred, well-off, and the struggling artist. Doesn't play, babe. You'd be better off dropping the whole thing and concentrating on planting your flowers. Isn't that what you're doing these days?"

He could make her angry, she thought, but he wasn't going to shake her from her purpose. "My sisters' lives were threatened, my home has been broken into. Idiots are sneaking in my garden and digging up my rosebushes." She stood, tall and slim and furious. "I have no intention of dropping the whole thing."

"Your business." He flicked the cigarette away before jumping effortlessly onto the pier. It shook and swayed beneath them. He was taller than she remembered, and she had to angle her chin to keep her eyes level. "Just don't expect to suck me into it."

"All right then. I'll just stop wasting my time and yours."

He waited until she'd stepped off the pier. "Suzanna." He liked the way it sounded when he said it. Soft and feminine and old-fashioned. "You ever learn to drive?"

Eyes stormy, she took a step back toward him. "Is that what this is all about?" she demanded. "You're still steaming because you fell off that stupid motorcycle and bruised your inflated male ego?"

"That wasn't the only thing that got bruised—or scraped, or lacerated." He remembered the way she'd looked. God, she couldn't have been more than sixteen. Rushing out of her car, her hair windblown, her face pale, her eyes dark and drenched with concern and fear.

And he'd been sprawled on the side of the road, his twenty-year-old pride as raw as the skin the asphalt had abraded.

"I don't believe it," she was saying. "You're still mad, after what, twelve years, for something that was clearly your own fault."

"My fault?" He tipped the bottle toward her. "You're the one who ran into me."

"I never ran into you or anyone. You fell."

"If I hadn't ditched the bike, you would have run into me. You weren't looking where you were going."

"I had the right of way. And you were going entirely too fast."

"Bull." He was starting to enjoy himself. "You were checking that pretty face of yours in the rearview mirror."

"I certainly was not. I never took my eyes off the road."

"If you'd had your eyes on the road, you wouldn't have run into me."

"I didn't—" She broke off, swore under her breath. "I'm not going to stand here and argue with you about something that happened twelve years ago."

"You came here to try to drag me into something that happened eighty years ago."

"That was an obvious mistake." She would have left it at that, but a very big, very wet dog came bounding across the lawn. With two happy barks, the animal leaped, planting both muddy feet on Suzanna's shirt and sending her staggering back.

"Sadie, down!" As Holt issued the terse command, he caught Suzanna before she hit the ground. "Stupid bitch."

"I beg your pardon?"

"Not you, the dog." Sadie was already sitting, thumping her dripping tail. "Are you all right?" He still had his arms around her, bracing her against his chest.

"Yes, fine." He had muscles like rock. It was impossible not to notice. Just as it was impossible not to notice that his breath fluttered along her temple, that he smelled very male. It had been a very long time since she had been held by a man.

Slowly he turned her around. For a moment, a moment too long, she was face-to-face with him, caught in the circle of his arms. His gaze flicked down to her mouth, lingered. A gull wheeled overhead, banked, then soared out over the water. He felt her heart thud against his. Once, twice, three times.

"Sorry," he said as he released her. "Sadie still sees herself as a cute little puppy. She got your shirt dirty."

"Dirt's my business." Needing time to recover, she crouched down to rub the dog's head. "Hi, there, Sadie."

Holt pushed his hands into his pockets as Suzanna acquainted herself with his dog. The bottle lay where he'd tossed it, spilling its contents onto the lawn. He wished to God she didn't look so beautiful, that her laugh as the dog lapped at her face didn't play so perfectly on his nerves.

In that one moment he'd held her, she'd fit into his arms as he'd once imagined she would. His hands fisted inside his pockets because he wanted to touch her. No, that wasn't even close. He wanted to pull her inside the cottage, toss her onto the bed and do incredible things to her.

"Maybe a man who owns such a nice dog isn't all bad." She tossed a glance over her shoulder and the cautious smile died on her lips. The way he was looking at her, his eyes so dark and fierce, his bony face so set had the breath backing up in her lungs. There was violence trembling around him. She'd had a taste of violence from a man, and the memory of it made her limbs weak.

Slowly he relaxed his shoulders, his arms, his hands. "Maybe he isn't," he said easily. "But it's more a matter of her owning me at this point."

Suzanne found it more comfortable to look at the dog than the master. "We have a puppy. Well, he's growing by leaps and bounds so he'll be as big as Sadie soon. In fact, he looks a great deal like her. Did she have a litter a few months ago?"

"No."

"Hmm. He's got the same coloring, the same shaped face. My brother-in-law found him half-starved. Someone had dumped him, I suppose, and he'd managed to get up to the cliffs."

"Even I draw the line at abandoning helpless puppies."

"I didn't mean to imply—" She broke off because a new thought had jumped into her mind. It was no crazier than looking for missing emeralds. "Did your grandfather have a dog?"

"He always had a dog, used to take it with him wherever he went. Sadie's one of the descendants."

Carefully she got to her feet again. "Did he have a dog named Fred?"

Holt's brows drew together. "Why?"

"Did he?"

Holt was already sure he didn't like where this was leading. "The first dog he had was called Fred. That was before the First World War. He did a painting of him. And when Fred exercised the right *de seigneur* around the neighborhood, my grandfather took a couple of the puppies."

Suzanne rubbed suddenly damp hands on her jeans. It took all of her control to keep her voice low and steady. "The day before Bianca died, she brought a puppy home to her children. A little black puppy she called Fred." She saw his eyes change and knew she had his attention, and his interest. "She'd found him out on the cliffs—the cliffs where she went to meet Christian." She moistened her lips as Holt continued to stare at her and say nothing. "My great-grandfather wouldn't allow the dog to stay. They argued about it, quite seriously. We were able to locate a maid who'd worked there, and she'd heard the whole thing. No one was sure what happened to that dog. Until now."

"Even if that's true," Holt said slowly, "it doesn't change the bottom line. There's nothing I can do for you."

"You can think about it, you can try to remember if he ever said anything, if he left anything behind that could help."

"I've got enough to think about." He paced a few feet away. He didn't want to be involved with anything that would bring him into contact with her again and again.

Suzanna didn't argue. She could only stare at the long, jagged scar that ran from his shoulder to nearly his waist. He turned, met her horrified eyes and stiffened.

"Sorry, if I'd known you were coming to call, I'd have put on a shirt."

"What—" She had to swallow the block of emotion in her throat. "What happened to you?"

"I was a cop one night too long." His eyes stayed steady on hers. "I can't help you, Suzanna."

She shook away the pity he obviously would detest. "You won't."

"Whatever. If I'd wanted to dig around in other people's problems, I'd still be on the force."

"I'm only asking you to do a little thinking, to let us know if you remember anything that might help."

He was running out of patience. Holt figured he'd already given her more than her share for one day. "I was a kid when he died. Do you really think he'd have told me if he'd had an affair with a married woman?"

"You make it sound sordid."

"Some people don't figure adultery's romantic." Then he shrugged. It was nothing to him either way. "Then again, if one of the partners turns out to be a washout, I guess it's tough to come down on the other for looking someplace else."

She looked away at that, closing in on a private pain. "I'm not interested in your views on morality, Holt. Just your memory. And I've taken up enough of your time."

He didn't know what he'd said to put that sad, injured look in her eyes. But he couldn't let her leave with that haunting him. "Look, I think you're reaching at straws here, but if anything comes to mind, I'll let you know. For Sadie's ancestor's sake."

"I'd appreciate it."

"But don't expect anything."

With a half laugh she turned to walk to her truck. "Believe me, I won't." It surprised her when he crossed the lawn with her.

"I heard you started a business."

"That's right." She glanced around the yard. "You could use me."

The faint sneer came again. "I ain't the rosebush type."

"The cottage is." Unoffended, she fished her keys out of her pocket. "It wouldn't take much to make it charming."

"I'm not in the market for posies, babe. I'll leave the puttering around the rose garden to you."

She thought of the aching muscles she took home with her every night and climbed into the truck to slam the door. "Yes, puttering around the garden is something we women do best. By the way, Holt, your grass needs fertilizer. I'm sure you have plenty to spread around."

She gunned the engine, set the shift in reverse and pulled out.

Chapter Two

The children came rushing out of the house, followed by a big-footed black dog. The boy and the girl skimmed down the worn stone steps with the easy balance and grace of youth. The dog tripped over his own feet and somersaulted. Poor Fred, Suzanna thought as she climbed out of the truck. It didn't look as though he would ever outgrow his puppy clumsiness.

"Mom!" Each child attached to one of Suzanna's jean-clad legs. At six, Alex was already tall for his age and dark as a gypsy. His sturdy tanned legs were scabbed at the knees and his bony elbows were scraped. Not from clumsiness, Suzanna thought, but from derring-do. Jenny, a year younger and blond as a fairy princess, carried the same badges of honor. Suzanna forgot her irritation and fatigue the moment she bent to kiss them.

"What have you two been up to?"

"We're building a fort," Alex told her. "It's going to be impregnant."

"Impregnable," Suzanna corrected, tweaking his nose.

"Yeah, and Sloan said he could help us with it on Saturday."

"Can you?" Jenny asked.

"After work." She bent to pet Fred, who was trying to push his way through the children for his rightful share of affection. "Hello, boy. I think I met one of your relatives today."

"Does Fred have relatives?" Jenny wanted to know.

"It certainly looked that way." She walked over to sit with the children on the steps. It was a luxury to sit, to smell the sea and flowers, to have a child under each arm. "I think I met his cousin Sadie."

"Where? Can she come to visit? Is she nice?"

"In the village," Suzanna said, answering Alex's rapid-fire questions in turn. "I don't know, and yes, she's very nice. Big, like Fred's going to be when he grows into his feet. What else did you do today?"

"Loren and Lisa came over," Jenny told her. "We killed hundreds of marauders."

"Well, we can all sleep easy tonight."

"And Max told us a story about storming the beach at Normally."

Chuckling, Suzanna kissed the top of Jenny's head. "I think that was Normandy."

"Lisa and Jenny played dolls, too." Alex gave his sister a brotherly smirk.

"She wanted to. She got the brand-new Barbie and her car for her birthday."

"It was a Ferrari," Alex said importantly, but didn't want to admit that he and Loren had played with it when the girls were out of the room. He inched closer to toy with his mother's ponytail. "Loren and Lisa are going to Disney World next week."

Suzanna bit back a sigh. She knew her children dreamed of going to that enchanted kingdom in central Florida. "We'll go someday."

"Soon?" Alex prompted.

She wanted to promise, but couldn't. "Someday," she repeated. The weariness was back when she rose to take each child by the hand. "You guys run and tell Aunt Coco I'm home. I need to shower and change. Okay?"

"Can we go to work with you tomorrow?"

She gave Jenny's hand a quick squeeze. "Carolanne's watching the shop tomorrow. I have site work." She felt their disappointment as keenly as her own. "Next week. Go ahead now," she said as she opened the massive front door. "And I'll look at your fort after dinner."

Satisfied with that, they barreled down the hall with the dog at their heels.

They didn't ask for much, Suzanna thought as she climbed the curving stairs to the second floor. And there was so much more she wanted to give them. She knew they were happy and safe and secure. They had a huge family who loved them. With one of her sisters married, and two others engaged, her children had men in their lives. Maybe uncles didn't replace a father, but it was the best she could do.

They hadn't heard from Baxter Dumont for months. Alex hadn't even rated a card on his birthday. The child support check was late again—as it was every month. Bax was too sharp a lawyer to neglect the payment completely, but he made certain it arrived weeks after its due date. To test her, she knew. To see if she would beg for it. Thank God she hadn't needed to yet.

The divorce had been final for a year and a half, but he continued to take out his feelings for her on the children—the only truly worthwhile thing they had made together.

Perhaps that was why she had yet to get over the nagging disillusionment, the sense of betrayal and loss and inadequacy. She no longer loved him. That love had died before Jenny had been born. But the hurt... Suzanna shook her head. She was working on it.

She stepped into her room. Like most of the rooms in The Towers, Suzanne's bedroom was huge. The house had been built in the early 1900s by her great-grandfather. It had been a showpiece, a testament to his vanity, his taste for the opulent and his need for status. It was five stories of somber granite with fanciful peaks and parapets, two spiraling towers and layering terraces. The interior was lofty ceilings, fancy woodwork, maze-like hallways. Part castle, part manor house, it had served first as summer home, then as permanent residence.

Through the years and financial reversals, the house had fallen on hard times. Suzanna's room, like the others, showed cracks in the plaster. The floor was scarred, the roof leaked and the plumbing had a mind of its own. As one, the Calhouns loved their family home. Now that the west wing was under renovation, they hoped it would be able to pay its own way.

She went to the closet for a robe, thinking that she'd been one of the lucky ones. She'd been able to bring her children here, into a real home, when their own had crumbled. She hadn't had to interview strangers to care for them while she made a living. Her father's sister, who had raised Suzanna and her sisters after their parents had died, was now caring for Suzanna's children. Though Suzanna was aware that Alex and Jenny were a handful, she knew there was no one better suited for the task than Aunt Coco.

And one day soon they would find Bianca's emeralds, and everything would settle back to what passed for normal in the Calhoun household.

"Suze." Lilah gave the door a quick knock then poked her head in. "Did you see him?"

"Yes, I saw him."

"Terrific." Lilah, her red hair curling to her waist, strolled in. She stretched out diagonally on the bed, plumping a pillow against the tiered headboard. Easily she settled into her favorite position. Horizontal. "So tell me."

"He hasn't changed much."

"Oh-oh."

"He was abrupt and rude." Suzanna pulled the T-shirt over her head. "I think he considered shooting me for trespassing. When I tried to explain what was going on, he sneered." Remembering that look, she tugged down the zipper of her jeans. "Basically, he was obnoxious, arrogant and insulting."

"Mmm. Sounds like a prince."

"He thinks we made the whole thing up to get publicity for The Towers when we open the retreat next year."

"What a crock." That stirred Lilah enough to have her sitting up. "Max was nearly killed. Does he think we're crazy?"

"Exactly." With a nod, Suzanna dragged on her robe. "I couldn't begin to guess why, but he seems to have a grudge against the Calhouns in general."

Lilah gave a sleepy smile. "Still stewing because you knocked him off his motorcycle."

"I did not—" On an oath, Suzanna gave up. "Never mind, the point is I don't think we're going to get any help from him." After pulling the band out of her hair, she ran her hands through it. "Though after the business with the dog, he did say he'd think about it."

"What dog?"

"Fred's cousin," she said over her shoulder as she walked into the bath to turn on the shower.

Lilah came to the doorway just as Suzanna was pulling the curtain closed. "Fred has a cousin?"

Over the drum of the water, Suzanna told her about Sadie, and her ancestors.

"But that's fabulous. It's just one more link in the chain. I'll have to tell Max."

With her eyes closed, Suzanna stuck her head under the shower. "Tell him he's on his own. Christian's grandson isn't interested."

He didn't want to be. Holt sat on the back porch, the dog at his feet, and watched the water turn to indigo in twilight.

There was music here, the symphony of insects in the grass, the rustle of wind, the countermelody of water against wood. Across the bay, Bar Island began to fade and merge into dusk. Nearby someone was playing a radio, a lonely alto sax solo that suited Holt's mood.

This was what he wanted. Quiet, solitude, no responsibilities. He'd earned it, hadn't he? he thought as he tipped the beer to his lips. He'd given ten years of his life to other people's problems, their tragedies, their miseries.

He was burned out, bone-dry and tired as hell.

He wasn't even sure he'd been a good cop. Oh, he had citations and medals that claimed he had been. But he also had a twelve-inch scar on his back that reminded him he'd nearly been a dead one.

Now he just wanted to enjoy his retirement, repair a few motors, scrape some barnacles, maybe do a little boating. He'd always been good with his hands and knew he could make a decent living repairing boats. Running his own business, at his own pace, in his own way. No reports to type, no leads to follow up, no dark alleys to search.

No knife-wielding junkies springing out of the shadows to rip you open and leave you bleeding on the littered concrete.

Holt closed his eyes and took another pull of beer. He'd made up his mind during the long, painful hospital stay. There would be no more commitment in his life, no more trying to save the world from itself. From that point on, he would start looking out for himself. Just himself.

He'd taken the money he'd inherited and had come home, to do as little as possible with the rest of his life. Sun and sea in the summer, roaring fires and howling winds in the winter. It wasn't so damn much to ask.

He'd been settling in, feeling pretty good about himself. Then she'd come along.

Hadn't it been bad enough that he'd looked at her and felt—Lord, the way he'd felt when he'd been twenty years old. Churned up and hungry. He was still hung up on her.

The lovely, and unattainable, Suzanna Calhoun of the Bar Harbor Calhouns. The princess in the tower. She'd lived high up in her castle on the cliffs. And he had lived in a cottage on the edge of the village. His father had been a lobsterman, and Holt had often delivered a catch to the Calhoun's back door—never going beyond the kitchen. But he'd sometimes heard voices or laughter or music. And he had wondered and wanted.

Now she had come to him. But he wasn't a love-struck boy any longer. He was a realist. Suzanna was out of his league, just as she had always been. Even if it had been different, he wasn't interested in a woman who had home and hearth written all over her.

As far as the emeralds went, there was nothing he could do to help her. Nothing he wanted to do.

He'd known about the emeralds, of course. That particular story had made national press. But the idea that his grandfather had been involved, had loved and been loved by a Calhoun woman. That was fascinating.

Even with the coincidence about the dogs, he wasn't sure he believed it. Holt hadn't known his grandmother, but his grandfather had been the hero of his childhood. He'd been the dashing and mysterious figure who had gone off to foreign places, come back with fabulous stories. He'd been the man who had been able to perform magic with a canvas and brush.

He could remember climbing up the stairs to the studio as a child to watch the tall man with the snow-white hair at work. Yet it had seemed more like combat than work. An elegant and passionate duel between his grandfather and the canvas.

They would take long walks, the young boy and the old man, along the shore, across the rocks. Up on the cliffs. With a sigh, Holt sat back. Very often they had walked to the cliffs just below The Towers. Even as a child he'd understood that as his grandfather had looked out to sea, he had gone someplace else.

Once, they had sat on the rocks there and his grandfather had told him a story about the castle on the cliffs, and the princess who'd lived there.

Had he been talking about The Towers, and Bianca?

Restless, Holt rose to go inside. Sadie glanced up, then settled her head on her front paws again as the screen door slammed.

The cottage suited him more than the home he'd grown up in. That had been a neat and soulless place with worn linoleum and dark paneled walls. Holt had sold it after his mother's death three years before. Recently he'd used the profits for some repairs and modernization of the cottage, but preferred keeping the old place much as it had been in his grandfather's day.

It was a boxy house, with plaster walls and wood floors. The original stone fireplace had been pointed up, and Holt looked forward to the first cool night when he could try it out.

The bedroom was tiny, almost an afterthought that jutted out from the main structure. He liked lying in bed at night and listening to rain drumming on the tin roof. The stairs to his grandfather's studio had been reinforced, as well as the railing that skirted along the open balcony. He climbed up now, to look at the wide, airy space, dim with twilight.

Now and then he thought about putting skylights in the angled roof, but he never considered refinishing the floor. The dark old wood was splattered with paint that had dripped from brush or palette. There were streaks of carmine and turquoise, drops of emerald green and canary yellow. His grandfather had preferred the vivid, the passionate, even the violent in his work.

Against one wall, canvases were stacked, Holt's legacy from a man who had only begun to find critical and financial success in his last years. They would, he knew, be worth a hefty sum. Yet as he never considered sanding the paint from the floors, he had never considered selling this part of his inheritance.

Crouching down, he began to look through the paintings. He knew them all, had studied them countless times, wondering how he could have come from a man with such vision and talent. Holt turned over the portrait, knowing that was why he had come up here.

The woman was as beautiful as a dream—the fine-featured oval face, the alabaster skin. Rich red-gold hair was swept up off a graceful neck. Full, soft lips were curved, just a little. But it was the eyes that drew Holt, as they always had. They were green, like a misty sea. It wasn't their color that pulled at him, but the expression in them, the look, the emotion that had been captured by his grandfather's brush and skill.

Such quiet sadness. Such inner grief. It was almost too painful to look at, because to look too long was to feel. He had seen that expression today, in Suzanna's eyes.

Could this be Bianca? he wondered. The resemblance was there, in the shape of the face, the curve of the mouth. The coloring was certainly wrong and the similarities slight. Except the eyes, he thought. When he looked at them, he thought of Suzanna.

Because he was thinking of her too much, he told himself. He rose, but he didn't turn the portrait back to the wall. He stood staring at it for a long time, wondering if his grandfather had loved the woman he'd painted.

It was going to be another hot one, Suzanna thought. Though it was barely seven, the air was already sticky. They needed rain, but the moisture hung in the air and stubbornly refused to fall.

Inside her shop, she checked on the refrigerated blooms and left a note for Carolanne to push the carnations by selling them at half price. She checked the soil in the hanging pots of impatiens and geraniums, then moved on to the display of gloxinia and begonias.

Satisfied, she took her sprayer out to drench the flats of annuals and perennials. The rosebushes and peonies were moving well, she noted. As were the yews and junipers.

By seven-thirty, she was checking on the greenhouse plants, grateful that her inventory was dwindling. What didn't sell, she would winter over. She would also take cuttings for next year's plants. But winter, and that quiet work, was months away.

By eight her pickup was loaded, and she was on her way to Seal Harbor. She would put in a full day's work there on the grounds of a newly constructed home. The buyers were from Boston, and wanted their summer home to have an established yard, complete with shrubs, trees and flower beds.

It would be hot, sweaty work, Suzanne mused. But it would also be quiet. The Andersons were in Boston this week, so she would have the yard to herself. She liked nothing better than working with the soil and living things, tending something she had planted and watching it grow and thrive.

Like her children, she thought with a smile. Her babies. Every time she put them to bed at night or watched them run in the sunlight, she knew that nothing that had happened to her before, nothing that would happen to her in the future would dim that glow of knowing they were hers.

The failed marriage had left her shaken and uncertain, and there were times she still had terrible doubts about herself as a woman. But not as a mother. Her children had the very best she could give them. The bond nourished her, as well as them.

Over the past two years, she'd begun to believe that she could be a success in business. Her flair for gardening had been her only useful skill and had been a kind of salvation during the last months of her dying marriage. In desperation she had sold her jewelry, taken out a loan and had plunged into Island Gardens.

It had made her feel good to use her maiden name. She hadn't wanted any frivolous or clever name for the business, but something straightforward. The first year had been rough—particularly when she'd been pouring every cent she could spare into legal fees to fight a custody suit.

The thought of that, the memory of it, still made her blood run cold. She couldn't have lost them.

Bax hadn't wanted the children, but he'd wanted to make things difficult for her. When it had been over, she'd lost fifteen pounds, countless hours of sleep and had been up to her neck in debt. But she had her children. The ugly battle had been won, and the price meant nothing.

Gradually she was pulling out. She'd gained back a few of the pounds, had caught up a bit on her sleep and was slowly, meticulously hacking away at the debt. In the two years since she'd opened the business, she'd earned a reputation as dependable, reasonable and imaginative. Two of the resorts had tried her out, and it looked as though they'd be negotiating long-term contracts.

That would mean buying another truck, hiring on full-time labor. And maybe, just maybe, that trip to Disney World.

She pulled up in the driveway of the pretty Cape Cod house. Now, she reminded herself, it meant getting to work.

The grounds took up about a half acre and were gently sloped. She had had three in-depth meetings with the owners to determine the plan. Mrs. Anderson wanted plenty of spring flowering trees and shrubs, and the long-term privacy factor of evergreens. She wanted to enjoy a perennial bed that was carefree and full of summer color. Mr. Anderson didn't want to spend his summers maintaining the yard, particularly the side portion, which fell in a more dramatic grade. There, Suzanna would use ground covers and rockeries to prevent erosion.

By noon, she had measured off each area with stakes and strings. The hardy azaleas were planted. Two long-blooming fairy roses flanked the flagstone walk and were already sweetening the air. Because Mrs. Anderson had expressed a fondness for lilacs, Suzanna placed a trio of compact shrubs near the master bedroom window, where the next spring's breezes would carry the scent indoors.

The yard was coming alive for her. It helped her ignore the aching muscles in her arms as she drenched the new plants with water. Birds were chirping, and somewhere in the near distance, a lawn mower was putting away.

One day, she would drive by and see that the fast-growing hedge roses she had planted along the fence had spread and bloomed until they covered the chain link. She would see the azaleas bloom in the spring and the maple leaves go red in the fall, and know that she'd been part of that.

It was important, more important than she could admit to anyone, that she leave a mark. She needed that to remind herself that she wasn't the weak and useless woman who had been so callously tossed aside.

Dripping with sweat, she picked up her water bottle and shovel and headed around to the front of the house again. She'd put in the first of the flowering almonds and was digging the hole for the second when a car pulled into the driveway behind her truck. Resting on her shovel, Suzanna watched Holt climb out.

She let out a little huff of breath, annoyed that her solitude had been invaded, and went back to digging.

"Out for a drive?" she asked when his shadow fell over her.

"No, the girl at the shop told me where to find you. What the hell are you doing?"

"Playing canasta." She shoveled some more dirt. "What do you want?"

"Put that shovel down before you hurt yourself. You've got no business digging ditches."

"Digging ditches is my business—more or less. Now, what do you want?"

He watched her dig for another ten seconds before he snatched the shovel away from her. "Give me that damn thing and sit down."

Patience had always been her strong point, but she was hard-pressed to find it now. Working at it, she adjusted the brim of the fielder's cap she wore. "I'm on a schedule, and I have six more trees, two rosebushes and twenty square feet of ground cover to plant. If you've got something to say, fine. Talk while I work."

He jerked the shovel out of her reach. "How deep do you want it?" She only lifted a brow. "How deep do you want the hole?"

She skimmed her gaze down, then up again. "I'd say a little more than six feet would be enough to bury you in."

He grinned, surprising her. "And you used to be so sweet." Plunging the shovel in, he began to dig. "Just tell me when to stop."

Normally she repaid kindness with kindness. But she was going to make an exception. "You can stop right now, I don't need any help. And I don't want the company."

"I didn't know you had a stubborn streak." He glanced up as he tossed dirt aside. "I guess I had a hard time getting past that pretty face." That pretty face, he noted, was flushed and damp and had shadows of fatigue under the eyes. It annoyed the hell out of him. "I thought you sold flowers."

"I do. I also plant them."

"Even I know that thing there is a tree."

"I plant those, too." Giving up, she took out a bandanna and wiped at her neck. "The hole needs to be wider, not deeper."

He shifted to accommodate her. Maybe he needed to do a little reevaluating. "How come you don't have anybody doing the heavy work for you?"

"Because I can do it myself."

Yes, there was stubbornness in the tone, and just a touch of nastiness. He liked her better for it. "Looks like a two-man job to me."

"It is a two-man job—the other man quit yesterday to be a rock star. His band got a gig down in Brighton Beach."

"Big time."

"Hmm. That's fine," she said, and turned to heft the three-foot tree by its balled roots. As Holt frowned at her, she lifted it, then set it carefully in the hole.

"Now I guess I fill it back in."

"You've got the shovel," she pointed out. As he worked, she dragged a bag of peat moss closer and began to mix it with the soil.

Her nails were short and rounded, he noted as she dug her already grimed fingers into the soil. There was no wedding ring on her finger. In fact, she wore no jewelry at all, though she had hands that were meant to wear beautiful things.

She worked patiently, her head down, her cap shielding her eyes. He could see the nape of her neck and wondered what it would be like to press his lips there. Her skin would be hot now, and damp. Then she rose, switching on the garden hose to drench the dirt.

"You do this every day?"

"I try to take a day or two in the shop. I can bring the kids in with me." With her feet, she tamped down the damp earth. When the tree was secure, she spread a thick lawyer of mulch, her moves competent and practiced. "Next spring, this will be covered with blooms." She wiped the back of her wrist over her brow. The little tank top she wore had a line of sweat down the front and back that only emphasized her fragile build. "I really am on a schedule, Holt. I've got some aspens and white pine to plant out in back, so if you need to talk to me, you're going to have to come along."

He glanced around the yard. "Did you do all this today?"

"Yes. What do you think?"

"I think you're courting sunstroke."

A compliment, she supposed, would have been too much to ask. "I appreciate the medical evaluation." She put a hand on the shovel, but he held on. "I need this."

"I'll carry it."

"Fine." She loaded the bags of peat and mulch into a wheelbarrow. He swore at her, tossed the shovel on top then nudged her away to push the wheelbarrow himself.

"Where out back?"

"By the stakes near the rear fence."

She frowned after him when he started off, then followed him. He began digging without consulting her so she emptied the wheelbarrow and headed back to her truck. When he glanced up, she was pushing out two more trees. They planted the first one together, in silence.

He hadn't realized that putting a tree in the ground could be soothing, even rewarding work. But when it stood, young and straight in the dazzling sunlight, he felt soothed. And rewarded.

"I was thinking about what you said yesterday," he began when they set the second tree in its new home.

"And?"

He wanted to swear. There was such patience in the single word, as if she'd known all along he would bring it up. "And I still don't think there's anything I can do, or want to do, but you may be right about the connection."

"I know I'm right about the connection." She brushed mulch from her hands to her jeans. "If you came out here just to tell me that, you've wasted a trip."

She rolled the empty wheelbarrow to the truck. She was about to muscle the next two trees out of the bed when he jumped up beside her.

"I'll get the damn things out." Muttering, he filled the wheelbarrow and rolled it back to the rear of the yard. "He never mentioned her to me. Maybe he knew her, maybe they had an affair, but I don't see how that helps you."

"He loved her," Suzanna said quietly as she picked up the shovel to dig. "That means he knew how she felt, how she thought. He might have had an idea where she would have hidden the emeralds."

"He's dead."

"I know." She was silent a moment as she worked. "Bianca kept a journal—at least we're nearly certain she did, and that she hid it away with the necklace. Christian might have kept one, too."

Annoyed, he grabbed the shovel again. "I never saw it."

She suppressed the urge to snap at him. However much it might grate, he could be a link. "I suppose most people keep a private journal in a private place. Or he might have kept some letters from her. We found one Bianca wrote him and was never able to send."

"You're chasing windmills, Suzanna."

"This is important to my family." She set the white pine carefully in the hole. "It's not the monetary value of the emeralds. It's what they meant to her."

He watched her work, the competent and gentle hands, the surprisingly strong shoulders. The delicate curve of her neck. "How could you know what they meant to her?"

She kept her eyes down. "I can't explain that to you in any way you'd understand or accept."

"Try me."

"We all seem to have some kind of bond with her—especially Lilah." She didn't look up when she heard him digging the next hole. "We'd never seen the emeralds, not even a photograph. After Bianca died, Fergus, my great-grandfather, destroyed all pictures of her. But Lilah...she drew a sketch of them one night. It was after we'd had a séance."

She did look up then and caught his look of amused disbelief. "I know how it sounds," she said, her voice stiff and defensive. "But my aunt believes in that sort of thing. And after that night, I think she may be right to. My youngest sister, C.C. had an...experience during the séance. She saw them—the emeralds. That's when Lilah drew the sketch. Weeks later, Lilah's fiancé found a picture of the emeralds in a library book. They were exactly as Lilah had drawn them, exactly as C.C. had seen them."

He said nothing for a moment as he set the next tree in place. "I'm not much on mysticism. Maybe one of your sisters saw the picture before, and had forgotten about it."

"If any of us had seen a picture, we wouldn't have forgotten. Still, the point is that all of us feel that finding the emeralds is important."

"They might have been sold eighty years ago."

"No. There was no record. Fergus was a maniac about keeping his finances." Unconsciously she arched her back, rolled her shoulders to relieve the ache. "Believe me, we've been through every scrap of paper we could find."

He let it drop, mulling it over as they planted the last of the trees.

"You know the bit about the needle in the haystack?" he asked as he helped her spread mulch. "People don't really find it."

"They would if they kept looking." Curious, she sat back on her heels to study him. "Don't you believe in hope?"

He was close enough to touch her, to rub the smudge of dirt from her cheek or run a hand down the ponytail. He did neither. "No, only in what is."

"Then I'm sorry for you." They rose together, their bodies nearly brushing. She felt something rush along her skin, something race through her blood, and automatically stepped back. "If you don't believe in what could be, there isn't any use in planting trees, or having children or even watching the sun set."

He'd felt it, too. And resented and feared it every bit as much as she. "If you don't keep your eye on what's real, right now, you end up dreaming your life away. I don't believe in the necklace, Suzanna, or in ghosts, or in eternal love. But if and when I'm certain that my grandfather was involved with Bianca Calhoun, I'll do what I can to help you."

She gave a half laugh. "You don't believe in hope or love, or anything else apparently. Why would you agree to help us?"

"Because if he did love her, he would have wanted me to." Bending, he picked up the shovel and handed it back to her. "I've got things to do."

Chapter Three

Suzanna pulled up to the shop, pleased that she had to squeeze between a station wagon and a hatchback in the graveled parking area. There were a few people wandering around the flats of annuals, and a young couple deliberating over the climbing roses. A woman, hugely pregnant, strolled about, carrying a tray of mixed pots. The toddler by her side held a single geranium like a flag.

Inside, Carolanne was ringing up a sale and flirting with the young man who held a ceramic urn of pink double begonias. "Your mother will love them," she said, and swept her long lashes over doe-colored eyes. "There's nothing like flowers for a birthday. Or anytime. We're having a special on carnations." She smiled and tossed her long, curling brown hair. "If you have a girlfriend."

"Well, no. . ." He cleared his throat. "Not really. Right now."

"Oh." Her smile warmed several degrees. "That's too bad." She gave him his change and a long look. "Come back anytime. I'm usually here."

"Sure. Thanks." He shot a glance over his shoulder, trying to keep her in sight, and nearly ran over Suzanna. "Oh. Sorry."

"That's all right. I hope your mother enjoys them." Chuckling, she joined the pert brunette at the cash register. "You're amazing."

"Wasn't he cute? I love it when they blush. Well." She turned her smile on Suzanna. "You're back early."

"It didn't take as long as I thought." She didn't feel it was necessary to add she'd had unexpected and unwanted help. Carolanne was a hard worker, a skilled salesperson, and an inveterate gossip. "How are things here?"

"Moving along. All this sunshine must be inspiring people to beef up their gardens. Oh, Mrs. Russ was back. She liked the primroses so much, she made her husband build her another window box so she could buy more. Since she was in the mood, I sold her two hibiscus—and two of those terra-cotta pots to put them in."

"I love you. Mrs. Russ loves you, and Mr. Russ is going to learn to hate you." At Carolanne's laugh, Suzanna looked out through the glass. "I'll go and see if I can help those people decide which roses they want."

"The new Mr. and Mrs. Halley. They both wait tables over at Captain Jack's, and just bought a cottage. He's studying to be an engineer, and she's going to start teaching at the elementary school in September."

Shaking her head, Suzanna laughed. "Like I said, you're amazing."

"No, just nosy." Carolanne grinned. "Besides, people buy more if you talk to them. And boy, do I love to talk."

"If you didn't, I'd have to close up shop."

"You'd just work twice as hard, if that's possible." She waved a hand before Suzanna could protest. "Before you go, I asked around to see if anyone needed any part-time work." Carolanne lifted her hands. "No luck yet."

It wasn't any use moaning, Suzanna thought. "This late in the season, everyone's already working."

"If Tommy the creep Parotti hadn't jumped ship—"

"Honey, he had a chance to make a break and do something he's always wanted to do. We can't blame him for that."

"You can't," Carolanne muttered. "Suzanna, you can't keep doing all the site work yourself. It's too hard."

"We're getting by," she said absently, thinking of the help she'd had that day. "Listen, Carolanne, after we deal with these customers, I have another delivery to make. Can you handle things until closing?"

"Sure." Carolanne let out a sigh. "I'm the one with a stool and a fan, you're the one with the pick and the shovel."

"Just keep pushing the carnations."

An hour later, Suzanna pulled up at Holt's cottage. It wasn't just impulse, she told herself. And it wasn't because she wanted to pressure him. Lecturing herself, she climbed out of the truck. It certainly wasn't because she wanted his company. But she was a Calhoun, and Calhouns always paid their debts.

She walked up the steps to the porch, again thinking it was a charming place. A few touches—morning glories climbing up the railing, a bed of columbine and larkspur, with some snapdragons and lavender.

Day lilies along that slope, she thought as she knocked. A border of impatiens. Miniature roses under the windows. And there, where the ground was rocky and uneven, a little herb bed, set off with spring bulbs.

It could be a fairy-tale place—but the man who lived there didn't believe in fairy tales.

She knocked again, noting that his car was there. As she had before, she walked around the side, but he wasn't in the boat this time. With a shrug, she decided she would do what she'd come to do.

She'd already picked the spot, between the water and the house, where the shrub could be seen and enjoyed through what she'd determined was the kitchen window. It wasn't much, but it would add some color to the empty backyard. She wheeled around what she needed, then began to dig.

Inside his work shed, Holt had the boat engine broken down. Rebuilding it would require concentration and time. Which was just what he needed. He didn't want to think about the Calhouns, or tragic love affairs, or responsibilities.

He didn't even glance up when Sadie rose from her nap on the cool cement and trotted outside. He and the dog had an understanding. She did as she chose, and he fed her.

When she barked, he kept on working. As a watchdog, Sadie was a bust. She barked at squirrels, at the wind in the grass, and in her sleep. A year before there'd been an attempted burglary in his house in Portland. Holt had relieved the would-be thief of his stereo equipment while Sadie had napped peacefully on the living room rug.

But he did look up, he did stop working when he heard the low, feminine laughter. It skimmed along his skin, light and warm. When he pushed away from the workbench, his stomach was already in knots. When he stood in the doorway and looked at her, the knots yanked tight.

Why wouldn't she leave him alone? he wondered, and shoved his hands into his pockets. He'd told her he'd think about it, hadn't he? She had no business coming here again.

They didn't even like each other. Whatever she did to him physically was his problem, and so far he'd managed quite nicely to keep his hands off her.

Now here she was, standing in his yard, talking to his dog. And digging a hole.

His brows drew together as he stepped out of the shed. "What the hell are you doing?"

Her head shot up. He saw her eyes, big and blue and alarmed. Her face, flushed from the heat and her work, went very pale. He'd seen that kind of look before—the quick, instinctive fear of a cornered victim. Then it was gone, fading so swiftly he nearly convinced himself he'd imagined it. Color seeped slowly into her cheeks again as she managed to smile.

"I didn't think you were here."

He stayed where he was and continued to scowl. "So, you decided to dig a hole in my yard."

"I guess you could say that." Steady now, annoyed with herself for the instinctive jolt, she plunged the shovel in again, braced her foot on it and deepened the hole. "I brought you a bush."

Damned if he was going to take the shovel from her this time and dig the hole himself. But he did cross to her. "Why?"

"To thank you for helping me out today. You saved me a good hour."

"So you use it to dig another hole."

"Uh-huh. There's a breeze off the water today." She lifted her face to it for a moment. "It's nice."

Because looking at her made his palms sweat, he scowled down at the tidy shrub pregnant with sassy yellow blooms. "I don't know how to take care of a bush. You put it there, you're condemning it to death row."

With a laugh, she scooped out the last of the dirt. "You don't have to do much. This one's very hardy, even when it's dry, and it'll bloom for you into the fall. Can I use your hose?"

"What?"

"Your hose?"

"Yeah." He raked a hand through his hair. He hadn't a clue how he was supposed to react. It was certainly the first time anyone had given him flowers—unless you counted the batch the guys at the precinct had brought in when he'd been in the hospital. "Sure."

At ease with her task, she continued to talk as she went to the outside wall to turn on the water. "It'll stay neat. It's a very well behaved little bush and won't get over three feet." She petted Sadie, who was circling the bush and sniffing. "If you'd like something else instead . . ."

He wasn't going to let himself be touched by some idiotic plant or her misplaced gratitude. "It doesn't matter to me. I don't know one from the other."

"Well, this is a *hypericum kalmianum.*"

His lips quirked into what might have been a smile. "That tells me a lot."

Chuckling, she set it in place. "A sunshine shrub in layman's terms." Still smiling, she tilted her head back to look at him. If she didn't know better, she'd have thought he was embarrassed. Fat chance. "I thought you could use some sunshine. Why don't you help me plant it? It'll mean more to you then."

He'd said he wasn't going to get sucked in, and damn it, he'd meant it. "Are you sure this isn't your idea of a bribe? To get me to help you out?"

Sighing a little, she sat back on her heels. "I wonder what makes someone so cynical and unfriendly. I'm sure you have your reasons, but they don't apply here. You did me a favor today, and I'm paying you back. Very simple. Now if you don't want the bush, just say so. I'll give it to someone else."

He lifted a brow at the tone. "Is that how you keep your kids in line?"

"When necessary. Well, what's it to be?"

Maybe he was being too hard on her. She'd made a gesture and he was slapping it back in her face. If she could be casually friendly, so could he. "I've already got a hole in my yard," he pointed out then knelt beside her. The dog lay down in the sunlight to watch. "We might as well put something in it."

And that, she supposed, was his idea of a thank-you. "Fine."

"So how old are your kids?" Not that he cared, he told himself. He was just making conversation.

"Five and six. Alex is the oldest, then Jenny." Her eyes softened as they always did when she thought of them. "They're growing up so fast, I can hardly keep up."

"What made you come back here after the divorce?"

Her hands tensed in the soil, then began to work again. It was a small and quickly concealed gesture, but he had very sharp eyes. "Because it's home."

There was a tender spot, he thought and eased around it. "I heard you're going to turn The Towers into a hotel."

"Just the west wing. That's C.C.'s husband's business."

"It's hard to picture C.C. married. The last time I saw her she was about twelve."

"She's grown up now, and beautiful."

"Looks run in the family."

She glanced up, surprised, then back down again. "I think you've just said something nice."

"Just stating a fact. The Calhoun sisters were always worth a second look." To please himself, he reached out to toy with the tip of her ponytail. "Whenever guys got together, the four of you were definitely topics of conversation."

She laughed a little, thinking how easy life had been back then. "I'm sure we'd have been flattered."

"I used to look at you," Holt said slowly. "A lot."

Wary, she lifted her head. "Really? I never noticed."

"You wouldn't have." His hand dropped away again. "Princesses don't notice peasants."

Now she frowned, not only at the words but at the clipped tone. "What a ridiculous thing to say."

"It was easy to think of you that way, the princess in the castle."

"A castle that's been crumbling for years," she said dryly. "And as I recall, you were too busy swaggering around and juggling girls to notice me."

He had to grin. "Oh, between the swaggering and juggling, I noticed you all right."

Something in his eyes set off a little warning bell. It might have been some time since she'd heard that particular sound, but she recognized it and heeded it. She looked down again to firm the dirt around the bush.

"That was a long time ago. I imagine we've both changed quite a bit."

"Can't argue with that." He pushed at the dirt.

"No, don't shove at it, press it down—firm, but gentle." Scooting closer, she put her hands over his to show him. "All it needs is a good start, and then—"

She broke off when he turned his hands over to grip hers.

They were close, knees brushing, bodies bent toward each other. He noted that her hands were hard, callused, a direct and fascinating contrast to the soft eyes and tea rose complexion. There was a strength in her fingers that would have surprised him if he hadn't seen for himself how hard she worked. For reasons he couldn't fathom, he found it incredibly erotic.

"You've got strong hands, Suzanna."

"A gardener's hands," she said, trying to keep her voice light. "And I need them to finish planting this bush."

He only tightened his grip when she tried to draw away. "We'll get to it. You know, I've thought about kissing you for fifteen years." He watched the faint smile fade away from her face and the alarm shoot into her eyes. He didn't mind it. It might be best for both of them if she was afraid of him. "That's a long time to think about anything."

He released one hand, but before she could let out a sigh of relief, he had cupped the back of her neck. His fingers were firm, his grip determined. "I'm just going to get it out of my system."

She didn't have time to refuse. He was quick. Before she could deny or protest, his mouth was on hers, covering and conquering. There was nothing soft about him. His mouth, his hands, his body when he pulled her against him, were hard and demanding. The swift frisson of fear had her lifting a hand to push against his shoulder. She might as well have tried to move a boulder.

Then the fear turned to an ache. She fisted her hand against him, forced to fight herself now rather than him.

She was taut as a wire. He could feel her nerves sizzle and snap as he clamped her against him. He knew it was wrong, unfair, even despicable, but damn it, he needed to wipe out this fever that continued to burn in him. He needed to convince himself that she was just another woman, that his fantasies of her were only remnants of a boy's foolish dreams.

Then she shuddered. A soft, yielding sound followed. And her lips parted beneath his in irresistible and avid invitation. Swearing, he plunged, dragging her head back by the hair so that he could take more of what she so mindlessly offered.

Her mouth was a banquet, and he too racked with hunger to stem the greed. He could smell her hair, fresh as rainwater, her skin, seductively musky with heat and labor, and the rich and primitive fragrance of earth newly turned. Each separate scent slammed into his system, pumping through his blood, roaring through his head to churn a need he'd hoped to dispel.

She couldn't breathe, or think. All of the weighty and worrisome cares she carried in her vanished. In their place, rioting sensations sprinted. The tensed ripple of muscle under her fingers, the hot and desperate taste of his mouth, the thunder of her heartbeat that raced with dizzying speed. She was wrapped around him now, her fingers digging in, her body straining, her mouth as urgent and impatient as his.

It had been so long since she had been touched. So long since she had tasted a man's desire on her lips. So long since she had wanted any man. But she wanted now—to feel his hands on her, rough and demanding, to have his body cover hers on the soft, sunny grass. To be wild and willful and wanton until this clawing ache was soothed.

The sheer power of that want ripped through her, tearing through her lips in a sobbing moan.

His fingers were curled into her shirt, had nearly ripped it aside before he caught himself, cursed himself. And released her. Her shallow ragged breaths were both condemnation and seduction as he forced himself to pull away. Her eyes had gone to cobalt and were wide with shock.

Small wonder, he thought in livid self-disgust. The woman had nearly been shoved to the ground and ravished in broad daylight.

Her lashes lowered before he could see the shame.

"I hope you feel better now."

"No." His hands were far from steady, so he curled them into fists. "I don't."

She didn't look at him, couldn't. Nor could she afford to think, just at this moment, of what she had done. To comfort herself she began to spread mulch around the newly planted bush. "If it stays dry, you'll have to water this regularly until it's established."

For a second time, he gripped her hands. This time she jolted. "Aren't you going to belt me?"

Using well-honed control, she relaxed and looked up. There was something in her eyes, something dark and passionate, but her voice was very calm. "There doesn't seem to be much point in that. I'm sure you're of the opinion that a woman like me would be . . . needy."

"I wasn't thinking about your needs when I kissed you. It was a purely selfish act, Suzanna. I'm good at being selfish."

Because his grip was light, she slipped her hands from under his. "I'm sure you are." She brushed her palms on her thighs before she rose. The only thought in her head was of getting away, but she made herself load the wheelbarrow calmly. Until he gripped her arm and whirled her around.

"What the hell is this?" His eyes were stormy, his voice as rough as his hands. He wanted her to rage at him—needed it to soothe his conscience. "I all but took you on the ground, without giving a hell of a lot of consideration to whether you'd have liked it or not, and now you're going to load up your cart and go away?"

She was very much afraid she would have liked it. That was why it was imperative that she stay very calm and very controlled. "If you want to pick a fight or a casual lover, Holt, you've come to the wrong person. My children are expecting me home, and I'm very tired of being grabbed."

Yes, her voice was calm, he thought, even firm, but her arm was trembling lightly under his hold. There was something here, he realized, some secrets she held behind those sad and beautiful eyes. The same stubbornness that had had him pursuing his gold shield made it essential that he discover them.

"Grabbed in general, or just by me?"

"You're the one doing the grabbing." Her patience was wearing thin. The Calhoun temper was always difficult to control. "I don't like it."

"That's too bad, because I have a feeling I'm going to be doing a lot more of it before we're through."

"Maybe I haven't made myself clear. We are through." She shook loose and grabbed the handles of the wheelbarrow.

He simply put his weight on it to stop her. He wasn't sure if she realized she'd just issued an irresistible challenge. His grin came slowly. "Now you're getting mad."

"Yes. Does that make you feel better?"

"Quite a bit. I'd rather have you claw at me than crawl off like a wounded bird."

"I'm not crawling anywhere," she said between her teeth. "I'm going home."

"You forgot your shovel," he told her, still grinning.

She snatched it up and tossed it into the wheelbarrow with a clatter. "Thanks."

"You're welcome."

He waited until she'd gone about ten feet. "Suzanna."

She slowed but didn't stop, and tossed a look over her shoulder. "What?"

"I'm sorry."

Her temper eased a bit as she shrugged. "Forget it."

"No." He dipped his hands into his pockets and rocked back on his heels. "I'm sorry I didn't kiss you like that fifteen years ago."

Swearing under her breath, she quickened her pace. When she was out of sight, he glanced back at the bush. Yeah, he thought, he was sorry as hell, but planned to make up for lost time.

She needed some time to herself. That wasn't a commodity Suzanna found very often in a house as filled with people as The Towers. But just now, with the moon on the rise and the children in bed, she took a few precious moments alone.

It was a clear night, and the heat of the day had been replaced by a soft breeze that was scented with the sea and roses. From her terrace she could see the dark shadow of the cliffs that always drew her. The distant murmur of water was a lullaby, as sweet as the call of a night bird from the garden.

Tonight it wouldn't ease her into sleep. No matter how tired her body was, her mind was too restless. It didn't seem to matter how often she told herself she had nothing to worry about. Her children were safely tucked into bed, dreaming about the day's adventures. Her sisters were happy. Each one of them had found her place in the world, just as each one of them had found a mate who loved her for who and what she was. Aunt Coco was happy and healthy and looking forward to the day when she would become head chef of The Towers Retreat.

Her family, always Suzanna's chief concern, was content and settled. The Towers, the only real home she'd ever known, was no longer in danger of being sold, but would remain the Calhoun home. It was pointless to worry about the emeralds. The family was doing all that could be done to find the necklace.

If they hadn't been exploring every avenue, she would never have gone to Holt Bradford. Her fingers curled on the stone wall. That, she thought, had been a useless exercise. He was Christian Bradford's grandson, but he didn't feel the connection. It was obvious that the past held no interest for him. He thought only about the moment, about himself, about his own comfort and pleasures.

Catching herself, Suzanna sighed and forced herself to relax her hands. If only he hadn't made her so angry. She despised losing her temper, and it had come dangerously close to breaking loose that day. It was her own fault, and her own problem that something else had broken loose.

Needs. She didn't want to need anyone but her family—the family she could love and depend on and worry about. She'd already learned a painful lesson about needing a man, one man. She didn't intend to repeat it.

He'd kissed her on impulse, she reminded herself. It had been a kind of dare to himself. There had certainly been no affection in it, no softness, no romance. The fact that it had stirred her was strictly chemical. She'd cut herself off from men for more than two years. And the last year or so of her marriage—well, there had been no affection, softness or romance there, either. She'd learned to do without those things when it came to men. She could continue to do without them.

If only she hadn't responded to him so... blatantly. He might as well have knocked her over the head with a club and dragged her into a cave by the hair for all the finesse he'd shown. Yet she had thrown herself into the moment, clinging to him, answering those hard and demanding lips with a fervor she'd never been able to show her own husband.

By doing so, she'd humiliated herself and amused Holt. Oh, the way he had grinned at her at the end had had her steaming for hours afterward. That was her problem, too, she thought now. Just as it was her problem that she could still taste him.

Perhaps she shouldn't be so hard on herself. As embarrassing as the moment had been, it had proved something. She was still alive. She wasn't the cold shell of a woman that Bax had tossed so carelessly aside. She could feel, and want.

Closing her eyes, she pressed a hand to her stomach. Want too much, it seemed. It was like a hunger, and the kiss, like a crust of bread after a long fast, had stirred the juices. She could be glad of that—to feel something again besides remorse and disillusionment. And feeling it, she could control it. Pride would prevent her from avoiding Holt. Just as pride would save her from any new humiliation.

She was a Calhoun, she reminded herself. Calhoun women went down fighting. If she had to deal with Holt again in order to widen the trail to the emeralds, then she would deal with him. She would never, never let herself be dismissed and destroyed by a man again. He hadn't seen the last of her.

"Suzanna, there you are."

Her thoughts scattered as she turned to see her aunt striding through the terrace doors. "Aunt Coco."

"I'm sorry, dear, but I knocked and knocked. Your light was on so I just peeked in."

"That's all right." Suzanna slipped an arm around Coco's sturdy waist. This was a woman she'd loved for most of her life. A woman who had been mother and father to her for more than fifteen years. "I was lost in the night, I guess. It's so beautiful."

Coco murmured an agreement and said nothing for a moment. Of all of her girls, she worried most about Suzanna. She had watched her ride away, a young bride radiant with hope. She had been there when Suzanna had come back, barely four years later, a pale, devastated woman with two small children. In the years since, she'd been proud to see Suzanna gain her feet, devoting herself to the difficult task of single parenthood, working hard, much too hard, to establish her own business.

And she had waited, painfully, for the sad and haunted look that clouded her niece's eyes, to finally fade forever.

"Couldn't you sleep?" Suzanna asked her.

"I haven't even thought about sleep yet." Coco let out a huff of breath. "That woman is driving me out of my mind."

Suzanna managed not to smile. She knew *that woman* was her Great-Aunt Colleen, the eldest of Bianca's children, and the sister of Coco's father. The rude, demanding and perpetually cranky woman had descended on them a week before. Coco was certain the move had been made with the sole purpose of making her life a misery.

"Did you hear her at dinner?" Tall and stately in her draping caftan, Coco began to pace. Her complaints were issued in an indignant whisper. Colleen might have been well past eighty, her bedroom may have been two dozen feet away, but she had ears like a cat. "The sauce was too rich, the asparagus too soft. The idea of her telling *me* how to prepare coq au vin. I wanted to take that cane and wrap it around her—"

"Dinner was superb, as always," Suzanna soothed. "She has to complain about something, Aunt Coco, otherwise her day wouldn't be complete. And as I recall, there wasn't a crumb left on her plate."

"Quite right." Coco drew in a deep breath, releasing it slowly. "I know I shouldn't let the woman get on my nerves. The fact is, she's always frightened me half to death. And she knows it. If it wasn't for yoga and meditation, I'm sure I'd have already lost my sanity. As long as she was living on one of those cruise ships, all I had to do was send her an occasional duty letter. But actually living under the same roof." Coco couldn't help it—she shuddered.

"She'll get tired of us soon, and sail off down the Nile or the Amazon or whatever."

"It can't be too soon for me. I'm afraid she's made up her mind to stay until we find the emeralds. Which is what this is all about anyway." Coco calmed herself enough to stand at the wall again. "I was using my crystal to meditate. So soothing, and after an evening with Aunt Colleen—" She broke off because she was clenching her teeth. "In any case, I was just drifting along, when thoughts and images of Bianca filled my head."

"That's not surprising," Suzanne put in. "She's on all of our minds."

"But this was very strong, dear. Very clear. There was such melancholy. I tell you, it brought tears to my eyes." Coco pulled a handkerchief out of her caftan. "Then suddenly, I was thinking of you, and that was just as strong and clear. The connection between you and Bianca was unmistakable. I realized there had to be a reason, and thinking it through, I believe it's because of Holt Bradford." Coco's eyes were shining now with discovery and enthusiasm. "You see, you've spoken to him, you've bridged the gap between Christian and Bianca."

"I don't think you can call my conversations with Holt a bridge to anything."

"No, he's the key, Suzanna. I doubt he understands what information he might have, but without him, we can't take the next step. I'm sure of it."

With a restless move of her shoulders, Suzanna leaned against the wall. "Whatever he understands, he isn't interested."

"Then you have to convince him otherwise." She put a hand on Suzanna's and squeezed. "We need him. Until we find the emeralds, none of us will feel completely safe. The police haven't been able to find that miserable thief, and we don't know what he may try next time. Holt is our only link with the man Bianca loved."

"I know."

"Then you'll see him again. You'll talk to him."

Suzanna looked toward the cliffs, toward the shadows. "Yes, I'll see him again."

I knew she would come back. However unwise, however wrong it might have been, I looked for her every afternoon. On the days she did not come to the cliffs, I would find myself staring up at the peaks of The Towers, aching for her in a way I had no right to ache for another man's wife. On the days she walked toward me, her hair like melted flame, that small, shy smile on her lips, I knew a joy like no other.

In the beginning, our conversations were polite and distant. The weather, unimportant village gossip, art and literature. As time passed, she became more at ease with me. She would speak of her children, and I came to know them through her. The little girl, Colleen, who liked pretty dresses and yearned for a pony. Young Ethan who only wanted to run and find adventure. And little Sean, who was just learning to crawl.

It took no special insight to see that her children were her life. Rarely did she speak of the parties, the musicals, the social gatherings I knew she at-

tended almost nightly. Not at all did she speak of the man she had married.

I admit I wondered about him. Of course, it was common knowledge that Fergus Calhoun was an ambitious and wealthy man, one who had turned a few dollars into an empire during the course of his life. He commanded both respect and fear in the business world. For that I cared nothing.

It was the private man who obsessed me. The man who had the right to call her wife. The man who lay beside her at night, who touched her. The man who knew the texture of her skin, the taste of her mouth. The man who knew how it felt to have her move beneath him in the dark.

I was already in love with her. Perhaps I had been from the moment I had seen her walking with the child through the wild roses.

It would have been best for my sanity if I had chosen another place to paint. I could not. Already knowing I would have no more of her, could have no more than a few hours of conversation, I went back. Again and again.

She agreed to let me paint her. I began to see, as an artist must see, the inner woman. Beyond her beauty, beyond her composure and breeding was a desperately unhappy woman. I wanted to take her in my arms, to demand that she tell me what had put that sad and haunted look in her eyes. But I only painted her. I had no right to do more.

I have never been a patient or a noble man. Yet with her, I found I could be both. Without ever touching me, she changed me. Nothing would be the same for me after that summer—that all too brief summer when she would come, to sit on the rocks and look out to sea.

Even now, a lifetime later, I can walk to those cliffs and see her. I can smell the sea that never changes, and catch the drift of her perfume. I have only to pick a wild rose to remember the fiery lights of her hair. Closing my eyes, I hear the murmur of the water on the rocks below and her voice comes back as clear and as sweet as yesterday.

I am reminded of the last afternoon that first summer, when she stood beside me, close enough to touch, as distant as the moon.

"We leave in the morning," she said, but didn't look at me. "The children are sorry to go."

"And you?"

A faint smile touched her lips but not her eyes. "Sometimes I wonder if I've lived before. If my home was an island like this. The first time I came here, it was as if I had been waiting to see it again. I'll miss the sea."

Perhaps it was only my own needs that made me think, when she glanced at me, that she would miss me, as well. Then she looked away again and sighed.

"New York is so different, so full of noise and urgency. It's hard to believe such a place exists when I stand here. Will you stay on the island through the winter?"

I thought of the cold and desolate months ahead and cursed fate for taunting me with what I could never have. "My plans change with my mood." *I said it lightly, fighting to keep the bitterness out of my voice.*

"I envy you your freedom." *She turned away then to walk back to where her nearly completed portrait rested on my easel.* "And your talent. You've made me more than what I am."

"Less." *I had to curl my hands into fists to keep from touching her.* "Some things can never be captured with paint and canvas."

"What will you call it?"

"Bianca. Your name is enough."

She must have sensed my feelings, though I tried desperately to hold them in myself. Something came into her eyes as she looked at me, and the look held longer than it should. Then she stepped back, cautiously, like a woman who had wandered too close to the edge of a cliff.

"One day you'll be famous, and people will beg for your work."

I couldn't take my eyes off her, knowing I might never see her again. "I don't paint for fame."

"No, and that's why you'll have it. When you do, I'll remember this summer. Goodbye, Christian."

She walked away from me—for what I thought was the last time—away from the rocks, through the wild grass and the flowers that fight through both for the sun.

Chapter Four

Coco Calhoun McPike didn't believe in leaving things up to chance—particularly when her horoscope that day had advised her to take a more active part in a family matter and to visit an old acquaintance. She felt she could do both by paying an informal call on Holt Bradford.

She remembered him as a dark, hot-eyed boy who had delivered lobster and loitered around the village, waiting for trouble to happen. She also remembered that he had once stopped to change a flat for her while she'd been struggling on the side of the road trying to figure out which end of the jack to put under the bumper. He'd refused—stiffly, she recalled—her offer of payment and had hopped back on his motorcycle and ridden off before she'd properly thanked him.

Proud, defiant, rebellious, she mused as she maneuvered her car into his driveway. Yet, in a grudging sort of way, chivalrous. Perhaps if she was clever—and Coco thought that she was—she could play on all of those traits to get what she wanted.

So this had been Christian Bradford's cottage, she mused. She'd seen it before, of course, but not since she'd known of the connection between the families. She paused for a moment. With her eyes closed she tried to *feel* something. Surely there was some remnant of energy here, something that time and wind hadn't washed away.

Coco liked to consider herself a mystic. Whether it was a true evaluation, or her imagination was ripe, she was certain she did feel some snap of passion in the air. Pleased with it, and herself, she trooped to the house.

She'd dressed very carefully. She wanted to look attractive, of course. Her vanity wouldn't permit otherwise. But she'd also wanted to look distinguished and just the tiniest bit matronly. She felt the old and classic Chanel suit in powder blue worked very well.

She knocked, putting what she hoped was a wise and comforting smile on her face. The wild barking and the steady stream of curses from within had her placing a hand on her breast.

Five minutes out of the shower, his hair dripping and his temper curdled, Holt yanked open the door. Sadie bounded out. Coco squeaked. Good reflexes had Holt snatching the amorous dog by the collar before she could send Coco over the porch railing.

"Oh my." Coco looked from dog to man, juggling the plate of double-fudge brownies. "Oh, goodness. What a very *large* dog. She certainly does look like our Fred, and I'd so hoped he'd stop growing soon. Why you could practically *ride* her if you liked, couldn't you?" She beamed a smile at Holt. "I'm so sorry, have I interrupted you?"

He continued to struggle with the dog, who'd gotten a good whiff of the brownies and wanted her share. Now. "Excuse me?"

"I've interrupted," Coco repeated. "I know it's early, but on days like this I just can't stay in bed. All this sun and twittering birds. Not to mention the sawing and hammering. Do you suppose she'd like one of these?" Without waiting for an answer, Coco took one of the brownies off the plate. "Now you sit and behave."

With what was certainly a grin, Sadie stopped straining, sat and eyed Coco adoringly.

"Good dog." Sadie took the treat politely then padded back into the house to enjoy it. "Well, now." Pleased with the situation, Coco smiled at Holt. "You probably don't remember me. Goodness, it's been years."

"Mrs. McPike." He remembered her, all right, though the last time he'd seen her, her hair had been a dusky blond. It had been ten years, he thought, but she looked younger. She'd either had a first-class face-lift or had discovered the fountain of youth.

"Why, yes. It's so flattering to be remembered by an attractive man. But you were hardly more than a boy the last time. Welcome home." She offered the plate of brownies.

And left him no choice but to accept it and ask her in.

"Thanks." He studied the plate as she breezed inside. Between plants and brownies, the Calhouns were making a habit of bearing gifts. "Is there something I can do for you?"

"To tell you the truth, I've just been dying to see the place. To think this is where Christian Bradford lived, and worked." She sighed. "And dreamed of Bianca."

"Well, he lived and worked here anyway."

"Suzanna tells me you're not quite convinced they loved each other. I can appreciate your reluctance to fall right in with the story, but you see, it's a part of my family history. And yours. Oh, what a glorious painting!"

She crossed the room to a misty seascape hung above the stone fireplace. Even through the haze of fog, the colors were ripe and vivid, as though the vitality and passion were fighting to free themselves from the thin graying curtain. Turbulent whitecaps, the black and toothy edge of rock, the gloom-crowned shadows of islands marooned in a cold, dark sea.

"It's powerful," she murmured. "And, oh, lonely. It's his, isn't it?"

"Yes."

She let out a shaky sigh. "If you'd like to see that view, you've only to walk on the cliffs beneath The Towers. Suzanna walks there, sometimes with the children, sometimes alone. Too often alone." Shaking off the mood, Coco turned back. "My niece seems to feel that you're not particularly interested in confirming Christian and Bianca's relationship, and helping to find the emeralds. I find that difficult to believe."

Holt set the plate aside. "It shouldn't be, Mrs. McPike. But what I told your niece was that if and when I was convinced there had been a connection of any importance, I'd do what I could to help. Which, as I see it, is next to nothing."

"You were a police officer, weren't you?"

Holt hooked his thumbs in his pockets, not trusting the change of subject. "Yeah."

"I have to admit I was surprised when I heard you'd chosen that profession, but I'm sure you were well suited to the job."

The scar on his back seemed to twinge. "I used to be."

"And you'd have solved cases, I suppose."

His lips curved a little. "A few."

"So you'd have looked for clues and followed them up until you found the right answer." She smiled at him. "I always admire the police on television who solve the mystery and tidy everything up before the end of the show."

"Life's not tidy."

On certain men, she thought, a sneer was not at all unattractive. "No, indeed not, but we could certainly use someone on our side who has your experience." She walked back toward him, and she was no longer smiling. "I'll be frank. If I had known what trouble it would cause my family, I might have let the legend of the emeralds die with me. When my brother and his wife were killed, and left their girls in my care, I was also left the responsibility of passing along the story of the Calhoun emeralds—when the time was right. By doing what I consider my duty, I've put my family in danger. I'll do anything in my power, and use anyone I can, to keep them from being hurt. Until those emeralds are found, I can't be sure my family is safe."

"You need the police," he began.

"They're doing what they can. It isn't enough." Reaching out, she put a hand on his. "They aren't personally involved, and can't possibly understand. You can."

Her faith and her obstinate logic made him uneasy. "You're overestimating me."

"I don't think so." Coco held his hand another moment, then gave it a brief squeeze before releasing it. "But I don't mean to nag. I only came so I could add my input to Suzanna's. She has such a difficult time pushing for what she wants."

"She does well enough."

"Well, I'm glad to hear it. But with her work and Mandy's wedding, and everything else that's been going on, I know she hasn't had time to speak with you again for the last couple of days. I tell you, our lives have been turned upside down for the last few months. First C.C.'s wedding, and the renovations, now Amanda and Sloan—and Lilah already setting a date to marry Max." She paused and hoped to look wistful. "If I could only find some nice man for Suzanna, I'd have all my girls settled."

Holt didn't miss the speculative look. "I'm sure she'll take care of that herself when she's ready."

"Not when she doesn't give herself a moment to look. And after what that excuse for a man did to her." She cut herself off there. If she started on Baxter Dumont, it would be difficult to stop. And it would hardly be proper conversation. "Well, in any case, she keeps herself too busy with her business and her children, so I like to keep my eye out for her. You're not married, are you?"

At least no one could accuse her of being subtle, Holt thought, amused. "Yeah. I've got a wife and six kids in Portland."

Coco blinked, then laughed. "It was a rude question," she admitted. "And before I ask another, I'll leave you alone." She started for the door, pleased that he had enough manners to accompany her and open it for her. "Oh, by the way, Amanda's wedding is Saturday, at six. We're holding the reception at the ballroom in The Towers. I'd like for you to come."

The unexpected curve had him hesitating. "I really don't think it's appropriate."

"It's more than appropriate," she corrected. "Our families go back quite a long way, Holt. We'd very much like to have you there." She started toward her car then turned, smiling again. "And Suzanna doesn't have an escort. It seems a pity."

The thief called himself by many names. When he had first come to Bar Harbor in search of the emeralds, he had used the name Livingston and had posed as a successful British businessman. He had only been partially successful and had returned under the guise of Ellis Caufield, a wealthy eccentric. Due to bad luck and his partner's fumbling, he'd had to abandon that particular cover.

His partner was dead, which was only a small inconvenience. The thief now went under the name of Robert Marshall and was developing a certain fondness for this alter ego.

Marshall was lean and tanned and had a hint of a Boston accent. He wore his dark hair nearly shoulder length and sported a drooping mustache. His eyes were brown, thanks to contact lenses. His teeth were slightly bucked. The oral device had cost him a pretty penny, but it had also changed the shape of his jaw.

He was very comfortable with Marshall, and delighted to have signed on as a laborer on The Towers renovation. His references had been forged and had added to his overhead. But the emeralds would be worth it. He intended to have them, whatever the price.

Over the past months they had gone from being a job to an obsession. He didn't just want them. He needed them. He found the risk of working so close to the Calhouns only added spice to the game. He had, in fact, passed within three feet of Amanda when she had come into the west wing to talk to Sloan O'Riley. Neither of them, who had known him only as Livingston, had given him a second glance.

He did his job well, hauling equipment, cleaning up debris. And he worked without complaint. He was friendly with his co-workers, even joining them occasionally for a beer after work.

Then he would go back to his rented house across the bay and plan.

The security at The Towers posed no problem—not when it would be so easy for him to disengage it from the inside. By working for the Calhouns, he could stay close, he could be certain he would hear about any new developments in their search for the necklace. And with care and skill, he could do some searching on his own.

The papers he had stolen from them had offered no real clue as yet. Unless it came from the letter he'd discovered. One that had been written to Bianca and signed only "Christian." A love letter, Marshall mused as he stacked lumber. It was something he had to look into.

"Hey, Bob. Got a minute?"

Marshall looked up and gave his foreman an affable smile. "Sure, nothing but minutes."

"Well, they need some tables moved into the ballroom for that wedding tomorrow. You and Rick give the ladies a hand."

"Right."

Marshall strolled along, fighting back a trembling excitement at being free to walk through the house. He took his instructions from a flustered Coco, then hefted his end of the heavy hunt table to move it up to the next floor.

"Do you think he'll come?" C.C. asked Suzanna as they finished washing down the glass on the mirrored walls.

"I doubt it."

C.C. brushed back her short cap of black hair as she stood aside to search for streaks. "I don't see why he wouldn't. And maybe if we all gang up on him, he'll break down and join ranks."

"I don't think he's a joiner." Suzanna glanced around and saw the two men struggling in with the table. "Oh, it goes against that wall. Thanks."

"No problem," Rick managed through gritted teeth. Marshall merely smiled and said nothing.

"Maybe if he sees the picture of Bianca and hears the tape from the interview Max and Lilah had with the maid who used to work here back then, he'll pitch in. He's Christian's only surviving family."

"Hey!" Rick muffled a curse when Marshall bobbled the table.

"I don't think he's big on family feeling," Suzanna put in. "One thing that hasn't changed about Holt Bradford is that he's still a loner."

Holt Bradford. Marshall committed the name to memory before he called across the room. "Is there anything else we can do for you ladies?"

Suzanna glanced over her shoulder with an absent smile. "No, not right now. Thanks a lot."

Marshall grinned. "Don't mention it."

"Some lookers, huh?" Rick muttered as they walked back out.

"Oh, yeah." But Marshall was thinking of the emeralds.

"I tell you, bud, I'd like to—" Rick broke off when two other women and a young boy came to the top of the stairs. He gave them both a big, toothy smile. Lilah gave him a lazy one in return and kept walking.

"Man, oh, man," Rick said with a hand to his heart. "This place is just full of babes."

"Pardon the leers," Lilah said mildly. "Most of them don't bite."

The slim strawberry blonde gave a weak smile. At the moment a couple of leering carpenters were the least of her worries. "I really don't want to get in the way," she began in a soft Southwestern drawl. "I know what Sloan said, but I really think it would be best if Kevin and I checked into a hotel for the night."

"This late in the season, you couldn't check into a tent. And we want you here. All of us. Sloan's family is our family now." Lilah smiled down at the dark-haired boy who was gawking at everything in sight. "It's a wild place, isn't it? Your uncle's making sure it doesn't come crashing down on our heads." She walked into the ballroom.

Suzanna was standing on a ladder, polishing glass, while C.C. sat on the floor, hitting the low spots. Lilah bent to the boy. "I was supposed to be in on this," she whispered. "But I played hooky."

The idea made him laugh, and the laughter, so much like Alex's, had Suzanna glancing over.

She was expecting them. Their arrival had been anticipated for weeks. But seeing them here, knowing who they were, had her nerves jolting.

The woman wasn't just Sloan's sister, nor was the boy just his nephew. A short time before, Suzanna had learned that Megan O'Riley had been her husband's lover, and the boy his child. The woman who was staring at her now, the boy's hand gripped in hers, had been only seventeen when Baxter had charmed her into bed and seduced her with vows of love and promises of marriage. And all the while, he had been planning to marry Suzanna.

Which one of us, Suzanna wondered, had been the other woman?

It didn't matter now, she thought, and she climbed down. Not when she could see the nerves so clearly in Megan O'Riley's eyes, the tension in the set of her body, and the courage in the angle of her chin.

Lilah made introductions so smoothly that an outsider might have thought there was nothing but pleasantries in the ballroom. As Suzanna offered a hand, all Megan could think was that she had overdressed. She felt stiff and foolish in the trim bronze-colored suit, while Suzanna seemed so relaxed and lovely in faded jeans.

This was the woman she had hated for years, for taking away the man she'd loved and stealing the father of her child. Even after Sloan had explained Suzanna's innocence, even knowing the hate had been wasted, Megan couldn't relax.

"I'm so glad to meet you." Suzanna put both hands over Megan's stiff one.

"Thank you." Feeling awkward, Megan drew her hand away. "We're looking forward to the wedding."

"So are we all." After a bracing breath, Suzanna let herself look down at Kevin, the half brother to her children. Her heart melted a little. He was taller than her son, and a full year older. But they had both inherited their father's dark good looks. Unconsciously Suzanna reached out to brush back the lock of hair that fell, the twin of Alex's, over Kevin's brow.

Megan's arm came around his shoulders in an instinctive move of defense. Suzanna let her hand drop to her side.

"It's nice to meet you, Kevin. Alex and Jenny could hardly sleep last night knowing you'd be here today."

Kevin gave her a fleeting smile, then glanced up at his mother. She'd told him he was going to meet his half brother and sister, and he wasn't too sure he was happy about it. He didn't think his mother was, either.

"Why don't we go down and find them?" C.C. put a hand on Suzanna's shoulder, gently rubbing. Megan noted that Lilah had already flanked her sister's other side. She didn't blame them for sticking together against an outsider, and her chin came up to prove it.

"It might be best if we—"

She never got to finish. Alex and Jenny came clattering down the hall to burst into the room, breathless and flushed. "Is he here?" Alex demanded. "Aunt Coco said he was, and we want to see—" He cut himself off, skidding to a halt on the freshly polished floor.

The two boys eyed each other, interested and cautious, like two terriers. Alex wasn't sure he was pleased that his new brother was bigger than he was, but he'd already decided it would be neat to have something besides a sister.

"I'm Alex and this is Jenny," Alex said, taking over introductions. "She's only five."

"Five and a half," Jenny put in, and marched up to Kevin. "And I can beat you up if I have to."

"Jenny, I don't think that'll be necessary." Suzanna spoke mildly, but the lifted brows said it all.

"Well, I could," Jenny muttered, still sizing him up. "But Mom says we have to be nice 'cause we're family."

"Do you know any Indians?" Alex demanded.

"Yeah." Kevin was no longer gripping his mother's hand for dear life. "Lots of them."

"Want to see our fort?" Alex asked.

"Yeah." He sent a pleading glance at his mother. "Can I?"

"Well, I—"

"Lilah and I'll take them out." C.C. gave Suzanna's shoulder a final squeeze.

"They'll be fine," Suzanna assured Megan as her sisters hustled the children along. "Sloan designed the fort, so it's sturdy." She picked up her rag again to run it through her hands. "Does Kevin know?"

"Yes." Megan turned her purse over and over in restless hands. "I didn't want him to meet your children without understanding." She took a deep breath and prepared to launch into the speech she'd prepared. "Mrs. Dumont—"

"Suzanna. This is hard for you."

"I don't imagine it's easy, or comfortable for either of us. I wouldn't have come," she continued, "if it hadn't been so important to Sloan. I love my brother, and I won't do anything to spoil his wedding, but you must see that this is an impossible situation."

"I can see it's a painful one for you. I'm sorry." Her hands lifted then fell. "I wish I had known sooner, about you, about Kevin. It's unlikely that I could have made any difference as far as Bax is concerned, but I wish I had known." She glanced down at the rag she was gripping too tightly, then put it aside. "Megan, I realize that while you were giving birth to Kevin, alone, I was in Europe, honeymooning with Kevin's father. You're entitled to hate me for that."

Megan could only stare and shake her head. "You're nothing like I expected. You were supposed to be cool and remote and resentful."

"It would be hard to resent a seventeen-year-old girl who was betrayed and left alone to raise a child. I wasn't much older than that when I married Bax. I understand how charming he could be, how persuasive. And how cruel."

"I thought we'd live happily ever after," Megan said with a sigh. "Well, I grew up quickly, and I learned fast." She let out another long breath as she studied Suzanna. "I hated you, for having everything I thought I wanted. Even when I'd stopped loving him, it helped get me through to hate you. And I was terrified of meeting you."

"That's something else we have in common."

"I can't believe I'm here, talking to you like this." To relieve her nerves she wandered around the ballroom. "I imagined it so many times all those years ago. I'd face you down, demand my rights." She gave a soft laugh. "Even today, I had a whole speech planned out. It was very sophisticated, very mature—maybe just a little vicious. I didn't want to believe that you hadn't known about Kevin, that you'd been a victim, too. Because it was so much easier to think of myself as the only one who'd been betrayed. Then your children came in." She closed her eyes. "How do you deal with the hurt, Suzanna?"

"I'll let you know when I figure it out."

Smiling a little, Megan glanced out of the window. "It hasn't affected them. Look."

Suzanna walked over. Down in the yard she could see her children, and Megan's son, climbing into the plywood fort.

Holt gave it a lot of thought. Up until the moment when he dragged the suit out of his closet, he'd been certain he wasn't going. What the devil was he supposed to do at a society wedding? He didn't like socializing or making small talk or picking at those tiny little canapés. You never knew what the hell was in them anyway.

He didn't like strangling himself with a tie or having to iron a shirt.

So why was he doing it?

He loosened the hated knot of the tie and frowned at himself in the dusty mirror over the bureau. Because he was an idiot and couldn't resist an invitation to the castle on the cliffs. Because he was twice an idiot and wanted to see Suzanna again.

It had been over a week since they had planted the yellow bush. A week since he'd kissed her. And a week since he'd admitted that one kiss, however turbulent, wasn't going to be enough.

He wanted to get a handle on her and thought the best way was to observe her in the midst of the family she seemed to love so much. He wasn't quite sure if she was the cool and remote princess of his youth, the hot-blooded woman he'd held in his arms or the vulnerable one whose eyes were haunting his dreams.

Holt was a man who liked to know exactly what he was up against, whether it was a suspect, a dinky motor or a woman. Once he had Suzanna pegged, he'd move at his own pace.

He didn't want to admit that she'd gotten to him with her fervent belief in the connection between his grandfather and her ancestor. More, he hated to admit that the visit by Coco McPike had made him feel guilty and responsible.

He wasn't going to the wedding to help anyone, he reminded himself. He wasn't making any commitments. He was going to please himself. This time he didn't have to stop at the kitchen door.

It wasn't a long drive, but he took his time, drawing it out. His first glimpse of The Towers bounced him back a dozen years. It was, as it had always been, a fanciful place, a maze of contrasts. It was built of somber stone, yet it was flanked with romantic towers. From one angle, it seemed formidable, from another graceful. At the moment, there was scaffolding on the west side, but instead of looking unsightly, it simply looked productive.

The sloped lawn was emerald green and guarded by gnarled and dignified trees, dashed with fragile and fragrant flowers. There was already a crowd of cars, and Holt felt foolish handing over the keys to his rusted Chevy to the uniformed valet.

The wedding was to take place on the terrace. Since it was about to begin, Holt kept well to the back of the crowd of people. There was organ music, very stately. He had to force himself not to drag at his tie and light a cigarette. There were a few murmured comments and sighs as the bridesmaids started down a long white runner spread over the lawn.

He barely recognized C.C. as the stunning goddess in the long rose-colored dress. Yeah, the Calhoun girls had always been lookers, he thought, and skimmed his gaze over the woman who walked behind her. Her dress was the color of sea foam, but he hardly noticed. It was the face—the face in the portrait in his grandfather's loft. Holt let out the breath between his teeth. Lilah Calhoun was a dead ringer for her great-grandmother. And Holt wasn't going to be able to deny the connection any longer.

He stuffed his hands into his pockets, wishing he hadn't come after all. Then he saw Suzanna.

This was the princess of his youthful imagination. Her pale gold hair fell in soft curls to her shoulders under a fingertip veil of misty blue. The dress of the same color flowed around her, skirts billowing in the breeze as she walked. She carried flowers in her hands; more were scattered in her hair. When she passed him, her eyes as soft and dreamy as the dress, he felt a longing so deep, so intense, he could barely keep from speaking her name.

He remembered nothing about the brief and lovely ceremony except how her face had looked when the first tear slipped down her cheek.

As it had been so many years ago, the ballroom was filled with light and music and flowers. As for the food, Coco had outdone herself. The guests were treated to lobster croquettes, steamship round, salmon mousse and champagne by the bucket. Dozens of chairs had been set up in corners and along the mirrored walls, and the terrace doors had been thrown open to allow the guests to spill outside.

Holt held himself apart, sipping the cold, frothy wine and using the time to observe. As his first visit to The Towers, it was quite a show, he decided. Mirrors tossed back the reflection of women in pastel dresses as they stood or sat or were lured out to dance. Music and the scent of gardenias filled the air.

The bride was stunning, tall and regal in white lace, her face luminous as she danced with the big, bronzed man who was now her husband. They looked good together, Holt thought idly. The way people were meant to, he supposed, when they were in love. He saw Coco dancing with a tall, fair man who looked as if he'd been born in a tuxedo.

Then he looked back, as he already had several times, at Suzanna. She was leaning over now, saying something to a dark-haired little boy. Her son? Holt wondered. It was obvious the kid was on the verge of some kind of rebellion. He was shuffling his feet and tugging at the bow tie. He had

Holt's sympathy. There couldn't be anything much worse for a kid on a summer evening then being stuck in a mini tuxedo and having to hang around with adults. Suzanna whispered something in his ear, then tugged on it. The boy's mutinous expression turned into a grin.

"Still brooding in corners, I see."

Holt turned and was once again struck by Lilah Calhoun's resemblance to the woman his grandfather had painted. "Just watching the show."

"It is worth the price of a ticket. Max." Lilah laid a hand on the arm of the tall, lanky man at her side. "This is Holt Bradford, whom I was madly in love with for about twenty-four hours some fifteen years ago."

Holt's brow lifted. "You never told me."

"Of course not. At the end of the day I decided I didn't want to be in love with the surly, dangerous sort after all. This is Max Quartermain, the man I'm going to love for the rest of my life."

"Congratulations." Holt took Max's offered hand. Firm grip, Holt mused, steady eyes and a slightly embarrassed smile. "You're the teacher, right?"

"I was. And you're Christian Bradford's grandson."

"That's right," Holt agreed, and his voice had cooled.

"Don't worry, we're not going to hound you as long as you're a guest." Studying him, Lilah ran a fingertip around the rim of her glass. "We'll do that later. I'll have Max show you the scar he got while we were having our little publicity stunt."

"Lilah." Max's voice was soft with an underlying command.

Lilah merely shrugged and sipped champagne. "You remember C.C." She gestured as her sister joined them.

"I remember a gangly kid with engine grease on her face." He relaxed enough to smile. "You look good."

"Thanks. My husband, Trent. Holt Bradford."

It was Coco's dance partner, Holt noted as the two men summed each other up during the polite introductions.

"And the bride and groom," Lilah announced, toasting the couple before she drank again.

"Hello, Holt." Though she was still glowing, Amanda's eyes were steady and watchful. "I'm glad you could come." As she introduced Sloan, Holt realized he'd been surrounded quite neatly. They didn't press. No, the emeralds were never mentioned. But they'd joined ranks, he thought, in a solid wall of determination he had to admire, even as he resented it.

"What is this, a family meeting?" Suzanna hurried up. "You're supposed to be mingling, not huddling in a corner. Oh. Holt." Her smile wavered a bit. "I didn't know you were here."

"Your aunt invited me."

"Yes, I know, but—" She broke off and put her hostess's smile back in place. "I'm glad you could make it."

Like hell, he thought and lifted his glass. "It's been...interesting so far."

At some unspoken signal, her family drifted away, leaving them alone in the corner beside a tub of gardenias. "I hope they didn't make you uncomfortable."

"I can handle it."

"That may be, but I wouldn't want you badgered at my sister's wedding."

"But it doesn't bother you if it's someplace else."

Before she could retort, small impatient hands were tugging at her skirt. "Mom, when can we have the cake?"

"When Amanda and Sloan are ready to cut it." She skimmed a finger down Alex's nose.

"But we're hungry."

"Then go over to the buffet table and stuff your little face."

He giggled at that but didn't relent. "The cake—"

"Is for later. Alex, this is Mr. Bradford."

Not particularly interested in meeting another adult who would pat his head and tell him what a big boy he was, Alex pouted up at Holt. When he was offered a very manly handshake, he perked up a bit.

"Are you the policeman?"

"I used to be."

"Did you ever get shot in the head?"

Holt muffled a chuckle. "No, sorry." For some reason he felt as though he'd lost face. "I did catch one in the leg once."

"Yeah?" Alex brightened. "Did it bleed and bleed?"

He had to grin. "Buckets."

"Wow. Did you shoot lots of bad guys?"

"Dozens of them."

"Okay! Wait a minute." He raced off.

"I'm sorry," Suzanna began. "He's going through a murder-and-mayhem stage."

"I'm sorry I didn't get shot in the head."

She laughed. "Oh, that's all right, you made up for it by telling him you shot lots of bad guys." She wondered, but didn't ask, if he'd been telling the truth.

"Suzanna, would—"

"Hey." Alex skidded to a halt, with two other children in tow. "I told them how you got shot in the leg."

"Did it hurt?" Jenny wanted to know.

"Some."

"It bled and bled," Alex said with relish. "This is Jenny, she's my sister. And this is my brother, Kevin."

Suzanna wanted to kiss him. She wanted to pull Alex up in her arms and smother him with kisses for accepting so easily what adults had made so complicated. Instead, she brushed a hand over his hair.

The three of them bombarded Holt with questions until Suzanna called a halt. "I think that's enough gore for now."

"But, Mom—"

"But, Alex," she mimicked. "Why don't you go get some punch?"

Since it seemed like a pretty good idea, they trooped off.

"Quite a brood," Holt murmured, then looked back at Suzanna. "I thought you had two kids."

"I do."

"Seems to me I just saw three."

"Kevin is my ex-husband's son," she said coolly. "Now, if you'll excuse me."

He put a hand on her arm. Another secret, he thought, and decided he would dig up that answer, as well. Not now. Now he was going to do something he'd thought about doing since he'd seen her walk down the white satin runner in the floaty blue dress.

"Would you like to dance?"

Chapter Five

She couldn't quite relax in his arms. She told herself it was foolish, that the dance was just a casual social gesture. But his body was so close, so firm, the hand at her back so possessive. It reminded her too clearly of the moment he had pulled her against him to send her soaring into a kiss.

"It's quite a house," he said, and gave himself the pleasure of feeling her hair against his cheek. "I always wondered what it was like inside."

"I'll have to give you a tour sometime."

He could feel her heart thud against his. Experimenting, he skimmed his hand up her spine. The rhythm quickened. "I'm surprised you haven't been back to nag me."

There was annoyance in her eyes as she drew her head back. "I have no intention of nagging you."

"Good." He brushed his thumb over her knuckles and felt her tremble. "But you will come back."

"Only because I promised Aunt Coco."

"No." He increased the pressure on her spine and brought her an inch closer. "Not only because of that. You wonder what it would be like, the same way I've wondered half my life."

A little line of panic followed his fingers up her spine. "This isn't the place."

"I choose my own ground." His lips hovered bare inches from hers. He watched her eyes darken and cloud. "I want you, Suzanna."

Her heart had leaped up to throb in her throat so that her voice was husky and uneven. "Am I supposed to be flattered?"

"No. You'd be smart to be scared. I won't make things easy on you."

"What I am," she said with more control, "is uninterested."

His lips curved. "I could kiss you now and prove you wrong."

"I won't have a scene at my sister's wedding."

"Fine, then come to my place tomorrow morning."

"No."

"All right then." He lowered his head. She turned hers away so that his lips brushed her temple, then nibbled on her ear.

"Stop it. My children—"

"Should hardly be shocked to see a man kiss their mother." But he did stop, because his knees were going weak. "Tomorrow morning, Suzanna. There's something I need to show you. Something of my grandfather's."

She looked up again, struggling to steady her pulse. "If this is some sort of game, I don't want to play."

"No game. I want you, and this time I'll have you. But there is something of my grandfather's you have the right to see. Unless you're afraid to be alone with me."

Her spine stiffened. "I'll be there."

The next morning, Suzanna stood on the terrace with Megan. They watched their children race across the lawn with Fred.

"I wish you could stay longer."

With a half laugh, Megan shook her head. "I'm surprised to say I wish I could, too. I have to be back at work tomorrow."

"You and Kevin are welcome here anytime. I want you to know that."

"I do." Megan shifted her gaze to meet Suzanna's. There was a sadness there she understood, though she rarely allowed herself to feel it. "If you and the kids decide to visit Oklahoma, you've got a home with us. I don't want to lose touch. Kevin needs to know this part of his family."

"Then we won't." She stooped to pick up a rose petal that had drifted from a bouquet to float to the terrace. "It was a beautiful wedding. Sloan and Mandy are going to be happy—and we'll have nieces and nephews in common."

"God, the world's a strange place." Megan took Suzanna's hand. "I'd like to think we can be friends, not only for our children's sakes or for Sloan and Amanda."

Suzanna smiled. "I think we already are."

"Suzanna!" Coco signaled from the kitchen door. "A phone call for you." She was chewing her lip when Suzanna reached her. "It's Baxter."

"Oh." Suzanna felt the simple pleasure of the morning drain. "I'll take it in the other room."

She braced herself as she walked down the hallway. He couldn't hurt her any longer, she reminded herself. Not physically, not emotionally. She slipped into the library, took a long, steadying breath, then picked up the phone.

"Hello, Bax."

"I suppose you considered it sly to keep me waiting on the phone."

And there it was again, she thought, that clipped, critical tone that had once made her shiver. Now she only sighed. "I'm sorry. I was outside."

"Digging in the garden, I suppose. Are you still pretending to make a living pruning rosebushes?"

"I'm sure you didn't call to see how my business is going."

"Your business, as you call it, is nothing to me but a slight embarrassment. Having my ex-wife selling flowers on the street corner—"

"Clouds your image, I know." She passed a hand over her hair. "We're not going to go through that again, are we?"

"Quite the little shrew these days." She heard him murmur something to someone else, then laugh. "No, I didn't call to remind you you're making a fool of yourself. I want the children."

Her blood turned to ice. "What?"

The shaky whisper pleased him enormously. "I believe it states quite clearly in the custody agreement that I'm entitled to two weeks during the summer. I'll pick them up on Friday."

"You...but you haven't—"

"Don't stammer, Suzanna. It's one of your more annoying traits. If you didn't comprehend, I'll repeat. I'm exercising my parental rights. I'll pick the children up on Friday, at noon."

"You haven't seen them in nearly a year. You can't just pick them up and—"

"I most certainly can. If you don't choose to honor the agreement, I'll simply take you back to court. It isn't legal or wise for you to try to keep the children from me."

"I've never tried to keep them from you. You haven't bothered with them."

"I have no intention of rearranging my schedule to suit you. Yvette and I are going to Martha's Vineyard for two weeks, and have decided to take the children. It's time they saw something of the world besides the little corner you hide in."

Her hands were shaking. She gripped the receiver more tightly. "You didn't even send Alex a card on his birthday."

"I don't believe there's anything in the agreement about birthday cards," he said shortly. "But it is very specific on visitation rights. Feel free to check with your lawyer, Suzanna."

"And if they don't want to go?"

"The choice isn't theirs—or yours." But his, he thought, which was exactly as he preferred it. "I wouldn't try to poison them against me."

"I don't have to," she murmured.

"See that they're packed and ready. Oh, and Suzanna, I've been reading quite a bit about your family lately. Isn't it odd that there wasn't any mention of an emerald necklace in our settlement agreement?"

"I didn't know it existed."

"I wonder if the courts would believe that."

She felt tears of frustration and rage fill her eyes. "For God's sake, didn't you take enough?"

"It's never enough, Suzanna, when you consider how very much you disappointed me. Friday," he said. "Noon." And hung up.

She was trembling. Even when she lowered carefully into a chair, she couldn't stop. She felt as though she'd been jerked back five years, into that terrible helplessness. She couldn't stop him. She'd read the custody agreement word for word before signing it, and he was within his rights. Oh, technically she could have demanded more notice, but that would only postpone the inevitable. If Bax had made up his mind, she couldn't change it. The more she fought, the more she argued, the harder he would twist the knife.

And the more difficult he would make it on the children.

Her babies. Rocking, she covered her face with her hands. It was only for a short time—she could survive it. But how would they feel when she shipped them off, giving them no choice?

She would have to make it sound like an adventure. With the right tone, the right words, she could convince them this was something they wanted to do. Pressing her lips together, she rose. But not now. She would never be able to convince them of anything but her own turmoil if she spoke with them now.

"Damn place is like Grand Central Station." The familiar thump of a cane nearly had Suzanna sinking back into the chair again. "People coming and going, phone ringing. You'd think nobody ever got married before." Suzanna's Great-Aunt Colleen, her magnificent white hair swept back and diamonds glittering at her ears, stopped in the doorway. "I'll have you know those little monsters of yours tracked dirt up the stairs."

"I'm sorry."

Colleen only huffed. She enjoyed complaining about the children, because she had grown so fond of them. "Hooligans. The one blessed day of the week there's not hammering and sawing every minute, and there's packs of children shrieking through the house. Why the hell aren't they in school?"

"Because it's July, Aunt Colleen."

"Don't see what difference that makes." Her frown deepened as she studied Suzanna. "What's the matter with you, girl?"

"Nothing. I'm just a little tired."

"Tired my foot." She recognized the look. She'd seen it before—the weary desperation and helplessness—in her own mother's eyes. "Who was that on the phone?"

Suzanna's chin came up. "That, Aunt Colleen, is none of your business."

"Well, you've climbed on your high horse." And it pleased her. She preferred that her grandniece bite back rather than take a slap. Besides, she'd just badger Coco until she learned what was going on.

"I have an appointment," Suzanna said as steadily as possible. "Would you mind telling Aunt Coco that I've gone out?"

"So now I'm a messenger boy. I'll tell her, I'll tell her," Colleen muttered, waving her cane. "It's high time she fixed me some tea."

"Thank you. I won't be long."

"Go out and clear your head," Colleen said as Suzanna started by. "There's nothing a Calhoun can't handle."

Suzanna sighed and kissed Colleen's thin cheek. "I hope you're right."

She didn't allow herself to think. She left the house and climbed into her pickup, telling herself she would handle whatever needed to be handled— but she would calm herself first.

She had become very skilled at pulling in her emotions. A woman couldn't sit in a courtroom with her children's futures hanging in the balance and not learn control.

It was possible to feel panic or rage or misery and function normally. When she was certain she could, she would speak with the children.

There was an appointment to be kept. Whatever Holt had to show her might distract her enough to help her keep control of her emotions until they leveled.

She thought she was calm when she pulled up at his house. As she got out of the truck, she combed a hand through her windblown hair. When she realized she was gripping her keys too hard she deliberately relaxed her fingers. She slid the keys into her pocket and knocked.

The dog sent up a din. Holt had one hand on Sadie's collar as he opened the door. "You made it. I thought I might have to come after you."

"I told you I'd be here." She stepped inside. "What do you have to show me?"

When he was sure Sadie would do no more than sniff and whine for attention, he released her. "Your aunt showed a lot more interest in the cottage."

"I'm a little pressed for time." After giving the dog an absent pat, she stuck her hands into the pockets of her baggy cotton slacks. "It's very nice." She glanced around, took in nothing. "You must be comfortable here."

"I get by," he said slowly, his eyes keen on her face. There wasn't a trace of color in her cheeks. Her eyes were too dark. He'd wanted to make her aware of him, maybe uncomfortably aware, but he hadn't wanted to make her sick with fear at the thought of seeing him again.

"You can relax, Suzanna." His voice was curt and dismissive. "I'm not going to jump you."

Her nerves stretched taut on the thin wire of control. "Can we just get on with this?"

"Yeah, we can get on with it, as soon as you stop standing there as if you're about to be chained and beaten. I haven't done anything—yet—to make you look at me that way."

"I'm not looking at you in any way."

"The hell you're not. Damn it, your hands are shaking." Furious, he grabbed them. "Stop it," he demanded. "I'm not going to hurt you."

"It has nothing to do with you." She yanked her hands away, hating the fact that she couldn't stop them from trembling. "Why should you think that anything I feel, any way I look depends on you? I have my own life, my own feelings. I'm not some weak, terrified woman who falls apart because a man raises his voice. Do you really think I'm afraid of you? Do you really think you could hurt me after—"

She broke off, appalled. She'd been shouting, and the furious tears were still burning her eyes. Her stomach was clenched so tight she could hardly breathe. Sadie had retreated to a corner and sat quivering. Holt stood a foot away, staring at her, eyes narrowed in speculation.

"I have to go," she managed, and bolted for the door. His hand slapped the wood and held it shut. "Let me go." When her voice broke, she bit down on her lip. She struggled with the door then whirled on him, eyes blazing. "I said let me go."

"Go ahead," he said with surprising calm, "take a punch at me. But you're not going anywhere while you're churned up like this."

"If I'm churned up, it's my own business. I told you, this has nothing to do with you."

"Okay, so you're not going to hit me. Let's try another release valve." He put his hands firmly on either side of her face and covered her mouth with his.

It wasn't a kiss meant to soothe or comfort. It did neither. This was raw and turbulent emotion and matched her own feelings completely.

Her arms were caught between them, her hands still fisted. Her body trembled; her skin heated. At the first flicker of response, he dived into the rough, desperate kiss until he was certain the only thing she was thinking about was him.

Then he took a moment longer, to please himself. She was a volcano waiting to erupt, a storm ready to blow. Her pent-up passion packed a punch more stunning than her fist could have. He intended to be around for the explosion, but he could wait.

When he released her, she leaned back against the door, her eyes closed, breath hitching. Watching her, he realized he'd never seen anyone fight so hard for control.

"Sit down." She shook her head. "All right, stand." With a dismissive shrug, he moved away to light a cigarette. "Either way you're going to tell me what set you off."

"I don't want to talk to you."

He sat on the arm of a chair and blew out a stream of smoke. "Lots of people haven't wanted to talk to me. But I usually find out what I want to know."

She opened her eyes. They were dry now, which relieved him considerably. "Is this an interrogation?"

With another shrug, he brought the cigarette to his lips again. It wouldn't do her any good if he caved in and offered soft words. He wasn't even sure he had them. "It can be."

She thought about pulling the door open and leaving. But he would only stop her. She'd learned the hard way that there were some battles a woman couldn't win.

"It isn't worth it," she said wearily. "I shouldn't have come while I was upset, but I thought I got myself under control."

"Upset about what?"

"It isn't important."

"Then it shouldn't be a problem to tell me."

"Bax called. My ex-husband." To comfort herself she began to roam the room.

Holt studied the tip of his cigarette, reminding himself that jealousy was out of place. "Looks like he can still stir you up."

"One phone call. One, and I'm back under his thumb." There was a bitterness in her voice he hadn't expected from her. He said nothing. "There's nothing I can do. Nothing. He's going to take the children for two weeks. I can't stop him."

Holt let out an impatient breath. "For God's sake, is that what all this hysteria's about? So the kids go off with Daddy for a couple of weeks." Disgusted, he crushed out his cigarette. And to think he'd been worried about her. "Save the vindictive-wife routine, babe. He's got a right."

"Oh yes, he's got the right." Her voice shook with an emotion so deep that Holt's head snapped up again. "Because it says so on a piece of paper. And he was there when they were conceived, so that makes him their father. Of course, that doesn't mean he has to love them, or worry about them or struggle to raise them without malice. It doesn't mean he has to remember Christmas or birthdays. It's just as Bax told me on the phone. There's nothing in the custody agreement that obligates him to send birthday cards. But it does obligate me to turn the children over to him when he has the whim."

There were tears threatening again, but she refused them. Tears in front of a man never brought anything but humiliation. "Do you think this is about me? He can't hurt me anymore. But my children don't deserve to be used so that he can try to pay me back for being so much less than he wanted."

Holt felt something hot and lethal spread in his gut. "He did a good job on you, didn't he?"

"That isn't the point. Alex and Jenny are the point. Somehow I have to convince them that the father who hasn't bothered to contact them in months, who could barely tolerate them when they lived under the same roof, is going to take them on a wonderful two-week vacation." Suddenly tired, she pushed her hands through her hair. "I didn't come here to talk about this."

"Yes, you did." Calmer, Holt lit another cigarette. If he didn't do something with his hands, he was going to touch her again, and he wasn't sure either of them could handle it. "I'm not family, so I'm safe. You can dump on me and figure I won't lose any sleep over it."

She smiled a little. "Maybe you're right. Sorry."

"I didn't ask for an apology. How do the kids feel about him?"

"He's a stranger."

"Then they probably don't have any preset expectations. Seems to me they might think of the whole thing as an adventure—and that you're letting him push your buttons. If he is using them to get to you, he hit bull's-eye."

"I'd already come to those same conclusions myself. I needed to vent some excess frustration." She tried a smile again. "Usually I just pull some weeds."

"I think kissing me worked better."

"It was different anyway."

He tapped out his cigarette and rose. The hell with what they could handle. "Is that the best description you can come up with?"

"Off the top of my head. Holt," she began when he slid his arms around her.

"Yeah?" He nipped at her chin, then her mouth.

"I don't want to be held." But she did, too much.

"That's too bad." His arms tightened, bringing her closer.

"You asked me to come here so you could..." She made a little sound of distress when he closed his teeth over her earlobe. "You could show me something of your grandfather's."

"That's right." Her skin smelled like the air high on the cliffs—laced with the sea and wildflowers and hot summer sunlight. "I also asked you here so I could get my hands on you again. We'll just take one thing at a time."

"I don't want to get involved." But even as she said it, her mouth was moving to meet his.

"Me, either." He changed the angle and sucked on her bottom lip.

"This is just—oh—chemistry." Her fingers tangled in his hair.

"You bet." His rough-palmed hands slipped under her shirt to explore.

"It can't go anywhere."

"It already is."

He was right about that, as well. For one brief moment she let herself fall into the kiss, into the heat. She needed something, someone. If she couldn't have comfort or compassion, she would take desire. But the more she took, the more her body strained for something just out of reach. Something she couldn't afford to want or need again.

"This is too fast," she said breathlessly, and struggled away. "I'm sorry, I realize it must seem as though I'm sending you mixed signals."

He was watching her eyes, just her eyes, as his body pulsed. "I think I can sort them out."

"I don't want to start something I won't be able to finish." She moistened her lips still warm from his. "And I have too many responsibilities, too much to worry about right now to even think about having..."

"An affair?" he finished. "You're going to have to think about it." With his eyes still on hers, he gathered her hair in his hand. "Go ahead, take a few days. I can afford to be patient as long as I get what I want. And I want you.''

Nerves skittered along her spine. ''Just because I find you attractive, physically, doesn't mean I'm going to jump into bed with you.''

''I don't much care whether you jump, crawl or have to be dragged. We can decide on the method later.'' Before she could think of a name to call him, he grinned, kissed her then stepped back. ''Now that that's settled, I'll take you up and show you the portrait.''

''If you think it's settled because you—what portrait?''

''You take a look, then tell me.''

He led the way up into the loft. Torn between curiosity and fury, Suzanna followed him. The only thing she was certain of at the moment was that since she'd met Holt Bradford again, her emotions had been on a roller coaster. All she wanted out of life was a nice smooth, uneventful ride.

''He worked up here.''

The simple statement captured her attention and her interest. ''Did you know him well?''

''I don't think anyone did.'' Holt moved over to open a tilt-out window. ''He came and went pretty much as he pleased. He'd come back here for a few days, or a few months. I'd sit up here sometimes and watch him work. If he got tired of me hanging around, he'd send me out with the dog, or into the village for ice cream.''

''There's still paint on the floor.'' Unable to resist, Suzanna bent down to touch. She glanced up, met Holt's eyes and understood.

He'd loved his grandfather. These splotches of paint, more than the cabin itself, were memories. She reached a hand out for his, rising when their fingers linked. Then she saw the portrait.

The canvas was tilted against the wall, its frame old and ornate. The woman looked back at her, with eyes full of secrets and sadness and love.

''Bianca,'' Suzanna said, and let her own tears come. ''I knew he must have painted her. He'd have had to.''

''I wasn't certain until I saw Lilah yesterday.''

''He never sold it,'' Suzanna murmured. ''He kept it, because it was all he had left of her.''

''Maybe.'' He wasn't entirely comfortable that the exact thought had occurred to him. ''I've got to figure there was something between them. I don't see how that helps you get any closer to the emeralds.''

''But you'll help.''

''I said I would.''

''Thank you.'' She turned to face him. Yes, he would help, she thought. He wouldn't break his word no matter how much it annoyed him to keep it.

''The first thing I have to ask you, is if you'll bring the portrait to The Towers so my family can see it. It would mean a great deal to them.''

* * *

At Suzanna's insistence, they took Sadie as well. She rode in the back of the pickup, grinning into the wind. When they arrived at The Towers, they saw Lilah and Max sitting out on the lawn. Fred, spotting the truck, tore across the yard, then came to a stumbling halt when Sadie leaped nimbly out of the back.

Body aquiver, he approached her. The dogs gave each other a thorough sniffing over. With a flick of her tail, Sadie pranced across the yard. She sent Fred one come-hither look over her shoulder that had him scrambling after her.

"Looks like love at first sight for old Fred," Lilah commented as she walked with Max to the truck. "We wondered where you'd gone." She ran a hand down Suzanna's arm, letting her know without words that she knew about the call from Bax.

"Are the kids around?"

"No, they went into the village with Megan and her parents to help Kevin pick out some souvenirs before they leave."

With a nod, Suzanna took her hand. "There's something you have to see." Stepping back, she gestured. Through the open door of the truck, Lila saw the painting. Her fingers tightened on her sister's.

"Oh, Suze."

"I know."

"Max, can you see?"

"Yes." Gently he kissed the top of her head and looked at the portrait of a woman who was the double for the one he loved. "She was beautiful. This is a Bradford." He glanced at Holt with a shrug. "I've been studying your grandfather's work for the past couple of weeks."

"You've had this all along," Lilah began.

Holt let the accusation in the tone roll off him. "I didn't know it was Bianca until I saw you yesterday."

She subsided, studying his face. "You're not as nasty as you'd like people to think. Your aura's much too clear."

"Leave Holt's aura alone, Lilah," Suzanna said with a laugh. "I want Aunt Coco to see this. Oh, I wish Sloan and Mandy hadn't left on their honeymoon."

"They'll only be gone two weeks," Lilah reminded her.

Two weeks. Suzanna struggled to keep the smile in place as Holt carried the portrait inside.

The moment she saw it, Coco wept. But that was only to be expected. Holt had propped the painting on the love seat in the parlor, and Coco sat in the wing chair, drenching her handkerchief.

"After all this time. To have part of her back in this house."

Lilah touched her aunt's shoulder. "Part of her has always been in the house."

"Oh, I know, but to be able to look at her." She sniffled. "And see you."

"He must have loved her so much." Damp eyed, C.C. rested her head on Trent's shoulder. "She looks just as I imagined her, just as I knew she looked that night when I felt her."

Holt kept his hands in his pocket. "Look, sentiment and séances aside, it's the emeralds you need. If you want my help, then I need to know everything."

"Séance." Coco dried her eyes. "We should hold another one. We'll hang the portrait in the dining room. With that to focus on we're bound to be successful. I've got to check the astrological charts." She got up and hurried out of the room.

"And she's off and running," Suzanna murmured.

Trent nodded. "Not to discredit Coco, but it might be best if I filled in Holt in a more conventional way."

"I'll make some coffee." Suzanna sent one last glance at the portrait before heading for the kitchen.

There wasn't so very much Trent could tell him, she thought as she ground beans. Holt already knew about the legend, the research they'd done, the danger her sisters had faced. It was possible that he might make more of it, with his training, than they had. But would he care, even a fraction of the amount her family did?

She understood that emotional motivation could change lives. And that without it, nothing worthwhile could be accomplished.

He had passion. But could his passions run deeper than a physical need? Not for her, she assured herself, measuring the coffee carefully. She'd meant what she'd said about not wanting to become involved. She couldn't afford to love again.

She was afraid he was right about an affair. If she couldn't be strong enough to resist him, she hoped she could be strong enough to hold her heart and her body separate. It couldn't be wrong to need to be touched and wanted. Perhaps by giving herself to him, in a physical way, she could prove to herself that she wasn't a failure as a woman.

God, she wanted to feel like a woman again, to experience that rush of pleasure and release. She was nearly thirty, she thought, and the only man with whom she'd been intimate had found her wanting. How much longer could she go on wondering if he was right?

She jolted when hands came down on her shoulders.

Slowly, aware of how easily she paled, Holt turned her to face him. "Where were you?"

"Oh. Up to my ears weeding pachysandra."

"That's a pretty good lie if you'd put more flare into it." But he let it go. "I'm going to run down and talk with Lieutenant Koogar. Rain check the coffee."

"All right, I'll drive you down."

"I'm hitching a ride with Max and Trent."

Her brow lifted. "Men only, I take it."

"Sometimes it works better that way." He rubbed a thumb over the line between her brows in a gentle gesture that surprised them both. Catching himself, he dropped his hand again. "You worry too much. I'll be in touch."

"Thank you. I won't forget what you're doing for us."

"Forget it." He hauled her against him and kissed her until she went limp. "I'd rather you remember that."

He strode out, and she sank weakly into a chair. She wouldn't have any choice but to remember it.

Chapter Six

He wasn't playing good samaritan, Holt assured himself. After getting a clearer handle on the situation, he was doing what he felt was best. Somebody had to keep an eye on her until Livingston was under wraps. The best way to keep an eye on her was to stick close.

Swinging into the graveled lot, he pulled up next to her pickup. He saw that she was outside the shop with customers, so amused himself by roaming around.

He'd driven by Island Gardens before but had never stopped in. There hadn't been any reason to. There were a lot of thriving blossoms crowded on wooden tables or sitting in ornamental pots. Though he couldn't tell one from the other, he could appreciate their appeal. Or maybe it was the fact that the air smelled like Suzanna.

It was obvious she knew what she was doing here, he reflected. There was a tidiness to the place, enhanced by a breezy informality that invited browsers to browse even as it tempted them to buy.

Colorful pictures were set up here and there, describing certain flowers, their planting instructions and maintenance. Along the side of the main building were stacks of fifty- and hundred-pound bags of planting medium and mulch.

He was looking over a tray of snapdragons when he heard a rustle in the bush behind him. He tensed automatically, and his fingers jerked once toward the weapon he no longer wore. Letting out a quiet breath, he cursed himself. He had to get over this reaction. He wasn't a cop anymore, and no one was likely to spring at his back with an eight-inch buck knife.

He turned his head slightly and spotted the young boy crouched behind a display of peonies. Alex grinned and popped up. "I got you!" He danced gleefully around the peonies. "I was a pygmy and I zapped you with my poison blow dart."

"Lucky for me I'm immune to pygmy poison. If it'd been Ubangi poison, I would've been a goner. Where's your sister?"

"In the greenhouse. Mom gave us seeds and stuff, but I got bored. It's okay for me to come out here," he said quickly, knowing how fast adults could make things tough for you. "As long as I don't go near the street or knock over anything."

He wasn't about to give the kid a hard time. "Have you killed many customers today?"

"It's pretty slow. 'Cause it's Monday, Mom says. That's why we can come to work with her and Carolanne can have the day off."

"You like coming here?"

Holt wasn't sure how it had happened, but he and the boy were walking among the flats of flowers, and Alex's hand was in his.

"Sure, it's neat. We get to plant things. Like, see those?" He pointed at an edging of multicolored flowers that sprang up beside the gravel. "Those are zinnias, and I planted them myself, so I get to water them and stuff. Sometimes we get to carry things to the car for people, and they give you quarters."

"Sounds like a good deal."

"And Mom closes up at lunchtime and we walk down the street and get pizza and play the video games. We get to come almost every Monday. Except—" He broke off and kicked at the gravel.

"Except what?"

"Next week we'll have to be on vacation, and Mom won't come."

Holt looked down at the boy's bent head and wondered what the hell to do. "I, ah, guess she's pretty busy here."

"Carolanne or somebody could work, and she could come. But she won't."

"Don't you figure she'd go with you if she could?"

"I guess." Alex kicked at the gravel again and, when Holt didn't scold, kicked a third time. "We have to go to somebody named Martha's yard, with my father and his new wife. Mom says it'll be fun, and we'll go to the beach and have ice cream."

"Sounds pretty good."

"I don't want to go. I don't see how come I have to. I want to go to Disney World with Mom."

When the little voice broke, Holt let out a deep breath and crouched down. "It's tough having to do things you don't want to. I guess you'll have to look after Jenny while you're gone."

Alex shrugged and sniffled. "I guess. She's scared to go. But she's only five."

"She'll be okay with you. Tell you what, I'll look after your mom while you're gone."

"Okay." Feeling better, Alex wiped his nose with the back of his hand. "Can I see on your leg where they shot you?"

"Sure." Holt pointed to a scar about six inches above his kneecap on his left leg.

"Wow." Since Holt didn't seem to mind, Alex ran a fingertip over it. "I guess since you were a policeman and all, you'll take good care of Mom."

"Sure I will."

Suzanna wasn't sure what she felt when she saw Holt and her son, dark heads bent close. But she knew something warm stirred when Holt lifted a hand and brushed it through Alex's hair.

"Well, what's all this?"

Both males looked over then back at each other to exchange a quick and private look before Holt rose. "Man talk," he said, and gave Alex's hand a squeeze.

"Yeah." Alex pushed out his chest. "Man talk."

"I see. Well, I hate to interrupt, but if you want pizza, you'd better go wash your hands."

"Can he come?" Alex asked.

"His name," Suzanna said, "is Mr. Bradford."

"His name is Holt." Holt sent Alex a wink and got a grin in return.

"Can he?"

"We'll see."

"She says that a lot," Alex confided, then raced off to find his sister.

"I suppose I do." Suzanna sighed then turned back to Holt. "What can I do for you?"

She was wearing her hair loose, with a little blue cap over it that made her look about sixteen. Holt suddenly felt as foolish and awkward as a boy asking for his first date.

"Do you still need part-time help?"

"Yes, without any luck." She began to pinch off begonias. "All the high school and college kids are set for the summer."

"I can give you about four hours a day."

"What?"

"Maybe five," he continued as she stared at him. "I've got a couple of repair jobs, but I call my own hours."

"You want to work for me?"

"As long as I only have to haul and plant the things. I ain't selling flowers."

"You can't be serious."

"I mean it. I won't sell them."

"No, I mean about working for me at all. You've already started up your own business, and I can't afford to pay more than minimum wage."

His eyes went very dark, very fast. "I don't want your money."

Suzanna blew the hair out of her eyes. "Now, I am confused."

"Look, I figured we could trade off. I'll do some of the heavy work for you, and you can fix up my yard some."

Her smile bloomed slowly. "You'd like me to fix up your yard?"

Women always made things complicated, he thought and stuffed his hands into his pockets. "I don't want you to go crazy or anything. A couple more bushes maybe. Now do you want to make a deal or don't you?"

Her smile turned to a laugh. "One of the Andersons' neighbors admired our team effort. I'm scheduled to start tomorrow." She held out a hand. "Be here at six."

He winced. "A.M.?"

"Exactly. Now, how about lunch?"

He put his hand in hers. "Fine. You're buying."

Good God, the woman worked like an elephant. She worked like two elephants, Holt corrected as the sweat poured down his back. He had a pick or shovel in his hand so often, he might as well be on a chain gang.

It should've been cooler up here on the cliffs. But the lawn they were landscaping—attacking, he thought as he brought the pick down again—was nothing but rock.

In the three days he'd worked with her, he'd given up trying to stop her from doing any of the heavy work. She only ignored him and did as she pleased. When he went home in the midafternoon, every muscle twinging, he wondered how in holy hell she kept it up.

He couldn't put in more than four or five hours and juggle his own jobs. But he knew she worked eight to ten every day. It wasn't difficult to see that she was throwing herself into her work to keep from thinking about the fact that the kids were leaving the next day.

He brought the pick down again, hit rock. The shock sang up his arms. At the low, steady swearing, Suzanna glanced up from her own work. "Why don't you take a break. I can finish that."

"Did you bring the dynamite?"

The smile touched her lips for only a moment. "No, really. Go get a drink out of the cooler. We're nearly ready to plant."

"Fine." He hated to admit that the whole business was wearing him out. There were blisters on top of his blisters, his muscles felt as though he'd gone ten rounds with the champ—and lost. Wiping his face and neck dry, he walked over to the cooler they'd set in the shade of a beech tree. As he pulled out a ginger ale, he heard the pick ring against the rocky soil. It was no use telling her she was crazy, he thought as he guzzled down the cold liquid. But he couldn't help it.

"You're a lunatic, Suzanna. This is the kind of work they give to people with numbers across their chest."

"What we have here," she said in a thick Southern drawl, "is a failure to communicate."

Her quote of the line from *Cool Hand Luke* made him grin, but only for an instant. "Stark, raving mad," he continued, watching her swing the pick. "What the hell do you think's going to grow in that rock?"

"You'd be surprised." She took a moment to wipe at the sweat that was dripping in her eyes. "See those lilies on the bank there?" She gave a little grunt as she dislodged a rock. "I planted them two years ago in September."

He glanced at the profusion of tall, colorful flowers with grudging admiration. He had to admit that they were an improvement over the rough, rocky soil, but was it worth it?

"The Snyders gave me my first real job." She hefted a rock and tossed it into the wheelbarrow. Stretching her back, she listened to the fat bees buzzing in the gaillardia. "A sympathy job, seeing as they were friends of the family and poor Suzanna needed a break." Her breath whooshed out as she struck soil, and she blinked away the little red dots in front of her eyes. "Surprised them that I knew what I was doing, and I've been working here on and off ever since."

"Great. Would you put that damn thing down a minute?"

"Almost done."

"You won't be done until you keel over. Who's going to see a few posies wilting all the way up here?"

"The Snyders will see them, their guests will see them." She shook her head to clear a haze brought on by the heat. "The photographer from *New England Gardens* will see them." Lord, the bees were loud, she thought as the buzzing filled her head. "And nothing's going to wilt. I'm putting in pinks and campanula and some coreopsis, some lavender for scent and monarda for the hummingbirds." She pressed a hand to her head, ran it over her eyes. "In September we'll plant some bulbs. Dwarf irises and windflowers. Some tuberoses and..." She staggered under a hot wave of dizziness. Holt made the dash from shade to sun as the pick slid out of her hands. When he grabbed her she seemed to melt into his arms.

Cursing her helped relieve the fright as he carried her over and laid her down under the tree. Her body was like hot wax he could all but pour onto the cool grass. "That's it." He plunged his hand into the cooler then rubbed icy water over her face. "You're finished, do you understand? If I see a pick in your hands again, I'll murder you."

"I'm all right." Her voice was weak, but the irritation was clear enough. "Just a little too much sun." The water on her face felt heavenly, even if his hands were a bit rough. She took the ginger ale from him and drank carefully.

"Too much sun," he was ranting, "too much work. And not enough food or sleep from the look of you. You're a mess, Suzanna, and I'm tired of it."

"Thank you very much." She pushed his hands away and leaned back against the tree. She needed a minute, she'd admit. But she didn't need a lecture. "I should have taken a break," she said in disgust. "I know better, but I've got things on my mind."

"I don't care what you've got on your mind." God, she was white as a sheet. He wanted to hold her until the color came back into her cheeks, to stroke her hair until she was strong and rested again. But the concern came out in fury. "I'm taking you home and you're going to bed."

Steadier, she set the bottle aside. "I think you're forgetting who works for whom."

"When you pass out on me, I take over."

"I didn't pass out," she said irritably. "I got dizzy. And nobody takes over for me, not now, not ever again. Stop splashing water in my face, you're going to drown me."

She was recovering fast enough, he thought, but it didn't cool his temper. "You're stubborn, hardheaded and just plain stupid."

"Fine. If you've finished yelling at me, I'm going to take my lunch break." She knew she had to eat. She didn't mind being stubborn or hardheaded, but she did mind being stupid. Which, she thought as she snatched a sandwich out of the cooler, was exactly what she had been to skip breakfast.

"Maybe I haven't finished yelling."

She shrugged as she unwrapped the sandwich. "Then you can yell while I eat. Or you can stop wasting time and have some lunch."

He considered dragging her to the truck. He liked the idea, but the benefits would only be short-term. Short of tying her up and locking her in a room, he couldn't stop her from working herself into the ground.

At least she was eating, he reflected. And the color had seeped back into her cheeks. Maybe there was another tack to getting his way. Casually he took out a sandwich.

"I've been thinking about the emeralds."

The change in topic and attitude surprised her. "Oh?"

"I read the transcript Max put together from the interview with Mrs. Tobias, the maid. And I listened to the tape."

"What do you think?"

"I think she's got a good memory, and that she was impressed by Bianca. From her viewpoint, the setup was that Bianca was unhappy in her marriage, devoted to her children and in love with my grandfather. She and Fergus were already on shaky ground when they had the blowout over the dog. We'll figure that was the straw that broke it. She decided to leave him, but she didn't go that night. Why?"

"Even if she'd finally made the decision," Suzanna said slowly, "there would have been arrangements to make. She'd have had to consider the children." This she understood all too well. "Where could she take them, how could she be certain she could provide for them. Even if the marriage was a disaster, she would have to plan carefully how to tell them she was taking them away from their father."

"So when Fergus left for Boston after they fought, she started to work it out. We have to figure she went to my grandfather, because he ended up with the dog."

"She loved him," Suzanna murmured. "She would have gone to him first. And he loved her, so he would have wanted to go away with her and the children."

"If we go with that, we take it to the next step. She went back to The Towers to pack, to get the kids together. But instead of meeting my grandfather and riding off into the sunset, she takes a jump out of the tower window. Why?''

"She was in turmoil." With her eyes half-closed, Suzanna stared into the sunlight. "She was about to take a step that would end her marriage, separate her children from their father. Break her vows. It's so difficult, so frightening. Like dying. Maybe she thought she was a failure, and when her husband came home, and she had to face him and herself, she couldn't."

Holt ran a hand over her hair. "Is that what it was like for you?"

Her shoulders stiffened. "We're talking about Bianca. And I don't see what her reasons for killing herself have to do with the emeralds."

Holt took his hand away. "First we decide why she hid them, then we go for where."

Slowly she relaxed again. "Fergus gave them to her when their first son was born. Not their first child. A girl didn't rate." She took another sip of her ginger ale and washed away some of her own bitterness. "She would have resented that, I think. To be rewarded—like a prize mare—for producing an heir. But, they were hers because the child was hers."

Because her eyes were heavy, she let them drift closed. "Bax gave me diamonds when Alex was born. I didn't feel guilty about selling them to start the business. Because they were mine. She might have felt the same way. The emeralds would have bought a new life for her, for the children."

"Why did she hide them?"

"To make certain he didn't find them if he stopped her from leaving. So that she knew she'd have something of her own."

"Did you hide your diamonds, Suzanna?"

"I put them in Jenny's diaper bag. The last place Baxter would look." With a half laugh, she plucked at the grass. "That sounds so melodramatic."

But he wasn't smiling or sneering, she noted. He was frowning out at the dianthiums where the bees hovered and hummed. "It sounds damn smart to me. She spent a lot of time in the tower, right?"

"We've looked there."

"We'll look again, and take her bedroom apart."

"Lilah will love that." Suzanna closed her eyes again. The food and the shade were making her sleepy. "It's her bedroom now. And we've looked there, too."

"I haven't."

"No." She decided it wouldn't hurt to stretch out while they finished talking it through. The grass was blissfully cool and soft. "If we found her journal, we'd know the answers. Mandy went through every book in the library, just in case it got mixed in like the purloined letter."

He began to stroke her hair again. "We'll take another look."

"Mandy wouldn't have missed anything. She's too organized."

"I'd rather check over old ground than depend on a séance."

She made a sound that was half laugh and half sigh. "Aunt Coco'll talk you into it." Her voice grew heavy with fatigue. "We need to plant the pinks first."

"Okay." He'd moved his hands down and was gently massaging her shoulders.

"It'll trail right over the rocks and down the bank. It doesn't give up," she murmured, and was asleep.

"You're telling me."

He left her there in the shade and walked back into the sunlight.

The grass was tickling her cheek when she woke. She'd rolled over onto her stomach and had slept like a stone. Groggy, she opened her eyes. She saw Holt sitting back against the tree, his legs crossed at the ankles. He was watching her as he brought a cigarette to his lips.

"I must have dozed off."

"You could say that."

"Sorry." She pushed herself up on her elbow. "We were talking about the emeralds."

He flicked the cigarette away. "We've talked enough for now." In one swift move, he hooked his hands under her arms and pulled her against him. Before she was fully awake, she was in his lap and his mouth was on hers.

He'd watched her sleep. And as he had watched her sleep, the need to touch her had boiled inside him until his blood was like lava. She'd looked so perfect, the sleeping princess, creamy skin dappled by hazy shade, her cheek resting on her hand, her hand on the grass.

He'd wanted those soft, warm lips under his, to feel that long, fragile body molded to him, to hear that quick little catch in her breathing. So he took, feverishly.

Disarmed, disoriented, she struggled back. Her blood had gone from slow and cool to rapid and hot. Her body, relaxed by sleep, was now taut as a bow. She dragged in a single ragged breath. All she could see was his face, his eyes dark and dangerous, his mouth hard and hungry. Then all was a blur as his lips brushed down on hers again.

She let him take what he seemed to need to take so desperately. Under the shade of the beech she pressed against him, answering each demand. When the dizziness came again, she reveled in it. This was not a weakness she had to fight. It was one she had wanted to feel as long as she could remember.

On an oath, he buried his face at her throat where her pulse jackhammered. Nothing and no one had ever made him feel like this. Frantic and shaky. Each time his mouth came back to hers it was with a new edge of desperation, each keener than the last. Dozens of sensations knifed into him, all sharp and deadly. He wanted to shove her aside, walk away before they cut him to ribbons. He wanted to roll with her on the cool, soft grass and drive out all the aches and jagged needs.

But her arms were around him, her hands moving restlessly through his hair while her body trembled. Then her cheek was against his, nuzzling there in a gesture that was almost unbearably sweet.

"What are we going to do?" she murmured. Wanting comfort, she turned her lips to his skin and sighed.

"I think we both know the answer to that."

Suzanna closed her eyes. It was so simple for him. She rested against him a moment, listening to the bees buzz in the flowers. "I need time."

He put his hands on her shoulders, pushing her back until they were face-to-face. "I may not be able to give it to you. We're not children anymore, and I'm tired of wondering what it would be like."

She let out a shaky breath. The turmoil wasn't only hers, she realized. She could feel it, shimmering out of him. "If you ask for more than I can give, we'll both be disappointed. I want you." She bit back a gasp when his fingers tightened. "But I can't make another mistake."

His eyes darkened and narrowed. "Do you want promises?"

"No," she said quickly. "No, I don't. But I have to keep the ones I made to myself. If I come to you, I have to be sure it's not just something I want, but something I can live with." Reaching out, she laid a hand on his cheek. "The one thing I can promise you is that if we're lovers, I won't regret it."

He couldn't argue, not when she looked at him that way. "When," he corrected.

"When," she said with a nod, then rose. Her legs weren't as shaky as she'd thought they would be. She felt stronger. *When,* she thought again. Yes, she'd already accepted that it was only a matter of time. "But for now, we'll have to take things as they come. We've got a job to finish."

"It's finished." He pulled himself to his feet as she turned.

The plants were in place, the ground smoothed and mulched. Where there had only been rocks and thin, thirsty soil were bright hopeful young flowers and tender green leaves.

"How?" she began, already hurrying over to study his work.

"You slept three hours."

"Three—" Appalled, she looked back at him. "You should have woken me up."

"I didn't," he said simply. "Now I've got to get back, I'm running late."

"But you shouldn't have—"

"It's done." Impatience shimmered around him. "Do you want to rip the damn things out and do it yourself?"

"No." As she studied him she realized he wasn't just angry, he was embarrassed. Not only had he done something sweet and considerate, but he'd spent three hours planting what he still sneeringly called posies.

So he stood there, she thought, looking very male and ruffled in the streaming sun, the charming rockery at his feet and his rough, clever hands stuffed in his pockets. Thank me and I'll snarl, he seemed to say.

It was then, facing him on the rocky slope, that she realized what she had refused to admit in his arms. What she had insisted was only passion and need. She loved him. Not just for the hot-blooded kisses or the demanding hands. But for the man beneath. The man who would run a careless hand over her son's hair or answer her little girl's incessant questions. The man who would leave paint splattered on the floor in memory of his grandfather.

The one who would plant flowers for her while she slept.

As she continued to stare, Holt shifted uncomfortably. "Look, if you're going to faint again, I'm going to leave you where you fall. I haven't got time to play nursemaid."

A smile moved slowly, beautifully over her face, confusing him. She loved him for that, too—that snapping impatience that covered the compassion. She would need time to think, of course. Time to adjust. But for now, for this moment, she could simply hold tight to this rush of feeling and be content.

"You did a good job."

He glanced back at the flowers, certain he'd rather cut out his tongue than admit how much he'd enjoyed the work. "You stick them in and cover them up." He moved his shoulders in dismissal. "I put the tools and stuff in the truck. I've got to go."

"I put the Bryce job off until Monday. Tomorrow—I have to be home tomorrow."

"All right. See you later."

As he walked off to his car, Suzanna knelt down to touch the fragile new blooms.

In the cottage near the water, the man who called himself Marshall completed a thorough search. He found a few things of minor interest. The ex-cop liked to read and didn't cook. There were shelves of well-worn books in the bedroom, and only a few scattered supplies in the kitchen. He kept his medals in a box tossed in the bottom of a drawer, and a loaded .32 at the ready in the nightstand.

After rifling through a desk, Marshall discovered that Christian's grandson had made a few shrewd investments. He found it amusing that a former Vice cop had had the sense to create a tidy nest egg. He also found it interesting that training had caused Holt to write up a detailed report on everything he knew about the Calhoun emeralds.

His temper threatened as he read of the interview with the former servant—the servant that Maxwell Quartermain had located. That grated. Quartermain should have been working for him. Or he should have been dead. Marshall was tempted to wreck the place, to toss furniture, break lamps. To give in to an orgy of destruction.

But he forced himself to stay calm. He didn't want to tip his hand. Not yet. Perhaps he hadn't found anything particularly enlightening, but he knew as much as the Calhouns did.

Very carefully, he put the papers back in place, shut the drawers. The dog was beginning to bark out in the yard. He detested dogs. Sneering at the sound, he rubbed at the scar on his leg where the little Calhoun mutt had bitten him. They would have to pay for that. They would all have to pay.

And so they would, he thought. When he had the emeralds.

He left the cottage precisely as he had found it.

I will not write of the winter. That is not a memory I wish to relive. But I did not leave the island. Could not leave it. She was never out of my mind in those months. In the spring, she remained with me. In my dreams.

And then, it was summer.

It isn't possible for me to write how I felt when I saw her running to me. I could paint it, but I could never find the words. I haunted those cliffs, waiting for her, hoping for her. It had become easy to convince myself that it would be enough just to see her, just to speak with her again. If she would only walk down the slope, through the wildflowers and sit on the rocks with me.

Then all at once, she was calling my name, running, her eyes so filled with joy. She was in my arms, her mouth on mine. And I knew she had suffered as I had suffered. She loved as I loved.

We both knew it was madness. Perhaps I could have been stronger, could have convinced her to go and leave me. But something had changed in her over the winter. No longer would she be content with only emptiness, as I learned her marriage was for her. Her children, so dear to her, could not forge a bond between her and the husband who wanted only obedience and duty. Yet I could not allow her to give herself to me, to take the step that could cause her guilt or shame or regret.

So we met, day after day on the cliffs, in all innocence. To talk and laugh, to pretend the summer was endless. Sometimes she brought the children, and it was almost as if we were a family. It was reckless, but somehow we didn't believe anything could touch us while we stood, cupped between sky and sea, with the peaks of the house far up at our backs.

We were happy with what we had. There have been no happier days in my life before or since. Love like that has no beginning or end. It has no right or wrong. In those bright summer days, she was not another man's wife. She was mine.

A lifetime later, I sit here in this aging body and look out at the water. Her face, her voice, come so clearly to me.

She smiled. "I used to dream of being in love."

I had taken the pins from her hair so that my hands could lose themselves in it. A small, precious pleasure. "Do you still?"

"Now I don't have to." She bent toward me, to touch her lips to mine. "I'll never have to dream again. Only wish."

I took her hand to kiss it, and we watched an eagle soar. "There's a ball tonight. I'll wish you were there, to waltz with me."

I got to my feet, drew her to hers and began to dance with her through the wild roses. "Tell me what you'll wear, so I can see you."

Laughing, she lifted her face to mine. "I shall wear ivory silk with a low bodice that bares my shoulders and a draped beaded skirt that catches the light. And my emeralds."

"A woman shouldn't look sad when she speaks of emeralds."

"No." She smiled again. "These are very special. I've had them since Ethan was born, and I wear them to remind me."

"Of what?"

"That no matter what happens, I've left something behind. The children are my real jewels." As a cloud came over the sun she pressed her head to my shoulder. "Hold me closer, Christian."

Neither of us spoke of the summer that was so quickly coming to an end, but I know we both thought of it at that moment when my arms held her tight and our hearts beat together in the dance. The fury of what I was soon to lose again rushed through me.

"I would give you emeralds, and diamonds, sapphires." I crushed my mouth to hers. "All that and more, Bianca, if I could."

"No." She brought her hands to my face, and I saw the tears sparkling in her eyes. "Only love me," she said.

Only love me.

Chapter Seven

Holt was home for less than three minutes when he knew someone had broken in. He might have turned in his shield, but he still had cop's eyes. There was nothing obviously out of place—but an ashtray was closer to the edge of the table, a chair was pulled at a slightly different angle to the fireplace, a corner of the rug was turned up.

Braced and at alert, he moved from the living room into the bedroom. There were signs here, as well. He noted them—the fractional rearrangement of the pillows, the different alignment of the books on the shelves—as he crossed to get his gun from the drawer. After checking the clip, he took his weapon with him as he searched the house.

Thirty minutes later, he replaced the gun. His face was set, his eyes flat and hard. His grandfather's canvases had been moved, not much, but enough to tell Holt that someone had touched them, studied them. And that was a violation he couldn't tolerate.

Whoever had tossed the place had been a pro. Nothing had been taken, little had been disturbed, but Holt was certain every inch of the cottage had been combed.

He was also certain who had done the combing. That meant that Livingston, by whatever guise he was using, was still close. Close enough, Holt thought, that he had discovered the Bradford connection to the Calhouns. And the emeralds.

Now, he decided as he dropped a hand on the head of the dog who whined at his feet, it was personal.

He went through the kitchen door to sit on the porch with his dog and a beer and watch the water. He would let his temper cool and his mind drift, sorting through all the pieces of the puzzle, arranging and rearranging until a picture began to form.

Bianca was the key. It was her mind, her emotions, her motivations he had to tap into. He lit a cigarette, resting his crossed ankles on the porch rail as the light began to soften and pearl toward twilight.

A beautiful woman, unhappily married. If the current crop of Calhoun women were anything to go by, Bianca would also have been strong willed, passionate and loyal. And vulnerable, he added. That came through strongly in the eyes of the portrait, just as it came through strongly in Suzanna's eyes.

She'd also been on the upper rungs of society's ladder, one of the privileged. A young Irishwoman of good family who had married extremely well.

Again, like Suzanna.

He drew on the cigarette, absently stroking Sadie's ears when she nuzzled her head into his lap. His gaze was drawn toward the little yellow bush, the slice of sunshine Suzanna had given him. According to the interview with the former maid, Bianca had also had a fondness for flowers.

She had had children, and by all accounts had been a good and devoted mother, while Fergus had been a strict and disinterested father. Then Christian Bradford had come into the picture.

If Bianca had indeed taken him as a lover, she had also taken an enormous social risk. Like Caesar's wife, a woman in her position was expected to be unblemished. Even a hint of an affair—particularly with a man beneath her station—and her reputation would have been in tatters.

Yet she had become involved.

Had it all grown to be too much for her? Holt wondered. Had she been eaten up by guilt and panic, hidden the emeralds away as some kind of last-ditch show of defiance, only to despair at the thought of the disgrace and scandal of divorce. Unable to face her life, she had chosen death.

He didn't like it. Shaking his head, Holt blew out a slow stream of smoke. He just didn't like the rhythm of it. Maybe he was losing his objectivity, but he couldn't see Suzanna giving up and hurling herself onto the cliffs. And there were too many similarities between Bianca and her great-granddaughter.

Maybe he should try to get inside Suzanna's head. If he understood her, maybe he could understand her star-crossed ancestor. Maybe, he admitted with a pull on the beer, he could understand himself. His feelings for her seemed to undergo radical changes every day, until he no longer knew exactly what he felt.

Oh, there was desire, that was clear enough. But it wasn't simple. He'd always counted on it being simple.

What made Suzanna Calhoun Dumont tick? Her kids, Holt thought immediately. No contest there, though the rest of her family ran a dead heat. Her business. She would work herself ragged making it run. But Holt suspected that her thirst to succeed in business doubled right back around to her children and family.

Restless, he rose to pace the length of the porch. A whippoorwill came to roost in the old wind-bent maple and lifted its voice in its three-note call.

Roused, the insects began to whisper in the grass. The first firefly, a lone sentinel, flickered near the water that lapped the bank.

This, too, was something he wanted. The simple quiet of solitude. But as he stood, looking out into the night, he thought of Suzanna. Not just the way she had felt in his arms, the way she made his blood swim. But what it would be like to have her beside him now, waiting for moonrise.

He needed to get inside her head, to make her trust him enough to tell him what she felt, how she thought. If he could make the link with her, he would be one step closer to making it with Bianca.

But he was afraid he was already in too deep. His own thoughts and feelings were clouding his judgment. He wanted to be her lover more than he had ever wanted anything. To sink into her, to watch her eyes darken with passion until that sad, injured look was completely banished. To have her give herself to him the way she had never given herself to anyone—not even the man she had married.

Holt pressed his hands to the rail, leaned out into the growing dark. Alone, with night to cloak him, he admitted that he was following the same pattern as his grandfather.

He was falling in love with a Calhoun woman.

It was late before he went back inside. Later still before he slept.

Suzanna hadn't slept at all. She had lain awake all night trying not to think about the two small suitcases she had packed. When she managed to get her mind off that, it had veered toward Holt. Thoughts of him only made her more restless.

She'd been up at dawn, rearranging the clothes she'd already packed, adding a few more things, checking yet again to be sure she had included a few of their favorite toys so that they wouldn't feel homesick.

She'd been cheerful at breakfast, grateful that her family had been there to add support and encouragement. Both children had been whiny, but she'd nearly joked them out of it by noon.

By one, her nerves had been frayed and the children were cranky again. By two she was afraid Bax had forgotten the entire thing, then was torn between fury and hope.

At three the car had come, a shiny black Lincoln. Fifteen horrible minutes later, her children were gone.

She couldn't stay home. Coco had been so kind, so understanding, and Suzanna had been afraid they would both dissolve into puddles of tears. For her aunt's sake as much as her own, she decided to go to work.

She would keep herself busy, Suzanna vowed. So busy that when the children got back, she hardly would have noticed they'd been gone.

She stopped by the shop, but Carolanne's sympathy and curiosity nearly drove her over the edge.

"I don't mean to badger you," Carolanne apologized when Suzanna's responses became clipped. "I'm just worried about you."

"I'm fine." Suzanna was selecting plants with almost obsessive care. "And I'm sorry for being short with you. I'm feeling a little rough today."

"And I'm being too nosy." Always good-natured, Carolanne shrugged. "I like the salmon-colored ones," she said as Suzanna debated over the group of New Guinea impatiens. "Listen, if you want to blow off some steam, just call me. We can have a girls' night out."

"I appreciate that."

"Anytime," Carolanne insisted. "It'll be fine. That's a really nice grouping," she added as Suzanna began to load her choices into the truck. "Are you putting in another bed?"

"Paying off a debt." Suzanna climbed into the truck, gave a wave then drove off. On the way to Holt's, she busied her mind by designing and redesigning the arrangement for the flower bed. She'd already scouted out the spot, bordering the front porch so he could enjoy it whenever he came or went from the cottage. Whether he wanted to or not.

The job would take her the rest of the day, then she would unwind by walking along the cliffs. Tomorrow she would put in a full day at the shop, then spend the cool of the evening working the gardens at The Towers.

One by one, the days would pass.

She didn't bother to announce herself after she'd parked the truck, but set right to work staking out the bed. The result was not what she'd hoped for. As she dug and hoed and worked the soil there was no soothing response. Her mind didn't empty of worries and fill with the pleasure of planting. Instead a headache began to work nastily behind her eyes. Ignoring it, she wheeled over a load of planting medium and dumped it. She was raking it smooth when Holt stepped out.

He'd watched her from the window for nearly ten minutes, hating the fact that the strong shoulders were slumped and her eyes dull with sadness.

"I thought you were taking the day off."

"I changed my mind." Without glancing up, she rolled the wheelbarrow back to the truck and loaded it with flats of plants.

"What the hell are all of those?"

"Your paycheck." She started with snapdragons, delphiniums and bright shasta daisies. "This was the deal."

Frowning, he came down a couple of steps. "I said maybe you could put in a couple of bushes."

"I'm putting in flowers." She packed down the soil. "Anyone with an ounce of imagination can see that this place is crying for flowers."

So she wanted to fight, he noted, rocking back on his heels. Well, he could oblige her. "You could have asked before you dug up the yard."

"Why? You'd just sneer and make some nasty macho remark."

He came down another step. "It's my yard, babe."

"And I'm planting flowers in it. *Babe.*" She tossed her head up. Yeah, she was mad enough to spit nails, he noted. And she was also miserable.

"If you don't want to bother to give them any water or care, then I will. Why don't you go back inside and leave me to it?"

Without waiting for a response, she went back to work. Holt took a seat while she added lavender and larkspur, dahlias and violas. He smoked lazily, noting that her hands were as sure and graceful as usual.

"Planting posies doesn't seem to be improving your mood today."

"My mood is just fine. In fact, it's dandy." She snapped a sprig off some freesia and swore. "Why shouldn't it be, just because I had to watch Jenny get in that damn car with tears running down her cheeks? Just because I had to stand there and smile when Alex looked back at me, his little mouth quivering and his eyes begging me not to make him go."

When her eyes filled, she shook the tears away. "And I had to stand there and take it when Bax accused me of being an overprotective, smothering mother who was turning his children, *his* children into timid weaklings."

She hacked her spade into the dirt. "They're not timid or weak," she said viciously. "They're just children. Why shouldn't they be afraid to go with him, when they hardly know him? And with his wife who stood there in her silk suit and Italian heels looking distressed and helpless. She won't have a clue what to do if Jenny has a bad dream or Alex gets a stomachache. And I just let them go. I just stood there and let them get in that awful car with two strangers. So I'm feeling just fine. I'm feeling terrific."

She sprang up to shove the wheelbarrow back to the truck. When she came back to do the mulching, he was gone. She forced herself to do the work carefully, reminding herself that at least here, over this one thing, she had control.

Holt came back, dragging the hose from around the other side of the house and holding two beers. "I'll water them. Have a beer."

Swiping a hand over her brow, she frowned at the bottles. "I don't drink beer."

"That's all I've got." He shoved one into her hand, then pushed the lever for the sprayer. "I think I can handle this part by now," he said dryly. "Why don't you have a seat?"

Suzanna walked to the steps and sat. Because she was thirsty she took one long sip, then rested her chin on her hand and watched him. He'd learned not to drown the plants, or pound them with a heavy spray. She let out a little sigh, then sipped again.

No words of sympathy, she thought. No comforting pats or claims to understand just how she felt. Instead, he'd given her exactly what she'd needed, a silent wall to hurl her misery and anger against. Did he know he'd helped her? She couldn't be sure. But she knew she had come here, to him, not only to plant flowers, not only to get out of the house, but because she loved him.

She hadn't given herself time to think about that, not since the feeling had opened and bloomed inside of her. Nor had she given herself a chance to wonder what it would mean to either of them.

It wasn't something she wanted. She wanted never to love again, never to risk hurt and humiliation at a man's hands again. But it had happened.

She hadn't looked for it. She had looked only for peace of mind, for security for her children, for simple contentment for herself. Yet she had found it.

And what would his reaction be if she told him. Would it please his ego? Would it shock or appall or amuse? It didn't matter, Suzanna told herself as she slipped an arm around the dog who had come to join her. For now, perhaps for always, the love was hers. She no longer expected emotions to be shared.

Holt shut off the spray. The colorful bed added charm to the simple wooden cottage. It even pleased him that he recognized some of the blooms by name. He wasn't going to ask her about the ones that were unfamiliar. But he'd look them up.

"It looks pretty good."

"They're mostly perennials," she said in the same casual tone. "I thought you might find it rewarding to see them come back year after year."

He might, but he also thought he would remember, much too vividly, how hurt and unhappy she'd looked when she'd planted them. He didn't dare dwell on how much it upset him to picture Alex and Jenny climbing tearfully into a car and driving away.

"They smell okay."

"That's the lavender." She took a deep breath of it herself before rising. "I'll go around and turn off the hose." She'd nearly turned the corner when he called her name.

"Suzanna. They'll be all right."

Not trusting her voice, she nodded and continued around back. She was crouched down, the dog's face in hers when he joined her.

"You know, if you put some day lilies and some sedum on that bank, you'd solve most of the erosion problem."

He cupped a hand under her elbow to pull her to her feet. "Is working the only thing you use to take your mind off things?"

"It does the job."

"I've got a better idea."

Her heart gave a quick jolt. "I really don't—"

"Let's go for a ride."

She blinked. "A ride?"

"In the boat. We've got a couple of hours before dark."

"A ride in the boat," she said, unaware that she amused him with her long, relieved sigh. "I'd like that."

"Good." He took her hand and pulled her to the pier. "You cast off." When the dog jumped in beside him, Suzanna realized this was an old routine. For a man who didn't want to appear to have any sentiment, it was a telling thing that he took a dog along for company when he set out to sea.

The engine roared to life. Holt waited only until Suzanna had climbed on board before he headed into the bay.

The wind slapped against her face. Laughing, she clapped a hand to her cap to keep it from flying off. After she'd pulled it on more securely, she joined him at the wheel.

"I haven't been out on the water in months," she shouted over the engine.

"What's the use of living on an island if you never go out on the water?"

"I like to watch it."

She turned her head and caught the bright glint of window glass from the secluded houses on Bar Island. Overhead gulls wheeled and screamed. Sadie barked at them, then settled on the boat cushions with her head on the side so that the wind could send her ears flying.

"Has she ever jumped out?" Suzanna asked him.

He glanced back at the dog. "No. She just looks stupid."

"You'll have to bring her by the house again. Fred hasn't been the same since he met her."

"Some women do that to a man." The salt breeze was carrying her scent to him, wrapping it around his senses so that he drew her in with every breath. She was standing close, braced against the boat's motion. The expression in her eyes was still far off and troubled, and he knew she wasn't thinking of him. But he thought of her.

He moved expertly through the bay traffic, keeping the speed slow and steady as he maneuvered around other boats, passed a hotel terrace where guests sat under striped umbrellas drinking cocktails or eating an early dinner. Far to starboard, the island's three-masted schooner streamed into port with its crowd of waving tourists.

Then the bay gave way to the sea and the water became less serene. The cliffs roared up into the sky. Arrogantly, defiantly, The Towers sat on its ridge overlooking village and bay and sea. Its somber gray stone mirrored the tone of the rain clouds out to the west. Its old, wavy glass glinted with fanciful rainbows. Like a mirage, there were streaks and blurs of color that was Suzanna's garden.

"Sometimes when I went lobstering with my father, I'd look up at it." And think of you. "Castle Calhoun," Holt murmured. "That's what he called it."

Suzanna smiled, shading her eyes with the flat of her hand as she studied the imposing house on the cliffs. "It's just home. It's always been home. When I look up at it I think of Aunt Coco trying out some new recipe in the kitchen and Lilah napping in the parlor. The children playing in the yard or racing down the stairs. Amanda sitting at her desk and working her meticulous way through the mounds of bills it takes to hold a home together. C.C. diving under the hood of the old station wagon to see if she could make a miracle happen and get one more year out of the engine. Sometimes I see my parents laughing at the kitchen table, so young, so alive, so full of plans." She turned around to keep the house in sight. "So many things have changed, and will change. But the house is still there. It's comforting. You'd understand that or you wouldn't have chosen to live in Christian's cottage, with all his memories."

He understood exactly, and it made him uneasy. "Maybe I just like having a place on the water."

Suzanna watched Bianca's tower disappear before she shifted to face him. "Sentiment doesn't make you weak, Holt."

He frowned out over the water. "I could never get close to my father. We came at everything from different directions. I never had to explain or justify anything I felt or wanted to my grandfather. He just accepted. I guess I figured there was a reason he left me the place when he died, even though I was only a kid."

It moved her in a very soft, very lovely way that he had shared even that much with her. "So you came back to it. We always come back to what we love." She wanted to ask him more, what his life had been like during the span of years he'd been away. Why he had turned his back on police work to repair boat motors and props. Had he been in love, or had his heart broken? But he hit the throttle and sent the boat streaking out over the wide expanse of water.

He hadn't come out to think deep thoughts, to worry or to wonder. He had come to give her, and himself, an hour of relaxation, a respite from reality. Wind and speed worked that particular miracle for him. It always had. When he heard her laugh, when she tossed her face up into the sun, he knew he'd chosen well.

"Here, take the wheel."

It was a challenge. She could hear the dare in his voice, see it in his eyes when he grinned at her. Suzanna didn't hesitate, but took his place at the helm.

She gloried in the control, in the power vibrating under her fingertips. The boat sliced through the water like a blade, racing to nowhere. There was only sea and sky and unlimited freedom. The Atlantic roughened, adding a dash of danger. The air took on a bite that shivered along the skin and made each breath a drink of icy wine.

Her hands were firm and competent on the wheel, her body braced and ready. The wistful look in her eyes had been replaced by a bright fearlessness that quickened his blood. Her face was flushed with excitement, dampened by the spray. She didn't look like a princess now, but like a queen who knew her own power and was ready to wield it.

He let her race where she chose, knowing that she would end where he had wanted her for most of his life. He wouldn't wait another day. Not even another hour.

She was breathless and laughing when she gave him the wheel again. "I'd forgotten what it was like. I haven't handled a boat in five years."

"You did all right." He kept the speed high as he turned the boat in a wide half circle.

Still laughing, she rubbed her hands over her arms. "Lord, it's freezing."

He glanced toward her and felt the punch low in his gut. She was glowing—her eyes as blue as the sky and only more vital, the thin cotton pants and blouse plastered against her slender body, her hair streaming out from under the cap.

When his palms grew damp and unsteady on the wheel, he looked away. Not falling in love, he realized. He'd stopped falling and had hit the ground with a fatal smack. "There's a jacket in the cabin."

"No, it feels wonderful." She closed her eyes and let the sensations hammer her. The wild wind, the golden evening sun, the smell of salt and sea and the man beside her, the roar of the motor and the churning wake. They might have been alone, completely, with nothing but excitement and speed, with either of them free to take the wheel and spear off into that fabulous aloneness.

She didn't want to go back. Suzanna drank deeply of the tangy air and thought how liberating it would be to race and race in no direction at all, then to drift wherever the current took her.

But the air was already warming. They were no longer alone. She heard the long, droning horn of a tourist boat as Holt cut the speed and glided toward the harbor.

This too was lovely, she thought. Coming home. Knowing your place, certain of your welcome. She let out a little sigh at the simple familiarity. The blue water of Frenchman Bay deepening now with evening, the buildings crowded with people, the clang of buoys. It was all the more comforting after the frantic race to nowhere.

They said nothing as he navigated across the bay and circled around to drift to his pier. But she was relaxed when she jumped out to secure the lines, when she ran her hands over the dog who leaned against her legs, begging for attention.

"You're quite the sailor, aren't you, girl?" She crouched down to give the dog a good rub. "I think she wants to go again."

Holt stepped nimbly to the dock and stood a foot apart. "There's a storm coming in."

Suzanna glanced up and saw that the clouds were blowing slowly but determinedly inland. "You're right. We can certainly use the rain." Foolish, she thought, to feel awkward now and start talking of the weather. She rose, uncertain of her moves now that he was standing here, tension in every line of his body, his eyes dark and intent on hers. "Thanks for the ride. I really enjoyed it."

"Good." The pier swayed when he started forward. Suzanna took two steps back and felt better when her feet hit solid ground.

"If you get a chance, maybe you can bring Sadie to visit Fred this weekend. He'll be lonely without the kids around."

"All right."

She was halfway across the yard, and he was still a foot away. If it hadn't seemed so paranoid, she would have said he was stalking her. "The bush is doing well." She ran her fingers over it as she passed. "But you really need to feed this lawn. I could recommend a simple and inexpensive program."

His lips curved slightly, but his eyes stayed on hers. "You do that."

"Well, I . . . it's getting late. Aunt Coco—"

"Knows you're a big girl." He took her arm to hold her still. "You're not going anywhere tonight, Suzanna."

Perhaps if she'd been wiser or more experienced, she would have gauged his mood before he touched her. There was no mistaking it now, not when his fingers had closed over her with taut possession, not when his needs, and his intention of satisfying them, were so clear in those deep gray eyes.

She wished she could have been so certain of her own mood and her own needs.

"Holt, I told you I needed time."

"Time's up," he said simply, with an underlying edge that had her pulse jerking.

"This isn't something I intend to take casually."

Heat flashed into his eyes. From miles away came the violent rumble of thunder. "There's nothing casual about it. We both know that."

She did know it, and the knowledge was terrifying. "I think—"

He swore and swept her into his arms. "You think too much."

The moment the shock wore off she began to struggle. By then he had already carried her onto the back porch. "Holt. I won't be pressured." The screen door slammed behind them. Didn't he know she was afraid? That she was so afraid if she took this step he would find her dull, shrug her off and leave her shattered? "I'm not going to be rushed into this."

"If you had your way, it would take another fifteen years." He kicked open the door to the bedroom then dropped her onto the bed. It wasn't what he had planned, but he was too knotted up with terror and longings to struggle with soft words.

She was off the bed in a shot to stand beside it, slim and straight as an arrow. The lowering light, already gathering gloom, crept through the window at her back. "If you think you can cart me in here and throw me on the bed—"

"That's exactly what I've done." His eyes stayed hard on hers as he pulled his shirt over his head. "I'm tired of waiting, Suzanna, and I'm damn tired of wanting you. We're going to do this my way."

It had been like this for her before, she thought as her heart sank to her stomach like a stone. Only then it had been Bax, ordering her into bed, peeling off his clothes before he climbed on top of her to take his marital rights, quick and hard and without affection. And after, there would come his derision and disgust for her.

"Your way's hardly new," she said tightly. "And it doesn't interest me. I'm not obligated to go to bed with you, Holt. To let you demand and take and tell me I'm not good enough to satisfy. I'm not going to be used again, by anyone."

He caught her arms before she could storm from the room, dragged her struggling and swearing against him to crush his heated mouth to hers. The force of it sent her reeling. She would have stumbled away if his arms hadn't banded her so tightly.

Over the fear and the anger her own needs swelled. She wanted to scream at him for pulling them from her, for leaving her raw and naked and defenseless. But she could only hold on.

He yanked her away, arm's length, his breath already ragged and shallow. Her eyes were dark as midnight and held as many secrets. He would uncover them; that he promised himself. One by one he would learn them all. And tonight, he would begin.

"No one is going to be used here, and I'm only going to take what you give." His tensed fingers flexed on her arms. "Look at me, Suzanna. Look at me and tell me you don't want me, and I'll let you go."

Her lips parted on a shaky breath. She loved him, and she was no longer a girl who could hold love to herself like a comforting pillow in the night. If she was not as strong as she hoped and able to hold her heart and body separate, then she had no choice but to unite them. If that heart was broken, she would survive.

Hadn't she promised them both there would be no regrets?

She lifted a hand to his gently though she expected no gentleness in return. The choice was one she made freely.

"I can't tell you I don't want you. There's no need to wait any longer."

Chapter Eight

If his nerves hadn't been so tangled, if the need hadn't been so acute, he might have been able to show her tenderness. If his blood hadn't been so hot, desire so greedy, he would have tried to give her some romance. But he was certain if he didn't possess now, possess quickly, he would shatter into hundreds of jagged shards of desperation.

So his mouth was fevered with impatience, his hands rough with urgency. At the first potent taste he understood she was already his. But it wasn't enough. Maybe it could never be enough.

She didn't tremble or hesitate. The vulnerability was cloaked inside a generosity that urged him to take his fill. As her hands roamed restlessly over his back he felt only her hunger, and none of her doubt.

He pushed the cap from her hair, then yanked the band from it so that his hands could take fistfuls of honey-colored silk. And the hands that gripped were unsteady, even as his mouth ruthlessly devoured hers.

She opened for him, releasing a soft and sultry moan of pleasure as his tongue plunged to duel with hers. He wanted so badly, and that want vibrating from him aroused her own. She had risen on her toes, unaware that she was fighting to meet him flare for flare. Her body was quaking with passions long suppressed.

And there was fear in that, fear in not knowing what would become of her if she lost that last toehold on control. She had to show him that she could give pleasure, make him enjoy and continue to want. If she fumbled now, lessened her grip on proving herself a woman, might he not find her less than his fantasy?

Yet she had never been wanted like this. Not like this with the violence of desire pulsing in the air so that every breath was like breathing temptation. She strained against him, hoping what she had to give would be enough while her system jolted along the battering tide of sensations.

His mouth raced over her face, down her throat where his teeth and the rough stubble of beard scraped. And his hands—Lord, his hands were fast and lethal.

She had to keep her head, but her knees were watery and her mind was spinning from the onslaught. Desperately she dug her nails into his back as she struggled away from the edge and tried to remember what a man would like.

She was quivering like a plucked bow, so tensed and wired he thought she might snap in two in his hands. She was holding back. The knowledge that she could do so when he was half-crazed brought on a kind of virulent fury. He tore the blouse aside as he pushed her onto the bed.

"Damn you, I want it all." Breath heaving, he encircled her wrists and dragged her arms over her head. "I'll have it all." When his mouth swooped down to capture hers, her hands strained under his grip, her pulse jittering in quick, rabbit jumps under his fingers.

His body was like a furnace, hot damp flesh fusing with hers in a way that made her shudder from the sheer wonder of it. Like iron, his fingers clamped hers still while his free hand raked over her in a merciless assault. She could feel the anger, taste the frustrated and furious desire. Desperate, she tried to pull in a breath to beg him to wait, to give her a moment, but all she could manage were jagged moans.

The wind kicked the curtains aside, letting dusk pour through. The first drops of rain hit the roof, sounding to her sensitized ears like gunshots that echoed the war he was waging on her. Again thunder rumbled, closer now, warning of a reckless power.

When his mouth found her breast, he let out a hot groan of pleasure. Here she was as soft as a summer breeze and as potent as whiskey. As she writhed beneath him, he dampened and tugged on the taut nipple, losing himself in the taste and texture while her heartbeat hammered against his mouth.

And she wanted as he wanted. He could feel the urgent excitement raging through her, hear it in her quick, sobbing breaths. Her hips arched and plunged against his until he was senseless. He ranged lower, his teeth nipping at her rib cage, his tongue laying a line of wet heat over her belly.

Her hands were free now and her fingers gripped his hair, then tore at the bedspread. She couldn't breathe. She needed to tell him. Her body was too full of aches and heat. She needed . . .

She needed.

Someone cried out. Suzanna heard the quick desperate sound, felt it tear from her own throat as her body arched up. Whole worlds exploded inside of her with a roar more huge than the thunder that stalked just overhead. Stunned, she lay shuddering under him as he lifted his head to stare at her.

Her eyes were dark, her face flushed with fresh fever. Beneath his, her body shook with aftershocks even as her hands slipped limply from his back to the ravaged bed. He hadn't guessed what it would do to him to see that kind of dazed pleasure on her face.

But he knew he wanted more.

He was driving her up again before she could recover. Now she could only embrace the speed and the thrill of danger. As the rain began to pound, she rolled with him, too giddy to be shocked by her own greed. Her hands were as rough and ready as his now, her mouth as merciless. When he dragged the slacks down her legs, her quick gasp was one of triumph. Her fingers were equally impatient as they yanked the denim over his hips, as they streaked and pressed over slick, heated flesh.

She wanted to touch as urgently as she needed to be touched. To possess even as she was possessed. She craved the madness, the turbulent hunger she hadn't known she could feel, and this tempestuous desire that reared up like a wild wolf to consume.

There was no thought of control now, not from either of them. When he sent her racing up again, then again, she rode each slashing crest only frantic for more. More was what he wanted to give her, and what he wanted to take. As the blood fired through his veins he drove himself into her, claiming possession in a frenzy of speed and heat. She matched him, beat for wild beat, the long, nurturing fingers digging into his hips.

They were alone again, but this time the sea was violently churning and the air was flaming hot. Here, at last was the power and the freedom. The speed was reckless, the journey a glorious risk. She felt him shudder, bury his face in her hair as he reached the end. Suzanna locked tight around him, and followed.

He'd wondered what it would be like for fifteen years. From boy to man he had dreamed about her, imagined her, wanted her. None of his fantasies had come close. She had been like a volcano, smoldering and shuddering, then erupting hot. Now she lay like warm wax beneath him, her body meltingly soft with passions spent. Her hair smelled of sun and sea. He thought he could stay just so for eternity, molded against her with the rain drumming on the roof and the wind blowing the curtains.

But he wanted to see her.

When he shifted, she made a small sound of protest and reached out. He said nothing, only kissed her until she relaxed again. Her eyes were drifting shut when he turned the lamp beside the bed on low.

Lord, she was beautiful, with her hair fanned out on the pillows, her skin glowing, her mouth soft and full. She tensed, but he ignored her discomfort as he took a long, silent study of the rest of her.

"Like I said," he murmured when his eyes came back to hers. "The Calhoun women are all lookers."

She didn't know what she was supposed to say or how she was expected to act. She knew that he had taken her to a new place, an extraordinary place, but she had no idea if he had experienced the same mind-spinning ride. Then he frowned and her stomach twisted. With his eyes narrowed, he traced a finger down her throat, over the swell of her breasts.

"I should have shaved," he said abruptly, hating the fact that he'd scraped and reddened her skin. "You could have told me I was hurting you."

"I guess I didn't notice."

"Sorry." He touched his lips gently to her throat. Her look of dazed surprise made him feel like an idiot. When he rolled away, she reached out tentatively for his hand.

"You didn't hurt me," she said softly. "It was wonderful." And she waited, hopeful that he would tell her the same.

"I've got to let the dog in." His voice was rough, but he gave her fingers a quick squeeze before he left the room.

Suzanna heard it now, the whining howls, the scratching at the screen. She told herself it wasn't a rejection. It only meant that he could go from passion to practicality more quickly than she. They had shared something, something vital. She could cling to that. She sat up, more than a little amazed to see the state of the bed. The spread was a heap on the floor, the sheets a tangled knot at the foot. Her clothes—what was left of them—were scattered with his.

She rose and, uncomfortable naked, tugged on his shirt before she lifted her own. One button out of five remained, hanging by a thread. Laughing, she hugged it to herself. To have been wanted like that. With a little sigh, she bent down to search for her buttons. Maybe now he could be cool and collected, maybe his life hadn't been changed as hers had, but she had been wanted, desperately. She would never forget it.

"What are you doing?"

She looked up to see him standing in the doorway. Obviously walking around buck naked didn't concern him in the least, she thought and felt her steady pulse jerk and dance again. He looked angry. She wished she understood what she had done, or hadn't done, to put that scowl on his face.

"My blouse," she said. "I found the buttons." She gripped them in one hand, the thin cotton in the other. "Do you have a needle and thread?"

"No." Didn't she know what she did to him, standing there in nothing but his shirt, her hair tousled, her eyes heavy? Did she want him to get down on his knees and beg?

"Oh." She swallowed and tried to smile. "Well, I can fix it at home. If I could just borrow your shirt. I'd better get back."

He closed the door behind him. "No," he said again, and crossed the room to take her.

The rain stopped at dawn, leaving the air washed clean. Suzanna awoke to the lazy music of water dripping from the gutters. Before her mind had adjusted to where she was, her mouth was captured in a hot, hungry kiss. Her body catapulted from sleep to desire in one breathless leap.

He'd awakened wanting her. That burning need wouldn't ease no matter how much he took, how willingly she gave. There were no words, none he knew, that could express what she had come to mean to him. From a boy's fantasy to a man's salvation.

He could only show her.

He covered her. He filled her. Watching her face in the watery morning sunlight, he knew he would never be content unless she was with him.

"You're mine." He threw the words out like a curse as her body shuddered beneath his. "Say it." His hands fisted on the sheets and he buried his face against her throat. "Damn it, Suzanna, say it."

She could say nothing but his name as he dragged her over the edge.

When her hands slid limply from his back, he rolled over, locking her close so that she lay over him. He could be content with her head resting on his heart. He told himself that he'd already pushed her hard and fast enough. But he'd wanted badly to hear the words.

His hands were fisted in her hair. As if, she thought dizzily, he would yank her back if she tried to move. Her body felt achy and bruised and glorious. She smiled, listening to the rapid thud of his heart and the liquid beauty of morning bird song.

Her eyes flew open, her head up. He did pull her hair, but more from reflex than intent. "It's morning," Suzanna said.

"That usually happens when the sun comes up."

"No, I—ouch."

"Sorry," he muttered, and reluctantly released her hair.

"I must have fallen asleep."

"Yeah." He ran his hands up and down her back. He liked the long, smooth feel of it. "You dozed off before I could interest you in another round."

Her color fluctuated, but when she tried to scramble up, he held her firmly in place.

"Going somewhere?"

"I have to get home. Aunt Coco must be frantic."

"She knows where you are." Because it was easier to keep her in place, he reversed positions again and began to nibble at her throat. Nothing could have pleased him more than feeling the instant quickening of her pulse under his lips. "And in all likelihood, she's got a pretty good idea what you've been up to."

Without much hope of dislodging him, she pushed at his shoulder. "I didn't tell her where I was going."

"I called her last night when I let Sadie in. Scratch my back, will you? Base of the spine."

She obliged automatically, even while her thoughts spun. "You—you told my aunt that I . . ."

"I told her you were with me. I figure she could put the rest together. That's good. Thanks."

Suzanna let out a long breath. Oh yes, Aunt Coco wouldn't have any trouble adding two and two. And there was absolutely no reason to feel uncomfortable or embarrassed. But she was both. Not only relating to her aunt but to the man whose naked body was spread over hers.

It had been one thing to face him at night. But the morning...

He lifted his head to study her. "What's the problem?"

"Nothing." When he lifted a brow she shifted in what passed for a shrug. "It's just that I'm not sure what to do now. I've never done this before."

He grinned at her. "How'd you get two kids?"

"I don't mean that I've never ... I mean I've never ..."

His grin only widened. "Well, get used to it, babe." Considering, he trailed a finger over her jawline. "Want me to help you out with morning-after etiquette?"

"I want you to stop leering at me."

"No, you see that's part of the form." He replaced his trailing finger with a light nip of his teeth. "I'm supposed to leer at you in the morning so you don't start feeling that you look like a hag."

"A—" The word caught in her throat. "A hag?"

"And you're supposed to tell me I was incredible."

Her brow lifted. "I am?"

"That, and any other superlatives you can come up with. Then—" he rolled her over again "—you're supposed to go fix me breakfast, to show me your talents are versatile."

"I can't tell you how grateful I am that you're filling me in on the procedure."

"No problem. And after you fix me breakfast, you should seduce me back into bed."

She laughed and pressed her cheek to his in a move that disarmed and delighted him. "I'll have to practice up on that, but I could probably handle a couple of scrambled eggs."

"Let me know if you find any."

"Have you got a robe?"

"What for?"

She looked up again. He was still leering. "Never mind." Sliding away, she instinctively turned her back as she groped on the floor for his shirt. "And what do you do while I'm fixing breakfast?"

He caught the ends of her hair, let them shift through his fingers. "I watch you."

And he enjoyed it, seeing her move around his kitchen, his shirt skimming her thighs with the scent of coffee ripening the air and her voice low and amused as she spoke to the dog.

She felt more at ease here, with familiar chores. The bush they had planted was a cloud of sunlight outside the window, and the breeze still smelled of rain.

"You know," she said as she grated cheese into the eggs, "you could use more than a toaster, one pot and a skillet."

"Why?" He kicked back in the chair and took a comfortable drag on his cigarette.

"Well, some people actually use this room to prepare entire meals."

"Only if they haven't heard of take-out." He saw that the coffee had dripped through and rose to pour them both a cup. "What do you take in this?"

"Just black. I need the kick."

"If you ask me, what you need is more sleep."

"I have to be at work in an hour or so." With the bowl of eggs in her hands, she stopped to stare out of the window. He recognized the look in her eyes and rubbed a hand over her shoulder.

"Don't."

"I'm sorry." She turned to the stove to pour the beaten eggs into the skillet. "I can't help but wonder what they're doing, if they're having a good time. They've never been away before."

"Hasn't he taken them for a weekend?"

"No, just a couple of afternoons that weren't terribly successful." She made an effort to shake the mood as she stirred the eggs. "Well, there's only thirteen days left to go."

"You're not helping them or yourself by getting worked up." His impotence grated as he fought to massage the tension from her shoulders.

"I'm fine. I will be fine," she corrected. "I've got more than enough to keep me busy for the next couple of weeks. And with the kids gone, I can put in more time trying to find the emeralds."

"You leave that to me."

She glanced over her shoulder. "This is a team effort, Holt. It always has been."

"I'm involved now, and I'll handle it."

She dished the eggs up as carefully as she chose her words. "I appreciate your help. All of us do. But they're called the Calhoun emeralds for a reason. Two of my sisters have been threatened because of them."

"Exactly my point. You're out of your league with Livingston, Suzanna. He's smart and he's brutal. He won't ask you nicely to get out of his way."

Turning, she handed him his plate. "I'm accustomed to smart, brutal men, and I've already spent enough of my life being afraid."

"What's that supposed to mean?"

"Just what I said." She lifted her plate, and the mug of coffee. "I won't let some thief intimidate me or make me afraid to do what's best for myself and my family."

But Holt was shaking his head. That wasn't the answer he'd wanted. "Are you afraid of Dumont? Physically?"

Her gaze wavered then leveled. "We're talking about the emeralds." She tried to move by him, but Holt blocked her path. His eyes had gone dark, but when he spoke his voice was softer, more controlled than she had ever heard it.

"Did he hit you?"

Her color deepened, then raced away from her cheeks. "What?"

"I want to know if Dumont ever hit you."

Nerves were tightening her throat. No matter how quiet his voice, there was a terrible gleam of violence in his eyes. "The eggs are getting cold, Holt, and I'm hungry."

He fought back the urge to hurl the plate against the wall. He sat, waited for her to take the seat across from him. She looked very frail and very composed in the stream of sunlight. "I want an answer, Suzanna." He picked up his coffee and sipped as she toyed with her food. He knew how to wait and how to push.

"No." Her voice was flat as she took the first bite. "He never hit me."

"Just knocked you around?" He kept his voice casual and ate without tasting. Her gaze flicked up to his, then away.

"There are a lot of ways to intimidate and demoralize, Holt. After that, humiliation is a snap." Picking up a slice of toast, she buttered it carefully. "You're nearly out of bread."

"What did he do to you?"

"Let it go."

"What," he repeated slowly, "did he do to you?"

"He made me face facts."

"Such as?"

"That I was pitifully inadequate as a wife of a corporate lawyer with social and political ambitions."

"Why?"

She slammed down the knife. "Is this how you interrogate suspects?"

Anger, he thought. That was better. "It's a simple question."

"And you want a simple answer? Fine. He married me because of my name. He thought there was a bit more money as well as prestige attached to it, but the Calhoun name was more than adequate. Unfortunately it became quickly apparent that I wasn't the social boon he'd imagined. My dinner party conversation was pedestrian at best. I could be dressed up to look the part of the prominent wife of a politically ambitious attorney, but I could never quite pull it off. It was, as he told me often, a huge disappointment that I couldn't get it through my head what was expected of me. That I was boring, in the drawing room, the dining room and the bedroom."

She sprang up to scrape the rest of her meal into Sadie's bowl. "Does that answer your question?"

"No." Holt pushed his plate away and pulled out a cigarette. "I'd like to know how he convinced you that you were at fault."

Keeping her back to him, she straightened. "Because I loved him. Or I loved the man I thought I'd married, and I wanted, very badly, to be the woman he'd be proud of. But the harder I tried, the more I failed. Then I had Alex, and it seemed...I had done something so incredible. I'd brought that beautiful baby into the world. And it was so easy, so natural for me to be a mother. I never had any doubts, any missteps. I was so happy, so focused on the child and the family we'd begun, that I didn't realize that Bax was discreetly finding more exciting companionship. Not until I found out I was going to have Jenny."

"So he cheated on you." His voice was deceptively mild. "What did you do about it?"

She didn't turn around, but began to run water in the sink to wash the dishes. "You can't understand what it's like to be betrayed that way. To already feel as though you're inadequate. To be carrying a man's child and find out that you've already been replaced."

"No, I can't. But it seems to me I'd be ticked off."

"Was I angry?" She nearly laughed. "Yes, I was angry, but I was also...wounded. I don't like to remember how easy it was for him to shatter me. Alex was only a few months old, and Jenny hadn't been planned. But I was so happy to be pregnant. He didn't want her. Nothing he'd done to me before had hurt or shocked me the way his reaction did when I told him I was pregnant again. He wasn't angry so much as...irked." She decided on a half laugh and plunged her hands into the soapy water.

"He had a son," she continued, "so the Dumont name would continue. He didn't intend to clutter up his life with children, and he certainly didn't want to have to drag me around the social wheel a second time while I was fat and tired and unattractive. The most practical solution was to terminate the pregnancy. We fought horribly about that. It was the first time I'd had the nerve to stand up to him—which only made it worse. Bax was used to getting his own way, he always had. Since he couldn't force me to do what he wanted, he paid me back, expertly."

Calmer now, she set the dish aside to drain and began to wash out the skillet. "He was still discreet publicly with his affairs, but he made sure I knew about them, and how sadly I compared to the women he slept with. He took my name off the checking and charge accounts so that I had to ask him whenever I needed money. That was one of his more subtle humiliations. The night Jenny was born, he was with another woman. He made certain I knew about that when he came to the hospital so the press could snap his picture while he played the proud father."

Holt hadn't moved. He didn't trust himself to move. "Why did you stay with him?"

"At first, because I kept hoping I would wake up beside the man I'd fallen in love with. Then, when I started to consider that my marriage was a failure, I had one child and was pregnant with another." She picked up a cloth and began to dry the dishes. "And I stayed because for a long time, a very long time I was convinced he was right about me. I wasn't clever and witty and sharp. I wasn't sexy or seductive. So the least I could be was loyal. When I realized I couldn't even be that, I had to consider the effect on the children. They weren't to be hurt. I couldn't have stood it if dissolving my marriage to Bax had hurt them. One day, I suddenly understood that it was all for nothing, that I was not only wasting my life but probably doing more harm to Alex and Jenny by pretending there was a marriage. Bax paid little attention to his son, and none at all to his daughter. He spent a great deal more time with his lover than he did with his family."

She sighed, set the dishes down. "So I hid my diamonds in Jenny's diaper bag and asked for a divorce." When she turned, the weariness was back on her face. "Does that answer your question?"

Very slowly, his eyes on hers, he rose. "Did it ever occur to you, did it ever once cross your mind that he was inadequate, that he was a failure? That he was a spoiled, selfish bastard?"

Her lips curved a little. "Well, the last part certainly occurred to me. It also occurs to me that my little story is one-sided. I imagine Bax's view of our relationship would differ from mine, and not without some merit."

"He's still pushing your buttons," Holt said with barely suppressed fury. "So you're not clever? I guess anyone could manage to raise two kids and run a business. Dull, too?" He took a step toward her, only more furious when he saw her instinctive move to brace. "Yeah, I don't know when I've been so bored by anyone, but then most men are bored with women with brains and guts, especially when they're softhearted and hardheaded. Nothing puts me to sleep faster than a woman who'll sweat all day to make sure her kids are provided for. God knows you're not sexy. I just didn't have anything better to do last night than to spend it going crazy over you."

He'd trapped her against the sink with his body and with an anger so ripe she could almost taste it. "You asked and I answered. I don't know what you want me to say now."

"I want you to say you don't give a damn about him." He grabbed her by the shoulders, his face close to hers. "I want you to tell me what I told you to tell me when I was inside you, when I was so full of you I couldn't breathe. You're mine, Suzanna. Nothing that happened before counts because you're mine now. That's what I want to hear."

His hands slipped down to clamp over her wrists. Even as she opened her mouth to speak he saw the quick wince of pain. Swearing, he looked down and saw the bruises he'd already put on her. He jerked back as if she'd slapped him.

"Holt—"

He raised a hand to silence her, turning away until he could clear the red haze of fury from his mind. He'd put marks on her skin. It had been done in passion and without intention, but that didn't erase them. By putting them there, he was no better than the man who had bruised her soul.

He jammed his hands into his pockets before he turned. "I've got things to do."

"But—"

"We got off the track, Suzanna. My fault. I know you have to get to work, and so do I."

So that was that, she thought. She'd bared her soul, now he would walk away. "All right. I'll see you on Monday."

With a nod, he headed for the back door, then swore, stopping with his hand on the screen. "Last night meant something to me. Do you understand that?"

She let out a quiet breath. "No."

His hand curled into a fist on the screen. "You're important to me. I care about you, and having you here, this way, is...I need you. Is that clear enough?"

She studied him—a fist on the door, impatience in his eyes, his body rigid with passions she couldn't quite understand. It was enough, she realized. For now it was more than enough.

"Yes, I think it's clear."

"I don't want it to end there." He turned his head, and his eyes were dark and fierce again. "It's not going to end there."

She continued to study his face, keeping her voice calm. "Are you asking me to come back?"

"You know damn well—" He cut himself off and closed his eyes. "Yes, I'm asking you to come back. And I'm asking you to think about spending time with me that isn't at work or in bed. If that doesn't spell it out for you, then—"

"Would you like to come to dinner?"

He gave her a blank stare. "What?"

"Would you like to come to dinner, tonight? Maybe we could take a drive after."

"Yeah." He dragged a hand through his hair, not sure if he was relieved or uneasy that it had been so simple. "That would be good."

Yes, it would be good, she thought and smiled. "I'll see you about seven then. Bring Sadie if you like."

Chapter Nine

It wasn't candlelight and moonbeams, Suzanna thought, but it was a romance. She hadn't believed she would find it again, or want it. Flexing her back as she drove up the curving road to The Towers, she smiled.

Of course, a relationship with Holt Bradford was lined with rough edges, but it had its softer moments. She'd had a lovely time discovering them over the past few days. And nights.

There was the way he'd shown up at the shop once or twice, just before lunchtime. He hadn't said anything about the children, or her missing the routine—just that he'd come into the village for some parts and felt like eating.

Or how he'd come up behind her at odd moments to rub the tension out of her shoulders. The evening he'd surprised her after a particularly grueling day by dragging her and a wicker basket filled with cold chicken into the boat.

He was still demanding, often abrupt, but he never made her feel less than what she wanted to be. When he loved her, he loved her with an urgency and ferocity that left no doubt as to his desire.

No, she hadn't been looking for romance, she thought as she parked the truck behind Holt's car. But she was terribly glad she'd found it.

The moment she opened the door, Lilah pounced. "I've been waiting for you."

"So I see." Suzanna lifted a brow. Lilah was still in her park service uniform. Knowing her schedule, Suzanna was sure her sister had been home nearly an hour. As a matter of routine, Lilah should have been in her most comfortable clothes and spread out dozing on the handiest flat surface. "What's up?"

"Can you do anything with that surly hulk you've gotten tangled up with?"

"If you mean Holt, not a great deal." Suzanna pulled off her cap to run her hands through her hair. "Why?"

"Right now, he's upstairs, taking my room apart inch by inch. I couldn't even change my clothes." She aimed a narrowed glance up the steps. "I told him we'd already looked there, and that if I'd been sleeping in the same room as the emeralds all these years, I'd know it."

"And he ignored you."

"He not only ignored me, he kicked me out of my own bedroom. And Max." She let out a hiss of breath and sat on the stairs. "Max grinned and said it was a damn good idea."

"Want to gang up on them?"

A wicked gleam came into Lilah's eyes. "Yeah." She rose then swung an arm over Suzanna's shoulders as they started up. "You're really serious about him, aren't you?"

"I'm taking it one step at a time."

"Sometimes when you love someone it's better to take it by leaps and bounds." Then she yawned and swore. "I missed my nap. It'd be satisfying if I could say I disliked that pushy jerk, but I can't. There's something too solid and steady under the bad manners."

"You've been looking at his aura again."

Lilah laughed and stopped at the top of the stairs. "He's a good guy, as much as I'd like to belt him right now. It's good to see you happy again, Suze."

"I haven't been unhappy."

"No, just not happy. There's a difference."

"I suppose there is. Speaking of happy, how are the wedding plans coming?"

"Actually, Aunt Coco and the relative from hell are in the kitchen arguing over them right now." She turned laughing eyes to her sister. "And having a delightful time. Our Great-Aunt Colleen is pretending she simply wants to make certain the event will live up to the Calhoun reputation, but the fact is, she's getting a big kick out of making guest lists and shooting down Aunt Coco's menus."

"As long as she's entertained."

"Wait until she gets hold of you," Lilah warned. "She has some very creative ideas for floral arrangements."

"Terrific." Suzanna stopped in Lilah's doorway. Holt was definitely hard at work. Never particularly ordered, Lilah's room looked as though someone had scooped up every piece of furniture and dropped it down again like pick-up sticks. At the moment, he had his head in the fireplace, and Max was crawling on the floor.

"Having fun, boys?" Lilah said lazily.

Max looked up and grinned. She was mad, all right, he thought. He'd learned to handle and enjoy her temper. "I found that other sandal you've been looking for. It was under the cushion of the chair."

"There's good news." She lifted a brow, noting that Holt was now sitting on Lilah's hearth, looking at Suzanna. And Suzanna was looking at him. "You need a break, Max."

"No, I'm fine."

"You definitely need a break." She walked in to take his hand and pull him to his feet. "You can come back and help Holt invade my privacy later."

"I told you she wouldn't like it," Suzanna said when Lilah dragged Max from the room.

"That's too bad."

With her hands on her hips she surveyed the damage. "Did you find anything?"

"Not unless you count the two odd earrings and one of those lacy things we found behind the dresser." He tilted his head. "You got any of those lacy things?"

"Not really." She looked down at her sweaty T-shirt. "Up until a few days ago, I didn't think I'd need any."

"You've got a real nice way of wearing denim, babe." He rose, and since she wasn't coming any closer, moved to her. "And..." He ran his hands over her shoulders, down her back to her hips. "I get a real charge out of taking it off you." He kissed her hard, in the deep and urgent way she'd come to expect. Then he nipped her bottom lip and grinned. "But anytime you want to borrow one of those lacy things from Lilah..."

She laughed and gave him a quick, affectionate hug, the kind she gave so freely that never failed to warm him from the inside out. "Maybe I'll surprise you. How long have you been here?"

"I came straight from the site. Did you get the rest of those whatdo-youcallits in?"

"Russian olives, yes." And her back was still aching. "You were a lot of help on the retaining wall."

"You were out of your mind to think you could build that thing on your own."

"I had a part-time laborer when I contracted."

He shook his head and went back to searching the fireplace. "You may be tough, Suzanna, but you're not equipped to haul around lumber and swing a sledgehammer."

"I'd have done it—"

"Yeah." He glanced around. "I know." He tested another brick. "It did look pretty good."

"It looked terrific. And since you didn't swear at me more than half a dozen times when you were hefting landscape timbers, why don't I reward you?"

"Oh, yeah?" He lost his interest in the bricks.

"I'll go get you a beer."

"I'd rather have—"

"I know." She laughed as she walked out. "But you'll have to settle for a beer. For now."

It felt good, she thought, to be able to joke like that. Not to be embarrassed or edgy. There was no need to feel anything but content, knowing he cared for her. In time, they might have something deeper.

Full of energy and hope, she rounded the last step and turned into the hall. All at once, there was chaos. She heard the dogs first, Fred and Sadie, barking fiendishly, then the clatter of feet on the porch and two high bellowing shouts.

"Mom!" Both Jenny and Alex yelled the single syllable as they burst into the house.

The rich and fast joy came first as she bent to scoop them up in her arms. Laughing, she smothered them both with kisses as the dogs dashed in mad circles.

"Oh, I missed you. I missed you both so much. Let me look at you." When she drew them back arm's length, her smile faltered. They were both on the edge of tears. "Baby?"

"We wanted to come home." Jenny's voice trembled as she buried her face against her mother's shoulder. "We hate vacation."

"Shh." She stroked Jenny's hair as Alex rubbed a fist under his eyes.

"We were unmanageable and bad," he said in a trembly voice. "And we don't care, either."

"Just the attitude I've come to expect," Bax said as he walked through the open front door. Jenny's arms tightened around Suzanna's neck, but Alex turned and threw out his Calhoun chin.

"We didn't like the dumb party, and we don't like you, either."

"Alex!" Her tone sharp, she dropped a hand on his shoulder. "That's enough. Apologize."

His lips quivered, but the stubborn gleam remained in his eyes. "We're sorry we don't like you."

"Take your sister upstairs," Bax said tightly. "I want to speak with your mother in private."

"You and Jenny go in the kitchen." Suzanna brushed a hand over Alex's cheek. "Aunt Coco's there."

Bax took a careless swipe at Fred with his foot. "And take these damn mutts with you."

"Chéri?" This from the svelte brunette who continued to hover in the doorway.

"Yvette." Keeping her arms around the children, Suzanna rose. "I'm sorry, I didn't see you."

The Frenchwoman waved distracted hands. "I beg your pardon, it's so confusing, I see. I just wondered—Bax, the children's bags?"

"Have the driver bring them in," he snapped. "Can't you see I'm busy?"

Suzanna sent the frazzled woman a look of sympathy. "He can just leave them here in the hall. If you'd like to come into the parlor...go see Aunt Coco," she told the children. "She'll be so happy you're back."

They went, holding each other's hand, with the dogs prancing at their heels.

"If you could spare a moment of your time," Bax said, then cast a glance up and down her work clothes, "out of your obviously fascinating day."

"The parlor," she repeated and turned. She struggled for calm, knowing it was essential. Whatever had caused him to change his plans and bring the children home a full week early was undoubtedly going to fall on her head. That she could handle. But the fact that the children had been upset was a different matter.

"Yvette—" Suzanna gestured to a chair "—can I get you something?"

"Oh, if you would be so kind. A brandy?"

"Of course. Bax?"

"Whiskey, a double."

She went to the liquor cabinet and poured, grateful her hands were steady. As she served Yvette, she thought she caught a glance of apology and embarrassment.

"Well, Bax, would you like to tell me what happened?"

"What happened began years ago when you had the mistaken idea you could be a mother."

"Bax," Yvette began, and was rounded on.

"Get out on the terrace. I prefer to do this privately."

So that hadn't changed, Suzanna thought. She gripped her hands together as Yvette crossed the room and exited through the glass doors.

"At least this little experiment should have rid her of the notion of having a child."

"Experiment?" Suzanna repeated. "Your visit with the children was an experiment?"

He sipped at the whiskey and watched her. He was still a striking man with a charmingly boyish face and fair hair. But temper, as it always had, added an edge to his looks that was anything but appealing.

"My reasons for taking the children are my concern. Their unforgivable behavior is yours. They haven't any conception of how to act in public and in private. They have the manners and dispositions of heathens and as little control. You've done a poor job, Suzanna, unless it was your intention to raise two miserable brats."

"Don't think you can stand here and speak about them that way in my house." Eyes dangerously bright, she walked toward him. "I don't give a damn if they fit your standards or not. I want to know why you've brought them back this way."

"Then listen," he suggested, and shoved her into a chair. "Your precious children don't have a clue what's expected of a Dumont. They were loud and unmanageable in restaurants, whiny and fidgety on the drive. When corrected they became defiant or sulky. At the resort, among several of my acquaintances, their behaviour was an embarrassment."

Too incensed for fear, Suzanna pulled herself out of the chair. "In other words, they were children. I'm sorry your plans were upset, Baxter, but it's difficult to expect a five- and six-year-old to present themselves as socially correct on all occasions. Even more difficult when they're thrust into a situation that wasn't any of their doing. They don't know you."

He swirled whiskey, swallowed. "They're perfectly aware that I'm their father, but you've seen to it that they have no respect for that relationship."

"No, you've seen to it."

Deliberately he set the whiskey aside. "Do you think I don't know what you tell them? Sweet, harmless little Suzanna." She stepped back automatically, pleasing him.

"I don't tell them anything about you," she said, furious with herself for retreating.

"Oh, no? Then you didn't mention the fact that they had a bastard brother out in Oklahoma?"

So that was it, she realized, struggling to settle. "Megan O'Riley's brother married my sister. There was no way to keep the situation a secret, even if I had wanted to."

"And you just couldn't wait to sling my name around." He gave her another shove that sent her stumbling back.

"The boy's their half brother. They accept that, and they're too young to understand what a despicable thing you did."

"My affairs are mine. Don't you forget it." Gripping her shoulders, he pushed her up against the wall. "I have no intention of letting you get away with your pitiful plots for revenge."

"Take your hands off me." She twisted, but he forced her back again.

"When I'm damn good and ready. Let me warn you, Suzanna. I won't have you spreading my private business around. If even a hint of this gets out, I'll know where it started, and you know who'll pay for it."

She kept herself rigid, kept her eyes steady. "You can't hurt me anymore."

"Don't count on it. You make sure your children keep this business of half brothers to themselves. If it's mentioned again—" he tightened his grip and jerked her up on her toes "—ever, you'll be very sorry."

"Take your threats and get out of my house."

"Yours?" He closed a hand around her throat. "Remember, it's only yours because I didn't want this crumbling anachronism. Push me, and I'll have you back in court in a heartbeat. And I'll have it all this time. Those children might benefit from a nice, Swiss boarding school, which is exactly where they'll be if you don't watch your step."

He saw her eyes change, but it wasn't the fear he'd expected. It was fury. She lifted a hand, but before she could strike out, he was jerked away and tumbling to the floor. She watched Holt drag him up again by the collar then send him crashing into a Louis Quinze table.

She'd never seen murder in a man's eyes before, but she recognized it in Holt's as he pounded a fist into Baxter's face.

"Holt, don't—"

She started forward only to have her arm gripped with surprising strength. "Let him alone," Colleen said, her mouth grim, her eyes bright.

He wanted to kill him, and might have, if the man had fought back. But Bax slumped in his hold, nose and mouth seeping blood. "You listen to me, you bastard." Holt slammed him against the wall. "Put your hands on her again, and you're dead."

Shaken, hurting, Bax fumbled for a handkerchief. "I can have you arrested for assault." Holding the cloth to his nose, he looked around and saw his wife standing inside the terrace doors. "I have a witness. You assaulted me and threatened my life." It was his first taste of humiliation, and he detested it. His glance veered toward Suzanna. "You'll regret this."

"No, she won't," Colleen put in before Holt could give in to the satisfaction of smashing his fist into the sneering mouth. "But you will, you miserable, quivering, spineless swine." She leaned heavily on her cane as she walked toward him. "You'll regret it for what's left of your worthless life if you ever lay hands on any member of my family again. Whatever you think you can do to us, I can do only more viciously to you. If you're unclear about my abilities, my name is Colleen Theresa Calhoun, and I can buy and sell you twice over."

She studied him, a pitiful man in a rumpled suit, bleeding into a silk handkerchief. "I wonder what the governor of your state—who happens to be my godchild—will have to say if I mention this scene to him." She gave a slow, satisfied nod when she saw she was understood. "Now get your miserable hide out of my house. Young man—" she inclined her head to Holt "—you'll be so kind as to show our guest to the door."

"My pleasure." Holt dragged him into the hall. The last thing Suzanna saw when she ran from the house was Yvette's fluttering hands.

"Where did she go?" Holt demanded when he found Colleen alone in the parlor.

"To lick her wounds, I suppose. Get me a brandy. Damn it, she'll keep a minute," she muttered when he hesitated. Colleen eased herself into a chair and waited for her heart rate to settle. "I knew she'd had a difficult time, but I wasn't fully aware of the extent of it. I've had this Dumont looked into since the divorce." She took the brandy and drank deeply. "Pitiful excuse for a man. I still wasn't aware he had abused her. I should have been, the first time I saw that look in her eyes. My mother had the same look." She closed her own and leaned back. "Well, if he doesn't want to see his political ambitions go up in smoke, he'll leave her be." Slowly she opened her eyes and gave Holt a steely look. "You did well for yourself—I admire a man who uses his fists. I only regret I didn't use my cane on him."

"I think you did better. I just broke his nose, you scared the—"

"I certainly did." She smiled and drank again. "Damn good feeling, too." She noted that Holt was staring at the open terrace doors, his hands still fisted. Suzanna could do worse, she thought and swirled the remaining brandy. "My mother used to go to the cliffs. You might find Suzanna there. Tell her the children are having cookies and spoiling their dinner."

She had gone to the cliffs. She didn't know why when she'd needed to run, that she had run there. Only for a moment, she promised herself. She would only need a moment alone.

She sat on a rock, covered her face and wept out the bitterness and shame.

He found her like that, alone and sobbing, the wind carrying off the sounds of her grief, the sea pounding restlessly below. He didn't know where to begin. His mother had always been a sturdy woman, and whatever tears she had shed, had been shed in private.

Worse, he could still see Suzanna pushed against the wall, Dumont's hand on her throat. She'd looked so fragile, and so brave.

He stepped closer, laid a hesitant hand on her hair. "Suzanna."

She was up like a shot, choking back tears, wiping them from her damp face. "I have to get back in. The children—"

"Are in the kitchen stuffing themselves with cookies. Sit down."

"No, I—"

"Please." He sat, easing her down beside him. "I haven't been here in a long time. My grandfather used to bring me. He used to sit right here and look out to sea. Once he told me a story about a princess in the castle up on the ridge. He must have been talking about Bianca, but later, when I remembered it, I always thought of you."

"Holt, I'm so sorry."

"If you apologize, you're only going to make me mad."

She swallowed another hot ball of tears. "I can't stand that you saw, that anyone saw."

"What I saw was you standing up to a bully." He turned her face to his. When he saw the fading red marks on her throat, he had to force back an oath. "He's never going to hurt you again."

"It was his reputation. The children must have talked about Kevin."

"Are you going to tell me?"

She did, as clearly as she was able. "When Sloan told me," she finished, "I knew it was important that the children understand they had a brother. What Bax doesn't realize is that I never thought about him, never cared. It was the children who mattered, all of them. The family."

"No, he wouldn't understand that. Or you." He brought her hand to his lips to kiss it gently. The stunned look on her face had him scowling out to sea. "I haven't been Mr. Sensitivity myself."

"You've been wonderful."

"If I had you wouldn't look like I hit you with a rock when I kiss your hand."

"It just isn't your style."

"No." He shrugged and dug out a cigarette. "I guess it's not." Then he changed his mind and slipped an arm around her shoulders instead. "Nice view."

"It's wonderful. I've always come here, to this spot. Sometimes..."

"Go ahead."

"You'll just laugh at me, but sometimes it's as if I can almost see her. Bianca. I can feel her, and I know she's here, waiting." She rested her head on his shoulder and shut her eyes. "Like right now. It's so warm and real. Up in the tower, her tower, it's bittersweet, more of a longing. But here, it's anticipation. Hope. I know you think I'm crazy."

"No." When she started to shift, he pulled her closer so that her head nestled back on his shoulder. "No, I can't. Not when I feel it, too."

From the west tower, the man who called himself Marshall watched them through field glasses. He didn't worry about being disturbed. The family no longer came above the second floor in the west wing, and the crew had knocked off thirty minutes before. He'd hoped to take advantage of the time that Sloan O'Riley was away with his new bride on his honeymoon to move more freely around the house. The Calhouns were so accustomed to seeing men in tool belts that they rarely gave him a second glance.

And he was interested, very interested in Holt Bradford, finding it fascinating that he was being drawn into this generation of Calhouns. It pleased him that he could continue his work right under the nose of an ex-cop. Such irony added to his vanity.

He would continue to keep tabs, he thought, while the cop completed his search. And he would be there to take what was his the moment the treasure was found. Whoever was in the way would simply be eliminated.

Suzanna spent all evening with her children, soothing ruffled feathers and trying to turn their unhappy experience into a silly misadventure. By the time she got them tucked into bed, Jenny was no longer clinging and Alex had rebounded like a rubber ball.

"We had to ride in the car for hours and hours." He bounced on his sister's bed while Suzanna smoothed Jenny's sheets. "And they had dumb music on the radio the *whole* time. People were singing like this." He opened his mouth wide and let out what he thought passed for an operatic aria. "And you couldn't understand a word."

"Not like that, like this." Jenny let out a screech that could have shattered crystal. "And we had to be quiet and appreciate."

Suzanna held her temper and tweaked her daughter's nose. "Well, you appreciated that it was awful, didn't you?"

That made Jenny giggle and reach up for another kiss. "Yvette said we could play a word game, but he said it gave him a headache, so she went to sleep."

"And that's what you should do, right now."

"I liked the hotel," Alex continued, hoping to postpone the inevitable. "We got to jump on the beds when nobody was looking."

"You mean like you do in your room?"

He grinned. "They had little bars of soap in the bathroom, and they put candy on your pillow at night."

Suzanna cocked her head. "You can forget that idea, toadface."

After Jenny was settled with her nightlight and army of stuffed animals, Suzanna carried Alex to his room. He didn't let her pick him up and cuddle often anymore, but tonight, he seemed to need it as much as she did.

"You've been eating bricks again," she murmured, and nuzzled his neck.

"I had five bricks for lunch." He flew out of her arms and onto the bed. She wrestled with him until he was breathless. He flopped back, laughing, then leaped out of bed again.

"Alex—"

"I forgot."

"You've already stretched it tonight, kid. In the bed or I'll have you cooked over a slow fire."

He pulled something out of the jeans he'd been wearing when he'd come home. "I saved it for you."

Suzanna took the flattened, broken chocolate wrapped in gold paper. It was more than a little melted, certainly inedible and more precious than diamonds.

"Oh, Alex."

"Jenny had one, too, but she lost it."

"That's all right." She brought him close for a fierce hug. "Thanks. I love you, you little worm."

"I love you, too." It didn't embarrass him to say it as it sometimes did, and he cuddled against her a moment longer. When his mother tucked him into bed, he didn't complain when she stroked his hair. "Night," he said, ready to sleep.

"Good night." She left him alone, weeping a little over the smashed mint. In her room, she opened the little case that had once held her diamonds, and tucked her son's gift inside.

She undressed then slipped into a thin white nightgown. There was paperwork waiting on her desk in the corner, but she knew her mind and nerves were still too rattled. To soothe herself, she opened the terrace doors and, taking her brush, walked outside to feel the night.

There was an owl hooting, crickets singing, the quiet whoosh of the sea. Tonight the moon was gilded and its light clear as glass. Smiling to herself, she lifted her face to it and skimmed the brush lazily through her hair.

Holt had never seen anything more beautiful than Suzanna brushing her hair in the moonlight. He knew he made a poor Romeo and was deathly afraid he'd make a fool of himself trying, but he had to give her something, to somehow show her what it meant to have her in his life.

He came out of the garden and started up the stone steps. He moved quietly, and she was dreaming. She didn't know he was there until he said her name.

"Suzanna."

She opened her eyes and saw him standing only a foot away, his hair ruffled by the breeze, his eyes dark in the shimmering light. "I was thinking about you. What are you doing here?"

"I went home, but . . . I came back." He wanted her to go on brushing her hair, but was certain the request would sound ridiculous. "Are you all right?"

"I'm fine, really."

"The kids?"

"They're fine, too. Sleeping. I didn't even thank you before. Maybe it's petty, but now that I've had a chance to settle, I can admit I really enjoyed seeing Bax's nose bleed."

"Anytime," Holt said, and meant it.

"I don't think it'll be necessary again, but I appreciate it." She reached out to touch his hand, and pricked her finger on a thorn. "Ow."

"That's a hell of a start," he mumbled, and thrust the rose at her. "I brought you this."

"You did?" Absurdly touched, she brushed the petals to her cheek.

"I stole it out of your garden." He stuck his hands into his pockets and wished for a cigarette. "I don't guess it counts."

"It certainly does." She had had two gifts that night, she thought, from the two men she loved. "Thank you."

He shrugged and wondered what to do next. "You look nice."

She smiled and glanced down at the simple white gown. "Well, it's not lacy."

"I watched you brushing your hair." His hand came out of his pocket of its own volition to touch. "I just stood there, down at the edge of the garden and watched you. I could hardly breathe. You're so beautiful, Suzanna."

Now it was she who couldn't breathe. He'd never looked at her just this way. His voice had never sounded so quiet. There was a reverence in it, as in the hand that stroked over her hair.

"Don't look at me like that." His fingers tightened in her hair and he had to force them to relax again. "I know I've been rough with you."

"No, you haven't."

"Damn it, I have." He fought against a welling impatience as she only stared at him. "I've pushed you around and grabbed on. I ripped your blouse."

A smile touched her lips. "When I sewed the buttons back on I remembered that night, and what it felt like to be needed that way." More than a little baffled, she shook her head. "I'm not fragile, Holt."

Couldn't she see how wrong she was? Didn't she know how she looked right now, her hair smooth and shining in the moonlight, the thin white gown flowing down?

"I want to be with you tonight." He slid his hand down to touch her cheek. "Let me love you tonight."

She couldn't have denied him anything. When he lifted her to carry her in, she pressed her lips to his throat. But his mouth didn't turn hot and ready to hers. He laid her down carefully, took the brush and rose from her to set it on the nightstand. Then he turned the lights low.

When his mouth came to hers at last, it was soft as a whisper. His hands didn't race to excite, but moved with exquisite patience to seduce.

He felt her confusion, heard it in the unsteady murmur of his name, but he only rubbed his lips over hers, tracing the shape with his tongue. His strong hands moved with an artist's grace over the tensed slope of her shoulders.

"Trust me." He took his mouth on a slow, quiet journey over her face. "Let go and trust me, Suzanna. There's more than one way." Over her jaw, down the line of her throat, back to her trembling lips his mouth whispered. "I should have showed you before."

"I can't..." Then his kiss had her sinking, deep, deeper still into some thick velvet haze. She couldn't right herself. Didn't want to. Surely this endless, echoing tunnel was paradise.

He touched, hardly touching at all, and left her weak. His mouth, gliding like a cool breeze over her flesh was rapture. She could hear him murmur to her, incredible promises, soft, lovely words. There was passion in them, in the fingertips that seemed designed only to bring her pleasure, yet this was a passion to give she had never expected.

He stroked her through the thin cotton, delighting in the liquid movements of her body beneath his hands. He could watch her face in the lamplight, feed on that alone, knowing she was steeped in him, in what he offered her. There was no need to strap down greed, desire was no less, but it had taken a different hue.

When she sighed, he brought his lips back to hers to swallow the flavor of his name.

He undressed her slowly, bringing the gown down inch by inch, wallowing in the delight of warming newly bared skin. Fascinated with each tremor he brought her, he lingered. Then took her gently over the first crest.

Unbearably sweet. Each movement, each sigh. Exquisitely tender. Every touch, every murmur. He had imprisoned her in a world of silk, gently bringing dozens of pulses to a throbbing ache that was like music. Never had she been more aware of her body than now as he explored it so thoroughly, so patiently.

At last she felt his flesh against hers, the warm, hard body she had come to crave. Opening heavy eyes, she looked. Lifting weighted limbs, she touched.

He hadn't known a need could be so strong yet so quiet. She enfolded him. He slipped into her. For both, it was like coming home.

I could not have foreseen that the day would be my last with her. Would I have looked more closely, held more tightly? The love could have been no greater, but could it have been treasured more completely?

There is no answer.

We found the little dog, cowering and half-starved in the rocks by our cliffs. Bianca found such pleasure in him. It was foolish, I suppose, but I think we both felt this was something we could share, since we had found him together.

We called him Fred, and I must admit I was sad to see him go when it was time for her to return to The Towers. Of course it was right that she take the orphaned pup to her children so that they could make him a family. I went home alone, to think of her, to try to work.

When she came to me, I was stunned that she should have taken such a risk. Only once before had she been to the cottage, and we had not dared chance that again. She was frantic and overwrought. Under her cloak, she carried the puppy. Because she was pale as a ghost, I made her sit and poured her brandy.

She told me, as I sat, hardly daring to speak, of the events that had taken place since we'd parted.

The children had fallen in love with the dog. There had been laughter and light hearts until Fergus had returned. He refused to have the dog, a stray mutt, in his home. Perhaps I could have forgiven him for that, thought of him only as a rigid fool. Bianca told me that he had ordered the dog destroyed, holding firm even on the tears and pleas of his children.

On the girl, young Colleen, he had been the hardest. Fearing a harsher, perhaps a physical reprisal, Bianca had sent the children and the dog up to their nanny.

The argument that had followed was bitter. She did not tell me all, but her tremors and the flash of fear in her eyes said enough. In his fury, he had threatened and abused her. It was then I saw in the light of my lamp, the marks on her throat where his hands had squeezed.

I would have gone then. I would have killed him. But her terror stopped me. Never before and never again in my life have I felt a rage such as that. To love as I loved, to know that she had been hurt and frightened. There are times I wish to God I had gone, and had killed. Perhaps things would have been different. But I'll never be sure.

I didn't leave her, but stayed while she wept and told me that he had gone to Boston, and that when he returned he intended to bring a new governess of his choosing. He had accused her of being a poor mother, and would take the care and control of the children from her.

If he had threatened to cut out her heart, he could not have done more damage. She would not see her children raised by a paid servant, overseen by a cold, ambitious father. She feared most for her daughter, knowing if nothing was done, Colleen would one day be bartered off into marriage—even as her mother had been.

It was this great fear that forced her decision to leave him.

She knew the risks, the scandal, the position she would be giving up. Nothing could sway her. She would take her children away where she knew they would be safe. Her wish was for me to go with them, but she did not beg or call upon my love.

She did not need to.

I would make the arrangements the next day, and she would prepare the children. Then she asked me to make her mine.

For so long I had wanted her. Yet I had promised myself I would not take her. That night I broke one promise, and I made another. I would love her eternally.

I still remember how she looked, her hair unbound, her eyes so dark. Before I touched her I knew how she would feel. Before I laid her in my bed, I knew how she would look there. Now it is only a dream, the sweetest memory of my life. The sound of the water and the crickets, the smell of wildflowers.

In that timeless hour, I had everything a man could want. She was beauty and love and promise. Seductive and innocent, shy and wanton. Even now, I can taste her mouth, smell her skin. And ache for her.

Then she was gone. What I had thought was a beginning was an end.

I took what money I had, sold paints and canvases for more and bought four tickets on the evening train. She did not come. There was a storm brewing. Hot lightning, vicious thunder, heavy wind. I told myself it was the weather that turned my blood so cold. But God help me, I think I knew. There was such a sharp, terrifying pain, such unreasonable fear. It consumed me.

For the first time, and the last, I went to The Towers. The rain began to slash as I beat on the door. The woman who answered was hysterical. I would have pushed past her, run through the house calling for Bianca, but at that moment, the police arrived.

She had jumped from the tower, thrown herself through the window onto the rocks. This is unclear now, as it was even then. I remember running, shouting for her over the howling wind. The lights of the house were blinding, slashing through the gloom. Men were already scrambling on the ridge and below with lanterns. I stood, looking down at her. My love. Taken from me. Not by her own hand. I could never accept that. But gone. Lost.

I would have leaped off that ridge myself. But she stopped me. I will swear it was her voice that stopped me. Instead, I sat on the ground, the rain pouring over me.

I could not join her then. Somehow I would have to live out my life without her. I have done so, and perhaps some good has come from the time I have spent here. The boy, my grandson. How Bianca would have loved him. There are times I take him to our cliffs and I'm sure she's there with us.

There are still Calhouns in The Towers. Bianca would have wanted that. Her children's children, and theirs. Perhaps one day another lonely young woman will walk those cliffs. I hope her fate is a kinder one.

I know, in my heart, that it is not ended yet. She waits for me. When my time comes at last, I will talk with Bianca again. I will love her as I once promised. Eternally.

Chapter Ten

Holt waited for Trent in the pergola along the seawall. Lighting a cigarette, he looked over the wide lawn to The Towers. One of the gargoyles
along the center peak had lost its head while the other sat grinning down,
more charming than ferocious. There were clematis—he recognized it
now—and roses climbing up to the first terrace. The old stone glowered in
the hazy sunlight. There was really no other word for it, but the flowers
gave it a kind of magical, Sleeping Beauty aura. Towers and turrets speared
up, arrogant of form, dignified with age.

Scaffolding bracketed the west end, and the high whine of a power saw
cut the air. A lift truck was parked under the balcony, its mechanism
groaning as it hefted its load of equipment to a trio of bare-backed men.
A radio jolted out tough rock.

Maybe it was right and just that the house held so tenaciously to the past
even while it accepted the present, Holt mused. If it was possible for stone
and mortar to absorb emotion and memory, The Towers had done so. Already he felt as though it harbored some of his.

The windows of the room where he had spent most of the night with
Suzanna winked back at him. He remembered every second of those
hours, every sigh, every movement. He also remembered that he had confused her. No, tenderness wasn't his style, he thought, but it had been easy
with her.

She hadn't asked him for softness. She hadn't asked him for anything.
Was that why he felt compelled to give? Without trying, she had tapped
into something inside him he hadn't known was there—and was still more
than a little uncomfortable with. Finding it, feeling it left him as vulnerable as she. He'd yet to work out the right way to tell her.

She deserved the music, the candlelight, the flowers. She deserved the
soft poetic words. He was going to try to give them to her, no matter how
big a fool it made him feel.

In the meantime, he had a job to do. He was going to find those damn emeralds for her. And he was going to put Livingston behind bars.

Holt tossed the cigarette away as he saw Trent come out of the house. In the pergola, they would have relative privacy. The clatter of construction echoed in countertime to the beat and drum of waves. Whatever they said wouldn't carry above ten feet. Anyone looking out of the house would see two men sharing a late-afternoon beer, away from the women.

Trent stepped inside and offered a bottle.

"Thanks." Holt leaned negligently against a post and lifted the beer. "Did you get the list?"

"Yeah." Trent took a seat on one of the stone benches so that he could watch the house as he drank. "We've only signed on four new men in the last month."

"References?"

"Of course." The faint annoyance in his tone was instinctive. "Sloan and I are well aware of security."

Holt merely shrugged. "A man liked Livingston wouldn't have any problem getting references. They'd cost him." Holt drank deeply. "But he'd get them."

"You'd know more about that sort of thing than I." Trent's eyes narrowed as he watched two of the men replacing shingles on the roof of the west wing. "But I have a hard time buying that he could be here, working right under our noses."

"Oh, he's here." Holt took out another cigarette, lighted it, then took a thoughtful drag. "Whoever tossed my place knew about the connection almost as soon as you did. Since none of you go around talking about the situation at cocktail parties, he'd have heard something here, in the house. He didn't sign on at the start of the job, because he was busy elsewhere. But the last few weeks..." He paused as the children ran out, dogs in tow, to race to their fort. "He wouldn't just sit and wait, not as long as there's a possibility you could knock out a wall and have the emeralds fall into your hand. And where better to keep an eye on things than inside?"

"It fits," Trent admitted. "But I don't like the idea of my wife, or any of the others, being that close." He thought of C.C., the baby she carried, and his eyes darkened. "If there's a chance you're right, I want to move on it."

"Give me the list, and I'll check it out. I've still got connections." Holt's gaze remained on the children. "He's not going to hurt any of them. That's a fact."

Trent nodded. He was a businessman and had never done anything more violent than a little boxing in college. But he would do whatever it took to protect his wife and unborn child. "I filled Max in, and Sloan and Amanda decided to break off their honeymoon. They should be here in a couple of hours."

That was good, Holt thought. It was best having the family all in one place. "What did Sloan tell her?"

"That there was some problem with the job." More comfortable now that wheels were in motion, Trent grinned a little. "If she finds out he's stringing her along, there'll be hell to pay."

"The less the women know, the better."

This time Trent laughed. "If any of them heard you say that, you'd lose three layers of skin. They're a tough bunch."

Holt thought of Suzanna. "They think they are."

"No, they are. It took me quite a while to accept it. Individually they're strong—velvet-coated steel. Not to mention stubborn, impulsive and feverishly loyal. Together..." Trent smiled again. "Well, I'll admit I'd rather face a pair of sumo wrestlers than the Calhoun women on a roll."

"When it's over, they can be as mad as they want."

"As long as they're safe," Trent finished, and noted that Holt was watching the children. "Great kids," he commented.

"Yeah. They're okay."

"They've got a hell of a mother." Trent drank contemplatively. "Too bad they don't have a real father."

Even the thought of Baxter Dumont made Holt's blood boil. "How much do you know about him?"

"More than I like. I know he put Suzanna through hell. He nearly broke her with the custody suit."

"Custody suit?" Stunned, Holt looked back. "He went after the kids?"

"He went after her," Trent corrected. "What better way? She doesn't talk about it. I got the story from C.C. Apparently he was annoyed that she filed for the divorce. Not good for his image, particularly since he's got his eye on a senate seat. He dragged her through a long, ugly court battle, trying to prove she was unstable and unfit."

"Bastard." Choking on rage, Holt turned away to flick the cigarette onto the rocks.

"He didn't want them. The idea was to ship them off to a boarding school. Or that was the threat. He backed off when Suzanna made the settlement."

His hands were on the stone rail now, fingers digging in. "What settlement?"

"She gave him damn near everything. He dropped the case so the arrangements could be made privately. He got the house, all the property, along with a chunk of her inheritance. She could have fought it, but she and the kids were already an emotional mess. She didn't want to take any chances with them, or put them through any more stress."

"No, she wouldn't." Holt drank in a futile attempt to wash the bitterness from his throat. "He's not going to hurt her or the kids anymore. I'll see to it."

"I thought you would." Trent rose, satisfied. He pulled a list out of his pocket and exchanged it for Holt's empty bottle. "Let me know what you find out."

"Yeah."

"The séance tonight." Trent saw Holt grimace and laughed again. "It may surprise you."

"The only thing that surprises me is that Coco talked me into it."

"If you plan on sticking around, you'll have to get used to being talked into all manner of things."

He was going to stick around, all right, Holt thought as Trent walked away. He just needed to find the right way to tell Suzanna. After glancing at the names on the list, Holt tucked it away. He'd make a couple of calls and see what he could dig up.

As he started across the lawn, the dogs galloped up to him, Fred devotedly pressing to Sadie's side. When they stopped jumping long enough to be petted, Fred lapped frantically at her face. Sadie tolerated it, then turned away and ignored him.

"They've got a name for women like you," Holt told her.

"Remember the Alamo!" Alex shouted. He stood spread legged on the roof of his fort, a plastic sword in his hand. Because he counted on his challenge being answered, his eyes gleamed as they met Holt's. "You'll never take us alive."

"Oh yeah?" Unable to resist, Holt moved closer. "What makes you think I want you, monkey brain?"

"'Cause we're the patriots and you're the evil invaders."

Jenny popped her head through an opening that served as a window. Before Holt could evade it, he was hit dead center of the chest with a splat of water from her pistol. Alex let out a triumphant hoot as Holt scowled down at his shirt.

"I suppose you know," Holt said slowly, "this means war."

As Jenny shrieked, he grabbed her and pulled her through the window. To her delight, he held her upside down so that her two blond ponytails brushed the grass.

"He's taken a hostage!" Alex bellowed. "Death to the last man." He scrambled inside then burst out of the doorway, brandishing his sword. Holt barely had time to right Jenny before the little missile plowed into him. "Off with his head," Alex chanted, echoed by his sister. Holt let his body go lax and took them both to the ground with him.

There were screams and giggles as he wrestled with them. It wasn't as easy as he'd supposed. They were both agile and slick, wriggling out of his hold to attack. He found himself at a disadvantage as Alex sat on his chest and Jenny found a spot on his ribs to tickle.

"I'm going to have to get rough," he warned them. When he took a spray of water in the face, he swore, making them both howl with laughter. A quick roll and he dislodged the pistol, then snatched it up to drench them both. With shrieks and giggles, they fell on him.

It was a wet and messy battle, and when he finally managed to pin them, they were all out of breath.

"I massacred you both," Holt managed. "Say uncle." Jenny poked a finger in his ribs, making him twitch. In defense he lowered his cheek to her neck and rubbed a day's worth of stubble over her skin.

"Uncle, uncle, uncle!" She screamed, gurgling with laughter. Satisfied, he used the same weapon on Alex until victorious, he rolled over and lay stomach down on the grass.

"You killed us," Alex admitted, not displeased. "But you're morally wounded."

"Yeah, but I think you mean mortally."

"Are you going to take a nap?" Jenny climbed onto his back to bounce. "Lilah sleeps in the grass sometimes."

"Lilah sleeps anywhere," Holt muttered.

"You can take a nap in my bed if you want," she invited, then pressed a curious finger on the edge of the scar she saw beneath his hitched-up T-shirt. "You have a hurt on your back."

"Uh-huh."

Alex was already scrambling to look. "Can I see?"

Holt tensed automatically, then forced himself to relax. "Sure."

As Alex pushed up the shirt, both children's eyes widened. It wasn't like the neat little scar they had both admired on his leg. This was long and jagged and mean, slashing from the waist so high up on his back they couldn't push the shirt up enough to see the end of it.

"Gee," was all Alex could think to say. He swallowed, then gamely touched a finger to the scar. "Did you get in a big fight?"

"Not exactly." He remembered the pain, the incredible flash of white heat. "One of the bad guys got me," he said, and hoped it would satisfy. When he felt Jenny's little mouth lower to his back, he went very still.

"Does it feel better now?" she asked.

"Yeah." He had to let out a long breath to steady his voice. "Thanks." Turning over, he sat up to brush a hand through her hair.

Suzanna stood a few feet away, watching them with her heart in her throat. She'd seen the battle from the kitchen doorway. It had touched her to see how easily Holt had joined in the game with her children. She'd been smiling when she'd started out to join them—then she had watched Jenny and Alex examining the scar on Holt's back, and Jenny's kiss to make it better. She had seen the look of ragged emotion on Holt's face when he'd turned to sweep his hand over her little girl's hair.

Now the three of them were on the grass, Jenny cuddled on his lap, Alex's arm slung affectionately around his shoulder. She took a moment to make certain her eyes were dry before she continued toward them.

"Is the war over?" she asked, and three pair of eyes lifted.

"He won," Alex told her.

"It doesn't look as though it was an easy victory." She scooped Jenny up when the girl lifted her arms. "You're all wet."

"He blasted us—but I got him first."

"That's my girl."

"And he's ticklish," Jenny confided. "*Real* ticklish."

"Is that so?" Suzanna sent Holt a slow smile. "I'll keep that in mind. Now you two scat. I noticed nobody put away the game you were playing."

"But, Mom—" Alex had his excuses ready, but she stopped them with a look.

"If you don't clean it up, I will," she said mildly. "But then I'll have your share of strawberry shortcake tonight."

That was a tough one. Alex agonized over it for a minute, then caved in. "I'll do it. Then I get Jenny's share."

"Do not." Jenny sprinted toward the house with her brother giving chase.

"Very smooth, Mom," Holt commented as he rose.

"I know their weaknesses." She put her arms around him, surprising and pleasing him. It was very rare for her to make the first move. "You're all wet, too."

"Sniper fire, but I picked them off like flies." Bringing her closer, he rested his cheek on her hair. "They're terrific kids, Suzanna. I'm, ah..." He didn't know how to tell her he'd fallen in love with them, any more than he knew how to tell her he'd fallen in love with their mother. "I'm getting you wet." Feeling awkward, he drew away.

Smiling, she touched a hand to his cheek. "Want to take a walk?"

He thought of the list in his pocket. It could wait an hour, he decided, and took her hand.

He'd known she would head to the cliffs. It seemed right that they would walk there as the shadows lengthened and the air cooled toward evening. She talked a little of the job she'd finished that day, he of the hull he'd repaired. But their minds weren't on work.

"Holt." She looked out to sea, her hand in his. "Will you tell me why you resigned from the force?" She felt his fingers stiffen, but didn't turn.

"It's done," he said flatly. "There's nothing to tell."

"The scar on your back—"

"I said it's done." He withdrew and pulled out a cigarette.

"I see." She absorbed the rejection. "Your past and your personal feelings about it are none of my business."

He took an impatient drag. "I didn't say that."

"You certainly did. You have the right to know all there is to know about me. I'm supposed to trust you with everything, unquestioningly. But I'm not to pry into what's yours."

He turned angry eyes on her. "What is this, some kind of test?"

"Call it what you like," she tossed back. "I'd hoped you trusted me by now, that you cared enough to let me in."

"I do care, damn it. Don't you know it still rips me up to remember it? Ten years of my life, Suzanna. Ten years." He whirled away to flick the cigarette over the edge.

"I'm sorry." Instinctively she put her hands on his shoulders to soothe. "If anyone knows how painful it is to dredge up old wounds, it's me. Why don't we go back? I'll see if I can find you a clean shirt."

"No." His jaw was clenched, his body tight as a spring. "You want to know, you've got a right. I tossed it in because I couldn't handle it. I spent ten years telling myself I could make a difference, that none of the crap I had to wade through would affect me. I could rub shoulders with dealers and pimps and victims all day and not lose any sleep at night. If I had to kill somebody, it was line of duty. Not something you want to think about too much, but something you live with. I saw a few cops burn out along the way, but it wasn't going to happen to me.''

She said nothing, just continued to rub at the knotted muscles of his shoulders while she waited for him to go on. He kept looking out to sea, smelling her, and the dusky scent of the wild roses that were at peak.

"Vice takes you into the pits, Suzanna. You get so you understand the people you're trying to wipe out. You think like them. You have to when you go under, or you don't come out again. There are things I'm never going to tell you, because I do care. Ugly things, and I just . . .'' He closed his eyes, and jammed his hands into his pockets. "I just didn't want to see it anymore. I was already thinking about coming back here—just sort of kicking it around.''

Suddenly weary, he lifted his hands to rub the heels over his eyes. "I was tired, Suzanna, and I wanted to live like a normal person again. The kind who doesn't strap on a gun every day or make deals with slime in back rooms. We were on a routine investigation, looking for a small-time dealer who we thought we could pressure information out of. Doesn't matter why,'' he said impatiently. "Anyway, we got a tip where to find him, and when we cornered him in this little dive, he snapped. Turned out the jerk had about twenty thousand in coke strapped under his clothes, and more than a couple lines in his system. He panicked. He dragged some half-stoned woman with him and bolted.''

His palms were beginning to sweat, so he wiped them against his jeans. "My partner and I separated to cut him off. He pulled the woman out in the alley. With us on either end, he didn't have any hope of getting away. I had my weapon out. It was dark. The garbage had turned.''

He could still smell it, rank and fetid, as the sweat began to run down his back. "I could hear my partner coming up the other side, and hear the woman crying. He'd sliced her up a little and she was balled up on the concrete. I couldn't be sure how bad she was hurt. I remember thinking the creep was going to be up for more than distribution. Then he jumped me. He had the knife in before I could get off a shot.''

He could still feel it ripping through his flesh, still smell his own blood. "I knew I was dead, and I kept thinking that I wouldn't be able to come home. That I was going to die in that damn alley with the stink of that garbage. I killed him as I went down. That's what they told me. I don't remember. The thing I remember next was waking up in the hospital feeling like I'd been sliced in half and sewn back together. I told myself that if I made it, I was coming back here. Because I knew if I had to walk down another alley, I wouldn't come back out.''

Suzanna had her arms tight around him now, her cheek pressed against his back. "Do you think because you came home instead of facing another alley, you failed?''

"I don't know."

"I did, for a long time. No one had put a knife in my back, but I came to understand that if I stayed with Bax, if I'd kept that promise, part of me would die. I chose survival, do you think I should be ashamed of that?"

"No." He turned, taking her shoulder. "No."

She lifted her hands to cup his face. In her eyes was understanding, and the sympathy he couldn't have accepted even a week before. "Neither do I. I hate what happened to you, but I'm glad it brought you here." Offering comfort, she touched her lips to his. Slowly, with a sweetness that was unbearably moving, she felt him let go.

His body relaxed against hers even as he pulled her closer. His mouth softened even as it heated. Here, at last, was the next level. There was not only passion, not only tenderness, but trust. As the wind whispered through the wild grass and the bright, brave flowers, she thought she heard something else, something so quiet and lovely that it brought tears to her eyes. When he lifted his head, when she saw his face, she knew he'd heard it, too. She smiled.

"We're not alone here," she murmured. "They must have stood in this same spot, holding each other like this. Wanting each other like this." Filled with the moment, she pressed his hand to her lips. "Holt, do you believe that fate and time can run in a circle?"

"I'm beginning to."

"They still come here, to wait. I wonder if they ever find each other. I think they will, if we can make things right." She kissed him again, then slipped an arm around his waist. "Let's go home. I have a feeling it's going to be an interesting evening."

"Suzanna," he began as they started back. "After the séance..." He trailed off, looking pained, and made her laugh.

"Don't worry, at The Towers we only have friendly ghosts."

"Right. Just don't expect me to put much stock in chanting and trances, but anyway, I was wondering if after—look, I know you don't like to leave the kids, but I thought you could come back to my place for a little while. There's some stuff I want to talk to you about."

"What stuff?"

"Just—stuff," he said lamely. If he was going to ask her to marry him, he wanted to do it right. "I'd appreciate it if you could get away for an hour or two."

"All right, if it's important. Is it about the emeralds?"

"No. It's...I'd rather wait, okay? Listen, I've got a couple of things to do before we start calling up spirits."

"Aren't you going to stay for dinner?"

"I can't. I'll be back." As they came up the slope and passed the stone wall, he pulled her against him for a brief hard kiss. "See you later."

She frowned after him and might have pursued, but her name was called from the second-level terrace. Shading her eyes, she saw her sister.

"Amanda!" With a laugh, she raced across the lawn and up the stone steps. "What are you doing back?" She gathered the new bride into her arms and squeezed. "You look wonderful—but you were supposed to be gone nearly another week. Is anything wrong?"

"No, nothing." She kissed both of Suzanna's cheeks. "Come on, I'll fill you in."

"Where are we going?"

"Bianca's tower. Family meeting."

They climbed up, then went inside to ascend the narrow circular stairs that led to the tower. C.C. and Lilah were already waiting.

"Aunt Coco?" Suzanna asked.

"We'll let her know what we discuss," Amanda answered. "But it would look too suspicious if we pulled her up here now."

With a nod, Suzanna took a seat on the floor at Lilah's feet. "So I take it this is women only?"

"No more than they deserve," C.C. said, and crossed her arms. "They've been skulking off to have their boy's club meetings for days now. It's time we set things straight."

"Max has definitely got something up his sleeve," Lilah put in. "He's acting much too innocent. And, he's been hanging around the construction crew for the last couple of days."

"I don't suppose he wants to learn how to set tile," Suzanna murmured.

"If he did, he'd have twenty books on it by now." Lilah rolled her shoulders and leaned back. "And this afternoon when I got home from work, I saw Trent and Holt powwowing in the pergola. Somebody who didn't know better might have thought they were just hanging out and having a beer, but something was going on."

"So they know something they're not telling us." Thoughtful, Suzanna drummed her fingers on her knees. She'd had a feeling something was going on, but Holt had done such a good job of distracting her, she hadn't acted on it.

"Sloan had a long, mumbling conversation with Trent on the phone two days ago. He claimed there was some problem with materials that he had to see to personally." Tossing her hair, Amanda gave a sniff. "And he thought I was stupid enough to buy it. He wanted to get back because they're on to something—and they want to keep the little women out of the way."

"Fat chance," C.C. muttered. "I'm for marching downstairs right now and demanding they tell us whatever they know. If Trent thinks I'm going to sit around twiddling my thumbs while he handles Calhoun business, he's got another think coming."

"Bamboo shoots and brass knuckles," Lilah mused, not terribly displeased with the image. "That'll just make them more stubborn. Male egos on the line, ladies. Get out your hard hats and flak jackets."

Suzanna laughed and patted her leg. "You've got a point. Let's see what we know... Sloan gets called back so they must think they're getting close. I can't see them being secretive if they thought they'd hit on the location of the emeralds."

"Neither can I." Because she thought best on her feet, Amanda paced. "Remember how stiff-necked they got when we decided to look for the yacht Max had jumped off? Sloan threatened to...what was it? Hog-tie," she said viciously. "Yes, that was it. He threatened to hog-tie me if I so much as thought about trying to find Livingston on my own."

"Trent won't even discuss Livingston with me," C.C. added, then wrinkled her nose. "It isn't good for me to be upset in my delicate condition."

From her sprawled perch on the window seat, Lilah gave a hoot. "I'd like to see any man go through childbirth then have the nerve to call a woman delicate."

"Holt says that Livingston is out of our league. *Ours*," Suzanna explained, making a circular motion with her finger. "Not his."

"Jerk." C.C. plopped down on the window seat beside Lilah. "So are we agreed? They've got a line on Livingston and they're keeping it to themselves."

The vote was unanimous.

"Now, we need to find out what they know." Amanda stopped pacing and tapped her foot. "Suggestions?"

"Well..." Suzanna looked down at her nails and smiled. "I say divide and conquer. The four of us should be able to dig information out of them—each in our own way. Then we rendezvous here, tomorrow, same time, and put the pieces together."

"I like it." Lilah sat up to put a hand on Suzanna's shoulder. "The poor guys haven't got a chance."

Suzanna reached up to lay her hand on Lilah's as Amanda and C.C. added theirs. "And when it's over," she said, "maybe they'll realize the Calhoun women take care of their own."

Chapter Eleven

Holt had never felt more ridiculous in his life. He was about to take part in a séance. If that wasn't bad enough, before the night was over, he was going to ask the woman who was currently laughing at him, to be his wife.

"It isn't a firing squad." Chuckling, Suzanna patted his cheek. "Relax."

"Damn foolishness is what it is." From the foot of the table, Colleen scowled at everyone in general. "The idea of talking to spirits. Hogwash. And you—" She stabbed a finger toward Coco. "Not that you ever kept an ounce of sense in that flighty head of yours, but I'd have thought even you would know better than to raise these girls on such bilge."

"It isn't bilge." As always, the steely gaze made Coco tremble, but she felt fairly safe with the length of the table between them. "You'll see after we begin."

"What I see is a table full of dolts." Though her face remained in stern lines, Colleen's heart melted as she looked up at the portrait of her mother, which had been hung over the fireplace. "I'll give you ten thousand for it."

Holt shrugged. She'd been dogging him for days about buying the painting. "It isn't for sale."

"If you think you're going to hose me, young man, you're mistaken. I know a hustle."

He grinned at her. He would have bet his last nickel she'd hustled plenty herself. "I'm not selling it."

"It's worth more, anyway," Lilah put in, unable to resist. "Isn't that right, Professor?"

"Well, actually, yes." Max cleared his throat. "Christian Bradford's early work is increasing in value. At Sotheby's two years ago, one of his seascapes went for thirty-five thousand."

"What are you," Colleen snapped, "his agent?"

Max swallowed a grin. "No, ma'am."

"Then hush. Fifteen thousand, and not a penny more."

Holt ran his tongue around his teeth. "Not interested."

"Maybe if we got on with the matter at hand." Coco held her breath, waiting for her aunt's wrath to fall. When Colleen only muttered and scowled, she relaxed. "Amanda, dear, light the candles. Now we must all try to empty our minds of all worries, all doubts. Concentrate on Bianca." When the candles were glowing, and the chandelier extinguished, she gave a last glance around the table. "Join hands."

Holt grumbled under his breath but took Suzanna's hand in his right, Lilah's in his left.

"Focus on the picture," Coco whispered, closing her eyes to bring it into her mind since it was behind her on the wall. Tingles of anticipation raced up and down her spine. "She's close to us, very close to us. She wants to help."

Holt let his mind drift because it helped him forget what he was doing. He tried to imagine what it would be like when he and Suzanna were alone in the cottage. He'd bought candles. Not the sturdy type he kept in the kitchen drawer for power outages, but slender white tapers that smelled of jasmine.

There was champagne chilling beside the six-pack in his refrigerator, and two new clear flutes beside his coffee mugs. Even now the jeweler's box was burning a hole in his hip pocket.

Tonight, he thought, he'd take the step. The words would come exactly as he planned. The music would be playing. She would open the box, look inside....

Her hands were draped with emeralds. He frowned, giving himself a little shake. That wasn't right. He hadn't bought her emeralds. But the image focused so clearly. Suzanna on her knees holding emeralds. Three glittering tiers flanked by icy diamonds and centered by a glowing tear-drop stone of dreamy green.

The Calhoun necklace. He felt the chill on his neck and ignored it. He'd seen the picture Max had found in the old library book. He knew what the emeralds looked like. It was the atmosphere, the humming silence and the flickering candles that made him think of them. That made him see them.

He didn't believe in visions. But when he closed his eyes to clear it from his mind, it seemed imprinted there. Suzanna kneeling on the floor with emeralds dripping from her fingers.

He felt a hand on his shoulder and looked around. There was no one there, only shadows and light thrown by the candles. But the feeling remained, with an urgency that had his hackles rising.

It was crazy, he told himself. And it was time to put an end to the whole insane business.

"Listen," he began. And the portrait of Bianca crashed to the floor.

Coco gave a piping squeak and jolted out of the chair. "Oh, my. Oh, my goodness," she murmured, patting her speeding heart.

Amanda was already racing forward. "Oh, I hope it isn't damaged."

"I don't think it will be." Lilah released Holt's hand. "Do you?"

The clear and steady gaze made him uncomfortable. Ignoring her, he turned to Suzanna. Her hand was like ice in his. "What is it? What's wrong?"

"Nothing." But she gave a quick shudder. "I think you'd better check the portrait."

He rose to go over where the others were crouched. As he did, Suzanna looked down the length of the table at her great-aunt. Colleen's white skin had paled like glass. Her eyes were dark and damp. Without a word, Suzanna rose and poured her a brandy. "It's going to be all right," she murmured, laying a hand on the thin shoulder.

"The frame cracked." Sloan ran a finger along it before he rose. "Funny that it would fall that way. Those nails are sturdy."

Holt started to shrug it off, but when he bent closer to where the frame had separated from the backing, he went very still. "There's something between the canvas and the back." Hefting the portrait, he laid it face-down on the table. "I need a knife."

Sloan pulled out his pocketknife and offered it. Holt made a long thin slit just beneath the cracked frame and slid out several sheets of paper.

"What is it?" The question was muffled as Coco had her hands pressed to her mouth.

"It's my grandfather's writing." The emotion sprang up strong and fast. It churned in Holt's eyes as he lifted them to Suzanna's. "It looks like a kind of diary. It's dated 1965."

"Sit down, dear." Coco put a comforting hand on his shoulder. "Trent, would you pour the brandy? I'll brew some tea for C.C."

He did need to sit, and he hoped the drink would steady him. For now, he could only stare at the papers and see his grandfather. Sitting on the back porch of the cottage, watching the water. Standing in his loft, slashing paint on canvas. Walking on the cliffs, telling a young boy stories.

When Suzanna came back to lay a hand on his, he turned his palm up and gripped her fingers. "It's been there all this time, and I didn't know."

"You weren't meant to know," she said quietly. "Until tonight." When he looked at her again, she curled her fingers tight around his. "Some things we just have to take on faith."

"Something happened tonight. Something upset you."

"I'll tell you. Not yet."

Composed, Coco brought in the tea, then took her seat. "Holt, whatever your grandfather wrote belongs to you. No one here will ask you to share it. If after you read it, you feel you prefer to keep it to yourself, we'll understand."

He glanced down at the papers again, then lifted the first sheet. "We'll read it together." He took a long breath, kept Suzanna's hand tight in his. " 'The moment I saw her, my life changed.' "

No one spoke as Holt read through his grandfather's memories. But around the table, hands linked again. There was no sound but his voice and the wind breathing through the trees outside the windows. When he was finished, the room remained silent.

Lilah spoke first, her voice thick with tears while others slid down her cheeks. "He never stopped loving her. Always, even though he made a life for himself, he loved her."

"How he must have felt, to come here that night and find out she was gone." Amanda leaned her head on Sloan's shoulder.

"But he was right." Suzanna watched one of her tears drop on the back of Holt's hand. "She didn't take her own life. She couldn't have. Not only did she love him too much, but she would have tolerated anything to protect her children."

"No, she didn't jump." Colleen whispered the words. She lifted her snifter with a trembling hand, then set it down again. "I've never spoken of that night, not to anyone. Through the years I've sometimes thought what I saw was a dream. A terrible, terrible nightmare."

Determined, she cleared her blurred vision and strengthened her voice. "He understood her, her Christian. He couldn't have written about her that way and not have known her heart. She was beautiful, but she was also kind and generous. I have never been loved as I was loved by my mother. And I have never hated as I hated my father."

She straightened her shoulders. Already the burden had lessened. "I was too young to understand her unhappiness or her desperation. In those days a man ruled his home, his family, as he chose. No one dared to question my father. But I remember the day she brought the puppy home, the little puppy my father would not have in his home. She did send us upstairs, but I hid at the top and listened. I had never heard her raise her voice to him before. Oh, she was valiant. And he was cruel. I didn't understand the names he called her. Then."

She paused to drink again, for her throat was dry and the memory bitter. "She defended me against him, knowing as even I knew he barely tolerated me, a female. When he left the house after the argument, I was glad. I prayed that night he would never come back. The next day, my mother told me we were going to take a trip. She hadn't told my brothers yet, but I was the eldest. She wanted me to understand that she would take care of us, that nothing bad would happen.

"Then, he came back. I knew she was upset, even frightened. I was to stay in my room until she came for me. But she didn't come. It grew late, and there was a storm. I wanted my mother." Colleen pressed her lips together. "She wasn't in her room, so I went up to the tower where she often spent her time. I heard them as I crept up the stairs. The door was open and I heard them. The terrible argument. He was raging, crazed with fury. She told him that she would no longer live with him, that she wanted nothing from him but her children and her freedom."

Because Colleen was shaking, Coco rose and walked down to take her hand.

"He struck her. I heard the slap and raced to the door. But I was afraid, too afraid to go in. She had a hand to her cheek, and her eyes were blazing. Not with fear, with fury. I will always remember that there was no fear in her at the end. He threatened her with scandal. He screamed at her that if she left his house, she would never lay eyes on any of his children again. She would never ruin his reputation. She would never throw an obstacle in the path of his ambitions."

Though her lips trembled, Colleen lifted her chin. "She did not beg. She did not weep. She hurled words back at him like thunderbolts." Fisting a hand, she pressed it to her mouth to smother her own tears. "She was magnificent. Her children would never be taken from her, and scandal be damned. Did he think she cared what people thought of her? Did he think she feared his power to have society shun her? She would take her children and she would make a life where both she and they could be loved. And I think it was that which drove him mad. The idea that she would choose another man over him. Over him. Fergus Calhoun. That she would toss his money and power and position back at him, rather than bow to his wishes. He grabbed her, lifting her from her feet, shaking her, screaming into her face while his own purpled with rage. I think I screamed then, and hearing me, she began to fight. When she struck him, he threw her aside. I heard the crash of the glass. He ran to it, roaring for her, but she was gone. How long he stood there while the wind and rain poured in, I don't know. When he turned his face was white, his eyes glazed. He walked past me without even seeing me. I went inside, over to the broken window and looked down until Nanny came and carried me away."

Coco pressed a kiss to the white hair, then gently stroked. "Come with me, dear. I'll take you upstairs. Lilah will bring you a nice cup of tea."

"Yes, I'll be right there." Lilah wiped her cheeks dry. "Max?"

"I'll come with you." He slipped an arm around her waist as Coco led Bianca's daughter from the room.

"Poor little girl," Suzanna murmured, and let her head rest on Holt's shoulder as he drove away from The Towers. "To have seen something so horrible, to have had to live with it all of her life. I think of Jenny—"

"Don't." He put a firm hand over hers. "You got out. Bianca didn't." He waited a moment. "You knew, didn't you? Before Colleen told us the story."

"I knew she hadn't committed suicide. I can't explain how, but tonight, I knew. It was as if she was standing right behind me."

He thought of the sensation of having a hand on his shoulder. "Maybe she was. After a night like this, it's hard for me to convince myself the picture falling off the wall was a coincidence."

Suzanna closed her eyes. "It was beautiful, what your grandfather wrote about her. If we never find the emeralds, we have that—we'll know she had that. To love that way," she said on a sigh. "It hardly seems possible. I don't want to think of the tragedy or sadness, but of the time they had together. Dancing in the wild roses."

He'd never danced with her in the sunlight, Holt thought. Or read her poetry or promised her eternal love.

When they reached the cottage, Sadie leaped out the back window of the car to race around the yard and sniff at the flower bed she'd planted for him. When Holt leaned across her, Suzanna looked down in surprise.

"What are you doing?"

"I'm opening the door for you." He shoved it open. "If I'd gotten out to do it, you wouldn't have waited."

Amused, Suzanna stepped out. "Thank you."

"You're welcome." When he reached the house, he unlocked the front door, then held that open. Keeping her face sober, Suzanna inclined her head as she slipped past him.

"Thank you."

Holt just let the screen slam shut. Brow lifted, Suzanna scanned the room.

"You've done something different."

"I cleaned it up," he muttered.

"Oh. It looks nice. You know, Holt, I've been meaning to ask you if you think Livingston is still on the island."

"Why? Did something happen?"

His response was much too abrupt, Suzanna noted and moved casually around the room. "No, I've just been wondering where he may be staying, what his next move might be." She ran a fingertip down one of the candles he'd bought. "Any ideas?"

"How should I know?"

"You're the expert on crime."

"And I told you to leave Livingston to me."

"And I told you I couldn't do that. Maybe I'll start poking around on my own."

"Try it and I'll handcuff you and lock you in a closet."

"The urban counterpart to hog-tying," she murmured. "I wouldn't have to try it if you'd tell me what you know. Or what you think."

"What brought this up now?"

She moved her shoulder. "Since we have a little time to ourselves, I thought we could talk about it."

"Look, why don't you just sit down?" He pulled out his lighter.

"What are you doing?"

"I'm lighting candles." His nerves were stretching like taffy. "What does it look like I'm doing?"

She did sit, and steepled her hands. "Since you're so cranky, I have to assume that you do know something."

"You don't have to assume anything except your ticking me off." He stalked to the stereo.

"How close are you?" she asked as a bluesy sax filled the air.

"I'm nowhere." Since that was a lie, he decided to temper it with part of the truth. "I think he's in the area because he broke in here and took a look around a couple weeks ago."

"What?" She catapulted out of the chair. "A couple of weeks ago, and you didn't tell me?"

"What were you going to do about it?" he countered. "Pull out a magnifying glass and deer-hunter's hat?"

"I had a right to know."

"Now you know. Just sit down, will you? I'll be back in a minute."

He stalked out and she began to pace. Holt knew more than he was saying, but at least she'd annoyed a piece from him. Livingston was close, close enough that he'd known Holt might have something of interest. The fact that Holt was wound like a top at the moment made her think something more was working on him. It shouldn't be difficult, she thought, now that she already had him irritated, to push a little more out of him.

The candles were scented, she noted, and smiled to herself. She couldn't imagine that he'd bought jasmine candles on purpose. Especially a half a dozen of them. She traced a finger over the calla lilies he'd stuck—not very artistically—in a vase. Maybe working with flowers was getting to him, she thought. He wasn't pretending so hard not to like them.

When he came back in, she smiled then looked puzzled. "Is that champagne?"

"Yeah." And he was thoroughly disgusted. He'd imagined she'd be charmed. Instead she questioned everything. "Do you want some or not?"

"Sure." The curt invitation was so typical she didn't take offense. After he'd poured, she tapped her glass absently against his. "Now, if you're sure it was Livingston who broke in, I think—"

"One more word," he said with dangerous calm. "One more word about Livingston and I'll pour the rest of the bottle over your hard head."

She sipped, knowing she'd have to be careful if she didn't want to waste a bottle of champagne and end up with sticky hair. "I'm only trying to get a clear picture."

He let out what was close to a roar of frustration and spun away. Champagne sloshed over his glass as he paced. "She wants a clear picture, and she's blind as a bat. I shoveled two months' worth of dust out of this place. I bought candles and flowers. I had to listen to some jerk try to teach me about wine. That's the picture, damn it."

She'd wanted to irritate information from him, not infuriate him. "Holt—"

"Just sit down and shut up. I should have known this would get screwed up. God knows why I tried to do it this way."

A light dawned, and she smiled. He'd set the stage, but she'd been too focused on her own scheme to take note. "Holt, it's very sweet of you to do all of this. I'm sorry if I didn't seem to appreciate it. If you wanted me to come here tonight so we could make love—"

"I don't want to make love with you." He swore, viciously. "Of course I want to make love with you, but that's not it. I'm trying to ask you to marry me, damn it, so will you sit *down!*"

Since her legs had dissolved from knees to toe, she slid into a chair.

"This is perfect." He gulped down champagne and started pacing again. "Just perfect. I'm trying to tell you that I'm crazy about you, that I don't think I can live without you, and all you can do is ask me what I'm doing and nag me about some obsessed jewel thief."

Cautiously she brought the glass to her lips. "Sorry."

"You should be sorry," he said bitterly. "I was ready to make a fool of myself tonight for you, and you won't even let me do that. I've been in love with you nearly half my life. Even when I moved away, I couldn't get you out of my mind. You spoiled every other woman for me. I'd start to get close to someone, and then...they weren't you. They just weren't you, and I'd never even gotten past your back door."

In love. The two words reeled in her head. *In love.* "I thought you didn't even like me."

"I couldn't stand you." He raked his free hand through his hair. "Every time I looked at you I wanted you so much I couldn't breathe. My mouth would go dry and my stomach would knot, and you'd just smile and keep walking." His dark and turbulent eyes locked on hers. "I wanted to strangle you. You run into me and knock me off my bike and I'm lying there bleeding and—and mortified. You're leaning over me, smelling like heaven and running your hands over me to see if anything was broken. One more minute of that and I'd have dragged you onto the asphalt with me." He rubbed his hand over his face. "Lord, you were only sixteen."

"You swore at me."

His face was a picture of anger and disgust. "Damn right, I swore at you. You were better off with that than with what I wanted to do to you." He was calming, little by little. He sipped again but kept pacing. "I talked myself into believing it was just an adolescent fantasy. Even a crush, and that was tough to swallow. Then you came walking across my yard. I looked at you and my throat went dry, my stomach knotted up. We were both past being adolescents."

He set his glass down, noting that she was gripping hers with both hands. Her eyes were huge and fixed on his. Cursing both of them, he fumbled for a cigarette then tossed it aside.

"I'm not good at this, Suzanna. I thought I could pull it off. Set the mood, you know? And after you'd had enough champagne, I'd convince you I could make you happy."

She couldn't relax her grip. She tried but couldn't. "I don't need champagne and candlelight, Holt."

He smiled a little. "Babe, you were born for it. I could lie to you and tell you I'll remember to give it to you every night. But I won't."

She looked down at her glass and wondered if she was ready to take this sort of chance again. Loving him was one thing. Being loved by him was incredible. But marriage... "Why don't you just tell me the truth then?"

He walked over to sit on the arm of the couch and face her. "I love you. I've never felt about anyone the way I feel about you. Whatever happens, I'll never feel like this about anyone else again. There's no taking back what's happened to either of us in the last few years, but maybe we can make things better for both of us. For the kids."

Her eyes changed, darkened. "It may never be easy. Bax would always be their legal father."

"He wouldn't be the one who loved them." When her eyes filled, he shook his head. No, she hadn't needed candlelight and champagne to make her vulnerable and open to his needs. Only a mention of her children. "I won't use them to get to you. I know I could, but first it has to be between you and me. Maybe I'm stuck on them, and I want to—I think I could be pretty good at being their father, but I don't want you to marry me for them."

She took a deep breath. Odd, her fingers had relaxed on the stem of the glass without her being aware. "I never wanted to love anyone again. And I certainly never wanted to get married." Her lips curved. "Until you." Setting the glass aside, she reached for his hand. "I can't claim to have loved you as long, but you couldn't love me more than I love you."

He didn't settle for her hand, but pulled her into his arms. When he at last managed to tear his mouth from hers, he buried his face in her hair. "Don't tell me you need to think about it, Suzanna."

"I don't need to think about it." She couldn't remember the last time her heart and mind had been so at peace. "I'll marry you."

Before the words were out of her mouth, she was tumbling with him onto the couch. She was laughing as they tugged at each other's clothes, laughing still when the frantic movements sent them rolling onto the floor.

"I knew it." She nipped his bare shoulder. "You did bring me here to make love."

"Can I help it if you can't keep your hands off me?" He trailed a necklace of quick kisses around her throat.

She smiled, tilting her head to give him easy access. "Holt, did you really think about pulling me down on the street after you'd fallen off your bike."

"After you'd run into me," he corrected, nuzzling her ear. "Yeah. Let me show you what I had in mind."

Later they lay like rag dolls on the floor, a tangle of limbs. When she could manage it, she lifted her head from his chest. "It was much better that we didn't try that twelve years ago."

Lazily he opened his eyes. She was smiling down at him, her hair brushing his shoulders, the candlelight glowing in her eyes. "Much better. I wouldn't have had any skin left on my back."

She chuckled then shifted to trace the shape of his face. "You always scared me a little. Looking so dark and dangerous. And, of course, the girls used to talk about you."

"Oh, yeah? What did they say?"

"I'll tell you when you're sixty. You could probably use it then." He pinched her, but she only laughed then rested her cheek on his. "When you're sixty, we'll be an old married couple with grandchildren."

He liked the thought of it. "And you still won't be able to keep your hands off me."

"And I'll remind you of the night you asked me to marry you, when you gave me flowers and candlelight, then shouted at me and raged up and down the room, making me love you even more."

"If that's all it takes, you'll be delirious about me by the time I'm sixty."

"I already am." She lowered her mouth to his.

"Suzanna." He drew her closer, started to roll her under him, then swore. "It's your own fault," he said as he nudged her aside.

"What?"

"You were supposed to be sitting over there, dazed by my romantic abilities." He fought to untangle his jeans and pull the jeweler's box from the pocket. "Then I was going to get down on one knee."

Eyes wide, she stared at the box, then at him. "You were not."

"Yes, I was. I was going to feel like an idiot, but I was going to do it. You've got no one to blame but yourself that we're lying naked on the floor. Here."

"You bought me a ring," she whispered.

"There could be a frog in there for all you know." Impatient with her, he flipped up the top himself. "I didn't want to give you diamonds." He shrugged when she said nothing, only stared into the box. "I figured you'd already had those. I thought about emeralds, but those are something you will have. And this is more like your eyes."

When the tears blurred her vision, the light refracted. There were diamonds, tiny, lovely stones in a heart shape about the deep and brilliant sapphire. They weren't cold, as the ones she had sold, but warmed by the rich blue fire they encircled.

Holt watched the first tear fall with a great deal of discomfort. "If you don't like it, we can take it back. You can pick out what you want."

"It's beautiful." She dashed a tear away with the back of her hand. "I'm sorry. I hate to cry. It's just so beautiful, and you bought it for me because you love me. And when I put it on—" she lifted drenched eyes to his "—I'm yours."

He dropped his brow to hers. Those were the words he'd wanted. The ones he'd needed. Taking the ring from the box, he slipped it onto her finger. "You're mine." He kissed her fingers, then her lips. "I'm yours." Bringing her close again, he remembered his grandfather's words. "Eternally."

Chapter Twelve

Suzanna took the children to the shop with her in the morning. She couldn't tell the rest of her family the news until she'd gauged Alex's and Jenny's feelings. The day was bright and hot. Knowing it would be a busy one, she arrived a full hour before opening. Because they wanted to check the herbs they had planted, she took them into the greenhouse to look at the tender shoots.

She let them argue for a while over whose plants would be the biggest or the best, supervising as they gave the shoots their morning drink.

"Do you guys like Holt?" she asked casually, nerves drumming.

"He's neat." Alex was tempted to turn the sprayer on his sister, but he'd gotten in trouble the last time he'd indulged himself.

"He plays with us sometimes." Jenny danced from foot to foot, waiting her turn. "I like when he throws me up in the air."

"I like him, too." Suzanna relaxed a little.

"Does he throw you up in the air?" Jenny wanted to know.

"No." With a laugh, Suzanna ruffled her hair.

"He could. He's got big muscles." Reluctantly Alex passed the sprayer to his sister. "He let me feel them." Screwing up his face, Alex flexed his own. Obliging, Suzanna pinched the tiny biceps.

"Wow. You're pretty tough."

"That's what he said."

"I was wondering..." Suzanna wiped nervous hands on her jeans. "How would you feel if he lived with us, all the time?"

"That'd be good," Jenny decided. "He plays with us even when we don't ask."

One down, Suzanna thought and turned to her son. "Alex?"

He shuffled his feet, frowning a little. "Are you going to get married like C.C. and Amanda?"

Sharp little devil, she thought, and crouched down. "I was thinking about it. What do you think?"

"Do I have to wear a dumb tuxedo again?"

She smiled and stroked his cheek. "Probably."

"Is he going to be our uncle, like Trent and Sloan and Max?" Jenny asked.

Suzanna got up to turn off the spray before answering her daughter. "No. He'd be your stepfather."

Brother and sister exchanged looks. "Would he still like us?"

"Of course he would, Jenny."

"Would we have to go away and live someplace else?"

She sighed and combed a hand through Alex's hair. "No. He would come to live with us at The Towers, or maybe we'd go and live with him at his cottage. We'd be a family."

Alex thought it over. "Would he be Kevin's stepfather, too?"

"No." She had to kiss him. "Megan's Kevin's mom, and maybe one day she'll fall in love and get married. Then Kevin will have a father."

"Did you fall in love with Holt?" Jenny asked.

"Yes, I did." She felt Alex shift uncomfortably and smiled. "I'd like to marry him so we could all live together. But Holt and I both wanted to see how you felt about it."

"I like him," Jenny announced. "He lets me ride on his shoulders."

Alex shrugged, a bit more cautious. "Maybe it's okay."

Concerned, Suzanna rose. "We can talk about it some more. Let's go set up."

They stepped out of the greenhouse just as Holt pulled up in the graveled lot. He knew he'd told her he'd wait until lunchtime, but he hadn't been able to. He'd awakened realizing he'd rather face another alley than those two kids who could so easily reject him. He stuffed his hands into his pockets and tried to look casual.

"Hi."

"Hi." Suzanna wanted to reach out to him, but her children held her hands.

"I thought I'd drop by and . . . how's it going?"

Jenny gave him a shy smile and huddled closer to her mother. "Mom says you're going to get married and be our stepfather and live with us."

Holt had to knock back an urge to shuffle his feet. "That's the plan."

Alex tightened his fingers around Suzanna's as he stared up at Holt. "Are you going to yell at us?"

After a quick glance at Suzanna, Holt stooped down until he was eye to eye with the boy. "Maybe. If you need it."

Alex trusted that answer more than he would have an unqualified no. "Do you hit?" He remembered the swats he'd received during his vacation. They'd insulted more than hurt, but he still resented it.

Holt put a hand under the boy's chin and held it firm. "No," he said, and the look in his eyes made Alex believe. "But I might hang you up by your thumbs, or boil you in oil. If I get really mad, I'll stake you to an anthill."

Alex's lips twitched, but he wasn't finished with the interrogation. "Are you going to make Mom cry like he did?"

"Alex," Suzanna began, but Holt cut her off.

"I might sometimes, if I'm stupid. But not on purpose. I love her a lot, so I want to make her happy. Sometimes I might screw up."

Alex frowned and considered. "Are you going to do all that kissing stuff? Since Trent and Sloan and Max came, there's always kissing."

"Yeah." Holt's face relaxed into a smile. "I'm going to do all that kissing stuff."

"But you won't like it," Alex said, hopeful. "You'll just do it 'cause Mom likes it."

"Sorry, I like it, too."

"Jeez," Alex muttered, deflated.

"Do it now." Jenny danced and giggled. "Do it now so I can see."

Willing to oblige, Holt straightened and pulled Suzanna close. When he took his lips from Suzanna's, Alex was red faced and Jenny was clapping. "I hate to tell you," Holt said soberly. "but one day you'll like it, too."

"Uh-uh. I'd rather eat dirt."

With a laugh, Holt hoisted him up, relieved and delighted when Alex slung a friendly arm around his neck. "Tell me that in ten years."

"I like it," Jenny insisted, and tugged on his leg. "I like it now. Kiss me." He hauled her in his other arm and kissed her tiny, waiting lips. She smiled, big blue eyes beaming. "You kissed Mom different."

"That's 'cause she's the mom and you're the kid."

She liked the way he smelled, the way his arm supported her. When she rubbed a hand over his cheek, she was a little disappointed that it was smooth today. "Can I call you Daddy?" she asked, and Holt felt his heart lurch in his chest.

"I—ah—sure. If you want."

"Daddy's for babies," Alex said in disgust. "But you can be Dad."

"Okay." He looked over at Suzanna. "Okay."

Holt wished he could have spent the day with them, but there were things that had to be done. He had a family now—it still dazed him—and he meant to protect them. He'd already put in calls to his contacts in Portland and was awaiting the rundowns on the four names from Trent's list. While he waited, he put in calls to the Department of Motor Vehicles, the credit bureau and the Internal Revenue, stretching it a bit by giving his old badge number and rank.

Between information and instinct, he whittled the four names down to two. While he waited for another call back, he read over his grandfather's diary.

He understood the feelings beneath the words, the longing, the devotion. He understood the rage his grandfather had felt when he'd learned the woman he loved had suffered abuse by the hands of the man she'd married. Was it coincidence or fate that his relationship with Suzanna had so many similarities to that of their ancestors? At least this time, the tale would have a happy ending.

Suzanna's diamonds, he thought, drumming his fingers on the pages. Bianca's emeralds. Suzanna had hidden her jewels, the one material thing she felt belonged to her from the marriage, as security for her children. He had to believe Bianca had done the same.

So, where was the equivalent of Jenny's diaper bag? he wondered.

When the phone rang, he snatched it up on the first ring. Before he hung up again, Holt had little doubt he had his man. Going into the bedroom, he checked his weapon, balancing the familiar weight in his hand. He strapped it to his calf.

Fifteen minutes later, he was walking through the chaos of construction in the west wing. He found Sloan in what was a nearly completed two-level suite. There was a smell of new lumber and male sweat. Sloan, in a tool belt and jeans, was supervising the construction of a new staircase.

"I didn't know architects swung hammers," Holt commented.

Sloan grinned. "I got a personal interest in this job."

Nodding, Holt scanned the crew. "Which one's Marshall?"

Alerted, Sloan unbuckled the tool belt. "He's up on the next level."

"I'd like to have a little talk with him."

Sloan's eyes flashed, but he merely nodded again. "I'll go with you." He waited until they were out of range of the crew. "You think he's the one?"

"Robert Marshall didn't apply for a Maine driver's license until six weeks ago. He's never paid taxes under the name and social security number he's using. Employers don't usually check with the DMV or IRS when they hire a laborer."

Sloan swore and flexed his fingers. He could still see Amanda racing along the terrace pursued by a man holding a gun. "I get first crack at him."

"I appreciate the sentiment, but you'll have to strap it in."

The hell he would, Sloan thought, and signaled the foreman. "Marshall," he said briefly.

"Bob?" The foreman pulled out a bandanna to wipe his neck. "You just missed him. I had him drive Rick into Emergency. Rick took a pretty good slice out of his thumb, figured he needed stitches."

"How long ago?" Holt demanded.

"'Bout twenty minutes, I guess. Told them to take the rest of the day, since we're knocking off at four." He stuffed the bandanna back into his pocket. "Problem?"

"No." Sloan bit down on temper. "Let me know if Rick's okay."

"Sure thing." He shouted at one of the carpenters, then lumbered off.

"I need an address," Holt said.

"Trent's got the paperwork." They started out. "Are you going to turn it over to Lieutenant Koogar?"

"No," Holt said simply.

"Good."

They found Trent in the office he'd thrown together on the first floor, a stack of files at his fingertips, a phone at his ear. He took one look at the two men. "I'll get back to you," he said into the phone and hung up. "Who is it?"

"He's using the name Robert Marshall." Holt pulled out a cigarette. "Foreman let him go early. I want an address."

Saying nothing, Trent crossed to a file cabinet to pull out a folder. "Max is upstairs. He has a stake in this, too."

Holt skimmed the information in Marshall's file. "Then get him. We'll do this together."

The apartment Marshall had listed was on the edge of the village. The woman who opened the door after Holt's third booming knock was bent and withered and out of sorts.

"What? What?" she demanded. "I'm not buying any encyclopedias or vacuum cleaners."

"We're looking for Robert Marshall," Holt told her.

"Who? Who?" She peered through the thick lenses of her glasses.

"Robert Marshall," he repeated.

"I don't know any Marshalls," she grumbled. "There's a McNeilly next door and a Mitchell down below, but no Marshalls. I don't want to buy any insurance, either."

"We're not selling anything," Trent said in his most patient voice. "We're looking for a man named Robert Marshall who lives at this address."

"I told you there's no Marshalls here. I live here. Lived here for fifteen years, since that worthless clot I married passed on and left me with nothing but bills. I know you," she said abruptly, pointing a gnarled finger at Sloan. "Saw your picture in the paper." Reaching to the table beside the door, she hefted an iron bookend. "You robbed a bank."

"No, ma'am." Later, Sloan thought, much later, he might find the whole business amusing. "I married Amanda Calhoun."

The woman held on to the bookend while she considered. "One of the Calhoun girls. That's right. The youngest one—no, not the youngest one, the next one." Satisfied, she set the bookend down again. "Well, what do you want?"

"Robert Marshall," Holt said again. "He gave this building and this apartment as his address."

"Then he's a liar or a fool, because I've lived here for fifteen years ever since that no-account husband of mine caught pneumonia and died. Here one day, gone the next." She snapped her bent fingers. "And good riddance."

Thinking it was a dead end, Holt glanced at Sloan. "Give her a description."

"He's about thirty, six feet tall, trim, black hair, shoulder length, big droopy moustache."

"Don't know him. The boy downstairs, the Pierson boy's got hair past his shoulders. A disgrace if you ask me. Bleaches it, too, just like a girl. He's no more'n sixteen. You'd think his mother would make him cut that hair, but no. Plays the music so loud I have to bang on the floor."

"Excuse me," Max put in and described the man he had known as Ellis Caufield.

"Sounds like my nephew. Lives in Rochester with his second wife. Sells used cars."

"Thanks." Holt wasn't surprised the thief had given a phony address, but he was annoyed. As they came out of the building, he dug a quarter from his pocket.

"I guess we wait until morning," Max was saying. "He doesn't know we're onto him, so he'll show up for work."

"I'm finished waiting." Holt headed for a phone booth. After dropping in the coin, he punched in numbers. "This is Detective Sergeant Bradford, Portland P.D., badge number 7375. I need a cross-check." He reeled off the phone number from Marshall's file. Then he held on with a cop's patience while the operator set her computer to work. "Thanks." He hung up and turned to the three men. "Bar Island," he said. "We'll take my boat."

While their men prepared to sail across the bay, the Calhoun women met in Bianca's tower. "So," Amanda began, pad and pencil at the ready. "What do we know?"

"Trent's been cross-checking the personnel files," C.C. supplied. "He claimed there was some hitch in withholding taxes, but that's bull."

"Interesting," Lilah mused. "Max stopped me from going over to the west wing this morning. I'd wanted to see how things were going, and he made all kinds of lame excuses why I shouldn't distract the men while they were working."

"And Sloan shoved a couple of files into a drawer, and locked it when I came into the room last night." Amanda tapped her pencil on the pad. "Why wouldn't they want us to know if they're checking up on the crews?"

"I think I have an idea," Suzanna said slowly. She'd been chewing it over most of the day. "Last night I found out that Holt's cottage had been broken into and searched."

Her three sisters pounced on that, hammering her with questions.

"Just wait." She lifted a hand. "He was irritated with me, which is why it came out. He was even more irritated that it had. But he did tell me, because he wanted to scare me into backing off, that he was certain it was Livingston."

"Which means," Amanda concluded, "that our old friend knows Holt's connected. Who else knows besides us?" In her organized way, she began to list names.

"Oh, stop fussing," Lilah said with a negligent wave of her hand. "No one knows except the family. None of us have mentioned it outside of this house."

"Maybe he found out the same way Max did," C.C. suggested. "From the library."

"Max checked out the books." Lilah shook her head. "Maybe he found the information in the papers he stole from us."

"It's possible." Amanda noted it down. "But he's had the papers for weeks. When did he break into the cottage?"

"A couple weeks ago, but I don't think he made the connection that way. I think he got it from us."

There was an instant argument. Suzanna stood, throwing up both hands to cut it off. "Listen, we're agreed that none of us have discussed this outside of the house. And we're agreed that the men are trying to keep us from finding out they're checking out the crews. Which means—"

"Which means," Amanda interrupted and shut her eyes. "The bastard's working for us. Like a fly on the wall, so he can pick up little pieces of information, poke around the house. We're so used to seeing guys hauling lumber, we wouldn't give him a second look."

"I think Holt already came to that conclusion." Suzanna lifted her hands again. "The question is, what do we do about it?"

"We give the construction boys a thrill tomorrow, and visit the west wing." Lilah straightened from the window seat. "I don't care what he's made himself look like this time, I'll know him if I get close enough." With that settled, she sat back. "Now, Suzanna, why don't you tell us when bad boy Bradford asked you to marry him?"

Suzanna grinned. "How did you know?"

"For an ex-cop, he's got great taste in jewelry." She took Suzanna's hand to show off the ring to her other sisters.

"Last night," she said as she was hugged and kissed and wept over. "We told the kids this morning."

"Aunt Coco's going to go through the roof." C.C. gave Suzanna another squeeze. "All four of us in a matter of months. She'll be in matchmaker heaven."

"All we need now is to get that creep behind bars and find the emeralds." Amanda dashed a tear away. "Oh, no! Do you realize what this means?"

"It means you have to organize another wedding," Suzanna answered.

"Not just that. It means we're going to be stuck with Aunt Colleen at least until the last handful of rice gets tossed."

Holt returned to The Towers in a foul mood. They'd found the house. Empty. They had no doubt that Livingston was living there. Bending the law more than a little, he had broken in and given the place as meticulous a search as Livingston had given his cottage. They'd found the stolen

Calhoun papers, the lists the thief had made and a copy of the original blueprints of The Towers.

They'd also found a typed copy of each woman's weekly schedule, along with handwritten comments that left no doubt as to the fact that Livingston had followed and observed each one of them. There was a well-ordered inventory of the rooms he had searched and the items he'd felt valuable enough to steal.

They had waited an hour for his return, then uneasy about leaving the women alone, had phoned in the information to Koogar. While the police staked out the rented house on Bar Island, Holt and his companions returned to The Towers.

It was only a matter of waiting now. That was something he had learned to do well in his years on the force. But now it wasn't a job, and every moment grated.

"Oh, my dear, dear boy." Coco flew at him the moment he stepped into the house. He caught her by her sturdy hips as she covered his face with kisses.

"Hey," was all he could manage as she wept against his shoulder. Her hair, he noted, was no longer gleaming black but fire-engine red. "What'd you do to your hair?"

"Oh, it was time for a change." She drew back to blow her nose into her hankie, then fell into his arms again. Helpless, he patted her back and looked at the grinning men around him for assistance.

"It looks okay," he assured her, wondering if that was what she was weeping about. "Really."

"You like it?" She pulled back again, fluffing at it. "I thought I needed a bit of dash, and red's so cheerful." She buried her face in the soggy hankie. "I'm so happy," she sobbed. "So very happy. I had hoped, you see. And the tea leaves indicated that it would all work out, but I couldn't help but worry. She's had such a dreadful time, and her sweet little babies, too. Now everything's going to be all right. I'd thought it might be Trent, but he and C.C. were so perfect. Then Sloan and Amanda. Then almost before I could blink, our dear Max and Lilah. Is it any wonder I'm overwhelmed?"

"I guess not."

"To think, all those years ago when you'd bring lobsters to the back door. And that time you changed a tire for me and were too proud to even let me thank you. And now, now, you're going to marry my baby."

"Congratulations." Trent grinned and slapped Holt on the back while Max dug out a fresh handkerchief for Coco.

"Welcome to the family." Sloan offered a hand. "I guess you know what you're getting into."

Holt studied the weeping Coco. "I'm getting the picture."

"Stop all that caterwauling." Colleen clumped down the stairs. "I could hear you wailing all the way up in my room. For heaven's sake, take that mess into the kitchen." She gestured with her cane. "Pour some tea into her until she pulls herself together. Out, all of you," she added. "I want to talk to this boy here."

Like rats deserting a sinking ship, Holt thought as they left him alone. Gesturing for him to follow, Colleen strode into the parlor.

"So, you think you're going to marry my grand-niece."

"No. I am going to marry her."

She sniffed. Damned if she didn't like the boy. "I'll tell you this, if you don't do better by her than that scum she had before, you'll answer to me." She settled into a chair. "What are your prospects?"

"My what?"

"Your prospects," she said impatiently. "Don't think you're going to latch on to my money when you latch on to her."

His eyes narrowed, pleasing her. "You can take your money and—"

"Very good," she said with an approving nod. "How do you intend to keep her?"

"She doesn't need to be kept." He whirled around the room. "And she doesn't need you or anyone else poking into her business. She's managed just fine on her own, better than fine. She came out of hell and managed to put her life together, take care of the kids and start a business. The only thing that's going to change is that she's going to stop working herself into the ground, and the kids'll have someone who wants to be their father. Maybe I won't be able to give her diamonds and take her to fancy dinner parties, but I'll make her happy."

Colleen tapped her fingers on the head of her cane. "You'll do. If your grandfather was anything like you, it's no wonder my mother loved him. So…" She started to rise, then saw the portrait over the mantel. Where her father's stern face had been was her mother's lovely one. "What's that doing there?"

Holt dipped his hands into his pockets. "It seemed to me that was where it belonged. That's where my grandfather would have wanted it."

Colleen eased herself back into the chair. "Thank you." Her voice was strained, but her eyes remained fierce. "Now go away. I want to be alone."

He left her, amazed that he was growing fond of her. Though he didn't look forward to another scene, he started toward the kitchen to ask Coco where he could find Suzanna.

But he found her himself, following the music that drifted down the hall. She was sitting at a piano, playing some rich, haunting melody he didn't recognize. Though the music was sad, there was a smile on her lips and one in her eyes. When she looked up, her fingers stilled, but the smile remained.

"I didn't know you played."

"We all had lessons. I was the only one they stuck with." She reached out a hand for his. "I was hoping we'd have a minute alone, so I could tell you how wonderful you were with the kids this morning."

With his fingers meshed with hers, he studied the ring he'd given her. "I was nervous." He laughed a little. "I didn't know how they'd take it.

When Jenny asked if she could call me Daddy...it's funny how fast you can fall in love. Suzanna." He kept toying with her hands, studying the ring. "I think I understand now what a parent would feel, what he'd go through to make sure his kids were safe. I'd like to have more. I know you'd need to think about it, and I don't want you to feel that I would care less about Alex and Jenny."

"I don't have to think about it." She pressed a kiss to his cheek. "I've always wanted a big family."

He drew her close so her head rested on his shoulder. "Suzanna, do you know where the nursery was when Bianca lived here?"

"On the third floor of the east wing. It's been used as a storeroom as long as I can remember." She straightened. "You think she hid the necklace there?"

"I think she hid them somewhere Fergus wouldn't look, and I can't see him spending a lot of time in the nursery."

"No, but you'd think someone would have come across them. I don't know why I say that," she corrected. "The place is filled with boxes and old furniture. The Tower's version of a garage sale."

"Show me."

It was worse than he'd imagined. Even overlooking the cobwebs and dust, it was a mess. Boxes, crates, rolled-up rugs, broken tables, shadeless lamps stood, sat or reclined over every inch of space. Speechless, he turned to Suzanna who offered a sheepish grin.

"A lot of stuff collects in eighty-odd years," she told him. "Most of what's valuable's been culled out, and a lot of that was sold when we were—well, when things were difficult. This floor's been closed off for a long time, since we couldn't afford to heat it. We had to concentrate on keeping up the living space. Once we got everything under some kind of control, we were going to kind of attack the other sections a room at a time."

"You need a bulldozer."

"No, just time and elbow grease. We had plenty of the latter, but not nearly enough of the former. Over the last couple of months, we've gone through a lot of the old rooms, inch by inch, but it's a slow process."

"Then we might as well get started."

They worked for two grueling and dirty hours. They found a tattered parasol, an amazing collection of nineteenth-century erotica, a trunk full of musty clothes from the twenties and a box of warped phonograph records. There was also a crate filled with toys, a miniature locomotive, a sad, faded rag doll, assorted yo-yos and tops. Among them were a set of lovely old fairy-tale prints that Suzanna set aside.

"For our nursery," she told him. "Look." She held up a yellow christening gown. "It might have been my grandfather's."

"You'd have thought this stuff would have been packed up with more care."

"I don't think Fergus ran a very tidy household after Bianca died. If any of this stuff belonged to his children, I'd wager the nanny bundled it away. He wouldn't have cared enough."

"No." He pulled a cobweb out of her hair. "Listen, why don't you take a break?"

"I'm fine."

It was useless to remind her that she'd been working all day, so he used another tactic. "I could use a drink. You think Coco's got anything cold in the refrigerator—maybe a sandwich to go with it?"

"Sure. I'll go check."

He knew that her aunt would insist on putting the quick meal together, and Suzanna would get that much time to sit and do nothing. "Two sandwiches," he added, and kissed her.

"Right." She rose, stretching her back. "It's sad to think about those three children, lying in here at night knowing their mother wasn't going to come and tuck them in again. Speaking of which, I'd better tuck in my own before I come back."

"Take your time." He was already headfirst in another crate.

She started out, thinking wistfully of Bianca's babies. Little Sean, who'd barely have been toddling, Ethan, who would grow up to father her father, Colleen, who was even now downstairs surely finding fault with something Coco had done. How the woman had ever been a sweet little girl . . .

A little girl, Suzanna thought, stopping on the second-floor landing. The oldest girl who would have been five or six when her mother died. Suzanna detoured and knocked on her great-aunt's door.

"Come in, damn it. I'm not getting up."

"Aunt Colleen." She stepped, amused to see the old woman was engrossed in a romance novel. "I'm sorry to disturb you."

"Why? No one else is."

Suzanna bit the tip of her tongue. "I was just wondering, the summer . . . that last summer, were you still in the nursery with your brothers?"

"I wasn't a baby, no need for a nursery."

"So you had your own room," Suzanna prompted, struggling to contain the excitement. "Near the nursery?"

"At the other end of the east wing. There was the nursery, then Nanny's room, the children's bath, and the three rooms kept for children of guests. I had the corner room at the top of the stairs." She frowned down at her book. "The next summer, I moved into one of the guest rooms. I didn't want to sleep in the room my mother had decorated for me, knowing she wouldn't come back to it."

"I'm sorry. When Bianca told you that you were going away, did she come to your room?"

"Yes. She let me pick out a few of my favorite dresses, then she packed them herself."

"Then after—I suppose they were unpacked again."

"I never wore those dresses again. I never wanted to. Shoved the trunk under my bed."

"I see." So there was hope. "Thank you."

"Moth-eaten by now," Colleen grumbled as Suzanna went out again. She thought of her favorite white muslin with its blue satin sash and with a sigh got up to walk to the terrace.

Dusk was coming early, she thought. Storm brewing. She could smell it in the wind, see it in the bad-tempered clouds already blocking the sun.

Suzanna raced up the stairs again. The sandwiches would have to wait. She pushed open the door of Colleen's old room. It too had been consigned to storage, but being smaller than the nursery wasn't as cramped. The wallpaper, perhaps the same that Bianca had picked for her daughter, was faded and spotted, but Suzanna could still see the delicate pattern of rosebuds and violets.

She didn't bother with the cases or boxes, but dragged or pushed them aside. She was looking for a traveling trunk, suitable for a young girl. What better place? she thought as she pushed aside a crate marked Winter Draperies. Fergus hadn't cared for his daughter. He would hardly have bothered to look through a trunk of dresses, particularly when that trunk had been shoved out of sight by a traumatized young girl.

It had no doubt been opened in later years. Perhaps someone—Suzanna's own mother?—had shaken out a dress or two, then finding them quaint but useless, had designated them to storage.

It could be anywhere, of course, she mused. But what better place to start than the source?

Her heart pounded dully as she stumbled across an old leather-strapped truck. Pulling it open, she found bolts of material carefully folded in tissue. But no little girl's dresses. And no emeralds.

Because the light was growing dim, she rose and started toward the door. She would get Holt, and a flashlight, before continuing. In the gloom, she rapped her shin sharply. Swearing, she looked down and saw the small trunk.

It had once been a glistening white, but now it was dull with age and dust. It had been shoved to the side, piled with other boxes and nearly hidden by them and a faded tapestry. Kneeling in the half-light, Suzanna uncovered it. She flexed her unsteady fingers then opened the lid.

There was a smell of lavender, sealed inside perhaps for decades. She lifted the first dress, a frilly white muslin, going ivory with time and banded by a faded blue satin sash. Suzanna set it carefully aside and drew out another. There were leggings and ribbons, pretty bows and a lacy nightie. And there, at the bottom, beside a small stuffed bear, a box and a book.

Suzanna put a trembling hand to her lips, then slowly reached down to lift the book.

Her journal, she thought as tears misted her eyes. Bianca's journal. Hardly daring to breathe, she turned the first page.

Bar Harbor June 12, 1912
I saw him on the cliffs, overlooking Frenchman Bay

Suzanna let out an unsteady breath and laid the book in her lap. This was not for her to read alone. It would wait for her family. Heart pounding, she reached down to take the box from the trunk. She knew before she opened it. She could feel the change in the room, the trembling of the air. As the first tear slid down her cheek, she opened the lid and uncovered Bianca's emeralds.

They pulsed like green suns, throbbing with life and passion. She lifted the necklace, the glorious three tiers, and felt the heat on her hands. Hidden eighty years before, in hope and desperation, they were now free. The gloom that filled the room was no match for them.

As she knelt, the necklace dripping from her fingers, she reached into the box and took out the matching earrings. Strange, she thought. She'd all but forgotten them. They were lovely, exquisite, but the necklace dominated. It was made to dominate.

Stunned, she stared down at the power in her hands. They weren't just gems, she realized. They were far from being simply beautiful stones. They were Bianca's passions and hopes and dreams. From the time she had placed them in the box until now, when they had been lifted out by her descendant, they had waited to see the light again.

"Oh, Bianca."

"A charming sight."

Her head jerked up at the voice. He stood in the doorway, hardly more than a shadow. When he stepped into the room, she saw the glint of the gun in his hand.

"Patience pays off," Livingston said. "I watched you and the cop go into the room down the hall. I've been losing quite a bit of sleep wandering these rooms at night."

As he came closer, she stared at him. He didn't look like the man she remembered. His coloring was wrong, even the shape of his face. She rose very slowly, clutching the book and earrings in one hand, the necklace in the other.

"You don't recognize me. But I know you. I know all of you. You're Suzanna, just one of the Calhouns who owes me quite a bit."

"I don't know what you're talking about."

"Three months of my time, and not a little trouble. Then there was the loss of Hawkins, of course. He wasn't much of a partner, but he was mine. Just as those are mine." He looked down at the necklace and his mouth watered. They dazzled him. More than he had dreamed, more than he had imagined. Everything he wanted. His fingers trembled lightly on the gun as he reached out. Suzanna jerked away. He lifted a brow. "Do you really think you can keep them from me? They're meant to be mine. And when they are, everything they are will be mine."

He stepped closer, and as she looked around for the best route of escape, his hand closed over her hair. "Some stones have power," he told her softly. "Tragedy seeps into them, making them stronger. Death and grief. It hones them. Hawkins didn't understand that, but he was a simple man."

And the one she was facing was a mad one. "The necklace belongs to the Calhouns. It always has. It always will."

He jerked her hair hard and fast. She would have yelped, but the gun was now pressed against the racing pulse in her throat. "It belongs to me. Because I've been clever enough, I've been determined enough to wait for it. The moment I read about it, I knew. Now tonight, it's done."

She wasn't certain what she would have done—given it to him, tried to reason. But at the moment, her little girl moved into the doorway. "Mom." Her voice trembled as she rubbed her eyes. "It's thundering. You're supposed to come get me when it thunders."

It happened fast. He turned, swinging the gun. With all her strength, Suzanna hurled herself at him, blocking his aim. "Run!" she screamed to Jenny. "Run down the hall to Holt." She shoved, and raced after her daughter. The decision had to be made the minute she hit the doorway. As she watched Jenny streak toward the right and—she hoped—safety, Suzanna plunged in the opposite direction.

He would follow her, not the child, she told herself. Because she still had the necklace. The next decision had to be made at the steps. To go down to her family and risk them. Or to go up, alone.

She was halfway up the stairs when she heard him pounding behind her. She jerked in shock as a bullet plowed into the plaster an inch from her shoulder.

Breathless, she streaked up, only now hearing the boom of thunder that had frightened Jenny and made her look for her mother. Her single thought was to put as much distance between the madman behind her and her child. Her feet clattered on the winding metal staircase that led to Bianca's tower.

His fingers darted through the open treads and snatched at her ankle. With a sound of terror and fury, she kicked out, dislodging them, then stumbled up the rest of the way. The door was shut. She nearly wept as she threw her weight against the thick wood. It gave, with painful slowness, then allowed her to fall inside. But before she could slam it closed, he was hurtling in.

She braced, certain it would be only seconds before she felt the bullet. He was panting, sweating, his eyes glazed. At the corner of his mouth, a muscle ticked and jerked. "Give it to me." The gun shook as he advanced on her. A flash of lightning had him looking wildly around the shadowy room. "Give it to me now."

He's afraid, she realized. Of this room. "You've been in here before."

He had, only once, and had run out again, terrified. There was something here, something that hated him. It crawled cold as ice along his skin. "Give me the necklace, or I'll just kill you and take it."

"This was her room," Suzanna murmured, keeping her eyes on his. "Bianca's room. She died when her husband threw her from that window."

Unable to resist, he looked at the glass, dark with gloom, then away again.

"She still comes here, to wait, and to watch the cliffs." She heard, as she had known she would, the sound of Holt racing up the steps. "She's here now. Take them." She held the emeralds out. "But she won't let you leave with them."

His face was bone white and sheened with sweat as he reached for the necklace. He gripped it, but rather than the heat Suzanna had felt, he felt only cold. And a terror.

"They're mine now." He shivered and stumbled.

"Suzanna," Holt said quietly from the doorway. "Move away from him." His weapon was drawn, gripped in both hands. "Move away," he repeated. "Slow."

She took one step back, then two, but Livingston paid no attention to her. He was wiping his gun hand over his dry lips.

"It's over," Holt told him. "Drop the gun, kick it aside." But Livingston continued to stare at the necklace, breathing raggedly. "Drop it." Braced, Holt moved closer. "Get out, Suzanna."

"No, I'm not leaving you."

He didn't have time to swear at her. Though he was prepared to kill, he could see that the man was no longer concerned with his weapon, or with escape. Instead, Livingston merely stared down at the emeralds and trembled.

With his eyes trained on Livingston, Holt reached up to grasp the wrist of his gun hand. "It's over," he said again.

"It's mine." Wild with rage and fear, Livingston lunged. He fired once into the ceiling before Holt disarmed him. Even then he struggled, but the struggle was brief. With the next crash of thunder, he howled, striking out wildly even as the others raced into the room. Disoriented or terrified, stunned by Holt's blow to his jaw or no longer sane, he whirled.

There was the crash of breaking glass. Then a sound Suzanna would never forget. A man's horrified scream. Even as Holt leaped forward to try to save him, Livingston pinwheeled through the broken window and tumbled to the rain swept rock below.

"My God." Suzanna pressed back against the wall, her hands over her mouth to stop her own screams. There were arms around her, a babble of voices.

Her family poured into the tower room. She bent to her children, pressing kisses on their cheeks. "It's all right," she soothed. "It's all right now. There's nothing to be afraid of." She looked up at Holt. He stood facing her, the black space at his back, the glitter of emeralds at his feet. "Everything's all right now. I'm going to take you downstairs."

Holt pushed the gun back in its holster. "We'll take them down."

An hour later, when the children were soothed and sleeping, he took her by the arm and pulled her out on the terrace. All the fear and rage he'd felt since Jenny had run crying down the hallway came pouring out.

"What the hell do you think you were doing?"

"I had to keep him away from Jenny." She thought she was calm, but her hands began to shake. "I suddenly had an idea about the emeralds. It was so simple, really. And I found them. Then he was there—and Jenny. He had a gun, and God, oh God, I thought he would kill her."

"All right, all right," Holt said. Suzanna didn't choke back the tears this time, but clung to him as they shuddered out of her. "The kids are fine, Suzanna. Nobody's going to hurt them. Or you."

"I didn't know what else to do. I wasn't trying to be brave or stupid."

"You were both. I love you." He framed her face in his hands and kissed her. "Did he hurt you?"

"No." She sniffled a little and wiped her eyes. "He chased me up there, and then . . . he snapped. You saw how he was when you came in."

"Yeah." Two feet away from her, with a gun in his hand. Holt's fingers tightened on her shoulders. "Don't you ever scare me like that again."

"It's a deal." She rubbed her cheek against his, for comfort and for love. "It's really over now, isn't it?"

He kissed the top of her head. "It's just beginning."

Epilogue

It was late when the family gathered together in the parlor. The police had finally finished and left them alone. They were drawn together, a solid, united front beneath the portrait of Bianca.

Colleen sat, a dog at her feet, the emeralds in her lap. She had shed no tears when Suzanna had explained how and where she had found them, but took comfort in having that small, precious memory of her mother.

There was no talk of death.

Holt keep Suzanna close, his arm firm around her. The storm had passed, and the moon had risen. The parlor was washed with light. The only sound was Suzanna's soft, clear voice as she read from Bianca's journal.

She turned the last page and spoke of Bianca's thoughts as she'd prepared to hide the emeralds.

"'I didn't think of their monetary value as I took them out, held them in my hands and watched them gleam in the light of the lamp. They would be a legacy for my children, and their children, a symbol of freedom, and of hope. And with Christian, of love.

"'As dawn broke, I decided to put them, together with this journal, in a safe place until I joined Christian again.'"

Slowly, quietly Suzanna closed the book. "I think she's with him now. That they're with each other."

She smiled when Holt's fingers gripped hers. Looking around the room, she saw her sisters, the men they loved, her aunt smiling through tears, and Bianca's daughter, gazing up at the portrait that had been painted with unconquerable love.

"It was Bianca, more than the emeralds, who brought us all together. I like to think that by finding them, by bringing them back, we've helped them find each other."

Beyond the house, the moon glimmered on the cliffs far above where the sea churned and fought with the rocks. The wind whispered through the wild roses and warmed the lovers who walked there.

Win an exciting weekend for two
in New York City at the

NEW YORK
Marriott.
MARQUIS

including return airfare and tickets
to a Broadway Show!

You and a guest could be on your way to the
Big Apple, courtesy Harlequin Enterprises
and the New York Marriott Marquis! See
Official Sweepstakes Rules for more details.

NEW YORK BLOCKBUSTER SWEEPSTAKES
OFFICIAL ENTRY FORM

To enter, complete an Official Entry Form or a 3" x 5" card by hand printing "New York Blockbuster Sweepstakes," your
name and address, and mail to: **in the U.S.:** New York Blockbuster Sweepstakes, P.O. Box 9076, Buffalo, NY 14269-9076,
or **in Canada:** New York Blockbuster Sweepstakes, P.O. Box 637, Fort Erie, Ontario, L2A 5X3. Limit one entry per outer
mailing envelope. Entries must be received no later than 1/31/97. No liability is assumed for lost, late, damaged,
nondelivered or misdirected mail.

NEW YORK BLOCKBUSTER SWEEPSTAKES
OFFICIAL ENTRY FORM

Name: _____

Address: _____

City: _____

State/Province: _____

Zip/Postal Code: _____

KNL

NEW YORK BLOCKBUSTER SWEEPSTAKES
OFFICIAL RULES—NO PURCHASE NECESSARY

To enter, complete an Official Entry Form or 3" x 5" card by hand printing the words "New York Blockbuster Sweepstakes" and your name and address thereon and mailing it in the U.S. to: New York Blockbuster Sweepstakes, P.O. Box 9076, Buffalo, NY 14269-9076, or in Canada to: New York Blockbuster Sweepstakes, P.O. Box 637, Fort Erie, Ontario L2A 5X3. Limit: One entry per outer mailing envelope. Entries must be received no later than 1/31/97. No liability is assumed for lost, late, damaged, nondelivered or misdirected mail. Entries are void if they are in whole or in part illegible, incomplete or damaged.

One winner will be selected in a random drawing to be conducted no later than 2/28/97 from among all eligible entries received. Prize consists of a 3 day/2 night weekend for two (Friday-Sunday) including round-trip air transportation from commercial airport nearest winner's home, two nights hotel accommodations (one room double occupancy), at the New York Marriott Marquis Hotel, and a pair of theater tickets to a major Broadway show (approx. prize value: $2,400 U.S.). Travelers must provide their own transportation to and from the commercial airport nearest winner's home; are responsible for taxes, tips and incidentals; must execute and return a Release of Liability prior to travel; and must depart and return prior to 12/31/97.

Sweepstakes offer is open only to residents of the U.S. (except Puerto Rico) and Canada who are 18 years of age or older, except employees and immediate family members of Harlequin Enterprises, Limited, their affiliates, subsidiaries, and all agencies, entities and persons connected with the use, marketing or conduct of this sweepstakes. All federal, state, provincial, municipal and local laws apply. Offer void wherever prohibited by law. Taxes and/or duties are the sole responsibility of the winner. Any litigation within the province of Quebec respecting the conduct and awarding of prize may be submitted to the Régie des alcools des courses et des jeux. Prize is guaranteed to be awarded; winner will be notified by mail. No substitution for prize is permitted. Odds of winning are dependent on the number of eligible entries received.

Potential winner must sign and return an Affidavit of Eligibility within 30 days of notification. In the event of non-compliance within this time period, prize may be awarded to an alternate winner. If prize or prize notification is returned as undelivered, prize may be awarded to an alternate winner. By acceptance of his/her prize, winner consents to use of his/her name, photograph or likeness for the purpose of advertising, trade and promotion on behalf of Harlequin Enterprises, Limited, without further compensation unless prohibited by law. In order to win a prize, a resident of Canada will be required to correctly answer a time-limited arithmetical skill-testing question by mail.

For the name of the winner (available after 3/31/97), send a separate stamped, self-addressed envelope to: New York Blockbuster Sweepstakes 4815 Winner, P.O. Box 4200, Blair, NE 68009-4200 U.S.A.

NYTRULE-T

C(THE)OUSINS

Olivia Okrent and her cousins grew up spending their summers at the family's country estate, unaware that dark secrets and haunting betrayals would one day be their legacy.

Now the cousins have lives and families of their own, getting together only for special occasions. But when lies and infidelities threaten her comfortable life, Olivia is faced with a choice that may separate her from her family, once and for all.

by

RONA JAFFE

Available this December at your favorite retail outlet.

Enjoy these wonderful books by
NORA ROBERTS
One of Silhouette's favorite authors.
Order today:

Silhouette Special Edition®

| #09872 | §CONVINCING ALEX | $3.50 | ☐ |

§Those Wild Ukrainians miniseries

Language of Love

#51040	TREASURES LOST	$3.59	☐
#51039	THE PLAYBOY PRINCE	$3.59	☐
#51032	GABRIEL'S ANGEL	$3.59	☐
#51031	ONE SUMMER	$3.59	☐
#51026	THE RIGHT PATH	$3.59	☐

(limited quantities available on certain titles)

TOTAL AMOUNT	$
POSTAGE & HANDLING	$
($1.00 for one book, 50¢ for each additional)	
APPLICABLE TAXES**	$_____
TOTAL PAYABLE	$_____

(check or money order—please do not send cash)

To order, complete this form and send it, along with a check or money order for the total above, payable to Silhouette Books, to: **In the U.S.:** 3010 Walden Avenue, P.O. Box 9077, Buffalo, NY 14269-9077; **In Canada:** P.O. Box 636, Fort Erie, Ontario, L2A 5X3.

Name: _____

Address: _____ City: _____

State/Prov.:_____ Zip/Postal Code: _____

**New York residents remit applicable sales taxes.
  Canadian residents remit applicable GST and provincial taxes. SNRBACK7-T